SACRED SONGS

SACRED SONGS
THE MAHABHARATA'S MANY GITAS

BIBEK DEBROY

Published by
Rupa Publications India Pvt. Ltd 2023
7/16, Ansari Road, Daryaganj
New Delhi 110002

Sales centres:
Bengaluru Chennai
Hyderabad Jaipur Kathmandu
Kolkata Mumbai Prayagraj

Copyright © Bibek Debroy 2023

All rights reserved.
No part of this publication may be reproduced, transmitted,
or stored in a retrieval system, in any form or by any means,
electronic, mechanical, photocopying, recording or otherwise,
without the prior permission of the publisher.

P-ISBN: 978-93-5702-509-6
E-ISBN: 978-93-5702-511-9

First impression 2023

10 9 8 7 6 5 4 3 2 1

Printed in India

This book is sold subject to the condition that it shall not, by way of trade or
otherwise, be lent, resold, hired out, or otherwise circulated,
without the publisher's prior consent, in any form of binding
or cover other than that in which it is published.

For Kyoko and Subrahmanyam Jaishankar

CONTENTS

Introduction		ix
1.	Shounaka Gita	1
2.	Kashyapa Gita	15
3.	Dharma Vyadha Gita	25
4.	Yaksha Prashna	105
5.	Nahusha Gita	123
6.	Sanatsujata	141
7.	Utathya Gita	169
8.	Vamadeva Gita	188
9.	Kamanda, Rishabha and Yama Gita	202
10.	Shadaja Gita	240
11.	Pingala Gita	251
12.	Putra Gita	263
13.	Shamyaka Gita	272
14.	Manki and Bodhya Gitas	277
15.	Ajagara Gita	290
16.	Srigala Gita	298
17.	Vichakhnu Gita	309
18.	Harita Gita	313
19.	Vritra Gita	318
20.	Parashara Gita	340
21.	Hamsa Gita	396
22.	Yajnavalkya Gita	406

23.	Kama Gita	462
24.	Anu Gita	467
25.	Pandava Gita	659
Acknowledgements		683

INTRODUCTION

The Bhagavat Gita, one of Hinduism's most important texts, encapsulates the essence of the vedanta tradition of Hinduism, along with the Upanishads and the Brahmasutra.[1] It has been translated innumerable times into English, the first being Charles Wilkins's translation in 1785.[2] 'Gita', as the Bhagavat Gita is popularly known, simply means 'something that was sung'. Therefore, though most people identify the usage of this word with the Bhagavat Gita, it should not be surprising that there are other texts that also bear the name 'Gita'. In fact, there is an entire corpus of Gita literature. Admittedly, the Bhagavat Gita is the most important in this corpus, but it is not the only one.

The number of texts in this corpus of Gita literature is somewhere between fifty and sixty. These other Gita texts are from the Mahabharata, the Puranas[3] and the Ramayana, and some are stand-alone. How does one arrive at this number between

---

[1] The Brahmasutra was composed by Badarayana, identified often with Krishna Dvaipayana Vedavyasa. Grammatically, the Bhagavat Gita should be referred to as the Bhagavat Gita or Bhagavadgita, not Bhagavad Gita. Deviating from what has come to be accepted practice, in this book, we will thus refer to it as Bhagavat Gita, not Bhagavad Gita. There are many strands and beliefs within Hinduism, for instance, in the six *darshana*s (schools) of samkhya, yoga, nyaya, vaisheshika, mimamsa and vedanta. They are not contradictory, and supplement one another. However, specifically, vedanta highlights identity between the *jivatman* and the *paramatman*. The jivatman is the *atman* in living beings, while the paramatman is the universal atman.

[2] *Bhagvat-Geeta, or Dialogues of Kreeshna and Arjoon,* Charles Wilkins (trans.), C. Nourse, London, 1785. The preface was written by Warren Hastings. Among several translations of this work, there is also *The Bhagavad Gita*, Bibek Debroy (trans.), New Delhi, Penguin India, 2005.

[3] In this case, the Mahapuranas.

fifty and sixty? A listing of such Gitas is available on a website of Sanskrit documents.[4] A few additional Gitas and their texts are present in the Indian Institute of Technology (IIT) Kanpur Gita supersite.[5] This volume is only about the Mahabharata Gitas, not the others.

The Puranas, Ramayana and Other Gitas

After composing the Mahabharata, Krishna Dvaipayana Vedavyasa is believed to have composed eighteen Mahapuranas, or major Puranas, and, of course, the Hari Vamsha, regarded as a sequel to the Mahabharata. The Mahabharata is believed to have 100,000 *shlokas*. Collectively, the eighteen Mahapuranas have 400,000 shlokas—a gigantic corpus. The Ramayana and the Mahabharata, together with the Puranas, are known as the Itihasa Purana, sometimes referred to as the fifth Veda.

Examples of Gitas from the Mahapuranas are the Agastya Gita, Rudra Gita and Putra Gita from the Varaha Purana; the Avadhuta Gita from the Padma Purana; the Uttara Gita and Rama Gita from the Brahmanda Purana; the Uddhava Gita, Aila Gita, Kapila Gita, Karuna Gita, Jayanteya Gita, Pranaya Gita, Bhikshu Gita, Bhramara Gita, Mahishi Gita, Yugala Gita, Shruti Gita and Venu Gita from the Bhagavata Purana; the Brahma Gita, Guru Gita and Suta Gita from the Skanda Purana; the Yama Gita from the Vishnu Purana; and the Vyasa Gita from the Kurma Purana. There are other Gitas not from the Mahapuranas but from minor Puranas, known as Upapuranas, and these number up to 200. Examples of those are the Ribhu Gita

---

[4]'Giitaa', *Sanskrit Documents*, https://tinyurl.com/54ejhx4t. Accessed on 16 June 2023. This website also has the texts of these Gitas. There are minor typos in the texts, typically involving न and ण, or स and ष. But this is an excellent resource. When these Gitas are from the Mahabharata, there will be variations from the texts we have used, since ours is from Bhandarkar Oriental Research Institute's (BORI's) Critical Edition (CE).

[5]'Other Gitas', *Gita Supersite*, https://tinyurl.com/mr35vedh. Accessed on 16 June 2023.

from the Shiva Rahasya Purana; the Ganesha Gita from the Ganesha Purana; the Shankara Gita from the Vishnudharmottara Purana; and the Devi Gita from the Devi Bhagavata Purana.

There are some Gitas from the Ramayana texts, though not from the Valmiki Ramayana. 'Texts' is in the plural, as one shouldn't form the impression that the Valmiki Ramayana is the only Ramayana in Sanskrit. For instance, the Yogavasishtha Ramayana and the Adhyatma Ramayana are also Ramayana texts in Sanskrit.[6] The Vasishtha Gita (spoken by Vasishtha to Rama) and Siddha Gita (spoken by the siddhas)[7] are from the Yogavasishtha Ramayana, and the Vibhishana Gita (spoken by Vibhishana to Rama) and Rama Gita (a dialogue between Rama and Lakshmana) are from the Adhyatma Ramayana.

Finally, there are stand-alone Gita texts such as the Ashtavakra Gita, Kashyapa Gita, Garbha Gita, Gayatri Gita, Tulasi Gita, Pandava Gita, Pingala Gita and Vanara Gita. In general, these Gita texts have not been translated into English, except in rare instances, when their source texts have been translated. Obviously, something like the Ashtavakra Gita (a dialogue between Sage Ashtavakra and King Janaka) is an exception to this rule. As an important text of *advaita* (non-dual) vedanta, the Ashtavakra Gita has been translated into English multiple times.

As stated earlier, this volume is a translation and annotation of only Mahabharata Gitas. As a very rough order of magnitude, around 30 per cent of the sixty Gitas will be translated in this volume.

The Text: Critical Edition

The Mahabharata, in which the Bhagavat Gita is embedded, has eighteen major sections or Parvas. These are not equal in length. The

---

[6]Strictly speaking, Adhyatma Ramayana is part of some versions of the Brahmanda Purana.
[7]Siddhas are those who have obtained *siddhi* or success.

eighteen Parvas of the Mahabharata are: (1) Adi Parva; (2) Sabha Parva; (3) Aranyaka (Vana) Parva; (4) Virata Parva; (5) Udyoga Parva; (6) Bhishma Parva; (7) Drona Parva; (8) Karna Parva; (9) Shalya Parva; (10) Souptika Parva; (11) Stri Parva; (12) Shanti Parva; (13) Anushasana Parva; (14) Ashvamedhika Parva; (15) Ashramavasika Parva; (16) Mousala Parva; (17) Mahaprasthanika Parva; and (18) Svargarohana Parva. This eighteen-Parva classification is reasonably familiar. However, there are indications within the Mahabharata that a 100-Parva classification preceded this eighteen-Parva classification. Vestiges of this classification remain in the present text. Hence, a Parva has subsections, which are also known as Parvas. To avoid confusion, let us call these sub-parvas. Thus, the Shanti Parva has the Raja Dharma, Apad Dharma and Moksha Dharma sub-parvas. Of course, a few slimmer Parvas do not have such subdivisions.

The different versions or recensions of the Sanskrit Mahabharata differ from each other in some details. Between 1919 and 1966, the Bhandarkar Oriental Research Institute (BORI), Pune, published what is known as the Critical Edition (CE). Since the Mahabharata was not composed at one point in time, ranging roughly between 500 BCE to 500 CE, a range of 1,000 years,[8] there were naturally additions and embellishments to the original text over this period. The CE tried to identify and weed these out. This sought to eliminate later interpolations, unifying the text across more than 1,200 various regional versions. In the foreword to the CE,[9] R.N. Dandekar wrote,

> It may, however, be emphasized that the constituted text as presented here by no means claims to be the text of *Ur-Mahabharata*, that ideal but impossible desideratum. But, at the same time, it does claim, with due modesty, to represent the most ancient text of the *Mahabharata* that can

---

[8] As opposed to the dating of the Kurukshetra War itself.
[9] Eliminating the prolegomena, introductions, critical apparatus and text-critical notes.

be reconstructed on the basis of all available manuscript and allied evidence. In a sense, it is the ancestor of all extant manuscripts of the Epic.[10]

The inference that this is the original text is a subjective matter, with no certitude associated with the proposition. It is necessary to clearly state this, since the CE has been criticized on grounds of commission and omission (of shlokas), mostly the latter.

There have been attempts to identify later text and distinguish it from older text, such as by examining the evolution of the Sanskrit language. But all such attempts are inherently subjective. One of them was by M.R. Yardi.[11] Using statistical analysis, he identified five different authors at different points in time for the Mahabharata. According to him, it was one of these later authors who created the Parva classification. Yardi's work is not the last word on the subject, but it did lead to the identification of five authors of the Mahabharata, that is, the CE version of the Mahabharata. These five are Vaishampayana, Suta, Souti, the composer of Hari Vamsha and the author who classified the epic into Parvas. There is no need to presume, as we often tend to do, that the eighteen- or 100-Parva classification was part of the original form of the Mahabharata.

Within this eighteen-Parva classification of the epic, the Bhishma Parva relates to the period during the Kurukshetra War when Bhishma was the commander of the Kourava forces. Within the Bhishma Parva, there is a sub-parva known as the Bhagavat Gita sub-parva, with 994 shlokas and twenty-seven chapters.[12] The customary text, or standard text one encounters, of the Bhagavat Gita has 700 shlokas and eighteen chapters and is embedded in

---

[10]Dandekar, R.N., 'Foreword', *The Mahabharata, Text as Constituted in Its Critical Edition, Volume I*, Bhandarkar Oriental Research Institute, Poona, 1971.
[11]Yardi, M.R., *The Mahabharata: Its Genesis and Growth (A Statistical Study)*, Bhandarkar Oriental Research Institute, Poona, 1986.
[12]All references are to the CE. This is Section 63 in the CE.

the Bhagavat Gita sub-parva of the Bhishma Parva.[13] The first nine chapters of the sub-parva are about preliminaries and preparations for the war, and the tenth chapter, which follows seamlessly from the ninth, is the familiar first chapter of the Bhagavat Gita, with the famous words—'*Dharmakshetre kurukshetre*'—addressed by Dhritarashtra to Sanjaya.

This underlines an important point: the Bhagavat Gita cannot, and should not, be read independently of the Mahabharata and the corpus of other Gitas in the Mahabharata. They form part of the same whole. One cannot accept the Bhagavat Gita and reject the rest of the Mahabharata.[14] The Bhagavat Gita is an integral part of the Mahabharata and not delinked from it; it is not to be read in isolation. The notions and philosophy that figure in the text—yoga, samkhya, vedanta, *tapas* and *pancharatra* doctrines[15]—mesh perfectly with their usage in the rest of the Mahabharata. Therefore, it is not surprising that shlokas from the Bhagavat Gita also figure elsewhere in the Mahabharata, sometimes exactly, sometimes with minor variations. This bolsters the argument that one should read the Mahabharata Gitas.

Given their importance and close association with the Bhagavat Gita, it is surprising that these Mahabharata Gitas have not been translated into English, except when the entire Mahabharata has been translated.[16] The sole exception is a translation of the

---

[13]Because of the numbering of verses in Chapter 1, some versions have 701 shlokas.
[14]Yardi undertook a similar study as that of the Mahabharata for the Bhagavat Gita—he tested for multiple authors of the Bhagavat Gita. He concluded there was a single author for the entire Bhagavat Gita. Of the five authors of the Mahabharata, the author of the Bhagavat Gita was identified to be Souti. See Yardi, M.R., *The Bhagavadgita as a Synthesis*, Bhandarkar Oriental Research Institute, Poona, 1991; Yardi, M.R., 'Theories of Multiple Authorship of the Bhagavadgita', *Annals of the Bhandarkar Oriental Research Institute, Diamond Jubilee Volume*, 1977–78.
[15]Tapas can imperfectly be translated as austerities. The English word does not capture the nuance of scorching and purification. Pancharatra rites are the rites performed over five days.
[16]There are three unabridged translations of the Mahabharata in English—*The Mahabharata of Krishna-Dwaipayana Vyasa Translated into English Prose*, Kisari

Sanatsujata and the Anu Gita, done together with the Bhagavat Gita, by Kashinath Telang many years ago.¹⁷

What Makes a Gita: Grounds for Selection

The text followed in this translation of the Mahabharata Gitas is the CE. Some of the Gitas we have chosen to translate are familiar. An example is the Yaksha Prashna. Most people are familiar with the questions asked by the yaksha and the answers given by Yudhishthira. If expected questions and answers are missing in this translation, it is because we have followed the CE, which has excised those shlokas. The CE contains shlokas from all periods in the thousand-year span.

Having decided to translate the Mahabharata Gitas, how does one define which is a Gita? Since the Bhagavat Gita is a discourse narrated by Krishna to Arjuna, should one use the filter of conversation—that to be described as a Gita, the text must be a dialogue between Krishna and Arjuna? This would result in only the Anu Gita qualifying as a Gita—none of the others would qualify. There would also exclude the Kama Gita, spoken by Krishna, but to Yudhishthira and not to Arjuna. Another approach would be with the four objectives of human existence, or *purushartha*s, which are *dharma*, *artha*, *kama* and *moksha*. Should the filter be the pursuit of these purusharthas? Defined thus, the entire Mahabharata must be included, as it is about these purusharthas. Should one choose a more obvious filter and consider only the text that is explicitly described as a Gita in the CE? This would identify (0) Bhagavat Gita; (1) Utathya Gita; (2) Vamadeva Gita; (3) Shamyaka Gita;

Mohan Ganguli (trans.), Bharata Press, Calcutta, 1883–96; *A Prose English Translation of the Mahabharata*, Manmatha Nath Dutt (trans.), H.C. Dass, Calcutta, 1895; *The Mahabharata*, Bibek Debroy (trans.), Penguin, 2015. Of these, the Debroy translation follows the CE.

[17] *The Bhagavadgita, with the Sanatsugatiya and the Anu Gita*, K.T. Telang (trans.), Sacred Books of the East, Vol. 8, F. Max Muller (ed.), second edition, Clarendon Press, Oxford, 1898.

(4) Manki Gita; (5) Vichakhnu Gita; (6) Harita Gita; (7) Vritra Gita; (8) Parashara Gita; and (9) Anu Gita.

We could also consider a non-CE version of the Mahabharata. However, there is a problem with using this obvious-sounding filter. Descriptions of 'Gita' occur not in the text, but in titles of Parvas, sub-parvas, chapters and in colophons appended at the end of sections. All these were added later, over that space of one thousand years. As such, this filter is not a good one. This is the reason why any listing of Gitas based on titles and colophons tends to contain more than nine entries, as happens with the Sanskrit documents website. They fit with the broad contours of what a Gita should contain, even if they are not explicitly described as a 'Gita'. Accordingly, we have included (10) Shounaka Gita; (11) Kashyapa Gita; (12) Dharma Vyadha Gita; (13) Nahusha Gita; (14) Kamanda, Rishabha and Yama Gita; (15) Shadaja Gita; (16) Pingala Gita; (17) Putra Gita; (18) Ajagara Gita; (19) Srigala Gita; (20) Hamsa Gita; (21) Yajnavalkya Gita; and (22) Kama Gita. It seems to us, however, that though technically not Gitas, Yaksha Prashna and Sanatsujata are very much in the spirit of Gita and directly facilitate understanding of the purusharthas.

To this list of twenty-four, we have added a twenty-fifth on somewhat weaker grounds. The Pandava or Prapanna Gita is not part of the Mahabharata text, CE or otherwise. The nature of this text is also completely different from that of the other Gitas, as it is just a collection of shlokas addressed to Krishna by various people. The justification for including it is that these shlokas are largely spoken by protagonists from the Mahabharata. Thus, in some sense, this text is identified with the Mahabharata as all the characters, including Krishna, are from the Mahabharata.

Table 1 shows that these Gitas are concentrated in those Parvas of the Mahabharata that are reflective in nature, without a preponderance of incidents. Therefore, there are several Gitas in Aranyaka (Vana) Parva, which are about the time the Pandavas spent in exile in the forest, and the most in Shanti Parva, which is known as the book of peace. After the Kurukshetra War is over, this is where Bhishma, lying on his bed of arrows, instructs Yudhishthira and his brothers. The table lists the name of the Parva, the sub-parva and the number of the chapter in that particular Parva, following the CE. The number of chapters and shlokas in the Gita are also indicated. It shows that the length of the Gitas varies enormously, from a slim Vichakhnu Gita to the Anu Gita, which is almost one-and-a-half times the length of the Bhagavat Gita.

A Note on the Text

Unlike the Telang translation, this volume has both Sanskrit and English, and the Sanskrit (in Devanagari) is sourced from the CE. An attempt has been made to translate word by word, shloka by shloka. There are a few instances where one shloka spills over into the next. It is only in such cases that the translation has combined shlokas. The translation naturally follows the language and style used in the Mahabharata translation, which has been tweaked here and there to convey the sense more clearly, with an alternative choice of words. Since the use of diacritical marks has been avoided in English, names have been rendered into English as phonetically as possible, even if that runs against customary practice. Thus, the use of Goutama, and not Gautama, and Droupadi, not Draupadi. But the presence of the Sanskrit text should not give rise to any confusion.

A final word of caution is also in order. With texts that focus on dharma, artha, kama and moksha, there can be alternative interpretations, and the interpretation used might not be the only one possible. But this is a translation, not a commentary. We have chosen the most natural interpretation, which need not always be the only possible one. This becomes even more of an issue when the text is difficult to understand, as with the Yajnavalkya Gita. Through footnotes, we have attempted to make everything as clear as possible to the reader.

In the translation, the Gitas are listed in the way they occur in the Mahabharata, chronologically, so to speak.

Table 1
Relevant Gitas and Their Details

Gita	Parva, Chapter(s)	Sub-parva	Number of Chapters	Number of Shlokas
Shounaka (शौनक)	Aranyaka, 2	Aranyaka	1	66
Kashyapa (काश्यप)	Aranyaka, 30	Kairata	1	50
Dharma Vyadha (धर्मव्याध)	Aranyaka, 197–206	Markandeya Samasya	10	412
Yaksha Prashna (यक्षप्रश्न)	Aranyaka, 297	Araneya	1	74
Nahusha (नहुष)	Aranyaka, 177–8	Ajagara	2	83
Sanatsujata (सनत्सुजात)	Udyoga, 42–5	Sanatsujata	4	121
Utathya (उतथ्य)	Shanti, 91–2	Raja Dharma	2	94
Vamadeva (वामदेव)	Shanti, 93–5	Raja Dharma	3	70
Kamanda, Rishabha and Yama (कामन्द, ऋषभ, यम)	Shanti, 123–7	Raja Dharma	5	189
Shadaja (षडज)	Shanti, 161	Apad Dharma	1	48
Pingala (पिङ्गल)	Shanti, 168	Moksha Dharma	1	53
Putra (पुत्र)	Shanti, 169	Moksha Dharma	1	37
Shamyaka (शम्याक)	Shanti, 170	Moksha Dharma	1	23
Manki and Bodhya (मङ्कि, बोध्य)	Shanti, 171	Moksha Dharma	1	61
Ajagara (अजगर)	Shanti, 172	Moksha Dharma	1	37
Srigala (शृगाल)	Shanti, 173	Moksha Dharma	1	52

Vichakhnu (विचख्नु)	Shanti, 257	Moksha Dharma	1	13
Harita (हारीत)	Shanti, 269	Moksha Dharma	1	20
Vritra (वृत्र)	Shanti, 270–1	Moksha Dharma	2	103
Parashara (पराशर)	Shanti, 279–87	Moksha Dharma	9	286
Hamsa (हंस)	Shanti, 288	Moksha Dharma	1	45
Yajnavalkya (याज्ञवल्क्य)	Shanti, 298–306	Moksha Dharma	9	283
Kama (काम)	Ashvamedhika, 13	–	1	21
Anu (अनु)	Ashvamdedhika, 16–50	–	35	996
Pandava/Prapanna Gita (पाण्डव/प्रपन्न)	–	–	1	83

1

SHOUNAKA GITA

The Shounaka Gita is from Aranyaka (Vana) Parva of the Mahabharata. The word '*aranya*' means 'forest', and in the eighteen-Parva classification of the Mahabharata, the Aranyaka Parva comes third. This Parva is about the Pandavas' sojourn in the forest. After Yudhishthira lost the gambling match with Duryodhana, the Pandavas were exiled to the forest for twelve years, with an additional year to be spent in disguise. Hence, they had to leave the palace. A sub-parva of Aranyaka Parva is also known as Aranyaka Parva, and the Shounaka Gita is from this sub-parva. The Shounaka Gita is contained within the second chapter of Aranyaka Parva, which has a total of seventy-nine shlokas. When the Pandavas leave for the forest, the brahmanas follow them. As Yudhishthira grieves the loss of his kingdom and self-respect, a learned brahmana named Shounaka consoles him. His words, with sixty-six shlokas, constitutes the Shounaka Gita. Shounaka essentially tells Yudhishthira that all miseries result from attachment. If one gets rid of attachment, sorrows vanish. There are many places where the Bhagavat Gita also talks about renouncing attachment (2.48, 2.57, 2.62, 3.7, 3.19, 3.25, 3.26, 3.34, 4.23, 5.10, 5.21, 13.22, 14.7, 14.8, 14.9, 18.5, 18.6, 18.7).

वैशंपायन उवाच

इत्युक्त्वा स नृपः शोचन्निषसाद महीतले ।
तमध्यात्मरतिर्विद्वाञ्छौनको नाम वै द्विजः ।
योगे सांख्ये च कुशलो राजानमिदमब्रवीत् ॥ (1)

Vaishampayana said, 'Saying this, the grieving king sat down on the ground. There was a learned *dvija*[1] named Shounaka, who was devoted to knowledge about *adhyatma*.[2] He was accomplished in samkhya and yoga, and he spoke to the king.'

शोकस्थानसहस्राणि भयस्थानशतानि च ।
दिवसे दिवसे मूढमाविशन्ति न पण्डितम् ॥ (2)

'[Shounaka said,] "Every day, there are a thousand reasons for grief and a hundred reasons for fear that make a foolish person enter delusion. But not a person who is learned."'

न हि ज्ञानविरुद्धेषु बहुदोषेषु कर्मसु ।
श्रेयोघातिषु सज्जन्ते बुद्धिमन्तो भवद्विधाः ॥ (3)

'"Intelligent ones like you do not get caught in karma,[3] which has many taints and is counter to *jnana*,[4] so that welfare is destroyed."'

अष्टाङ्गां बुद्धिमाहुर्यां सर्वश्रेयोविघातिनीम् ।
श्रुतिस्मृतिसमायुक्तां सा राजंस्त्वय्यवस्थिता ॥ (4)

---

[1]The word 'dvija' means twice-born, once at the time of birth and the second time when the sacred thread is worn. It refers to brahmanas, but is also applied to any of the three upper *varna*s.
[2]Knowledge about adhyatma means knowledge about the self.
[3]Karma means action, the fruits of that action and also the consequent destiny.
[4]Jnana means knowledge. Jnana and *vijnana* are often used as synonyms. However, sometimes, a distinction is drawn between the two terms. Jnana is knowledge acquired from texts and the guru, while vijnana is knowledge obtained through self-introspection.

"'O King! The eight[5] forms of intelligence spoken about exist in you. This is the best of everything and destroys obstructions. This is in conformity with the Shrutis and Smritis.'"[6]

अर्थकृच्छ्रेषु दुर्गेषु व्यापत्सु स्वजनस्य च ।
शारीरमानसैर्दुःखैर्न सीदन्ति भवद्विधाः ॥ (5)

"'When calamities that are difficult to cross arise because of penury or hardship, or are caused by the deeds of relatives, those like you do not suffer physically or mentally.'"

श्रूयतां चाभिधास्यामि जनकेन यथा पुरा ।
आत्मव्यवस्थानकरा गीताः श्लोका महात्मना ॥ (6)

"'Listen. I will recount to you the shlokas that the great-souled Janaka[7] chanted in earlier times to impart stability to one's atman.'"

मनोदेहसमुत्थाभ्यां दुःखाभ्यामर्दितं जगत् ।
तयोर्व्याससमासाभ्यां शमोपायमिमं शृणु ॥ (7)

"'"The world is afflicted by two kinds of misery—that arising from the mind and that from the body. Listen to the means of pacifying these two, individually and together.'"

व्याधेरनिष्टसंस्पर्शाच्छ्रमादिष्टविवर्जनात् ।
दुःखं चतुर्भिः शारीरं कारणैः संप्रवर्तते ॥ (8)

"'"Physical sorrow results from four kinds of reasons—disease, the touch of something harmful, labour and separation from desired things.'"

---

[5]Yoga has eight elements—*yama* (restraint), *niyama* (rituals), *asana* (posture), *pranayama* (breathing), *pratyahara* (withdrawal), *dharana* (retention), *dhyana* (meditation) and *samadhi* (liberation)—comprising Ashtanga Yoga (yoga with eight forms).
[6]Shrutis have no human origin. They are revealed texts, like the Vedas. Smritis like these Gitas have human composers and were passed down through a process of verbal transmission, explaining use of the word '*smriti*', which means memory and retention.
[7]A royal sage (*rajarshi*), not to be confused with Janaka who was Sita's father. All kings of these lineage (in Videha) were known as Janaka.

तदाशुप्रतिकाराच्च सततं चाविचिन्तनात् ।
आधिव्याधिप्रशमनं क्रियायोगद्वयेन तु ॥ (9)

'"'Mental and physical pain can always be swiftly pacified through treatment or by not thinking about them. These are the two courses of action.'"'

मतिमन्तो ह्यतो वैद्याः शमं प्रागेव कुर्वते ।
मानसस्य प्रियाख्यानैः संभोगोपनयैर्नृणाम् ॥ (10)

'"'That is the reason intelligent physicians first try to pacify mental pain of men by recounting agreeable accounts and offering objects that bring pleasure.'"'

मानसेन हि दुःखेन शरीरमुपतप्यते ।
अयःपिण्डेन तप्तेन कुम्भसंस्थमिवोदकम् ॥ (11)

'"'Just as a hot iron ball affects the water in a pot, mental grief afflicts the body.'"'

मानसं शमयेत्तस्माज्ज्ञानेनाग्निमिवाम्बुना ।
प्रशान्ते मानसे दुःखे शरीरमुपशाम्यति ॥ (12)

'"'Just as water quenches fire, the mind is pacified through jnana. When mental grief is pacified, the body is also pacified.'"'

मनसो दुःखमूलं तु स्नेह इत्युपलभ्यते ।
स्नेहातु सज्जते जन्तुर्दुःखयोगमुपैति च ॥ (13)

'"'The root of all mental ailments is seen to be affection. Affection makes a creature attached, and that leads to misery.'"'

स्नेहमूलानि दुःखानि स्नेहजानि भयानि च ।
शोकहर्षौ तथायासः सर्वं स्नेहात्प्रवर्तते ॥ (14)

'"'Attachment is the root of all unhappiness, and attachment causes fear. Every kind of unhappiness and happiness and effort results from attachment.'"'

स्नेहात्करणरागश्च प्रजज्ञे वैषयस्तथा ।
अश्रेयस्कावुभावेतौ पूर्वस्तत्र गुरुः स्मृतः ॥ (15)

'"It is affection that gives birth to attachment to material objects. Both are harmful, but the former is said to be more serious."'[8]

कोटराग्निर्यथाशेषं समूलं पादपं दहेत् ।
धर्मार्थिनं तथाल्पोऽपि रागदोषो विनाशयेत् ॥ (16)

'"A fire in the hollow trunk burns down the entire tree, right down to the roots. Similarly, the evil of attachment, no matter how small, destroys those in search of dharma and artha."'

विप्रयोगे न तु त्यागी दोषदर्शी समागमात् ।
विरागं भजते जन्तुर्निर्वैरो निष्परिग्रहः ॥ (17)

'"He who has renounced is not non-attached. But a creature who can see the faults[9] from proximity is non-attached, bears no hatred and receives nothing."'

तस्मात्स्नेहं स्वपक्षेभ्यो मित्रेभ्यो धनसंचयात् ।
स्वशरीरसमुत्थं तु ज्ञानेन विनिवर्तयेत् ॥ (18)

'"Therefore, by using jnana, one should withdraw from affection towards one's allies, one's friends, the riches one has accumulated and everything that arises from one's own body."'[10]

ज्ञानान्विते मुख्येषु शास्त्रज्ञेषु कृतात्मसु ।
न तेषु सज्जते स्नेहः पद्मपत्रेष्विवोदकम् ॥ (19)

'"Like water on a lotus leaf, one who possesses the jnana of the foremost sacred texts controls his atman and is not touched by affection."'

---

[8]Affection is a more serious evil than attachment for material objects since it leads to attachment.
[9]One who can see the faults of attachment, without necessarily renouncing it.
[10]The text does not say one's own body, but everything arising from one's own body. Therefore, it goes beyond the physical body and covers all material and physical interactions, with other individuals and objects.

रागाभिभूतः पुरुषः कामेन परिकृष्यते ।
इच्छा संजायते तस्य ततस्तृष्णा प्रवर्तते ॥ (20)

'"'A man overwhelmed with attachment is attracted by desire. From the desire that is created, thirst originates.'"'[11]

तृष्णा हि सर्वपापिष्ठा नित्योद्वेगकरी नृणाम् ।
अधर्मबहुला चैव घोरा पापानुबन्धिनी ॥ (21)

'"'Thirst is wicked in every way and always makes men anxious. It is terrible and leads to a lot of *adharma*. It binds one in sin.'"'

या दुस्त्यजा दुर्मतिभिर्या न जीर्यति जीर्यतः ।
योऽसौ प्राणान्तिको रोगस्तां तृष्णां त्यजतः सुखम् ॥ (22)

'"'Those who are evil-minded find it extremely difficult to give up this thirst. It does not decay when the body decays. It is like a fatal disease. He who discards this thirst becomes happy.'"'

अनाद्यन्ता तु सा तृष्णा अन्तर्देहगता नृणाम् ।
विनाशयति संभूता अयोनिज इवानलः ॥ (23)

'"'This thirst has no beginning and no end. It destroys men from inside their bodies. It arises like a fire that has no origin.'"'

यथैधः स्वसमुत्थेन वह्निना नाशमृच्छति ।
तथाकृतात्मा लोभेन सहजेन विनश्यति ॥ (24)

'"'Like kindling is destroyed by the fire that it has created, one who does not control himself is destroyed by his natural avarice.'"'

राजतः सलिलादग्नेश्चोरतः स्वजनादपि ।
भयमर्थवतां नित्यं मृत्योः प्राणभृतामिव ॥ (25)

'"'Just as those who are alive are always scared at the prospect of death, those with riches are always scared of the king,[12] water, fire, thieves and relatives.'"'

---

[11] The thirst for material possessions.
[12] The king imposed taxes. In addition, the king was the source of punishment, in case the riches were acquired illegally.

यथा ह्यामिषमाकाशे पक्षिभि: श्वापदैर्भुवि ।
भक्ष्यते सलिले मत्स्यैस्तथा सर्वेण वित्तवान् ॥ (26)

'"A piece of meat is devoured by birds in the sky, on the ground by predatory beasts and in the water by fish. But one with riches is devoured everywhere."'

अर्थ एव हि केषांचिदनर्थो भविता नृणाम् ।
अर्थश्रेयसि चासक्तो न श्रेयो विन्दते नर: ।
तस्मादर्थागमा: सर्वे मनोमोहविवर्धना: ॥ (27)
कार्पण्यं दर्पमानौ च भयमुद्वेग एव च ।
अर्थजानि विदु: प्राज्ञा दु:खान्येतानि देहिनाम् ॥ (28)

'"To some men, riches are the source of disaster. A man who is addicted to the superiority of riches will never attain superiority. Therefore, the acquisition of riches always increases the delusion of the mind and is the source of miserliness, insolence, vanity, fear and anxiety. The wise ones know that riches are the source of misery for embodied beings."'

अर्थस्योपार्जने दु:खं पालने च क्षये तथा ।
नाशे दु:खं व्यये दु:खं घ्नन्ति चैवार्थकारणात् ॥ (29)

'"There is misery in earning wealth, preserving it and its decay. Its destruction brings unhappiness. Its expenditure brings unhappiness. Even then, people kill for riches."'

अर्था दु:खं परित्यक्तुं पालिताश्चापि तेऽसुखा: ।
दु:खेन चाधिगम्यन्ते तेषां नाशं न चिन्तयेत् ॥ (30)

'"There is unhappiness in giving up wealth. But there is unhappiness in preserving it too. Since its possession brings such misery, one should not think about its loss."'

असंतोषपरा मूढा: संतोषं यान्ति पण्डिता: ।
अन्तो नास्ति पिपासाया: संतोष: परमं सुखम् ।
तस्मात्संतोषमेवेह धनं पश्यन्ति पण्डिता: ॥ (31)

"'"The foolish are always dissatisfied, the learned find contentment. There is no end to thirst. Contentment is supreme happiness. Therefore, learned ones see that contentment is wealth."'"

अनित्यं यौवनं रूपं जीवितं द्रव्यसंचयः ।
ऐश्वर्यं प्रियसंवासो गृध्येदेषु न पण्डितः ॥ (32)

"'"A learned person knows that youth, beauty, life, accumulation of riches, prosperity and association with loved ones are temporary and never craves for these."'"

त्यजेत् संचयांस्तस्मात्तज्जं क्लेशं सहेत कः ।
न हि संचयवान्कश्चिद्दृश्यते निरुपद्रवः ॥ (33)

"'"Therefore, who will pursue accumulation of riches and consequent unhappiness? One who has accumulated riches is never seen to be without difficulties."'"

अतश्च धर्मिभिः पुंभिरनीहार्थः प्रशस्यते ।
प्रक्षालनाद्धि पङ्कस्य दूरादस्पर्शनं वरम् ॥ (34)

"'"For this reason, men who follow dharma do not praise those who possess wealth in this world. It is better to avoid mud from a distance than to touch it and wash later."'"[13]

युधिष्ठिरैवमर्थेषु न स्पृहां कर्तुमर्हसि ।
धर्मेण यदि ते कार्यं विमुक्तेच्छो भवार्थतः ॥ (35)

"'O Yudhishthira! Therefore, you should not desire riches. If you wish to act in accordance with dharma, free yourself from riches.'"

युधिष्ठिर उवाच

नार्थोपभोगलिप्सार्थमियमर्थेप्सुता मम ।
भरणार्थं तु विप्राणां ब्रह्मन्काङ्क्षे न लोभतः ॥ (36)

---

[13] The text does not state this explicitly, but this seems to be the place where Janaka's quote ends.

'Yudhishthira replied, "O Brahmana! I do not desire riches because I wish to enjoy them after acquisition. I do not desire them out of avarice, but so that I can support the brahmanas."'

कथं ह्यास्मद्विधो ब्रह्मन्वर्तमानो गृहाश्रमे ।
भरणं पालनं चापि न कुर्यादनुयायिनाम् ॥ (37)

'"O Brahmana! How can those like us, who are in the householder stage,[14] fail to support and sustain those who follow?"'[15]

संविभागो हि भूतानां सर्वेषामेव शिष्यते ।
तथैवापचमानेभ्यः प्रदेयं गृहमेधिना ॥ (38)

'"It is taught that one must divide among all beings. One who is a householder should give to those who do not cook."'[16]

तृणानि भूमिरुदकं वाक्चतुर्थी च सूनृता ।
सतामेतानि गेहेषु नोच्छिद्यन्ते कदाचन ॥ (39)

'"The homes of virtuous men should never lack four things—grass, ground, water and welcoming words."'

देयमार्तस्य शयनं स्थितश्रान्तस्य चासनम् ।
तृषितस्य च पानीयं क्षुधितस्य च भोजनम् ॥ (40)

'"Those who are afflicted must be given a bed.[17] Those who are tired of standing must be given a seat.[18] Those who are thirsty must be given a drink, and those who are hungry must be given food."'

चक्षुर्दद्यान्मनो दद्याद्वाचं दद्याच्च सूनृताम् ।
प्रत्युद्गम्याभिगमनं कुर्यान्न्यायेन चार्चनम् ॥ (41)

---

[14] In the four-ashram classification, the householder stage is called *garhasthya*. The others are *brahmacharya*, *vanaprastha* and *sannyasa*.
[15] 'Those who follow' refers to the brahmanas who followed the Pandavas when they left for their exile. As householders, the Pandavas should have provided sustenance to those brahmanas but were no longer in a position to do so.
[16] Ascetics do not cook for themselves. Anything one possesses should be shared among all beings and not be used only for one's own narrow, selfish needs.
[17] This corresponds to grass or straw in the previous shloka.
[18] This corresponds to ground in the previous shloka.

"'One's eyesight must be given.[19] One's mind must be given. One's pleasant words must be given. One must stand up to greet the guest and offer proper homage.'"

अग्निहोत्रमनड्वांश्च ज्ञातयोऽतिथिबान्धवा: ।
पुत्रदारभृताश्चैव निर्दहेयुरपूजिता: ॥ (42)

"'*Agnihotra*,[20] bulls, kin, guests, relatives, sons, wives and servants burn down those who do not offer homage.'"

नात्मार्थं पाचयेदन्नं न वृथा घातयेत्पशून् ।
न च तत्स्वयमश्नीयाद्विधिवद्यन्न निर्वपेत् ॥ (43)

"'No one should cook food only for one's own self, nor should animals be killed in vain.[21] No one should eat food oneself, without having offered it in the proper fashion.'"

श्वभ्यश्च श्वपचेभ्यश्च वयोभ्यश्चावपेद्भुवि ।
वैश्वदेवं हि नामैतत्सायंप्रातर्विधीयते ॥ (44)

"'In the morning and evening, it is recommended that food should be spread out on the ground for dogs, *shvapacha*s,[22] birds and the vishvadevas.'"[23]

विघसाशी भवेत्तस्मान्नित्यं चामृतभोजन: ।
विघसं भृत्यशेषं तु यज्ञशेषं तथामृतम् ॥ (45)

---

[19]To the guest, in the sense of paying attention to them.
[20]Agnihotra is the fire sacrifice.
[21]Without offering them as sacrifices.
[22]Shvapachas are often equated with chandalas or outcasts. 'Shvapacha' is sometimes translated as dog-eater, but this does not follow. Unlike others, shvapachas kept dogs and were accompanied by them. 'Shvapacha' can also mean someone who cooks in the company of dogs or cooks for dogs.
[23]Vishva is regarded to have ten gods as sons—Vasu, Satya, Kratu, Daksha, Kala, Kama, Dhriti, Kuru, Pururava and Madravashva. Alternatively, the food offerings on the ground are for the vishvadevas (counted as one), Agni, Soma, Dhanvantari, Kuhu, Anumati, Prajapati, heaven and earth.

'"Always eating food that is left after servants have eaten is like partaking of *amrita*.²⁴ What is left at the end of a sacrifice is also like amrita."'

एतां यो वर्तते वृत्तिं वर्तमानो गृहाश्रमे ।
तस्य धर्म परं प्राहुः कथं वा विप्र मन्यसे ॥ (46)

'"It is said that one who leads the life of a householder, while following these practices, follows supreme dharma. O Brahmana! What do you think?"'

शौनक उवाच

अहो बत महत्कष्टं विपरीतमिदं जगत् ।
येनापत्रपते साधुरसाधुस्तेन तुष्यति ॥ (47)

'Shounaka replied, "Alas! It is a great misery that the world is full of contradictions. The wicked find satisfaction in that which scares the virtuous."'

शिश्नोदरकृतेऽप्राज्ञः करोति विघसं बहु ।
मोहरागसमाक्रान्त इन्द्रियार्थवशानुगः ॥ (48)

'"Overwhelmed by delusion and attachment, under the subjugation of gratification of the senses, foolish men do many things for the penis and the stomach."'

ह्रियते बुध्यमानोऽपि नरो हारिभिरिन्द्रियैः ।
विमूढसंज्ञो दुष्टाश्वैरुद्भ्रान्तैरिव सारथिः ॥ (49)

'"Like a charioteer who has lost control over wicked and confused horses, even an intelligent man is confused in his understanding and is led astray by the senses."'

षडिन्द्रियाणि विषयं समागच्छन्ति वै यदा ।
तदा प्रादुर्भवत्येषां पूर्वसंकल्पजं मनः ॥ (50)

---

²⁴'Amrita' can loosely be translated as nectar, ambrosia. It arose as a result of the churning of the ocean and bestowed immortality. Here, the meaning is that of immortality.

'"When any of the six senses[25] comes close to an object, prior resolution springs up in the mind and manifests itself through them."'

मनो यस्येन्द्रियग्रामविषयं प्रति चोदितम् ।
तस्यौत्सुक्यं संभवति प्रवृत्तिश्चोपजायते ॥ (51)

'"When the mind is directed towards enjoying the objects of the senses, eagerness is created and inclination is generated."'

ततः संकल्पवीर्येण कामेन विषयेषुभिः ।
विद्धः पतति लोभाग्नौ ज्योतिर्लोभात्पतंगवत् ॥ (52)

'"That resolution is the seed of desire towards an object and, pierced, one falls into the flames of avarice, like a moth in its greed for a lamp."'

ततो विहारैराहारैर्मोहितश्च विशां पते ।
महामोहमुखे मग्नो नात्मानमवबुध्यते ॥ (53)

'"O Lord of the Earth! Thus, immersed in the mouth of great delusion and deluded by pleasure and food, he does not know his own atman."'

एवं पतति संसारे तासु तास्विह योनिषु ।
अविद्याकर्मतृष्णाभिर्भ्राम्यमाणोऽथ चक्रवत् ॥ (54)
ब्रह्मादिषु तृणान्तेषु हूतेषु परिवर्तते ।
जले भुवि तथाकाशे जायमानः पुनः पुनः ॥ (55)

'"He descends into *samsara*,[26] from one womb to another. As a result of ignorance, karma and thirst, he is whirled around, as if on a wheel, changing from one being to another—from Brahma to a blade of grass, born repeatedly in water, on the ground and in the sky."'

अबुधानां गतिस्त्वेषा बुधानामपि मे शृणु ।
ये धर्मे श्रेयसि रता विमोक्षरतयो जनाः ॥ (56)

---

[25] The mind and the five senses of hearing, touch, sight, taste and smell.
[26] The cycle of birth, death and rebirth.

'"This is the path of those who do not know. Hear about that of people who know, those who are devoted to superior dharma and seek to liberate themselves."'

यदिदं वेदवचनं कुरु कर्म त्यजेति च ।
तस्माद्धर्मानिमान्सर्वान्नाभिमानात्समाचरेत् ॥ (57)

'"These are the words of the Vedas. Perform karma but also renounce it. Therefore, one should not practise any dharma because of pride."'

इज्याध्ययनदानानि तपः सत्यं क्षमा दमः ।
अलोभ इति मार्गोऽयं धर्मस्याष्टविधः स्मृतः ॥ (58)

'"It has been said that there is an eight-fold path of dharma—sacrifices, studying, gifts, austerities, truthfulness, forbearance, self-control and lack of avarice."'

तत्र पूर्वश्चतुर्वर्गः पितृयानपथे स्थितः ।
कर्तव्यमिति यत्कार्यं नाभिमानात्समाचरेत् ॥ (59)

'"Of these, the first four are established in *pitriyana*.[27] One should always act because a deed has to be done, not because of pride."'

उत्तरो देवयानस्तु सद्भिराचरितः सदा ।
अष्टाङ्गेनैव मार्गेण विशुद्धात्मा समाचरेत् ॥ (60)
सम्यक्संकल्पसंबन्धात्सम्यक्चेन्द्रियनिग्रहात् ।
सम्यग्व्रतविशेषाच्च सम्यक्च गुरुसेवनात् ॥ (61)
सम्यगाहारयोगाच्च सम्यक्वाध्ययनागमात् ।
सम्यक्कर्मोपसंन्यासात्सम्यक्चित्तनिरोधनात् ।
एवं कर्माणि कुर्वन्ति संसारविजिगीषवः ॥ (62)

'"The latter four represent *devayana*,[28] always followed by those who are virtuous. One whose atman is pure should always travel along these eight paths—through correct resolution and association, correct restraint of the senses, correct observance of the specific vows, correct serving of gurus, correct regulation of food, correct

---

[27] The way of the ancestors. Along this path, one has to be reborn.
[28] The way of devas. Along this path, one is freed and does not have to be reborn again.

studying of the sacred texts, correct renunciation of rituals and correct restraining of thoughts. Those who wish to conquer samsara undertake karma in this way."

रागद्वेषविनिर्मुक्ता ऐश्वर्यं देवता गताः ।
रुद्राः साध्यास्तथादित्या वसवोऽथाश्विनावपि ।
योगैश्वर्येण संयुक्ता धारयन्ति प्रजा इमाः ॥ (63)

"'It is because they are united by the powers of yoga and free from attachment and hatred that devas like the rudras, the sadhyas, adityas, vasus and Ashvins are able to sustain beings and possess prosperity.'"

तथा त्वमपि कौन्तेय शममास्थाय पुष्कलम् ।
तपसा सिद्धिमन्विच्छ योगसिद्धिं च भारत ॥ (64)

"'O Kounteya! O Descendant of the Bharata Lineage! Like them, you must attain complete equanimity. You must seek to obtain siddhi[29] in austerities and siddhi in yoga.'"

पितृमातृमयी सिद्धिः प्राप्ता कर्ममयी च ते ।
तपसा सिद्धिमन्विच्छ द्विजानां भरणाय वै ॥ (65)

"'Through your karma, you have already obtained siddhi for your father and your mother. To sustain the dvijas, you must now seek siddhi in your austerities.'"

सिद्धा हि यद्यदिच्छन्ति कुर्वते तदनुग्रहात् ।
तस्मात्तपः समास्थाय कुरुष्वात्ममनोरथम् ॥ (66)

"'Those who obtain such siddhi can obtain whatever they wish because of that. Therefore, practise austerities. Accomplish everything that you desire.'"

Thus ends the Shounaka Gita.

---

[29]Siddhi also means acquisition of powers.

2

KASHYAPA GITA

Like the Shounaka Gita, the Kashyapa Gita is from Aranyaka Parva but from Kairata sub-parva. *Kirata*s are mountain-dwellers who make a living through hunting. This section is named so because Shiva assumes the form of a kirata and fights Arjuna to test him when the Pandavas, in exile, are in the forest of Kamyaka. Later, Arjuna proceeds to heaven to obtain weapons from Indra. The setting for the Kashyapa Gita is a conversation between Droupadi and Yudhishthira. Droupadi is full of anger at the hardships the Pandavas have to face and is thirsting for revenge. Droupadi exhorts Yudhishthira to not forgive the Kouravas. The Kashyapa Gita has a single chapter with fifty shlokas. Though this is known as the Kashyapa Gita, only a few shlokas are actually spoken by Kashyapa. The rest are spoken by Yudhishthira and the message is that of conquering anger. There are many places where the Bhagavat Gita also talks about conquering anger (2.56, 2.62, 2.63, 3.36, 3.37, 4.10, 5.23, 16.21).

युधिष्ठिर उवाच

क्रोधो हन्ता मनुष्याणां क्रोधो भावयिता पुनः ।
इति विद्धि महाप्राज्ञे क्रोधमूलौ भवाभवौ ॥ (1)

Yudhishthira said, 'Anger destroys men and anger again leads to their prosperity. O Immensely Intelligent One! Know therefore that both creation and destruction find their source in anger.'

यो हि संहरते क्रोधं भावस्तस्य सुशोभने ।
यः पुनः पुरुषः क्रोधं नित्यं न सहते शुभे ।
तस्याभावाय भवति क्रोधः परमदारुणः ॥ (2)

'O Extremely Beautiful One! He who restrains his anger obtains prosperity. O Auspicious One! But a man who never controls his anger does not obtain prosperity. The terrible anger contributes to his destruction.'

क्रोधमूलो विनाशो हि प्रजानामिह दृश्यते ।
तत्कथं मादृशः क्रोधमुत्सृजेल्लोकनाशनम् ॥ (3)

'It has been seen that anger is the root of destruction of all beings. How can someone like me indulge in anger, when it brings about the destruction of worlds?'

क्रुद्धः पापं नरः कुर्यात्क्रुद्धो हन्याद्गुरूनपि ।
क्रुद्धः परुषया वाचा श्रेयसोऽप्यवमन्यते ॥ (4)

'An angry man commits sin. An angry man may even kill his gurus. An angry man dishonours his betters with harsh words.'

वाच्यावाच्ये हि कुपितो न प्रजानाति कर्हिचित् ।
नाकार्यमस्ति क्रुद्धस्य नावाच्यं विद्यते तथा ॥ (5)

'When angered, one does not know what should be said and what should not be said. There is nothing that an angry person cannot do or say.'

हिंस्यात्क्रोधादवध्यांश्च वध्यान्संपूजयेदपि ।
आत्मानमपि च क्रुद्धः प्रेषयेद्यमसादनम् ॥ (6)

'From anger, one can cause violence to someone who should not be killed or honour someone who should be killed. An angry person can even send himself to Yama's abode.'

एतान्दोषान्प्रपश्यद्भिर्भर्जितः क्रोधो मनीषिभिः ।
इच्छद्भिः परमं श्रेय इह चामुत्र चोत्तमम् ॥ (7)

'On witnessing these taints, learned ones have said that anger must be conquered if one wishes for supreme welfare in this world and excellence in the world hereafter.'

तं क्रोधं वर्जितं धीरैः कथमस्मद्विधश्चरेत् ।
एतद्द्रौपदि संधाय न मे मन्युः प्रवर्धते ॥ (8)

'Those who are patient have discarded anger. O Droupadi! Thinking about this, why should someone like me also not act accordingly? Therefore, my anger does not increase.'

आत्मानं च परं चैव त्रायते महतो भयात् ।
क्रुध्यन्तमप्रतिक्रुध्यन्द्वयोरेष चिकित्सकः ॥ (9)

'One who does not retaliate in rage against someone who is angry saves himself and the other person from great fear. He is like a physician for both.'

मूढो यदि क्लिश्यमानः क्रुध्यतेऽशक्तिमान्नरः ।
बलीयसां मनुष्याणां त्यजत्यात्मानमन्ततः ॥ (10)

'An incapable man may be oppressed by men who are stronger. But if he is angered, in his folly, he brings about his own destruction.'

तस्यात्मानं सन्त्यजतो लोका नश्यन्त्यनात्मनः ।
तस्माद्द्रौपद्यशक्तस्य मन्योर्नियमनं स्मृतम् ॥ (11)

'In the hereafter, there is no world for one who does not control one's own atman and one destroys oneself. O Droupadi! It has, therefore, been said that a person who is incapable[1] should control his anger.'

विद्वांस्तथैव यः शक्तः क्लिश्यमानो न कुप्यति ।
स नाशयित्वा क्लेष्टारं परलोके च नन्दति ॥ (12)

'Even if capable, a learned person is not angry when oppressed. Having destroyed what causes hardship, he finds delight in the next world.'

---

[1] Incapable of countering.

तस्मादबलवता चैव दुर्बलेन च नित्यदा ।
क्षन्तव्यं पुरुषेणाहुरापत्स्वपि विजानता ॥ (13)

'Therefore, it is said a man who knows, strong or weak, always forgives, even if he faces hardships.'

मन्योर्हि विजयं कृष्णे प्रशंसन्तीह साधवः ।
क्षमावतो जयो नित्यं साधोरिह सतां मतम् ॥ (14)

'O Krishnaa![2] The virtuous always praise those who have conquered anger. The virtuous hold the view that victory always comes to the forgiving and the good.'

सत्यं चानृतत: श्रेयो नृशंसाच्चानृशंसता ।
तमेवं बहुदोषं तु क्रोधं साधुविवर्जितम् ।
मादृश: प्रसृजेत्कस्मात्सुयोधनवधादपि ॥ (15)

'Truth is superior to falsehood and lack of cruelty to cruelty. For the sake of killing someone like Suyodhana,[3] how can someone like me generate anger, which has many faults and is shunned by the virtuous?'

तेजस्वीति यमाहुर्वै पण्डिता दीर्घदर्शिन: ।
न क्रोधोऽभ्यन्तरस्तस्य भवतीति विनिश्चितम् ॥ (16)

'It has been determined that learned and far-sighted ones call someone energetic when he has no anger inside him.'

यस्तु क्रोधं समुत्पन्नं प्रज्ञया प्रतिबाधते ।
तेजस्विनं तं विद्वांसो मन्यन्ते तत्त्वदर्शिन: ॥ (17)

'If a person uses wisdom to check the anger that has arisen, those who know the truth think that he is energetic.'

क्रुद्धो हि कार्यं सुश्रोणि न यथावत्प्रपश्यति ।
न कार्यं न च मर्यादां नर: क्रुद्धोऽनुपश्यति ॥ (18)

---

[2]'Krishnaa' is one of Droupadi's names.
[3]Duryodhana is often addressed as Suyodhana in the Mahabharata.

'O One with Beautiful Hips! An angry person cannot see the course of action accurately. An angry man does not see his tasks or his limits.'

हन्त्यवध्यानपि क्रुद्धो गुरूनरूक्षैस्तुदत्यपि ।
तस्मात्तेजसि कर्तव्ये क्रोधो दूरात्प्रतिष्ठित: ॥ (19)

'An angry person kills those who should not be killed. He exhibits harshness towards his gurus. Therefore, it is the duty of any energetic person to keep anger at a distance.'

दाक्ष्यं ह्यमर्ष: शौर्यं च शीघ्रत्वमिति तेजस: ।
गुणा: क्रोधाभिभूतेन न शक्या: प्राप्तुमञ्जसा ॥ (20)

'A person overwhelmed by rage is not capable of obtaining qualities like accomplishment, tolerance, valour, swiftness and energy.'

क्रोधं त्यक्त्वा तु पुरुष: सम्यक्तेजोऽभिपद्यते ।
कालयुक्तं महाप्राज्ञे क्रुद्धैस्तेज: सुदु:सहम् ॥ (21)

'By forsaking anger, a man can obtain his true energy. O Immensely Wise One! But it is extremely difficult for an angry one to exhibit his energy when the time is right.'

क्रोधस्त्वपण्डितै: शश्वतेज इत्यभिधीयते ।
रजस्तल्लोकनाशाय विहितं मानुषान्प्रति ॥ (22)

'Those who are not learned always think that anger is energy. *Rajas*[4] has been given to humans for the destruction of the world.'

तस्माच्छश्वत्यजेत्क्रोधं पुरुष: सम्यगाचरन् ।
श्रेयान्स्वधर्मानपगो न क्रुद्ध इति निश्चितम् ॥ (23)

'Therefore, a person who wishes to act appropriately must always renounce anger. It is certain that it is better to give up one's own dharma than succumb to anger.'

---

[4]The three *gunas* are *sattva,* rajas and *tamas.* Rajas is the quality of passion, sattva of purity and tamas of ignorance.

यदि सर्वमबुद्धीनामतिक्रान्तममेधसाम् ।
अतिक्रमो मद्विधस्य कथं स्वित्स्यादनिन्दिते ॥ (24)

'All those who possess no intelligence or have limited intelligence transgress this. O Unblemished One! How can someone like me do this?'

यदि न स्युर्मनुष्येषु क्षमिणः पृथिवीसमाः ।
न स्यात्संधिर्मनुष्याणां क्रोधमूलो हि विग्रहः ॥ (25)

'If men who are equal to the earth in forgiveness did not exist, there would be no peace among men but dissension caused by anger.'

अभिषक्तो ह्याभिषजेदाहन्याद्गुरुणा हतः ।
एवं विनाशो भूतानामधर्मः प्रथितो भवेत् ॥ (26)

'If injured ones return the injury, and those afflicted by gurus return the affliction, the outcome will be a destruction of beings and establishment of adharma.'

आक्रुष्टः पुरुषः सर्वः प्रत्याक्रोशेदनन्तरम् ।
प्रतिहन्याद्धतश्चैव तथा हिंस्याच्च हिंसितः ॥ (27)
हन्युर्हि पितरः पुत्रान्पुत्राश्चापि तथा पितॄन् ।
हन्युश्च पतयो भार्याः पतीन्भार्यास्तथैव च ॥ (28)
एवं संकुपिते लोके जन्म कृष्णे न विद्यते ।
प्रजानां संधिमूलं हि जन्म विद्धि शुभानने ॥ (29)

'O Krishnaa! O One with Beautiful Face! If every man who is abused immediately abuses back, if one who is injured returns violence with violence, if fathers kill their sons and sons kill their fathers, if husbands kill their wives and wives kill their husbands, then there can be no birth in a world thus angered. Know that the birth of all beings is conditional on conciliation.'

ताः क्षीयेरन्प्रजाः सर्वाः क्षिप्रं द्रौपदि तादृशे ।
तस्मान्मन्युर्विनाशाय प्रजानामभवाय च ॥ (30)

'O Droupadi! All beings will be swiftly destroyed in such a situation. Thus, anger leads to the destruction and non-existence of all beings.'

यस्मातु लोके दृश्यन्ते क्षमिण: पृथिवीसमा: ।
तस्माज्जन्म च भूतानां भवश्च प्रतिपद्यते ॥ (31)

'It is because people as forgiving as the earth are seen in this world that beings are born and there is existence.'

क्षन्तव्यं पुरुषेणेह सर्वास्वापत्सु शोभने ।
क्षमा भवो हि भूतानां जन्म चैव प्रकीर्तितम् ॥ (32)

'O Beautiful One! In this world, a man must be forgiving in all his difficulties. It has been said that the birth of all beings results from forgiveness.'

आक्रुष्टस्ताडित: क्रुद्ध: क्षमते यो बलीयसा ।
यश्च नित्यं जितक्रोधो विद्वानुत्तमपूरुष: ॥ (33)

'If a man is insulted and oppressed by a stronger person, but always pacifies his rage and controls his anger, he is learned and excellent.'

प्रभाववानपि नरस्तस्य लोका: सनातना: ।
क्रोधनस्त्वल्पविज्ञान: प्रेत्य चेह च नश्यति ॥ (34)

'Such a man has influence in the eternal worlds. But one who has little knowledge and falls prey to anger is destroyed in this world and in the next one.'

अत्राप्युदाहरन्तीमा गाथा नित्यं क्षमावताम् ।
गीता: क्षमावता कृष्णे काश्यपेन महात्मना ॥ (35)

'O Krishnaa! Regarding this, the great-souled and forgiving Kashyapa sang this chant about those who are eternally forgiving and it is cited.'

क्षमा धर्म: क्षमा यज्ञ: क्षमा वेदा: क्षमा श्रुतम् ।
यस्तामेवं विजानाति स सर्वं क्षन्तुमर्हति ॥ (36)

'"Forgiveness is dharma. Forgiveness is sacrifice. Forgiveness is the Vedas. Forgiveness is the Shrutis. He who knows this is capable of forgiving everything."'

क्षमा ब्रह्म क्षमा सत्यं क्षमा भूतं च भावि च ।
क्षमा तपः क्षमा शौचं क्षमया चोद्धृतं जगत् ॥ (37)

'"Forgiveness is the *brahman*. Forgiveness is the truth. Forgiveness is the past and the future. Forgiveness is austerity. Forgiveness is purity. Forgiveness holds up the entire world."'

अति ब्रह्मविदां लोकानति चापि तपस्विनाम् ।
अति यज्ञविदां चैव क्षमिणः प्राप्नुवन्ति तान् ॥ (38)

'"Forgiving ones attain worlds obtained by ascetics who know the brahman and by those who know about sacrifices."'

क्षमा तेजस्विनां तेजः क्षमा ब्रह्म तपस्विनाम् ।
क्षमा सत्यं सत्यवतां क्षमा दानं क्षमा यशः ॥ (39)

'"Forgiveness is the energy of the energetic. Forgiveness is the brahman of the ascetics. Forgiveness is the truth of those who are truthful. Forgiveness is donation. Forgiveness is fame."'

तां क्षमामीदृशीं कृष्णे कथमस्मद्विधस्त्यजेत् ।
यस्यां ब्रह्म च सत्यं च यज्ञा लोकाश्च विष्ठिताः ।
भुज्यन्ते यज्वनां लोकाः क्षमिणामपरे तथा ॥ (40)

'O Krishnaa! The brahman, truth, sacrifices and the worlds are established in forgiveness. How can someone like me give up something like that? Those who perform sacrifices enjoy their worlds, and those who forgive enjoy other worlds.'

क्षन्तव्यमेव सततं पुरुषेण विजानता ।
यदा हि क्षमते सर्वं ब्रह्म संपद्यते तदा ॥ (41)

'A man with knowledge must always forgive. Whoever forgives everything attains the brahman. This world belongs to those who forgive.'

क्षमावतामयं लोकः परश्चैव क्षमावताम् ।
इह संमानमृच्छन्ति परत्र च शुभां गतिम् ॥ (42)

'This world is for those who forgive and the next world is for those who forgive too. They are honoured here and attain an auspicious destination in the hereafter.'

येषां मन्युर्मनुष्याणां क्षमया निहतः सदा ।
तेषां परतरे लोकास्तस्मात्क्षान्तिः परा मता ॥ (43)

'Men who always destroy their rage and intolerance through forgiveness obtain the supreme worlds in the hereafter. Therefore, forgiveness is considered supreme.'

इति गीताः काश्यपेन गाथा नित्यं क्षमावताम् ।
श्रुत्वा गाथाः क्षमायास्त्वं तुष्य द्रौपदि मा क्रुधः ॥ (44)

'In praise of those who are always forgiving, Kashyapa sang this chant. O Droupadi! Now that you have heard this chant about forgiveness, do not be angered and be content.'

पितामहः शांतनवः शमं संपूजयिष्यति ।
आचार्यो विदुरः क्षत्ता शममेव वदिष्यतः ।
कृपश्च संजयश्चैव शममेव वदिष्यतः ॥ (45)

'Our grandfather,[5] Shantanu's son, always worships peace. The Acharya[6] and Kshatta Vidura also speak about peace. Kripa and Sanjaya speak about peace too.'

सोमदत्तो युयुत्सुश्च द्रोणपुत्रस्तथैव च ।
पितामहश्च नो व्यासः शमं वदति नित्यशः ॥ (46)

'Somadatta, Yuyutsu, Drona's son[7] and our grandfather Vyasa always speak about peace.'

एतैर्हि राजा नियतं चोद्यमानः शमं प्रति ।
राज्यं दातेति मे बुद्धिर्न चेल्लोभानशिष्यति ॥ (47)

---

[5]Bhishma.
[6]Drona.
[7]Ashvatthama.

'Always urged by them towards being forgiving, I think the King[8] will return the kingdom. If he does not return the kingdom to me because of avarice, I think he will be destroyed.'

कालोऽयं दारुण: प्राप्तो भरतानामभूतये ।
निश्चितं मे सदैवैतत्पुरस्तादपि भामिनि ॥ (48)

'A terrible time has arrived. It will lead to the destruction of the Bharatas.[9] O Beautiful One! I am certain that this has been decreed by destiny earlier.'

सुयोधनो नार्हतीति क्षमामेवं न विन्दति ।
अर्हस्तस्याहमित्येव तस्मान्मां विन्दते क्षमा ॥ (49)

'Suyodhana is undeserving of forgiveness and, therefore, he finds none. I deserve it and, therefore, forgiveness has possessed me.'

एतदात्मवतां वृत्तमेष धर्म: सनातन: ।
क्षमा चैवानृशंस्यं च तत्कर्तास्म्यहमञ्जसा ॥ (50)

'Forgiveness and lack of cruelty are eternal dharma and the conduct of those who have control over their own selves. Therefore, that is the way I will act.'

Thus ends the Kashyapa Gita.

---

[8]Duryodhana.
[9]King Bharata, the son of Dushyanta and Shakuntala, was a common ancestor of both the Kouravas and the Pandavas. Therefore, both the Kouravas and the Pandavas are known as Bharatas, and, in the course of the Kurukshetra War, there was great destruction on both sides.

3

DHARMA VYADHA GITA

In Aranyaka Parva, there is a sub-parva known as Markandeya Samasya Parva. This contains a long conversation between the Pandavas and Sage Markandeya. The word *'samasya'* means the completion or filling up of that which is incomplete. In the course of this conversation, Markandeya tells the Pandavas about a hunter (*vyadha*) who follows dharma called Dharma Vyadha, which gives the Gita its name. Dharma Vyadha Gita has ten chapters, with 412 shlokas. This is an important Gita, because it tells us about the dharma followed by a householder, in this case, a hunter. It tells us about the importance of following one's own dharma. A householder ends up teaching an ascetic about the true meaning of dharma. While the Bhagavat Gita mentions *svadharma*, acting in accordance with one's own dharma (3.35, 18.47), given the context, it does not have much that is directly about an average householder, as opposed to kshatriyas fighting on the battlefield. In the Dharma Vyadha Gita, a hunter, abhorred and criticized for violence, instructs the learned sage Koushika about following svadharma.

Chapter 1

मार्कण्डेय उवाच
कश्चिद्द्विजातिप्रवरो वेदाध्यायी तपोधनः ।
तपस्वी धर्मशीलश्च कौशिको नाम भारत ॥ (1)

Markandeya said, 'O Descendant of the Bharata Lineage! There was a foremost among dvijas by the name of Koushika. He studied the Vedas and was rich in austerities. He was an ascetic and followed dharma in his conduct.'

साङ्गोपनिषदान्वेदानधीते द्विजसत्तमः ।
स वृक्षमूले कस्मिंश्चिद्वेदानुच्चारयन्स्थितः ॥ (2)

'That supreme among dvijas studied the Vedas, together with the Angas and the Upanishads.[1] One day, he was seated under a tree and was reciting the Vedas.'

उपरिष्टाच्च वृक्षस्य बलाका संन्यलीयत ।
तया पुरीषमुत्सृष्टं ब्राह्मणस्य तदोपरि ॥ (3)

'A female crane was perched on the tree. At that time, it released some excrement on top of the brahmana.'

तामवेक्ष्य ततः क्रुद्धः समपध्यायत द्विजः ।
भृशं क्रोधाभिभूतेन बलाका सा निरीक्षिता ॥ (4)

'The dvija was angered. Overcome by terrible anger, he glanced at the crane, and, struck by the gaze, it fell to the ground.'

अपध्याता च विप्रेण न्यपतद्धसुधातले ।
बलाकां पतितां दृष्ट्वा गतसत्त्वामचेतनाम् ।
कारुण्यादभिसंतप्तः पर्यशोचत तां द्विजः ॥ (5)

---

[1] The Angas mean the six Vedangas of *shiksha* (articulation and pronunciation), *chhanda* (prosody), *vyakarana* (grammar), *nirukta* (etymology), *jyotisha* (astronomy) and *kalpa* (rituals).

'On seeing that the crane had fallen down on the ground, struck by his gaze and bereft of its senses, the brahmana was tormented by compassion and grieved.'

अकार्यं कृतवानस्मि रागद्वेषबलात्कृतः ।
इत्युक्त्वा बहुशो विद्वान्ग्रामं भैक्षाय संश्रितः ॥ (6)

'"Overcome by the force of rage and hatred, I have done what I should not have done." Uttering these words several times, the learned one went to a village to beg for alms.'

ग्रामे शुचीनि प्रचरन्कुलानि भरतर्षभ ।
प्रविष्टस्तत्कुलं यत्र पूर्वं चरितवांस्तु सः ॥ (7)

'O Bull of the Bharata Lineage! He wandered around the pure households that were in the village. Roaming around, he entered a household that he had visited before.'

देहीति याचमानो वै तिष्ठेत्युक्तः स्त्रिया ततः ।
शौचं तु यावत्कुरुते भाजनस्य कुटुम्बिनी ॥ (8)
एतस्मिन्नन्तरे राजन्क्षुधासंपीडितो भृशम् ।
भर्ता प्रविष्टः सहसा तस्या भरतसत्तम ॥ (9)

'He said, "Please give to one who seeks." And the lady replied, "Wait." O King! O Supreme among the Bharata Lineage! While the housewife was cleaning the vessel, her husband suddenly returned and entered, suffering from great hunger.'

सा तु दृष्ट्वा पतिं साध्वी ब्राह्मणं व्यपहाय तम् ।
पाद्यमाचमनीयं च ददौ भर्त्रे तथासनम् ॥ (10)

'On seeing her husband, the virtuous lady neglected the brahmana. She gave her husband water for washing the feet and rinsing the mouth, and a seat.'

प्रह्वा पर्यचरच्चापि भर्तारमसितेक्षणा ।
आहारेणाथ भक्ष्यैश्च वाक्यैः सुमधुरैस्तथा ॥ (11)

'The dark-eyed one first waited on her husband. She gave him tasty food to eat and addressed him with extremely sweet words.'

उच्छिष्टं भुञ्जते भर्तुः सा तु नित्यं युधिष्ठिर ।
दैवतं च पतिं मेने भर्तुश्चित्तानुसारिणी ॥ (12)

'O Yudhishthira! She always ate food that had been left over by her husband. Always following her husband's inclinations, she thought her husband to be divine.'

न कर्मणा न मनसा नात्यश्नान्नापि चापिबत् ।
तं सर्वभावोपगता पतिशुश्रूषणे रता ॥ (13)

'In deeds, thoughts, eating, drinking or any other way, all her sentiments were devoted to serving her husband.'

साध्वाचारा शुचिर्दक्षा कुटुम्बस्य हितैषिणी ।
भर्तुश्चापि हितं यत्तत्सततं सानुवर्तते ॥ (14)

'She was virtuous in conduct, pure and accomplished, striving for the welfare of the household. She always followed that which would ensure her husband's welfare.'

देवतातिथिभृत्यानां श्वश्रूश्वशुरयोस्तथा ।
शुश्रूषणपरा नित्यं सततं संयतेन्द्रिया ॥ (15)

'She always served devas, *atithi*s,[2] servants, her father-in-law and mother-in-law. She was always in control of her senses.'

सा ब्राह्मणं तदा दृष्ट्वा संस्थितं भैक्षकाङ्क्षिणम् ।
कुर्वती पतिशुश्रूषां सस्मारार्थ शुभेक्षणा ॥ (16)

'While the one with the auspicious eyes was thus tending to her husband, she remembered the brahmana was standing there, desiring alms.'

---

[2] The word 'atithi' used here signifies more than an ordinary guest. Atithi = *a* + *tithi*, 'tithi' being a lunar day. There are those who are expected to eat on a given tithi. They are known and expected guests. An expected guest is not an atithi—an atithi is an unexpected guest. A householder eats only after such unexpected atithis have been fed.

व्रीडिता साभवत्साध्वी तदा भरतसत्तम ।
भिक्षामादाय विप्राय निर्जगाम यशस्विनी ॥ (17)

'O Supreme among the Bharata Lineage! The virtuous lady was ashamed. The illustrious one emerged, bringing alms for the brahmana.'

ब्राह्मण उवाच

किमिदं भवति त्वं मां तिष्ठेत्युक्त्वा वराङ्गने ।
उपरोधं कृतवती न विसर्जितवत्यसि ॥ (18)

'The brahmana said, "O One with the Beautiful Limbs! What is this? You asked me to wait. Having requested me, you did not release me."'

मार्कण्डेय उवाच

ब्राह्मणं क्रोधसंतप्तं ज्वलन्तमिव तेजसा ।
दृष्ट्वा साध्वी मनुष्येन्द्र सान्त्वपूर्वं वचोऽब्रवीत् ॥ (19)

Markandeya continued, 'O Indra among Men! On seeing that the brahmana was burning with rage and seemingly blazing with energy, the virtuous lady pacified him and spoke these words.'

क्षन्तुमर्हसि मे विप्र भर्ता मे दैवतं महत् ।
स चापि क्षुधितः श्रान्तः प्राप्तः शुश्रूषितो मया ॥ (20)

'"O Brahmana! You should pardon me. My husband is my greatest divinity. He had returned hungry and exhausted, and I served him."'

ब्राह्मण उवाच

ब्राह्मणा न गरीयांसो गरीयांस्ते पतिः कृतः ।
गृहस्थधर्मे वर्तन्ती ब्राह्मणानवमन्यसे ॥ (21)

'The brahmana replied, "Brahmanas are not superior and you have made your husband superior.[3] While following the dharma of a householder, you are showing disrespect to a brahmana."'

---

[3] Through her action, she has indicated that she takes her husband to be superior to brahmanas.

इन्द्रोऽप्येषां प्रणमते किं पुनर्मानुषा भुवि ।
अवलिप्ते न जानीषे वृद्धानां न श्रुतं त्वया ।
ब्राह्मणा ह्यग्निसदृशा दहेयुः पृथिवीमपि ॥ (22)

'"Even Indra bows down to such a person, not to speak of men on earth. O Proud One! Do you not know and have you not heard from the elders? A brahmana is like a fire and can even burn down the earth."'

स्त्र्युवाच

नावजानाम्यहं विप्रान्देवैस्तुल्यान्मनस्विनः ।
अपराधमिमं विप्र क्षन्तुमर्हसि मेऽनघ ॥ (23)

'The lady replied, "I have not shown disrespect to brahmanas. They are spirited and are equals of devas. O Brahmana! O Unblemished One! You should pardon my transgression."'

जानामि तेजो विप्राणां महाभाग्यं च धीमताम् ।
अपेयः सागरः क्रोधात्कृतो हि लवणोदकः ॥ (24)

'"I know the energy of immensely fortunate and intelligent brahmanas. In their anger, they made the waters of the ocean salty and undrinkable."'[4]

तथैव दीप्ततपसां मुनीनां भावितात्मनाम् ।
येषां क्रोधाग्निरद्यापि दण्डके नोपशाम्यति ॥ (25)

'"In that way, there are sages who are blazing ascetics and have cleansed their atmans. The fire of their anger has still not been pacified in Dandaka."'[5]

ब्राह्मणानां परिभवाद्व्रातापिश्च दुरात्मवान् ।
अगस्त्यमृषिमासाद्य जीर्णः क्रूरो महासुरः ॥ (26)

---

[4] Brihaspati had cursed the ocean to this effect.
[5] Dandaka was born into the Ikshvaku lineage. He coveted Bhargava's daughter and was cursed by Bhargava that his kingdom would become a wasteland. This is Dandaka Aranya or Dandaka forest.

'"Because he oppressed brahmanas, the evil-souled, cruel and great asura Vatapi was digested by Rishi Agastya."'[6]

प्रभावा बहवश्चापि श्रूयन्ते ब्रह्मवादिनाम् ।
क्रोध: सुविपुलो ब्रह्मन्प्रसादश्च महात्मनाम् ॥ (27)

'"I have heard a lot about the powers of those who speak about the brahman. O Brahmana! Their anger is extremely great. But so are the favours of those great-souled ones."'

अस्मिंस्त्वतिक्रमे ब्रह्मन्क्षन्तुमर्हसि मेऽनघ ।
पतिशुश्रूषया धर्मो य: स मे रोचते द्विज ॥ (28)

'"O Brahmana! O Unblemished One! You should pardon this transgression of mine. O Dvija! The dharma of serving my husband appeals to me."'

दैवतेष्वपि सर्वेषु भर्ता मे दैवतं परम् ।
अविशेषेण तस्याहं कुर्यां धर्मं द्विजोत्तम ॥ (29)

'"Among devas, my husband is the supreme divinity. O Supreme among Dvijas! I must particularly follow that dharma."'

शुश्रूषाया: फलं पश्य पत्युर्ब्राह्मण यादृशम् ।
बलाका हि त्वया दग्धा रोषात्तद्विदितं मम ॥ (30)

'"O Brahmana! Behold the fruits of serving my husband. It is known to me that you burnt down a crane through your anger."'

क्रोध: शत्रु: शरीरस्थो मनुष्याणां द्विजोत्तम ।
य: क्रोधमोहौ त्यजति तं देवा ब्राह्मणं विदु: ॥ (31)

'"O Supreme among Dvijas! Anger is an enemy that resides in the bodies of men. Devas know him to be a brahmana who has discarded delusion and anger."'

यो वदेदिह सत्यानि गुरुं सन्तोषयेत च ।
हिंसितश्च न हिंसेत तं देवा ब्राह्मणं विदु: ॥ (32)

---

[6] Agastya ate and digested Vatapi.

"'Devas know him to be a brahmana who speaks the truth in this world, satisfies his guru and is not violent even when he has been harmed.'"

जितेन्द्रियो धर्मपरः स्वाध्यायनिरतः शुचिः ।
कामक्रोधौ वशे यस्य तं देवा ब्राह्मणं विदुः ॥ (33)

"'Devas know him to be a brahmana who has conquered his senses, is devoted to dharma, is always engaged in studying, is pure and is in control of desire and anger.'"

यस्य चात्मसमो लोको धर्मज्ञस्य मनस्विनः ।
सर्वधर्मेषु च रतस्तं देवा ब्राह्मणं विदुः ॥ (34)

"'Devas know him to be a brahmana who looks upon the world as towards his own self, knows about dharma, is spirited and is devoted to all forms of dharma.'"

योऽध्यापयेदधीयीत यजेद्वा याजयीत वा ।
दद्याद्वापि यथाशक्ति तं देवा ब्राह्मणं विदुः ॥ (35)

"'Devas know him to be a brahmana who studies, teaches, sacrifices, officiates at the sacrifices of others and donates according to his capacity.'"

ब्रह्मचारी च वेदान्यो अधीयीत द्विजोत्तम ।
स्वाध्याये चाप्रमत्तो वै तं देवा ब्राह्मणं विदुः ॥ (36)

"'O Supreme among Dvijas! Devas know him to be a brahmana who is a *brahmachari*,[7] teaches the Vedas to others and is not distracted in the course of his self-studies.'"

यद्ब्राह्मणानां कुशलं तदेषां परिकीर्तयेत् ।
सत्यं तथा व्याहरतां नानृते रमते मनः ॥ (37)

"'What ensures the welfare of brahmanas has been recounted in this way—always speaking the truth, with the mind not rejoicing in falsehood.'"

---

[7] A person who follows the path of the brahman, sometimes understood as a person who follows celibacy or is a celibate student.

धनं तु ब्राह्मणस्याहुः स्वाध्यायं दममार्जवम् ।
इन्द्रियाणां निग्रहं च शाश्वतं द्विजसत्तम ।
सत्यार्जवे धर्ममाहुः परं धर्मविदो जनाः ॥ (38)

"'O Supreme among Dvijas! The eternal wealth of brahmanas is said to be in studying, self-control, uprightness and restraint of the senses. People who know dharma say that truth and uprightness are the supreme dharma.'"

दुर्ज्ञेयः शाश्वतो धर्मः स तु सत्ये प्रतिष्ठितः ।
श्रुतिप्रमाणो धर्मः स्यादिति वृद्धानुशासनम् ॥ (39)

"'While eternal dharma is difficult to fathom, it is based on truth. The injunctions of the aged are that the proof of dharma is in the Shrutis.'"

बहुधा दृश्यते धर्मः सूक्ष्म एव द्विजोत्तम ।
भवानपि च धर्मज्ञ स्वाध्यायनिरतः शुचिः ।
न तु तत्त्वेन भगवन्धर्मान्वेत्सीति मे मतिः ॥ (40)

"'O Supreme among Dvijas! Dharma can be seen in many ways and it is subtle. You also know dharma. You are devoted to studying and are pure. O Illustrious One! In my view, you do not know the true nature of dharma.'"

मातापितृभ्यां शुश्रूषुः सत्यवादी जितेन्द्रियः ।
मिथिलायां वसन्व्याधः स ते धर्मान्प्रवक्ष्यति ।
तत्र गच्छस्व भद्रं ते यथाकामं द्विजोत्तम ॥ (41)

"'There is a hunter who lives in Mithila. He serves his father and his mother. He is truthful and has conquered his senses. He will tell you about dharma. O Fortunate One! O Supreme among Dvijas! If you so wish, go there.'"

अत्युक्तमपि मे सर्वं क्षन्तुमर्हस्यनिन्दित ।
स्त्रियो ह्यवध्याः सर्वेषां ये धर्मविदुषो जनाः ॥ (42)

'"O Unblemished One! If I have spoken excessively, you should pardon me. All the ones who know dharma say that women must not be killed."'

ब्राह्मण उवाच

प्रीतोऽस्मि तव भद्रं ते गत: क्रोधश्च शोभने ।
उपालम्भस्त्वया ह्युक्तो मम नि:श्रेयसं परम् ।
स्वस्ति तेऽस्तु गमिष्यामि साधयिष्यामि शोभने ॥ (43)

'The brahmana replied, "O Fortunate One! O Beautiful One! I am pleased with you and my anger has gone. The reprimands uttered by you have been extremely beneficial for me. O Beautiful One! May you be fortunate. I will go and strive."'

मार्कण्डेय उवाच

तया विसृष्टो निर्गम्य स्वमेव भवनं ययौ ।
विनिन्दन्स द्विजोऽऽत्मानं कौशिको नरसत्तम ॥ (44)

Markandeya continued, 'O Supreme among Men! Having taken her leave, the dvija Koushika reprimanded himself and left for his own dwelling.'

Chapter 2

मार्कण्डेय उवाच

चिन्तयित्वा तदाश्चर्यं स्त्रिया प्रोक्तमशेषत: ।
विनिन्दन्स द्विजोऽऽत्मानमागस्कृत इवाबभौ ॥ (1)

Markandeya said, 'The dvija thought about all the extraordinary things the woman had told him. He censured himself, as if he had been guilty.'

चिन्तयान: स धर्मस्य सूक्ष्मां गतिमथाब्रवीत् ।
श्रद्दधानेन भाव्यं वै गच्छामि मिथिलामहम् ॥ (2)

'Then, thinking about the subtle course of dharma, he said, "I must have faith. I must go to Mithila."'

कृतात्मा धर्मवित्तस्यां व्याधो निवसते किल ।
तं गच्छाम्यहमद्यैव धर्मं प्रष्टुं तपोधनम् ॥ (3)

'"A hunter who knows dharma, one who has cleansed his atman, dwells there. I will go there today, and ask the one who is rich in austerities about dharma."'

इति संचिन्त्य मनसा श्रद्दधानः स्त्रिया वचः ।
बलाकाप्रत्ययेनासौ धर्म्यैश्च वचनैः शुभैः ।
संप्रतस्थे स मिथिलां कौतूहलसमन्वितः ॥ (4)

'Thus, he thought in his mind, trusting the lady's words, made certain by the auspicious one's words about dharma and her knowledge of the death of the crane. Filled with curiosity, he left for Mithila.'

अतिक्रामन्नरण्यानि ग्रामांश्च नगराणि च ।
ततो जगाम मिथिलां जनकेन सुरक्षिताम् ॥ (5)

'He passed through many forests, villages and cities and arrived in Mithila, protected extremely well by Janaka.'[8]

धर्मसेतुसमाकीर्णां यज्ञोत्सववतीं शुभाम् ।
गोपुराट्टालकवतीं गृहप्राकारशोभिताम् ॥ (6)

'It was an auspicious city, rich in sacrifices and festivals. It was full of *dharmasetu*s.[9] It was adorned with turrets, mansions, houses and ramparts.'

प्रविश्य स पुरीं रम्यां विमानैर्बहुभिर्वृताम् ।
पण्यैश्च बहुभिर्युक्तां सुविभक्तमहापथाम् ॥ (7)

---

[8] The king of Mithila, which was the capital of the kingdom of Videha. All kings of Videha were known as Janaka.
[9] Dharmasetus are religious institutions. The word 'setu' means an institution.

'He entered the beautiful city, surrounded by many *vimana*s.[10] There were many large roads, laid out well, lined with many wares.'

अश्वै रथैस्तथा नागैर्यानैश्च बहुभिर्वृताम् ।
हृष्टपुष्टजनाकीर्णां नित्योत्सवसमाकुलाम् ॥ (8)

'It was crowded with large numbers of horses, chariots, elephants and vehicles. It was full of people who were happy and well-fed. It was always full of festivities.'

सोऽपश्यद्बहुवृत्तान्तां ब्राह्मण: समतिक्रमन् ।
धर्मव्याधमपृच्छच्च स चास्य कथितो द्विजै: ॥ (9)

'As he passed, the brahmana saw many other things there. He asked about Dharma Vyadha and was told about him by dvijas.'

अपश्यत्तत्र गत्वा तं सूनामध्ये व्यवस्थितम् ।
मार्गमाहिषमांसानि विक्रीणन्तं तपस्विनम् ।
आकुलत्वात् क्रेतृणामेकान्ते संस्थितो द्विज: ॥ (10)

'He went there and saw the ascetic seated in the midst of a slaughterhouse. The ascetic was selling the meat of deer and buffaloes. It was crowded with a large number of buyers and the dvija waited.'

स तु ज्ञात्वा द्विजं प्राप्तं सहसा संभ्रमोत्थित: ।
आजगाम यतो विप्र: स्थित एकान्त आसने ॥ (11)

'On getting to know that the dvija had arrived, the hunter quickly arose and went to where the brahmana was standing alone.'

व्याध उवाच

अभिवादये त्वा भगवन्स्वागतं ते द्विजोत्तम ।
अहं व्याधस्तु भद्रं ते किं करोमि प्रशाधि माम् ॥ (12)

'The hunter said, "O Illustrious One! O Supreme among Dvijas! I salute you. Welcome. O Fortunate One! I am only a hunter. Tell me what I can do for you."'

---

[10]Vimana means a celestial vehicle as well as a palace or mansion.

एकपत्न्या यदुक्तोऽसि गच्छ त्वं मिथिलामिति ।
जानाम्येतदहं सर्वं यदर्थं त्वमिहागतः ॥ (13)

'"I know everything about the devoted wife telling you, 'Go to Mithila.' I know the reason why you have come here."'

मार्कण्डेय उवाच

श्रुत्वा तु तस्य तद्वाक्यं स विप्रो भृशहर्षितः ।
द्वितीयमिदमाश्चर्यमित्यचिन्तयत द्विजः ॥ (14)

Markandeya said, 'Hearing his words, the brahmana was extremely delighted. Second, the dvija thought that this was wonderful.'

अदेशस्थं हि ते स्थानमिति व्याधोऽब्रवीद्द्विजम् ।
गृहं गच्छाव भगवन्यदि रोचयसेऽनघ ॥ (15)

'The hunter told the dvija, "O Illustrious One! O Unblemished One! This place is not an appropriate place for you. If it pleases you, let us go home."'

बाढमित्येव संहृष्टो विप्रो वचनमब्रवीत् ।
अग्रतस्तु द्विजं कृत्वा स जगाम गृहान्प्रति ॥ (16)

'The brahmana was extremely delighted at these words and agreed. Making the dvija precede him, the hunter went towards his house.'

प्रविश्य च गृहं रम्यमासनेनाभिपूजितः ।
पाद्यमाचमनीयं च प्रतिगृह्य द्विजोत्तमः ॥ (17)

'On entering the house, he hounoured him and gave him a beautiful seat. The supreme among dvijas accepted the water offered for washing the feet and for rinsing the mouth.'

ततः सुखोपविष्टस्तं व्याधं वचनमब्रवीत् ।
कर्मैतद्वै न सदृशं भवतः प्रतिभाति मे ।
अनुतप्ये भृशं तात तव घोरेण कर्मणा ॥ (18)

'Once he was comfortably seated, he spoke these words to the hunter: "It seems to me that a task like this is not appropriate for you. O Son![11] I am extremely sorry that you have to perform this terrible task."

व्याध उवाच

कुलोचितमिदं कर्म पितृपैतामहं मम ।
वर्तमानस्य मे धर्मे स्वे मन्युं मा कृथा द्विज ॥ (19)

'The hunter replied, "This is the right occupation for my family, followed by my father and my grandfather. O Dvija! Do not be intolerant at me being engaged in my own dharma."'

धात्रा तु विहितं पूर्वं कर्म स्वं पालयाम्यहम् ।
प्रयत्नाच्च गुरू वृद्धौ शुश्रूषेऽहं द्विजोत्तम ॥ (20)

'"The creator has earlier decided that this should be my karma and I am performing it. O Supreme among Dvijas! I take care of and serve my aged gurus."'[12]

सत्यं वदे नाभ्यसूये यथाशक्ति ददामि च ।
देवातिथिभृत्यानामवशिष्टेन वर्तये ॥ (21)

'"I speak the truth. I do not envy. I donate according to my capacity. I live on what is left after offering to devas, atithis and servants."'

न कुत्सयाम्यहं किंचिन्न गर्हे बलवत्तरम् ।
कृतमन्वेति कर्तारं पुरा कर्म द्विजोत्तम ॥ (22)

'"I do not speak ill of anyone, nor do I censure someone more powerful. O Supreme among Dvijas! The karma performed earlier always follows the doer."'

कृषिगोरक्ष्यवाणिज्यमिह लोकस्य जीवनम् ।
दण्डनीतिस्त्रयी विद्या तेन लोका भवन्त्युत ॥ (23)

---

[11] The word used is *'tata'*. It means both son (and is also used for someone junior) and father (and is also used for someone senior). Here, it is used as 'son'.
[12] Gurus as in the parents, in this case.

'"In this world, the means of livelihood are agriculture, animal husbandry and trade. Governance and the three forms of knowledge also exist in this world."'[13]

कर्म शूद्रे कृषिर्वैश्ये संग्रामः क्षत्रिये स्मृतः ।
ब्रह्मचर्यं तपो मन्त्राः सत्यं च ब्राह्मणे सदा ॥ (24)

'"It has been said that tasks are for shudras, agriculture for vaishyas and fighting for kshatriyas. Brahmanas must always be engaged in brahmacharya, austerities, mantras and the truth."'

राजा प्रशास्ति धर्मेण स्वकर्मनिरताः प्रजाः ।
विकर्माणश्च ये केचितान्युनक्ति स्वकर्मसु ॥ (25)

'"A king governs in accordance with dharma and subjects are engaged in their own tasks. He must redirect those who are engaged in contrary tasks to their own tasks."'

भेतव्यं हि सदा राज्ञां प्रजानामधिपा हि ते ।
मारयन्ति विकर्मस्थं लुब्धा मृगमिवेषुभिः ॥ (26)

'"The king is the lord and must always be feared by the subjects. He must kill those who are engaged in contrary tasks, like a greedy deer is killed with arrows."'

जनकस्येह विप्रर्षे विकर्मस्थो न विद्यते ।
स्वकर्मनिरता वर्णाश्चत्वारोऽपि द्विजोत्तम ॥ (27)

'"O Brahmana Rishi! O Supreme among Dvijas! Under Janaka, there is no one who performs contrary tasks. All the four varnas are engaged in their own tasks."'

स एष जनको राजा दुर्वृत्तमपि चेत्सुतम् ।
दण्ड्यं दण्डे निक्षिपति तथा न ग्लाति धार्मिकम् ॥ (28)

---

[13] The three forms of knowledge are the first three Vedas, excluding Atharva Veda. The text uses the expression '*danda niti*', which can loosely be translated as governance, the policy for punishment.

'"King Janaka is such that even if his son was to be evil in conduct, he would chastise him with the rod. But he does not cause suffering to those who follow dharma."'

सुयुक्तचारो नृपतिः सर्वं धर्मेण पश्यति ।
श्रीश्च राज्यं च दण्डश्च क्षत्रियाणां द्विजोत्तम ॥ (29)

'"Using spies well, the King sees that there is dharma everywhere. O Supreme among Dvijas! Prosperity, the kingdom and punishment belong to kshatriyas."'

राजानो हि स्वधर्मेण श्रियमिच्छन्ति भूयसीम् ।
सर्वेषामेव वर्णानां त्राता राजा भवत्युत ॥ (30)

'"Through following their own dharma, kings can wish for great prosperity. For all the varnas, the king is the saviour."'

परेण हि हतान्ब्रह्मन्वराहमहिषानहम् ।
न स्वयं हन्मि विप्रर्षे विक्रीणामि सदा त्वहम् ॥ (31)

'"O Brahmana! I sell boars and buffaloes that have been killed by others. O Brahmana Rishi! I do not kill them myself, but always sell them."'

न भक्षयामि मांसानि ऋतुगामी तथा ह्यहम् ।
सदोपवासी च तथा नक्तभोजी तथा द्विज ॥ (32)

'"I do not eat flesh. I lie with my wife during her season. O Dvija! I always fast during the day and eat at night."'

अशीलश्चापि पुरुषो भूत्वा भवति शीलवान् ।
प्राणिहिंसारतश्चापि भवते धार्मिकः पुनः ॥ (33)

"A person born into ill conduct may become a person with good conduct. Even if born as someone who causes violence to animals, he may follow dharma."

व्यभिचारान्नरेन्द्राणां धर्मः संकीर्यते महान् ।
अधर्मो वर्धते चापि संकीर्यन्ते तथा प्रजाः ॥ (34)

'"The deviations of Indras among men can cause great decay in dharma. Then, adharma increases and subjects decay."'

उरुण्डा वामना: कुब्जा: स्थूलशीर्षास्तथैव च ।
क्लीबाश्चान्धाश्च जायन्ते बधिरा लम्बचूचुका: ।
पार्थिवानामधर्मत्वात्प्रजानामभव: सदा ॥ (35)

'"Those who are stunted, dwarfs and hunchbacked, those with large heads, eunuchs, the blind and the deaf, and those with elongated nipples are born then. Because of the adharma practised by kings, subjects always endure hardships.'

स एष राजा जनक: सर्वं धर्मेण पश्यति ।
अनुगृह्णन्प्रजा: सर्वा: स्वधर्मनिरता: सदा ॥ (36)

'"But King Janaka is one who looks at everyone with eyes of dharma. He favours all subjects who are always devoted to their own dharma."'

ये चैव मां प्रशंसन्ति ये च निन्दन्ति मानवा: ।
सर्वान्सुपरिणीतेन कर्मणा तोषयाम्यहम् ॥ (37)

'"Whether men praise me or criticize me, I satisfy all of them with tasks that are performed well."'

ये जीवन्ति स्वधर्मेण संभुञ्जन्ते च पार्थिवा: ।
न किंचिदुपजीवन्ति दक्षा उत्थानशीलिन: ॥ (38)

'"Kings who enjoy and live their lives according to their own dharma, without depending on others for a livelihood, are accomplished and always rise."'

शक्त्यान्नदानं सततं तितिक्षा धर्मनित्यता ।
यथार्हं प्रतिपूजा च सर्वभूतेषु वै दया ।
त्यागान्नान्यत्र मर्त्यानां गुणास्तिष्ठन्ति पूरुषे ॥ (39)

'"Constant donation of food according to one's ability, forbearance, constant devotion to dharma, reverence towards those who deserve it, compassion towards all beings and renunciation—when these qualities exist, they, and nothing else, distinguish a man among mortals.'"

मृषावादं परिहरेत्कुर्यात्प्रियमयाचितः ।
न च कामान्न संरम्भान्न द्वेषाद्धर्ममुत्सृजेत् ॥ (40)

"'One should give up false speech and perform what is agreeable, even if not asked. One should not discard dharma out of desire, rashness or hatred.'"

प्रिये नातिभृशं हृष्येदप्रिये न च संज्वरेत् ।
न मुह्येदर्थकृच्छ्रेषु न च धर्मं परित्यजेत् ॥ (41)

"'One should not rejoice excessively at something agreeable, or be anxious at something disagreeable. One should not be deluded because of hardships over artha and abandon dharma.'"

कर्म चेत्किंचिदन्यत्स्यादितरन्न समाचरेत् ।
यत्कल्याणमभिध्यायेत्तत्रात्मानं नियोजयेत् ॥ (42)

"'If one commits a reprehensible act, one should not commit it again. One should engage oneself in what ensures welfare.'"

न पापं प्रति पापः स्यात्साधुरेव सदा भवेत् ।
आत्मनैव हतः पापो यः पापं कर्तुमिच्छति ॥ (43)

"'Evil should not be countered with evil. One should always be virtuous. A wicked person who wishes to commit an evil act destroys himself.'"

कर्म चौतदसाधूनां वृजिनानामसाधुवत् ।
न धर्मोऽस्तीति मन्वानाः शुचीनवहसन्ति ये ।
अश्रद्दधाना धर्मस्य ते नश्यन्ति न संशयः ॥ (44)

"'Deceitful deeds and acting like wicked people are not virtuous. Those who think there is dharma in this, those who laugh at purity and those who are disrespectful towards dharma—there is no doubt that they will be destroyed.'"

महादृतिरिवाध्मातः पापो भवति नित्यदा ।
मूढानामवलिप्तानामसारं भाषितं भवेत् ।
दर्शयत्यन्तरात्मानं दिवा रूपमिवांशुमान् ॥ (45)

"'A wicked person is always greatly inflated, like a bag full of air. Whenever a foolish person speaks, he is seen to have no substance. Like the sun reveals forms during the day, he reveals what is inside himself.'"

न लोके राजते मूर्खः केवलात्मप्रशंसया ।
अपि चेह मृजा हीनः कृतविद्यः प्रकाशते ॥ (46)

"'A fool only praises himself but cannot shine in this world. However, even if he has not performed ablutions, a learned one's radiance shines through.'

अब्रुवन्कस्यचिन्निन्दामात्मपूजामवर्णयन् ।
न कश्चिद्गुणसंपन्नः प्रकाशो भुवि दृश्यते ॥ (47)

"'He does not criticize anyone, nor does he describe himself as deserving of worship. A person who doesn't possess qualities is not seen to shine on earth.'"

विकर्मणा तप्यमानः पापाद्विपरिमुच्यते ।
नैतत्कुर्यां पुनरिति द्वितीयात्परिमुच्यते ॥ (48)

"'One who is tormented by perverse deeds is freed from those sins. If he avers that he will not commit it again, he is freed from a second sin.'"

कर्मणा येन तेनेह पापाद्विजवरोत्तम ।
एवं श्रुतिरियं ब्रह्मन्धर्मेषु परिदृश्यते ॥ (49)

"'O Foremost among Supreme Dvijas! One can also be freed from the sin through karma. O Brahmana! This is what can be seen in the Shrutis about dharma.'"

पापान्यबुद्ध्वेह पुरा कृतानि प्रागधर्मशीलो विनिहन्ति पश्चात् ।
धर्मो ब्रह्मनुदते पूरुषाणां यत्कुर्वते पापमिह प्रमादात् ॥ (50)

'"One who has ignorantly committed sins earlier can destroy them later by placing dharma at the forefront and being devoted to it. O Brahmana! Even if sins have been committed out of distraction, dharma can absolve men."'

पापं कृत्वा हि मन्येत नाहमस्मीति पूरुषः ।
चिकीर्षेदेव कल्याणं श्रद्दधानोऽनसूयकः ॥ (51)

'"After committing a sin, a person should think, 'I was not the man who committed it.' He should desire to do what is beneficial. He should be faithful and without malice."'

वसनस्येव छिद्राणि साधूनां विवृणोति यः ।
पापं चेत्पुरुषः कृत्वा कल्याणमभिपद्यते ।
मुच्यते सर्वपापेभ्यो महाभ्रैरिव चन्द्रमाः ॥ (52)

'"This is how virtuous people cover the holes in their garments. After committing a sin, a man can still obtain what is beneficial. He can be freed from all sins, like the moon from large clouds."'

यथादित्यः समुद्यन्वै तमः सर्वं व्यपोहति ।
एवं कल्याणमातिष्ठन्सर्वपापैः प्रमुच्यते ॥ (53)

'"Like the sun rises and dispels the darkness in every direction, establishment in what is beneficial ensures freedom from all sin."'

पापानां विद्ध्यधिष्ठानं लोभमेव द्विजोत्तम ।
लुब्धाः पापं व्यवस्यन्ति नरा नातिबहुश्रुताः ।
अधर्मा धर्मरूपेण तृणैः कूपा इवावृताः ॥ (54)

'"O Supreme among Dvijas! Know that avarice is the foundation of all wickedness. Men who are not too learned are goaded by avarice and resort to sin. Just as wells are covered by grass, evil ones cloak their adharma in the form of dharma."'

तेषां दमः पवित्राणि प्रलापा धर्मसंश्रिताः ।
सर्वं हि विद्यते तेषु शिष्टाचारः सुदुर्लभः ॥ (55)

'"Those who possess self-control, those whose conversation is pure, those who resort to dharma and those who exhibit virtuous conduct—everyone knows that these are difficult to find."'

मार्कण्डेय उवाच

स तु विप्रो महाप्राज्ञो धर्मव्याधमपृच्छत ।
शिष्टाचारं कथमहं विद्यामिति नरोत्तम ।
एतन्महामते व्याध प्रब्रवीहि यथातथम् ॥ (56)

Markandeya said, 'Then the immensely wise brahmana asked Dharma Vyadha, "O Best of Men! How will I know virtuous conduct? O Immensely Intelligent Hunter! Please tell me this exactly."'

व्याध उवाच

यज्ञो दानं तपो वेदाः सत्यं च द्विजसत्तम ।
पञ्चैतानि पवित्राणि शिष्टाचारेषु नित्यदा ॥ (57)

'The hunter replied, "O Best among Dvijas! Sacrifices, donations, austerities, the Vedas and truthfulness—these are the five sacred things that always characterize good conduct.

कामक्रोधौ वशे कृत्वा दम्भं लोभमनार्जवम् ।
धर्म इत्येव सन्तुष्टास्ते शिष्टाः शिष्टसंमताः ॥ (58)

'"Having controlled desire and anger, having discarded arrogance, greed and deceit, those who are satisfied with dharma become virtuous and are honoured by the virtuous."'

न तेषां विद्यतेऽवृत्तं यज्ञस्वाध्यायशीलिनाम् ।
आचारपालनं चैव द्वितीयं शिष्टलक्षणम् ॥ (59)

'"Those who perform sacrifices and are engaged in studying will never lack a means of livelihood. They follow good conduct, and this is the second characteristic of those who are virtuous."'

गुरुशुश्रूषणं सत्यमक्रोधो दानमेव च ।
एतच्चतुष्टयं ब्रह्मञ्छिष्टाचारेषु नित्यदा ॥ (60)

"'O Brahmana! Serving gurus, truthfulness, lack of anger and donations—these four are always present in those who are virtuous.'"

शिष्टाचारे मन: कृत्वा प्रतिष्ठाप्य च सर्वश: ।
यामयं लभते तुष्टिं सा न शक्या ह्वतोऽन्यथा ॥ (61)

"'One can obtain satisfaction by fixing one's mind on virtuous conduct in every way. That confers contentment. It is impossible for it to be otherwise.'"

वेदस्योपनिषत्सत्यं सत्यस्योपनिषद्दम: ।
दमस्योपनिषत्त्याग: शिष्टाचारेषु नित्यदा ॥ (62)

"'The Vedas are established in truth. Truth is established in self-control. Self-control is established in renunciation. These always constitute virtuous conduct.'"

ये तु धर्ममसूयन्ते बुद्धिमोहान्विता नरा: ।
अपथा गच्छतां तेषामनुयातापि पीड्यते ॥ (63)

"'Men with deluded intelligence abuse dharma. They follow a path that should not be traversed and cause suffering.'"

ये तु शिष्टा: सुनियता: श्रुतित्यागपरायणा: ।
धर्म्यं पन्थानमारूढा: सत्यधर्मपरायणा: ॥ (64)

"'Both those who are virtuous, well-controlled, devoted to the Shrutis and those who renounce ascend onto the path of dharma and are devoted to truth and dharma.'"

नियच्छन्ति परां बुद्धिं शिष्टाचारान्विता नरा: ।
उपाध्यायमते युक्ता: स्थित्या धर्मार्थदर्शिन: ॥ (65)

"'They control the supreme intelligence. These are men who follow virtuous conduct. They are obedient to their preceptors. They base themselves on insight about dharma and artha.'"

नास्तिकान्भिन्नमर्यादान्क्रूरान्पापमतौ स्थितान् ।
त्यज तान्ज्ञानमाश्रित्य धार्मिकानुपसेव्य च ॥ (66)

'"Avoid non-believers. They transgress boundaries. They are cruel and are established in wicked intelligence. Avoid them. Resort to jnana and serve those who follow dharma."'

कामलोभग्रहाकीर्णां पञ्चेन्द्रियजलां नदीम् ।
नावं धृतिमयीं कृत्वा जन्मदुर्गाणि संतर ॥ (67)

'"Using the boat of fortitude, cross the impassable river that has the five senses as its waters and is infested with the crocodiles of desire and avarice and, thus, overcome birth."'[14]

क्रमेण संचितो धर्मो बुद्धियोगमयो महान् ।
शिष्टाचारे भवेत्साधू रागः शुक्लेव वाससि ॥ (68)

'"Dharma is gradually accumulated through yoga and great intelligence. It adorns those with virtuous conduct, like a good colour on a white garment."'

अहिंसा सत्यवचनं सर्वभूतहितं परम् ।
अहिंसा परमो धर्मः स च सत्ये प्रतिष्ठितः ।
सत्ये कृत्वा प्रतिष्ठां तु प्रवर्तन्ते प्रवृत्तयः ॥ (69)

'"Non-violence and truthfulness in speech ensure the greatest welfare for all beings. Non-violence is supreme dharma and it is established in truth. Truth provides the foundation, based on which such conduct flourishes."'

सत्यमेव गरीयस्तु शिष्टाचारनिषेवितम् ।
आचारश्च सतां धर्मः सन्तश्चाचारलक्षणाः ॥ (70)

'"Truth is supreme and is served by those who possess virtuous conduct. Dharma is the conduct of the virtuous, and the sign of the virtuous is in their conduct."'

यो यथाप्रकृतिर्जन्तुः स्वां स्वां प्रकृतिमश्नुते ।
पापात्मा क्रोधकामादीन्दोषानाप्नोत्यनात्मवान् ॥ (71)

---

[14] This indicates samsara.

'"Every being is bound by its own nature and has to enjoy its respective nature. An evil-souled person has no control over his own self and suffers from the sins of anger, desire and so on."'

आरम्भो न्याययुक्तो यः स हि धर्म इति स्मृतः ।
अनाचारस्त्वधर्मेति एतच्छिष्टानुशासनम् ॥ (72)

'"It has been said that dharma is that which has been begun according to good policy. The virtuous have instructed that bad conduct is adharma."'

अक्रुध्यन्तोऽनसूयन्तो निरहंकारमत्सराः ।
ऋजवः शमसंपन्नाः शिष्टाचारा भवन्ति ते ॥ (73)

'"Those not prone to anger, those who do not hate, those who are without ego, those who are without envy, those who are upright and full of serenity are characterized by good conduct."'

त्रैविद्यवृद्धाः शुचयो वृत्तवन्तो मनस्विनः ।
गुरुशुश्रूषवो दान्ताः शिष्टाचारा भवन्त्युत ॥ (74)

"Those who have aged with the three Vedas, those who are pure in behaviour and spirited and those who are controlled and serve their gurus, possess good conduct."'

तेषामदीनसत्त्वानां दुष्कराचारकर्मणाम् ।
स्वैः कर्मभिः सत्कृतानां घोरत्वं संप्रणश्यति ॥ (75)

'"It is extremely difficult to emulate the karma of those who don't lack in spirit. Through their own good karma, they destroy anything terrible."'

तं सदाचारमाश्चर्यं पुराणं शाश्वतं ध्रुवम् ।
धर्मं धर्मेण पश्यन्तः स्वर्गं यान्ति मनीषिणः ॥ (76)

'"That good conduct is wonderful, ancient, eternal and certain. This is dharma. Learned ones who use dharma to see in this way go to heaven."'

आस्तिका मानहीनाश्च द्विजातिजनपूजकाः ।
श्रुतवृत्तोपसंपन्नाः ते सन्तः स्वर्गगामिनः ॥ (77)

'"They are believers. They are devoid of pride. They worship those who are dvijas. Those virtuous ones possess learning and good conduct and go to heaven."'

वेदोक्तः परमो धर्मो धर्मशास्त्रेषु चापरः ।
शिष्टाचीर्णश्च शिष्टानां त्रिविधं धर्मलक्षणम् ॥ (78)

'"The dharma stated in the Vedas is supreme. The Dharmashastras are the second.[15] Good conduct of virtuous ones is another. These are the three signs of dharma."'

पारणं चापि विद्यानां तीर्थानामवगाहनम् ।
क्षमा सत्यार्जवं शौचं शिष्टाचारनिदर्शनम् ॥ (79)

'"The signs of good conduct are seen to be the accomplishment of knowledge, bathing in *tirthas*,[16] forbearance, truthfulness, uprightness and purity."'

सर्वभूतदयावन्तो अहिंसानिरताः सदा ।
परुषं न प्रभाषन्ते सदा सन्तो द्विजप्रियाः ॥ (80)

'"The virtuous are compassionate towards all beings, always practise non-violence, never utter harsh words and do what is agreeable to dvijas."'

शुभानामशुभानां च कर्मणां फलसंचये ।
विपाकमभिजानन्ति ते शिष्टाः शिष्टसंमताः ॥ (81)

'"Those who know about the accumulation of the fruits of auspicious and inauspicious karma are virtuous. They know about the consequences and are honoured by those who are virtuous."'

---

[15]The Dharmashastras are sacred texts that deal with customs, practices, law and ethical conduct. They belong to the Smriti tradition, that is, they have specific authors.
[16]Tirthas are places of pilgrimage, typically those where one descends into water.

न्यायोपेता गुणोपेताः सर्वलोकहितैषिणः ।
सन्तः स्वर्गजितः शुक्लाः संनिविष्टाश्च सत्पथे ॥ (82)

'"They follow good policy, possess qualities and desire the welfare of everyone. These virtuous and pure ones conquer heaven. They are firmly established on the path of virtue."'

दातारः संविभक्तारो दीनानुग्रहकारिणः ।
सर्वभूतदयावन्तस्ते शिष्टाः शिष्टसंमताः ॥ (83)

'"Those who donate, share, show favours to the dejected and are compassionate towards all beings are the virtuous. They are honoured by the virtuous."'

सर्वपूज्याः श्रुतधनास्तथैव च तपस्विनः ।
दाननित्याः सुखाँल्लोकानाप्नुवन्तीह च श्रियम् ॥ (84)

'"They are worshipped by everyone. They possess the wealth of learning and are ascetics. They always donate. They obtain happy worlds and prosperity in this world."'

पीडया च कलत्रस्य भृत्यानां च समाहिताः ।
अतिशक्त्या प्रयच्छन्ति सन्तः सद्भिः समागताः ॥ (85)

'"Even if their wives and servants suffer, virtuous ones control themselves, and give in excess of their capacity when good people arrive."'

लोकयात्रां च पश्यन्तो धर्मात्महितानि च ।
एवं सन्तो वर्तमाना एधन्ते शाश्वतीः समाः ॥ (86)

'"Even when they follow the ways of the world, they look at dharma and what is beneficial within their own selves. Such virtuous ones prosper for years that amount to eternity."'

अहिंसा सत्यवचनमानृशंस्यमथार्जवम् ।
अद्रोहो नातिमानश्च ह्रीस्तितिक्षा दमः शमः ॥ (87)
धीमन्तो धृतिमन्तश्च भूतानामनुकम्पकाः ।
अकामद्वेषसंयुक्तास्ते सन्तो लोकसत्कृताः ॥ (88)

"'Non-violence, truthfulness in speech, lack of cruelty, uprightness, absence of hatred, lack of excessive pride, modesty, forbearance, self-control, serenity, intelligence, fortitude, compassion towards all beings and the absence of desire and hatred characterize the virtuous, and they are honoured by the world.'"

त्रीण्येव तु पदान्याहुः सतां वृत्तमनुत्तमम् ।
न द्रुह्येच्चैव दद्याच्च सत्यं चैव सदा वदेत् ॥ (89)

"'It is said that three things single out the excellent trail of the virtuous—non-injury, compassion and constant truthfulness in speech.'"

सर्वत्र च दयावन्तः सन्तः करुणवेदिनः ।
गच्छन्तीह सुसंतुष्टा धर्म्यं पन्थानमुत्तमम् ।
शिष्टाचारा महात्मानो येषां धर्मः सुनिश्चितः ॥ (90)

"'The virtuous are those who are compassionate towards everyone. They feel pity. They obtain satisfaction in this world and traverse the supreme path of dharma. Those great-souled ones possess good conduct and have firmly established themselves in dharma.'"

अनसूया क्षमा शान्तिः संतोषः प्रियवादिता ।
कामक्रोधपरित्यागः शिष्टाचारनिषेवणम् ॥ (91)

"'They have no envy. They forgive. They are serene. They are satisfied. They speak pleasantly. They have discarded desire and anger. They follow the conduct of the good.'"

कर्मणा श्रुतसंपन्नं सतां मार्गमनुत्तमम् ।
शिष्टाचारं निषेवन्ते नित्यं धर्मेष्वतन्द्रिताः ॥ (92)

"'Their deeds are in accordance with the Shrutis. They follow the supreme path of the virtuous. They follow good conduct and are always devoted to dharma, never wavering.'"

प्रज्ञाप्रासादमारुह्य मुह्यतो महतो जनान् ।
प्रेक्षन्तो लोकवृत्तानि विविधानि द्विजोत्तम ।
अतिपुण्यानि पापानि तानि द्विजवरोत्तम ॥ (93)

"'They ascend to the mansion of wisdom and see the great masses who are deluded. O Supreme among Dvijas! O Foremost among the Best of Dvijas! They observe the world in all its different pursuits, the extremely sacred deeds, as well as the evil ones.'"

एतत्ते सर्वमाख्यातं यथाप्रज्ञं यथाश्रुतम् ।
शिष्टाचारगुणान्ब्रह्मन्पुरस्कृत्य द्विजर्षभ ॥ (94)

"'O Brahmana! O Bull among Dvijas! This is the entire account, as I have learnt it and as I have heard it, about the revered qualities and conduct of the virtuous.'"

Chapter 3

मार्कण्डेय उवाच

स तु विप्रमथोवाच धर्मव्याधो युधिष्ठिर ।
यदहं ह्याचरे कर्म घोरमेतदसंशयम् ॥ (1)

Markandeya said, 'O Yudhishthira! Thus did Dharma Vyadha speak to the brahmana. "There is no doubt that the deeds that I perform are terrible."'

विधिस्तु बलवान्ब्रह्मन्दुस्तरं हि पुराकृतम् ।
पुराकृतस्य पापस्य कर्मदोषो भवत्ययम् ।
दोषस्यैतस्य वै ब्रह्मन्विघाते यत्नवानहम् ॥ (2)

"'O Brahmana! But destiny is powerful. And it is impossible to overcome deeds committed earlier. The sins committed earlier are the taints of karma. O Brahmana! I have endeavoured to destroy this taint.'"

विधिना विहिते पूर्वं निमित्तं घातको भवेत् ।
निमित्तभूता हि वयं कर्मणोऽस्य द्विजोत्तम ॥ (3)

"'When destiny has already killed something earlier, the killer is only the instrument. O Supreme among Dvijas! We are only instruments of our karma.'"

येषां हतानां मांसानि विक्रीणामो वयं द्विज ।
तेषामपि भवेद्धर्म उपभोगेन भक्षणात् ।
देवतातिथिभृत्यानां पितृणां प्रतिपूजनात् ॥ (4)

'"O Dvija! We sell the meat of those who have been killed. It is only their dharma that they should be enjoyed and eaten so as to honour devas, atithis, servants and ancestors."

ओषध्यो वीरुधश्चापि पशवो मृगपक्षिण: ।
अन्नाद्यभूता लोकस्य इत्यपि श्रूयते श्रुति: ॥ (5)

'"It has been heard in the Shrutis that plants, creepers, animals, deer and birds are the decreed food for all beings."'[17]

आत्ममांसप्रदानेन शिबिरौशीनरो नृप: ।
स्वर्गं सुदुर्लभं प्राप्त: क्षमावान्द्विजसत्तम ॥ (6)

'"O Supreme among Dvijas! The compassionate king Shibi Aushinara obtained a heaven that is extremely difficult to attain by offering his own flesh."'[18]

राज्ञो महानसे पूर्वं रन्तिदेवस्य वै द्विज ।
द्वे सहस्रे तु वध्येते पशूनामन्वहं तदा ॥ (7)

'"O Dvija! Earlier, in King Rantideva's great kitchen, two thousand sacrificial animals were slaughtered every day."'[19]

समांसं ददतो ह्यन्नं रन्तिदेवस्य नित्यश: ।
अतुला कीर्तिरभवन्नृपस्य द्विजसत्तम ।
चातुर्मास्येषु पशवो वध्यन्त इति नित्यश: ॥ (8)

---

[17]While this translation is correct, the word '*pashu*' is used for a domestic sacrificial animal and '*mriga*' for a wild animal that is hunted.
[18]To save a dove from a hawk, King Shibi gave up some of his own flesh in exchange.
[19]Rantideva was a king of the Lunar dynasty, known for his generosity and the slaughter of animals as sacrifices. The river Charmanvati (Chambal) turned red with blood, and it is named after the hides of the sacrificed animals.

"'Rantideva always gave food with meat. O Supreme among Dvijas! The king's fame is unmatched. He always killed sacrificial animals at *chaturmasya*.'"[20]

अग्नयो मांसकामाश्च इत्यपि श्रूयते श्रुतिः ।
यज्ञेषु पशवो ब्रह्मन्वध्यन्ते सततं द्विजैः ।
संस्कृताः किल मन्त्रैश्च तेऽपि स्वर्गमवाप्नुवन् ॥ (9)

"'It has been heard in the Shrutis that fire desires meat. O Brahmana! Dvijas always kill animals at sacrifices. They[21] are purified through *mantra*s, and we have heard that they go to heaven.'"

यदि नैवाग्नयो ब्रह्मन्मांसकामाभवन्पुरा ।
भक्ष्यं नैव भवेन्मांसं कस्यचिद्द्विजसत्तम ॥ (10)

"'O Brahmana! O Supreme among Dvijas! If the fire had not desired meat earlier, who would have eaten it now?'"

अत्रापि विधिरुक्तश्च मुनिभिर्मांसभक्षणे ।
देवतानां पितॄणां च भुङ्क्ते दत्वा तु यः सदा ।
यथाविधि यथाश्रद्धं न स दुष्यति भक्षणात् ॥ (11)

"'Even now, sages have articulated rules on the eating of meat. "If a person always eats after offering to devas and ancestors, in accordance with the rules and with faith, no sin attaches to him from the act of eating."'"

अमांसाशी भवत्येवमित्यपि श्रूयते श्रुतिः ।
भार्यां गच्छन्ब्रह्मचारी ऋतौ भवति ब्राह्मणः ॥ (12)

"'It has been heard in the Shrutis that such a person is an equal of one who does not eat meat. A brahmana who has intercourse with his wife during her season is equal to a brahmachari.'"

---

[20] Seasonal festivals occurring every four months, during the months of Kartika, Phalguna and Ashada.
[21] The sacrificed animals.

सत्यानृते विनिश्चित्य अत्रापि विधिरुच्यते ।
सौदासेन पुरा राज्ञा मानुषा भक्षिता द्विज ।
शापाभिभूतेन भृशमत्र किं प्रतिभाति ते ॥ (13)

'"The rules that differentiate truth from falsehood are recited even now. O Dvija! In earlier times, King Soudasa ate humans. He had been overtaken by a terrible curse. How does that appear to you?"'

स्वधर्म इति कृत्वा तु न त्यजामि द्विजोत्तम ।
पुराकृतमिति ज्ञात्वा जीवाम्येतेन कर्मणा ॥ (14)

'"O Supreme among Dvijas! I do this according to my own dharma in this way and do not give it up. Knowing that this is due to my earlier deeds, I perform this task for my livelihood."'

स्वकर्म त्यजतो ब्रह्मन्नधर्म इह दृश्यते ।
स्वकर्मनिरतो यस्तु स धर्म इति निश्चयः ॥ (15)

'"O Brahmana! In this world, it is seen that it is adharma to give up one's own karma. It is certainly dharma to adhere to one's own karma."'

पूर्वं हि विहितं कर्म देहिनं न विमुञ्चति ।
धात्रा विधिरयं दृष्टो बहुधा कर्मनिर्णये ॥ (16)

'"Karma committed earlier never releases an embodied creature.[22] The creator's ordinances foresaw the determination of these many different forms of karma."'

द्रष्टव्यं तु भवेत्प्राज्ञ क्रूरे कर्मणि वर्तता ।
कथं कर्म शुभं कुर्यां कथं मुच्ये पराभवात् ।
कर्मणस्तस्य घोरस्य बहुधा निर्णयो भवेत् ॥ (17)
दाने च सत्यवाक्ये च गुरुशुश्रूषणे तथा ।
द्विजातिपूजने चाहं धर्मे च निरतः सदा ।
अतिवादातिमानाभ्यां निवृत्तोऽस्मि द्विजोत्तम ॥ (18)

---

[22] Karma follows a being into its next birth.

"'O Wise One! It must be examined how a person engaged in cruel karma can engage in auspicious karma, so that he becomes free from being overpowered. O Supreme among Dvijas! It has been determined that there are many ways of freeing oneself from terrible karma—donations, truthfulness in speech, service of gurus, worship of dvijas and refraining from excessive self-praise and pride. I have always devoted myself to this dharma.'"

कृषिं साध्विति मन्यन्ते तत्र हिंसा परा स्मृता ।
कर्षन्तो लाङ्गलै: पुंसो घ्नन्ति भूमिशयान्बहून् ।
जीवानन्यांश्च बहुशस्तत्र किं प्रतिभाति ते ॥ (19)

"'Agriculture is thought to be virtuous. But it has been said that there is great violence in it. Through tilling with the plough, men kill many beings that lie inside the ground and many other hundreds of beings. How does that appear to you?'"

धान्यबीजानि यान्याहुर्ब्रीह्यादीनि द्विजोत्तम ।
सर्वाण्येतानि जीवानि तत्र किं प्रतिभाति ते ॥ (20)

"'O Supreme among Dvijas! *Vrihi*[23] and other seeds of grains are all living organisms. How does that appear to you?'"

अध्याक्रम्य पशूंश्चापि घ्नन्ति वै भक्षयन्ति च ।
वृक्षानथौषधीश्चैव छिन्दन्ति पुरुषा द्विज ॥ (21)

"'O Dvija! Men hunt, kill and eat animals. They also cut trees and plants.'"

जीवा हि बहवो ब्रह्मन्वृक्षेषु च फलेषु च ।
उदके बहवश्चापि तत्र किं प्रतिभाति ते ॥ (22)

"'O Brahmana! There are many living beings in trees and fruit. There are many in water too. How does that appear to you?'"

सर्वं व्याप्तमिदं ब्रह्मन्प्राणिभि: प्राणिजीवनै: ।
मत्स्या ग्रसन्ते मत्स्यांश्च तत्र किं प्रतिभाति ते ॥ (23)

---

[23] A kind of rice.

"'O Brahmana! Everything is pervaded by living beings. There is life in living beings. Fish devour fish. How does that appear to you?'"

सत्त्वैः सत्त्वानि जीवन्ति बहुधा द्विजसत्तम ।
प्राणिनोऽन्योन्यभक्षाश्च तत्र किं प्रतिभाति ते ॥ (24)

"'O Supreme among Dvijas! Living beings live on other living beings in many ways. Living beings devour each other. How does that appear to you?'"

चङ्क्रम्यमाणा जीवांश्च धरणीसंश्रितान्बहून् ।
पद्भ्यां घ्नन्ति नरा विप्र तत्र किं प्रतिभाति ते ॥ (25)

"'O Brahmana! Through the mere act of walking, men trample with their feet and kill many beings that are on the ground. How does that appear to you?'"

उपविष्टाः शयानाश्च घ्नन्ति जीवाननेकशः ।
ज्ञानविज्ञानवन्तश्च तत्र किं प्रतिभाति ते ॥ (26)

"'Even those who possess jnana and vijnana kill many beings when they are seated or lying down. How does that appear to you?'"

जीवैर्ग्रस्तमिदं सर्वमाकाशं पृथिवी तथा ।
अविज्ञानाच्च हिंसन्ति तत्र किं प्रतिभाति ते ॥ (27)

"'The entire earth and the sky are full of living beings. One causes injury to them unknowingly. How does that appear to you?'"

अहिंसेति यदुक्तं हि पुरुषैर्विस्मितैः पुरा ।
के न हिंसन्ति जीवान्वै लोकेऽस्मिन्द्विजसत्तम ।
बहु संचिन्त्य इह वै नास्ति कश्चिदहिंसकः ॥ (28)

"'It is surprising that men in earlier times spoke of non-violence. O Supreme among Dvijas! In this world, who does not injure living beings? After thinking a lot about this, there is no one who does not cause violence.'"

अहिंसायां तु निरता यतयो द्विजसत्तम ।
कुर्वन्त्येव हि हिंसां ते यत्नादल्पतरा भवेत् ॥ (29)

"'O Supreme among Dvijas! Even ascetics who are devoted to non-violence cause violence, though their efforts make it less.'"

आलक्ष्याश्चैव पुरुषाः कुले जाता महागुणाः ।
महाघोराणि कर्माणि कृत्वा लज्जन्ति वै न च ॥ (30)

"'It can be seen that there are men who possess great qualities and who have been born in noble lineages. Nevertheless, they perform extremely terrible karma and are not ashamed.'"

सुहृदः सुहृदोऽन्यांश्च दुर्हृदश्चापि दुर्हृदः ।
सम्यक्प्रवृत्तान्पुरुषान्न सम्यगनुपश्यतः ॥ (31)

"'Well-wishers do not look kindly on well-wishers. Ill-wishers look kindly on ill-wishers. Men who are proper in conduct do not look kindly on those who are like them.'"

समृद्धैश्च न नन्दन्ति बान्धवा बान्धवैरपि ।
गुरूंश्चैव विनिन्दन्ति मूढाः पण्डितमानिनः ॥ (32)

"'Relatives are not delighted when relatives become prosperous. Foolish ones, priding themselves as learned, criticize gurus.'"

बहु लोके विपर्यस्तं दृश्यते द्विजसत्तम ।
धर्मयुक्तमधर्मं च तत्र किं प्रतिभाति ते ॥ (33)

"'O Supreme among Dvijas! There are many things in this world that are seen to be contrary. Dharma is laced with adharma. How does that appear to you?'"

वक्तुं बहुविधं शक्यं धर्माधर्मेषु कर्मसु ।
स्वकर्मनिरतो यो हि स यशः प्राप्नुयान्महत् ॥ (34)

"'It is possible to say many kinds of things about the dharma or adharma of karma. But he who is devoted to his own karma attains great fame.'"

Chapter 4

मार्कण्डेय उवाच
धर्मव्याधस्तु निपुणं पुनरेव युधिष्ठिर ।
विप्रर्षभमुवाचेदं सर्वधर्मभृतां वर: ॥ (1)

Markandeya said, 'O Yudhishthira! The accomplished Dharma Vyadha, supreme among those who uphold all forms of dharma, then again spoke to the brahmana rishi.'

श्रुतिप्रमाणो धर्मो हि वृद्धानामिति भाषितम् ।
सूक्ष्मा गतिर्हि धर्मस्य बहुशाखा ह्यनन्तिका ॥ (2)

'"The seniors have said that the proof of dharma is in the Shrutis. But the course of dharma is subtle. It has many branches and is infinite."'

प्राणात्यये विवाहे च वक्तव्यमनृतं भवेत् ।
अनृतं च भवेत्सत्यं सत्यं चैवानृतं भवेत् ॥ (3)

'"When life is at risk or at the time of marriage, one should utter a falsehood. Falsehood becomes truth, and truth becomes falsehood."'

यद्भूतहितमत्यन्तं तत्सत्यमिति धारणा ।
विपर्ययकृतोऽधर्म: पश्य धर्मस्य सूक्ष्मताम् ॥ (4)

'"Whatever ensures the welfare of beings is held to be the truth. Acting in a contrary way is adharma. Behold the subtlety of dharma."'

यत्करोत्यशुभं कर्म शुभं वा द्विजसत्तम ।
अवश्यं तत्समाप्नोति पुरुषो नात्र संशय: ॥ (5)

'"O Supreme among Dvijas! Whether a man performs auspicious deeds or inauspicious ones, there is no doubt that he certainly reaps the fruits."'

विषमां च दशां प्राप्य देवान्गर्हति वै भृशम् ।
आत्मनः कर्मदोषाणि न विजानात्यपण्डितः ॥ (6)

"A person who is not learned does not know the taints of his acts. On confronting a calamitous state, he censures devas severely."

मूढो नैकृतिकश्चापि चपलश्च द्विजोत्तम ।
सुखदुःखविपर्यासो यदा समुपपद्यते ।
नैनं प्रज्ञा सुनीतं वा त्रायते नैव पौरुषम् ॥ (7)

"O Supreme among Dvijas! Foolish, deceitful and fickle ones do not possess the wisdom, good policy or manliness to save themselves when their happiness or unhappiness happen to be reversed."

यो यमिच्छेद्यथा कामं तं तं कामं समश्नुयात् ।
यदि स्यादपराधीनं पुरुषस्य क्रियाफलम् ॥ (8)

"A man will obtain whatever he desires, as long as the fruits of his deeds and his desires are not dependent on anything else."

संयताश्चापि दक्षाश्च मतिमन्तश्च मानवाः ।
दृश्यन्ते निष्फलाः सन्तः प्रहीणाः सर्वकर्मभिः ॥ (9)

"Controlled, accomplished, intelligent and virtuous men can be seen to be obstructed and unsuccessful in all their tasks."

भूतानामपरः कश्चिद्धिंसायां सततोत्थितः ।
वञ्चनायां च लोकस्य स सुखेनेह जीवति ॥ (10)

"But there may be another who is always ready to injure another being. He deceives people. He lives happily in this world."

अचेष्टमानमासीनं श्रीः कंचिदुपतिष्ठति ।
कश्चित्कर्माणि कुर्वन्हि न प्राप्यमधिगच्छति ॥ (11)

"A person attains prosperity without even trying. In this world, there is another who undertakes karma and does not obtain what he strives for."

देवानिष्ट्वा तपस्तप्त्वा कृपणैः पुत्रगृद्धिभिः ।
दशमासधृता गर्भे जायन्ते कुलपांसनाः ॥ (12)

'"Tormented ones worship devas and torment themselves through austerities, desiring a son. After bearing for ten months in the womb, a stain on the lineage is born."'

अपरे धनधान्यैश्च भोगैश्च पितृसंचितैः ।
विपुलैरभिजायन्ते लब्धास्तैरेव मङ्गलैः ॥ (13)

'"Others enjoy the riches, grain and objects of pleasure accumulated in immense quantities by their fathers, obtained through auspicious means."'

कर्मजा हि मनुष्याणां रोगा नास्त्यत्र संशयः ।
आधिभिश्चैव बाध्यन्ते व्याधैः क्षुद्रमृगा इव ॥ (14)

'"There is no doubt that disease here is the result of earlier karma performed by men. Like small animals bound by hunters, ailments tie them down."'

ते चापि कुशलैर्वैद्यैर्निपुणैः संभृतौषधैः ।
व्याधयो विनिवार्यन्ते मृगा व्याधैरिव द्विज ॥ (15)

'"O Dvija! Just as hunters hunt deer, competent physicians who have skillfully accumulated medicines can keep ailments away."'

येषामस्ति च भोक्तव्यं ग्रहणीदोषपीडिताः ।
न शक्नुवन्ति ते भोक्तुं पश्य धर्मभृतां वर ॥ (16)

'"Those who have food to eat are afflicted by the evils of indigestion. O Supreme among Those Who Uphold Dharma! Behold. One is unable to eat."'

अपरे बाहुबलिनः क्लिश्यन्ते बहवो जनाः ।
दुःखेन चाधिगच्छन्ति भोजनं द्विजसत्तम ॥ (17)

'"O Supreme among Dvijas! There are many others with strength in their arms. They suffer because they can find food after misery."'

इति लोकमनाक्रन्दं मोहशोकपरिप्लुतम् ।
स्रोतसासकृदाक्षिप्तं ह्रियमाणं बलीयसा ॥ (18)

"'Thus the world is helplessly flooded with weeping, delusion and sorrow, repeatedly tossed and washed away by powerful currents.'"

न म्रियेयुर्न जीर्येयुः सर्वे स्युः सार्वकामिकाः ।
नाप्रियं प्रतिपश्येयुर्वशित्वं यदि वै भवेत् ॥ (19)

"'If everyone was master over everything, there would be no death and no decay. All objects of desire would be obtained and one would not see anything disagreeable.'"

उपर्युपरि लोकस्य सर्वो गन्तुं समीहते ।
यतते च यथाशक्ति न च तद्वर्तते तथा ॥ (20)

"'Everyone would obtain greatness in superior worlds. Even if a person tries according to capacity, it does not happen.'"

बहवः संप्रदृश्यन्ते तुल्यनक्षत्रमङ्गलाः ।
महच्च फलवैषम्यं दृश्यते कर्मसंधिषु ॥ (21)

"'There are many who are seen to be born under the same auspicious *nakshatra*.[24] But a great difference in fruits is seen because of the association with karma.'"

न कश्चिदीशते ब्रह्मन्स्वयंग्राहस्य सत्तम ।
कर्मणां प्राकृतानां वै इह सिद्धिः प्रदृश्यते ॥ (22)

"'O Brahmana! O Excellent One! No one can determine what he gets. In general, natural karma is seen to lead to siddhi in this world.'"

यथा श्रुतिरियं ब्रह्मञ्जीवः किल सनातनः ।
शरीरमध्रुवं लोके सर्वेषां प्राणिनामिह ॥ (23)

---

[24] A nakshatra is an asterism. It is not necessarily a star, since some nakshatras are constellations. Along the zodiac, there are twenty-seven, sometimes twenty-eight, nakshatras.

'"O Brahmana! It has been said in the Shrutis that the jivatman is certainly eternal, but the bodies of all living beings in this world are not permanent."'

वध्यमाने शरीरे तु देहनाशो भवत्युत ।
जीव: संक्रमतेऽन्यत्र कर्मबन्धनिबन्धन: ।। (24)

'"Therefore, when the body dies, only the body is destroyed. Fettered by the bonds of karma, the jivatman moves elsewhere."'

ब्राह्मण उवाच

कथं धर्मभृतां श्रेष्ठ जीवो भवति शाश्वत: ।
एतदिच्छाम्यहं ज्ञातुं तत्त्वेन वदतां वर ।। (25)

'The brahmana asked, "O Best among Those Who Uphold Dharma! O Supreme among Those Who Are Eloquent! In what way is the jivatman eternal? I wish to know about this in detail."'

व्याध उवाच

न जीवनाशोऽस्ति हि देहभेदे मिथ्यैतदाहुर्म्रियतेति मूढा: ।
जीवस्तु देहान्तरित: प्रयाति दशार्धतैवास्य शरीरभेद: ।। (26)

'The hunter replied, "The jivatman does not perish when the body is destroyed. Only foolish ones falsely aver that it dies. The jivatman leaves for another body. The five elements lead to a difference in the body."'

अन्यो हि नाश्नाति कृतं हि कर्म स एव कर्ता सुखदु:खभागी ।
यत्तेन किंचिद्धि कृतं हि कर्म तदश्नुते नास्ति कृतस्य नाश: ।। (27)

'"No one except the doer enjoys the karma. Resultant happiness and unhappiness are enjoyed by the doer alone. Any karma done must be enjoyed, what has been done is not destroyed."'

अपुण्यशीलाश्च भवन्ति पुण्या नरोत्तमा: पापकृतो भवन्ति ।
नरोऽनुयातस्त्विह कर्मभि: स्वैस्तत: समुत्पद्यति भावितस्तै: ।। (28)

'"Those who have been inauspicious in conduct can become pure. The best of men can become sinners. A man is always pursued by his own karmas. Determined by these, he is born again."'

ब्राह्मण उवाच

कथं संभवते योनौ कथं वा पुण्यपापयो: ।
जाती: पुण्या ह्यपुण्याश्च कथं गच्छति सत्तम ॥ (29)

'The brahmana asked, "O Excellent One! How does formation in the womb occur? How does one become virtuous or wicked? How is one born as auspicious or inauspicious?"'

व्याध उवाच

गर्भाधानसमायुक्तं कर्मेदं संप्रदृश्यते ।
समासेन तु ते क्षिप्रं प्रवक्ष्यामि द्विजोत्तम ॥ (30)

'The hunter replied, "It is seen that the act of conception is linked to karma. O Supreme among Dvijas! I will describe it to you quickly and briefly."'

यथा संभृतसंभार: पुनरेव प्रजायते ।
शुभकृच्छुभयोनीषु पापकृत्पापयोनिषु ॥ (31)

'"One is born again with the past accumulation, the auspicious in auspicious wombs and the evil in evil wombs."'

शुभै: प्रयोगैर्देवत्वं व्यामिश्रैर्मानुषो भवेत् ।
मोहनीयैर्विर्योनीषु त्वधोगामी च किल्बिषै: ॥ (32)

'"Through auspicious unions, one becomes a deva. Through mixed ones, one becomes human. Confounded because of unions with wrong species, one is tainted and descends."'[25]

जातिमृत्युजरादु:खै: सततं समभिद्रुत: ।
संसारे पच्यमानश्च दोषैरात्मकृतैर्नर: ॥ (33)

---

[25] That is, is born as inferior species.

"'It is because of the sins he performs that a man is cooked in samsara and always afflicted by birth, death, old age and miseries.'"

तिर्यग्योनिसहस्राणि गत्वा नरकमेव च ।
जीवाः संपरिवर्तन्ते कर्मबन्धनिबन्धनाः ॥ (34)

"'Tied by the bonds of earlier karma, beings wander through thousands of inferior births and even go to hell.'"

जन्तुस्तु कर्मभिस्तैस्तैः स्वकृतैः प्रेत्य दुःखितः ।
तदुःखप्रतिघातार्थमपुण्यां योनिमश्नुते ॥ (35)

"'Through the karma of one's own deeds, a being dies and suffers. To counter that earlier misery, it is born in an inauspicious womb.'"

ततः कर्म समादत्ते पुनरन्यन्नवं बहु ।
पच्यते तु पुनस्तेन भुक्त्वापथ्यमिवातुरः ॥ (36)

"'Then it again accumulates a large amount of new karma. It is cooked again, like a diseased person who has eaten unwholesome food.'"

अजस्रमेव दुःखार्तोऽदुःखितः सुखसंज्ञितः ।
ततोऽनिवृत्तबन्धत्वात्कर्मणामुदयादपि ।
परिक्रामति संसारे चक्रवद्बहुवेदनः ॥ (37)

"'Although it suffers innumerable miseries, it considers that unhappiness to have the signs of happiness. Therefore, the bonds are not loosened and a new karma arises again. Encircled by many miseries, it whirls around in samsara.'"

स चेन्निवृत्तबन्धस्तु विशुद्धश्चापि कर्मभिः ।
प्राप्नोति सुकृताँल्लोकान्यत्र गत्वा न शोचति ॥ (38)

"'By casting off those bonds of deeds and by undertaking pure karma, one can obtain the worlds of the virtuous, or go elsewhere, to a place where one does not grieve.'"

पापं कुर्वन्पापवृत्तः पापस्यान्तं न गच्छति ।
तस्मात्पुण्यं यतेत्कर्तुं वर्जयेत च पातकम् ॥ (39)

"'The sinful one who performs evil deeds never goes to where there is an end to sin. Therefore, one should perform auspicious deeds and avoid sin.'"

अनसूयु: कृतज्ञश्च कल्याणान्येव सेवते ।
सुखानि धर्ममर्थं च स्वर्गं च लभते नर: ॥ (40)

"'A man who is grateful and without malice, serving what is beneficial, obtains happiness, dharma, artha and heaven.'"

संस्कृतस्य हि दान्तस्य नियतस्य यतात्मन: ।
प्राज्ञस्यानन्तरा वृत्तिरिह लोके परत्र च ॥ (41)

"'The wise who strive to be clean, self-controlled and restrained and in control of themselves enjoy an unmatched existence in this world and in the next.'"

सतां धर्मेण वर्तेत क्रियां शिष्टवदाचरेत् ।
असंक्लेशेन लोकस्य वृत्तिं लिप्सेत वै द्विज ॥ (42)

"'Follow dharma; the virtuous conduct themselves and act in accordance with what is good. O Dvija! One should desire to adopt a conduct that does not cause hardships to people.'"

सन्ति ह्यागतविज्ञाना: शिष्टा: शास्त्रविचक्षणा: ।
स्वधर्मेण क्रिया लोके कर्मण: सोऽप्यसंकर: ॥ (43)

"'There are virtuous people who possess vijnana. They are good and accomplished in the sacred texts. In this world, they act in accordance with their own dharma, without mixing it up.'"

प्राज्ञो धर्मेण रमते धर्म चैवोपजीवति ।
तस्य धर्मादवाप्तेषु धनेषु द्विजसत्तम ।
तस्यैव सिञ्चते मूलं गुणान्पश्यति यत्र वै ॥ (44)

"'One who is wise finds pleasure in dharma. He lives his life on the basis of dharma. O Supreme among Dvijas! When he is rich in dharma, he sees its qualities and waters the roots.'"

धर्मात्मा भवति ह्येवं चित्तं चास्य प्रसीदति ।
स मैत्रजनसंतुष्ट इह प्रेत्य च नन्दति ॥ (45)

'"One with dharma in his atman is like this and his consciousness is pleased. He is satisfied with his friends. He finds delight here, and also after death."'

शब्दं स्पर्शं तथा रूपं गन्धानिष्टांश्च सत्तम ।
प्रभुत्वं लभते चापि धर्मस्यैतत्फलं विदुः ॥ (46)

'"O Excellent One! He obtains sound, touch, form and fragrance, as he wishes. He attains lordship. These are known to be the fruits of dharma."'

धर्मस्य च फलं लब्ध्वा न तृप्यति महाद्विज ।
अतृप्यमाणो निर्वेदमादत्ते ज्ञानचक्षुषा ॥ (47)

'"O Dvija! But having obtained the great fruits of dharma, he is not content. One who is dissatisfied uses the insight of jnana to become non-attached."'

प्रज्ञाचक्षुर्नर इह दोषं नैवानुरुध्यते ।
विरज्यति यथाकामं न च धर्मं विमुञ्चति ॥ (48)

'"With the eyes of wisdom, a man is not constrained by any sin. As he desires, he is radiant in dharma and becomes free."'

सर्वत्यागे च यतते दृष्ट्वा लोकं क्षयात्मकम् ।
ततो मोक्षे प्रयतते नानुपायादुपायतः ॥ (49)

'"Seeing that the world is naturally subject to decay, he renounces everything and strives for moksha,[26] using the right means and nothing else."'

एवं निर्वेदमादत्ते पापं कर्म जहाति च ।
धार्मिकश्चापि भवति मोक्षं च लभते परम् ॥ (50)

---

[26]Supreme liberation, freedom from samsara.

"'He, thus, gives up all evil deeds and obtains non-attachment. He is devoted to dharma and also obtains supreme moksha.'"

तपो निःश्रेयसं जन्तोस्तस्य मूलं शमो दमः ।
तेन सर्वानवाप्नोति कामान्यान्मनसेच्छति ॥ (51)

"'Austerities are the best course for beings and the foundation for that is tranquility and self-control. Through this, one can obtain everything that the mind desires.'"

इन्द्रियाणां निरोधेन सत्येन च दमेन च ।
ब्रह्मणः पदमाप्नोति यत्परं द्विजसत्तम ॥ (52)

"'O Supreme among Dvijas! Through restraining the senses, truthfulness and self-control, one obtains the supreme state of the brahman.'"

ब्राह्मण उवाच

इन्द्रियाणि तु यान्याहुः कानि तानि यतव्रत ।
निग्रहश्च कथं कार्यो निग्रहस्य च किं फलम् ॥ (53)

'The brahmana asked, "O One Who Is Firm in His Vows! What are spoken of as the senses? How can they be controlled and what are the fruits of this control?"'

कथं च फलमाप्नोति तेषां धर्मभृतां वर ।
एतदिच्छामि तत्त्वेन धर्म ज्ञातुं सुधार्मिक ॥ (54)

"'O Foremost among Those Who Uphold Dharma! What are the fruits obtained from this? O One Who Follows Dharma Well! I wish to know this truth about dharma.'"

Chapter 5

मार्कण्डेय उवाच

एवमुक्तस्तु विप्रेण धर्मव्याधो युधिष्ठिर ।
प्रत्युवाच यथा विप्रं तच्छृणुष्व नराधिप ॥ (1)

Markandeya said, 'O Yudhishthira! O Lord of Men! At these words of the brahmana, Dharma Vyadha replied to the brahmana. Listen to it.'

व्याध उवाच

विज्ञानार्थं मनुष्याणां मनः पूर्वं प्रवर्तते ।
तत्प्राप्य कामं भजते क्रोधं च द्विजसत्तम ॥ (२)

'The hunter replied, "O Supreme among Dvijas! The mind first operates in men and leads to perception. Because they have this, they serve desire and anger."'

ततस्तदर्थं यतते कर्म चारभते महत् ।
इष्टानां रूपगन्धानामभ्यासं च निषेवते ॥ (३)

'"For that purpose, they undertake great endeavours. They form the habit of serving the desired form and smell."'

ततो रागः प्रभवति द्वेषश्च तदनन्तरम् ।
ततो लोभः प्रभवति मोहश्च तदनन्तरम् ॥ (४)

'"Then comes attachment, and from this follows hatred. Avarice comes after that, followed by delusion."'

तस्य लोभाभिभूतस्य रागद्वेषहतस्य च ।
न धर्मे जायते बुद्धिर्व्याजाद्धर्मं करोति च ॥ (५)

'"When they are overwhelmed by avarice and battered by attachment and hatred, dharma is not generated in their intelligence. Instead, there is pretence about following dharma."'

व्याजेन चरते धर्ममर्थं व्याजेन रोचते ।
व्याजेन सिध्यमानेषु धनेषु द्विजसत्तम ।
तत्रैव रमते बुद्धिस्ततः पापं चिकीर्षति ॥ (६)

'"Dharma is practised in deceit. One finds pleasure in acquiring artha through deceit. O Supreme among Dvijas! One becomes successful in obtaining riches through deceit. Their intelligence finds pleasure in this, and evil becomes attractive."'

सुहृद्भिर्वार्यमाणश्च पण्डितैश्च द्विजोत्तम ।
उत्तरं श्रुतिसंबद्धं ब्रवीति श्रुतियोजितम् ॥ (7)

"'O Supreme among Dvijas! Well-wishers and learned ones urge for restraint. But one is ready with replies from the Shrutis and speaks of what is sanctioned by them.'"

अधर्मस्त्रिविधस्तस्य वर्धते रागदोषतः ।
पापं चिन्तयते चापि ब्रवीति च करोति च ॥ (8)

"'However, because of the faults of attachment, three kinds of adharma increase. There is sin in thought, speech and deed.'"

तस्याधर्मप्रवृत्तस्य गुणा नश्यन्ति साधवः ।
एकशीलाश्च मित्रत्वं भजन्ते पापकर्मिणः ॥ (9)

"'Flowing from addiction to adharma, all virtuous qualities are destroyed. Only those who are similar in conduct remain friends with such an evil-doer.'"

स तेनासुखमाप्नोति परत्र च विहन्यते ।
पापात्मा भवति ह्येवं धर्मलाभं तु मे शृणु ॥ (10)

"'As a consequence, unhappiness is reaped in this world and there is destruction in the next. All evil-souled ones are like this. Now hear from me about the gains from dharma.'"

यस्त्वेतान्प्रज्ञया दोषान्पूर्वमेवानुपश्यति ।
कुशलः सुखदुःखेषु साधूंश्चाप्युपसेवते ।
तस्य साधुसमारम्भाद्बुद्धिर्धर्मेषु जायते ॥ (11)

"'Through one's wisdom, one can foresee sins. One is skilful in differentiating happiness from unhappiness and consorts with virtuous people. By practising virtuous deeds, one's intelligence turns to dharma.'"

ब्राह्मण उवाच

ब्रवीषि सूनृतं धर्मं यस्य वक्ता न विद्यते ।
दिव्यप्रभावः सुमहानृषिरेव मतोऽसि मे ॥ (12)

'The brahmana said, "You have described the proper policy about dharma. There is no one else who can speak about it. It is my view that you are an extremely great rishi and your power is divine."'

व्याध उवाच

ब्राह्मणा वै महाभागाः पितरोऽग्रभुजः सदा ।
तेषां सर्वात्मना कार्यं प्रियं लोके मनीषिणा ॥ (13)

'The hunter replied, "The immensely fortunate brahmanas are always rendered offerings first, together with the ancestors. In this world, with all their hearts, learned ones do what is pleasing to them."'

यत्तेषां च प्रियं तत्ते वक्ष्यामि द्विजसत्तम ।
नमस्कृत्वा ब्राह्मणेभ्यो ब्राह्मीं विद्यां निबोध मे ॥ (14)

'"O Supreme among Dvijas! I will tell you what brings pleasure to them. After bowing in obeisance to brahmanas, I will tell you about the knowledge of the brahman. Listen to me."'

इदं विश्वं जगत्सर्वमजय्यं चापि सर्वशः ।
महाभूतात्मकं ब्रह्मान्नातः परतरं भवेत् ॥ (15)

'"O Brahmana! This entire universe, everything in this universe and everything that cannot be destroyed and the great elements have the brahman inside them. There is nothing beyond that."'

महाभूतानि खं वायुरग्निरापस्तथा च भूः ।
शब्दः स्पर्शश्च रूपं च रसो गन्धश्च तद्गुणाः ॥ (16)

'"The great elements are space, wind, fire, water and earth. Sound, touch, form, taste and smell are their qualities."'

तेषामपि गुणाः सर्वे गुणवृत्तिः परस्परम् ।
पूर्वपूर्वगुणाः सर्वे क्रमशो गुणिषु त्रिषु ॥ (17)

'"Each of these qualities has the attribute of following the preceding quality.[27] In due order, all of them follow the preceding qualities based on the three gunas."'

षष्ठस्तु चेतना नाम मन इत्यभिधीयते ।
सप्तमी तु भवेद्बुद्धिरहंकारस्तत: परम् ॥ (18)

'"It is said that the sixth quality is named consciousness, also called the mind. The seventh is intelligence, and *ahamkara*[28] follows that."'

इन्द्रियाणि च पञ्चैव रज: सत्त्वं तमस्तथा ।
इत्येष सप्तदशको राशिरव्यक्तसंज्ञक: ॥ (19)

'"There are five senses. There is sattva, rajas and tamas. These are the seventeen that constitute what is not manifest."'[29]

सर्वैरिहेन्द्रियार्थैस्तु व्यक्ताव्यक्तै: सुसंवृत: ।
चतुर्विंशक इत्येष व्यक्ताव्यक्तमयो गुण: ।
एतत्ते सर्वमाख्यातं किं भूयो श्रोतुमिच्छसि ॥ (20)

'"The manifest and the unmanifest are well-concealed within all the objects of the senses. Including the manifest and the unmanifest, there are twenty-four attributes.[30] I have told you everything. What else do you wish to hear?"'

---

[27] Space led to wind, wind led to fire, fire led to water and water led to earth. This is the sequence of creation, and the reverse is the sequence of dissolution. The quality of space is sound, the quality of wind is both touch and sound, the quality of fire is form, touch and sound and so on.
[28] Ahamkara is ego. Literally, it conveys the nuance of, 'I am the one who is doing.'
[29] The five elements, the five senses of perception, the five organs of action, the mind and intelligence.
[30] To the list of seventeen, one adds the five objects of the senses, ahamkara and the jivatman.

Chapter 6

मार्कण्डेय उवाच

एवमुक्तः स विप्रस्तु धर्मव्याधेन भारत ।
कथामकथयद्भूयो मनसः प्रीतिवर्धनीम् ॥ (1)

Markandeya said, 'O Descendant of the Bharata Lineage! This is what Dharma Vyadha told the brahmana, and the conversation between the two of them was pleasing to the mind.'

ब्राह्मण उवाच

महाभूतानि यान्याहुः पञ्च धर्मविदां वर ।
एकैकस्य गुणान्सम्यक्पञ्चानामपि मे वद ॥ (2)

'The brahmana said, "O Supreme among Those Who Know about Dharma! It is said that there are five great elements. Please tell me correctly about the qualities of these five."

व्याध उवाच

भूमिरापस्तथा ज्योतिर्वायुराकाशमेव च ।
गुणोत्तराणि सर्वाणि तेषां वक्ष्यामि ते गुणान् ॥ (3)

'The hunter answered, "Earth, water, fire, wind and space have separate qualities and I will tell you everything about their successive qualities."

भूमिः पञ्चगुणा ब्रह्मन्नुदकं च चतुर्गुणम् ।
गुणास्त्रयस्तेजसि च त्रयश्चाकाशवातयोः ॥ (4)

'"O Brahmana! Earth has five qualities, water has four qualities, fire has three qualities and wind and space together have three qualities."

शब्दः स्पर्शश्च रूपं च रसो गन्धश्च पञ्चमः ।
एते गुणाः पञ्च भूमेः सर्वेभ्यो गुणवत्तराः ॥ (5)

'"Sound, touch, form, taste and smell as the fifth—these are the five qualities of the earth, which has more qualities than the others."

शब्दः स्पर्शश्च रूपं च रसश्चापि द्विजोत्तम ।
अपामेते गुणा ब्रह्मन्कीर्तितास्तव सुव्रत ॥ (6)

'"O Supreme among Dvijas! O Brahmana! O One Who Is Firm in His Vows! Sound, touch, form and taste have been said to be the qualities of water."'

शब्दः स्पर्शश्च रूपं च तेजसोऽथ गुणास्त्रयः ।
शब्दः स्पर्शश्च वायौ तु शब्द आकाश एव च ॥ (7)

'"Sound, touch and form are the three qualities of fire. Sound and touch are the two qualities of air. Space only has sound."'

एते पञ्चदश ब्रह्मन्गुणा भूतेषु पञ्चसु ।
वर्तन्ते सर्वभूतेषु येषु लोकाः प्रतिष्ठिताः ।
अन्योन्यं नातिवर्तन्ते संपच्च भवति द्विज ॥ (8)

'"O Brahmana! Together, these fifteen qualities[31] exist in the five elements, and they are in all the beings who are established in the worlds. O Dvija! These five do not stand in opposition to one another, but exist in combination."'

यदा तु विषमीभावमाचरन्ति चराचराः ।
तदा देही देहमन्यं व्यतिरोहति कालतः ॥ (9)

'"However, when they are unbalanced in mobile and immobile objects, because of destiny, the atman moves from one body to another."'

आनुपूर्व्या विनश्यन्ति जायन्ते चानुपूर्वशः ।
तत्र तत्र हि दृश्यन्ते धातवः पाञ्चभौतिकाः ।
यैरावृतमिदं सर्वं जगत्स्थावरजङ्गमम् ॥ (10)

'"In due order, they are destroyed. They are created again in sequence. The five elements can be seen in everything, mobile and immobile, that this entire universe is encompassed by."'

---

[31] 5+4+3+2+1=15.

इन्द्रियैः सृज्यते यद्यत्तद्व्यक्तमिति स्मृतम् ।
अव्यक्तमिति विज्ञेयं लिङ्गग्राह्यमतीन्द्रियम् ॥ (11)

"'Whatever is created by the senses is known as the manifest. Whatever cannot be grasped by the senses is known to bear the signs of the unmanifest.'"

यथास्वं ग्राहकान्येषां शब्दादीनामिमानि तु ।
इन्द्रियाणि यदा देही धारयन्निह तप्यते ॥ (12)

"'Sound and others grasp an embodied being. Nurtured by the senses, he is tormented in this world.'"

लोके विततमात्मानं लोकं चात्मनि पश्यति ।
परावरज्ञः सक्तः सन्सर्वभूतानि पश्यति ॥ (13)

"'But if he can see the world extended in his atman and his atman extended in the world, he is then capable of seeing the superior and the inferior. Though still attached, he can see all beings.'"

पश्यतः सर्वभूतानि सर्वावस्थासु सर्वदा ।
ब्रह्मभूतस्य संयोगो नाशुभेनोपपद्यते ॥ (14)

"'He always sees all the elements in all their states. He is united with the brahman and never obtains that which is inauspicious.'"

ज्ञानमूलात्मकं क्लेशमतिवृत्तस्य मोहजम् ।
लोको बुद्धिप्रकाशेन ज्ञेयमार्गेण दृश्यते ॥ (15)

"'The envelope of difficulties resulting from delusion is overcome and the source of this is jnana about the atman. The world is illuminated with intelligence and the path of knowledge can be seen.'"

अनादिनिधनं जन्तुमात्मयोनिं सदाव्ययम् ।
अनौपम्यममूर्तं च भगवानाह बुद्धिमान् ।
तपोमूलमिदं सर्वं यन्मां विप्रानुपृच्छसि ॥ (16)

"'Intelligent ones have said that Bhagavan is an entity without a beginning and without an end. He creates himself and never decays. He is beyond comparison and is without manifestation. O

Brahmana! Everything that you have asked me has its foundation in austerities.'"

इन्द्रियाण्येव तत्सर्वं यत्स्वर्गनरकावुभौ ।
निगृहीतविसृष्टानि स्वर्गाय नरकाय च ॥ (17)

"'Everything about both heaven and hell is based on our senses. When restrained, they lead to heaven. When uncontrolled, they lead to hell.'"

एष योगविधि: कृत्स्नो यावदिन्द्रियधारणम् ।
एतन्मूलं हि तपस: कृत्स्नस्य नरकस्य च ॥ (18)

"'Everything in the mode of yoga is about the subjugation of the senses. This is the foundation for all austerities. It is also the root of hell.'"

इन्द्रियाणां प्रसङ्गेन दोषमृच्छत्यसंशयम् ।
संनियम्य तु तान्येव तत: सिद्धिमवाप्नुते ॥ (19)

"'By indulging in the senses, there is no doubt that one reaps sin. But by bringing them under control, one can obtain siddhi.'"

षण्णामात्मनि नित्यानामैश्वर्यं योऽधिगच्छति ।
न स पापै: कुतोऽनर्थैर्युज्यते विजितेन्द्रिय: ॥ (20)

"'If one controls these six[32] within one's self, one never suffers adversity and is not visited by sin. How can there be calamity when one has conquered the senses?'"

रथ: शरीरं पुरुषस्य दृष्टमात्मा नियन्तेन्द्रियाण्याहुरश्वान् ।
तैरप्रमत्त: कुशली सदश्वैर्दान्तै: सुखं याति रथीव धीर: ॥ (21)

"'It has been seen that a man's body is like a chariot. The senses have been spoken of as horses and the atman controls them. When these good horses are skilfully controlled, one is self-controlled and happy, like a steady charioteer.'"

---

[32] The mind and the five sense organs.

षण्णामात्मनि नित्यानामिन्द्रियाणां प्रमाथिनाम् ।
यो धीरो धारयेद्रश्मीन्स स्यात्परमसारथि: ॥ (22)

'"When the six horses of the senses are always controlled by the atman, one is like a supreme and steady charioteer, wielding the reins."'

इन्द्रियाणां प्रसृष्टानां हयानामिव वर्त्मसु ।
धृतिं कुर्वीत सारथ्ये धृत्या तानि जयेद्ध्रुवम् ॥ (23)

'"When the senses are uncontrolled, like horses along a road, the charioteer must steadily rein them in, and it is certain that victory will be achieved."'

इन्द्रियाणां हि चरतां यन्मनोऽनुविधीयते ।
तदस्य हरते बुद्धिं नावं वायुरिवाम्भसि ॥ (24)

'"But if the mind follows these senses, running wild, one loses one's intelligence, like a boat tossed on water by the wind."'[33]

येषु विप्रतिपद्यन्ते षट्सु मोहात्फलागमे ।
तेष्वध्यवसिताध्यायी विन्दते ध्यानजं फलम् ॥ (25)

'"O Brahmana! However, one who perseveres steadily on these six and is not deluded about obtaining fruits, meditating on the insight of learning, reaps fruits that are the outcome of dhyana."'

Chapter 7

मार्कण्डेय उवाच

एवं तु सूक्ष्मे कथिते धर्मव्याधेन भारत ।
ब्राह्मण: स पुन: सूक्ष्मं पप्रच्छ सुसमाहित: ॥ (1)

Markandeya said, 'O Descendant of the Bharata Lineage! Dharma Vyadha spoke about these subtle matters. Extremely attentively, the brahmana again asked him about a subtle matter.'

---

[33]This is almost identical to Bhagavat Gita 2.67.

ब्राह्मण उवाच

सत्त्वस्य रजसश्चैव तमसश्च यथातथम् ।
गुणांस्तत्त्वेन मे ब्रूहि यथावदिह पृच्छत: ॥ (2)

'The brahmana said, "Now please tell me exactly about the gunas of sattva, rajas and tamas. Please tell me accurately about what I have asked you."'

व्याध उवाच

हन्त ते कथयिष्यामि यन्मां त्वं परिपृच्छसि ।
एषां गुणान्पृथक्त्वेन निबोध गदतो मम ॥ (3)

'The hunter replied, "I will indeed tell you what you have asked me. I will tell you exactly about these separate gunas. Listen to my words."'

मोहात्मकं तमस्तेषां रज एषां प्रवर्तकम् ।
प्रकाशबहुलत्वाच्च सत्त्वं ज्याय इहोच्यते ॥ (4)

'"Tamas is characterized by delusion, while rajas motivates action. It is said that sattva is the best because of its immense powers of illumination."'

अविद्याबहुलो मूढ: स्वप्नशीलो विचेतन: ।
दुर्दृशीकस्तमोध्वस्त: सक्रोधस्तामसोऽलस: ॥ (5)

'"One who is extremely ignorant, foolish, prone to dreaming, bereft of senses, ugly, prone to anger, lazy and descends into darkness is under the influence of tamas."'

प्रवृत्तवाक्यो मन्त्री च योऽनुराग्यभ्यसूयक: ।
विवित्समानो विप्रर्षे स्तब्धो मानी स राजस: ॥ (6)

'"O Brahmana Rishi! A man who is ready in action and speech, affectionate, without malice, industrious, steady and proud is under the influence of rajas."'

प्रकाशबहुलो धीरो निर्विविन्त्सोऽनसूयक: ।
अक्रोधनो नरो धीमान्दान्तश्चैव स सात्त्विक: ॥ (7)

'"A man with great illumination, persevering, without attachment and without malice, without anger, intelligent and self-controlled, is under the influence of sattva."'

सात्त्विकस्त्वथ संबुद्धो लोकवृत्तेन क्लिश्यते ।
यदा बुध्यति बोद्धव्यं लोकवृत्तं जुगुप्सते ॥ (8)

'"When one with the illumination of sattva suffers from the difficulties of the world, when one has learnt everything that has to be learnt, one hates the ways of the world."'

वैराग्यस्य हि रूपं तु पूर्वमेव प्रवर्तते ।
मृदुर्भवत्यहंकार: प्रसीदत्यार्जवं च यत् ॥ (9)

'"Then a form of non-attachment first makes itself felt. Ahamkara becomes milder, and one is pleased at being upright."'

ततोऽस्य सर्वद्वंद्वानि प्रशाम्यन्ति परस्परम् ।
न चास्य संयमो नाम क्वचिद्भवति कश्चन ॥ (10)

'"Then all conflicts between contrary sentiments are pacified. Anything known as restraint in anything is never necessary."'

शूद्रयोनौ हि जातस्य सद्गुणानुपतिष्ठत: ।
वैश्यत्वं भवति ब्रह्मन्क्षत्रियत्वं तथैव च ॥ (11)

'"O Brahmana! One may be born as a shudra. But if he is established in his own good qualities, he will become a vaishya, and even a kshatriya."'

आर्जवे वर्तमानस्य ब्राह्मण्यमभिजायते ।
गुणास्ते कीर्तिता: सर्वे किं भूय: श्रोतुमिच्छसि ॥ (12)

'"Similarly, one who is upright in conduct will be born as a brahmana. Thus, I have told you everything about the gunas. What else do you wish to hear?"'

ब्राह्मण उवाच

पार्थिवं धातुमासाद्य शारीरोऽग्नि: कथं भवेत् ।
अवकाशविशेषेण कथं वर्तयतेऽनिल: ॥ (13)

'The brahmana asked, "What happens to the fire in the body when it is combined with the elements of the earth?[34] When it is expelled, how does the remaining wind behave?"'

मार्कण्डेय उवाच

प्रश्नमेतं समुद्दिष्टं ब्राह्मणेन युधिष्ठिर ।
व्याध: स कथयामास ब्राह्मणाय महात्मने ॥ (14)

Markandeya continued, 'O Yudhishthira! When the brahmana asked this question, the hunter replied to the great-souled brahmana.'

व्याध उवाच

मूर्धानमाश्रितो वह्नि: शरीरं परिपालयन् ।
प्राणो मूर्धनि चाग्नौ च वर्तमानो विचेष्टते ।
भूतं भव्यं भविष्यच्च सर्वं प्राणे प्रतिष्ठितम् ॥ (15)

'The hunter answered, "The fire resides in the head and protects the body. The fire is in the head and in *prana*[35] and motivates all action. Everything in the past, the present and the future is based on prana."'

श्रेष्ठं तदेव भूतानां ब्रह्मज्योतिरुपास्महे ।
स जन्तु: सर्वभूतात्मा पुरुष: स सनातन: ।
मनो बुद्धिरहंकारो भूतानां विषयश्च स: ॥ (16)

'"It is the best entity that exists in beings, and we worship this radiance of the brahman. It is the entity that exists in the atmans

---

[34]When the physical body dies.
[35]Prana is the breath of life or the life-force. The word is also used in a more specific sense. Prana draws breath into the body; *apana* exhales it. *Vyana* distributes it through the body and *samana* assimilates it. *Udana* gives rise to sound. But prana is also used as a general term, encompassing all five.

of all beings. It is the eternal Purusha. It is mind. It is intelligence. It is ahamkara. It is the seat in all beings.'"

एवं त्विह स सर्वत्र प्राणेन परिपाल्यते ।
पृष्ठतस्तु समानेन स्वां स्वां गतिमुपाश्रितः ॥ (17)

"'In this way, everything is protected through prana. Later, it goes in different respective directions, supported by samana.'"

बस्तिमूले गुदे चैव पावकः समुपाश्रितः ।
वहन्मूत्रं पुरीषं चाप्यपानः परिवर्तते ॥ (18)

"'There is a fire in the bladder and anus, and this is known as apana. It circles around and bears the excrement and urine.'"

प्रयत्ने कर्मणि बले य एकस्त्रिषु वर्तते ।
उदान इति तं प्राहुरध्यात्मविदुषो जनाः ॥ (19)

"'Learned people who know about adhyatma say that the three elements of endeavour, action and power are controlled by udana.'"

संधौ संधौ सन्निविष्टः सर्वेष्वपि तथानिलः ।
शरीरेषु मनुष्याणां व्यान इत्युपदिश्यते ॥ (20)

"'It has been said that the wind that exists in every joint of the human body is known as vyana.'"

धातुष्वग्निस्तु विततः स तु वायुसमीरितः ।
रसान्धातूंश्च दोषांश्च वर्तयन्परिधावति ॥ (21)

"'The fire that is in the elements of the body is distributed and fanned by these winds. It triggers the juices, elements and humours and circulates them.'"

प्राणानां संनिपातात्तु संनिपातः प्रजायते ।
ऊष्मा चाग्निरिति ज्ञेयो योऽन्नं पचति देहिनाम् ॥ (22)

"'Through the combination and friction of the pranas, fire is created. This should be known as the digestive fire, which enables embodied beings to digest food.'"

अपानोदानयोर्मध्ये प्राणव्यानौ समाहितौ ।
समन्वितस्त्वधिष्ठानं सम्यक्पचति पावक: ॥ (23)

"'Prana and vyana are placed between apana and udana, and the combined fire resulting from this leads to proper digestion."'

तस्यापि पायुपर्यन्तस्तथा स्यादगुदसंज्ञित: ।
स्रोतांसि तस्माज्जायन्ते सर्वप्राणेषु देहिनाम् ॥ (24)

"'It extends itself up to the anus, also described as the rectum. In all embodied beings with life, this bears the flow of anything not digested."'

अग्निवेगवह: प्राणो गुदान्ते प्रतिहन्यते ।
स ऊर्ध्वमागम्य पुन: समुत्क्षिपति पावकम् ॥ (25)

"'This prana bears the flow of the fire and strikes at the end of the anus. Then it again ascends and flings the fire upwards."'

पक्वाशयस्त्वधो नाभ्या ऊर्ध्वमामाशय: स्थित: ।
नाभिमध्ये शरीरस्य प्राणा: सर्वे प्रतिष्ठिता: ॥ (26)

"'The area above the navel is the region of undigested food. All the pranas are established at the centre of the navel in the body."'

प्रवृत्ता हृदयात्सर्वास्तिर्यगूर्ध्वमधस्तथा ।
वहन्त्यन्नरसान्नाड्यो दश प्राणप्रचोदिता: ॥ (27)

"'Ten arteries radiate from the heart upwards, downwards and sideways and, driven by prana, bear the juices of the food."'

योगिनामेष मार्गस्तु येन गच्छन्ति तत्परम् ।
जितक्लमासना धीरा मूर्ध्न्यात्मानमादधु: ।
एवं सर्वेषु विततौ प्राणापानौ हि देहिषु ॥ (28)

"'This is the path that practitioners of yoga traverse for what is beyond this. They are seated, having conquered exhaustion. They are persevering and raise their atmans up to their heads. In this way, prana and apana are spread in all embodied creatures."'

एकादशविकारात्मा कलासंभारसंभृतः ।
मूर्तिमन्तं हि तं विद्धि नित्यं कर्मजितात्मकम् ॥ (29)

'"The different components of a body go through eleven transformations.[36] Know that though a being is embodied, it is always subjugated by its own karma."'

तस्मिन्यः संस्थितो ह्यग्निर्नित्यं स्थाल्यामिवाहितः ।
आत्मानं तं विजानीहि नित्यं योगजितात्मकम् ॥ (30)

'"Know that the fire that is always inside is like that carried on a plate. Always conquer one's own self through yoga and know the atman."'

देवो यः संस्थितस्तस्मिन्नब्बिन्दुरिव पुष्करे ।
क्षेत्रज्ञं तं विजानीहि नित्यं त्यागजितात्मकम् ॥ (31)

'"Always conquering one's own self through renunciation, know *kshetrajna*, the divinity established like a drop inside the lotus."'[37]

जीवात्मकानि जानीहि रजः सत्त्वं तमस्तथा ।
जीवमात्मगुणं विद्धि तथात्मानं परात्मकम् ॥ (32)

'"Know that sattva, rajas and tamas are the attributes of life in this world. These gunas are attributes of life. Know the jivatman and the paramatman beyond."'

सचेतनं जीवगुणं वदन्ति स चेष्टते चेष्टयते च सर्वम् ।
ततः परं क्षेत्रविदो वदन्ति प्राकल्पयद्यो भुवनानि सप्त ॥ (33)

'"They say that consciousness is the quality of life. It is the doer, and action marks everything. Those who know about the *kshetra* say that the supreme one created the seven worlds before the *kalpa* started."'[38]

---

[36]This is a reference to the five senses of perception, the five organs of action and the mind.
[37]The heart is being compared to a lotus. 'Kshetra' means field and is used for the physical body. 'Kshetrajna' is someone who knows the body, and is an expression used for the jivatman.
[38]There are actually fourteen worlds (*lokas*)—seven above the earth, including the

एवं सर्वेषु भूतेषु भूतात्मा न प्रकाशते ।
दृश्यते त्वर्ग्यया बुद्ध्या सूक्ष्मया ज्ञानवेदिभिः ॥ (34)

'"In this way, the atman that is in all beings is not manifest in beings. It can be seen, using the intelligence, by foremost ones who possess the subtle jnana of insight."'

चित्तस्य हि प्रसादेन हन्ति कर्म शुभाशुभम् ।
प्रसन्नात्मात्मनि स्थित्वा सुखमानन्त्यमश्नुते ॥ (35)

'"Through serenity in consciousness, they destroy auspicious and inauspicious karma. Establishing the tranquil jivatman in the paramatman, they obtain infinite bliss."'

लक्षणं तु प्रसादस्य यथा तृप्तः सुखं स्वपेत् ।
निवाते वा यथा दीपो दीप्येत्कुशलदीपितः ॥ (36)

'"The sign of serenity is that one is content and sleeps happily, like the secure radiance of a lamp ignited by one who is skilled in handling lamps."'

पूर्वरात्रे परे चैव युञ्जानः सततं मनः ।
लघ्वाहारो विशुद्धात्मा पश्यन्नात्मानमात्मनि ॥ (37)

'"One should control one's mind in the first half of the night and the later part of the night. After eating lightly, purifying oneself, one sees the paratman in one's jivatman."'

प्रदीप्तेनेव दीपेन मनोदीपेन पश्यति ।
दृष्ट्वात्मानं निरात्मानं तदा स तु विमुच्यते ॥ (38)

'"This is like seeing the shining light of a lamp with the lamp of one's mind. One who sees the atman beyond one's own self is freed."'

---

earth, and seven below. This is a reference to the seven above—*bhuloka, bhuvarloka, svarloka, maharloka, janaloka, tapoloka* and *satyaloka*. 'Kalpa' is a cycle of creation, occurring during Brahma's day. When Brahma wakes up, there is creation. When it is night for Brahma and he goes to sleep, there is destruction.

सर्वोपायैस्तु लोभस्य क्रोधस्य च विनिग्रहः ।
एतत्पवित्रं यज्ञानां तपो वै संक्रमो मतः ॥ (39)

'"Avarice and anger must be controlled by all means. Austerities are held to be the sacrifices for purification and the means of crossing over."'

नित्यं क्रोधात्तपो रक्षेच्छ्रियं रक्षेत मत्सरात् ।
विद्यां मानापमानाभ्यामात्मानं तु प्रमादतः ॥ (40)

'"One must always protect austerities from anger. One must protect one's prosperity from envy, one's learning from vanity and insults and one's atman from distraction."'

आनृशंस्यं परो धर्मः क्षमा च परमं बलम् ।
आत्मज्ञानं परं ज्ञानं परं सत्यव्रतं व्रतम् ॥ (41)

'"Non-violence is the greatest dharma. Forgiveness is the greatest strength. Jnana about the atman is the supreme jnana. The vow of truthfulness is the supreme vow."'

सत्यस्य वचनं श्रेयः सत्यं ज्ञानं हितं भवेत् ।
यद्भूतहितमत्यन्तं तद्वै सत्यं परं मतम् ॥ (42)

'"Truthful speech is best. True jnana ensures welfare. It is held that the extreme welfare of all beings is the supreme truth."'

यस्य सर्वे समारम्भाः निराशीर्बन्धनाः सदा ।
त्यागे यस्य हुतं सर्वं स त्यागी स च बुद्धिमान् ॥ (43)

"One whose acts are always performed without being tied down by wishes, one who has renounced everything and offered it as oblation is one who has truly renounced. He is intelligent."[39]

यतो न गुरुरप्येनं च्यावयेदुपपादयन् ।
तं विद्याद्ब्रह्मणो योगं वियोगं योगसंज्ञितम् ॥ (44)

---

[39] Though the exact words are not used, there is a similarity with Bhagavat Gita 4.19. The person renounces the fruits of action and, in that sense, even renounces the acts.

"'This is union with the brahman, something that cannot be taught or explained by a guru. This renunciation is known as yoga.'"

न हिंस्यात्सर्वभूतानि मैत्रायणगतश्चरेत् ।
नेदं जीवितमासाद्य वैरं कुर्वीत केनचित् ॥ (45)

"'There should not be violence towards any being. One must traverse the path of friendliness. Having obtained this life, one must never practise enmity.'"

आकिंचन्यं सुसंतोषो निराशित्वमचापलम् ।
एतदेव परं ज्ञानं सदात्मज्ञानमुत्तमम् ॥ (46)

"'Self-negation, extreme satisfaction, lack of wishes and steadfastness lead to supreme jnana. Constant knowledge of the atman is supreme jnana.'"

परिग्रहं परित्यज्य भव बुद्ध्या यतव्रत: ।
अशोकं स्थानमातिष्ठेन्निश्चलं प्रेत्य चेह च ॥ (47)

"'One should renounce one's possessions. One should use one's intelligence to be steady in one's vows. One then attains a firm place that is without sorrow, in this world and in the next.'"

तपोनित्येन दान्तेन मुनिना संयतात्मना ।
अजितं जेतुकामेन भाव्यं सङ्गेष्वसङ्गिना ॥ (48)

"'The self-controlled sage who has restrained himself and is always devoted to austerities will be unvanquished if he gives up the desire to conquer and becomes non-attached to attachments.'"

गुणागुणमनासङ्गमेककार्यमनन्तरम् ।
एतद्ब्राह्मण ते वृत्तमाहुरेकपदं सुखम् ॥ (49)

"'Those that are regarded as qualities are no longer qualities in him. After this, he continuously embarks on a single task. O Brahmana! This is said to be the conduct that alone bestows bliss.'"

परित्यजति यो दु:खं सुखं चाप्युभयं नर: ।
ब्रह्म प्राप्नोति सोऽत्यन्तमसङ्गेन च गच्छति ॥ (50)

'"Such a man renounces both happiness and unhappiness. He transcends all attachment and obtains the brahman."'

यथाश्रुतमिदं सर्वं समासेन द्विजोत्तम ।
एतत्ते सर्वमाख्यातं किं भूयः श्रोतुमिच्छसि ॥ (51)

'"O Supreme among Dvijas! I have briefly told you everything that I have heard. That is all. What else do you desire to hear?"'

Chapter 8

मार्कण्डेय उवाच

एवं संकथिते कृत्स्ने मोक्षधर्मे युधिष्ठिर ।
दृढं प्रीतमना विप्रो धर्मव्याधमुवाच ह ॥ (1)

Markandeya said, 'O Yudhishthira! When all this about the dharma of moksha had been told to the brahmana, he was extremely pleased in his mind. He spoke to Dharma Vyadha.'

न्याययुक्तमिदं सर्वं भवता परिकीर्तितम् ।
न तेऽस्त्यविदितं किंचिद्धर्मेष्विह हि दृश्यते ॥ (2)

'"You have described everything to me, with all the arguments. It can be seen that there is nothing about dharma that you do not know."'

व्याध उवाच

प्रत्यक्षं मम यो धर्मस्तं पश्य द्विजसत्तम ।
येन सिद्धिरियं प्राप्ता मया ब्राह्मणपुंगव ॥ (3)

'The hunter replied, "O Supreme among Dvijas! With your own eyes, behold my dharma. O Bull among Brahmanas! It is through this that I have achieved siddhi."

उत्तिष्ठ भगवन्क्षिप्रं प्रविश्याभ्यन्तरं गृहम् ।
द्रष्टुमर्हसि धर्मज्ञ मातरं पितरं च मे ॥ (4)

"'O Illustrious One! Arise and swiftly enter the inner part of my house. O One Who Knows about Dharma! You should see my mother and my father.'"

मार्कण्डेय उवाच

इत्युक्त: स प्रविश्याथ ददर्श परमार्चितम् ।
सौधं हृद्यं चतु:शालमतीव च मनोहरम् ॥ (5)

Markandeya continued, 'At these words, the brahman entered and saw an extremely beautiful house. It was lovely and white-washed, and was divided into four parts.'

देवतागृहसंकाशं दैवतैश्च सुपूजितम् ।
शयनासनसंबाधं गन्धैश्च परमैर्युतम् ॥ (6)

'It was like a residence of devas and was greatly revered by devas. It had excellent seats and beds and was fragrant with perfumes.'

तत्र शुक्लाम्बरधरौ पितरावस्य पूजितौ ।
कृताहारौ सुतुष्टौ तावुपविष्टौ वरासने ।
धर्मव्याधस्तु तौ दृष्ट्वा पादेषु शिरसापतत् ॥ (7)

'After having eaten, the hunter's revered parents were comfortably seated on excellent seats. They were content and were dressed in white garments. One seeing them, Dharma Vyadha prostrated himself, his head touching their feet.'

वृद्धावूचतु:

उत्तिष्ठोत्तिष्ठ धर्मज्ञ धर्मस्त्वामभिरक्षतु ।
प्रीतौ स्वस्तव शौचेन दीर्घमायुरवाप्नुहि ।
सत्पुत्रेण त्वया पुत्र नित्यकालं सुपूजितौ ॥ (8)

'The aged ones said, "O One Who Knows about Dharma! Arise, arise. May dharma protect you. We are pleased with your purity. May you be well and have a long life. O Son! You have always been a good son. You have worshipped us for a long time."'

न तेऽन्यदैवतं किंचिद्दैवतेष्वपि वर्तते ।
प्रयतत्वाद्द्विजातीनां दमेनासि समन्वितः ॥ (9)

"'You have not acknowledged a divinity even among devas themselves. Through efforts, you have attained the self-control of dvijas.'"

पितुः पितामहा ये च तथैव प्रपितामहाः ।
प्रीतास्ते सततं पुत्र दमेनावां च पूजया ॥ (10)

"'O Son! Your fathers, grandfathers and great-grandfathers have always been pleased with you, because of your self-control and your worship.'"

मनसा कर्मणा वाचा शुश्रूषा नैव हीयते ।
न चान्या वितथा बुद्धिर्दृश्यते सांप्रतं तव ॥ (11)

"'In thought, deed and words, you have never deviated from serving. Now it seems to us that you have no other thought in your mind.'"

जामदग्न्येन रामेण यथा वृद्धौ सुपूजितौ ।
तथा त्वया कृतं सर्वं तद्दिशिष्टं च पुत्रक ॥ (12)

"'O Son! Like Jamadagni's son, Rama,[40] you have done everything to worship your aged parents well. Indeed, you have been special in what you have done.'"

मार्कण्डेय उवाच

ततस्तं ब्राह्मणं ताभ्यां धर्मव्याधो न्यवेदयत् ।
तौ स्वागतेन तं विप्रमर्चयामासतुस्तदा ॥ (13)

Markandeya continued, 'Then Dharma Vyadha introduced the brahmana to them, and they welcomed and honoured the brahmana.'"

---

[40]Parashurama.

प्रतिगृह्य च तां पूजां द्विजः पप्रच्छ तावुभौ।
सपुत्राभ्यां सभृत्याभ्यां कच्चिद्वां कुशलं गृहे।
अनामयं च वां कच्चित्सदैवेह शरीरयोः॥ (14)

'The dvija accepted the honours and asked them, "Is everything well in your household, with your sons and your servants? Are you physically well, without any disease?"'

वृद्धावूचतुः

कुशलं नो गृहे विप्र भृत्यवर्गे च सर्वशः।
कच्चित्त्वमप्यविघ्नेन संप्राप्तो भगवन्निह॥ (15)

'The aged ones replied, "O Brahmana! Everything is well at home and the servants are fine too. O Illustrious One! Did you face any impediments in coming here?"'

मार्कण्डेय उवाच

बाढमित्येव तौ विप्रः प्रत्युवाच मुदान्वितः।
धर्मव्याधस्तु तं विप्रमर्थवद्वाक्यमब्रवीत्॥ (16)

Markandeya continued, 'The brahmana happily said that he hadn't faced any problems. Dharma Vyadha then spoke these words of great import to the brahmana.'

पिता माता च भगवन्नेतौ मे दैवतं परम्।
यदैवतेभ्यः कर्तव्यं तदेताभ्यां करोम्यहम्॥ (17)

'"O Illustrious One! These two, my father and my mother, are the supreme divinities for me, and I do for them what is undertaken for devas."'

त्रयस्त्रिंशद्यथा देवाः सर्वे शक्रपुरोगमाः।
संपूज्याः सर्वलोकस्य तथा वृद्धाविमौ मम॥ (18)

'"All the thirty-three devas have Shakra[41] at the forefront. Just as they are worshipped by all the worlds, I tend to these two aged ones."'

---

[41] Indra.

उपहारानाहरन्तो देवतानां यथा द्विजाः ।
कुर्वन्ते तद्वदेताभ्यां करोम्यहमतन्द्रितः ॥ (19)

"'Just as dvijas collect offerings for devas, I attentively act for these two.'"

तौ मे परमं ब्रह्मन्पिता माता च दैवतम् ।
एतौ पुष्पैः फलै रत्नैस्तोषयामि सदा द्विज ॥ (20)

"'O Brahmana! These two, my father and my mother, are my supreme divinities. O Dvija! I constantly satisfy them with flowers, fruits and gems.'"

एतावेवाग्नयो मह्यं यान्वदन्ति मनीषिणः ।
यज्ञा वेदाश्च चत्वारः सर्वमेतौ मम द्विज ॥ (21)

"'For me, they are like the fires the learned ones speak about. O Dvija! They are everything to me—sacrifices and the four Vedas.'"

एतदर्थं मम प्राणा भार्या पुत्राः सुहृज्जनाः ।
सपुत्रदारः शुश्रूषां नित्यमेव करोम्यहम् ॥ (22)

"'My life, my wife, my sons and my well-wishers are for them. With my sons and my wife, I constantly serve them.'"

स्वयं च स्नापयाम्येतौ तथा पादौ प्रधावये ।
आहारं संप्रयच्छामि स्वयं च द्विजसत्तम ॥ (23)

"'I bathe them myself and wash their feet. O Supreme among Dvijas! I give them food myself.'"

अनुकूलाः कथा वच्मि विप्रियं परिवर्जयन् ।
अधर्मेणापि संयुक्तं प्रियमाभ्यां करोम्यहम् ॥ (24)

"'I only speak pleasant things to them, avoiding the unpleasant. So as to bring pleasure to them, I even do that which is tinged with adharma.'"

धर्ममेव गुरुं ज्ञात्वा करोमि द्विजसत्तम ।
अतन्द्रितः सदा विप्र शुश्रूषां वै करोम्यहम् ॥ (25)

'"O Supreme among Dvijas! O Brahmana! Knowing dharma to be my preceptor, I constantly and tirelessly serve them."'

पञ्चैव गुरवो ब्रह्मन्पुरुषस्य बुभूषतः ।
पिता मातग्निरात्मा च गुरुश्च द्विजसत्तम ॥ (26)

'"O Brahmana! O Supreme among Dvijas! A man is adorned through five preceptors—the father, the mother, the fire, himself and the guru."'

एतेषु यस्तु वर्तेत सम्यगेव द्विजोत्तम ।
भवेयुरग्नयस्तस्य परिचीर्णास्तु नित्यशः ।
गार्हस्थ्ये वर्तमानस्य धर्म एष सनातनः ॥ (26)

'"O Supreme among Dvijas! If they are served properly, they always remain for him, like well-tended fires. That is the eternal dharma for those who are in garhasthya."'

Chapter 9

मार्कण्डेय उवाच

गुरू निवेद्य विप्राय तौ मातापितरावुभौ ।
पुनरेव स धर्मात्मा व्याधो ब्राह्मणमब्रवीत् ॥ (1)

Markandeya continued, 'Having introduced his father and mother as his gurus to the brahmana, the hunter, with dharma in his atman, again spoke to the brahmana.'

प्रवृत्तचक्षुर्जातोऽस्मि संपश्य तपसो बलम् ।
यदर्थमुक्तोऽसि तया गच्छस्व मिथिलामिति ॥ (2)
पतिशुश्रूषपरया दान्तया सत्यशीलया ।
मिथिलायां वसन्व्याधः स ते धर्मान्प्रवक्ष्यति ॥ (3)

'"Behold. I have obtained insight through the strength of my austerities. Thus, the wife, who was devoted to her husband, self-controlled and truthful in conduct, told you to go to Mithila—because a hunter who resides there would tell you about dharma."'

ब्राह्मण उवाच

पतिव्रतायाः सत्यायाः शीलाढ्यायाया यतव्रत ।
संस्मृत्य वाक्यं धर्मज्ञ गुणवानसि मे मतः ॥ (4)

'The brahmana said, "O One Who Knows about Dharma! O One Who Is Firm in Vows! I remember the words of the wife, truthful, virtuous in conduct and devoted to her husband. It is my view that you possess the qualities."'

व्याध उवाच

यत्तदा त्वं द्विजश्रेष्ठ तयोक्तो मां प्रति प्रभो ।
दृष्टमेतत्तया सम्यगेकपत्न्या न संशयः ॥ (5)

'The hunter replied, "O Best among Dvijas! O Lord! There is no doubt that what you have said about me was completely foreseen by that faithful wife."'

त्वदनुग्रहबुद्ध्या तु विप्रैतद्दर्शितं मया ।
वाक्यं च शृणु मे तात यत्ते वक्ष्ये हितं द्विज ॥ (6)

'"O Brahmana! It is to exhibit favours towards your intelligence that I showed you these things. O Tata!⁴² O Dvija! Now listen to the beneficial words I will tell you."'

त्वया विनिकृता माता पिता च द्विजसत्तम ।
अनिसृष्टोऽसि निष्क्रान्तो गृहात्ताभ्यामनिन्दित ।
वेदोच्चारणकार्यार्थमयुक्तं तत्त्वया कृतम् ॥ (7)

"O Supreme among Dvijas! You have ignored your mother and father. O Unblemished One! You left the house without their permission for the sake of studying the meaning and chanting of the Vedas."

तव शोकेन वृद्धौ तावन्धौ जातौ तपस्विनौ ।
तौ प्रसादयितुं गच्छ मा त्वा धर्मोऽत्यगान्महान् ॥ (8)

---

⁴²Since Dharma Vyadha is instructing, it is right that he should address Koushika as 'tata' in the sense of 'son'.

'"Out of grief for you, your aged parents have turned blind and have become ascetics. Go and seek their favour, else great dharma will forsake you."'

तपस्वी त्वं महात्मा च धर्मे च निरत: सदा ।
सर्वमेतदपार्थं ते क्षिप्रं तौ संप्रसादय ॥ (9)

'"You are an ascetic. You are great souled. You are always devoted to dharma. But all of this will be futile unless you please them quickly."'

श्रद्धस्व मम ब्रह्मन्नान्यथा कर्तुमर्हसि ।
गम्यतामद्य विप्रर्षे श्रेयस्ते कथयाम्यहम् ॥ (10)

'"O Brahmana! You should trust my words and not act against them. Go to them. O Brahmana Rishi! I am telling you this for your own welfare."'

ब्राह्मण उवाच

यदेतदुक्तं भवता सर्वं सत्यमसंशयम् ।
प्रीतोऽस्मि तव धर्मज्ञ साध्वाचार गुणान्वित ॥ (11)

'The brahmana said, "O One Who Knows about Dharma! O One Who Possesses Qualities and Virtuous Conduct! There is no doubt that everything that you have said is true. I am pleased with you."'

व्याध उवाच

दैवतप्रतिमो हि त्वं यस्त्वं धर्ममनुव्रत: ।
पुराणं शाश्वतं दिव्यं दुष्प्रापमकृतात्मभि: ॥ (12)

'The hunter replied, "You are the equal of devas, and you have always followed the dharma that is ancient, eternal and divine, difficult to access for those who have not cleansed their atmans."'

अतन्द्रित: कुरु क्षिप्रं मातापित्रोर्हि पूजनम् ।
अत: परमहं धर्मं नान्यं पश्यामि कंचन ॥ (13)

"'Go swiftly to your mother and your father and worship them attentively. Beyond that, there is no other supreme dharma that I can see.'"

ब्राह्मण उवाच

इहाहमागतो दिष्ट्या दिष्ट्या मे संगतं त्वया ।
ईदृशा दुर्लभा लोके नरा धर्मप्रदर्शका: ॥ (14)

'The brahmana said, "It is through good fortune that I came here. It is through good fortune that I met you. Men like you, exponents of dharma, are difficult to find in this world."'

एको नरसहस्रेषु धर्मविद्विद्यते न वा ।
प्रीतोऽस्मि तव सत्येन भद्रं ते पुरुषोत्तम ॥ (15)

"'Among one thousand men, one may find someone who is learned in dharma, or one may not. O Fortunate One! O Supreme among Men! I am pleased with your truth.'"

पतमानो हि नरके भवतास्मि समुद्धृत: ।
भवितव्यमथैवं च यद्दृष्टोऽसि मयानघ ॥ (16)

"'I was descending into hell and you have saved me. O Unblemished One! It had been destined and that is the reason I met you.'"

राजा ययातिर्दौहित्रै: पतिततस्तारितो यथा ।
सद्भि: पुरुषशार्दूल तथाहं भवता त्विह ॥ (17)

"'O Tiger among Men! King Yayati fell and was rescued by his daughter's virtuous sons.[43] Like that, I have now been saved by you.'"

मातापितृभ्यां शुश्रूषां करिष्ये वचनात्तव ।
नाकृतात्मा वेदयति धर्माधर्मविनिश्चयम् ॥ (18)

---

[43] The daughter in question is Madhavi, whose sons saved Yayati from the wrath of Sage Galava. In order for Yayati to please Galava and give him the horses he wanted, Madhavi had sons through several kings.

"'Acting in accordance with your words, I will serve my mother and my father. One who has not cleansed his atman does not know how to differentiate between dharma and adharma.'"

दुर्ज्ञेय: शाश्वतो धर्म: शूद्रयोनौ हि वर्तता ।
न त्वां शूद्रमहं मन्ये भवितव्यं हि कारणम् ।
येन कर्मविपाकेन प्राप्तेयं शूद्रता त्वया ॥ (19)

"'The eternal dharma is incomprehensible to one who has been as a shudra. I do not regard you as a shudra. There must be some reason in destiny. Perhaps you obtained the status of a shudra because of some ripening of karma.'"

एतदिच्छामि विज्ञातुं तत्त्वेन हि महामते ।
कामया ब्रूहि मे तथ्यं सर्वं त्वं प्रयतात्मवान् ॥ (20)

"'O Immensely Intelligent One! I wish to know the truth about this. O One Who Has Controlled His Atman! If you so desire, please tell me everything accurately.'"

व्याध उवाच

अनतिक्रमणीया हि ब्राह्मणा वै द्विजोत्त ।
शृणु सर्वमिदं वृत्तं पूर्वदेहे ममानघ ॥ (21)

'The hunter replied, "O One Born as a Dvija! No brahmana should be crossed. O Unblemished One! Hear everything that had happened to me in an earlier body."'

अहं हि ब्राह्मण: पूर्वमासं द्विजवरात्मज ।
वेदाध्यायी सुकुशलो वेदाङ्गानां च पारग: ।
आत्मदोषकृतैर्ब्रह्मन्नवस्थां प्राप्तवानिमाम् ॥ (22)

"'O Son of Foremost among Dvijas! I was a brahmana earlier. I studied the Vedas, became accomplished and was skilled in the Vedangas. O Brahmana! But it was because of my own sins that I have been reduced to my present state.'"

कश्चिद्राजा मम सखा धनुर्वेदपरायणः ।
संसर्गाद्धनुषि श्रेष्ठस्ततोऽहमभवं द्विज ॥ (23)

'"There was a king who was my friend and he was skilled in *dhanurveda*.[44] O Dvija! Because of association with him, I also became supreme in wielding the bow."'

एतस्मिन्नेव काले तु मृगयां निर्गतो नृपः ।
सहितो योधमुख्यैश्च मन्त्रिभिश्च सुसंवृतः ।
ततोऽभ्यहन्मृगांस्तत्र सुबहूनाश्रमं प्रति ॥ (24)

'"Once, the king went out hunting. He was surrounded by his ministers and was with his foremost warriors. Near a hermitage, he killed many deer."'

अथ क्षिप्तः शरो घोरो मयापि द्विजसत्तम ।
ताडितश्च मुनिस्तेन शरेणानतपर्वणा ॥ (25)

'"O Supreme among Dvijas! I also shot a terrible arrow, with a plume that was bent downwards. That arrow struck a sage."'

भूमौ निपतितो ब्रह्मन्नुवाच प्रतिनादयन् ।
नापराध्याम्यहं किंचित्केन पापमिदं कृतम् ॥ (26)
मन्वानस्तं मृगं चाहं संप्राप्तः सहसा मुनिम् ।
अपश्यं तमृषिं विद्धं शरेणानतपर्वणा ।
तमुग्रतपसं विप्रं निष्टनन्तं महीतले ॥ (27)

'"O Brahmana! He fell down on the ground and screamed, 'I am innocent. Who has perpetrated this evil deed?' Still thinking him to be a deer, I rushed towards him and suddenly reached the sage. I saw that the rishi had been pierced by my arrow with a plume that was bent downwards. The brahmana, fierce in his austerities, was dying on the ground."'

अकार्यकरणाच्चापि भृशं मे व्यथितं मनः ।
अजानता कृतमिदं मयेत्यथ तमब्रुवम् ।

---

[44] The science of fighting with the bow, the skill of fighting. However, 'dhanurveda' meant learning about all weapons, not just a bow and arrows.

क्षन्तुमर्हसि मे ब्रह्मन्निति चोक्तो मया मुनिः ॥ (28)

'"My mind was extremely distressed to see that I had performed an act that should not be performed. I told him, 'I performed this act out of ignorance. Please pardon me. O Brahmana! I should be forgiven.' I said this to the sage."'

ततः प्रत्यब्रवीद्वाक्यमृषिर्मां क्रोधमूर्छितः ।
व्याधस्त्वं भविता क्रूर शूद्रयोनाविति द्विज ॥ (29)

'"But the rishi was senseless with rage and replied with these words: 'O Cruel One! O Dvija! You will be born as a vyadha and will be born from a shudra womb.'"'

Chapter 10

व्याध उवाच

एवं शप्तोऽहमृषिणा तदा द्विजवरोत्तम ।
अभिप्रसादयमृषिं गिरा वाक्यविशारदम् ॥ (1)

'The hunter said, "O Supreme among Foremost of Dvijas! When I had thus been cursed by the rishi, I spoke to the one who was eloquent with words, so as to placate him."'

अजानता मयाकार्यमिदमद्य कृतं मुने ।
क्षन्तुमर्हसि तत्सर्वं प्रसीद भगवन्निति ॥ (2)

'"O Sage! I performed this act out of ignorance today. O Illustrious One! You should pardon everything. Please show me your favour."'

ऋषिरुवाच

नान्यथा भविता शाप एवमेतदसंशयम् ।
आनृशंस्यादहं किंचित्कर्तानुग्रहमद्य ते ॥ (3)

'"The rishi replied, 'There is no doubt that the curse that I have pronounced cannot be negated. But because of my mildness, I will now show you a slight favour.'"'

शूद्रयोनौ वर्तमानो धर्मज्ञो भविता ह्यसि ।
मातापित्रोश्च शुश्रूषां करिष्यसि न संशयः ॥ (4)

'"'Even when you are born from the womb of a shudra, you will know about dharma. There is no doubt that you will serve your mother and your father.'"'

तया शुश्रूषया सिद्धिं महतीं समवाप्स्यसि ।
जातिस्मरश्च भविता स्वर्गं चैव गमिष्यसि ।
शापक्षयान्ते निर्वृत्ते भवितासि पुनर्द्विजः ॥ (5)

'"'Through your service to them, you will achieve great siddhi. You will remember your earlier birth, and you will go to heaven. When the curse has run its course, you will again become a dvija.'"'

व्याध उवाच

एवं शप्तः पुरा तेन ऋषिणास्म्युग्रतेजसा ।
प्रसादश्च कृतस्तेन ममैवं द्विपदां वर ॥ (6)

'The hunter said, "In this way, in earlier times, I was cursed by the rishi who was fierce in his energy. O Supreme among Bipeds! But he showed me his favour too."'

शरं चोद्धृतवानस्मि तस्य वै द्विजसत्तम ।
आश्रमं च मया नीतो न च प्राणैर्व्ययुज्यत ॥ (7)

'"O Supreme among Dvijas! I took the arrow out of his body. His life had not left him, and I carried him to the hermitage."'

एतत्ते सर्वमाख्यातं यथा मम पुराभवत् ।
अभितश्चापि गन्तव्यं मया स्वर्गं द्विजोत्तम ॥ (8)

'"I have thus told you the details of everything that befell me earlier. O Supreme among Dvijas! I will go to heaven hereafter."'

ब्राह्मण उवाच

एवमेतानि पुरुष दुःखानि च सुखानि च ।
प्राप्नुवन्ति महाबुद्धे नोत्कण्ठां कर्तुमर्हसि ।
दुष्करं हि कृतं तात जानता जातिमात्मनः ॥ (9)

'The brahmana replied, "O Greatly Intelligent One! All men are subject to unhappiness and happiness in this way. You should, therefore, not be anxious about this. O Father! You have performed an extremely difficult task and have learnt about your earlier life."'

कर्मदोषश्च वै विद्वन्नात्मजातिकृतेन वै ।
कंचित्कालं मृष्यतां वै ततोऽसि भविता द्विज: ।
सांप्रतं च मतो मेऽसि ब्राह्मणो नात्र संशय: ॥ (10)

'"O Learned One! The stain of your evil karma is because of the lineage you have been born into. After some futile time has passed, you will become a dvija again. There is no doubt that I take you to be a brahmana even now."'

ब्राह्मण: पतनीयेषु वर्तमानो विकर्मसु ।
दाम्भिको दुष्कृतप्राय: शूद्रेण सदृशो भवेत् ॥ (11)

'"A brahmana who performs perverse karma is certain to meet with downfall. One who is proud and an evil-doer is the equal of a shudra."'

यस्तु शूद्रो दमे सत्ये धर्मे च सततोत्थित: ।
तं ब्राह्मणमहं मन्ये वृत्तेन हि भवेद्द्विज: ॥ (12)

'"A shudra who is controlled, truthful and devoted to dharma always rises. I take him to be a brahmana who is a dvija because of his conduct."'

कर्मदोषेण विषमां गतिमाप्नोति दारुणाम् ।
क्षीणदोषमहं मन्ये चाभितस्त्वां नरोत्तम ॥ (13)

'"Through the blemishes of perverse karma, one attains a terrible end. O Supreme among Men! I think that all of your sins have now been destroyed."'

कर्तुमर्हसि नोत्कण्ठां त्वद्विधा ह्यविषादिन: ।
लोकवृत्तान्तवृत्तज्ञा नित्यं धर्मपरायणा: ॥ (14)

"'You should not be anxious on this account. Someone like you should not be miserable. You know about the ways of conduct in the world. You are always devoted to dharma.'"

व्याध उवाच

प्रज्ञया मानसं दुःखं हन्याच्छारीरमौषधैः ।
एतद्विज्ञानसामर्थ्यं न बालैः समतां व्रजेत् ॥ (15)

'The hunter replied, "Like physical pain is destroyed with medicines, mental pain is destroyed with wisdom. This capacity for knowledge does not come equally to those who are fools."'

अनिष्टसंप्रयोगाच्च विप्रयोगात्प्रियस्य च ।
मानुषा मानसैर्दुःखैर्युज्यन्ते अल्पबुद्धयः ॥ (16)

"'Men of limited intelligence are overcome by mental distress when they are confronted with the unpleasant and separated from the pleasant.'"

गुणैर्भूतानि युज्यन्ते वियुज्यन्ते तथैव च ।
सर्वाणि नैतदेकस्य शोकस्थानं हि विद्यते ॥ (17)

"'All beings are united with qualities and similarly, separated from them. Everyone is subject to this, and there is no reason for grief.'"

अनिष्टेनान्वितं पश्यंस्तथा क्षिप्रं विरज्यते ।
ततश्च प्रतिकुर्वन्ति यदि पश्यन्त्युपक्रमम् ।
शोचतो न भवेत्किंचित्केवलं परितप्यते ॥ (18)

"'When one sees something harmful, one should swiftly withdraw. One should take counter measures if one sees it coming. Nothing can be done for one who only sorrows. He laments.'"

परित्यजन्ति ये दुःखं सुखं वाप्युभयं नराः ।
त एव सुखमेधन्ते ज्ञानतृप्ता मनीषिणः ॥ (19)

"'Men who give up both happiness and unhappiness are learned ones who are satisfied with jnana. They obtain happiness.'"

असंतोषपरा मूढा: संतोषं यान्ति पण्डिता: ।
असंतोषस्य नास्त्यन्तस्तुष्टिस्तु परमं सुखम् ।
न शोचन्ति गताध्वान: पश्यन्त: परमां गतिम् ॥ (20)

'"Foolish ones are dissatisfied. The learned are satisfied. There is no end to dissatisfaction. Satisfaction is supreme happiness. Those who do not grieve have gone along that path and have attained the supreme destination."'

न विषादे मन: कार्यं विषादो विषमुत्तमम् ।
मारयत्यकृतप्रज्ञं बालं क्रुद्ध इवोरग: ॥ (21)

'"One should not immerse one's mind in grief. Grief is a terrible poison. Like an angry serpent, it kills those who are foolish and have not attained wisdom."'

यं विषादोऽभिभवति विषमे समुपस्थिते ।
तेजसा तस्य हीनस्य पुरुषार्थो न विद्यते ॥ (22)

'"If a person is overcome with sorrow when difficulties surface, his energy is destroyed and he does not accomplish the objectives of human existence."'[45]

अवश्यं क्रियमाणस्य कर्मणो दृश्यते फलम् ।
न हि निर्वेदमागम्य किंचित्प्राप्नोति शोभनम् ॥ (23)

'"The fruits of the karma we have done can certainly be seen. One who falls prey to despair does not obtain that which is good."'

अथाप्युपायं पश्येत् दु:खस्य परिमोक्षणे ।
अशोचन्नारभेतैव युक्तश्चाव्यसनी भवेत् ॥ (24)

'"Instead, one should look for means to free oneself from misery. One should not start to sorrow, but seek to eliminate the hardship."'

भूतेष्वभावं संचिन्त्य ये तु बुद्धे: परं गता: ।
न शोचन्ति कृतप्रज्ञा: पश्यन्त: परमां गतिम् ॥ (25)

---

[45] The *purushartha*s or objectives of human existence are dharma, artha, kama and moksha.

'"If one thinks about the nature of all beings, one obtains supreme intelligence. One should not sorrow. One should obtain wisdom. One should look towards the supreme objective."'

न शोचामि च वै विद्वन्कालाकाङ्क्षी स्थितोऽस्म्यहम् ।
एतैर्निदर्शनैर्ब्रह्मन्नावसीदामि सत्तम ॥ (26)

'"I do not sorrow. Learned ones do not either. I am here, waiting for the time to pass. O Brahmana! O Excellent One! That is the sign of me not being depressed."'

ब्राह्मण उवाच

कृतप्रज्ञोऽसि मेधावी बुद्धिश्च विपुला तव ।
नाहं भवन्तं शोचामि ज्ञानतृप्तोऽसि धर्मवित् ॥ (27)

'The brahmana said, "You have attained wisdom. You are learned. You possess great intelligence. You are content in jnana. You know about dharma. I am not grieving on account of you."'

आपृच्छे त्वां स्वस्ति तेऽस्तु धर्मस्त्वा परिरक्षतु ।
अप्रमादस्तु कर्तव्यो धर्मे धर्मभृतां वर ॥ (28)

'"I wish to take my leave from you. May you be fortunate. May dharma protect you. O Supreme among Those Who Uphold Dharma! May you not deviate in your duty towards dharma."'

मार्कण्डेय उवाच

बाढमित्येव तं व्याधः कृताञ्जलिरुवाच ह ।
प्रदक्षिणमथो कृत्वा प्रस्थितो द्विजसत्तमः ॥ (29)

Markandeya continued, 'Joining his hands in salutation, the hunter granted leave. The supreme among dvijas performed *pradakshina*[46] around him and departed.'

---

[46]Pradakshina is a special kind of circumambulation, where the entity being circumambulated is always on the right.

स तु गत्वा द्विजः सर्वां शुश्रूषां कृतवांस्तदा ।
मातापितृभ्यां वृद्धाभ्यां यथान्यायं सुसंशितः ॥ (30)

'When he returned, the dvija assiduously served his mother, his father and the elders in accordance with the prescribed rules.'

एतत्ते सर्वमाख्यातं निखिलेन युधिष्ठिर ।
पृष्टवानसि यं तात धर्मं धर्मभृतां वर ॥ (31)
पतिव्रताया माहात्म्यं ब्राह्मणस्य च सत्तम ।
मातापित्रोश्च शुश्रूषा व्याधे धर्मश्च कीर्तितः ॥ (32)

'O Yudhishthira! O Son! O Foremost among Those Who Uphold Dharma! O Excellent One! I have thus told you everything that you asked me about—the faithful wife, the greatness of brahmanas and serving the mother and the father, recounted by Dharma Vyadha.'

युधिष्ठिर उवाच

अत्यद्भुतमिदं ब्रह्मन्धर्माख्यानमनुत्तमम् ।
सर्वधर्मभृतां श्रेष्ठ कथितं द्विजसत्तम ॥ (33)

Yudhishthira replied, 'O Brahmana! O Supreme among Dvijas! This excellent account of dharma is extraordinary, as recounted by the best among all those who uphold dharma.'

सुखश्रव्यतया विद्वन्मुहूर्तमिव मे गतम् ।
न हि तृप्तोऽस्मि भगवञ्छृण्वानो धर्ममुत्तमम् ॥ (34)

'O Learned One! This is pleasant to hear, and it seemed to me that only an instant has passed. O Illustrious One! But I am still not satisfied with hearing about excellent dharma.'

Thus ends the Dharma Vyadha Gita.

4

YAKSHA PRASHNA

In the Aranyaka Parva, there is a sub-parva known as Araneya Parva, a derivative of the word '*arani*', meaning wood used for kindling. While the Pandavas are in the forest and nearing the end of the period of exile, a brahmana whose kindling wood has been lost requests them to pursue a deer. That is how the sub-parva is named. In Yaksha Prashna, the Pandavas are asked questions by a yaksha.[1] Failing to answer the yaksha's questions, Nakula, Sahadeva, Arjuna and Bhima are killed, but are restored to life when Yudhishthira answers the yaksha's questions correctly. The entire Araneya Parva is about this incident, but the section 'Yaksha Prashna' refers to the conversation between the yaksha and Yudhishthira, when the latter answers the questions asked by the former. This consists of a single chapter with seventy-four shlokas.[2] All of this was an attempt by Dharma, the divinity who was Yudhishthira's father, to test Yudhishthira's adherence to dharma. Disguising himself as a deer, it was he who stole the kindling wood. One by one, the Pandava brothers go in search of the wood. Thirsty, they want to drink water from a lake, guarded by the yaksha in the form of a crane. Not bothering to answer the crane's question, one by one, they are killed. Strictly speaking,

---

[1] Yakshas are a semi-divine race, often described as Kubera's attendants.
[2] Many people are familiar with Yaksha's questions and Yudhishthira's replies. This translation is based on the CE. Since the CE excised some shlokas, some of those familiar questions (and answers) are missing in this translation.

the yaksha asks several questions, not one. Therefore, it should be called यक्षप्रश्ना, in the plural, and not यक्षप्रश्न, in the singular.

वैशंपायन उवाच ।

स ददर्श हतान्भ्रातॄँल्लोकपालानिव च्युतान् ।
युगान्ते समनुप्राप्ते शक्रप्रतिमगौरवान् ॥ (1)

Vaishampayana[3] said, 'He[4] saw his dead brothers, as glorious as Shakra, like dislodged *lokapalas*[5] when the end of the *yuga*[6] has arrived.'

विनिकीर्णधनुर्बाणं दृष्ट्वा निहतमर्जुनम् ।
भीमसेनं यमौ चोभौ निर्विचेष्टान्गतायुषः ॥ (2)

'He saw Arjuna dead, with his bow and arrows scattered, and Bhimasena and the twins motionless and bereft of life.'

स दीर्घमुष्णं निःश्वस्य शोकबाष्पपरिप्लुतः ।
बुद्ध्या विचिन्तयामास वीराः केन निपातिताः ॥ (3)
नैषां शस्त्रप्रहारोऽस्ति पदं नेहास्ति कस्यचित् ।
भूतं महदिदं मन्ये भ्रातरो येन मे हताः ।
एकाग्रं चिन्तयिष्यामि पीत्वा वेत्स्यामि वा जलम् ॥ (4)
स्यात्तु दुर्योधनेनेदमुपांशुविहितं कृतम् ।
गान्धारराजरचितं सततं जिह्मबुद्धिना ॥ (5)
यस्य कार्यमकार्यं वा सममेव भवत्युत ।
कस्तस्य विश्वसेद्धीरो दुर्मतेरकृतात्मनः ॥ (6)
अथ वा पुरुषैर्गूढैः प्रयोगोऽयं दुरात्मनः ।
भवेदिति महाबुद्धिर्बहुधा तदचिन्तयत् ॥ (7)

'His eyes overflowed with tears and his warm sighs were long. Using his intelligence, he thought. "Who has killed these brave ones?

---

[3]Rishi Vaishampayana is recounting everything to King Janamejaya.
[4]Yudhishthira.
[5]Guardians of the world.
[6]Yuga is a measure of time, an era.

There are no marks of weapons striking them, nor are there any signs of footprints. I think it must be a great being that has killed my brothers in this way. I must reflect on this with concentration. Perhaps I will know after drinking the water. Perhaps this is a secret deed by Duryodhana, who does not know what should not be done and always follows the King of Gandhara,[7] deceitful in intelligence. No brave person can trust one who is evil-minded and whose atman has not been cleansed. Or perhaps that evil-souled one has employed secret servants." Thus, the immensely intelligent one thought in many ways.'

तस्यासीन्न विषेणेदमुदकं दूषितं यथा ।
मुखवर्णाः प्रसन्ना मे भ्रातृणामित्यचिन्तयत् ॥ (8)
एकैकशश्चौघबलानिमान्पुरुषसत्तमान् ।
कोऽन्यः प्रतिसमासेत कालान्तकयमादृते ॥ (9)

'But he did not think that the water was polluted with poison. He thought, "The faces of my brothers are healthy in complexion. These men are excellent and each one of them is capable of withstanding floods of armies. Who but Yama, the arbiter of destiny, can subjugate them?"'

एतेनाध्यवसायेन तत्तोयमव्यवगाढवान् ।
गाहमानश्च तत्तोयमन्तरिक्षात्स शुश्रुवे ॥ (10)

'Reflecting in this way, he immersed himself in the water. As he immersed himself in the water, he heard these words from the sky.'

यक्ष उवाच

अहं बकः शैवलमत्स्यभक्षो मया नीताः प्रेतवशं तवानुजाः ।
त्वं पञ्चमो भविता राजपुत्र न चेत्प्रश्नान्पृच्छतो व्याकरोषि ॥ (11)

'The yaksha said, "I am a crane that lives on aquatic plants and fish. I have conveyed your younger brothers to the land of the

---

[7]Shakuni.

dead. O Prince! If you do not answer my questions and do this,[8] you will be the fifth."

मा तात साहसं कार्षीर्मम पूर्वपरिग्रह: ।
प्रश्नानुक्त्वा तु कौन्तेय तत: पिब हरस्व च ॥ (12)

'"O Son! Do not be rash enough to do this. I have obtained possession of this earlier. O Kounteya! Answer my questions. Then drink and take the water."'

युधिष्ठिर उवाच

रुद्राणां वा वसूनां वा मरुतां वा प्रधानभाक् ।
पृच्छामि को भवान्देवो नैतच्छकुनिना कृतम् ॥ (13)

'Yudhishthira asked, "Are you the foremost among the rudras, the vasus or the maruts? I am asking you. Which deva are you? This is not the task of a bird."'

हिमवान्पारियात्रश्च विन्ध्यो मलय एव च ।
चत्वार: पर्वता: केन पातिता भूरितेजस: ॥ (14)

'"Who is the greatly energetic one who has brought these four mountains[9] down on the ground—Himalaya, Pariyatra, Vindhya and Malaya?"'

अतीव ते महत्कर्म कृतं बलवतां वर ।
यन्न देवा न गन्धर्वा नासुरा न च राक्षसा: ।
विषहेरन्महायुद्धे कृतं ते तन्महाद्भुतम् ॥ (15)

'"O Supreme among Strong Ones! You have performed an extremely great deed. Devas, gandharvas, asuras and rakshasas[10] are incapable of withstanding them in a great battle. You have accomplished something immensely extraordinary."'

---

[8]That is, drink the water.
[9]The four Pandavas.
[10]Gandharvas and rakshasas are semi-divine races, often described as Kubera's companions.

न ते जानामि यत्कार्यं नाभिजानामि काङ्क्षितम् ।
कौतूहलं महज्जातं साध्वसं चागतं मम ॥ (16)

'"I do not know your purpose, nor do I know what you want. I am greatly curious, but I am also overwhelmed by fright."'

येनास्मद्युद्विग्नहृदयः समुत्पन्नशिरोज्वरः ।
पृच्छामि भगवंस्तस्मात्को भवानिह तिष्ठति ॥ (17)

'"You are making my heart anxious and a fever is rising in my head. O Illustrious One! I am asking you. Who are you, established here?"'

यक्ष उवाच

यक्षोऽहमस्मि भद्रं ते नास्मि पक्षी जलेचरः ।
मयैते निहताः सर्वे भ्रातरस्ते महौजसः ॥ (18)

'The yaksha replied, "O Fortunate One! I am a yaksha. I am not an aquatic bird. It is I who killed all your greatly energetic brothers."'

वैशंपायन उवाच

ततस्तामशिवां श्रुत्वा वाचं स परुषाक्षराम् ।
यक्षस्य ब्रुवतो राजन्नुपक्रम्य तदा स्थितः ॥ (19)

Vaishampayana continued, 'O King![11] On hearing these inauspicious words spoken by the yaksha in a harsh voice, he approached nearby and stood there.'

विरूपाक्षं महाकायं यक्षं तालसमुच्छ्रयम् ।
ज्वलनार्कप्रतीकाशमधृष्यं पर्वतोपमम् ॥ (20)
वृक्षमाश्रित्य तिष्ठन्तं ददर्श भरतर्षभः ।
मेघगम्भीरया वाचा तर्जयन्तं महाबलम् ॥ (21)

'The bull of the Bharata lineage saw the yaksha, with malformed eyes and gigantic in form, as tall as a tala tree. He was as fiery as the fire and the sun and was invincible like a mountain. The

---

[11]King Janamejaya.

immensely strong one stood near a tree and censured him in a voice that was as deep as the roar of thunder.'

यक्ष उवाच

इमे ते भ्रातरो राजन्वार्यमाणा मयाऽसकृत् ।
बलात्तोयं जिहीर्षन्तस्ततो वै सूदिता मया ॥ (22)

'The yaksha said, "O King! These brothers of yours were repeatedly restrained by me. But they tried to drink the water by force, and I killed them."'

न पेयमुदकं राजन्प्राणानिह परीप्सता ।
पार्थ मा साहसं कार्षीर्मम पूर्वपरिग्रह: ।
प्रश्नानुक्त्वा तु कौन्तेय तत: पिब हरस्व च ॥ (23)

'"O King! This water should not be drunk by someone who desires his life. O Partha![12] Do not be rash. I have obtained possession of this earlier. O Kounteya! Answer my questions. Then drink and take."'[13]

युधिष्ठिर उवाच

नैवाहं कामये यक्ष तव पूर्वपरिग्रहम् ।
कामं नैतत्प्रशंसन्ति सन्तो हि पुरुषा: सदा ॥ (24)
यदात्मना स्वमात्मानं प्रशंसेतत्पुरुष: प्रभो ।
यथाप्रज्ञं तु ते प्रश्नान्प्रतिवक्ष्यामि पृच्छ माम् ॥ (25)

'Yudhishthira replied, "O Yaksha! I do not desire what you have possessed earlier. Virtuous men never praise such desires; men should not praise themselves either. O Lord! Ask me. I will answer according to my wisdom."'

यक्ष उवाच

किं स्विदादित्यमुनयति के च तस्याभितश्चरा: ।
कश्चौनमस्तं नयति कस्मिंश्च प्रतितिष्ठति ॥ (26)

---

[12]Partha means Pritha's (Kunti's) son, so Yudhishthira, Bhima and Arjuna are all 'Partha'.
[13]Take the water.

'The yaksha asked, "What makes the sun rise and who are those around him? What conveys him to setting and on what is he established?"'

युधिष्ठिर उवाच

ब्रह्मादित्यमुन्नयति देवास्तस्याभितश्चराः ।
धर्मश्चास्तं नयति च सत्ये च प्रतितिष्ठति ॥ (27)

'Yudhishthira replied, "Brahma makes the sun rise and devas remain around him. Dharma conveys him towards setting, and he is established on truth."'

यक्ष उवाच

केन स्विच्छ्रोत्रियो भवति केन स्विद्विन्दते महत् ।
केन द्वितीयवान्भवति राजन्केन च बुद्धिमान् ॥ (28)

'The yaksha asked, "How does one become learned? How does one attain greatness? O King! How does one obtain a second[14]? How does one become intelligent?"'

युधिष्ठिर उवाच

श्रुतेन श्रोत्रियो भवति तपसा विन्दते महत् ।
धृत्या द्वितीयवान्भवति बुद्धिमान्वृद्धसेवया ॥ (29)

'Yudhishthira replied, "One becomes learned through the Shrutis. One attains greatness through austerities. One obtains a second through fortitude. One becomes intelligent by serving the elders."'

यक्ष उवाच

किं ब्राह्मणानां देवत्वं कश्च धर्मः सतामिव ।
कश्चैषां मानुषो भावः किमेषामसतामिव ॥ (30)

---

[14] The word used is '*dvitiyavana*', meaning one who has a second. But the meaning remains obscure here. However, '*dvitiya*' also means the second in a family, that is, a son. Perhaps the sense is that one obtains a son through perseverance.

'The yaksha asked, "What is the divinity in brahmanas? What dharma of theirs is like that of the virtuous? What are their human traits? Which of their traits are like that of those without virtue?"'

युधिष्ठिर उवाच

स्वाध्याय एषां देवत्वं तप एषां सतामिव ।
मरणं मानुषो भावः परिवादोऽसतामिव ॥ (31)

'Yudhishthira replied, "Studying is their divine trait. Their austerities are like those of the virtuous. Mortality is their human trait. Slander is like the conduct of those without virtue."'

यक्ष उवाच

किं क्षत्रियाणां देवत्वं कश्च धर्मः सतामिव ।
कश्चौषां मानुषो भावः किमेषामसतामिव ॥ (32)

'The yaksha asked, "What is the divinity of kshatriyas? What dharma of theirs is like that of the virtuous? What are their human traits? Which of their traits are like that of those without virtue?"'

युधिष्ठिर उवाच

इष्वस्त्रमेषां देवत्वं यज्ञ एषां सतामिव ।
भयं वै मानुषो भावः परित्यागोऽसतामिव ॥ (33)

'Yudhishthira replied, "Arrows and weapons are their divine traits. Their sacrifices are like that of the virtuous. Fear is their human trait. Desertion is the conduct of those without virtue."'

यक्ष उवाच

किमेकं यज्ञियं साम किमेकं यज्ञियं यजुः ।
का चौका वृश्चते यज्ञं कां यज्ञो नातिवर्तते ॥ (34)

'The yaksha asked, "Which is the single sacrificial chant? What is the single sacrificial formula? What is the single thing sacrifices need? And what can sacrifices not transgress?"'

युधिष्ठिर उवाच

प्राणो वै यज्ञियं साम मनो वै यज्ञियं यजुः ।
वागेका वृश्चते यज्ञं तां यज्ञो नातिवर्तते ॥ (35)

'Yudhishthira replied, "Prana[15] is the sacrificial chant. The mind is the sacrificial formula. Speech is the single thing sacrifices need, and sacrifices cannot transgress it."'

यक्ष उवाच

किं स्विदापततां श्रेष्ठं किं स्विन्निपततां वरम् ।
किं स्वित्प्रतिष्ठमानानां किं स्वित्प्रवदतां वरम् ॥ (36)

'The yaksha asked, "What is the best among those that descend? What is supreme among those that are sown? What is the best among those that stand? What is supreme among those who speak?"'

युधिष्ठिर उवाच

वर्षमापततां श्रेष्ठं बीजं निपततां वरम् ।
गावः प्रतिष्ठमानानां पुत्रः प्रवदतां वरः ॥ (37)

'Yudhishthira replied, "Rain is the best among those that descend. Seeds are supreme among those that are sown. Cows are the best among those that stand. Sons are supreme among those who speak."'[16]

यक्ष उवाच

इन्द्रियार्थाननुभवन्बुद्धिमाँल्लोकपूजितः ।
संमतः सर्वभूतानामुच्छ्वसन्को न जीवति ॥ (38)

'The yaksha asked, "Who experiences the objects of the senses, is intelligent, is worshipped by the worlds, is revered by all beings and breathes, but is not alive?"'

---

[15]Used here in the sense of 'breath of life'.
[16]The CE uses the word '*pravadatam*', meaning those who speak. Some other versions use the word '*prasavatam*', meaning those who are born. Since the answer is a son, the latter fits better than the former.

युधिष्ठिर उवाच

देवतातिथिभृत्यानां पितॄणामात्मनश्च यः ।
न निर्वपति पञ्चानामुच्छ्वसन् स जीवति ॥ (39)

'Yudhishthira replied, "A person who does not render offerings to the five—devas, atithis, servants, ancestors and himself—breathes but is not alive."'

यक्ष उवाच

किं स्विद्गुरुतरं भूमेः किं स्विदुच्चतरं च खात् ।
किं स्विच्छीघ्रतरं वायोः किं स्विद्बहुतरं नृणाम् ॥ (40)

'The yaksha asked, "What is heavier than the earth? What is loftier than the sky? What is swifter than the wind? What is more numerous than men?"'

युधिष्ठिर उवाच

माता गुरुतरा भूमेः पिता उच्चतरश्च खात् ।
मनः शीघ्रतरं वायोश्चिन्ता बहुतरी नृणाम् ॥ (41)

'Yudhishthira replied, "The mother is heavier than the earth. The father is loftier than the sky. The mind is swifter than the wind. Thoughts are more numerous than men."'[17]

यक्ष उवाच

किं स्वित्सुप्तं न निमिषति किं स्विज्जातं न चोपति ।
कस्य स्विद्धृदयं नास्ति किं स्विद्वेगेन वर्धते ॥ (42)

'The yaksha asked, "What does not close its eyes while asleep? What does not move when it is born? What has no heart? What grows through speeding?"'

---

[17]The CE uses the word '*nrinam*', meaning men. Some other versions use the word '*trinam*', meaning grass. Grass does fit better than men.

युधिष्ठिर उवाच

मत्स्यः सुप्तो न निमिषत्यण्डं जातं न चोपति ।
अश्मनो हृदयं नास्ति नदी वेगेन वर्धते ॥ (43)

'Yudhishthira replied, "A fish does not close its eyes while asleep. An egg does not move when it is born. A stone has no heart. A river grows through speeding."'

यक्ष उवाच

किं स्वित्प्रवसतो मित्रं किं स्विन्मित्रं गृहे सतः ।
आतुरस्य च किं मित्रं किं स्विन्मित्रं मरिष्यतः ॥ (44)

'The yaksha asked, "Who is a friend to one who is away from home?[18] Who is a friend at home? Who is a friend to one who is sick? Who is a friend to one who is about to die?"'

युधिष्ठिर उवाच

सार्थः प्रवसतो मित्रं भार्या मित्रं गृहे सतः ।
आतुरस्य भिषङ् मित्रं दानं मित्रं मरिष्यतः ॥ (45)

'Yudhishthira replied, "A caravan is a friend to one who is away from home. A wife is a friend at home. A physician is a friend to one who is sick. Donations are a friend to one who is about to die."'[19]

यक्ष उवाच

किं स्विदेको विचरते जातः को जायते पुनः ।
किं स्विद्धिमस्य भैषज्यं किं स्विदावपनं महत् ॥ (46)

'The yaksha asked, "What roams around alone? What is born again after birth? What is a medicine for cold? What is the greatest place to sow in?"'

---

[18]That is, a traveller.
[19]Because donations ensure welfare in the worlds beyond death.

युधिष्ठिर उवाच

सूर्य एको विचरते चन्द्रमा जायते पुनः ।
अग्निर्हिमस्य भैषज्यं भूमिरापवनं महत् ॥ (47)

'Yudhishthira replied, "The sun travels alone. The moon is born again. Fire is the medication for cold. The earth is the greatest place to sow in."'

यक्ष उवाच

किं स्विदेकपदं धर्म्यं किं स्विदेकपदं यशः ।
किं स्विदेकपदं स्वर्ग्यं किं स्विदेकपदं सुखम् ॥ (48)

'The yaksha asked, "What is the single step to dharma? What is the single step to fame? What is the single step to heaven? What is the single step to happiness?"'

युधिष्ठिर उवाच

दाक्ष्यमेकपदं धर्म्यं दानमेकपदं यशः ।
सत्यमेकपदं स्वर्ग्यं शीलमेकपदं सुखम् ॥ (49)

'Yudhishthira replied, "Skill is the single step to dharma. Donations represent the single step to fame. Truth is the single step to heaven. Good conduct is the single step to happiness."'

यक्ष उवाच

किं स्विदात्मा मनुष्यस्य किं स्विद्दैवकृतः सखा ।
उपजीवनं किं स्विदस्य किं स्विदस्य परायणम् ॥ (50)

'The yaksha asked, "What is a man's atman? What is the friend given by destiny? What is the support of his life? What is his refuge?"'

युधिष्ठिर उवाच

पुत्र आत्मा मनुष्यस्य भार्या दैवकृतः सखा ।
उपजीवनं च पर्जन्यो दानमस्य परायणम् ॥ (51)

'Yudhishthira replied, "A son is a man's self.[20] The wife is the friend given by destiny. Rains are the support of his life. Donations are his refuge."'

यक्ष उवाच

धन्यानामुत्तमं किं स्विद्धनानां किं स्विदुत्तमम् ।
लाभानामुत्तमं किं स्वित्किं सुखानां तथोत्तमम् ॥ (52)

'The yaksha asked, "What is supreme among lauded objects? What is supreme among riches? What is the supreme gain? What is supreme happiness?"'

युधिष्ठिर उवाच

धन्यानामुत्तमं दाक्ष्यं धनानामुत्तमं श्रुतम् ।
लाभानां श्रेष्ठमारोग्यं सुखानां तुष्टिरुत्तमा ॥ (53)

'Yudhishthira replied, "Skill is supreme among objects that are lauded. Learning is supreme among riches. Good health is the supreme gain. Contentment is the supreme happiness."'

यक्ष उवाच

कश्च धर्मः परो लोके कश्च धर्मः सदाफलः ।
किं नियम्य न शोचन्ति कैश्च सन्धिर्न जीर्यते ॥ (54)

'The yaksha asked, "What is the supreme dharma in this world? What dharma always leads to fruits? What entity, when controlled, does not make people grieve? What alliance never decays?"'

युधिष्ठिर उवाच

आनृशंस्यं परो धर्मस्त्रयीधर्मः सदाफलः ।
मनो यम्य न शोचन्ति सन्धिः सद्भिर्न जीर्यते ॥ (55)

'Yudhishthira replied, "Non-violence is the supreme dharma. The dharma of the three[21] always leads to fruits. When the mind is

---

[20]This implies that a man is born in the form of his son.
[21]The three Vedas—Rig Veda, Sama Veda and Yajur Veda. Atharva Veda is often

controlled, people do not grieve. An alliance with the virtuous never decays."'

यक्ष उवाच

किं नु हित्वा प्रियो भवति किं नु हित्वा न शोचति ।
किं नु हित्वार्थवान्भवति किं नु हित्वा सुखी भवेत् ॥ (56)

'The yaksha asked, "If abandoned, what makes one pleasant? If abandoned, what does not lead to sorrow? If abandoned, what ensures prosperity? If abandoned, what makes one happy?"'

युधिष्ठिर उवाच

मानं हित्वा प्रियो भवति क्रोधं हित्वा न शोचति ।
कामं हित्वार्थवान्भवति लोभं हित्वा सुखी भवेत् ॥ (57)

'Yudhishthira replied, "The abandoning of pride makes one pleasant. If one abandons anger, one does not grieve. The abandoning of desire ensures prosperity. The abandoning of greed makes one happy."'

यक्ष उवाच

मृतः कथं स्यात्पुरुषः कथं राष्ट्रं मृतं भवेत् ।
श्राद्धं मृतं कथं वा स्यात्कथं यज्ञो मृतो भवेत् ॥ (58)

'The yaksha asked, "When is a man dead? When is a kingdom dead? When is a funeral ceremony dead? When is a sacrifice dead?"'

युधिष्ठिर उवाच

मृतो दरिद्रः पुरुषो मृतं राष्ट्रमराजकम् ।
मृतमश्रोत्रियं श्राद्धं मृतो यज्ञस्त्वदक्षिणः ॥ (59)

'Yudhishthira replied, "A poor man is dead. A kingdom without a king is dead. A funeral ceremony performed without a learned brahmana is dead. A sacrifice without *dakshina*[22] is dead."'

---

not included in the list.

[22]Daskhina is the sacrificial fee paid to an officiating priest at a sacrifice. It is

यक्ष उवाच

का दिक्किमुदकं प्रोक्तं किमन्नं पार्थ किं विषम् ।
श्राद्धस्य कालमाख्याहि ततः पिब हरस्व च ॥ (60)

'The yaksha asked, "What is the right direction? What is spoken of as water? O Partha! What is food and what is poison? What is the right time for a funeral ceremony? Then you can drink and take."'[23]

युधिष्ठिर उवाच

सन्तो दिग्जलमाकाशं गौरन्नं प्रार्थना विषम् ।
श्राद्धस्य ब्राह्मणः कालः कथं वा यक्ष मन्यसे ॥ (61)

'Yudhishthira replied, "The virtuous are the right direction. The sky is water. The cow is food. A request is poison. A brahmana is the best time for a funeral sacrifice.[24] O Yaksha! What do you think?"'

यक्ष उवाच

व्याख्याता मे त्वया प्रश्ना याथातथ्यं परन्तप ।
पुरुषं त्विदानीमाख्याहि यश्च सर्वधनी नरः ॥ (62)

'The yaksha said, "O Scorcher of Enemies! You have explained all my questions correctly. Tell me now. Who is a man? Which man possesses all riches?"'

युधिष्ठिर उवाच

दिवं स्पृशति भूमिं च शब्दः पुण्यस्य कर्मणा ।
यावत्स शब्दो भवति तावत्पुरुष उच्यते ॥ (63)

---

also the fee paid by a *shishya* (disciple) to his guru (preceptor) on the successful completion of studies.

[23]The water.

[24]*Brahma muhurta* refers to that specific time of the day that is regarded as being presided over by the brahman. It occurs towards the early part of the day, 48 minutes before the sun rises. Here, the word brahmana refers to brahma muhurta.

'Yudhishthira replied, "The reputation of auspicious deeds touches heaven and earth. As long as that reputation remains, one is said to be a man."'

तुल्ये प्रियाप्रिये यस्य सुखदुःखे तथैव च ।
अतीतानागते चोभे स वै सर्वधनी नरः ॥ (64)

'"One to whom the pleasant and the unpleasant, happiness and unhappiness and the past and the future are equal, is a man who possesses all riches."'

यक्ष उवाच

व्याख्यातः पुरुषो राजन्यश्च सर्वधनी नरः ।
तस्मात्त्वैको भ्रातृणां यमिच्छसि स जीवतु ॥ (65)

'The yaksha said, "O King! You have explained who is a man and which man possesses all riches. Therefore, one of your brothers, whichever one you wish, will live."'

युधिष्ठिर उवाच

श्यामो य एष रक्ताक्षो बृहच्छाल इवोद्गतः ।
व्यूढोरस्को महाबाहुर्नकुलो यक्ष जीवतु ॥ (66)

'Yudhishthira replied, "O Yaksha! Nakula is dark, with red eyes, mighty arms and a broad chest. He is as tall as a shala tree. Let him live."'

यक्ष उवाच

प्रियस्ते भीमसेनोऽयमर्जुनो वः परायणम् ।
स कस्मान्नकुलो राजन्सापत्नं जीवमिच्छसि ॥ (67)

'The yaksha said, "You love Bhimasena, and you depend on Arjuna. O King! Why do you then wish Nakula, who is your stepbrother, to be revived?"'

यस्य नागसहस्रेण दशसंख्येन वै बलम् ।
तुल्यं तं भीममुत्सृज्य नकुलं जीवमिच्छसि ॥ (68)

'"Bhima has strength equal to ten thousand elephants. Why do you discard him and wish for Nakula to live?"'

तथैनं मनुजाः प्राहुर्भीमसेनं प्रियं तव ।
अथ केनानुभावेन सापत्नं जीवमिच्छसि ॥ (69)

'"Similarly, people say that Bhimasena is your beloved. Out of what sentiments do you wish for your stepbrother to live?"'

यस्य बाहुबलं सर्वे पाण्डवाः समुपाश्रिताः ।
अर्जुनं तमपाहाय नकुलं जीवमिच्छसि ॥ (70)

'"All the Pandavas depend on the strength of Arjuna's arms. But you discard him and wish for Nakula to live."'

युधिष्ठिर उवाच

आनृशंस्यं परो धर्मः परमार्थाच्च मे मतम् ।
आनृशंस्यं चिकीर्षामि नकुलो यक्ष जीवतु ॥ (71)

'Yudhishthira replied, "Non-violence is the supreme dharma. It is my view that this is the supreme objective. I am attracted to non-violence. O Yaksha! Let Nakula live."'

धर्मशीलः सदा राजा इति मां मानवा विदुः ।
स्वधर्मान्न चलिष्यामि नकुलो यक्ष जीवतु ॥ (72)

'"Men know me as a king who always follows dharma in his conduct. I will not deviate from my own dharma. O Yaksha! Let Nakula live."'

यथा कुन्ती तथा माद्री विशेषो नास्ति मे तयोः ।
मातृभ्यां सममिच्छामि नकुलो यक्ष जीवतु ॥ (73)

'"Madri is like Kunti, and I see no difference between the two. I wish the same for both my mothers. O Yaksha! Let Nakula live."'

यक्ष उवाच

तस्य तेऽर्थाच्च कामाच्च आनृशंस्यं परं मतम् ।
तस्मात्ते भ्रातरः सर्वे जीवन्तु भरतर्षभ ॥ (74)

'The yaksha said, "O Bull of the Bharata lineage! Since you think that non-violence is superior to artha and kama, all of your brothers will be restored to life."'

Thus ends the Yaksha Prashna.

5

NAHUSHA GITA

The Nahusha Gita is from a sub-parva of Aranyaka Parva known as Ajagara Parva. '*Ajagara*' refers to a python. The word translates literally to something that swallows a goat (*aja*). When the Pandavas go to the origin of the Yamuna and the Dvaitavana lake, along the banks of Sarasvati, Bhima is captured by King Nahusha, who is in the form of a python—which gives this section its name. The highlight of this section is a dialogue between Yudhishthira and Nahusha in his python form. This part, consisting of two chapters and eighty-three shlokas, is known as the Nahusha Gita.

Chapter 1

वैशम्पायन उवाच

युधिष्ठिरस्तमासाद्य सर्पभोगाभिवेष्टितम् ।
दयितं भ्रातरं वीरमिदं वचनमब्रवीत् ॥ (1)

Vaishampayana said, 'On seeing his beloved brother encircled in the coils of the snake, Yudhishthira approached and addressed the brave one in these words.'

कुन्तीमातः कथमिमामापदं त्वमवाप्तवान् ।
कश्चायं पर्वताभोगप्रतिमः पन्नगोत्तमः ॥ (2)

'"O One Whose Mother Is Kunti![1] How has this calamity befallen you? Who is this supreme pannaga?[2] This serpent's body is like a mountain."'

स धर्मराजमालक्ष्य भ्राता भ्रातरमग्रजम् ।
कथयामास तत्सर्वं ग्रहणादि विचेष्टितम् ॥ (3)

'On seeing his elder brother Dharmaraja, he[3] told his brother everything that had happened and how he had come to be seized.'

युधिष्ठिर उवाच

देवो वा यदि वा दैत्य उरगो वा भवान्यदि ।
सत्यं सर्पो वचो ब्रूहि पृच्छति त्वां युधिष्ठिरः ॥ (4)

'Yudhishthira asked, "O Serpent! Yudhishthira is asking you. Speak the truth. Are you a deva, a daitya[4] or an uraga?"'

किमाहृत्य विदित्वा वा प्रीतिस्ते स्यादभुजङ्गम ।
किमाहारं प्रयच्छामि कथं मुञ्चेद्भवानिमम् ॥ (5)

'"O Serpent! Let it be known what must be brought to please you. What food will I give you? What must be done to free him?"'

सर्प उवाच

नहुषो नाम राजाहमासं पूर्वस्तवानघ ।
प्रथितः पञ्चमः सोमादायोः पुत्रो नराधिप ॥ (6)

'The serpent replied, "O Unblemished One! I was earlier a king named Nahusha, your ancestor. O Lord of Men! I was Ayu's famous son and was fifth in the line from Soma."'[5]

---

[1]Addressing Bhima.
[2]A 'pannaga' or 'naga' is not the same as an ordinary snake (*sarpa*), though naga/pannaga and sarpa are sometimes used synonymously. A pannaga/naga has semi-divine attributes and often resides in a distinct region. 'Uraga' is another term for pannaga/naga.
[3]Bhima.
[4]Diti and Danu, both daughters of Daksha, were married to Sage Kashyapa. Their respective sons were daityas and danavas, though the two terms are often used as synonyms. Loosely, daityas are the antithesis of devas.
[5]This is the Lunar dynasty, originating with Soma or Chandra, the Moon. Soma's

क्रतुभिस्तपसा चौव स्वाध्यायेन दमेन च ।
त्रैलोक्यैश्वर्यमव्यग्रं प्राप्तो विक्रमणेन च ॥ (7)

'"Through sacrifices, austerities, studying, self-restraint and valour, I obtained unrivalled prosperity in the three worlds."'

तदैश्वर्यं समासाद्य दर्पो मामगमत्तदा ।
सहस्रं हि द्विजातीनामुवाह शिबिकां मम ॥ (8)

'"Having attained that prosperity, insolence came over me. Thousands of dvijas carried my palanquin."'[6]

ऐश्वर्यमदमत्तोऽहमवमन्य ततो द्विजान् ।
इमामगस्त्येन दशामानीत: पृथिवीपते ॥ (9)

'"Intoxicated with my prosperity, I insulted those dvijas. O Lord of the Earth! I have been reduced to this state because of Agastya."'

न तु मामजहात्प्रज्ञा यावद्द्येति पाण्डव ।
तस्यैवानुग्रहाद्राजन्नगस्त्यस्य महात्मन: ॥ (10)

'"O Pandava! O King! But because of the favours of the great-souled Agastya, I have not lost my wisdom even now."'

षष्ठे काले ममाहार: प्राप्तोऽयमनुजस्तव ।
नाहमेनं विमोक्ष्यामि न चान्यमभिकामये ॥ (11)

'"I have obtained your younger brother as my food at the sixth point in time.[7] I will not free him, nor do I desire anything else."'

प्रश्नानुच्चारितांस्तु त्वं व्याहरिष्यसि चेन्मम ।
अथ पश्चाद्विमोक्ष्यामि भ्रातरं ते वृकोदरम् ॥ (12)

---

son was Budha, Budha's son was Pururava, Pururava's son was Ayu and Ayu's son was Nahusha. So Nahusha was fifth in the line.
[6]Nahusha dislodged Indra and became the ruler of Svarga, the world of devas. Insolent and proud, he made brahmanas carry his palanquin. When Nahusha's foot touched Agastya's body, the latter became enraged and cursed the former.
[7]Meaning, the sixth day. The python eats on every sixth day.

'"But if you answer the questions I ask you, I will subsequently free your brother Vrikodara."'[8]

युधिष्ठिर उवाच

ब्रूहि सर्प यथाकामं प्रतिवक्ष्यामि ते वच: ।
अपि चेच्छक्नुयां प्रीतिमाहर्तुं ते भुजङ्गम ॥ (13)

'Yudhishthira replied, "O Serpent! Tell me whatever you wish and I will reply. O Serpent! If I am capable of doing this, I will please you."'

वेद्यं यद्ब्राह्मणेनेह तद्भवान्वेत्ति केवलम् ।
सर्पराज तत: श्रुत्वा प्रतिवक्ष्यामि ते वच: ॥ (14)

'"You are aware of what only a brahmana can know in this world. O King of Snakes! On hearing your words, I will reply."'

सर्प उवाच

ब्राह्मण: को भवेद्राजन्वेद्यं किं च युधिष्ठिर ।
ब्रवीह्यतिमतिं त्वां हि वाक्यैरनुमिमीमहे ॥ (15)

'The serpent asked, "O King! O Yudhishthira! Who is a brahmana and what should he know? From what you have said, I imagine you know."'

युधिष्ठिर उवाच

सत्यं दानं क्षमा शीलमानृशंस्यं दमो घृणा ।
दृश्यन्ते यत्र नागेन्द्र स ब्राह्मण इति स्मृत: ॥ (16)

'Yudhishthira replied, "O Indra among Nagas! It is said that a brahmana is one in whom truthfulness, charity, forgiveness, good conduct, lack of cruelty, self-control and compassion can be seen."'

वेद्यं सर्प परं ब्रह्म निर्दु:खमसुखं च यत् ।
यत्र गत्वा न शोचन्ति भवत: किं विवक्षितम् ॥ (17)

---

[8]Another name for Bhima. 'Vrikodara' means one with a belly like a wolf.

"'O Serpent! He knows the supreme brahman, which is beyond happiness and unhappiness, and on attaining which, there is no sorrow. What else deserves to be said?'"

सर्प उवाच

चातुर्वर्ण्यं प्रमाणं च सत्यं च ब्रह्म चैव हि ।
शूद्रेष्वपि च सत्यं च दानमक्रोध एव च ।
आनृशंस्यमहिंसा च घृणा चैव युधिष्ठिर ॥ (18)

'The serpent said, "Truthfulness and understanding of the brahman can be found in all the four varnas. O Yudhishthira! Truthfulness, charity, lack of anger, lack of cruelty, non-violence and compassion can also be found among shudras."'

वेद्यं यच्चाथ निर्दुःखमसुखं च नराधिप ।
ताभ्यां हीनं पदं चान्यन्न तदस्तीति लक्षये ॥ (19)

"'O Lord of Men! You have said that the object of knowledge is beyond happiness and unhappiness. But nothing can be seen to exist that is devoid of either.'"

युधिष्ठिर उवाच

शूद्रे चैतद्भवेल्लक्ष्यं द्विजे तच्च न विद्यते ।
न वै शूद्रो भवेच्छूद्रो ब्राह्मणो न च ब्राह्मण: ॥ (20)

'Yudhishthira replied, "If these traits, not even found in a brahmana, are seen in a shudra, he is not a shudra. One in whom a brahmana's traits are not found is a shudra, not a brahmana."'

यत्रैतल्लक्ष्यतेसर्प वृत्तं स ब्राह्मण: स्मृत: ।
यत्रैतन्न भवेत्सर्प तं शूद्रमिति निर्दिशेत् ॥ (21)

"'O Serpent! It is said that one in whom such conduct is discerned is a brahmana. O Serpent! One in whom these do not exist is identified as a shudra.'"

यत्पुनर्भवता प्रोक्तं न वेद्यं विद्यतेति ह ।
ताभ्यां हीनमतीत्यात्र पदं नास्तीति चेदपि ॥ (22)

'"You have also said that the object of knowledge does not exist because there is nothing that is devoid of either.[9] Therefore, it does not exist."'

एवमेतन्मतं सर्प ताभ्यां हीनं न विद्यते ।
यथा शीतोष्णयोर्मध्ये भवेन्नोष्णं न शीतता ॥ (23)

'"O Serpent! It is your view that a state devoid of either does not exist. However, there is a state between cold and hot, which is neither cold nor hot."'

एवं वै सुखदुःखाभ्यां हीनमस्ति पदं क्वचित् ।
एषा मम मतिः सर्प यथा वा मन्यते भवान् ॥ (24)

'"Like that, there is something in between, which is neither happiness nor unhappiness. That is my view. O Serpent! What do you think?"'

सर्प उवाच

यदि ते वृत्ततो राजन्ब्राह्मणः प्रसमीक्षितः ।
व्यर्था जातिस्तदायुष्मन्कृतिर्यावन्न दृश्यते ॥ (25)

'The snake said, "O King! O one with a long life! If you assert that a brahmana is known by his conduct, then birth has no meaning if that kind of conduct cannot be seen."'

युधिष्ठिर उवाच

जातिरत्र महासर्प मनुष्यत्वे महामते ।
संकरात्सर्ववर्णानां दुष्परीक्ष्येति मे मतिः ॥ (26)

'Yudhishthira replied, "O Great Serpent! O Immensely Wise One! My view is that among men, birth is difficult to determine because of mixed birth among all the varnas."'

सर्वे सर्वास्वपत्यानि जनयन्ति यदा नराः ।
वाङ्मैथुनमथो जन्म मरणं च समं नृणाम् ॥ (27)

---

[9]Happiness and unhappiness.

'"Since all men beget children everywhere,¹⁰ all men are equal in speech, intercourse, birth and death."'

इदमार्षं प्रमाणं च ये यजामह इत्यपि ।
तस्माच्छीलं प्रधानेष्टं विदुर्ये तत्त्वदर्शिनः ॥ (28)

'"The proof of this can be found in the words of the rishis with insight about the truth, who said, 'We sacrifice' and so on, basing this primarily on good conduct."'¹¹

प्राङ्नाभिवर्धनात्पुंसो जातकर्म विधीयते ।
तत्रास्य माता सावित्री पिता त्वाचार्य उच्यते ॥ (29)

'"The birth rituals of a man are performed even before the navel chord has been severed. At that time, the mother is *savitri* and the father is spoken of as the acharya."'¹²

वृत्त्या शूद्र समो ह्येष यावद्वेदे न जायते ।
अस्मिन्नेवं मतिद्वैधे मनुः स्वायम्भुवोऽब्रवीत् ॥ (30)
कृतकृत्याः पुनर्वर्णा यदि वृत्तं न विद्यते ।
संकरस्तत्र नागेन्द्र बलवान्प्रसमीक्षितः ॥ (31)

'"Before initiation into knowledge of the Vedas has occurred, everyone is equally shudra by conduct. O Indra among Nagas! When there is a difference of opinion on this, Svayambhuva Manu¹³ has stated, 'What is done about rituals determines varna. If conduct doesn't exist, then mixed varnas dominate overwhelmingly.'"'

---

¹⁰Irrespective of the mother's varna.
¹¹That is, the right to sacrifice is based on conduct, and not on varna.
¹²The word 'savitri' means several things. It is a sacred mantra from the Rig Veda. It is also the ceremony of investiture with the sacred thread. The sense is that at the time of birth, the mother is more important than the father, and this birth ritual is the equivalent of the sacred thread ceremony.
¹³Each *manvantara* (era) is presided over by a sovereign known as Manu. It is because humans are descended from Manu that they are known as *manava*. There are fourteen manvantaras and fourteen Manus to preside over them. The present manvantara is the seventh and the Manu who presides over this is known as Vaivasvata because he was born from the sun (Vivasvat). Svayambhuva Manu was the first, thus known because he originated from Svayambhu (Brahma).

यत्रेदानीं महासर्प संस्कृतं वृत्तमिष्यते ।
तं ब्राह्मणमहं पूर्वमुक्तवान्भुजगोत्तम ॥ (33)

'"O Great Snake! O Supreme among Serpents! Since such mixed conduct is seen now, I told you earlier that I am a brahmana."'

सर्प उवाच

श्रुतं विदितवेद्यस्य तव वाक्यं युधिष्ठिर ।
भक्षयेयमहं कस्माद्भ्रातरं ते वृकोदरम् ॥ (33)

'The snake replied, "O Yudhishthira! I have now heard your words. You know what should be known. How can I devour your brother Vrikodara?"'

Chapter 2

युधिष्ठिर उवाच

भवानेतादृशो लोके वेदवेदाङ्गपारग: ।
ब्रूहि किं कुर्वत: कर्म भवेद्गतिरनुत्तमा ॥ (1)

'Yudhishthira asked, "In this world, there is no one as accomplished as you in the Vedas and the Vedangas. Please tell me. What is the karma through which one attains the supreme objective?"'

सर्प उवाच

पात्रे दत्त्वा प्रियाण्युक्त्वा सत्यमुक्त्वा च भारत ।
अहिंसानिरत: स्वर्गं गच्छेदिति मतिर्मम ॥ (2)

'The snake replied, "O Descendant of the Bharata Lineage! It is my view that one goes to heaven by giving to those who are worthy, speaking what is agreeable, speaking the truth and by always resorting to non-violence."'

युधिष्ठिर उवाच

दानाद्वा सर्प सत्याद्वा किमतो गुरु दृश्यते ।
अहिंसाप्रिययोश्चैव गुरुलाघवमुच्यताम् ॥ (3)

'Yudhishthira asked, "O Snake! Between donations and truthfulness, which is seen to be superior? Between non-violence and agreeable words, which is superior and which is inferior? Please tell me."'

सर्प उवाच

दाने रतत्वं सत्यं च अहिंसा प्रियमेव च ।
एषां कार्यगरीयस्त्वाद्दृश्यते गुरुलाघवम् ॥ (4)

'The snake replied, "The superiority or inferiority of devotion to donations, truthfulness, non-violence or agreeable words is determined by the effects of these deeds."'

कस्माच्चिद्दानयोगाद्धि सत्यमेव विशिष्यते ।
सत्यवाक्याच्च राजेन्द्र किंचिद्दानं विशिष्यते ॥ (5)

'"Sometimes, truthfulness is superior to donations. O Indra among Kings! Sometimes, donations are superior to truthfulness."'

एवमेव महेष्वास प्रियवाक्यान्महीपते ।
अहिंसा दृश्यते गुर्वी ततश्च प्रियमिष्यते ॥ (6)

'"O Mighty Archer! O Lord of the Earth! In that way, there are occasions when non-violence is seen to be superior to agreeable words and other occasions when agreeable words are superior."'

एवमेतद्व्वेद्राजन्कार्यापेक्षमनन्तरम् ।
यदभिप्रेतमन्यत्ते ब्रूहि यावद्ब्रवीम्यहम् ॥ (7)

'"O King! In this fashion, the superiority depends on the subsequent effects. If there is anything else that you wish to think of, tell me. I will explain."'

युधिष्ठिर उवाच

कथं स्वर्गं गतिः सर्प कर्मणां च फलं ध्रुवम् ।
अशरीरस्य दृश्येत विषयांश्च ब्रवीहि मे ॥ (8)

'Yudhishthira asked, "O Snake! How does one obtain a destination in heaven? What are seen to be the certain fruits of karma obtained by the one without a body?[14] Please explain these things to me."'

सर्प उवाच

तिस्रो वै गतयो राजन्परिदृष्टाः स्वकर्मभिः ।
मानुष्यं स्वर्गवासश्च तिर्यग्योनिश्च तत्त्रिधा ॥ (9)

'The snake replied, "O King! Depending on one's own karma, there are seen to be three destinations—human birth, residence in heaven and rebirth as inferior species. There are these three."'

तत्र वै मानुषाल्लोकाद्दानादिभिरतन्द्रितः ।
अहिंसार्थसमायुक्तैः कारणैः स्वर्गमश्नुते ॥ (10)

'"Because of unwavering attention to donations and deeds, based on reasons of non-violence in this human world, one obtains heaven."'

विपरीतैश्च राजेन्द्र कारणैर्मानुषो भवेत् ।
तिर्यग्योनिस्तथा तात विशेषश्चात्र वक्ष्यते ॥ (11)

'"O Indra among Kings! Because of contrary deeds, one is born as human or inferior species. O Son! I will tell you about the specifics."'

कामक्रोधसमायुक्तो हिंसा लोभसमन्वितः ।
मनुष्यत्वात्परिभ्रष्टस्तिर्यग्योनौ प्रसूयते ॥ (12)

'"One full of desire and anger, overcome by violence and avarice, is dislodged from a human state and is reborn as inferior species."'

---

[14] The jivatman.

तिर्यग्योन्यां पृथग्भावो मनुष्यत्वे विधीयते ।
गवादिभ्यस्तथाऽश्वेभ्यो देवत्वमपि दृश्यते ॥ (13)

'"It has separately been stated that one born as an inferior species can be reborn as a human. Thus, cattle and horses are seen to have obtained the status of devas."'

सोऽयमेता गती: सर्वा जन्तुश्चरति कार्यवान् ।
नित्ये महति चात्मानमवस्थापयते नृप ॥ (14)

'"Such is the destination of all beings, depending on what they have done. O King! One must always establish oneself in greatness."'

जातो जातश्च बलवान्भुङ्क्ते चात्मा स देहवान् ।
फलार्थस्तात निष्पृक्त: प्रजा लक्षणभावन: ॥ (15)

'"From one birth to another birth, the jivatman enjoys the powerful fruits that come from a body, though it is distinct. This is the characteristic of all created beings."'

युधिष्ठिर उवाच

शब्दे स्पर्शे च रूपे च तथैव रसगन्धयो: ।
तस्याधिष्ठानमव्यग्रो ब्रूहि सर्प यथातथम् ॥ (16)

'Yudhishthira asked, "O Snake! Tell me exactly how the atman is established in a body and experiences sound, touch, colour, taste and smell."'

किं न गृह्णासि विषयान्युगपत्त्वं महामते ।
एतावदुच्यतां चोक्तं सर्वं पन्नगसत्तम ॥ (17)

'"O Immensely Intelligent One! Do you also not simultaneously experience the objects of the senses? O Supreme among Pannagas! Please tell me everything that I have asked."'

सर्प उवाच

यदात्मद्रव्यमायुष्मन्देहसंश्रयणान्वितम् ।
करणाधिष्ठितं भोगानुपभुङ्क्ते यथाविधि ॥ (18)

'The snake replied, "O One with a Long Life! When the atman has resorted to a physical body and has established itself in control, it experiences each of those senses, depending on their characteristics."'

ज्ञानं चैवात्र बुद्धिश्च मनश्च भरतर्षभ ।
तस्य भोगाधिकरणे करणानि निबोध मे ॥ (19)

'"O Bull of the Bharata Lineage! Learn from me that because of that ownership, jnana, intelligence and the mind are faculties that determine the atman's enjoyment of the senses."'

मनसा तात पर्येति क्रमशो विषयानिमान् ।
विषयायतनस्थेन भूतात्मा क्षेत्रनिःसृतः ॥ (20)

'"O Son! Through the mind, the atman of a being experiences one after another, from one object to another object, the senses that flow out of the kshetra."'

अत्र चापि नरव्याघ्र मनो जन्तोर्विधीयते ।
तस्माद्युगपदस्यात्र ग्रहणं नोपपद्यते ॥ (21)

'"O Tiger among Men! Here, the mind is, thus, the cause of all perceptions among animals. It cannot experience multiple objects simultaneously."'

स आत्मा पुरुषव्याघ्र भ्रुवोरन्तरमाश्रितः ।
द्रव्येषु सृजते बुद्धिं विविधेषु परावराम् ॥ (22)

'"O Tiger among Men! The atman is established between the eyebrows. It creates the intelligence about different kinds of objects, superior and inferior."'

बुद्धेरुत्तरकालं च वेदना दृश्यते बुधैः ।
एष वै राजशार्दूल विधिः क्षेत्रज्ञभावनः ॥ (23)

'"O Tiger among Kings! According to the wise, different kinds of experience flow from this intelligence. These are thought to be the ways of the kshetrajna."'

युधिष्ठिर उवाच

मनसश्चापि बुद्धेश्च ब्रूहि मे लक्षणं परम् ।
एतदध्यात्मविदुषां परं कार्यं विधीयते ॥ (24)

'Yudhishthira said, "After this, please tell me, what are the specific characteristics that distinguish the mind and the intelligence? What is said to be the supreme task for those who know about adhyatma?"'

सर्प उवाच

बुद्धिरात्मानुगा तात उत्पातेन विधीयते ।
तदाश्रिता हि संज्ञैषा विधिस्तस्यैषिणे भवेत् ॥ (25)

'The snake replied, "O Son! Through various distractions, the intelligence is said to follow the atman. Though consciousness is dependent on it,[15] the balance is tilted."'

बुद्धेर्गुणविधिर्नास्ति मनस्तु गुणवद्भवेत् ।
बुद्धिरुत्पद्यते कार्यं मनस्तूत्पन्नमेव हि ॥ (26)

'"Intelligence is not subject to the different gunas. But the mind has these gunas. Tasks are created from the intelligence, but they are also generated in the mind."'

एतद्विशेषणं तात मनो बुद्ध्योर्मयेरितम् ।
त्वमप्यत्राभिसंबुद्धः कथं वा मन्यते भवान् ॥ (27)

'"O Son! I have thus distinguished between the mind and intelligence. But you yourself have understanding about this. What do you think?"'

युधिष्ठिर उवाच

अहो बुद्धिमतां श्रेष्ठ शुभा बुद्धिरियं तव ।
विदितं वेदितव्यं ते कस्मान्मामनुपृच्छसि ॥ (28)

---

[15]The atman.

'Yudhishthira replied, "O Best among Those Who Are Endowed with Intelligence! Your intelligence is auspicious. You know everything that there is to know. Why are you asking me?"'

सर्वज्ञं त्वां कथं मोह आविशत्स्वर्गवासिनम् ।
एवमद्भुतकर्माणिमिति मे संशयो महान् ॥ (29)

'"You know everything. You resided in heaven. You were the performer of extraordinary deeds. I have a great doubt. How did this delusion come over you?"'

सर्प उवाच

सुप्रज्ञमपि चेच्छूरमृद्धिर्मोहयते नरम् ।
वर्तमानः सुखे सर्वो नावैतीति मतिर्मम ॥ (30)

'The snake said, "Even an extremely wise and brave man is deluded by prosperity. It is my view that this is what happens to all those who are presently happy."'

सोऽहमैश्वर्यमोहेन मदाविष्टो युधिष्ठिर ।
पतितः प्रतिसंबुद्धस्त्वां तु संबोधयाम्यहम् ॥ (31)

'"O Yudhishthira! I became deluded because of my prosperity. I was intoxicated. Though enlightened, I descended into this state and am enlightening you now."'

कृतं कार्यं महाराज त्वया मम परन्तप ।
क्षीणः शापः सुकृच्छ्रो मे त्वया सम्भाष्य साधुना ॥ (32)

'"O Great King! O Scorcher of Enemies! You have performed a service towards me. Because of my conversation with a virtuous person, the curse, which led to great hardships, has decayed."'

अहं हि दिवि दिव्येन विमानेन चरन्पुरा ।
अभिमानेन मत्तः सर्वंचिन्नान्यमचिन्तयम् ॥ (33)

'"In earlier times, I used to roam around heaven in a celestial chariot. Intoxicated with my vanity, I thought of nothing else."'

ब्रह्मर्षिदेवगन्धर्वयक्षराक्षस किंनरा: ।
करान्मम प्रयच्छन्ति सर्वे त्रैलोक्यवासिन: ॥ (34)

'"*Brahmarshi*s, devas, gandharvas, yakshas, rakshasas, kinnaras and all the residents of the three worlds had to pay me tribute."'[16]

चक्षुषा यं प्रपश्यामि प्राणिनं पृथिवीपते ।
तस्य तेजो हराम्याशु तद्धि दृष्टिबलं मम ॥ (35)

'"O Lord of the Earth! Such was the power of my glance that whatever being my eyes happened to behold, the strength of my sight swiftly robbed him of his energy."'

ब्रह्मर्षीणां सहस्रं हि उवाह शिबिकां मम ।
स मामपनयो राजन्भ्रंशयामास वै श्रिय: ॥ (36)

'"Thousands of brahmarshis bore my palanquin. O King! This misconduct brought about my being dislodged from prosperity."'

तत्र ह्यगस्त्य: पादेन वहन्पृष्टो मया मुनि: ।
अदृष्टेन ततोऽस्म्युक्तो ध्वंस सर्पेति वै रुषा ॥ (37)

'"One day, when Sage Agastya was bearing me, my feet happened to touch him. In anger, destiny[17] then spoke these words, 'May you be destroyed. Become a snake.'"'

ततस्तस्माद्विमानाग्रात्प्रच्युतश्च्युतभूषण: ।
प्रपतन्बुबुधेऽऽत्मानं व्यालीभूतमधोमुखम् ॥ (38)

---

[16]Devas are shining ones, that is, gods. Gandharvas, celestial musicians, are a semi-divine race. Yakshas, rakshasas and kinnaras (kimpurushas) are also semi-divine species, with yakshas and rakshasas often described as Kubera's companions. There is a hierarchy of rishis, with *maharshis* placed above rishis and brahmarshis placed above maharshis.

[17]Agastya, in the form of destiny.

'"At that, I fell down from that supreme vimana.[18] I lost all my ornaments. While I was falling with my face down, I saw that I had become a predatory serpent."'[19]

अयाचं तमहं विप्रं शापस्यान्तो भवेदिति ।
अज्ञानात्संप्रवृत्तस्य भगवन्क्षन्तुमर्हसि ॥ (39)

'"Then I requested that brahmana, 'Please free me from this curse. O Illustrious One! I have transgressed in ignorance. You should pardon me.'"'

तत: स मामुवाचेदं प्रपतन्तं कृपान्वित: ।
युधिष्ठिरो धर्मराज: शापात्त्वां मोक्षयिष्यति ॥ (40)
अभिमानस्य घोरस्य बलस्य च नराधिप ।
फले क्षीणे महाराज फलं पुण्यमवाप्स्यसि ॥ (41)

'"At this, as I was falling, he was overcome by compassion and told me, 'Dharmaraja Yudhishthira will free you from this curse, once the fruits of your insolence and terrible strength have decayed. O Lord of Men! O Great King! You will then obtain auspicious fruits.'"'

ततो मे विस्मयो जातस्तद्दृष्ट्वा तपसो बलम् ।
ब्रह्म च ब्राह्मणत्वं च येन त्वाहमचूचुदम् ॥ (42)

'"On witnessing the strength of his austerities, there was wonder in me. That is the reason I asked you about the brahman and brahmanas."'

सत्यं दमस्तपोयोगमहिंसा दाननित्यता ।
साधकानि सदा पुंसां न जातिर्न कुलं नृप ॥ (43)

'"O King! Truthfulness, self-control, austerities, yoga, non-violence and constant donations are always the means for men, not birth or lineage."'

अरिष्ट एष ते भ्राता भीमो मुक्तो महाभुज: ।
स्वस्ति तेऽस्तु महाराज गमिष्यामि दिवं पुन: ॥ (44)

---

[18]Here, celestial vehicle.
[19]The word used is *vyala*, which means both predator and serpent.

'"Your mighty-armed brother, Bhima, is unharmed and has been freed. O Great King! May you be well. I will return to heaven again."'

वैशम्पायन उवाच

इत्युक्त्वाजगरं देहं त्यक्त्वा स नहुषो नृपः ।
दिव्यं वपुः समास्थाय गतस्त्रिदिवमेव ह ॥ (45)

Vaishampayana said, 'Having said this, King Nahusha discarded the body of an ajagara. Assuming a celestial form, he returned to heaven.'

युधिष्ठिरोऽपि धर्मात्मा भ्रात्रा भीमेन संगतः ।
धौम्येन सहितः श्रीमानाश्रमं पुनरभ्यगात् ॥ (46)

'The prosperous, Yudhishthira, with dharma in his atman, returned to the hermitage with his brother Bhima, accompanied by Dhoumya.'[20]

ततो द्विजेभ्यः सर्वेभ्यः समेतेभ्यो यथातथम् ।
कथयामास तत्सर्वं धर्मराजो युधिष्ठिरः ॥ (47)

'Dharmaraja Yudhishthira told the assembled dvijas everything that had happened, exactly as it had occurred.'

तच्छ्रुत्वा ते द्विजाः सर्वे भ्रातरश्चास्य ते त्रयः ।
आसन्सुव्रीडिता राजन्द्रौपदी च यशस्विनी ॥ (48)

'O King! On hearing this, all the dvijas, the other three brothers and the illustrious Droupadi were extremely ashamed.'

ते तु सर्वे द्विजश्रेष्ठाः पाण्डवानां हितेप्सया ।
मैवमित्यब्रुवन्भीमं गर्हयन्तोऽस्य साहसम् ॥ (49)

'All the foremost dvijas desired the welfare of the Pandavas. Censuring Bhima's rashness, they told him not to act in this way.'

---

[20]Dhoumya was the priest of the Pandavas.

पाण्डवास्तु भयान्मुक्तं प्रेक्ष्य भीमं महाबलम् ।
हर्षमाहारयांचक्रुर्विजह्रुश्च मुदा युता: ॥ (50)

'The Pandavas were extremely delighted at seeing the immensely strong Bhima freed from fear. They happily enjoyed themselves.'

Thus ends the Nahusha Gita.

6

SANATSUJATA

The Sanatsujata (also known as Sanatsujatiya) segment is not explicitly named as a Gita, but the teachings are representative of the Gita literature in the Mahabharata. When Kashinath Telang translated the Bhagavat Gita and the Anu Gita in 1882, he included the Sanatsujata.[1] It was important enough for Adi Shankaracharya to have written a commentary on it, and so was it for other commentators. The Sanatsujata segment is a sub-parva of Udyoga Parva, which is so named because it is about preparations for the Kurukshetra War. Sanatsujata obtains its name because of King Dhritarashtra's questioning of Sage Sanatsujata as advised by Vidura. Because Sanatsujata is the sage's name, the text is often known as Sanatsujatiya. The conversation between Sage Sanatsujata and Dhritarashtra goes on throughout the night and ends abruptly because the sage leaves when it is morning. After this, Dhritarashtra has to go to the assembly hall and the Sage is invited for the duration of the night. It is a beautiful exposition about knowledge of the brahman, about life and death, and indeed, about vedanta. The Sanatsujata segment is difficult to understand, and therefore, also

---

[1] *The Bhagavadgita, with the Sanatsugatiya and the Anu Gita*, K.T. Telang (trans.), Sacred Books of the East, Vol. 8, F. Max Muller (ed.), second edition, Clarendon Press, Oxford, 1898. Since we have followed BORI, there are some major differences between Telang's manuscript and our Sanskrit text. Telang's follows an academic style, with a lot of cross-referencing. We have avoided such crossreferencing and there are instances where our choice of words and interpretation differs from that of Telang but not in any substantive way.

difficult to translate. This segment of four chapters (Chapters 42–45 of Udyoga Parva) has 121 shlokas.

Chapter 1

वैशंपायन उवाच

ततो राजा धृतराष्ट्रो मनीषी संपूज्य वाक्यं विदुरेरितं तत् ।
सनत्सुजातं रहिते महात्मा पप्रच्छ बुद्धिं परमां बुभूषन् ॥ (1)

Vaishampayana said,[2] 'The intelligent king Dhritarashtra honoured the words that Vidura had spoken. Desiring supreme intelligence, the great-souled one privately questioned Sanatsujata.'

धृतराष्ट्र उवाच

सनत्सुजात यदीदं शृणोमि मृत्युर्हि नास्तीति तवोपदेशम् ।
देवासुरा ह्याचरन्ब्रह्मचर्यममृत्यवे तत्कतरन्नु सत्यम् ॥ (2)

'Dhritarashtra asked, "O Sanatsujata! I have heard about your teaching that death does not exist. Yet, the gods and the asuras observed brahmacharya for the sake of immortality. Which of these is true?"'

सनत्सुजात उवाच

अमृत्यु: कर्मणा केचिन्मृत्युर्नास्तीति चापरे ।
शृणु मे ब्रुवतो राजन्यथैतन्मा विशङ्कित्याः ॥ (3)

'Sanatsujata replied, "Some hold that karma ensures immortality. Others say that there is no death. O King! Listen to my words on this, so that you no longer have any doubts."'

उभे सत्ये क्षत्रियाद्यप्रवृत्ते मोहो मृत्यु: संमतो य: कवीनाम् ।
प्रमादं वै मृत्युमहं ब्रवीमि सदाप्रमादममृतत्वं ब्रवीमि ॥ (4)

---

[2]Sage Vaishampayana is narrating this to King Janameyjaya.

"'O Kshatriya! Both of these statements are prevalent and true. The wise regard delusion as death. I am also telling you that delusion is death. When no delusion exists, that is immortality.'"

प्रमादाद्वै असुरा: पराभवन्नप्रमादाद्ब्रह्मभूता भवन्ति ।
न वै मृत्युर्व्याघ्र इवत्ति जन्तून् ह्यस्य रूपमुपलभ्यते ह ॥ (5)

"'The asuras were vanquished because they were distracted. Had they not been distracted, they would have been immersed in the brahman. Death is not a tiger that consumes beings. Its form is not one that can be noticed.'"

यमं त्वेके मृत्युमतोऽन्यमाहुरात्मावसन्नममृतं ब्रह्मचर्यम् ।
पितृलोके राज्यमनुशास्ति देव: शिव: शिवानामशिवोऽशिवानाम् ॥ (6)

"'Some hold that Yama is death, but others do not hold that. Immortality is the atman's pursuit of brahmacharya. That deva[3] rules his kingdom in the world of the ancestors. He is auspicious towards those who are pure and is inauspicious towards those who are impure.'"

आस्यादेष नि:सरते नराणां क्रोध: प्रमादो मोहरूपश्च मृत्यु: ।
ते मोहितास्तद्दृशे वर्तमाना इत: प्रेतास्तत्र पुन: पतन्ति ॥ (7)

"'Through instructions issued from his mouth, men suffer death in the form of anger, distractedness and delusion. Being overcome by delusion, they leave for the hereafter and descend again.'"[4]

ततस्तं देवा अनु विप्लवन्ते अतो मृत्युर्मरणाख्यामुपैति ।
कर्मोदये कर्मफलानुरागास्तत्रानु यान्ति न तरन्ति मृत्युम् ॥ (8)

"'Following him, devas also go into a decline. Thus it is that Yama is also known by the name of Death. But there are those who are attached to the fruits of karma. Because of their karma, they go there,[5] crossing over beyond death.'"

---

[3]Yama.
[4]Meaning that they are born again and again.
[5]To heaven.

योऽभिध्यायन्नुत्पतिष्णून्निहन्यादनादरेणाप्रतिबुध्यमानः ।
स वै मृत्युमृत्युरिवाप्ति भूत्वा एवं विद्वान्यो विनिहन्ति कामान् ॥ (9)

'"There are learned ones who think and kill their desires, when these try to rise, realizing that these should not be respected. Because learned ones have killed their desires, though they assume the form of death, death cannot destroy them."'

कामानुसारी पुरुषः कामाननु विनश्यति ।
कामान्व्युदस्य धुनुते यत्किंचित्पुरुषो रजः ॥ (10)

'"A man who follows desires is destroyed, together with the desires. A man who conquers his desires withstands all taints."'

तमोऽप्रकाशो भूतानां नरकोऽयं प्रदृश्यते ।
गृह्णन्त इव धावन्ति गच्छन्तः श्वभ्रमुन्मुखाः ॥ (11)

'"Darkness appears to beings in the form of hell. Deluded, they eagerly rush towards it and fall into the pit."'[6]

अभिध्या वै प्रथमं हन्ति चैनं कामक्रोधौ गृह्य चैनं तु पश्चात् ।
एते बालान्मृत्यवे प्रापयन्ति धीरास्तु धैर्येण तरन्ति मृत्युम् ॥ (12)

'"The sense of ego kills such a person first. Desire and anger seize him and kill him later. Such childish ones are thus dispatched towards their death. But steady ones with fortitude can cross beyond death."'

अमन्यमानः क्षत्रिय किंचिदन्यन्नाधीयते तार्णं इवास्य व्याघ्रः ।
क्रोधाल्लोभान्मोहमयान्तरात्मा स वै मृत्युस्त्वच्छरीरे य एषः ॥ (13)

'"O Kshatriya! If a man thinks of nothing,[7] how can a tiger made out of straw attack him? If the atman is confused through anger and desire, then death exists within one's own body."'

एवं मृत्युं जायमानं विदित्वा ज्ञाने तिष्ठन्बिभेतीह मृत्योः ।
विनश्यते विषये तस्य मृत्यु मृत्योर्यथा विषयं प्राप्य मर्त्यः ॥ (14)

---

[6]They rush towards desire and fall into hell.
[7]That is, has no desire.

'"Know that this is how death is born. One who is established in jnana has no fear of death. If the object[8] is destroyed, so is death, just as mortal beings are destroyed when they confront death."'

धृतराष्ट्र उवाच

येऽस्मिन्धर्मान्नाचरन्तीह केचित्तथा धर्मान्केचिदिहाचरन्ति ।
धर्म: पापेन प्रतिहन्यते स्म उताहो धर्म: प्रतिहन्ति पापम् ॥ (15)

'Dhritarashtra asked, "There are some here who do not follow dharma. There are also some who follow dharma. Is dharma destroyed by evil or is evil destroyed by dharma?"'

सनत्सुजात उवाच

उभयमेव तत्रोपभुज्यते फलं धर्मस्यैवेतरस्य च ।
धर्मेणाधर्मं प्रणुदतीह विद्वान्धर्मो बलीयानिति तस्य विद्धि ॥ (16)

'Sanatsujata replied, "The fruits of both are enjoyed, that of dharma and of its opposite.[9] A learned one uses dharma to give up adharma. Know that dharma is stronger."'

धृतराष्ट्र उवाच

यानिमानाहु: स्वस्य धर्मस्य लोकान्द्विजातीनां पुण्यकृतां सनातनान् ।
तेषां परिक्रमान्कथयन्तस्ततोऽन्यान्नैतद्विद्वन्नैव कृतं च कर्म ॥ (17)

'Dhritarashtra said, "It is said that the eternal worlds are obtained by dvijas who perform pure deeds in accordance with dharma. O Learned One! It is said that there are different kinds of progress for them, depending on the karma that has been performed."'

सनत्सुजात उवाच

येषां बले न विस्पर्धा बले बलवतामिव ।
ते ब्राह्मणा इत: प्रेत्य स्वर्गलोके प्रकाशते ॥ (18)

---

[8]Object of desire.
[9]Dharma and adharma.

'Sanatsujata replied, "There are brahmanas who are not proud of their strength, unlike those who try to surpass the strong with strength. In the hereafter, they are radiant in the world of heaven."'

यत्र मन्येत भूयिष्ठं प्रावृषीव तृणोलपम् ।
अन्नं पानं च ब्राह्मणस्तज्जीवन्नानुसंज्वरेत् ॥ (19)

'"Wherever a brahmana thinks food and drink are sufficient to sustain life, like grass during the rainy season, he should live there, without anxiety."'

यत्राकथयमानस्य प्रयच्छत्यशिवं भयम् ।
अतिरिक्तमिवाकुर्वन्स श्रेयान्नेतरो जन: ॥ (20)

'"Where there is inauspicious danger, one should control the urge to speak. It is best not to act in excess, or try to establish superiority over other people."'

यो वाकथयमानस्य आत्मानं नानुसंज्वरेत् ।
ब्रह्मस्वं नोपभुञ्जेद्वा तदन्नं संमतं सताम् ॥ (21)

'"If a person does not cause torment by proclaiming his superiority and if he does not enjoy the property of a brahmana, then food offered by such a person is regarded as acceptable by the virtuous."'

यथा स्वं वान्तमश्नाति श्वा वै नित्यमभूतये ।
एवं ते वान्तमश्नन्ति स्ववीर्यस्योपजीवनात् ॥ (22)

'"A dog always eats its own vomit and causes injury to itself. Like that, those who proclaim their own valour eat their own vomit."'

नित्यमज्ञातचर्या मे इति मन्येत ब्राह्मण: ।
ज्ञातीनां तु वसन्मध्ये नैव विद्येत किंचन ॥ (23)

'"A brahmana thinks that his conduct should always be unknown. Even if he dwells among his relatives, nothing will be known about him."'

को ह्येवमन्तरात्मानं ब्राह्मणो हन्तुमर्हति ।
तस्माद्धि किंचित्क्षत्रिय ब्रह्मावसति पश्यति ॥ (24)

'"Who except a brahmana is capable of destroying his atman? O Kshatriya! It is because of such conduct that he can visualize the brahman that dwells inside him."'

अश्रान्तः स्यादनादानात्संमतो निरुपद्रवः ।
शिष्टो न शिष्टवत्स्यद्ब्राह्मणो ब्रह्मवित्कविः ॥ (25)

'"He is never exhausted. He is honoured because he does not receive from others. He never causes impediments. He is virtuous, even if he does not seem to be virtuous. Such a wise brahmana knows the brahman."'

अनाढ्या मानुषे वित्ते आढ्या वेदेषु ये द्विजाः ।
ते दुर्धर्षा दुष्प्रकम्प्या विद्यात्तान्ब्रह्मणस्तनुम् ॥ (26)

'"These brahmanas are not rich because of human wealth. They are rich because of the Vedas. They are difficult to assail. They are difficult to shake. Know that because of knowledge, they have the brahman in their bodies."'

सर्वान्स्विष्टकृतो देवान्विद्याद्य इह कश्चन ।
न समानो ब्राह्मणस्य यस्मिन्प्रयतते स्वयम् ॥ (27)

'"In this world, a person who honours devas and performs every kind of sacrifice is never the equal of a brahmana, even if he exerts himself."'[10]

यमप्रयतमानं तु मानयन्ति स मानितः ।
न मान्यमानो मन्येत नामानादभिसंज्वरेत् ॥ (28)

'"One who is honoured without exerting himself is truly honoured. When honoured, he does not think about it, nor does he suffer because he is not honoured."'

विद्वांसो मानयन्तीह इति मन्येत मानितः ।
अधर्मविदुषो मूढा लोकशास्त्रविशारदाः ।
न मान्यं मानयिष्यन्ति इति मन्येदमानितः ॥ (29)

---

[10]This is so because a true brahmana does not have to exert himself through sacrifices.

'"One who is honoured should think that only the learned show honours. If one is not honoured, one should not think that foolish ones, skilled in adharma and not adept in the ways of the world and the sacred texts, do not know how to honour a revered person."'

न वै मानं च मौनं च सहितौ चरत: सदा ।
अयं हि लोको मानस्य असौ मौनस्य तद्विदु: ॥ (30)

'"Honour and silence[11] can never travel together. Know that this world is that of honour and that one[12] is one of silence."'

श्री: सुखस्येह संवास: सा चापि परिपन्थिनी ।
ब्राह्मी सुदुर्लभा श्रीहि प्रज्ञाहीनेन क्षत्रिय ॥ (31)

'"Prosperity is the store of happiness in this world, though it runs counter to the objective.[13] O Kshatriya! For someone who is devoid of wisdom, the prosperity of the brahman is extremely difficult to obtain."'

द्वाराणि तस्या हि वदन्ति सन्तो बहुप्रकाराणि दुरावराणि ।
सत्यार्जवे ह्रीर्दमशौचविद्या: षण्मानमोहप्रतिबाधनानि ॥ (32)

'"Virtuous ones have spoken of many different kinds of doors, all difficult to uphold. There are six that counter pride and delusion—truthfulness, uprightness, modesty, self-control, purity and knowledge."'

Chapter 2

धृतराष्ट्र उवाच

ऋचो यजूंष्यधीते य: सामवेदं च यो द्विज: ।
पापानि कुर्वन्पापेन लिप्यते न स लिप्यते ॥ (1)

---

[11] The vow of silence.
[12] The next world.
[13] Prosperity characterizes this world and runs counter to the objective of the next world.

'Dhritarashtra asked, "A brahmana may have learnt the chants of the Rig Veda, the Yajur Veda and the Sama Veda. If he performs a sin, will he be tainted, or will he not be tainted?"'

सनत्सुजात उवाच

नैनं सामान्यृचो वापि न यजूंषि विचक्षण ।
त्रायन्ते कर्मण: पापान्न ते मिथ्या ब्रवीम्यहम् ॥ (2)

'Sanatsujata replied, "One who is accomplished in the chants of the Sama, the Rig and the Yajur will not be saved from his evil deeds. I am not uttering a falsehood to you."'

न छन्दांसि वृजिनात्तारयन्ति मायाविनं मायया वर्तमानम् ।
नीडं शकुन्ता इव जातपक्षाश्छन्दांस्येनं प्रजहत्यन्तकाले ॥ (3)

'"The metres do not save a deceitful one who has resorted to deceit from sin. When their wings have grown, birds flee a nest. Like that, the metres desert one whose time of destruction has come."'

धृतराष्ट्र उवाच

न चेद्भेदा वेदविदं शक्तास्त्रातुं विचक्षण ।
अथ कस्मात्प्रलापोऽयं ब्राह्मणानां सनातन: ॥ (4)

'Dhritarashtra asked, "O Learned One! If the Vedas are incapable of saving one who knows the Vedas, then why have the brahmanas perpetually talked about them?"'

सनत्सुजात उवाच

अस्मिँल्लोके तपस्तप्तं फलमन्यत्र दृश्यते ।
ब्राह्मणानामिमे लोका ऋद्धे तपसि संयता: ॥ (5)

'Sanatsujata replied, "The austerities performed in this world are seen to yield fruits in another. When they are controlled and rich in austerities, brahmanas obtain those worlds."

धृतराष्ट्र उवाच

कथं समृद्धमप्यृद्धं तपो भवति केवलम् ।
सनत्सुजात तद्ब्रूहि यथा विद्याम तद्वयम् ॥ (6)

'Dhritarashtra asked, "How can austerities become prosperous and how can they fail to do so? O Sanatsujata! Please tell me this, so that we may get to know."'

सनत्सुजात उवाच

क्रोधादयो द्वादश यस्य दोषास्तथा नृशंसादि षडत्र राजन् ।
धर्मादयो द्वादश चाततानाः शास्त्रे गुणा ये विदिता द्विजानाम् ॥ (7)
क्रोधः कामो लोभमोहौ विवित्साकृपासूया मानशोकौ स्पृहा च ।
ईर्ष्या जुगुप्सा च मनुष्यदोषा वर्ज्याः सदा द्वादशैते नरेण ॥ (8)

'Sanatsujata replied, "O King! There are twelve vices like anger and another six like cruelty. Dvijas who know about the sacred texts are knowledgeable about the qualities that prevent dharma—anger, desire, avarice, delusion, possessiveness, lack of compassion, discontent, pride, sorrow, lust, jealousy and aversion. These are the twelve human vices that a man must always avoid."'

एकैकमेते राजेन्द्र मनुष्यान्पर्युपासते ।
लिप्समानोऽन्तरं तेषां मृगाणामिव लुब्धकः ॥ (9)

'"O Indra among Kings! Every single one of them waits for a weakness in a man, like a hunter waits for a deer."'

विकत्थनः स्पृहयालुर्मनस्वी बिभ्रत्कोपं चपलोऽरक्षणश्च ।
एते प्राप्ताः षण्णरान्पापधर्मान्प्रकुर्वते नोत सन्तः सुदुर्गे ॥ (10)

'"Maligning others,[14] covetousness, vanity, vindictiveness, anger and fickleness—if these six vices are left uncontrolled, they incite men towards evil in dharma. They do not perform anything good in extremely difficult situations."'

---

[14]Alternatively, speaking well of themselves.

संभोगसंविद्विषमेधमानो दत्तानुतापी कृपणोऽबलीयान् ।
वर्गप्रशंसी वनितासु द्वेष्टा एतेऽपरे सप्त नृशंसधर्माः ॥ (11)

'"Scheming to enjoy, hatred, pride in deceit, regrets after giving, weakness of miserliness, praise of one's kin and hatred of women—these are the seven cruel kinds of adharma."'

धर्मश्च सत्यं च दमस्तपश्च अमात्सर्यं ह्रीस्तितिक्षानसूया ।
यज्ञश्च दानं च धृतिः श्रुतं च महाव्रता द्वादश ब्राह्मणस्य ॥ (12)

'"Dharma, truthfulness, self-control, austerities, lack of envy, modesty, patience, lack of malice, sacrifices, generosity, fortitude and learning—these are the twelve great vows for a brahmana."'

यस्त्वेतेभ्यः प्रवसेद्वादशेभ्यः सर्वामपीमां पृथिवीं प्रशिष्यात् ।
त्रिभिर्द्वाभ्यामेकतो वा विशिष्टो नास्य स्वमस्तीति स वेदितव्यः ॥ (13)

'"If one dwells with these twelve, one is capable of ruling the entire earth. Even if one is distinguished by the presence of three, two, or only one of these, know that one is not truly the lord of anything."'

दमस्त्यागोऽप्रमादश्च एतेष्वमृतमाहितम् ।
तानि सत्यमुखान्याहुर्ब्राह्मणा ये मनीषिणः ॥ (14)

'"Self-control, renunciation and lack of distraction—immortality is vested in these. Learned brahmanas say that truthfulness is the foremost."'

दमोऽष्टादशदोषः स्यात्प्रतिकूलं कृताकृते ।
अनृतं चाभ्यसूया च कामार्थौ च तथा स्पृहा ॥ (15)
क्रोधः शोकस्तथा तृष्णा लोभः पैशुन्यमेव च ।
मत्सरश्च विवित्सा च परितापस्तथा रतिः ॥ (16)
अपस्मारः सातिवादस्तथा संभावनात्मनि ।
एतैर्विमुक्तो दोषैर्यः स दमः सद्भिरुच्यते ॥ (17)

'"There are eighteen qualities that work against self-control—perversity in what is done or not done, falsehood, malice, desire, acquisitiveness, covetousness, anger, sorrow, thirst, greed, calumny, jealousy, possessiveness, regret, gloating, forgetfulness, slander and vanity. The virtuous say that one who is free from these vices is self-controlled."'

श्रेयांस्तु षड्विधस्त्याग: प्रियं प्राप्य न हृष्यति ।
अप्रिये तु समुत्पन्ने व्यथां जातु न चाच्छति ॥ (18)
इष्टान्दारांश्च पुत्रांश्च न चान्यं यद्वचो भवेत् ।
अर्हते याचमानाय प्रदेयं तद्वचो भवेत् ।
अप्यवाच्यं वदत्येव स तृतीयो गुण: स्मृत: ॥ (19)
त्यक्तैर्द्रव्यैर्यो भवति नोपयुङ्क्ते च कामत: ।
न च कर्मसु तद्धीन: शिष्यबुद्धिर्नरो यथा ।
सर्वैरेव गुणैर्युक्तो द्रव्यवानपि यो भवेत् ॥ (20)

"'There are six types of renunciation regarded as superior—lack of rejoicing when one obtains something pleasant; lack of misery when something unpleasant is generated; giving to worthy supplicants without being asked, even if it is a beloved wife or sons. One must give to a worthy recipient when one has given one's word, even if one is asked for what should not be asked. This is known as the third quality. Relinquishment of objects, non-enjoyment of desire and giving up the fruits of deeds[15] without any distress—a man then exhibits the intelligence of a shishya.[16] Even if he possesses objects, he possesses all the qualities."'

अप्रमादोऽष्टदोष: स्यात्तान्दोषान्परिवर्जयेत् ।
इन्द्रियेभ्यश्च पञ्चभ्यो मनसश्चैव भारत ।
अतीतानागतेभ्यश्च मुक्तो ह्येतै: सुखी भवेत् ॥ (21)

"'O Descendant of the Bharata Lineage! There are eight vices that lead to ignorance and these vices must be avoided—those that come from the five senses, the mind, the past and the future. A person who is freed from these is happy."'

---

[15]The list of six continues, but the enumeration of the six is not very clear.
[16]That is, he is ready to serve.

दोषैरेतैर्विमुक्तं तु गुणैरेतैः समन्वितम् ।
एतत्समृद्धमप्यृद्धं तपो भवति केवलम् ।
यन्मां पृच्छसि राजेन्द्र किं भूयः श्रोतुमिच्छसि ॥ (22)

'"Only austerities that are free from these vices, and are united with the qualities, become prosperous and successful. O Indra among Kings! This is what you asked me. What else do you wish to hear?"'

धृतराष्ट्र उवाच

आख्यानपञ्चमैर्वेदैर्भूयिष्ठं कथ्यते जनः ।
तथैवान्ये चतुर्वेदास्त्रिवेदाश्च तथापरे ॥ (23)

'Dhritarashtra said, "Some people have said that there are five Vedas, with ancient accounts as the fifth. Others say that they know four Vedas and still others say that they know three Vedas."'

द्विवेदाश्चैकवेदाश्च अनृचश्च तथापरे ।
तेषां तु कतमः स स्याद्यमहं वेद ब्राह्मणम् ॥ (24)

'"Others say that they know two Vedas and still others say that they know one Veda. There are others who know no hymns. Among these brahmanas, who should I regard as the best?"'

सनत्सुजात उवाच

एकस्य वेदस्याज्ञानाद्वेदास्ते बहवोऽभवन् ।
सत्यस्यैकस्य राजेन्द्र सत्ये कश्चिदवस्थितः ।
एवं वेदमनुसाद्य प्रज्ञां महति कुर्वते ॥ (25)

'Sanatsujata replied, "Because there is ignorance about the single Veda, many Vedas have been thought of. O Indra among Kings! There is one truth and only some are established in that truth. Understanding this, wisdom should be sought in the great one."'[17]

दानमध्ययनं यज्ञो लोभादेतत्प्रवर्तते ।
सत्यात्प्रच्यवमानानां संकल्पो वितथो भवेत् ॥ (26)

---

[17] The brahman or the paramatman.

"'If gifts, studying and sacrifices are out of greed, then the resolutions of those proud ones deviate from the truth.'"

ततो यज्ञः प्रतायेत सत्यस्यैवावधारणात् ।
मनसान्यस्य भवति वाचान्यस्योत कर्मणा ।
संकल्पसिद्धः पुरुषः संकल्पानधितिष्ठति ॥ (27)

"'Therefore, one should undertake a sacrifice only for the sake of the truth. When a man performs this with mind, speech and deeds, he is successful in his resolutions and is established in his resolutions.'"

अनैभृत्येन वै तस्य दीक्षितव्रतमाचरेत् ।
नामैतद्धातुनिर्वृत्तं सत्यमेव सतां परम् ।
ज्ञानं वै नाम प्रत्यक्षं परोक्षं जायते तपः ॥ (28)

"'Without doing this in private, one should be consecrated for a vow. The word '*satyam*' is derived from the root '*sat*' and is the supreme objective and truth. The results of jnana are direct. Those of austerities are generated indirectly.'"

विद्याद्बहु पठन्तं तु बहुपाठीति ब्राह्मणम् ।
तस्मात्क्षत्रिय मा मंस्था जल्पितेनैव ब्राह्मणम् ।
य एव सत्यान्नापैति स ज्ञेयो ब्राह्मणस्त्वया ॥ (29)

"'A brahmana who reads a lot should only be known as one who reads a lot. O Kshatriya! Therefore, do not regard a brahmana to be superior only because he talks. He who has not deviated from the truth should be known as a brahmana by you.'"

छन्दांसि नाम क्षत्रिय तान्यथर्वा जगौ पुरस्तादृषिसर्ग एषः ।
छन्दोविदस्ते य उ तानधीत्य न वेद्यवेदस्य विदुर्न वेद्यम् ॥ (30)

"'O Kshatriya! When the class of rishis was created in ancient times, Atharvan[18] chanted these hymns. Those who studied them were known as those who learnt hymns. But they do not know the One[19] who should be known through the Vedas.'"

---

[18]Ancient sage from whom the Atharva Veda is traced.
[19]The brahman or the paramatman.

न वेदानां वेदिता कश्चिदस्ति कश्चिद्वेदान्बुध्यते वापि राजन् ।
यो वेद वेदान् स वेद वेद्यं सत्ये स्थितो यस्तु स वेद वेदम् ॥ (31)

'"O King! There are some who know the Vedas and there are some who understand the Vedas. He who knows the Vedas knows what should be known. He who knows what should be known is established in truth."'

अभिजानामि ब्राह्मणमाख्यातारं विचक्षणम् ।
यश्छिन्नविचिकित्स: सन्नाचष्टे सर्वसंशयान् ॥ (32)

'"I know him to be a brahmana who explains with a sense of discrimination and is capable of removing doubts, having cured and dispelled all his own doubts."'

तस्य पर्येषणं गच्छेत्प्राचीनं नोत दक्षिणम् ।
नार्वाचीनं कुतस्तिर्यङ्नादिशं तु कथंचन ॥ (33)

'"The One can never be found by going to the east, or the south, or the west, or diagonally or in any direction at all."'

तूष्णींभूत उपासीत न चेष्टेन्मनसा अपि ।
अभ्यावर्तेत ब्रह्मास्य अन्तरात्मनि वै श्रितम् ॥ (34)

'"One should think about this while meditating in silence, being immobile even in one's thoughts. The brahman that is established in the inner atman will then manifest itself."'

मौनाद्धि स मुनिर्भवति नारण्यवसनान्मुनि: ।
अक्षरं तत्तु यो वेद स मुनि: श्रेष्ठ उच्यते ॥ (35)

'"He who maintains silence is a *muni*,[20] one does not become a muni by residing in the forest. He who knows the one without decay is said to be the supreme hermit."'

सर्वार्थानां व्याकरणाद्वैयाकरण उच्यते ।
प्रत्यक्षदर्शी लोकानां सर्वदर्शी भवेन्नर: ॥ (36)

---

[20]'Muni' means sage or hermit, with the same verbal root as '*mouna*' or silence.

"'One who knows the grammar behind everything is said to be a grammarian. But a man who can directly see all the worlds is a man who sees everything.'"

सत्ये वै ब्राह्मणस्तिष्ठन्ब्रह्म पश्यति क्षत्रिय ।
वेदानां चानुपूर्व्येण एतद्विद्धन्ब्रवीमि ते ॥ (37)

"'O Kshatriya! A brahmana who is established in the truth sees the brahman, by following in due order what is prescribed in the Vedas. This is exactly what I am telling you.'"

Chapter 3

धृतराष्ट्र उवाच

सनत्सुजात यदिमां परार्थां ब्राह्मीं वाचं प्रवदसि विश्वरूपाम् ।
परां हि कामेषु सुदुर्लभां कथां तद्ब्रूहि मे वाक्यमेतत्कुमार ॥ (1)

'Dhritarashtra said, "O Sanatsujata! You have spoken words deep in meaning, about the brahman, whose form is the universe. O Kumara![21] Please describe to me what is supreme and extremely rare among desired objects."'

सनत्सुजात उवाच

नैतद्ब्रह्म त्वरमाणेन लभ्यं यन्मां पृच्छस्यभिहृष्यस्यतीव ।
अव्यक्तविद्यामभिधास्ये पुराणीं बुद्ध्या च तेषां ब्रह्मचर्येण सिद्धाम् ॥ (2)

'Sanatsujata replied, "You have cheerfully asked me about the brahman, but it is not something that can be obtained in a hurry. I will tell you the ancient knowledge about the one who is not manifest. This can be successfully obtained when the intelligence reflects, through the practice of brahmacharya."'

---

[21]Youthful one or brahmachari.

धृतराष्ट्र उवाच

अव्यक्तविद्यामिति यत्सनातनीं ब्रवीषि त्वं ब्रह्मचर्येण सिद्धाम् ।
अनारभ्या वसतीहार्य काले कथं ब्राह्मण्यममृतत्वं लभेत ॥ (3)

'Dhritarashtra said, "You have said that the eternal knowledge about the one who is not manifest can be successfully obtained through the practice of brahmacharya. How should one reside at the time, so that one obtains the immortality of the brahman?"'[22]

सनत्सुजात उवाच

येऽस्मिँल्लोके विजयन्तीह कामान्ब्राह्मीं स्थितिमनुतितिक्षमाणा: ।
त आत्मानं निर्हरन्तीह देहान्मुञ्जादिषीकामिव सत्त्वसंस्था: ॥ (4)

'Sanatsujata replied, "Those who conquer their desires in this world while patiently establishing themselves in the brahman are firmly based on the truth. They pluck the atman out of the body, like a stalk of *munja* grass."'[23]

शरीरमेतौ कुरुत: पिता माता च भारत ।
आचार्यशास्ता या जाति: सा सत्या साजरामरा ॥ (5)

'"O Descendant of the Bharata Lineage! The father and the mother create the body. But the birth instructed by the preceptor is the true birth because that is free of age or death."'[24]

आचार्ययोनिमिह ये प्रविश्य भूत्वा गर्भ ब्रह्मचर्यं चरन्ति ।
इहैव ते शास्त्रकारा भवन्ति प्रहाय देहं परमं यान्ति योगम् ॥ (6)

'"Those who enter a preceptor's womb and become embryos there, observing brahmacharya, become learned in the sacred texts in this world and attain supreme yoga after they give up their bodies."'

य आवृणोत्यवितथेन कर्णावृतं कुर्वन्नमृतं संप्रयच्छन् ।
तं मन्येत पितरं मातरं च तस्मै न द्रुह्येत्कृतमस्य जानन् ॥ (7)

---

[22] How should one behave as a brahmachari?
[23] 'Munja' is a kind of rush or grass, used to make girdles for brahmanas.
[24] The preceptor is also like a father, and initiation into studies is like a second birth.

"'The preceptor fills the ears with the truth, practises truth and confers immortality. He should be regarded as the father and the mother. Knowing what he does, one should not cause him any injury.'"

गुरुं शिष्यो नित्यमभिमन्यमानः स्वाध्यायमिच्छेच्छुचिरप्रमत्तः ।
मानं न कुर्यान्न दधीत रोषमेष प्रथमो ब्रह्मचर्यस्य पादः ॥ (8)

"'A shishya must always honour his guru. Pure and without distraction, he should study. His pride should not be hurt, nor should he be angered at tasks he is asked to perform. This is the first quarter of brahmacharya.'"

आचार्यस्य प्रियं कुर्यात्प्राणैरपि धनैरपि ।
कर्मणा मनसा वाचा द्वितीयः पाद उच्यते ॥ (9)

"'Doing what pleases the preceptor, in deeds, thoughts and speech, even at the expense of life and riches, is said to be the second quarter.'"

समा गुरौ यथा वृत्तिर्गुरुपत्न्यां तथा भवेत् ।
यथोक्तकारी प्रियकृत्तृतीयः पाद उच्यते ॥ (10)

"'The conduct towards the guru's wife should be the same as that towards the guru, acting as one is instructed and performing what is agreeable. This is said to be the third quarter.'"

नाचार्यायेहोपकृत्वा प्रवादं प्राज्ञः कुर्वीत नैतदहं करोमि ।
इतीव मन्येत न भाषयेत स वै चतुर्थो ब्रह्मचर्यस्य पादः ॥ (11)

"'Taking oneself to be wise, one should never tell a preceptor that one will not do something. Even if one thinks this, one should not say it. This is the fourth quarter of brahmacharya.'"

एवं वसन्तं यदुपप्लवेद्धनमाचार्याय तदनुप्रयच्छेत् ।
सतां वृत्तिं बहुगुणामेवमेति गुरोः पुत्रे भवति च वृत्तिरेषा ॥ (12)

"'One should reside by presenting to the preceptor whatever objects one obtains. For those who are virtuous and possess many qualities, the conduct should be the same towards the guru's son.'"

एवं वसन्सर्वतो वर्धतीह बहून्पुत्रॉंल्लभते च प्रतिष्ठाम् ।
वर्षन्ति चास्मै प्रदिशो दिशश्च वसन्त्यस्मिन्ब्रह्मचर्ये जनाश्च ॥ (13)

'"When one resides in this way, one prospers in this world. One obtains many sons and fame. All the directions shower down upon him[25] and many people dwell with him in turn for the sake of brahmacharya."'

एतेन ब्रह्मचर्येण देवा देवत्वमाप्नुवन् ।
ऋषयश्च महाभागा ब्रह्मलोकं मनीषिणः ॥ (14)
गन्धर्वाणामनेनैव रूपमप्सरसामभूत् ।
एतेन ब्रह्मचर्येण सूर्यो अह्नाय जायते ॥ (15)

'"It is through such brahmacharya that devas attained divinity, the immensely fortunate and learned rishis attained Brahma's world and the gandharvas and the apsaras obtained their beauty. It is with such brahmacharya that the sun rises every day."'

य आशयेत्पाटयेच्चापि राजन्सर्वं शरीरं तपसा तप्यमानः ।
एतेनासौ बाल्यमत्येति विद्वान्मृत्युं तथा रोधयत्यन्तकाले ॥ (16)

'"O King! He who lies down and torments his entire body with austerities will transcend childishness and become learned. When his end comes, he will conquer death."'

अन्तवन्तः क्षत्रिय ते जयन्ति लोकाञ्जनाः कर्मणा निर्मितेन ।
ब्रह्मैव विद्वांस्तेन अभ्येति सर्वं नान्यः पन्था अयनाय विद्यते ॥ (17)

'"O Kshatriya! The worlds that people conquer through karma they have performed come to an end. But through knowledge, one obtains the complete brahman. There is no other path to traverse."'[26]

धृतराष्ट्र उवाच

आभाति शुक्लमिव लोहितमिव अथो कृष्णमथाञ्जनं काद्रवं वा ।
तद्ब्राह्मणः पश्यति योऽत्र विद्वान्कथंरूपं तदमृतमक्षरं पदम् ॥ (18)

---

[25] Shower riches.
[26] The last sentence is reminiscent of the Upanishads.

'Dhritarashtra asked, "Is the appearance white or red? Is the appearance dark—black like collyrium—or brown? In what form does a righteous and learned brahmana visualize the seat of that immortal and undecaying one?[27]"'

सनत्सुजात उवाच

नाभाति शुक्लमिव लोहितमिव अथो कृष्णमायसमर्कवर्णम् ।
न पृथिव्यां तिष्ठति नान्तरिक्षे नैतत्समुद्रे सलिलं बिभर्ति ॥ (19)

'Sanatsujata replied, "He does not appear as white or red, as black or with the complexion of iron, nor does he have the complexion of the sun. He is not established in the earth or the sky. He is not to be found in the waters of the ocean."'[28]

न तारकासु न च विद्युदाश्रितं न चाभ्रेषु दृश्यते रूपमस्य ।
न चापि वायौ न च देवतासु न तच्चन्द्रे दृश्यते नोत सूर्ये ॥ (20)

'"He does not find refuge in the stars or in the lightning. His form cannot be seen in the clouds. He cannot be found in the wind or devas, nor can he be seen in the moon or the sun."'

नैवर्क्षु तन्न यजुःषु नाप्यथर्वसु न चौव दृश्यत्यमलेषु सामसु ।
रथंतरे बार्हते चापि राजन्महाव्रते नैव दृश्येद्रुवं तत् ॥ (21)

'"He is not the mantras of the Rig Veda, the Yajur Veda or the Atharva Veda, nor can he be seen in the unblemished Sama Veda. O King! It is certain that he cannot be seen in great vows and in *rathantara* and *barhata*."'[29]

अपारणीयं तमसः परस्तात्तदन्तकोऽप्येति विनाशकाले ।
अणीयरूपं क्षुरधारया तन्महच्च रूपं त्वपि पर्वतेभ्यः ॥ (22)

'"He is the darkness that is impossible to cross. He is beyond death but can be seen inside, at the time of one's destruction. His form

---

[27] The appearance of brahman or the paramatman is being talked about in this shloka.
[28] These sentences are also reminiscent of the Upanishads.
[29] Rathantara is a metre that particularly occurs in the Sama Veda. Barhata, also called *brihati*, is a kind of metre.

is as thin as a razor's edge, but he is also larger in form than the mountains."'

सा प्रतिष्ठा तदमृतं लोकास्तद्ब्रह्म तद्यशः ।
भूतानि जज्ञिरे तस्मात्प्रलयं यान्ति तत्र च ॥ (23)

'"He is the foundation. He is immortality. He is the worlds. He is the brahman. He is fame. He is the source of all beings and at the time of dissolution, he is the one into whom they flow."'

अनामयं तन्महदुद्यतं यशो वाचो विकारान्कवयो वदन्ति ।
तस्मिञ्जगत्सर्वमिदं प्रतिष्ठितं ये तद्विदुरमृतास्ते भवन्ति ॥ (24)

'"He is without division and is gigantic. His fame soars up. The words of the wise say that he is without transformation. Everything in the universe is established in him. Those who know him become immortal."'

Chapter 4

सनत्सुजात उवाच

यत्तच्छुक्रं महज्ज्योतिर्दीप्यमानं महद्यशः ।
तद्वै देवा उपासन्ते यस्मादर्को विराजते ।
योगिनस्तं प्रपश्यन्ति भगवन्तं सनातनम् ॥ (1)

'Sanatsujata said, "He is the seed and is a great and blazing light. He is the resplendent one whose fame is great. He is the one whom devas worship. It is because of him that the sun shines. He is the one whom the yogis see. He is the eternal and illustrious one."'

शुक्राद्ब्रह्म प्रभवति ब्रह्म शुक्रेण वर्धते ।
तच्छुक्रं ज्योतिषां मध्येऽतप्तं तपति तापनम् ।
योगिनस्तं प्रपश्यन्ति भगवन्तं सनातनम् ॥ (2)

'"Everything originates with the brahman's seed. It is because of the brahman's seed that everything flourishes. It is because of the seed that stellar bodies burn in the middle of the sky and the sun obtains its radiance. He is the one whom the yogis see. He is the eternal and illustrious one."'

आपोऽथ अद्भ्य: सलिलस्य मध्ये उभौ देवौ शिश्रियातेऽन्तरिक्षे ।
स सध्रीची: स विषूचीर्वसाना उभे बिभर्ति पृथिवीं दिवं च ।
योगिनस्तं प्रपश्यन्ति भगवन्तं सनातनम् ॥ (3)

"'It is because of him that there is water in the middle of the ocean. It is because of him that the two divinities are in the firmament.[30] They hold up what flows in and what flows out, in the earth and in heaven.[31] He is the one whom the yogis see. He is the eternal and illustrious one."'

उभौ च देवौ पृथिवीं दिवं च दिशश्च शुक्रं भुवनं बिभर्ति ।
तस्माद्दिश: सरितश्च स्रवन्ति तस्मात्समुद्रा विहिता महान्त: ।
योगिनस्तं प्रपश्यन्ति भगवन्तं सनातनम् ॥ (4)

"'Both these divinities support earth and heaven. The seed bears the directions and the universe. The rivers flow from those directions and the great oceans are created from these. He is the one whom the yogis see. He is the eternal and illustrious one."'

चक्रे रथस्य तिष्ठन्तं ध्रुवस्याव्ययकर्मण: ।
केतुमन्तं वहन्त्यश्वास्तं दिव्यमजरं दिवि ।
योगिनस्तं प्रपश्यन्ति भगवन्तं सनातनम् ॥ (5)

"'Based on the wheels, the steady chariot ceaselessly works. He has a flaming crest and the celestial and ageless horses bear him in the sky.[32] He is the one whom the yogis see. He is the eternal and illustrious one."'

---

[30]The sun and the moon.
[31]This shloka is especially difficult to understand and translate. There is an allusion to the jivatman and the paramatman, and one can say the paramatman (the one yogis see) holds up both the jivatman and the breath of life, as well as heaven and earth.
[32]This is a reference to the horses and chariot of the sun.

न सादृश्ये तिष्ठति रूपमस्य न चक्षुषा पश्यति कश्चिदेनम् ।
मनीषयाथो मनसा हृदा च य एवं विदुरमृतास्ते भवन्ति ।
योगिनस्तं प्रपश्यन्ति भगवन्तं सनातनम् ॥ (6)

'"There is no form that is similar to his. He can never be seen with the eyes. Learned ones who get to know him through their minds and their hearts become immortal. He is the one whom the yogis see. He is the eternal and illustrious one."'

द्वादशपूगां सरितं देवरक्षितम् ।
मधु ईशन्तस्तदा संचरन्ति घोरम् ।
योगिनस्तं प्रपश्यन्ति भगवन्तं सनातनम् ॥ (7)

'"There is a terrible river with twelve flows protected by devas, and one drinks from it.[33] He is the one whom the yogis see. He is the eternal and illustrious one."'

तदर्धमासं पिबति संचित्य भ्रमरो मधु ।
ईशान: सर्वभूतेषु हविर्भूतमकल्पयत् ।
योगिनस्तं प्रपश्यन्ति भगवन्तं सनातनम् ॥ (8)

'"Like a bee, there are those who drink the honey only for half a month.[34] He is the lord who has ordained oblations for all beings. He is the one whom the yogis see. He is the eternal and illustrious one."'

हिरण्यपर्णमश्वत्थमभिपत्य अपक्षका: ।
ते तत्र पक्षिणो भूत्वा प्रपतन्ति यथादिशम् ।
योगिनस्तं प्रपश्यन्ति भगवन्तं सनातनम् ॥ (9)

---

[33] This is another shloka that is difficult to understand and translate. The twelve could be the twelve months, and the river could be symbolic of life. But the twelve probably means the five organs of perception, the five organs of action, intelligence and the mind.

[34] The image probably is that one only enjoys half the fruit of actions and has to be reborn for the other half. The bee stands for the jivatman.

"There is an ashvattha tree[35] with golden foliage. They alight like featherless birds there. Having obtained feathers, they fly out in different directions.[36] He is the one whom the yogis see. He is the eternal and illustrious one."

पूर्णात्पूर्णान्युद्धरन्ति पूर्णात्पूर्णानि चक्रिरे ।
हरन्ति पूर्णात्पूर्णानि पूर्णमेवावशिष्यते ।
योगिनस्तं प्रपश्यन्ति भगवन्तं सनातनम् ॥ (10)

"The complete is taken away from the complete. It is from the complete that the complete universe is created. The complete is taken away from the complete. But it is the complete that remains.[37] He is the one whom the yogis see. He is the eternal and illustrious one."

तस्माद्वै वायुरायातस्तस्मिंश्च प्रयत: सदा ।
तस्मादग्निश्च सोमश्च तस्मिंश्च प्राण आतत: ॥ (11)

"The wind flows from him and it is in him that it subsides. Agni and Soma were created from him. All life was created from him."

सर्वमेव ततो विद्यात्तद्द्रष्टुं न शक्नुम: ।
योगिनस्तं प्रपश्यन्ति भगवन्तं सनातनम् ॥ (12)

"He is everything. All knowledge flows from him. I am incapable of describing him. He is the one whom the yogis see. He is the eternal and illustrious one."

---

[35] The holy fig tree.
[36] The tree is symbolic of the brahman. The featherless birds are individual souls or jivatman. Originally, they are part of the brahman. But after having obtained feathers or individual characteristics, they are born as different beings. Alternatively, the feathers can stand for knowledge. Originally, they are without feathers and are without knowledge. But having alighted on the tree, they obtain the feathers of knowledge.
[37] The brahman is complete. The universe is also complete and is created from the brahman. But even after the universe has been created from the brahman, the brahman remains complete. This, too, is reminiscent of the Upanishads.

अपानं गिरति प्राणः प्राणं गिरति चन्द्रमाः ।
आदित्यो गिरते चन्द्रमादित्यं गिरते परः ।
योगिनस्तं प्रपश्यन्ति भगवन्तं सनातनम् ॥ (13)

'"Apana dissolves into prana, prana dissolves into the moon. The moon dissolves into the sun. The sun dissolves into the supreme. He is the one whom the yogis see. He is the eternal and illustrious one."'

एकं पादं नोत्क्षिपति सलिलाद्धंस उच्चरन् ।
तं चेत्सततमृत्विजं न मृत्युर्नामृतं भवेत् ।
योगिनस्तं प्रपश्यन्ति भगवन्तं सनातनम् ॥ (14)

'"When it ascends out of the water, the swan does not raise one foot. If it did raise that *ritvija*,[38] there would be no death or immortality.[39] He is the one whom the yogis see. He is the eternal and illustrious one."'

एवं देवो महात्मा स पावकं पुरुषो गिरन् ।
यो वै तं पुरुषं वेद तस्येहात्मा न रिष्यते ।
योगिनस्तं प्रपश्यन्ति भगवन्तं सनातनम् ॥ (15)

'"There is one great-souled divinity. He is the being who swallows the fire. If one knows this being, one's atman will never suffer. He is the one whom the yogis see. He is the eternal and illustrious one."'

यः सहस्रं सहस्राणां पक्षान्संतत्य संपतेत् ।
मध्यमे मध्य आगच्छेदपि चेत्स्यान्मनोजवः ।
योगिनस्तं प्रपश्यन्ति भगवन्तं सनातनम् ॥ (16)

---

[38] The word 'ritvija' means an officiating priest. That officiating priest stands for a leg that is submerged and is busy only performing sacrifices.
[39] That is, there would be no difference between death and immortality. Here, man is compared to a swan and man has four legs or parts (waking, dreaming, sleeping and *turiya*). Turiya is the fourth state in which one perceives union between the jivatman and the brahman. Ordinary people only perceive the first three parts and, therefore, one of the legs is hidden and not used. Wise ones perceive the fourth leg, too, and see no difference between death and immortality.

"'The thousands and thousands of wings that are spread out to fly must return to the centre, and what is in the centre, with the speed of thought.[40] He is the one whom the yogis see. He is the eternal and illustrious one.'"

न दर्शने तिष्ठति रूपमस्य चौनं पश्यन्ति सुविशुद्धसत्त्वाः ।
हितो मनीषी मनसाभिपश्ये द्वे तं श्रयेयुरमृतास्ते भवन्ति ।
योगिनस्तं प्रपश्यन्ति भगवन्तं सनातनम् ॥ (17)

"'His form is stationed beyond the range of sight. Only those who are extremely pure of heart can see him. A wise one desiring welfare sees him through the mind. Those who resort to him become immortal. He is the one whom the yogis see. He is the eternal and illustrious one.'"

गूहन्ति सर्पा इव गह्वराणि स्वशिक्षया स्वेन वृत्तेन मर्त्याः ।
तेषु प्रमुह्यन्ति जना विमूढा यथाध्वानं मोहयन्ते भयाय ।
योगिनस्तं प्रपश्यन्ति भगवन्तं सनातनम् ॥ (18)

"'Because of their own learning and their own conduct, mortals hide from him, behaving like snakes in their holes. But only foolish ones are deluded by this and, deceived and confounded, follow the road of fear. He is the one whom the yogis see. He is the eternal and illustrious one.'"

सदा सदासत्कृतः स्यान्न मृत्युरमृतं कुतः ।
सत्यानृते सत्यसमानबन्धने सतश्च योनिरसतश्चैक एव ।
योगिनस्तं प्रपश्यन्ति भगवन्तं सनातनम् ॥ (19)

"'There is neither existence, nor is there non-existence. Therefore, what source can give rise to death or immortality? Both existence and non-existence are based on the same truth. Existence and non-existence originate in the same womb. He is the one whom the yogis see. He is the eternal and illustrious one.'"

---

[40] The individual atmans must all return to the brahman.

न साधुना नोत असाधुना वा समानमेतद्दृश्यते मानुषेषु ।
समानमेतदमृतस्य विद्यादेवंयुक्तो मधु तद्वै परीप्सेत् ।
योगिनस्तं प्रपश्यन्ति भगवन्तं सनातनम् ॥ (20)

"'Among men, whether they are virtuous or wicked, these are not seen in the same way.[41] Having been united with the divine knowledge of immortality, one should taste that honey. He is the one whom the yogis see. He is the eternal and illustrious one.'"

नास्यातिवादा हृदयं तापयन्ति नानधीतं नाहुतमग्निहोत्रम् ।
मनो ब्राह्मीं लघुतामादधीत प्रज्ञानमस्य नाम धीरा लभन्ते ।
योगिनस्तं प्रपश्यन्ति भगवन्तं सनातनम् ॥ (21)

"'The heart is not tormented because of abuse.[42] Nor do lack of studying and lack of agnihotra matter. The mind becomes as light as the brahman. Those who are wise and persevering obtain him. He is the one whom the yogis see. He is the eternal and illustrious one.'"

एवं यः सर्वभूतेषु आत्मानमनुपश्यति ।
अन्यत्रान्यत्र युक्तेषु किं स शोचेत्ततः परम् ॥ (22)

"'Thus, one sees one's own atman in all beings, all engaged in various tasks. After this, why should there be any sorrow?'"

यथोदपाने महति सर्वतः संप्लुतोदके ।
एवं सर्वेषु वेदेषु ब्राह्मणस्य विजानतः ॥ (23)

"'When there is a great deal of water in a reservoir, it overflows in all directions. Like that, brahmanas who know, look at him in all the Vedas.'"[43]

---

[41] This is so because they do not possess wisdom and do not realize there is no difference between existence and non-existence. This is because, apparently, wise men also do not possess true wisdom.

[42] For such a wise man.

[43] The Vedas are being compared to the well filled up by the brahman. Those who know no longer need small wells. The words are almost identical to Bhagavat Gita 2.46.

अङ्गुष्ठमात्रः पुरुषो महात्मा न दृश्यतेऽसौ हृदये निविष्टः ।
अजश्चरो दिवारात्रमतन्द्रितश्च स तं मत्वा कविरास्ते प्रसन्नः ॥ (24)

"'The great-souled being is the size of a thumb. Though he resides in the heart, he cannot be seen. The lord is without origin. He roams ceaselessly, throughout night and day. Knowing this, a wise one is full of happiness.'"

अहमेवास्मि वो माता पिता पुत्रोऽस्म्यहं पुनः ।
आत्माहमपि सर्वस्य यच्च नास्ति यदस्ति च ॥ (25)

"'I am I. I am also the mother, the father and the son. I am the atman of everything, whether I exist or whether I do not exist.'"

पितामहोऽस्मि स्थविरः पिता पुत्रश्च भारत ।
ममैव यूयमात्मस्था न मे यूयं न वोऽप्यहम् ॥ (26)

"'O Descendant of the Bharata Lineage! I am the ancient grandfather,[44] the father and the son. You dwell in my atman. But you are not mine, and I am not yours.'"

आत्मैव स्थानं मम जन्म चात्मा वेदप्रोक्तोऽहमजरप्रतिष्ठः ॥ (27)

"'The atman is my foundation. The atman is my birth. I am the foundation, without decay, that the Vedas speak about.'"

अणोरणीयान्सुमनाः सर्वभूतेषु जागृमि ।
पितरं सर्वभूतानां पुष्करे निहितं विदुः ॥ (28)

"'I am subtler than the most subtle. With an excellent mind, I am awake in all beings. Know him to be the father of all beings, dwelling in the *pushkara*[45] in all beings.'"

Thus ends the Sanatasujata.

---

[44] Brahma.

[45] 'Pushkara' means a blue lotus. The lotus symbolizes the heart of a being. Alternatively, it also means a cage, and it can also symbolize the cages that bodies represent.

7

UTATHYA GITA

In the eighteen-Parva classification of the Mahabharata, Shanti Parva is the twelfth and the longest Parva. It is about peace after the Kurukshetra War is over, and has sections where Bhishma, lying on his bed of arrows, teaches Yudhishthira. It has three sub-parvas: Raja Dharma Parva, Apad Dharma Parva and Moksha Dharma Parva. The Utathya Gita consists of two chapters from Raja Dharma Parva and comprises ninety-four shlokas. The Raja Dharma Parva speaks of the dharma of 'rajas'—kings—also known as raja dharma. As a part of this Gita, Bhishma tells Yudhishthira what Utathya, an ancient rishi and the elder brother of Brihaspati (the guru of the gods), told King Mandhata, a famous king from the *surya vamsha* (the Solar dynasty), in a discourse about raja dharma. Raja dharma also features prominently in the Itihasa Purana corpus, particularly in Shanti Parva of the Mahabharata.

Chapter 1

भीष्म उवाच

यानङ्गिरा: क्षत्रधर्मानुतथ्यो ब्रह्मवित्तम: ।
मान्धात्रे यौवनाश्वाय प्रीतिमानभ्यभाषत ॥ (1)

Bhishma said, 'Utathya, the son of Angiras, was supreme among those who knew about the brahman. He affectionately told Mandhata, the son of Yuvanashva, about the dharma of kshatriyas.'

स यथानुशासनैनमुतथ्यो ब्रह्मवित्तमः ।
तत्ते सर्वं प्रवक्ष्यामि निखिलेन युधिष्ठिर ॥ (2)

'O Yudhishthira! I will tell you completely and in entirety what Utathya, supreme among those who knew about the brahman, instructed.'

उतथ्य उवाच

धर्माय राजा भवति न कामकरणाय तु ।
मान्धातरेवं जानीहि राजा लोकस्य रक्षिता ॥ (3)

'Utathya said, "The king exists for dharma, not for the sake of engaging in kama. O Mandhata! Know that the king is the protector of the world."'

राजा चरति वै धर्मं देवत्वायैव गच्छति ।
न चेद्धर्मं स चरति नरकायैव गच्छति ॥ (4)

'"If the king acts in accordance with dharma, then he advances towards a state of divinity.[1] If he follows adharma, he goes to hell."'

धर्मे तिष्ठन्ति भूतानि धर्मो राजनि तिष्ठति ।
तं राजा साधु यः शास्ति स राजा पृथिवीपतिः ॥ (5)

'"Beings are based on dharma. Dharma is based on the king. A virtuous king who rules in this way is a king who is a lord of the earth."'

राजा परमधर्मात्मा लक्ष्मीवान्पाप उच्यते ।
देवाश्च गर्हां गच्छन्ति धर्मो नास्तीति चोच्यते ॥ (6)

'"It is said that a king who has supreme dharma in his atman and is also prosperous but censures the devas does not truly possess dharma."'

अधर्मे वर्तमानानामर्थसिद्धिः प्रदृश्यते ।
तदेव मङ्गलं सर्वं लोकः समनुवर्तते ॥ (7)

---

[1] He goes to heaven.

'"When those who follow adharma are seen to be successful in their pursuit of artha, then everyone in the world thinks that this is auspicious and begins to follow them."'

उच्छिद्यते धर्मवृत्तमधर्मो वर्तते महान् ।
भयमाहुर्दिवारात्रं यदा पापो न वार्यते ॥ (8)

'"When sins are not restrained, dharma is uprooted, great adharma follows, and it is said that there is fear both during the day and the night."'

न वेदाननुवर्तन्ति व्रतवन्तो द्विजातयः ।
न यज्ञांस्तन्वते विप्रा यदा पापो न वार्यते ॥ (9)

'"Dvijas do not follow the Vedas and the vows. When sins are not restrained, brahmanas do not perform sacrifices."'

वध्यानामिह सर्वेषां मनो भवति विह्वलम् ।
मनुष्याणां महाराज यदा पापो न वार्यते ॥ (10)

'"O Great King! When sins are not restrained in this world, the minds of all men are confused, like those about to be slain."'

उभौ लोकावभिप्रेक्ष्य राजानमृषयः स्वयम् ।
असृजन्सुमहद्भूतमयं धर्मो भविष्यति ॥ (11)

'"Having looked at both the worlds,[2] the rishis created the king as an extremely great being, so that there would be dharma."'[3]

यस्मिन्धर्मो विराजेत तं राजानं प्रचक्षते ।
यस्मिन्विलीयते धर्मस्तं देवा वृषलं विदुः ॥ (12)

'"One in whom dharma shines is spoken of as a king.[4] If dharma disappears in someone, devas know that person to be a *vrishala*."'[5]

---

[2] This world and the next.
[3] This is a reference to the rishis creating Prithu as a king. The king is necessary to ensure that dharma flourishes, the virtuous are protected and the wicked are punished.
[4] The Sanskrit for shine here is *'virajate'*, which also means to appear beautiful.
[5] 'Vrishala' means a contemptible person, sometimes equated with shudra. *'Vrisha'*

वृषो हि भगवान्धर्मो यस्तस्य कुरुते ह्यलम् ।
वृषलं तं विदुर्देवास्तस्माद्धर्मं न लोपयेत् ॥ (13)

'"O Illustrious One! Dharma is a bull and the devas know one who does away with it as a vrishala. Therefore, dharma should not be destroyed."'

धर्मे वर्धति वर्धन्ति सर्वभूतानि सर्वदा ।
तस्मिन्ह्रसति हीयन्ते तस्माद्धर्मं प्रवर्धयेत् ॥ (14)

'"When dharma prospers, all beings always prosper and when it decays, they decay. Therefore, make dharma prosper."'

धनात्प्रवति धर्मो हि धारणाद्धेति निश्चयः ।
अकार्याणां मनुष्येन्द्र स सीमान्तकरः स्मृतः ॥ (15)

'"It is certain that dharma flows from the acquisition and preservation of wealth. O Indra among Men! It has been said that one should lay down the boundaries of what should not be done."'

प्रभवार्थं हि भूतानां धर्मः सृष्टः स्वयंभुवा ।
तस्मात्प्रवर्धयेद्धर्मं प्रजानुग्रहकारणात् ॥ (16)

'"Svayambhu[6] created dharma for the power of beings. Therefore, to show favours to subjects, propagate dharma."'

तस्माद्धि राजशार्दूल धर्मः श्रेष्ठ इति स्मृतः ।
स राजा यः प्रजाः शास्ति साधुकृत्पुरुषर्षभः ॥ (17)

'"O Tiger among Kings! That is the reason it has been said that dharma is the best. The bull among men who rules his subjects virtuously is a true king."'

कामक्रोधावनादृत्य धर्ममेवानुपालयेत् ।
धर्मः श्रेयस्करतमो राज्ञां भरतसत्तम ॥ (18)

---

means a bull as well as moral merit. '*Alam*' means enough. A person who relays enough of dharma is a vrishala.
[6]Brahma.

'"One should ignore desire and anger and rule in accordance with dharma. O Supreme among the Bharata Lineage![7] Dharma is the best task to be followed by a king."'

धर्मस्य ब्राह्मणा योनिस्तस्मात्तान्पूजयेत्सदा ।
ब्राह्मणानां च मान्धात: कामान्कुर्यादमत्सरी ॥ (19)

'"Brahmanas are dharma's womb and must always be worshipped. O Mandhata! Without any resentment, the desires of brahmanas must be followed."'

तेषां ह्याकामकरणाद्राज्ञ: संजायते भयम् ।
मित्राणि च न वर्धन्ते तथामित्रीभवन्त्यपि ॥ (20)

'"If one does not act so as to satisfy their wishes, this results in fear for the king. The friends do not increase and become his enemies."'

ब्राह्मणान्वै तदासूयाद्यदा वैरोचनो बलि: ।
अथास्माच्छीरपाक्रामद्यास्मिन्नासीत्प्रतापिनी ॥ (21)

'"Bali, Virochana's son, exhibited resentment towards brahmanas.[8] Because of this, the powerful Shri[9] was enraged and no longer resided with him."'

ततस्तस्मादपक्रम्य सागच्छत्पाकशासनम् ।
अथ सोऽन्वतपत्पश्चाच्छ्रियं दृष्ट्वा पुरंदरे ॥ (22)

---

[7]This is an inconsistency in the original because the words are being spoken to Mandhata, not Yudhishthira. Bharata and the Pandavas are from the Lunar dynasty. Mandhata was from the Solar dynasty. There was a lesser known Bharata in the Solar dynasty, but he came after Mandhata.
[8]Bali was an asura. He was deprived of the three worlds by Vishnu in his *vamana* (dwarf) incarnation. There are no stories to suggest that Bali was wicked or resentful towards brahmanas. Vishnu restored the three worlds to Indra, who had been deprived of them by Bali.
[9]Lakshmi, the goddess of prosperity.

'"Instead, she went to the chastiser of Paka.[10] Later, he[11] was tormented when he saw Shri with Purandara."'[12]

एतत्फलमसूयाया अभिमानस्य चाभिभो ।
तस्मादबुध्यस्व मान्धातर्मा त्वा जह्यात्प्रतापिनी ॥ (23)

'"O Lord! But this was the result of his pride and intolerance. O Mandhata! Therefore, understand that the powerful one can forsake you."'

दर्पो नाम श्रियः पुत्रो जज्ञेऽधर्मादिति श्रुतिः ।
तेन देवासुरा राजन्नीताः सुबहुशो वशम् ॥ (24)

'"The Shrutis say that adharma leads to the birth of Shri's son, named Darpa.[13] O King! He has caused the subjugation of devas and asuras on many occasions."'

राजर्षयश्च बहवस्तस्मादबुध्यस्व पार्थिव ।
राजा भवति तं जित्वा दासस्तेन पराजितः ॥ (25)

'"O King! Many rajarshis did not understand this either. Having conquered it, one becomes a king. One who is defeated becomes a slave."'[14]

स यथा दर्पसहितमधर्मं नानुसेवते ।
तथा वर्तस्व मान्धातश्चिरं चेत्स्थातुमिच्छसि ॥ (26)

'"Do not serve insolence and adharma. O Mandhata! If you wish to be established for a long time, follow this."'

मत्तात्प्रमत्तात्पोगण्डादुन्मत्ताच्च विशेषतः ।
तदभ्यासादुपावर्तादहितानां च सेवनात् ॥ (27)

---

[10]Indra killed a demon named Paka.
[11]Bali.
[12]Another name for Indra.
[13]Insolence.
[14]Alternatively, servant.

"'In particular, do not associate with those who are intoxicated,[15] careless, infantile and mad. Do not indulge in conduct that is harmful.'"

निगृहीतादमात्याच्च स्त्रीभ्यश्चैव विशेषतः ।
पर्वताद्विषमादुर्गाद्धस्तिनोऽश्वात्सरीसृपात् ॥ (28)

"'In particular, always make efforts to be careful of advisers who have been punished, women, mountains, uneven terrain, forts, elephants, horses and reptiles.'"

एतेभ्यो नित्ययत्तः स्यान्नक्तं चर्यां च वर्जयेत् ।
अत्यायं चातिमानं च दम्भं क्रोधं च वर्जयेत् ॥ (29)

"'Always control these. Do not wander around in the night. Abandon excessive pride, insolence and anger.'"

अविज्ञातासु च स्त्रीषु क्लीबासु स्वैरिणीषु च ।
परभार्यासु कन्यासु नाचरेन्मैथुनं नृपः ॥ (30)

"'The king should not indulge in sexual intercourse with unknown women, eunuchs, promiscuous women, the wives of others and maidens.'"[16]

कुलेषु पापरक्षांसि जायन्ते वर्णसंकरात् ।
अपुमांसोऽङ्गहीनाश्च स्थूलजिह्वा विचेतसः ॥ (31)

"'If there is a mixing of varnas, wicked rakshasas[17] are born in the family—eunuchs, those without limbs, those with thick tongues and idiots.'"

एते चान्ये च जायन्ते यदा राजा प्रमाद्यति ।
तस्माद्राज्ञा विशेषेण वर्तितव्यं प्रजाहिते ॥ (32)

---

[15]Probably in the sense of being intoxicated with insolence.
[16]The Sanskrit word used for maiden is '*kanya*', which also means 'virgin'. Maiden in the sense of an unmarried woman seems to fit better here.
[17]Here, the word 'rakshasa' is not to be understood as a species but as an evil person born in the family.

'"When the king is careless, these and others are born. Therefore, for the sake of the welfare of the subjects, the king must take special care."'

क्षत्रियस्य प्रमत्तस्य दोष: संजायते महान् ।
अधर्मा: संप्रवर्तन्ते प्रजासंकरकारका: ॥ (33)

'"When a kshatriya is careless, great sins result. Adharma is enhanced and this leads to a mixing of the subjects."'[18]

अशीते विद्यते शीतं शीते शीतं न विद्यते ।
अवृष्टिरतिवृष्टिश्च व्याधिश्चाविशति प्रजा: ॥ (34)

'"It is cold during the summer and it is not cold during the winter. There is no rain, or there is too much of rain. The subjects are penetrated by disease."'

नक्षत्राण्युपतिष्ठन्ति ग्रहा घोरास्तथापरे ।
उत्पाताश्चात्र दृश्यन्ते बहवो राजनाशना: ॥ (35)

'"Terrible nakshatras and planets are seen to rise. Many omens are seen, signifying the king's destruction."'

अरक्षितात्मा यो राजा प्रजाश्चापि न रक्षति ।
प्रजाश्च तस्य क्षीयन्ते ताश्च सोऽनु विनश्यति ॥ (36)

'"When the king does not protect his subjects, he is himself not protected. The subjects decay, and he also follows them towards destruction."'

द्वावाददाते ह्येकस्य द्वयोश्च बहवोऽपरे ।
कुमार्य: संप्रलुप्यन्ते तदाहुर्नृपदूषणम् ॥ (37)

'"Two seize the possessions of one and many others seize the possessions of two. Virgins are corrupted. These are said to be the sins of the king."'

---

[18] Mixing of the varnas.

ममैतदिति नैकस्य मनुष्येष्ववतिष्ठते ।
त्यक्त्वा धर्मं यदा राजा प्रमादमनुतिष्ठति ॥ (38)

'"Not a single man can say, 'This belongs to me.' This is what happens when the king is careless and abandons dharma."'

Chapter 2

उतथ्य उवाच

कालवर्षी च पर्जन्यो धर्मचारी च पार्थिवः ।
संपद्यदैषा भवति सा बिभर्ति सुखं प्रजाः ॥ (1)

'Utathya said, "When the king follows dharma, Parjanya[19] showers down at the right time. There is prosperity and the subjects shine in happiness."'

यो न जानाति निर्हन्तुं वस्त्राणां रजको मलम् ।
रक्तानि वा शोधयितुं यथा नास्ति तथैव सः ॥ (2)

'"He,[20] lacking this, is like a washerman who does not know how to wash dirty clothes, or one who washes away the dye in the process."'

एवमेव द्विजेन्द्राणां क्षत्रियाणां विशामपि ।
शूद्राश्चतुर्णां वर्णानां नानाकर्मस्ववस्थिताः ॥ (3)

'"It is the same with dvijas, kshatriyas, vaishyas and shudras who are no longer established in the various tasks of the four varnas."'

कर्म शूद्रे कृषिर्वैश्ये दण्डनीतिश्च राजनि ।
ब्रह्मचर्यं तपो मन्त्राः सत्यं चापि द्विजातिषु ॥ (4)

'"Labour is for shudras, agriculture for vaishyas and *dandaniti*[21] for kings. Brahmacharya, austerities, mantras and truth are for dvijas."'

---

[19] The god of rain, usually equated with Indra.
[20] The careless king.
[21] Administering reward and punishment.

तेषां यः क्षत्रियो वेद वस्त्राणामिव शोधनम् ।
शीलदोषान्विनिहन्तुं स पिता स प्रजापतिः ॥ (5)

'"Like cleaning clothes, among them, the kshatriya who knows good conduct and about restraining bad conduct is like a father and a lord of beings."'

कृतं त्रेता द्वापरश्च कलिश्च भरतर्षभ ।
राजवृत्तानि सर्वाणि राजैव युगमुच्यते ॥ (6)

'"O Bull of the Bharata Lineage![22] Krita, Treta, Dvapara and Kali[23] are all dependent on the conduct of kings. It is said that the king makes the *yuga*."'

चातुर्वर्ण्यं तथा वेदाश्चातुराश्रम्यमेव च ।
सर्वं प्रमुह्यते ह्येतद्यदा राजा प्रमाद्यति ॥ (7)

'"When the king is careless, the four varnas and the four Vedas and ashramas are all confused."'

राजैव कर्ता भूतानां राजैव च विनाशकः ।
धर्मात्मा यः स कर्ता स्याद्धर्मात्मा विनाशकः ॥ (8)

'"The king is the one who makes beings. The king is their destroyer. The one with dharma in his atman is a maker. The one with adharma in his atman is a destroyer."'

राज्ञो भार्याश्च पुत्राश्च बान्धवाः सुहृदस्तथा ।
समेत्य सर्वे शोचन्ति यदा राजा प्रमाद्यति ॥ (9)

'"When the king is careless, the king's wives, sons, relatives and well-wishers all sorrow together."'

हस्तिनोऽश्वाश्च गावश्चाप्युष्ट्राश्वतरगर्दभाः ।
अधर्मवृत्ते नृपतौ सर्वे सीदन्ति पार्थिव ॥ (10)

---

[22]This inconsistency occurs again.
[23]The four yugas, with dharma progressively declining from Krita (Satya) Yuga to Kali Yuga.

"'O Lord of the Earth! When the king follows adharma, all the elephants, horses, cattle, camels, mules and asses suffer.'"

दुर्बलार्थं बलं सृष्टं धात्रा मान्धातरुच्यते ।
अबलं तन्महद्भूतं यस्मिन्सर्वं प्रतिष्ठितम् ॥ (11)

"'O Mandhata! It is said that the creator created strength for the sake of the weak.[24] The foundation of everything is based on the weak.'"

यच्च भूतं स भजते भूता ये च तदन्वयाः ।
अधर्मस्थे हि नृपतौ सर्वे सीदन्ति पार्थिव ॥ (12)

"'O Lord of the Earth! When the king bases himself on adharma, beings who depend on him and others who depend on those beings all suffer.'"

दुर्बलस्य हि यच्चक्षुर्मुनेराशीविषस्य च ।
अविषह्यतमं मन्ये मा स्म दुर्बलमासदः ॥ (13)

"'I think that the glances of one who is weak, those of a sage and those of a virulent snake cannot be tolerated. Therefore, do not make the weak suffer.'"

दुर्बलांस्तात बुध्येथा नित्यमेवाविमानितान् ।
मा त्वां दुर्बलचक्षूंषि प्रदहेयुः सबान्धवम् ॥ (14)

"'O Son! Know that the weak should never be thought of as those who should be disregarded. Otherwise, the glances of the weak will burn you down, together with your relatives.'"

न हि दुर्बलदग्धस्य कुले किंचित्प्ररोहति ।
आमूलं निर्दहत्येव मा स्म दुर्बलमासदः ॥ (15)

"'If a family is burnt down by the weak, it is burnt down to the roots and nothing grows there. Therefore, do not make the weak suffer.'"

---

[24]This was done so that the weak could be protected.

अबलं वै बलाच्छ्रेयो यच्चातिबलवद्बलम् ।
बलस्याबलदग्धस्य न किंचिदवशिष्यते ॥ (16)

'"Weakness is superior to strength, since greater strength is superior to strength. When the strong is burnt down by the weak, there is nothing left."'

विमानितो हतोत्क्रुष्टस्त्रातारं चेन्न विन्दति ।
अमानुषकृतस्तत्र दण्डो हन्ति नराधिपम् ॥ (17)

'"If a humiliated and struck person cries out for succour and fails to find a man who tries to help him, the consequent punishment slays the lord of the earth."'

मा स्म तात बले स्थेया बाधिष्ठा मापि दुर्बलम् ।
मा त्वा दुर्बलचक्षूंषि धक्ष्यन्त्यग्निरिवाश्रयम् ॥ (18)

'"O Son! When you base yourself on strength, do not suppress the weak. Otherwise, the glances of the weak will burn you down, like a fire that consumes the foundation."'

यानि मिथ्याभिशस्तानां पतन्त्यश्रूणि रोदताम् ।
तानि पुत्रान्पशूंन्नन्ति तेषां मिथ्याभिशासताम् ॥ (19)

'"The tears shed by those who weep because they have been falsely accused slay the sons and animals of those who have made those false accusations."'

यदि नात्मनि पुत्रेषु न चेत्पौत्रेषु नप्तृषु ।
न हि पापं कृतं कर्म सद्य: फलति गौरिव ॥ (20)

'"If not on one's own self, it descends on the son. If not on the son, it descends on the son's son or the daughter's son. Like a cow, the fruits of an evil deed are not immediately reaped."'[25]

यत्राबलो वध्यमानस्त्रातारं नाधिगच्छति ।
महान्दैवकृतस्तत्र दण्ड: पतति दारुण: ॥ (21)

---

[25]One has to wait for a cow to have a calf before it can be milked.

"'When a weak person is slain and cannot find a protector, devas have arranged that a great and terrible punishment should descend.'"[26]

युक्ता यदा जानपदा भिक्षन्ते ब्राह्मणा इव ।
अभीक्ष्णं भिक्षुदोषेण राजानं घ्नन्ति तादृशाः ॥ (22)

"'Though they should not beg, when the residents of the countryside are forced to beg like brahmanas, it is as if that sin of begging slays the king.'"

राज्ञो यदा जनपदे बहवो राजपूरुषाः ।
अनयेनोपवर्तन्ते तद्राज्ञः किल्बिषं महत् ॥ (23)

"'When the many royal officers employed by the king in the countryside are engaged in wrong policy, a great sin devolves on the king.'"

यदा युक्ता नयन्त्यर्थान्कामादर्थवशेन वा ।
कृपणं याचमानानां तद्राज्ञो वैशसं महत् ॥ (24)

"'When those employed for good policy are overcome by reasons of desire and greed for riches and extract from those who are distressed and pleading, that is a great sin on the part of the king.'"

महावृक्षो जायते वर्धते च तं चैव भूतानि समाश्रयन्ति ।
यदा वृक्षश्छिद्यते दह्यते वा तदाश्रया अनिकेता भवन्ति ॥ (25)

"'A large tree sprouts and then grows. It offers refuge to beings. When the tree is severed or burnt down, those who have sought refuge in it are also rendered homeless.'"[27]

यदा राष्ट्रे धर्ममार्गं चरन्ति संस्कारान् वा राजगुणं ब्रुवाणाः ।
तैरेवाधर्मश्चरितो धर्ममोहात्तूर्णं जह्यात्सुकृतं दुष्कृतं च ॥ (26)

"'When those in the kingdom practise the foremost kinds of dharma and follow good conduct, the qualities of the king are spoken about.

---

[26]Descend on the king.
[27]The king is being compared to the tree and the royal officers to those who have made homes in the tree.

When they practise adharma and are confused about dharma, their good deeds swiftly turn to bad deeds.'"

यत्र पापा ज्यायमानाश्चरन्ति सतां कलिर्विन्दति तत्र राज्ञ: ।
यदा राजा शास्ति नरान्निशिष्यान् तद्राज्यं वर्धते भूमिपाल ॥ (27)

'"When the wicked are known to roam among the virtuous, the king suffers from *kali*[28] there. O Protector of the Earth! When the lord of the earth punishes men who should not be punished, the kingdom does not prosper."'

यश्चामात्यं मानयित्वा यथाहं मन्त्रे च युद्धे च नृपो नियुञ्ज्यात् ।
प्रवर्धते तस्य राष्ट्रं नृपस्य भुङ्क्ते महीं चाप्यखिलां चिराय ॥ (28)

'"When advisers are honoured in accordance with what they deserve and are engaged by the king for counsel and war, the kingdom of that king prospers. He enjoys the entire earth for a long period of time."'

अत्रापि सुकृतं कर्म वाचं चैव सुभाषिताम् ।
समीक्ष्य पूजयन्राजा धर्मं प्राप्नोत्यनुत्तमम् ॥ (29)

'"The king who looks towards good deeds and honours them with pleasant words obtains supreme dharma."'

संविभज्य यदा भुङ्क्ते न चान्यानवमन्यते ।
निहन्ति बलिनं दृप्तं स राज्ञो धर्म उच्यते ॥ (30)

'"When the king enjoys his own share and does not disregard others and slays those who are strong and insolent, that king is said to follow dharma."'

त्रायते हि यदा सर्वं वाचा कायेन कर्मणा ।
पुत्रस्यापि न मृष्येच्च स राज्ञो धर्म उच्यते ॥ (31)

'"When the king saves everyone in speech, body and deeds, and does not pardon his own son, that king is said to follow dharma."'

---

[28] In the sense of strife and discord.

यदा शारणिकान्राजा पुत्रवत्परिरक्षति ।
भिनत्ति न च मर्यादां स राज्ञो धर्म उच्यते ॥ (32)

'"When the king protects those who seek refuge, like his own son, and does not violate any agreements, that king is said to follow dharma."'

यदाप्तदक्षिणैर्यज्ञैर्यजते श्रद्धयान्वित: ।
कामद्वेषावनादृत्य स राज्ञो धर्म उच्यते ॥ (33)

'"When the king performs rites and sacrifices and faithfully gives away dakshina, disregarding his own desire and hatred, that king is said to follow dharma."'

कृपणानाथवृद्धानां यदाश्रु व्यपमार्ष्टि वै ।
हर्षं संजनयन्नृणां स राज्ञो धर्म उच्यते ॥ (34)

'"When he wipes away the tears of the distressed, those without protectors, the aged and the weak, and generates delight among men, that king is said to follow dharma."'

विवर्धयति मित्राणि तथारींश्चापकर्षति ।
संपूजयति साधूंश्च स राज्ञो धर्म उच्यते ॥ (35)

'"When his friends prosper and his enemies are brought down, when he worships the virtuous, that king is said to follow dharma."'

सत्यं पालयति प्राप्त्या नित्यं भूमिं प्रयच्छति ।
पूजयत्यतिथीन्भृत्यान्स राज्ञो धर्म उच्यते ॥ (36)

'"When he protects the truth and always gives away land, honouring guests and servants, that king is said to follow dharma."'

निग्रहानुग्रहौ चोभौ यत्र स्यातां प्रतिष्ठितौ ।
अस्मिँल्लोके परे चैव राजा तत्प्राप्नुते फलम् ॥ (37)

'"When favours and chastisement are both established in him, then that king obtains fruits in this world and in the next."'

यमो राजा धार्मिकाणां मान्धातः परमेश्वरः ।
संयच्छन्भवति प्राणान्नसंयच्छंस्तु पापकः ॥ (38)

'"O Mandhata! Yama Raja is the supreme lord for those who follow dharma. When he restrains himself, there is life. When he does not restrain himself, there are sinners."'

ऋत्विक्पुरोहिताचार्यान्सत्कृत्यानवमन्य च ।
यदा सम्यक्प्रगृह्णाति स राज्ञो धर्म उच्यते ॥ (39)

'"When he receives officiating priests, priests and preceptors properly, honouring them and not showing them disrespect, that king is said to follow dharma."'

यमो यच्छति भूतानि सर्वाण्येवाविशेषतः ।
तस्य राज्ञानुकर्तव्यं यन्तव्या विधिवत्प्रजा ॥ (40)

'"Yama controls all beings, without differentiating between them. It is the king's task to duly control subjects in this way."'

सहस्राक्षेण राजा हि सर्व एवोपमीयते ।
स पश्यति हि यं धर्म स धर्मः पुरुषर्षभ ॥ (41)

'"O Bull among Men! In every way, all kings are like the thousand-eyed one.[29] What he sees as dharma is dharma."'

अप्रमादेन शिक्षेथाः क्षमां बुद्धिं धृतिं मतिम् ।
भूतानां सत्त्वजिज्ञासां साध्वसाधु च सर्वदा ॥ (42)

'"You must be careful, learned, forgiving, intelligent, patient and wise, always testing the spirit of beings and separating the good from the wicked."'

संग्रहः सर्वभूतानां दानं च मधुरा च वाक् ।
पौरजानपदाश्चैव गोप्तव्याः स्वा यथा प्रजाः ॥ (43)

---

[29]Indra.

'"You must assuage all beings through gifts and pleasant words. You must protect the residents of the city and the countryside as if they are your own sons."'

न जात्वदक्षो नृपतिः प्रजाः शक्नोति रक्षितुम् ।
भारो हि सुमहांस्तात राज्यं नाम सुदुष्करम् ॥ (44)

'"O Son! A king who is not accomplished is incapable of protecting the subjects. What is known as the kingdom is an extremely great and difficult burden to bear."'

तद्दण्डविन्नृपः प्राज्ञः शूरः शक्नोति रक्षितुम् ।
न हि शक्यमदण्डेन क्लीबेनाबुद्धिनापि वा ॥ (45)

'"Wielding the rod, only a wise and brave king is capable of protecting it. One who is a eunuch and devoid of intelligence, is incapable of wielding the rod."'

अभिरूपैः कुले जातैर्दक्षैर्भक्तैर्बहुश्रुतैः ।
सर्वा बुद्धिः परीक्षेथास्तापसाश्रमिणाम् अपि ॥ (46)

'"There must be handsome ones born in noble lineages.[30] They must be accomplished, faithful and extremely learned. You must test the intelligence of all of these and also that of ascetics who live in hermitages."'

ततस्त्वं सर्वभूतानां धर्मं वेत्स्यसि वै परम् ।
स्वदेशे परदेशे वा न ते धर्मो विनश्यति ॥ (47)

'"In this way, you will know the supreme dharma of all beings and your dharma will not be destroyed in your country or in the lands of others."'

धर्मश्चार्थश्च कामश्च धर्म एवोत्तरो भवेत् ।
अस्मिँल्लोके परे चैव धर्मवित्सुखमेधते ॥ (48)

---

[30] As ministers and advisers.

"'Among dharma, artha and kama, dharma is the best. One who knows dharma enjoys happiness in this world and in the next.'"

त्यजन्ति दारान्ग्राणांश्च मनुष्याः प्रतिपूजिताः ।
संग्रहश्चैव भूतानां दानं च मधुरा च वाक् ॥ (49)

"'When men are honoured well in return, they abandon their chief wives.[31] People should be collected through gifts and pleasant words.'"

अप्रमादश्च शौचं च तात भूतिकरं महत् ।
एतेभ्यश्चैव मान्धातः सततं मा प्रमादिथाः ॥ (50)

"'O Son! Great prosperity follows from attentiveness and purity. O Mandhata! Always pay attention to these and do not be distracted.'"

अप्रमत्तो भवेद्राजा छिद्रदर्शी परात्मनोः ।
नास्य छिद्रं परः पश्येच्छिद्रेषु परमन्वियात् ॥ (51)

"'The king must be careful and look for weaknesses in his own self and that of the enemy. The enemy should not be able to see his weaknesses. But he must search out those of the enemy.'"

एतद्‌वृत्तं वासवस्य यमस्य वरुणस्य च ।
राजर्षीणां च सर्वेषां तत्त्वमप्यनुपालय ॥ (52)

"'This was the conduct of Vasava, Yama, Varuna and all the rajarshis. Follow that truly.'"

तत्कुरुष्व महाराज वृत्तं राजर्षिसेवितम् ।
आतिष्ठ दिव्यं पन्थानमह्नाय भरतर्षभ ॥ (53)

"'O Great King! Act in accordance with this conduct, followed by the rajarshis. O Bull of the Bharata Lineage![32] Ascend onto this divine path and remain on it.'"

---

[31] When men are rewarded for their loyalty, they are ready to give up what they hold dear, such as their chief wives.
[32] This inconsistency occurs again.

धर्मवृत्तं हि राजानं प्रेत्य चेह च भारत ।
देवर्षिपितृगन्धर्वा: कीर्तयन्त्यमितौजस: ॥ (54)

'"O Descendant of the Bharata Lineage![33] In this world and the next, *devarshi*s,[34] ancestors and gandharvas praise the conduct of infinitely energetic kings who act in accordance with dharma."'

भीष्म उवाच

स एवमुक्तो मान्धाता तेनोतथ्येन भारत ।
कृतवानविशङ्कस्तदेक: प्राप च मेदिनीम् ॥ (56)

Bhishma said, 'O Descendant of the Bharata Lineage! Mandhata was thus addressed by Utathya. Without any hesitation, he acted accordingly and obtained the earth.'

भवानपि तथा सम्यङ्मान्धातेव महीपति: ।
धर्मं कृत्वा महीं रक्षन्स्वर्गे स्थानमवाप्स्यसि ॥ (56)

'You should also act properly, like that lord of the earth. Observe dharma, protect the earth and obtain a place in heaven.'

Thus ends the Utathya Gita.

---

[33]This inconsistency occurs again.
[34]Divine rishis.

8

VAMADEVA GITA

The Vamadeva Gita consists of three chapters from Raja Dharma Parva, one of the three sub-parvas of Shanti Parva, and has ninety-four shlokas. In this, Bhishma tells Yudhishthira what Vamadeva told King Vasumana. The conversation follows seamlessly from the Utathya Gita. King Vasumana was the son of Haryashva, the king of Ayodhya. Ayodhya was the capital of Kosala, so a king of Ayodhya means a king of Kosala. Vasumana was a virtuous and generous king. There were many different sages named Vamadeva. Since Kosala is mentioned, this particular Vamadeva is probably the one described in Valmiki Ramayana as Dasharatha's priest and Vasishtha's friend. In any event, such names referred to an entire lineage rather than a specific individual.

Chapter 1

युधिष्ठिर उवाच

कथं धर्मे स्थातुमिच्छन्राजा वर्तेत धार्मिक: ।
पृच्छामि त्वा कुरुश्रेष्ठ तन्मे ब्रूहि पितामह ॥ (1)

Yudhishthira asked, 'How should a king who conducts himself in accordance with dharma, and who wishes to establish himself in dharma, behave? O Best of the Kuru Lineage! O Grandfather! I am asking you. Please tell me.'

भीष्म उवाच

अत्राप्युदाहरन्तीममितिहासं पुरातनम् ।
गीतं दृष्ट्यार्थतत्त्वेन वामदेवेन धीमता ॥ (2)

Bhishma replied, 'In this connection, an ancient history is recounted. The intelligent Vamadeva saw the exact truth about this and sang it.'

राजा वसुमना नाम कौसल्यो बलवाञ्शुचि: ।
महर्षिं परिपप्रच्छ वामदेवं यशस्विनम् ॥ (3)
धर्मार्थसहितं वाक्यं भगवन्ननुशाधि माम् ।
येन वृत्तेन वै तिष्ठन्न् च्यवेयं स्वधर्मत: ॥ (4)

'There was a king named Vasumana from Kosala. He was powerful and pure. He asked the illustrious maharishi Vamadeva. "O Illustrious One! Instruct me in words that are full of dharma and artha, so that I conduct myself in accordance with them and so that I remain established and do not deviate from my own dharma."'

तमब्रवीद्वामदेवस्तपस्वी जपतां वर: ।
हेमवर्णमुपासीनं ययातिमिव नाहुषम् ॥ (5)

'"The supreme among those who performed *japa*,[1]" the ascetic Vamadeva, replied to him, as he[2] was seated there, golden in complexion, like Yayati, the son of Nahusha.'

धर्ममेवानुवर्तस्व न धर्माद्विद्यते परम् ।
धर्मे स्थिता हि राजानो जयन्ति पृथिवीमिमाम् ॥ (6)

'"Follow dharma alone. There is nothing that is superior to dharma. Basing themselves on dharma, kings conquer this entire earth."'

अर्थसिद्धे: परं धर्मं मन्यते यो महीपति: ।
ऋतां च कुरुते बुद्धिं स धर्मेण विरोचते ॥ (7)

---

[1]Japa is meditation with silent chanting.
[2]Vasumana.

"'The lord of the earth who thinks that dharma is superior to success in the matter of artha, and who makes his intelligence truthful, finds delight in dharma.'"

अधर्मदर्शी यो राजा बलादेव प्रवर्तते ।
क्षिप्रमेवापयातोऽस्मादुभौ प्रथममध्यमौ ॥ (8)

"'If a king looks towards adharma and acts on the basis of force alone, he is swiftly dislodged from both the first and the second.'"[3]

असत्यापिष्ठसचिवो वध्यो लोकस्य धर्महा ।
सहैव परिवारेण क्षिप्रमेवावसीदति ॥ (9)

"'Because his advisers are wicked and evil, he slays dharma in this world and deserves to be swiftly killed, along with his relatives.'"

अर्थानामननुष्ठाता कामचारी विकत्थनः ।
अपि सर्वां महीं लब्ध्वा क्षिप्रमेव विनश्यति ॥ (10)

"'If he does not seek artha and is addicted to kama, and if he is boastful, even if he obtains the entire earth, he will swiftly perish.'"

अथाददानः कल्याणमनसूयुर्जितेन्द्रियः ।
वर्धते मतिमात्राजा स्रोतोभिरिव सागरः ॥ (12)

"'However, if a king concentrates on what is beneficial, is devoid of malice, conquers his senses and is intelligent, he flourishes, like an ocean into which streams flow.'"

न पूर्णोऽस्मीति मन्येत धर्मतः कामतोऽर्थतः ।
बुद्धितो मित्रतश्चापि सततं वसुधाधिपः ॥ (12)

"'For dharma, artha and kama, he must always think that he is not yet full.[4] The lord of the earth must possess friendliness in his mind.'"

एतेष्वेव हि सर्वेषु लोकयात्रा प्रतिष्ठिता ।
एतानि शृण्वँल्लभते यशः कीर्तिं श्रियः प्रजाः ॥ (13)

---

[3]Dharma and artha, respectively.
[4]That is, he must want more of these.

"'The entire progress of the worlds is established on all these. If he listens to this, he will obtain fame, glory, prosperity and subjects.'"

एवं यो धर्मसंरम्भी धर्मार्थपरिचिन्तकः ।
अर्थान्समीक्ष्यारभते स ध्रुवं महदश्नुते ॥ (14)

"'A person who is proud of dharma, who thinks about dharma and artha, who undertakes action only after thinking about artha, is certain to obtain greatness.'"

अदाता ह्यनतिस्नेहो दण्डेनावर्तयन्प्रजाः ।
साहसप्रकृतीराजा क्षिप्रमेव विनश्यति ॥ (15)

"'If the king does not give, is not extremely affectionate, if he always wields the rod over his subjects and if he is naturally rash, he will swiftly perish.'"

अथ पापं कृतं बुद्ध्या न च पश्यत्यबुद्धिमान् ।
अकीर्त्यापि समायुक्तो मृतो नरकमश्नुते ॥ (16)

"'The one without intelligence does not use his intelligence to see that he has committed a wicked deed. He is covered in ill-fame and after death, attains hell.'"

अथ मानयितुर्दातुः शुक्लस्य रसवेदिनः ।
व्यसनं स्वमिवोत्पन्नं विजिघांसन्ति मानवाः ॥ (17)

"'If he shows honour, donates, is pure and knows about good taste, men seek to destroy any hardships that he confronts as if those are their own.'"

यस्य नास्ति गुरुर्धर्मे न चान्याननुपृच्छति ।
सुखतन्त्रोऽर्थलाभेषु नचिरं महदश्नुते ॥ (18)

"'If he does not have a guru to tell him about dharma, if he does not ask others, if he only concentrates on happiness and obtaining riches, his greatness does not last long.'"

गुरुप्रधानो धर्मेषु स्वयमर्थान्ववेक्षिता ।
धर्मप्रधानो लोकेषु सुचिरं महदश्नुते ॥ (19)

"If he gives importance to his guru in matters connected with dharma, if he himself glances towards artha, if he places dharma at the forefront when dealing with people, his greatness lasts for a long time."

Chapter 2

वामदेव उवाच

यत्राधर्मं प्रणयते दुर्बले बलवत्तरः ।
तां वृत्तिमुपजीवन्ति ये भवन्ति तदन्वयाः ॥ (1)

'Vamadeva said, "When someone who is strong imposes adharma on those who are weak, those who earn a living from him[5] also follow that kind of conduct."'

राजानमनुवर्तन्ते तं पापाभिप्रवर्तकम् ।
अविनीतमनुष्यं तत्क्षिप्रं राष्ट्रं विनश्यति ॥ (2)

'"They follow the king, who implements the wicked practices. With those insolent men, that kingdom is swiftly destroyed."'

यद्वृत्तिमुपजीवन्ति प्रकृतिस्थस्य मानवाः ।
तदेव विषमस्थस्य स्वजनोऽपि न मृष्यते ॥ (3)

'"When men naturally earn a living from such evil conduct, when he[6] faces a difficulty, even his relatives do not cleanse it."'[7]

साहसप्रकृतिर्यत्र कुरुते किंचिदुल्बणम् ।
अशास्त्रलक्षणो राजा क्षिप्रमेव विनश्यति ॥ (4)

'"When the king is naturally rash, when he acts without any basis, when he does not follow the indications of the sacred texts, he is swiftly destroyed."'

---

[5]The king's officers.
[6]The king.
[7]That is, they do nothing to mitigate it.

योऽत्यन्ताचरितां वृत्तिं क्षत्रियो नानुवर्तते ।
जितानामजितानां च क्षत्रधर्मादपैति सः ॥ (5)

'"The kshatriya who does not follow the conduct that has been followed for a long time, meant both for those who win and for those who lose, deviates from the dharma of kshatriyas."'

द्विषन्तं कृतकर्माणं गृहीत्वा नृपती रणे ।
यो न मानयते द्वेषात्क्षत्रधर्मादपैति सः ॥ (6)

'"A king who is successful in his attempt to seize an enemy in battle and who does not then show respect to the enemy deviates from the dharma of kshatriyas."'

शक्तः स्यात्सुमुखो राजा कुर्यात्कारुण्यमापदि ।
प्रियो भवति भूतानां न च विभ्रश्यते श्रियः ॥ (7)

'"The king must be pleasant in speech. If he can, he must show compassion at a time of distress. He will then be loved by creatures and not be dislodged from his prosperity."'

अप्रियं यस्य कुर्वीत भूयस्तस्य प्रियं चरेत् ।
नचिरेण प्रियः स स्याद्यो‌ऽप्रियः प्रियमाचरेत् ॥ (8)

'"If someone has done something disagreeable, he should thereafter act agreeably towards him. If he acts in this pleasant way, a person who is not liked will soon be liked."'

मृषावादं परिहरेत्कुर्यात्प्रियमयाचितः ।
न च कामान्न संरम्भान्न द्वेषाद्धर्ममुत्सृजेत् ॥ (9)

'"He must avoid false words. Without being asked, he must avoid doing something disagreeable. For the sake of desire, anger or hatred, he should not abandon dharma."'

नापत्रपेत प्रश्नेषु नाभिभव्यां गिरं सृजेत् ।
न त्वरेत न चासूयेत्तथा संगृह्यते परः ॥ (10)

'"He should not be ashamed of questions, nor should he be careless in speaking words. He should not be hasty or malicious. That is how enemies are overcome."'

प्रिये नातिभृशं हृष्येदप्रिये न च संज्वरेत् ।
न मुह्येदर्थकृच्छ्रेषु प्रजाहितमनुस्मरन् ॥ (11)

'"He should not be unduly delighted at something agreeable, nor should he be anxious at something disagreeable. Remembering the welfare of subjects, he should not be deluded at a hardship in pursuit of artha."'

यः प्रियं कुरुते नित्यं गुणतो वसुधाधिपः ।
तस्य कर्माणि सिध्यन्ति न च संत्यज्यते श्रिया ॥ (12)

'"The lord of the earth who possesses qualities should always do what is pleasant. He obtains success in his deeds and prosperity does not desert him."'

निवृत्तं प्रतिकूलेभ्यो वर्तमानमनुप्रिये ।
भक्तं भजेत् नृपतिस्तद्वै वृत्तं सतामिह ॥ (13)

'"The king must always favour those who have stopped acting against him and are now favourably disposed, as he must favour those who are devoted. That is the conduct of the virtuous in this world."'

अप्रकीर्णेन्द्रियं प्राज्ञमत्यन्तानुगतं शुचिम् ।
शक्तं चैवानुरक्तं च युञ्ज्यान्महति कर्मणि ॥ (14)

'"There are those whose senses are not diverted. They are wise, extremely devoted and pure. They are capable and faithful. Such people must be employed for important tasks."'

एवमेव गुणैर्युक्तो यो न रज्यति भूमिपम् ।
भर्तुरर्थेष्वसूयन्तं न तं युञ्जीत कर्मणि ॥ (15)

'"There are those who may possess good qualities, but do not find delight in the lord of the earth. They are resentful of the master's prosperity. Such people should not be employed for tasks."'

मूढमैन्द्रियकं लुब्धमनार्यचरितं शठम् ।
अनतीतोपधं हिंस्रं दुर्बुद्धिमबहुश्रुतम् ॥ (16)

'"There are those who are foolish and addicted to their senses. They are greedy, ignoble in their conduct and fraudulent. They have failed the tests and are cruel. They are evil in intelligence and do not possess a great deal of learning."'

त्यक्तोपात्तं मद्यरतं द्यूतस्त्रीमृगयापरम् ।
कार्ये महति यो युञ्ज्याद्धीयते स नृपः श्रियः ॥ (17)

'"They have squandered away their possessions in drinking, gambling, women and hunting. If the king employs them in important tasks, prosperity does not remain with him."'

रक्षितात्मा तु यो राजा रक्ष्यान्यश्चानुरक्षति ।
प्रजाश्च तस्य वर्धन्ते ध्रुवं च महदश्नुते ॥ (18)

'"If the king protects himself and protects those who should be protected, then the subjects prosper and it is certain that he attains greatness."'

ये के चिद्भूमिपतयस्तान्सर्वानन्ववेक्षयेत् ।
सुहृद्भिरनभिख्यातैस्तेन राजा न रिष्यते ॥ (19)

'"One must use well-wishers who are not recognized to keep an eye on the acts of all the other lords of the earth. By this means, the king is not harmed."'

अपकृत्य बलस्थस्य दूरस्थोऽस्मीति नाश्वसेत् ।
श्येनानुचरितैर्ह्येते निपतन्ति प्रमाद्यतः ॥ (20)

'"When one has harmed a strong person, one should not be comforted because that person lives a long distance away. Following the conduct of hawks, such people swoop down when one is careless."'

दृढमूलस्त्वदुष्टात्मा विदित्वा बलमात्मनः ।
अबलानभियुञ्जीत न तु ये बलवत्तराः ॥ (21)

"'If one is firm in one's foundation, if one is not evil in one's atman and if one knows about one's strengths, one can engage with a weaker person but not with one who is stronger.'"

विक्रमेण महीं लब्ध्वा प्रजा धर्मेण पालयन् ।
आहवे निधनं कुर्याद्राजा धर्मपरायण: ॥ (22)

"'Having conquered the earth through valour, having protected the subjects through dharma, having been devoted to dharma, a king can be killed in battle.'"

मरणान्तमिदं सर्वं नेह किंचिदनामयम् ।
तस्माद्धर्मे स्थितो राजा प्रजा धर्मेण पालयेत् ॥ (23)

"'Everything ends in death. In this world, there is nothing without disease. Therefore, the king must be established in dharma and must protect the subjects in accordance with dharma.'"

रक्षाधिकरणं युद्धं तथा धर्मानुशासनम् ।
मन्त्रचिन्त्यं सुखं काले पञ्चभिर्वर्धते मही ॥ (24)

"'In the course of time, the earth prospers with five things—arrangements for protection, battle, rule according to dharma, thinking about counsel and happiness.'"

एतानि यस्य गुप्तानि स राजा राजसत्तम ।
सततं वर्तमानोऽत्र राजा भुङ्क्ते महीमिमाम् ॥ (25)

"'The king who protects these is supreme among kings. If a king is always engaged in these, he enjoys this earth.'"

नैतान्येकेन शक्यानि सातत्येनान्ववेक्षितुम् ।
एतेष्वाप्तान्प्रतिष्ठाप्य राजा भुङ्क्ते महीं चिरम् ॥ (26)

"'No single person is capable of paying attention to all of these together. That is the reason the king must engage these[8] and enjoy the earth for a long period of time.'"

---

[8] The ministers and advisers.

दातारं संविभक्तारं मार्दवोपगतं शुचिम् ।
असन्त्यक्तमनुष्यं च तं जनाः कुर्वते प्रियम् ॥ (27)

'"When a person is ready to give, ready to share, mild, upright and pure, and does not abandon men, people do things that are agreeable to him."'

यस्तु निःश्रेयसं ज्ञात्वा ज्ञानं तत्प्रतिपद्यते ।
आत्मनो मतमुत्सृज्य तं लोकोऽनुविधीयते ॥ (28)

'"When one knows what is beneficial and acts in accordance with that knowledge, when he gives up his own views, then people follow him."'

योऽर्थकामस्य वचनं प्रतिकूल्यान् मृष्यते ।
शृणोति प्रतिकूलानि विमना नचिरादिव ॥ (29)
अग्राम्यचरितां बुद्धिमत्यन्तं यो न बुध्यते ।
जितानामजितानां च क्षत्रधर्मादपैति सः ॥ (30)

'"When he does not tolerate words about artha and kama that are contrary, when he is distracted and listens to contrary views for a long period of time, when he does not comprehend the intelligence of foremost ones who are not ordinary in action, regardless of whether they have been defeated or not been defeated, he deviates from the dharma of kshatriyas."'

मुख्यानमात्यान्यो हित्वा निहीनान्कुरुते प्रियान् ।
स वै व्यसनमासाद्य गाधमार्तो न विन्दति ॥ (31)

'"If he abandons his foremost advisers and makes those who are inferior his loved ones, he confronts disaster. When he is distressed, he does not find succour."'

यः कल्याण गुणाञ्ज्ञातीन्द्वेषान्नैवाभिमन्यते ।
अदृढात्मा दृढक्रोधो नास्यार्थो रमतेऽन्तिके ॥ (32)

'"When he disrespects kin with beneficial qualities because of his hatred, when his atman is not firm, when his anger is firm, his prosperity doesn't remain close to him and give him delight."'

अथ यो गुणसंपन्नान्हृदयस्याप्रियानपि ।
प्रियेण कुरुते वश्यांश्चिरं यशसि तिष्ठति ॥ (33)

'"When he acts pleasantly so as to bring those with good qualities under his control, even though they are not dear to his heart, his fame is established for a long time."'

नाकाले प्रणयेदर्थान्नाप्रिये जातु संज्वरेत् ।
प्रिये नातिभृशं हृष्येद्युञ्येतारोग्यकर्मणि ॥ (34)

'"He must not pursue love and wealth at the wrong time. The unpleasant must not make him anxious. He should not be greatly delighted at something agreeable. He must be engaged in tasks that are healthy."'

के मानुरक्ता राजान: के भयात्समुपाश्रिता: ।
मध्यस्थ दोषा: के चौषामिति नित्यं विचिन्तयेत् ॥ (35)

'""Which men are devoted to the king? Which seek refuge because of fear? Who amongst them has the taint of actually being neutral?' Always think of these things."'

न जातु बलवान्भूत्वा दुर्बले विश्वसेत्क्वचित् ।
भारुण्डसदृशा ह्येते निपतन्ति प्रमाद्यत: ॥ (36)

'"If one is strong, one should never trust those who are weak. If one is careless, they will descend like *bharunda* birds."'[9]

अपि सर्वैर्गुणैर्युक्तं भर्तारं प्रियवादिनम् ।
अभिद्रुह्यति पापात्मा तस्माद्धि विभिषेज्जनात् ॥ (37)

'"If someone is wicked in his atman, he will act against a master who possesses all the qualities and is pleasant in speech. Therefore, one should be scared of such people."'

एतां राजोपनिषदं ययाति: स्माह नाहुष: ।
मनुष्यविजये युक्तो हन्ति शत्रूननुत्तमान् ॥ (38)

---

[9] Birds with sharp beaks, sometimes described as consuming corpses.

'"Yayati, the son of Nahusha, declared this teaching for kings: 'If one is engaged in conquering men, one can slay a supreme enemy.'"'

Chapter 3

वामदेव उवाच
अयुद्धेनैव विजयं वर्धयेद्वसुधाधिपः ।
जघन्यमाहुर्विजयं यो युद्धेन नराधिप ॥ (1)

'Vamadeva continued, "The lord of the earth should prosper through victories without battle. O Lord of Men! It is said that victory through a war is the worst."'

न चाप्यलब्धं लिप्सेत मूले नातिदृढे सति ।
न हि दुर्बलमूलस्य राज्ञो लाभो विधीयते ॥ (2)

'"If his foundations are not firm, he should not desire to obtain something. If the foundations are weak, a king's pursuit of gains is not recommended."'

यस्य स्फीतो जनपदः सम्पन्नः प्रियराजकः ।
सन्तुष्टपुष्टसचिवो दृढमूलः स पार्थिवः ॥ (3)

'"If the countryside is prosperous and wealthy, if the king is loved, if the advisers are satisfied and well-nourished, then the king's foundations are firm."'

यस्य योधाः सुसंतुष्टाः सान्त्विताः सूपधास्थिताः ।
अल्पेनापि स दण्डेन महीं जयति भूमिपः ॥ (4)

'"When the warriors are well-satisfied, content and well-entrenched, then the lord of the earth can conquer the earth with the slightest exertion of the rod."'

पौरजानपदा यस्य स्वनुरक्ताः सुपूजिताः ।
सधना धान्यवन्तश्च दृढमूलः स पार्थिवः ॥ (5)

"'If the residents of the city and the countryside are devoted to him, if they are honoured well, if they possess riches and grain, then the lord of the earth has a firm foundation.'"

प्रभावकालावधिकौ यदा मन्येत चात्मनः ।
तदा लिप्सेत मेधावी परभूमिं धनान्युत ॥ (6)

"'At the time when he thinks his own power is superior, that is when an intelligent one should desire the land and the riches of another.'"

भोगेष्वदयमानस्य भूतेषु च दयावतः ।
वर्धते त्वरमाणस्य विषयो रक्षितात्मनः ॥ (7)

"'When he ignores the objects of pleasure, when he is compassionate towards beings, when he protects his kingdom and his own self, he swiftly prospers.'"

तक्षत्यात्मानमेवैष वनं परशुना यथा ।
यः सम्यग्वर्तमानेषु स्वेषु मिथ्या प्रवर्तते ॥ (8)

"'When those on his side act well but he behaves falsely towards them, then he injures his own self, like a forest severed with an axe.'"

न वै द्विषन्तः क्षीयन्ते राज्ञो नित्यमपि घ्नतः ।
क्रोधं नियन्तुं यो वेद तस्य द्वेष्टा न विद्यते ॥ (9)

"'If a king is always engaged in killing, there is no end to those who hate him. But if he knows how to control his anger, those who hate him do not exist.'"

यदार्यजनविद्विष्टं कर्म तन्नाचरेद्बुधः ।
यत्कल्याणमभिध्यायेत्तत्रात्मानं नियोजयेत् ॥ (10)

"'A learned person does not engage in tasks that noble people hate. He engages himself in tasks that are beneficial.'"

नैनमन्येऽवजानन्ति नात्मना परितप्यते ।
कृत्यशेषेण यो राजा सुखान्यनुबुभूषति ॥ (11)

"'Then, even if a king adorns himself with acts of happiness, though tasks are incomplete, his own self is not tormented and others do not think disrespectfully of him.'"

इदं वृत्तं मनुष्येषु वर्तते यो महीपतिः ।
उभौ लोकौ विनिर्जित्य विजये संप्रतिष्ठते ॥ (12)

"'A lord of the earth who acts in this way towards men conquers both the worlds and is established in victory.'"

भीष्म उवाच

इत्युक्तो वामदेवेन सर्वं तत्कृतवान्नृपः ।
तथा कुर्वंस्त्वमप्येतौ लोकौ जेता न संशयः ॥ (13)

Bhishma concluded, 'Having been addressed in this way by Vamadeva, the king followed everything in what he did. If you act in this way, there is no doubt that you will conquer both the worlds.'

Thus ends the Vamadeva Gita.

9

KAMANDA, RISHABHA AND YAMA GITA

The Rishabha Gita actually consists of two chapters, with a conversation between Sage Rishabha and King Sumitra. It is the last section of Raja Dharma Parva within Shanti Parva and, consequently, part of the conversation between Yudhishthira and Bhishma, who is lying on the bed of arrows. However, there is a conversation between Sage Kamanda and King Angarishtha immediately before, and another one between Dhritarashtra and Duryodhana, describing an incident concerning Prahrada (or Prahlada) and Indra. Similarly, once the Rishabha Gita is over, there is a conversation between Sage Goutama and Yama. A narrow definition of the Rishabha Gita would break the continuity of both what comes before and after it. Therefore, this section has all five chapters, consisting of 189 shlokas, and we have called it Kamanda, Rishabha and Yama Gita. All these four conversations are about raja dharma, a theme that runs throughout Raja Dharma Parva of the Mahabharata, as instructed by Bhishma to Yudhishthira. Briefly, Bhishma marshals the arguments of others to make his case.

Chapter 1

युधिष्ठिर उवाच

तात धर्मार्थकामानां श्रोतुमिच्छामि निश्चयम् ।
लोकयात्रा हि कात्स्र्येन त्रिष्वेतेषु प्रतिष्ठिता ॥ (1)

Yudhishthira asked, 'O Father! I wish to hear what has been determined about dharma, artha and kama. All the progress in the world is based on these three.'

धमार्थकामाः किंमूलास्त्रयाणां प्रभवश्च कः ।
अन्योन्यं चानषुज्जन्ते वर्तन्ते च पृथक्पृथक् ॥ (2)

'What are the foundations of dharma, artha and kama and what is their power? They are sometimes connected with each other and sometimes, they exist separately.'

भीष्म उवाच

यदा ते स्युः सुमनसो लोकसंस्थार्थनिश्चये ।
कालप्रभवसंस्थासु सज्जन्ते च त्रयस्तदा ॥ (3)

Bhishma replied, 'When people are cheerful in their minds, having determined to pursue these for the establishment of the world, then these three originate through the force of destiny and unite with each other.'

धर्ममूलस्तु देहोऽर्थः कामोऽर्थफलमुच्यते ।
संकल्पमूलास्ते सर्वे संकल्पो विषयात्मकः ॥ (4)

'The foundation of the body is dharma, and artha is based on that. Kama is said to be the fruit of artha. Resolution is the foundation of everything and resolution is based on material objects.'

विषयाश्चैव कात्स्र्येन सर्व आहारसिद्धये ।
मूलमेतत्त्रिवर्गस्य निवृत्तिर्मोक्ष उच्यते ॥ (5)

'All material objects find success in everything being procured. These form the basis for the three objectives.[1] Withdrawal is said to be moksha.'

धर्मः शरीरसंगुप्तिर्धमार्थं चार्थ इष्यते ।
कामो रतिफलाश्चात्र सर्वे चौते रजस्वलाः ॥ (6)

'Dharma protects the body and artha is desired for the sake of dharma. Here, kama is for the fruit of sexual pleasure. But all these are nothing but dust.'[2]

संनिकृष्टांश्चरेदेनान्न चौनान्मनसा त्यजेत् ।
विमुक्तस्तमसा सर्वान्धर्मादीन्कामनैष्ठिकान् ॥ (7)

'One should follow whichever of these attracts and not discard them in one's mind. All these begin with dharma and end with kama[3] and one should renounce them only when one has freed oneself from tamas.'

श्रेष्ठबुद्धिस्त्रिवर्गस्य यदयं प्राप्नुयात्क्षणात् ।
बुद्ध्या बुध्येदिहार्थं न तद्ब्रह्म तु निकृष्टया ॥ (8)

'A man who is superior in intelligence can use his intelligence to attain as much of these three objectives in an instant as an inferior person can in an entire day.'

अपध्यानमलो धर्मो मलोऽर्थस्य निगूहनम् ।
संप्रमोदमलः कामो भूयः स्वगणुवर्तितः ॥ (9)

'Dharma is stained by evil thoughts. Artha is stained by secrecy. Kama is stained by excessive delight. Each can follow its qualities in excess.'

---

[1] The three objectives of dharma, artha and kama are based on the acquisition of material objects.
[2] The text uses the word *'rajasvala'*, meaning a menstruating woman. That imagery exists implicitly. Beyond that, 'rajas' means dust and also refers to the quality of passion.
[3] An indirect way of referring to dharma, artha and kama.

अत्राप्युदाहरन्तीमितिहासं पुरातनम् ।
कामन्दस्य च संवादमङ्गारिष्ठस्य चोभयो: ॥ (10)

'In this connection, an ancient history is recounted about a conversation between Kamanda and Angarishtha.'

कामन्दमृषिमासीनमभिवाद्य नराधिप: ।
अङ्गारिष्ठोऽथ पप्रच्छ कृत्वा समयपर्ययम् ॥ (11)

'The lord of men greeted Rishi Kamanda after he had been seated. Having observed the prescribed norms, Angarishtha questioned him.'

य: पापं कुरुते राजा काममोहबलात्कृत: ।
प्रत्यासन्नस्य तस्यर्षे किं स्यात्पापप्रणाशनम ॥ (12)

'"A king may be deluded by the force of kama and act sinfully. O Rishi! When such a situation arises, how can the sins be destroyed?"'

अधर्मो धर्म इति ह योऽज्ञानादाचरेदिह ।
तं चापि प्रथितं लोके कथं राजा निवर्तयेत् ॥ (13)

'"In ignorance, one may follow adharma, taking it to be dharma. How can a king restrain that which is celebrated in the world?"'

कामन्द उवाच
यो धर्मार्थौ समुत्सृज्य काममेवानुवर्तते ।
स धर्मार्थपरित्यागात्प्रज्ञानाशमिहाछति ॥ (14)

'Kamanda replied, "A man who disregards dharma and artha and follows kama destroys his own wisdom, because he has abandoned dharma and artha."'

प्रज्ञाप्रणाशको मोहस्तथा धर्मार्थनाशक: ।
तस्मान्नास्तिकता चैव दुराचारश्च जायते ॥ (15)

'"The delusion that destroys wisdom also destroys dharma and artha. From this is created bad conduct and the trait of not believing."'[4]

दुराचारान्यदा राजा प्रदुष्टान्न नियच्छति ।
तस्मादुद्विजते लोक: सर्पाद्वेश्मगतादिव ॥ (16)

'"When the king does not restrain wicked people from bad conduct, anxious people think that this is as if a snake has entered the house."'[5]

तं प्रजा नानुवर्तन्ते ब्राह्मणा न च साधव: ।
तत: संक्षयमाप्नोति तथा वध्यत्वमेति च ॥ (17)

'"The subjects do not follow him, nor do brahmanas and virtuous people. He confronts destruction and even deserves to be killed."'

अपध्वस्तस्त्ववमतो दु:खं जीवति जीवितम् ।
जीवेच्च यदपध्वस्तस्तच्छुद्धं मरणं भवेत् ॥ (18)

'"When one is disrespected, even if one remains alive, the misery is like that of being dead. Remaining alive with dishonour is like pure death."'

अत्रैतदाहुराचार्या: पापस्य च निबर्हणम् ।
सेवितव्या त्रयी विद्या सत्कारो ब्राह्मणेषु च ॥ (19)

'"On this, the preceptors have talked about means of destroying sin. He must serve the three forms of knowledge[6] and treat brahmanas well."'

महामना भवेद्धर्मे विवहेच्च महाकुले ।
ब्राह्मणांश्चापि सेवेत क्षमायुक्तान्मनस्विन: ॥ (20)

---

[4] The word used for such a person is '*nastika*', which does not mean atheist.
[5] The king is being compared to a snake.
[6] The three Vedas.

'"He must be great-minded and follow dharma. He must marry into a great lineage. He must serve brahmanas. He must be spirited and forgiving."'

जपेदुदकशीलः स्यात्सुमुखो नान्यदास्थितः ।
धर्मान्वितासंप्रविशेद्बहिः कृत्वैव दुष्कृतीन् ॥ (21)

'"Having undertaken ablutions with water, he must perform japa. He must be pleasant in appearance and not act in a contrary way. He must seek those who follow dharma and cast away those who perform wicked deeds."'

प्रसादयेन्मधुरया वाचाप्यथ च कर्मणा ।
इत्यस्मीति वदेन्नित्यं परेषां कीर्तयन्गुणान् ॥ (22)

'"He must please them[7] with sweet words and deeds and tell them, 'I belong to you.' He must always recount the good qualities of others."'

अपापो ह्येवमाचारः क्षिप्रं बहुमतो भवेत् ।
पापान्यपि च कृच्छ्राणि शमयेन्नात्र सशयः ॥ (23)

'"If his conduct is devoid of sin, he will quickly obtain great respect. There is no doubt that he will be able to negate all the wicked deeds he has committed."'

गुरवोऽपि परं धर्मं यद्ब्रूयुस्तत्तथा कुरू ।
गुरूणां हि प्रसादाद्धि श्रेयः परमवाप्स्यसि ॥ (24)

'"What is stated by the seniors is supreme dharma. Act accordingly. If you obtain the favours of the seniors, you will obtain the best and the supreme."'

---

[7] The virtuous people.

Chapter 2

युधिष्ठिर उवाच

इमे जना नरश्रेष्ठ प्रशंसन्ति सदा भुवि ।
धर्मस्य शीलमेवादौ ततो मे संशयो महान् ॥ (1)

Yudhishthira said, 'O Best of Men! These people on earth always praise the good conduct that flows from dharma. However, I have a great doubt about this.'

यदि तच्छक्यमस्माभिर्ज्ञातुं धर्मभृतां वर ।
श्रोतुमिच्छामि तत्सर्वं यथैतदुपलभ्यते ॥ (2)

'O Supreme among Those Who Uphold Dharma! If we are capable of knowing this, I wish to hear everything about this, exactly as comprehended.'

कथं नु प्राप्यते शीलं श्रोतुमिच्छामि भारत ।
किंलक्षणं च तत्प्रोक्तं ब्रूहि मे वदतां वर ॥ (3)

'O Descendant of the Bharata Lineage! How can good conduct be obtained? I wish to hear this. What are its signs? O Supreme among Eloquent Ones! Please tell me this.'

भीष्म उवाच

पुरा दुर्योधनेनेह धृतराष्ट्राय मानद ।
आख्यातं तप्यमानेन श्रियं दृष्ट्वा तथागताम् ॥ (4)
इन्द्रप्रस्थे महाराज तव स भ्रातृकस्य ह ।
सभायां चावहसनं तत्सर्वं शृणु भारत ॥ (5)

Bhishma replied, 'O One Who Grants Honours! O Great King! In earlier times, Duryodhana was tormented at the sight of your prosperity, when he went to Indraprastha with his brothers. He was laughed at in the assembly hall. He told Dhritarashtra about this. O Descendant of the Bharata Lineage! Listen to the entire account.'

भवतस्तां सभां दृष्ट्वा समृद्धिं चाप्यनुत्तमाम् ।
दुर्योधनस्तदासीनः सर्वं पित्रे न्यवेदयत् ॥ (6)

'Having witnessed your supreme prosperity in the assembly hall, Duryodhana seated himself and told his father everything.'

श्रुत्वा च धृतराष्ट्रोऽपि दुर्योधनवचस्तदा ।
अब्रवीत्कर्णसहितं दुर्योधनमिदं वचः ॥ (7)

'On hearing Duryodhana's words, Dhritarashtra spoke these words to Duryodhana, who was with Karna.'

किमर्थं तप्यसे पुत्र श्रोतुमिच्छामि तत्त्वतः ।
श्रुत्वा त्वामनुनेष्यामि यदि सम्यग्भविष्यसि ॥ (8)
यथा त्वं महदैश्वर्यं प्राप्तः परपुरंजय ।
किंकरा भ्रातरः सर्वे मित्राः संबन्धिनस्तथा ॥ (9)

'"O Son! Why are you tormented? I wish to hear the truth about this. O Conqueror of Enemy Cities! On hearing this, if it is proper, I will instruct you, so that you can also obtain great prosperity, with your servants, your brothers, all your friends and your kin."'

आच्छादयसि प्रावारानश्नासि पिशितौदनम् ।
आजानेया वहन्ति त्वां कस्माच्छोचसि पुत्रक ॥ (10)

'"You cover yourself in excellent garments. You eat rice mixed with meat. You are borne on good horses. O Son! Why are you grieving?"'

दुर्योधन उवाच

दश तानि सहस्राणि स्नातकानां महात्मनाम् ।
भुञ्जते रुक्मपात्रीषु युधिष्ठिरनिवेशने ॥ (11)

'Duryodhana replied, "In Yudhishthira's abode, ten thousand great-souled *snatakas*[8] eat from golden vessels."'

---

[8] A snataka is a brahmana who has completed brahmacharya and is about to step into the next stage of life. The word also means an assistant priest.

दृष्ट्वा च तां सभां दिव्यां दिव्यपुष्पफलान्विताम् ।
अश्वांस्तित्तिरकल्माषान्व्रतानि विविधानि च ॥ (12)
दृष्ट्वा तां पाण्डवेयानामृद्धिमिन्द्रोपमां शुभाम् ।
अमित्राणां सुमहतीमनुशोचामि मानद ॥ (13)

'"His divine assembly hall is full of celestial flowers and fruits. There are speckled horses of the *tittira* breed.[9] There are many kinds of gems. I saw all that. I saw the dazzling prosperity of the Pandaveyas,[10] my enemies, and it was like that of Indra. O One Who Grants Honours! On seeing this, I am grieving greatly."'

धृतराष्ट्र उवाच

यदीच्छसि श्रियं तात यादृशीं तां युधिष्ठिरे ।
विशिष्टां वा नरव्याघ्र शीलवान्भव पुत्रक ॥ (14)

'Dhritarashtra replied, "O Son! O Tiger among Men! O Son! If you desire prosperity that is like Yudhishthira's or superior to it, you must follow good conduct."'

शीलेन हि त्रयो लोका: शक्या जेतुं न संशय: ।
न हि किंचिदसाध्यं वै लोके शीलवतां भवेत् ॥ (15)

'"There is no doubt that the three worlds can be conquered through good conduct. For those who possess good conduct, there is nothing in the world that cannot be accomplished."'

एकरात्रेण मान्धाता त्र्यहेण जनमेजय: ।
सप्तरात्रेण नाभाग: पृथिवीं प्रतिपेदिवान् ॥ (16)

'"Mandhata obtained the earth in a single night, Janamejaya in three days and Nabhaga in seven nights."'

एते हि पार्थिवा: सर्वे शीलवन्तो दमान्विता: ।
अतस्तेषां गुणक्रीता वसुधा स्वयमागमत् ॥ (17)

---

[9] A special breed of horse, speckled in colour.
[10] This word also refers to the Pandavas.

"'All these kings possessed good conduct and self-control. Purchased by their good qualities, the earth presented herself of her own accord.'"

अत्राप्युदाहरन्तीममितिहासं पुरातनम् ।
नारदेन पुरा प्रोक्तं शीलमाश्रित्य भारत ॥ (18)

"'In this connection, an ancient history is recounted. O Descendant of the Bharata Lineage! In ancient times, Narada spoke about good conduct.'"

प्रह्लादेन हृतं राज्यं महेन्द्रस्य महात्मनः ।
शीलमाश्रित्य दैत्येन त्रैलोक्यं च वशीकृतम् ॥ (19)

"'Prahrada robbed the great-souled Indra of his kingdom. By resorting to good conduct, the daitya subjugated the three worlds.'"

ततो बृहस्पतिं शक्रः प्राञ्जलिः समुपस्थितः ।
उवाच च महाप्राज्ञः श्रेय इच्छामि वेदितुम् ॥ (20)

"'Shakra joined his hands in salutation and presented himself before Brihaspati. The immensely wise one said, 'I wish to know about what is beneficial.'"

ततो बृहस्पतिस्तस्मै ज्ञानं नैःश्रेयसं परम् ।
कथयामास भगवान्देवेन्द्राय कुरूद्वह ॥ (21)

"'At this, Brihaspati gave him the jnana that is best and supreme. O Extender of the Kuru Lineage! The illustrious one spoke about this to Indra of the devas.'"

एतावच्छ्रेय इत्येव बृहस्पतिरभाषत ।
इन्द्रस्तु भूयः पप्रच्छ क्व विशेषो भवेदिति ॥ (23)

"'Brihaspati told him about what was best. However, Indra again asked him about what was superior to that.'"

बृहस्पतिरुवाच

विशेषोऽस्ति महांस्तात भार्गवस्य महात्मनः ।
तत्रागमय भद्रं ते भूय एव पुरन्दर ॥ (23)

'"Brihaspati said, 'O Son! There is something that is greater than this. O Fortunate One! O Purandara! Go to the great-souled Bhargava[11] and he will tell you.'"'

धृतराष्ट्र उवाच

आत्मनस्तु ततः श्रेयो भार्गवात्सुमहायशाः ।
ज्ञानमागमयत्प्रीत्या पुनः स परमद्युतिः ॥ (24)

'Dhritarashtra said, "The immensely famous one[12] found out from Bhargava what was best for him. He was delighted at having obtained this jnana and regained his supreme radiance."'

तेनापि समनुज्ञातो भार्गवेण महात्मना ।
श्रेयोऽस्तीति पुनर्भूयः शुक्रमाह शतक्रतुः ॥ (25)

'"Having taken the permission of the great-souled Bhargava, Shatakratu[13] again asked Shukra about what was beneficial."'

भार्गवस्त्वाह धर्मज्ञः प्रह्रादस्य महात्मनः ।
ज्ञानमस्ति विशेषेण ततो हृष्टश्च सोऽभवत् ॥ (26)
स ततो ब्राह्मणो भूत्वा प्रह्रादं पाकशासनः ।
सृत्वा प्रोवाच मेधावी श्रेय इच्छामि वेदितुम् ॥ (27)

'"Bhargava, who knew about dharma, told him that the great-souled Prahrada possessed that superior jnana. Delighted at this, the chastiser of Paka[14] assumed the form of a brahmana and went to Prahrada. The intelligent one said, 'I wish to know what is beneficial.'"'

---

[11]Shukracharya, the preceptor of the demons.
[12]Indra.
[13]Indra's name, meaning the performer of one hundred sacrifices.
[14]Indra.

प्रह्लादस्त्वब्रवीद्विप्रं क्षणो नास्ति द्विजर्षभ ।
त्रैलोक्यराज्ये सक्तस्य ततो नोपदिशामि ते ॥ (28)

"'Prahrada told the brahmana, 'O Bull among Dvijas! I do not have the time. I am engaged in ruling the three worlds and am incapable of instructing you.'"

ब्राह्मणस्त्वब्रवीद्वाक्यं कस्मिन्काले क्षणो भवेत् ।
ततोपदिष्टमिच्छामि यद्यत्कार्यान्तरं भवेत् ॥ (29)

"'The brahmana spoke these words: 'When will there be time? When there is a break in your work, I wish to be instructed.'"

ततः प्रीतोऽभवद्राजा प्रह्लादो ब्रह्मवादिने ।
तथेत्युक्त्वा शुभे काले ज्ञानतत्त्वं ददौ तदा ॥ (30)

"'At this, King Prahrada, knowledgeable about the brahman, was delighted and agreed. At an auspicious time, he imparted that true jnana.'"

ब्राह्मणोऽपि यथान्यायं गुरुवृत्तिमनुत्तमाम् ।
चकार सर्वभावेन यद्वत्स मनसेच्छति ॥ (31)

"'As is proper, the brahmana observed supreme conduct towards the guru. In every kind of way, he did all that he[15] desired in his mind.'"

पृष्टश्च तेन बहुशः प्राप्तं कथमरिंदम ।
त्रैलोक्यराज्यं धर्मज्ञ कारणं तद्ब्रवीहि मे ॥ (32)

"'He often asked him, 'O Scorcher of Enemies! How did you obtain the kingdom of the three worlds? O One Who Knows about Dharma! Please tell me the reason.'"

प्रह्लाद उवाच

नासूयामि द्विजश्रेष्ठ राजास्मीति कदाचन ।
कव्यानि वदतां तात संयच्छामि वहामि च ॥ (33)

---

[15] Prahrada. Indra served Prahrada like a disciple seeking knowledge.

'"Prahrada replied, 'O Best among Dvijas! I never show any malice. I never say that I am the king. O Son! I control myself and implement what Kavya[16] says.'"

ते विस्रब्धाः प्रभाषन्ते संयच्छन्ति च मां सदा ।
ते मा कव्यपदे सक्तं शुश्रूषुमनसूयकम् ॥ (34)

'"Anything said by that trustworthy one is always implemented by me. Without any malice, I am devoted to serving at Kavya's feet.'"

धर्मात्मानं जितक्रोधं संयतं संयतेन्द्रियम् ।
समाचिन्वन्ति शास्तारः क्षौद्रं मध्विव मक्षिकाः ॥ (35)

'"I possess dharma in my atman. I have conquered anger. I have controlled myself and have restrained my senses. I have collected the teachings of those who have instructed, like bees collecting *kshoudra* honey.'"[17]

सोऽहं वाग्रपिष्टानां रसानामवलेहिता ।
स्वजात्यानधितिष्ठामि नक्षत्राणीव चन्द्रमाः ॥ (36)

'"I have licked the juices that have oozed out from the tongues of those eloquent ones. I have established myself amidst my species, like the moon amidst nakshatras.'"

एतत्पृथिव्याममृतमेतच्चक्षुरनुत्तमम् ।
यद्ब्राह्मणमुखे कव्यमेतच्छ्रुत्वा प्रवर्तते ॥ (37)

'"What flows from the mouth of a brahmana like Kavya is supreme insight and is like amrita on this earth. I have implemented what I have heard.'"

धृतराष्ट्र उवाच

एतावच्छ्रेय इत्याह प्रह्लादो ब्रह्मवादिनम् ।
शुश्रूषितस्तेन तदा दैत्येन्द्रो वाक्यमब्रवीत् ॥ (38)

---

[16]Shukracharya.

[17]A specific kind of honey from the sampangi plant, which belongs to the oleander family.

'Dhritarashtra said, "Prahrada, who knew about the brahman, spoke about what was beneficial in this way. Because of the servitude, the Indra among daityas[18] spoke these words."'

यथावद्गुरुवृत्त्या ते प्रीतोऽस्मि द्विजसत्तम ।
वरं वृणीष्व भद्रं ते प्रदातास्मि न संशयः ॥ (39)

'"O Supreme among Dvijas! I am pleased with your conduct towards your guru. O Fortunate One! Ask for a boon. There is no doubt that I will give it to you."'

कृतमित्येव दैत्येन्द्रमुवाच स च वै द्विजः ।
प्रह्रादस्त्वब्रवीत्प्रीतो गृह्यतां वर इत्युत ॥ (40)

'"The dvija told the Indra among the daityas that he had already obtained one.[19] Prahrada was delighted at this and asked him to accept another boon."'

ब्राह्मण उवाच

यदि राजन्प्रसन्नस्त्वं मम चेच्छसि चेद्धितम् ।
भवतः शीलमिच्छामि प्राप्तुमेष वरो मम ॥ (41)

'"The brahmana replied, 'O King! If you are pleased with me and wish to ensure my welfare, I wish to have the good conduct that you possess. Let me obtain that boon.'"'

धृतराष्ट्र उवाच

ततः प्रीतश्च दैत्येन्द्रो भयं चास्याभवन्महत् ।
वरे प्रदिष्टे विप्रेण नाल्पतेजायमित्युत ॥ (42)

'Dhritarashtra continued, "Though the Indra among the daityas was pleased at this, he also suffered from great fear.[20] But this was

---

[18]Meaning the king of the daityas, that is, Prahrada.
[19]Having been given the knowledge.
[20]He suffered from great fear as he could not refuse a brahmana, though he knew that it was Indra disguised as one. Therefore, he was scared that Indra would ask for all his prosperity as a boon.

the boon the brahmana had asked for and he was not one with limited energy."

एवमस्त्विति तं प्राह प्रह्लादो विस्मितस्तदा ।
उपाकृत्य तु विप्राय वरं दुःखान्वितोऽभवत् ॥ (43)

"'Though Prahrada was astounded at this, so as to do a good turn to the brahmana, he said he agreed to grant the boon. But he was miserable.'"

दत्ते वरे गते विप्रे चिन्तासीन्महती ततः ।
प्रह्लादस्य महाराज निश्चयं न च जग्मिवान् ॥ (44)

"'With the boon having been granted and the brahmana having departed, Prahrada began to think a lot. O Great King! However, he could not arrive at any conclusion.'"

तस्य चिन्तयतस्तात छाया भूतं महाद्युते ।
तेजो विग्रहवत्तात शरीरमजहात्तदा ॥ (45)

"'O Son! While he was thinking in this way, an immensely radiant light emerged. O Son! This shadow assumed a form made out of energy and left the body.'"

तमपृच्छन्महाकायं प्रह्लादः को भवानिति ।
प्रत्याह ननु शीलोऽस्मि त्यक्तो गच्छाम्यहं त्वया ॥ (46)
तस्मिन्द्विजवरे राजन्वत्स्याम्यहमनिन्दितम् ।
योऽसौ शिष्यत्वमागम्य त्वयि नित्यं समाहितः ।
इत्युक्त्वान्तर्हितं तद्वै शक्रं चान्वविशत्प्रभो ॥ (47)

"'Prahrada asked the immensely gigantic form, 'Who are you?' It replied, 'I am your good conduct. Since you have abandoned me, I will leave you. O King! I will go to that supreme among dvijas, the unblemished one who came here as your disciple and was always controlled.' O Lord! Having said this, it disappeared and penetrated Shakra.'"

तस्मिंस्तेजसि याते तु तादृग्रूपस्ततोऽपरः ।
शरीरान्निःसृतस्तस्य को भवानिति चाब्रवीत् ॥ (48)

धर्म प्रह्लाद मां विद्धि यत्रासौ द्विजसत्तम: ।
तत्र यास्यामि दैत्येन्द्र यत: शीलं ततो ह्यहम् ॥ (49)

'"After that energy had gone, another form emerged from his body. 'Who are you?' he asked. It replied, 'O Prahrada! Know me to be dharma. I will go that supreme among dvijas. O Indra among Daityas! Since good conduct has already gone there, I will also go there.'"'

ततोऽपरो महाराज प्रज्वलन्निव तेजसा ।
शरीरान्नि:सृतस्तस्य प्रह्लादस्य महात्मन: ॥ (50)

'"O Great King! After this, another mass of blazing energy emerged from the great-souled Prahrada's body."'

को भवानिति पृष्टश्च तमाह स महाद्युति: ।
सत्यमस्म्यसुरेन्द्रार्य यास्येऽहं धर्ममन्विह ॥ (51)

'"'Who are you?' he asked. The immensely radiant one replied, 'O Indra of the Asuras! I am truth and I will follow dharma and leave.'"'

तस्मिन्ननुगते धर्मं पुरुषे पुरुषोऽपर: ।
निश्चक्राम ततस्तस्मात्पृष्ठश्चाह महात्मना ।
वृत्तं प्रह्लाद मां विद्धि यत: सत्यं ततो ह्यहम् ॥ (52)

'"After this being had followed dharma, another being emerged. When this was questioned by the great-souled one, it replied, 'O Prahrada! Know me to be the *vritta*.[21] I exist where truth exists.'"'

तस्मिंगते महाश्वेत: शरीरात्तस्य निर्ययौ ।
पृष्टश्चाह बलं विद्धि यतो वृत्तमहं तत: ।
इत्युक्त्वा च ययौ तत्र यतो वृत्तं नराधिप ॥ (53)

'"When it had gone, a giant and white form emerged from his body. Asked, it said, 'Know me to be strength. I exist where there is

---

[21]The word 'vritta' has multiple meanings. It means a circular covering. It also means good conduct. Therefore, we can take it in the sense of the protective covering of good conduct.

covering.' O Lord Of Men! Having said this, it went where covering had gone.'"

ततः प्रभामयी देवी शरीरात्तस्य निर्ययौ ।
तामपृच्छत्स दैत्येन्द्रः सा श्रीरित्येवमब्रवीत् ॥ (54)
उषितास्मि सुखं वीर त्वयि सत्यपराक्रमे ।
त्वया त्यक्ता गमिष्यामि बलं यत्र ततो ह्यहम् ॥ (55)

"'A radiant goddess then emerged from the body. Asked by the Indra among the Daityas, she replied, 'I am Shri. O Brave One! Because of your truth and valour, I had dwelt happily with you. But I have been abandoned by you now and will go where strength is.'"

ततो भयं प्रादुरासीत्प्रह्लादस्य महात्मनः ।
अपृच्छत च तां भूयः क्व यासि कमलालये ॥ (56)
त्वं हि सत्यव्रता देवी लोकस्य परमेश्वरी ।
कश्चासौ ब्राह्मणश्रेष्ठस्तत्त्वमिच्छामि वेदितुम् ॥ (57)

"'At this, the great-souled Prahrada was terrified. He asked her again, 'O One Who Resides in a Lotus! Where are you going? You are a goddess who is always devoted to the truth. You are the supreme goddess of the worlds. Who was that best among brahmanas? I wish to know the truth.'"

श्रीरूवाच

स शक्रो ब्रह्मचारी च यस्त्वया चोपशिक्षितः ।
त्रैलोक्ये ते यदैश्वर्यं तत्तेनापहृतं प्रभो ॥ (58)

"'Shri replied, 'That was Shakra, in the form of a brahmachari. He is the one who has been instructed by you. O Lord! He has now robbed you of the prosperity of the three worlds.'"

शीलेन हि त्वया लोकाः सर्वे धर्मज्ञ निर्जिताः ।
तद्विज्ञाय महेन्द्रेण तव शीलं हृतं प्रभो ॥ (59)

"''O One Who Knows about Dharma! You conquered all the worlds through your good conduct. O Lord! Knowing this, the great Indra has robbed you of your good conduct.'"

धर्मः सत्यं तथा वृत्तं बलं चैव तथा ह्यहम् ।
शीलमूला महाप्राज्ञ सदा नास्त्यत्र संशयः ॥ (60)

'"O Immensely Wise One! Dharma, truth, covering, strength and I—there is no doubt that all of us find our foundations in good conduct."'

भीष्म उवाच

एवमुक्त्वा गता तु श्रीस्ते च सर्वे युधिष्ठिर ।
दुर्योधनस्तु पितरं भूय एवाब्रवीदिदम् ॥ (61)

Bhishma continued, 'O Yudhishthira! Having said this, Shri and all the others departed. Duryodhana again spoke to his father and uttered these words.'

शीलस्य तत्त्वमिच्छामि वेत्तुं कौरवनन्दन ।
प्राप्यते च यथा शीलं तमुपायं वदस्व मे ॥ (62)

'"O Descendant of the Kourava Lineage! I wish to know the true nature of good conduct. Tell me the means whereby I can acquire good conduct."'

धृतराष्ट्र उवाच

सोपायं पूर्वमुद्दिष्टं प्रह्रादेन महात्मना ।
सङ्क्षेपतस्तु शीलस्य शृणु प्राप्तिं नराधिप ॥ (63)

'Dhritarashtra replied, "The means have earlier been instructed by the great-souled Prahrada. O Lord of Men! Listen briefly to how good conduct can be obtained."'

अद्रोहः सर्वभूतेषु कर्मणा मनसा गिरा ।
अनुग्रहश्च दानं च शीलमेतत्प्रशस्यते ॥ (64)

'"There must be non-violence towards all beings, in deeds, thoughts and words. Compassion and generosity are praised as good conduct."'

यदन्येषां हितं न स्यादात्मनः कर्म पौरुषम् ।
अपत्रपेत वा येन न तत्कुर्यात्कथंचन ॥ (65)

'"For one's own sake, one must not commit a harsh act that causes harm to another, nor should one ever do something one is ashamed of."'

तत्तु कर्म तथा कुर्याद्येन श्लाघेत संसदि ।
एतच्छीलं समासेन कथितं कुरुसत्तम ॥ (66)

'"One should undertake tasks such that one is praised in assemblies. O Supreme among the Kuru Lineage! Briefly, this is said to be good conduct."'

यद्यप्यशीला नृपते प्राप्नुवन्ति क्वचिच्छ्रियम् ।
न भुञ्जते चिरं तात स मूलाश्च पतन्ति ते ॥ (67)

'"O Son! Even if a king who does not have good conduct obtains Shri, he will not enjoy her for a long time. He will fall down, along with the roots."'

एतद्विदित्वा तत्त्वेन शीलवान्भव पुत्रक ।
यदीच्छसि श्रियं तात सुविशिष्टां युधिष्ठिरात् ॥ (68)

'"O Son! Know this to be the true nature of good conduct. O Son! If you desire prosperity that is superior to that of Yudhishthira's, be like that."'

भीष्म उवाच

एतत्कथितवान्पुत्रे धृतराष्ट्रो नराधिप ।
एतत्कुरुष्व कौन्तेय ततः प्राप्स्यसि तत्फलम् ॥ (69)

Bhishma concluded, 'O Lord of Men! This is what Dhritarashtra told his son. O Kounteya! If you act in this way, you will obtain the fruits.'

Chapter 3

युधिष्ठिर उवाच

शीलं प्रधानं पुरुषे कथितं ते पितामह ।
कथमाशा समुत्पन्ना या च सा तद्वदस्व मे ॥ (1)

Yudhishthira said, 'O Grandfather! You have said that good conduct is the most important thing for a man. How does hope arise and what is its nature? Please tell me this.'

संशयो मे महानेष समुत्पन्नः पितामह ।
छेत्ता च तस्य नान्योऽस्ति त्वत्तः परपुरंजय ॥ (2)

'O Grandfather! This great doubt has arisen in me. O Conqueror of Enemy Cities! There is no one other than you who knows the truth and can dispel this.'

पितामहाशा महती ममासीद्धि सुयोधने ।
प्राप्ते युद्धे तु यद्युक्तं तत्कर्तायमिति प्रभो ॥ (3)

'O Grandfather! I had a great deal of hope about Suyodhana. O Lord! When the war was near, I thought that he would act as he had been asked to.'

सर्वस्याशा सुमहती पुरुषस्योपजायते ।
तस्यां विहन्यमानायां दुःखो मृत्युरसंशयम् ॥ (4)

'Great hope is generated in a man and it becomes everything. When that is destroyed, there is no doubt that he suffers a misery that is like death.'

सोऽहं हताशो दुर्बुद्धिः कृतस्तेन दुरात्मना ।
धार्तराष्ट्रेण राजेन्द्र पश्य मन्दात्मतां मम ॥ (5)

'Because of what he did, the evil-minded and evil-souled son of Dhritarashtra destroyed all my hopes. O Indra among Kings! See how foolish I have been.'

आशां महत्तरां मन्ये पर्वतादपि सद्रुमात् ।
आकाशादपि वा राजन्नप्रमेयैव वा पुनः ॥ (6)

'I think that hope is greater than a mountain with all its trees. O King! Or perhaps it is as immeasurable as the sky.'

एषा चैव कुरुश्रेष्ठ दुर्विचिन्त्या सुदुर्लभा ।
दुर्लभत्वाच्च पश्यामि किमन्यदुर्लभं ततः ॥ (7)

'O Best among the Kuru Lineage! It is extremely difficult to understand it[22] and it is extremely difficult to obtain. I can see it is extremely difficult to obtain. Is there anything more difficult to obtain than that?'

भीष्म उवाच

अत्र ते वर्तयिष्यामि युधिष्ठिर निबोध तत् ।
इतिहासं सुमित्रस्य निर्वृत्तमृषभस्य च ॥ (8)

Bhishma replied, 'O Yudhishthira! In this connection, listen to what happened. This is the history of what transpired between Sumitra and Rishabha.'

सुमित्रो नाम राजर्षिर्हैहयो मृगयां गतः ।
ससार स मृगं विद्ध्वा बाणेन नतपर्वणा ॥ (9)

'Among the Haihayas,[23] there was a rajarshi named Sumitra, and he went out on a hunt. Having pursued a deer, he pierced it with an arrow with drooping tufts.'

स मृगो बाणमादाय ययावमितविक्रमः ।
स च राजा बली तूर्णं ससार मृगमन्तिकात् ॥ (10)

---

[22]Hope.
[23]Haihaya was a famous dynasty, with Kartavirya Arjuna (killed by Parashurama) as its most famous king. While there were many branches of the Haihaya kingdom, at the zenith of its power, the capital was in Mahishmati (Maheshvara).

'The deer was infinite in its valour. In spite of being struck by the arrow, it continued to flee and the powerful king swiftly dashed towards the deer.'

ततो निम्नं स्थलं चैव स मृगोऽद्रवदाशुगः ।
मुहूर्तमेव राजेन्द्र समेन स पथागमत् ॥ (11)

'O Indra among Kings! The deer quickly fled through a hollow and, in an instant, began to run over flat terrain again.'

ततः स राजा तारुण्यादौरसेन बलेन च ।
ससार बाणासनभृत्सखड्गो हंसवत्तदा ॥ (12)

'The king was young, enterprising and strong. With arrows, a bow and a sword, he pursued it, like a swan.'

तीर्त्वा नदानदींश्चैव पल्वलानि वनानि च ।
अतिक्रम्याभ्यतिक्रम्य ससारैव वने चरन् ॥ (13)

'He plunged through large and small rivers, lakes and woods. Having crossed through places that were difficult to cross, he chased it into a forest.'

स तु कामान्मृगो राजन्नासाद्यासाद्य तं नृपम् ।
पुनरभ्येति जवनो जवेन महता ततः ॥ (14)

'O King! As it wished, the deer sometimes showed itself to the king and sometimes hid itself from the king. It would then speed on, acquiring greater speed.'

स तस्य बाणैर्बहुभिः समभ्यस्तो वनेचरः ।
प्रक्रीडन्निव राजेन्द्र पुनरभ्येति चान्तिकम् ॥ (15)

'He struck the resident of the forest with many arrows. O Indra among Kings! But it seemed to be playing with him and would again approach near.'

पुनश्च जवमास्थाय जवनो मृगयूथपः ।
अतीत्यातीत्य राजेन्द्र पुनरभ्येति चान्तिकम् ॥ (16)

'The leader of a herd of deer would then again speed up, resorting to greater speed. O Indra among Kings! It would forge ahead and then again appear nearby.'

तस्य मर्मच्छिदं घोरं सुमित्रोऽमित्रकर्शनः ।
समादाय शरश्रेष्ठं कार्मुकान्निरवासृजत् ॥ (17)

'Sumitra, the destroyer of enemies, affixed a foremost and terrible arrow that was capable of penetrating the inner organs and released it from his bow.'

ततो गव्यूतिमात्रेण मृगयूथपयूथपः ।
तस्य बानपथं त्यक्त्वा तस्थिवान्प्रहसन्निव ॥ (18)

'However, the leader of the herd of deer advanced far ahead, by a distance that was more than one *govyuti*,[24] beyond the reach of the arrow. It then stood there, seeming to laugh at the king.'

तस्मिन्निपतिते बाणे भूमौ प्रजलिते ततः ।
प्रविवेश महारण्यं मृगो राजाप्यथाद्रवत् ॥ (19)

'The blazing arrow fell down on the ground. When the deer had entered a great forest, the king pursued it there.'

प्रविश्य तु महारण्यं तापसानामथाश्रमम् ।
आससाद ततो राजा श्रान्तश्चोपाविशत्पुनः ॥ (20)

'Having entered the great forest, the king approached a hermitage of ascetics. He was tired and seated himself.'

तं कार्मुकधरं दृष्ट्वा श्रमार्तं क्षुधितं तदा ।
समेत्य ऋषयस्तस्मिन्पूजां चक्रुर्यथाविधि ॥ (21)

'The rishis approached and saw him there, with the bow in his hand, exhausted, afflicted and hungry. Following the prescribed rites, they honoured him.'

---

[24]Measure of distance. It is the distance at which a cow's bellow can he heard.

ऋषयो राजशार्दूलमपृच्छन्स्वं प्रयोजनम् ।
केन भद्रमुखार्थेन संप्राप्तोऽसि तपोवनम् ॥ (22)
पदातिर्बद्धनिस्त्रिंशो धन्वी बाणी नरेश्वर ।
एतदिच्छाम विज्ञातुं कुतः प्राप्तोऽसि मानद ।
कस्मिन्कुले हि जातस्त्वं किं नामासि ब्रवीहि नः ॥ (23)

'The rishis asked that tiger among kings what he wanted. "O Fortunate One! What is the reason behind your coming to this hermitage of ascetics? O Lord of Men! Though you are on foot, you have girded your sword and have a bow and arrows. O One Who Grants Honours! We wish to know where you have come from. What lineage were you born in? Tell us what your name is."'

ततः स राजा सर्वेभ्यो द्विजेभ्यः पुरुषर्षभ ।
आचख्यौ तद्यथान्यायं परिचर्यां च भारत ॥ (24)

'O Bull among Men! O Descendant of the Bharata Lineage! At this, the king told all the dvijas everything and also about the pursuit.'

हैहयानां कुले जातः सुमित्रो मित्रनन्दनः ।
चरामि मृगयूथानि निघ्नन्बाणैः सहस्रशः ।
बलेन महता गुप्तः सामात्यः सावरोधनः ॥ (25)

'"I have been born in the lineage of the Haihayas. I am Sumitra, the son of Mitra. I was roaming around, slaying herds of deer with thousands of arrows. I am protected by a large army and the advisers and *avarodhana*[25] are with me."'

मृगस्तु विद्धो बाणेन मया सरति शल्यवान् ।
तं द्रवन्तमनु प्राप्तो वनमेतद्यदृच्छया ।
भवत्सकाशे नष्टश्रीर्हताशः श्रमकर्शितः ॥ (26)

'"I pierced a deer with my arrow. Though pierced by my arrow, it ran away. While running after it as I desired, I arrived in this forest and near you. My prosperity has been destroyed. My hopes have been destroyed. I am suffering from exhaustion."'

---

[25]'Avarodhana' refers to women who lived in the inner quarters of a palace. They usually travelled with a king as part of the camp.

किं नु दुःखमतोऽन्यद्वै यदहं श्रमकर्शितः ।
भवतामाश्रमं प्राप्तो हताशो नष्टलक्षणः ॥ (27)

'"What can be a greater misery than this? I am suffering from exhaustion. I have arrived in your hermitage, with my hopes destroyed and all my signs[26] lost."'

न राज्यलक्षणत्यागो न पुरस्य तपोधनाः ।
दुःखं करोति तत्तीव्रं यथाशा विहता मम ॥ (28)

'"O Ones Rich in Austerities! Having to abandon the signs of the kingship or giving up the city does not cause me as fierce a misery as the dashing of my hopes."'

हिमवान्वा महाशैलः समुद्रो वा महोदधिः ।
महत्त्वान्नान्वपद्येतां रोदस्योरन्तरं यथा ।
आशायास्तपसि श्रेष्ठास्तथा नान्तमहं गतः ॥ (29)

'"The Himalayas, giant among mountains, and the ocean, the great store of water, are regarded as vast and so is the space between heaven and earth. O Best among Ascetics! But I cannot see any end to hope."'

भवतां विदितं सर्वं सर्वज्ञा हि तपोधनाः ।
भवन्तः सुमहाभागास्तस्मात्प्रक्ष्यामि संशयम् ॥ (30)

'"O Ones Rich in Austerities! Everything is known to you. You are omniscient. O Immensely Fortunate Ones! I am, therefore, presenting you with the doubt I have."'

आशावान्पुरुषो यः स्यादन्तरिक्षमथापि वा ।
किं नु ज्यायस्तरं लोके महत्त्वात्प्रतिभाति वः ।
एतदिच्छामि तत्त्वेन श्रोतुं किमिह दुर्लभम् ॥ (31)

'"Which seems to be greater in this world, the hope of a man or the sky? I wish to hear the truth about this. Which is more difficult to obtain?"'

---

[26]Of kingship.

यदि गुह्यं तपोनित्या न वो ब्रूतेह माचिरम् ।
न हि गुह्यमतः श्रोतुमिच्छामि द्विजपुङ्गवाः ॥ (32)

'"O Ones Who Are Always Engaged in Austerities! If this is not a secret, please tell me without any delay. O Bulls among Dvijas! If you do not regard this to be a secret, I wish to hear."'

भवत्तपोविघातो वा येन स्याद्विरमे ततः ।
यदि वास्ति कथायोगो योऽयं प्रश्नो मयेरितः ॥ (33)

'"However, if this causes an impediment in your austerities, I will desist. The question that I have asked should not lead to a long conversation."'

एतत्कारणसामर्ग्यं श्रोतुमिच्छामि तत्त्वतः ।
भवन्तो हि तपोनित्या ब्रूयुरेतत्समाहिताः ॥ (34)

'"These are all the reasons I wish to hear the truth about this. You are always engaged in austerities and are extremely controlled. You should tell me."'

Chapter 4

भीष्म उवाच

ततस्तेषां समस्तानामृषीणामृषिसत्तमः ।
ऋषभो नाम विप्रर्षिः स्मयन्निव ततोऽब्रवीत् ॥ (1)

Bhishma said, 'Then, among those assembled rishis, a brahmana rishi named Rishabha, supreme among rishis, smiled and spoke.'

पुराहं राजशार्दूल तीर्थान्यनुचरन्प्रभो ।
समासादितवान्दिव्यं नरनारायणाश्रमम् ॥ (2)

'"O Tiger among Kings! O Lord! In earlier times, I visited all the tirthas and arrived at the divine hermitage of Nara and Narayana."'

यत्र सा बदरी रम्या ह्रदो वैहायसस्तथा ।
यत्र चाश्वशिरा राजन्वेदान्पठति शाश्वतान् ॥ (3)

'"There is the badari[27] tree there, and there is the beautiful lake in the sky.[28] O King! Ashvashira[29] recites the eternal Vedas there."'

तस्मिन्सरसि कृत्वाहं विधिवत्तर्पणं पुरा ।
पितृणां देवतानां च ततोऽऽश्रममियां तदा ॥ (4)

'"In those ancient times, I first rendered the recommended offerings to ancestors and devas in that lake. I next went to the hermitage."'

रेमाते यत्र तौ नित्यं नरनारायणावृषी ।
अदूरादाश्रमं कं चिद्वासार्थमगमं ततः ॥ (5)

'"The rishis Nara and Narayana always find delight there. To find an abode, I went a little distance away from the hermitage."'

ततश्चीराजिनधरं कृशमुच्चमतीव च ।
अद्राक्षमृषिमायान्तं तनुं नाम तपोनिधिम् ॥ (6)

'"There, I saw an extremely emaciated rishi coming towards me. He was dressed in rags and hides and he was extremely tall. He was a store of austerities and his name was Tanu."'

अन्यैनरैर्महाबाहो वपुषाष्टगुणान्वितम् ।
कृशता चापि राजर्षे न दृष्टा तादृशी क्वचित् ॥ (7)

'"O Mighty-Armed One! O Rajarshi! Many other men have the eight qualities his form possessed.[30] But I have never seen anyone as lean as him."'

शरीरमपि राजेन्द्र तस्य कानिष्ठिकासमम् ।
ग्रीवा बाहू तथा पादौ केशाश्चाद्भुतदर्शनाः ॥ (8)

'"O Indra among Kings! His body was as thin as a little finger. His neck, arms, feet and hair were extraordinary to see."'

---

[27]The jujube tree.
[28]The celestial Ganga is believed to originate from this lake in the sky.
[29]With the head of a horse. Another incarnation of Vishnu.
[30]The eight qualities are intelligence, good conduct, self-control, studying, valour, restraint in speech, generosity and gratitude.

शिर: कायानुरूपं च कर्णौ नेत्रे तथैव च ।
तस्य वाक्चैव चेष्टा च सामान्ये राजसत्तम ॥ (9)

'"His head was as large as his body and so were his ears and his eyes. O Supreme among Kings! His speech and movement were feeble."'

दृष्ट्वाहं तं कृशं विप्रं भीत: परमदुर्मना: ।
पादौ तस्याभिवाद्याथ स्थित: प्राञ्जलिरग्रत: ॥ (10)

'"On seeing this extremely emaciated brahmana, I was scared and very distressed. I touched his feet and, joining my hands in salutation, stood before him."'

निवेद्य नामगोत्रं च पितरं च नरर्षभ ।
प्रदिष्टे चासने तेन शनैरहमुपाविशम् ॥ (11)

'"O Bull among Men! I told him my name, my *gotra*[31] and my father's name. Then I slowly sat down on the seat he showed me."'

तत: स कथयामास कथा धर्मार्थसंहिता: ।
ऋषिमध्ये महाराज तत्र धर्मभृतां वर: ॥ (12)

'"O Great King! In the midst of those rishis, that supreme upholder of dharma recounted stories that were full of dharma and artha."'

तस्मिंस्तु कथयत्येव राजा राजीवलोचन: ।
उपायाज्जवनैरश्वै: सबल: सावरोधन: ॥ (13)

'"While he was talking, a king arrived on swift horses, with an army and women. His eyes were like blue lotuses."'

स्मरन्पुत्रमरण्ये वै नष्टं परमदुर्मना: ।
भूरिद्युम्न पिता धीमान्रघुश्रेष्ठो महायशा: ॥ (14)

---

[31]Family name, denoting common lineage. This has to do with prohibiting endogamy, since marriage within the same gotra is not allowed.

'"Remembering his son, who had got lost in the forest, he was extremely distressed. He was the father of Bhuridyumna,[32] and he was intelligent and immensely illustrious, born in Raghu's lineage."'

इह द्रक्ष्यामि तं पुत्रं द्रक्ष्यामीहेति पार्थिवः ।
एवमाशाकृतो राजंश्चरन्वनमिदं पुरा ॥ (15)

'"The lord of the earth said, 'I will see my son here. It is here that I will see him.' In those ancient times, the king was roaming around, driven thus by hope."'

दुर्लभः स मया द्रष्टुं नूनं परमधार्मिकः ।
एकः पुत्रो महारण्ये नष्ट इत्यसकृत्तदा ॥ (16)
दुर्लभः स मया द्रष्टुमाशा च महती मम ।
तया परीतगात्रोऽहं मुमूर्षुर्नात्र संशयः ॥ (17)

'"It is also extremely unlikely that I will ever see the one who is supreme in dharma.[33] I have only one son and he has perished in the forest. It is extremely unlikely that I will see him, but hopes run high. There is no doubt that I will die and cast aside my body."'

एतच्छ्रुत्वा स भगवांस्तनुर्मुनिवरोत्तमः ।
अवाक्शिरा ध्यानपरो मुहूर्तमिव तस्थिवान् ॥ (18)

'"Hearing these words, the illustrious Tanu, supreme among excellent sages, lowered his head. For a muhurta,[34] he immersed himself in dhyana."'

तमनुध्यान्तमालक्ष्य राजा परमदुर्मनाः ।
उवाच वाक्यं दीनात्मा मन्दं मन्दमिवासकृत् ॥ (19)
दुर्लभं किं नु विप्रर्षे आशायाश्चैव किं भवेत् ।
ब्रवीतु भगवानेतद्यदि गुह्यं न तन्मयि ॥ (20)

'"On seeing him meditating, the king was greatly distressed. Cheerless in his mind and unhappy, he gently spoke these words.

---

[32]The son's name was Bhuridyumna.
[33]Referring to the son.
[34]A muhurta is a period of forty-eight minutes.

'O Brahmana Rishi! What is difficult to get and rarer than hope? O Illustrious One! If it is not a secret, please tell me.'"

महर्षिर्भगवांस्तेन पूर्वमासीद्विमानितः ।
बालिशां बुद्धिमास्थाय मन्दभाग्यतयात्मनः ॥ (21)

"'In the past, because of his misfortune and foolish intelligence, the illustrious maharshi had been insulted.'"[35]

अर्थयन्कलशं राजन्काञ्चनं वल्कलानि च ।
निर्विण्णः स तु विप्रर्षिर्निराशः समपद्यत ॥ (22)

"'O King! The brahmana rishi had asked for some riches, a golden pot and some bark for clothing, but his hopes had been belied and he had been distressed.'"

एवमुक्त्वाभिवाद्याथ तमृषिं लोकपूजितम् ।
श्रान्तो न्यषीदद्धर्मात्मा यथा त्वं नरसत्तम ॥ (23)

"'O Supreme among Men! Having spoken to the rishi, revered in the worlds, the one with dharma in his atman[36] worshipped him. But he[37] was exhausted and sat down.'"

अर्घ्यं ततः समानीय पाद्यं चैव महानृषिः ।
आरण्यकेन विधिना राज्ञे सर्वं न्यवेदयत् ॥ (24)

"'The great rishi brought him *arghya* and *padya*[38] and showed the king all the due honours, as is recommended for someone dwelling in the forest.'"

ततस्ते मुनयः सर्वे परिवार्य नरर्षभम् ।
उपाविशन्पुरस्कृत्य सप्तर्षय इव ध्रुवम् ॥ (25)

---

[35]It will become clear later that Bhuridyumna's father had insulted Tanu.
[36]Bhuridyumna's father.
[37]Tanu.
[38]Arghya is a gift offered to a guest. Padya is water for washing the feet.

'"All the sages surrounded that bull among men. They sat down, with him at the front, like the saptarshis around Dhruva."'[39]

अपृच्छंश्चैव ते तत्र राजानमपराजितम् ।
प्रयोजनमिदं सर्वमाश्रमस्य प्रवेशनम् ॥ (26)

'"They asked the unvanquished king about the complete reason behind his entering the hermitage."'

राजोवाच

वीरद्युम्न इति ख्यातो राजाहं दिक्षु विश्रुतः ।
भूरिद्युम्नं सुतं नष्टमन्वेष्टुं वनमागतः ॥ (27)

'"The king said, 'I am a king famous in all the directions by the name of Viradyumna. I have come to the forest to look for my son Bhuridyumna, who has got lost.'"'

एकपुत्रः स विप्राग्र्य बाल एव च सोऽनघ ।
न दृश्यते वने चास्मिंस्तमन्वेष्टुं चराम्यहम् ॥ (28)

'"O Foremost among Brahmanas! O Unblemished One! He is my only son. He cannot be seen in this forest and I have been roaming around, searching for him.'"

ऋषभ उवाच

एवमुक्ते तु वचने राज्ञा मुनिरधोमुखः ।
तूष्णीमेवाभवत्तत्र न च प्रत्युक्तवान्नृपम् ॥ (29)

'Rishabha said, "Having been thus addressed by the king, the sage[40] remained with his head lowered. He was silent and did not reply to the king."'

स हि तेन पुरा विप्रो राज्ञा नात्यर्थमानितः ।
आशाकृशं च राजेन्द्र तपो दीर्घं समास्थितः ॥ (30)

---

[39]The sages sat down around Tanu. Dhruva is the Pole Star and the saptarshis refers to the seven great sages as well as the constellation of Ursa Major.
[40]Tanu.

'"O Indra among Kings! In the past, insolent because of his prosperity, the king had insulted the brahmana. With his hopes belied, he[41] had engaged in austerities for a long time."'

प्रतिग्रहमहं राज्ञां न करिष्ये कथंचन ।
अन्येषां चैव वर्णानामिति कृत्वा धियं तदा ॥ (31)

'"He had made up his mind then, 'I will never accept anything from a king, or from any of the other varnas.'"'

आशा हि पुरुषं बालं लालापयति तस्थुषी ।
तामहं व्यपनेष्यामि इति कृत्वा व्यवस्थितः ॥ (32)

'"'Hope agitates men who are foolish. I will fling it away.' He had taken this pledge and had abided by it."'

राजोवाच

आशायाः किं कृशत्वं च किं चेह भुवि दुर्लभम् ।
ब्रवीतु भगवानेतत्त्वं हि धर्मार्थदर्शिवान् ॥ (33)

'"The king asked, 'Can hope be made to wear thin? Is there anything else on earth that is more difficult to get? O Illustrious One! You have seen the nature of dharma and artha. Please tell me.'"'

ऋषभ उवाच

ततः संस्मृत्य तत्सर्वं स्मारयिष्यन्निवाब्रवीत् ।
राजानं भगवान्विप्रस्ततः कृशतनुस्तनुः ॥ (34)
कृशत्वे न समं राजन्नाशाया विद्यते नृप ।
तस्या वै दुर्लभत्वातु प्रार्थिताः पार्थिवा मया ॥ (35)

'Rishabha said, "Remembering everything, the illustrious brahmana Tanu, emaciated in his body, reminded the king of the incident and said, 'O King! There is nothing as emaciated as hope. O Lord of Men! I have sought from many lords of the earth and have found nothing is as difficult to obtain.'"'

---

[41] Tanu.

राजोवाच

कृशाकृशे मया ब्रह्मन्गृहीते वचनात्तव ।
दुर्लभत्वं च तस्यैव वेदवाक्यमिव द्विज ॥ (36)

'"The king replied, 'O Brahmana! I have understood the purport of your words, about it being emaciated and also not emaciated[42] and also about the difficulty of obtaining. O Dvija! Your words are like the words of the Vedas.'"

संशयस्तु महाप्राज्ञ संजातो हृदये मम ।
तन्मे सत्तम तत्त्वेन वक्तुमर्हसि पृच्छतः ॥ (37)

'""O Immensely Wise One! However, a doubt has arisen in my heart. O Excellent One! I am asking you and you should tell me the truth about this.'"

त्वत्तः कृशतरं किं नु ब्रवीतु भगवानिदम् ।
यदि गुह्यं न ते विप्र लोकेऽस्मिन्किं नु दुर्लभम् ॥ (38)

'""O Illustrious One! Tell me, if it is not a secret, is there anyone more emaciated than you? O Brahmana! In this world, is there anything that is more difficult to get?'"[43]

कृशतनुरुवाच

दुर्लभोऽप्यथ वा नास्ति योऽर्थी धृतिमवाप्नुयात् ।
सुदुर्लभतरस्तात योऽर्थिनं नावमन्यते ॥ (39)

'"Krishatanu[44] replied, 'It is rarer to find a petitioner who is satisfied with what he has got.[45] O Son! It is rarer to find a person who does not disrespect a petitioner.'"

---

[42]Hope is strong, but it can be controlled. Therefore, hope can be emaciated. The objects one hopes for are difficult to get. Therefore, hope cannot be emaciated.
[43]That is, more difficult than the remarkable emaciation of the body.
[44]'Krisha' means emaciated, and the text here refers to Tanu as Krishatanu.
[45]While not obvious, this may refer to judicial procedures too.

संश्रुत्य नोपक्रियते परं शक्त्या यथार्हतः ।
सक्ता या सर्वभूतेषु साशा कृशतरी मया ॥ (40)

'"There are those who promise to help others according to capacity and as they deserve, but later do not do so, though they are able. However, even then, the hope that still remains in beings is thinner than I am."'

एकपुत्रः पिता पुत्रे नष्टे वा प्रोषिते तथा ।
प्रवृत्तिं यो न जानाति साशा कृशतरी मया ॥ (41)

'"There may be a father with a single son who is lost or absent from home. When one doesn't know what has happened to him, the hope that still remains is thinner than I am."'

प्रसवे चैव नारीणां वृद्धानां पुत्रकारिता ।
तथा नरेन्द्र धनिनामाशा कृशतरी मया ॥ (42)

'"There are aged women who desire to give birth. There are hopes among wealthy people. O Indra among Men! The hopes in them are thinner than I am."'

ऋषभ उवाच

एतच्छ्रुत्वा ततो राजन्स राजा सावरोधनः ।
संस्पृश्य पादौ शिरसा निपपात द्विजर्षभे ॥ (43)

'Rishabha said, "O King! Having heard this, the king and his women prostrated themselves and touched the feet of that bull among dvijas with their heads."'

राजोवाच

प्रसादये त्वा भगवन्पुत्रेणेच्छामि संगतिम् ।
वृणीष्व च वरं विप्र यमिच्छसि यथाविधि ॥ (44)

'"The king said, 'O Illustrious One! Through your favours, I desire to meet my son. O Brahmana! If you so wish, follow the rites and please grant me this boon.'"'

ऋषभ उवाच

अब्रवीच्च हि तं वाक्यं राजा राजीवलोचन: ।
सत्यमेतद्यथा विप्र त्वयोक्तं नास्त्यतो मृषा ॥ (45)

'Rishabha continued, "The king, with eyes like blue lotuses, spoke these words. 'O Brahmana! What you have said is true. There is nothing false in what you have said.'"

तत: प्रहस्य भगवांस्तनुर्धर्मभृतां वर: ।
पुत्रमस्यानयत्क्षिप्रं तपसा च श्रुतेन च ॥ (46)

'"The illustrious Tanu, supreme among the upholders of dharma, laughed at this. Through his austerities and his learning, he swiftly brought the son there."'

तं समानाय्य पुत्रं तु तदोपालभ्य पार्थिवम् ।
आत्मानं दर्शयामास धर्मे धर्मभृतां वर: ॥ (47)

'"Having brought the son there, he reprimanded the lord of the earth.[46] He was supreme among the upholders of dharma and showed himself to be none other than Dharma."'

संदर्शयित्वा चात्मानं दिव्यमद्भुतदर्शनम् ।
विपाप्मा विगतक्रोधश्चचार वनमन्तिकात् ॥ (48)

'"He exhibited his own self and it was divine and marvellous to behold. He was devoid of sin and devoid of anger, and left for the nearby forest."'

एतद्दृष्टं मया राजंस्ततश्च वचनं श्रुतम् ।
आशामपनयस्वाशु तत: कृशतरीमिमाम् ॥ (49)

'"O King! I saw this and I heard those words. Quickly dispel your hope, which is thinner than what he was."'

---

[46] He reprimanded because of what the king had done earlier.

भीष्म उवाच

स तत्रोक्तो महाराज ऋषभेण महात्मना ।
सुमित्रोऽपनयत्क्षिप्रमाशां कृशतरीं तदा ॥ (50)

Bhishma concluded, 'O Great King! Thus addressed by the great-souled Rishabha, Sumitra swiftly flung away his hope, which was extremely thin.'

एवं त्वमपि कौन्तेय श्रुत्वा वाणीमिमां मम ।
स्थिरो भव यथा राजन्हिमवानचलोत्तम: ॥ (51)

'O Kounteya! You have heard these words from me. O King! You should also be as steady as the Himalayas, supreme among mountains.'

त्वं हि द्रष्टा च श्रोता च कृच्छ्रेष्वर्थकृतेष्विह ।
श्रुत्वा मम महाराज न संतप्तुमिहार्हसि ॥ (52)

'You will see and hear those who face hardships because they pursue objectives. O Great King! Listen to me. You should not be tormented.'

Chapter 5

युधिष्ठिर उवाच

नामृतस्येव पर्याप्तिर्ममास्ति ब्रुवति त्वयि ।
तस्मात्कथय भूयस्त्वं धर्ममेव पितामह ॥ (1)

Yudhishthira said, 'Though you have spoken, I have not obtained enough of this amrita. O Grandfather! Therefore, speak to me again about dharma.'

भीष्म उवाच

अत्राप्युदाहरन्तीममितिहासं पुरातनम् ।
गौतमस्य च संवादं यमस्य च महात्मन: ॥ (2)

Bhishma replied, 'On this, an ancient history is recounted about a conversation between Goutama and the great-souled Yama.'

पारियात्रगिरिं प्राप्य गौतमस्याश्रमो महान् ।
उवास गौतमो यत्र कालं तदपि मे शृणु ॥ (3)

'Reaching Mount Pariyatra, Goutama resided there, in Goutama's great hermitage, for some time. Hear from me about this.'

षष्टिं वर्षसहस्राणि सोऽतप्यद्गौतमस्तपः ।
तमुग्रतपसं युक्तं तपसा भावितं मुनिम् ॥ (4)

'Goutama tormented himself through austerities for sixty thousand years. The cleansed and ascetic sage performed fierce austerities.'

उपयातो नरव्याघ्र लोकपालो यमस्तदा ।
तमपश्यत्सुतपसमृषिं वै गौतमं मुनिम् ॥ (5)

'O Tiger among Men! Yama, the guardian of the world, went to him there. As Sage Goutama performed those excellent austerities, he looked at the rishi.'

स तं विदित्वा ब्रह्मर्षिर्यममागतमोजसा ।
प्राञ्जलिः प्रयतो भूत्वा उपसपृप्तस्तपोधनः ॥ (6)

'Because of his energy, the brahmana rishi realized that Yama had arrived. The one who was rich in austerities joined his hands in salutation and advanced towards him.'

तं धमराजो दृष्ट्वैव नमस्कृत्य नरर्षभम् ।
न्यमन्त्रयत धर्मेण क्रियतां किमिति ब्रुवन् ॥ (7)

'Dharmaraja[47] looked towards that bull among men and bowed down before him. Dharma asked him, "What can I do for you?"'

---

[47]Yama.

गौतम उवाच

मातापितृभ्यामानानृण्यं किं कृत्वा समवाप्नुयात् ।
कथं च लोकानश्नाति पुरूषो दुर्लभांश्शुमान् ॥ (8)

'Goutama asked, "How can one free oneself of the debts due to the mother and the father? How can a man quickly obtain the radiant worlds, which are so difficult to obtain?"'

यम उवाच

तप:शौचवता नित्यं सत्यधर्मरतेन च ।
मातापित्रोरहरह: पूजनं कार्यमञ्जसा ॥ (9)

'Yama replied, "Austerities, purity, constant devotion to truth and dharma, worship of the mother and the father day after day are the tasks one should be attached to."'

अश्वमेधैश्च यष्टव्यं बहुभि: स्वाप्तदक्षिणै: ।
तेन लोकानुपाश्नाति पुरूषोऽद्भुतदर्शनान् ॥ (10)

'"One must perform many horse sacrifices, with adequate dakshina. A man will then obtain worlds that are extraordinary to behold."'

Thus ends the Kamanda, Rishabha and Yama Gita.

10

SHADAJA GITA

The second sub-parva of Shanti Parva, Apad Dharma Parva, speaks of the dharma that is allowed in times of calamity (*apad*), when deviations from the standard template of dharma are permitted. The Shadaja Gita occurs towards the end of Apad Dharma Parva and consists of a single chapter with forty-eight shlokas. Bhishma has just finished telling the Pandavas, and Nakula in particular, about the evolution of the sword as a weapon. The word '*shadaja*' means originating from six. The Shadaja Gita has individual views about dharma, emanating from the five Pandavas and Vidura.

वैशंपायन उवाच

इत्युक्तवति भीष्मे तु तूष्णींभूते युधिष्ठिरः ।
पप्रच्छावसरं गत्वा भ्रातॄन्विदुर पञ्चमान् ॥ (1)

Vaishampayana said, 'When Bhishma said this and became silent, Yudhishthira left his presence and asked his brothers, with Vidura as the fifth.'

धर्मे चार्थे च कामे च लोकवृत्तिः समाहिता ।
तेषां गरीयान्कतमो मध्यमः को लघुश्च कः ॥ (2)

'"The conduct of people is based on an aggregate of dharma, artha[1] and kama. Which of these is the most important? Which is medium and which is the least important?"'

कस्मिंश्चात्मा नियन्तव्यस्त्रिवर्गविजयाय वै ।
संतुष्टा नैष्ठिकं वाक्यं यथावद्वक्तुमर्हथ ॥ (3)

'"If one wishes to conquer all three categories together, which of these must one control? O Accomplished and Content Ones! You should speak accurately."'

ततोऽर्थगतितत्त्वज्ञः प्रथमं प्रतिभानवान् ।
जगाद विदुरो वाक्यं धर्मशास्त्रमनुस्मरन् ॥ (4)

'Vidura was foremost among those who knew the truth about the progress of artha. He possessed the illumination. Remembering the texts of dharma, he spoke these words.'

बहुश्रुत्यं तपस्त्यागः श्रद्धा यज्ञक्रिया क्षमा ।
भावशुद्धिर्दया सत्यं संयमश्चात्मसम्पदः ॥ (5)
एतदेवाभिपद्यस्व मा ते भूच्चलितं मनः ।
एतन्मूलौ हि धर्मार्थवेतदेकपदं हितम् ॥ (6)

'"A great deal of learning, austerities, renunciation, faith, rites of sacrifices, forgiveness, purification of sentiments, compassion, truthfulness, restraint and richness of the atman—these must be cultivated and the mind must not waver. These are the foundations of dharma and artha and can be subsumed in the single word of 'welfare'."'

धर्मेणैवर्षयस्तीर्णा धर्मे लोकाः प्रतिष्ठिताः ।
धर्मेण देवा दिविगा धर्मे चार्थः समाहितः ॥ (7)

'"The rishis crossed over through dharma. The worlds are established in dharma. Devas obtained heaven through dharma. Artha is submerged in dharma."'

---

[1] There is a typo in the CE; it says *ardha*, which has been corrected here.

धर्मो राजन्गुणश्रेष्ठो मध्यमो ह्यर्थ उच्यते ।
कामो यवीयानिति च प्रवदन्ति मनीषिण: ।
तस्माद्धर्मप्रधानेन भवितव्यं यतात्मना ॥ (8)

'"O King! Dharma is supreme in qualities. Artha is said to be medium. The learned ones say that kama is the least important. Therefore, a person must control his atman and make dharma the most important."'

समाप्तवचने तस्मिन्नर्थशास्त्रविशारद: ।
पार्थो वाक्यार्थतत्त्वज्ञो जगौ वाक्यमतन्द्रित: ॥ (9)

'When he stopped speaking, the attentive Partha,[2] who was accomplished in the texts about artha and knew the true meaning of words spoken about artha, uttered these words.'

कर्मभूमिरियं राजन्निह वार्ता प्रशस्यते ।
कृषिवाणिज्यगोरक्ष्यं शिल्पानि विविधानि च ॥ (10)

'"O King! This world is an arena for karma, and such conduct is praised—agriculture, trade, animal husbandry and many kinds of artisanship."'

अर्थ इत्येव सर्वेषां कर्मणामव्यतिक्रम: ।
न ऋतेऽर्थेन वर्तेते धर्मकामाविति श्रुति: ॥ (11)

'"Among all these tasks, there is nothing that transcends the need for artha. The Shrutis have said that without artha, dharma and kama cannot occur."'

विजयी ह्यर्थवान्धर्ममाराधयितुमुत्तमम् ।
कामं च चरितुं शक्तो दुष्प्रापमकृतात्मभि: ॥ (12)

'"A victorious person obtains artha and can pursue supreme dharma. He is capable of following kama, which is difficult for those with unclean atmans to obtain."'

---

[2] Arjuna in this case.

अर्थस्यावयवावेतौ धर्मकामाविति श्रुतिः ।
अर्थसिद्ध्या हि निर्वृत्तावुभावेतौ भविष्यतः ॥ (13)

'"The Shrutis say that dharma and kama take the form of artha. These two can be attained through the successful acquisition of artha."'

उद्भूतार्थं हि पुरुषं विशिष्टतरयोनयः ।
ब्रह्माणमिव भूतानि सततं पर्युपासते ॥ (14)

'"Those who have been born in superior lineages surround the man who possesses artha, just as the beings always worship Brahma."'

जटाजिनधरा दान्ताः पङ्कदिग्धा जितेन्द्रियाः ।
मुण्डा निस्तन्तवश्चापि वसन्त्यर्थार्थिनः पृथक् ॥ (15)

'"Those who have matted hair, are clad in deer skin, are controlled and have smeared themselves with mud, those who have conquered their senses, have shaved their heads, have no offspring and dwell separately—even they hanker after artha."'

काषायवसनाश्चान्ये श्मश्रुला ह्रीसुसंवृताः ।
विद्वांसश्चैव शान्ताश्च मुक्ताः सर्वपरिग्रहैः ॥ (16)

'"There are others who are bearded and attired in ochre garments, covering themselves well with humility. They are learned and tranquil. They are free and have given up all their possessions."'

अर्थार्थिनः सन्ति केचिदपरे स्वर्गकाङ्क्षिणः ।
कुलप्रत्यागमाश्चौके स्वं स्वं मार्गमनुष्ठिताः ॥ (17)

'"Even among them, some desire heaven and some others strive for artha. Some give up the practices of their lineages and are established in their own individual paths."'

आस्तिका नास्तिकाश्चैव नियताः संयमे परे ।
अप्रज्ञानं तमोभूतं प्रज्ञानं तु प्रकाशता ॥ (18)

'"There are believers and non-believers, completely engaged in supreme restraint.³ Lack of jnana is submerged in darkness, and jnana provides the radiance."'⁴

भृत्यान्भोगैर्द्विषो दण्डैर्यो योजयति सोऽर्थवान् ।
एतन्मतिमतां श्रेष्ठ मतं मम यथातथम् ।
अनयोस्तु निबोध त्वं वचनं वाक्यकण्ठयो: ॥ (19)

'"A person who possesses artha can maintain his servants in objects of pleasure and exert the rod against his enemies. O Best among Intelligent Ones! That is the reason my view is accurate. Now listen to the words of these two. Their throats are choking with words."'

ततो धर्मार्थकुशलौ माद्रीपुत्रावनन्तरम् ।
नकुल: सहदेवश्च वाक्यं जगदतु: परम् ॥ (20)

'Madri's sons, Nakula and Sahadeva, accomplished in dharma and artha, spoke these supreme words next.'

आसीनश्च शयानश्च विचरन्नपि च स्थित: ।
अर्थयोगं दृढं कुर्याद्योगैरुच्चावचैरपि ॥ (21)

'"Whether one is seated, lying down, roaming around or standing, through the pursuit of superior and inferior means, one must always attempt to firmly pursue the acquisition of artha."'

अस्मिंस्तु वै सुसंवृत्ते दुर्लभे परमप्रिये ।
इह कामानवाप्नोति प्रत्यक्षं नात्र संशय: ॥ (22)

'"This is hidden well, extremely difficult to obtain and is supremely loved. In this world, once one has obtained this, there is no doubt that one can directly obtain kama."'

योऽर्थो धर्मेण संयुक्तो धर्मो यश्चार्थसंयुत: ।
मध्विवामृतसंयुक्तं तस्मादेतौ मताविह ॥ (23)

---

³*Astika* and nastika should not be translated as theist and atheist. Astika is someone who believes in Vedas and their rituals. Nastika is the opposite. Atheist should be translated as *nirishvaravadi* in Sanskrit.
⁴Only some have truly renounced and have seen the light; others are still ignorant.

'"Artha is united with dharma, and dharma is united with artha. This is the way amrita is united with honey. Therefore, our view is the following."'

अनर्थस्य न कामोऽस्ति तथार्थोऽधर्मिण: कुत: ।
तस्मादुद्विजते लोको धर्मार्थाद्यो बहिष्कृत: ॥ (24)

'"There can be no kama without artha. How can there be dharma without artha? Thus, people are scared of those who are outside the pale of dharma and artha."'

तस्माद्धर्मप्रधानेन साध्योऽर्थ: संयतात्मना ।
विश्वस्तेषु च भूतेषु कल्पते सर्व एव हि ॥ (25)

'"Therefore, even if a person thinks that dharma is the most important, he must control his atman and seek to accomplish artha. If beings trust a person, then he can accomplish everything."'

धर्मं समाचरेत्पूर्वं तथार्थं धर्मसंयुतम् ।
तत: कामं चरेत्पश्चात्सिद्धार्थस्य हि तत्फलम् ॥ (26)

'"One must first pursue dharma and then artha that is in conformity with dharma. Kama should be pursued after that. These are the fruits of the successful pursuit of artha."'

विरेमतुस्तु तद्वाक्यमुक्त्वा तावश्विनो: सुतौ ।
भीमसेनस्तदा वाक्यमिदं वक्तुं प्रचक्रमे ॥ (27)

'Having spoken these words, the sons of the two Ashvins[5] stopped. Bhimasena then started to speak these words.'

नाकाम: कामयत्यर्थं नाकामो धर्ममिच्छति ।
नाकाम: कामयानोऽस्ति तस्मात्कामो विशिष्यते ॥ (28)

'"A person without kama does not desire artha. A person without kama does not desire dharma. A person without kama cannot follow the path of desire. Therefore, kama is superior."'

---

[5]Nakula and Sahadeva descended from the two Ashvins, the two physicians of the gods.

कामेन युक्ता ऋषयस्तपस्येव समाहिताः ।
पलाशफलमूलाशा वायुभक्षाः सुसंयताः ॥ (29)

"It is because they are united with kama that the rishis are controlled in their austerities. They eat palasha[6] leaves, fruits and roots. They subsist on air and are greatly restrained."

वेदोपवादेष्वपरे युक्ताः स्वाध्यायपारगाः ।
श्राद्धयज्ञक्रियायां च तथा दानप्रतिग्रहे ॥ (30)

"There are others who are engaged in chanting the Vedas; they are devoted to studying. They perform *shraddha*[7] and sacrifices and receive donations."

वणिजः कर्षका गोपाः कारवः शिल्पिनस्तथा ।
दैवकर्म कृतश्चैव युक्ताः कामेन कर्मसु ॥ (31)

"Merchants, farmers, herdsmen, craftsmen and artisans are engaged in the tasks of devas. But it is kama that drives the action."

समुद्रं चाविशन्त्यन्ये नराः कामेन संयुताः ।
कामो हि विविधाकारः सर्वं कामेन संततम् ॥ (32)

"Driven by kama, men enter the ocean. Kama has many different forms. Everything is driven by kama."

नास्ति नासीन्नाभविष्यद्भूतं कामात्मकात्परम् ।
एतत्सारं महाराज धर्मार्थावत्र संश्रितौ ॥ (33)

"There is nothing, there was nothing and there will be nothing that is beyond the simple fact of kama. O Great King! This is the essence and dharma and artha are dependent on it."

नवनीतं यथा दध्नस्तथा कामोऽर्थधर्मतः ।
श्रेयस्तैलं च पिण्याकाद्धृतं श्रेय उदश्वितः ॥ (34)

---

[6] The flame of the forest.
[7] Funeral rites.

'"Kama is to dharma and artha what butter is to curds. Oil is better than what is left of oilseeds after the extraction of oil. Ghee is better than what is left of milk after churning."'

श्रेय: पुण्यफलं काष्ठात्कामो धर्मार्थयोर्वर: ।
पुष्पतो मध्विव रस: कामात्संजायते सुखम् ॥ (35)

'"Auspicious fruits are better than wood. Kama is superior to both dharma and artha. Just as honey comes from the juice of flowers, like that, happiness is generated from kama."'

सुचारुवेषाभिरलंकृताभिर्मदोत्कटाभि: प्रियवादिनीभि: ।
रमस्व योषाभिरुपेत्य कामं कामो हि राजंस्तरसाभिपाती ॥ (36)

'"O King! Serve kama. Pleasure yourself with women who are attired in extremely beautiful garments and are ornamented, mad with intoxication and pleasant in speech. Kama will come to you swiftly."'

बुद्धिर्ममैषा परिषत्स्थितस्य मा भूद्विचारस्तव धर्मपुत्र ।
स्यात्संहितं सद्भिरफलगुसारं समेत्य वाक्यं परमानृशंस्यम् ॥ (37)

'"In this group, this is my view. O Dharma's Son! You should not reflect about this for a long time. If virtuous people paid heed to these beneficial words, which are not shallow in import, there would be the greatest lack of cruelty."'

धर्मार्थकामा: सममेव सेव्या यस्त्वेकसेवी स नरो जघन्य: ।
द्वयोस्तु दक्षं प्रवदन्ति मध्यं स उत्तमो यो निरतिस्त्रिवर्गे ॥ (38)

'"One must serve dharma, artha and kama in equal measure. If a man serves only one of these, he is the worst. A person who is accomplished in two is said to be medium. The superior person is engaged in all three categories."'

प्राज्ञ: सुहृच्चन्दनसारलिप्तो विचित्रमाल्याभरणैरुपेत: ।
ततो वच: संग्रहविग्रहेण प्रोक्त्वा यवीयान्विरराम भीम: ॥ (39)

'"He is wise. His well-wishers smear him with sandalwood paste. He is adorned in colourful garlands and ornaments." Having spoken these words, briefly and in detail, Bhima, the younger brother, stopped.'

ततो मुहूर्तादथ धर्मराजो वाक्यानि तेषाम् अनुचिन्त्य सम्यक् ।
उवाच वाचावितथं स्मयन्वै बहुश्रुतो धर्मभृतां वरिष्ठ: ॥ (40)

'For a muhurta,[8] Dharmaraja thought well about the words that had been spoken to him. Extremely learned and supreme among the upholders of dharma, he smiled and spoke these truthful words.'

नि:संशयं निश्चितधर्मशास्त्रा: सर्वे भवन्तो विदितप्रमाणा: ।
विज्ञातु कामस्य ममेह वाक्यमुक्तं यद्वै नैष्ठिकं तच्छ्रुतं मे ।
इह त्ववश्यं गदतो ममापि वाक्यं निबोधध्वमनन्यभावा: ॥ (41)

'"There is no doubt that all your determinations are based on the sacred texts of dharma and that you are acquainted with the proof. You have carefully spoken these words to me, and I have heard and got to know about kama. You have said that it is essential in this world. However, single-mindedly, listen to the sentiments in my words."'

यो वै न पापे निरतो न पुण्ये नार्थे न धर्मे मनुजो न कामे ।
विमुक्तदोष: समलोष्टकाञ्चन: स मुच्यते दु:खसुखार्थसिद्धे: ॥ (42)

'"A man who is engaged in neither good deeds nor evil ones, and not engaged in artha, dharma or kama, is freed from all taints and looks on gold and stones in the same way. He is successful in freeing himself from unhappiness and happiness."'

भूतानि जातीमरणान्वितानि जराविकारैश्च समन्वितानि ।
भूयश्च तैस्तै: प्रतिबोधितानि मोक्षं प्रशंसन्ति न तं च विद्म: ॥ (43)

'"Beings are born and they die. They face old age and decay. There have been repeated instructions on moksha, and it has been praised. But we do not know this."'

---

[8]Sometimes, a muhurta is understood to represent an instant.

स्नेहे नबद्धस्य न सन्ति तानीत्येवं स्वयंभूर्भगवानुवाच ।
बुधाश्च निर्वाणपरा वदन्ति तस्मान्न कुर्यात्प्रियमप्रियं च ॥ (44)

'"The illustrious Svayambhu has said that one not bound down by affection does not suffer these.[9] The learned ones have said that nirvana[10] is supreme. Therefore, one should not act in accordance with what is pleasant and what is unpleasant."'

एतत्प्रधानं न तु कामकारो यथा नियुक्तोऽस्मि तथा चरामि ।
भूतानि सर्वाणि विधिर्नियुङ्क्ते विधिर्बलीयानिति वित्त सर्वे ॥ (45)

'"However, a person who follows kama does not attach importance to this. I act wherever I have been engaged. All the beings have been appointed by destiny. Know that destiny is powerful in everything."'

न कर्मणाप्नोत्यनवाप्यमर्थं यद्भावि सर्वं भवतीति वित्त ।
त्रिवर्गहीनोऽपि हि विन्दतेऽर्थं तस्मादिदं लोकहिताय गुह्यम् ॥ (46)

'"One cannot attain the objective by undertaking karma. Know that whatever is going to happen will happen. Even if a person is devoid of the three categories, he can attain this objective.[11] Thus, this is the secret for the welfare of the worlds."'

ततस्तदर्घ्यं वचनं मनोनुगं समस्तमाज्ञाय ततोऽतिहेतुमत् ।
तदा प्रणेदुश्च जहर्षिरे च ते कुरुप्रवीराय च चक्रुरञ्जलीन् ॥ (47)

'These foremost words were pleasant to the mind and full of reason. They heard them and were delighted. They joined their hands in salutation to the foremost one among the Kuru lineage.'

सुचारुवर्णाक्षरशब्दभूषितां मनोनुगां निर्धुतवाक्यकण्टकाम् ।
निशम्य तां पार्थिव पार्थभाषितां गिरं नरेन्द्रा: प्रशशंसुरेव ते ।
पुनश्च पप्रच्छ सरिद्ध्रासुतं तत: परं धर्ममहीनसत्त्व: ॥ (48)

---

[9] Birth, death, old age and decay.
[10] Literally, extinction. Here, it is used synonymously with moksha.
[11] The objective being moksha. The three modes are dharma, artha and kama.

'Those words were extremely beautiful and adorned with letters, syllables and words. They were pleasing to the mind and devoid of thorns. O King! On hearing the words spoken by Partha,[12] those Indras among men applauded those words. The one who had never been dispirited[13] again questioned the son of the river[14] about supreme dharma.'

Thus ends the Shadaja Gita.

---

[12]Yudhishthira.
[13]Yudhishthira.
[14]Bhishma, Ganga's son.

11

PINGALA GITA

The Moksha Dharma Parva section of Shanti Parva is about moksha dharma, that is, the pursuit of moksha. The Pingala Gita is its first chapter, in which a brahmana comforts King Senajit[1] and tells him about the story of a courtesan named Pingala, after whom the Pingala Gita is named. Pingala was a courtesan from Avanti, alternatively Videha. There are different versions of the story told in the Puranas, not in the Mahabharata. The Mahabharata only has this passing mention. She earned her living as a public prostitute. However, when she turned old, there were no customers. She reflects on the wickedness of her life and turns to virtue. Consequently, she is born as a princess in her next life. The Pingala Gita has a single chapter with fifty-three shlokas.

युधिष्ठिर उवाच

धर्माः पितामहेनोक्ता राजधर्माश्रिताः शुभाः ।
धर्माश्रमाणां श्रेष्ठं वक्तुमर्हसि पार्थिव ॥ (1)

Yudhishthira said, 'O Grandfather! You have spoken about how one can resort to auspicious raja dharma. O King! You should tell me about the best dharma for those who are in the ashramas.'

---

[1] There were many kings named Senajit. We know nothing more about which King Senajit this was.

भीष्मो उवाच

सर्वत्र विहितो धर्म: स्वर्ग्य: सत्यफलं तप: ।
बहुद्वारस्य धर्मस्य नेहास्ति विफला क्रिया ॥ (2)

Bhishma replied, 'There are many doors to dharma and rites are never unsuccessful. Dharma, the path to heaven, truthfulness and fruits of austerities have been indicated everywhere.'

यस्मिन्यस्मिंस्तु विनये यो यो याति विनिश्चयम् ।
स तमेवाभिजानाति नान्यं भरतसत्तम ॥ (3)

'O Supreme among the Bharata Lineage! Whatever good policy one has thought of and has determined to observe should be understood as the only one, there being no other.'

यथा यथा च पर्येति लोकतन्त्रमसारवत् ।
तथा तथा विरागोऽत्र जायते नात्र संशय: ॥ (4)

'Whenever one reflects that the ways of the world are without substance, there is no doubt that non-attachment is generated.'

एवं व्यवसिते लोके बहुदोषे युधिष्ठिर ।
आत्ममोक्षनिमित्तं वै यतेत मतिमान्नर: ॥ (5)

'O Yudhishthira! When the ways of the world are like this, with many taints, an intelligent man must try to accomplish the objective of moksha for his atman.'

युधिष्ठिर उवाच

नष्टे धने वा दारे वा पुत्रे पितरि वा मृते ।
यया बुद्ध्या नुदेच्छोकं तन्मे ब्रूहि पितामह ॥ (6)

Yudhishthira asked, 'O Grandfather! When riches are destroyed and a wife, a son or a father dies, how can one use one's intelligence to dispel that sorrow? Please tell me that.'

भीष्म उवाच

नष्टे धने वा दारे वा पुत्रे पितरि वा मृते ।
अहो दुःखमिति ध्यायञ्छोकस्यापचितिं चरेत् ॥ (7)

Bhishma replied, 'When riches are destroyed and a wife, a son or a father dies, one laments in grief. However, one must act so as to dispel that sorrow through meditation.'

अत्राप्युदाहरन्तीममितिहासं पुरातनम् ।
यथा सेनजितं विप्रः कश्चिदित्यब्रवीद्वचः ॥ (8)
पुत्रशोकाभिसंतप्तं राजानं शोकविह्वलम् ।
विषन्नवदनं दृष्ट्वा विप्रो वचनमब्रवीत् ॥ (9)

'In this connection, an ancient history is recounted about the words that were spoken by a brahmana to Senajit, when the king was tormented by grief on account of his son and was distracted with misery. On seeing that his face was sorrowful, the brahmana spoke these words.'

किं नु खल्वसि मूढस्त्वं शोच्यः किमनुशोचसि ।
यदा त्वामपि शोचन्तः शोच्या यास्यन्ति तां गतिम् ॥ (10)

'"You are as dumb as a millstone. Why are you sorrowing? What are you grieving about? There are those who will sorrow over you and those mourners will also advance towards the same end."'

त्वं चैवाहं च ये चान्ये त्वां राजन्पर्युपासते ।
सर्वे तत्र गमिष्यामो यत एवागता वयम् ॥ (11)

'"O King! You, I and all the others who surround you, all of us will go to the place where we have come from."'

सेनजिदुवाच

का बुद्धिः किं तपो विप्र कः समाधिस्तपोधन ।
किं ज्ञानं किं श्रुतं वा ते यत्प्राप्य न विषीदसि ॥ (12)

'Senajit asked, "O Brahmana! O One Who Is Rich in Austerities! What intelligence, austerities, samadhi,[2] jnana and learning can be obtained, so that one does not succumb to lassitude?"'

ब्राह्मण उवाच

पश्य भूतानि दुःखेन व्यतिषक्तानि सर्वशः ।
आत्मापि चायं न मम सर्वा वा पृथिवी मम ॥ (13)

'The brahmana replied, "Behold. All beings are tied down in misery. For me, my atman is not mine. But the entire earth is mine."'

यथा मम तथान्येषामिति बुद्ध्या न मे व्यथा ।
एतां बुद्धिमहं प्राप्य न प्रहृष्ये न च व्यथे ॥ (14)

'"What is mine also belongs to others. Because of this intelligence, I am not pained. Having obtained this intelligence, I am neither delighted nor pained."'

यथा काष्ठं च काष्ठं च समेयातां महोदधौ ।
समेत्य च व्यपेयातां तद्वद्भूतसमागमः ॥ (15)

'"Just as a piece of wood approaches another piece of wood in the great ocean, comes together and drifts apart, that is the way beings encounter each other."'

एवं पुत्राश्च पौत्राश्च ज्ञातयो बान्धवास्तथा ।
तेषु स्नेहो न कर्तव्यो विप्रयोगो हि तैर्ध्रुवम् ॥ (16)

'"Sons, grandsons, kin and relatives are like that. One should not be attached to them, since separation from them is certain."'

अदर्शनादापतितः पुनश्चादर्शनं गतः ।
न त्वासौ वेद न त्वं तं कः सन्कमनुशोचसि ॥ (17)

---

[2] The state of ultimate immersion, the final stage of Ashtanga Yoga.

'"He[3] came from what cannot be seen. He has gone to what cannot be seen. He did not know you. You did not know him. Who are you? Who are you sorrowing over?"'

तृष्णार्तिप्रभवं दुःखं दुःखार्तिप्रभवं सुखम् ।
सुखात्संजायते दुःखमेवमेतत्पुनः पुनः ।
सुखस्यान्तरं दुःखं दुःखस्यान्तरं सुखम् ॥ (18)

'"Misery is an affliction created by thirst. Happiness is created by the affliction of sorrow. Then again, misery is repeatedly generated by joy. Unhappiness comes after happiness. Happiness comes after unhappiness."'

सुखात्त्वं दुःखमापन्नः पुनरापत्स्यसे सुखम् ।
न नित्यं लभते दुःखं न नित्यं लभते सुखम् ॥ (19)

'"Misery follows joy and is again followed by joy. Unhappiness is not permanently obtained, nor is happiness permanently obtained."'

नालं सुखाय सुहृदो नालं दुःखाय शत्रवः ।
न च प्रज्ञालमर्थानां न सुखानामलं धनम् ॥ (20)

'"Indeed, well-wishers are not the reason for happiness. Indeed, enemies are not the reason for unhappiness. Artha is not sufficient for wisdom, nor indeed are riches sufficient for happiness."'

न बुद्धिर्धनलाभाय न जाड्यमसमृद्धये ।
लोकपर्यायवृत्तान्तं प्राज्ञो जानाति नेतरः ॥ (21)

'"One cannot obtain riches through intelligence, nor is stupidity the reason for penury. It is only a wise person, and no one else, who understands the progress of the world."'

बुद्धिमन्तं च मूढं च शूरं भीरुं जडं कविम् ।
दुर्बलं बलवन्तं च भागिनं भजते सुखम् ॥ (22)

---

[3] Senajit's son.

'"The intelligent, the foolish, the brave, the coward, the dumb, the wise, the weak, the powerful—all of them enjoy their share of happiness because of destiny."'

धेनुर्वत्सस्य गोपस्य स्वामिनस्तस्करस्य च ।
पय: पिबति यस्तस्या धेनुस्तस्येति निश्चय: ॥ (23)

'"The cow simultaneously belongs to the calf, the cowherd, the master and the thief. But it is certain that the cow actually belongs to the person who drinks her milk."'[4]

ये च मूढतमा लोके ये च बुद्धे: परं गता: ।
ते नरा: सुखमेधन्ते क्लिश्यत्यन्तरितो जन: ॥ (24)

'"Those who are the most foolish in the world and those who have attained supreme intelligence—only these men can enjoy happiness. People who are in between suffer."'

अन्त्येषु रेमिरे धीरा न ते मध्येषु रेमिरे ।
अन्त्यप्राप्तिं सुखमाहुर्दु:खमन्तरमन्तयो: ॥ (25)

'"Patient ones find delight in the two extremes, not in the ones in the middle.[5] It is said that happiness is associated with the two extremes and unhappiness with ones in between."'

ये तु बुद्धिसुखं प्राप्ता द्वंद्वातीता विमत्सरा: ।
तान्नैवार्था न चानर्था व्यथयन्ति कदाचन ॥26॥

---

[4]The others have an illusory sense of owning the cow. One should not despair because of an illusory sense of ownership.
[5]This is a reference to the four states of consciousness—*jagrata* (wakefulness), *svapna* (dreaming), *sushupti* (deep sleep) and turiya (pure consciousness). The wise take delight in wakefulness and pure consciousness, not in dreaming or deep sleep. While the previous sentence has a reference to the most foolish, it is possible that this is meant to represent a state of wakefulness. Supreme intelligence is achieved by those who have pure consciousness.

'"Those who have obtained happiness through their intelligence and those who are free from opposite sentiments,[6] devoid of jealousy, are never distressed by prosperity or adversity."'

अथ ये बुद्धिमप्राप्ता व्यतिक्रान्ताश्च मूढताम् ।
तेऽतिवेलं प्रहृष्यन्ति संतापमुपयान्ति च ॥ (27)

'"However, there are also foolish people who have not obtained that intelligence. They have not been able to go beyond excessive delight and extreme torment."'

नित्यप्रमुदिता मूढा दिवि देवगणा इव ।
अवलेपेन महता परिदृब्धा विचेतसः ॥ (28)

'"There are foolish ones who are bereft of consciousness. They are immensely haughty because of their strength and are given to constant delight as if they are like devas in heaven."'

सुखं दुःखान्तमालस्यं दुःखं दाक्ष्यं सुखोदयम् ।
भूतिश्चैव श्रिया सार्धं दक्षे वसति नालसे ॥ (29)

'"However, because of their laziness, such happiness terminates in unhappiness. And because of skill, unhappiness can give rise to happiness. Riches and prosperity dwell with those who are accomplished, not with those who are lazy."'

सुखं वा यदि वा दुःखं द्वेष्यं वा यदि वा प्रियम् ।
प्राप्तं प्राप्तमुपासीत हृदयेनापराजितः ॥ (30)

'"Whether it is happiness or unhappiness, whether it is hated or agreeable—whatever has been obtained must be honoured with an unvanquished heart."'

शोकस्थानसहस्राणि हर्षस्थानशतानि च ।
दिवसे दिवसे मूढमाविशन्ति न पण्डितम् ॥ (31)

---

[6] Like happiness and unhappiness, pleasure and pain.

'"From one day to another day, there are a thousand reasons for misery and a hundred reasons for joy. Stupid people are submerged in these, but not those who are learned."'

बुद्धिमन्तं कृतप्रज्ञं शुश्रूसुमनसूयकम् ।
दान्तं जितेन्द्रियं चापि शोको न स्पृशते नरम् ॥ (32)

'"If a man is intelligent, accomplished in his wisdom, given to servitude[7] and lack of envy, and is self-controlled, having conquered his senses, sorrow cannot touch him."'

एतां बुद्धिं समास्थाय गुप्तचित्तश्चरेद्बुधः ।
उदयास्तमयज्ञं हि न शोकः स्प्रस्तुमर्हति ॥ (33)

'"A learned person resorts to this intelligence and guards his consciousness. Sorrow cannot touch a person who knows the origin and the end of everything."'[8]

यन्निमित्तं भवेच्छोकस्त्रासो वा दुःखमेव वा ।
आयासो वा यतोमूलस्तदेकाङ्गमपि त्यजेत् ॥ (34)

'"The reasons behind sorrow, fright, unhappiness and exertion must be severed from the roots, like casting aside one of the limbs of the body."'

यद्यत्यजति कामानां तत्सुखस्याभिपूर्यते ।
कामानुसारी पुरुषः कामाननु विनश्यति ॥ (35)

'"If objects of desire are cast aside, this fills one with happiness. Indeed, a man who follows desire is destroyed by that desire."'

यच्च कामसुखं लोके यच्च दिव्यं महत्सुखम् ।
तृष्णाक्षयसुखस्यैते नार्हतः सोदशीं कलाम् ॥ (36)

'"The happiness obtained from the pursuit of desire in this world or the great bliss obtained in heaven is not even one-sixteenth of the happiness obtained from the extinction of thirst."'

---

[7] Of elders, seniors and preceptors.
[8] The brahman.

पूर्वदेहकृतं कर्म शुभं वा यदि वाशुभम् ।
प्राज्ञं मूढं तथा शूरं भजते यादृशं कृतम् ॥ (37)

'"The karma committed in an earlier body, auspicious or inauspicious, and the consequences of those deeds are enjoyed by the wise, the foolish and the brave."'

एवमेव किलैतानि प्रियाण्येवाप्रियाणि च ।
जीवेषु परिवर्तन्ते दुःखानि च सुखानि च ॥ (38)

'"In this way, the pleasant and the unpleasant, unhappiness and happiness circulate among living beings."'

तदेवं बुद्धिमास्थाय सुखं जीवेद्गुणान्वितः ।
सर्वान्कामाञ्जुगुप्सेत सङ्गान्कुर्वीत पृष्ठतः ।
वृत्त एष हृदि प्रौढो मृत्युरेष मनोमयः ॥ (39)

'"Knowing this and resorting to this intelligence, a person with qualities lives in joy. He shuns all desire and turns his back on attachment. The wise regard this kind of conduct of the heart as mental death."'

यदा संहरते कामान्कूर्मोऽङ्गानीव सर्वशः ।
तदात्मज्योतिरात्मा च आत्मन्येव प्रसीदति ॥ (40)

'"A tortoise draws in all its limbs.[9] Like that, such a person draws in desire and finds pleasure in his own radiant atman."'

किंचिदेव ममत्वेन यदा भवति कल्पितम् ।
तदेव परितापार्थं सर्वं संपद्यते तदा ॥ (41)

'"Even if the slightest sense of ownership is thought of, that will give rise to repentance and pervade everything."'

न बिभेति यदा चायं यदा चास्मान्न बिभ्यति ।
यदा नेच्छति न द्वेष्टि ब्रह्म संपद्यते तदा ॥ (42)

---

[9] The first part of this is similar to Bhagavat Gita 2.58.

'"He is not frightened of anything. No one is frightened of him. He has no desire and no hatred. He is then immersed in the brahman."'[10]

उभे सत्यानृते त्यक्त्वा शोकानन्दौ भयाभये ।
प्रियाप्रिये परित्यज्य प्रशान्तात्मा भविष्यति ॥ (43)

'"He gives up truth and falsehood, sorrow and joy, fear and freedom from fear, pleasant and unpleasant. Having abandoned these, he is serene in his atman."'

यदा न कुरुते धीरः सर्वभूतेषु पापकम् ।
कर्मणा मनसा वाचा ब्रह्म संपद्यते तदा ॥ (44)

'"That patient person does not do anything wicked towards any being, in deeds, thoughts and words. He is then immersed in the brahman."'

या दुस्त्यजा दुर्मतिभिर्या न जीर्यति जीर्यतः ।
योऽसौ प्राणान्तिको रोगस्तां तृष्णां त्यजतः सुखम् ॥ (45)

'"He abandons the thirst[11] that is so difficult for the evil-minded to give up. Even when one ages, it is not digested. It is like a disease that brings an end to life. Having done this, he obtains happiness."'

अत्र पिङ्गलया गीता गाथाः श्रृयन्ति पार्थिव ।
यथा सा कृच्छ्रकालेऽपि लेभे धर्म सनातनम् ॥ (46)

'"O Lord of the Earth! On this, a verse sung by Pingala has been heard. This is about how she obtained eternal dharma at a time of hardship."'

संकेते पिङ्गला वेश्या कान्तेनासिद्धिनाकृता ।
अथ कृच्छ्रगता शान्तां बुद्धिमास्थापयत्तदा ॥ (47)

'"A prostitute named Pingala went to the place meant for a rendezvous but was rejected by her lover. In spite of facing that calamity, by resorting to her intelligence, she found peace."'

---

[10]There is a similarity with Bhagavat Gita 2.57.
[11]Desire.

पिङ्गलोवाच

उन्मत्ताहमनुन्मत्तं कान्तमन्ववसं चिरम् ।
अन्तिके रमणं सन्तं नैनमध्यगमं पुरा ॥ (48)

'"Pingala said, 'I have been crazy for a long time. In my madness, I have dwelt with my beloved. Because my beloved was nearby, I did not pursue the path of the virtuous earlier.'"

एकस्थूनं नवद्वारमपिधास्याम्यगारकम् ।
का हि कान्तमिहायान्तमयं कान्तेति मंस्यते ॥ (49)

'"This pillar has nine gates and I will cover it.[12] Even when he[13] approaches, which woman in this world regards him as a beloved?'"

अकामा: कामरूपेण धूर्ता नरकरूपिण: ।
न पुनर्वञ्चयिष्यन्ति प्रतिबुद्धास्मि जागृमि ॥ (50)

'"I have been thwarted in my desire. But, in the form of desire, those crafty ones[14] are like hell. They will not deceive me again. I know now and have woken up.'"

अनर्थोऽपि भवत्यर्थो दैवात्पूर्वकृतेन वा ।
संबुद्धाहं निराकारा नाहमद्याजितेन्द्रिया ॥ (51)

'"Depending on destiny and earlier deeds, adversity gives rise to prosperity. I have now conquered my senses and have obtained the realization that I am without form.'"

सुखं निराश: स्वपिति नैराश्यं परमं सुखम् ।
आशामनाशां कृत्वा हि सुखं स्वपिति पिङ्गला ॥ (52)

---

[12] The body is the pillar and the nine gates are the two eyes, two ears, one mouth, two nostrils, one anus and the genitals. It will be covered with knowledge.
[13] The brahman. The Sanskrit text does not gender brahman, but it is difficult to translate this into English without using the gender.
[14] Human lovers.

"'"I am without any hope and am happy. There is great happiness when there is nothing to hope. Having destroyed hope, Pingala sleeps in happiness."'"

भीष्म उवाच

एतैश्चान्यैश्च विप्रस्य हेतुमद्भि: प्रभाषितै: ।
पर्यवस्थापितो राजा सेनजिन्मुमुदे सुखम् ॥ (53)

Bhishma concluded, 'The learned brahmana spoke about these and other reasons. King Senajit was comforted and found joy and happiness.'

Thus ends the Pingala Gita.

12

PUTRA GITA

The Putra Gita occurs towards the beginning of Moksha Dharma Parva in Shanti Parva. It is a brief and single chapter, consisting of thirty-seven shlokas. In the course of this, Bhishma tells Yudhishthira about a conversation between a father and a son. Since the word for son is *putra*, this is known as the Putra Gita.

युधिष्ठिर उवाच

अतिक्रामति कालेऽस्मिन्सर्वभूतक्षयावहे ।
किं श्रेय: प्रतिपद्येत तन्मे ब्रूहि पितामह ॥ (1)

Yudhishthira asked, 'This time, which brings about the destruction of all beings, moves on. O Grandfather! What is the supreme benefit one should try for? Please tell me.'

भीष्म उवाच

अत्राप्युदाहरन्तीममितिहासं पुरातनम् ।
पितु: पुत्रेण संवादं तन्निबोध युधिष्ठिर ॥ (2)

Bhishma replied, 'In this connection, an ancient history is recounted. This is a conversation between a father and a son. O Yudhishthira! Listen to it.'

द्विजाते: कस्यचित्पार्थ स्वाध्यायनिरतस्य वै ।
बभूव पुत्रो मेधावी मेधावी नाम नामत: ॥ (3)

'O Partha! There was a certain dvija who was devoted to studying. He had an intelligent son named Medhavin.'[1]

सोऽब्रवीत्पितरं पुत्र: स्वाध्यायकरणे रतम् ।
मोक्षधर्मार्थकुशलो लोकतत्त्वविचक्षण: ॥ (4)

'The son was accomplished in the objective of moksha dharma and was also conversant with the true nature of the world. He spoke to his father, who was engaged in the act of studying.'

धीर: किं स्वित्तात कुर्यात्प्रजानन्निक्षिप्रं ह्यायुर्भ्रश्यते मानवानाम् ।
पितस्तदाचक्ष्व यथार्थयोगं ममानुपूर्व्या येन धर्मं चरेयम् ॥ (5)

'"O Father! Since the lifespan passes so quickly and men are destroyed, what should a patient person do? O Father! Tell me about proper yoga and about the due order in which one should follow dharma."'

वेदानधीत्य ब्रह्मचर्येण पुत्र पुत्रानिच्छेत्पावनार्थं पितृणाम् ।
अग्नीनाधाय विधिवच्चेष्टयज्ञो वनं प्रविश्याथ मुनिर्बुभूषेत् ॥ (6)

'The father replied, "O Son! In brahmacharya, one must study the Vedas. Then, one must desire sons, so that the ancestors can be purified. Next, one must accept the sacrificial fire and perform sacrifices, in accordance with the prescribed rites. Finally, one must enter the forest and strive to adorn oneself as a hermit."'

पुत्र उवाच

एवमभ्याहते लोके समन्तात्परिवारिते ।
अमोघासु पतन्तीषु किं धीर इव भाषसे ॥ (7)

'The son asked, "The world is surrounded from all sides and is afflicted. A fall is certain. How can you speak with such patience?"'

---

[1] The word *'medhavin'* means learned or intelligent.

पितोवाच

कथमभ्याहतोलोक: केन वा परिवारित: ।
अमोघा: का: पतन्तीह किं नु भीषयसीव माम् ॥ (8)

'The father replied, "How is the world afflicted? By what is it surrounded? Why is a fall certain? Why are you scaring me?"'

पुत्र उवाच

मृत्युनाभ्याहतो लोको जरया परिवारित: ।
अहोरात्रा: पतन्त्येते ननु कस्मान्न बुध्यसे ॥ (9)

'The son said, "The world is afflicted by death. It is surrounded by old age. Day and night, there is downfall. How can you not comprehend this?"'

यथाहमेतज्जानामि न मृत्युस्तिष्ठतीति ह ।
सोऽहं कथं प्रतीक्षिष्ये जालेनेपिहितश्चरन् ॥ (10)

'"I know that death does not wait for anyone.[2] How can I wait for it, as if my feet are bound in that net?"'

रात्र्यां रात्र्यां व्यतीतायामायुरल्पतरं यदा ।
गाधोदके मत्स्य इव सुखं विन्देत कस्तदा ।
तदेव बन्ध्यं दिवसमिति विद्याद्विचक्षण: ॥ (11)

'"As one night follows another night, the lifespan is decreased. Being like a fish in shallow water, how can one then obtain happiness? The discriminating person knows that every day is barren."'

अनवाप्तेषु कामेषु मृत्युरभ्योति मानवम् ।
शष्पाणीव विचिन्वन्तमन्यत्रगतमानसम् ।
वृकीवोरणमासाद्य मृत्युरादाय गच्छति ॥ (12)

'"Before all desires are satisfied, a human encounters death. It is as if a ram is inattentive and is roaming around, seeking out young grass, when a she-wolf grabs him and conveys him to death."'

---

[2] Death touches everyone.

अद्यैव कुरु यच्छ्रेयो मा त्वा कालोऽत्यगादयम् ।
अकृतेष्वेव कार्येषु मृत्युवैं संप्रकर्षति ॥ (13)

'"Do what is best today, lest you are overtaken by time. Death attracts, even if tasks are left incomplete."'

श्व:कार्यमद्य कुर्वीत पूर्वाह्णे चापराह्णिकम् ।
न हि प्रतीक्षते मृत्युः कृतं वास्य न वा कृतम् ।
को हि जानाति कस्याद्य मृत्युसेना निवेक्ष्यते ॥ (14)

'"Tomorrow's task should be done today, the afternoon's in the forenoon. Death does not wait to see if a task has been done or is yet undone. Who knows if he will be glanced at by death's soldiers today?"'

युवैव धर्मशील: स्यादनिमित्तं हि जीवितम् ।
कृते धर्मे भवेत्कीर्तिरिह प्रेत्य च वै सुखम् ॥ (15)

'"When one is young, one must accept the pursuit of dharma as the only reason for remaining alive.[3] Acting in accordance with dharma, one obtains fame in this world and happiness after death."'

मोहेन हि समाविष्ट: पुत्रदारार्थमुद्यत: ।
कृत्वा कार्यमकार्यं वा पुष्टिमेषां प्रयच्छति ॥ (16)

'"Overcome by delusion, one strives for the sake of sons and wives. In an attempt to provide them with sustenance, one performs desirable and undesirable acts."'

तं पुत्रपशुसंमत्तं व्यासक्तमनसं नरम् ।
सुप्तं व्याघ्रो महौघो वा मृत्युरादाय गच्छति ॥ (17)

'"A man thinks in his mind that sons and animals are important and is devoted to this. While he is thus asleep, death seizes him, like an extremely powerful tiger."'

---

[3] Instead of going through the four ashramas, which is what the father had suggested.

संचिन्वानकमेवैकं कामानामवितृप्तकम् ।
व्याघ्रः पशुमिवादाय मृत्युरादाय गच्छति ॥ (18)

'"He has still not been satisfied by seeking out objects of desire. Nevertheless, like a tiger grabbing an animal, death takes him away and departs."'

इदं कृतमिदं कार्यमिदमन्यत्कृताकृतम् ।
एवमीहासुखासक्तं कृतान्तः कुरुते वशे ॥ (19)

'"He is still thinking about the tasks that have been done, those which remain undone and those which have partly been done. While he is attached to happiness in this world, he comes under the subjugation of the Destroyer."'

कृतानां फलमप्राप्तं कर्मणां कर्मसङ्गिनम् ।
क्षेत्रापणगृहासक्तं मृत्युरादाय गच्छति ॥ (20)

'"This happens even before he has obtained the fruits of the karma that has been completed. He is attached to the field, the shop and the home and attached to karma, but death seizes him and departs."'

मृत्युर्जरा च व्याधिश्च दुःखं चानेककारणम् ।
अनुषक्तं यदा देहे किं स्वस्थ इव तिष्ठसि ॥ (21)

'"There is death, old age and disease and many other reasons for misery. All of them dwell in the body. How can you then remain as if you are healthy?"'

जातमेवान्तकोऽन्ताय जरा चान्वेति देहिनम् ।
अनुषक्ता द्वयेनैते भावाः स्थावरजङ्गमाः ॥ (22)

'"From the moment a person has been born, death and old age search him out, to bring about his end. Everything, mobile and immobile, is confronted by these two."'

मृत्योर्वा गृहमेवैतद्या ग्रामे वसतो रति: ।
देवानामेष वै गोष्ठो यदरण्यमिति श्रुति: ॥ (23)

'"The Shrutis have said that the pleasure[4] from attachment to dwelling in homes in villages and habitations is just like death. However, this can be contained in the forest."'

निबन्धनी रज्जुरेषा या ग्रामे वसतो रति: ।
छित्त्वैनां सुकृतो यान्ति नैनां छिन्दन्ति दुष्कृत: ॥ (24)

'"The attachment to residing in villages binds one down with ropes. The performer of good deeds can sever these. But the performer of evil deeds cannot sever these."'

न हिंसयति य: प्राणान्मनोवाक्कायहेतुभि: ।
जीवितार्थापनयनै: कर्मभिर्न स बध्यते ॥ (25)

'"A person who does not unnecessarily injure living beings through thoughts, words and deeds is not destroyed by those who seek to take away life and artha. He is not tied down by his karma."'

न मृत्युसेनामायान्तीं जातु कश्चित्प्रबाधते ।
ऋते सत्यमसंत्याज्यं सत्ये ह्यमृतमाश्रितम् ॥ (26)

'"When the soldiers of death advance, nothing can withstand them, with the exception of truth and the abandonment of falsehood. There is amrita in truth."'

तस्मात्सत्यव्रताचार: सत्ययोगपरायण: ।
सत्यागम: समो दान्त: सत्येनैवान्तकं जयेत् ॥ (27)

'"Therefore, one must follow the vow of truth and be devoted to the yoga of truth. There is delight, peace and tranquillity in truth. It is through truth that one triumphs over the Destroyer."'

---

[4]There is a problem with the text of the CE. It says *devaanam* (belonging to the gods), which makes it impossible to understand it. We have taken it as *devanam* and translated it as 'pleasure'.

अमृतं चैव मृत्युश्च द्वयं देहे प्रतिष्ठितम् ।
मृत्युमापद्यते मोहात्सत्येनापद्यतेऽमृतम् ॥ (28)

'"Both immortality and death exist in the body. Through delusion, one obtains death. Through truth, one obtains immortality."'

सोऽहं ह्यहिंस्र: सत्यार्थी कामक्रोधबहिष्कृत: ।
समदु:खसुख: क्षेमी मृत्युं हास्याम्यमर्त्यवत् ॥ (29)

'"That is the reason I do not cause injury and am pursuing the truth. I have cast aside desire and anger. I am impartial to happiness and unhappiness. I am tranquil and look on death as if I am immortal."'

शान्तियज्ञरतो दान्तो ब्रह्मयज्ञे स्थितो मुनि: ।
वाङ्मन:कर्मयज्ञश्च भविष्याम्युदगायने ॥ (30)

'"I will become a controlled hermit who will be devoted to sacrifices for peace, sacrifices for the brahman, sacrifices through words and sacrifices through deeds, thereby making myself wake up."'

पशुयज्ञै: कथं हिंस्रैर्मादृशो यष्टुमर्हति ।
अन्तवद्भिरूत प्राज्ञ: क्षेत्रयज्ञै: पिशाचवत् ॥ (31)

'"How can one perform such violent sacrifices that involve the slaughter of animals? How can a wise person act like a pishacha,[5] injure himself internally, and observe the sacrifices of kshatriyas?"'

यस्य वाङ्मनसी स्यातां सम्यक्प्रणिहिते सदा ।
तपस्त्यागश्च योगश्च स वै सर्वमवाप्नुयात् ॥ (32)

'"If a person is always single-minded in his words, thoughts, austerities, renunciation and yoga and follows these well, he obtains everything."'

नास्ति विद्यासमं चक्षुर्नास्ति विद्यासमं बलम् ।
नास्ति रागसमं दु:खं नास्ति त्यागसमं सुखम् ॥ (33)

---

[5] Pishachas are beings that live on flesh.

'"There is no sight that is equal to knowledge. There is no strength that is equal to knowledge. There is no misery that is like that of attachment. There is no happiness that is equal to renunciation."'

आत्मन्येवात्मना जात आत्मनिष्ठोऽप्रजोऽपि वा ।
आत्मन्येव भविष्यामि न मां तारयति प्रजा ॥ (34)

'"My atman has been generated from the atman.[6] Though I have no offspring, I will base myself on the atman.[7] My crossing over will come from the atman, not from offspring."'

नैतादृशं ब्राह्मणस्यास्ति वित्तं यथैकता समता सत्यता च ।
शीले स्थितिर्दण्डनिधानमार्जवं ततस्ततश्चोपरमः क्रियाभ्यः ॥ (35)

'"There are no riches for a brahmana that are equal to solitude, impartiality and truth. Basing himself on good conduct, not chastising anyone, resorting to uprightness, he performs the supreme rites."'

किं ते धनैर्बान्धवैर्वापि किं ते किं ते दारैर्ब्राह्मण यो मरिष्यति ।
आत्मानमन्विच्छ गुहां प्रविष्टं पितामहास्ते क्व गताः पिता च ॥ (36)

'"What do you have to do with riches? What do you have to do with relatives? What do you have to do with wives? O Brahmana! They will all die. Your atman is hidden inside a cave. Enter and seek it out. Where have your grandfather and your father gone?"'[8]

भीष्म उवाच

पुत्रस्यैतद्वचः श्रुत्वा यथाकार्षीत्पिता नृप ।
तथा त्वमपि वर्तस्व सत्यधर्मपरायणः ॥ (37)

---

[6] The first atman refers to the jivatman and the second atman to the paramatman, the brahman.

[7] The atman here stands for the brahman. Medhavin will shun the standard prescription of first having an offspring before embarking on vanaprastha and sannyasa.

[8] Reiterating the point that they are mortal.

Bhishma concluded, 'O King! Hearing the words of the son, the father acted accordingly. You should also conduct yourself in that way, observing the dharma of truth.'

Thus ends the Putra Gita.

13

SHAMYAKA GITA

The Shamyaka Gita occurs towards the beginning of Moksha Dharma Parva in Shanti Parva. It is a brief and single chapter, consisting of twenty-three shlokas. It is named after a chant by a brahmana named Shamyaka. A brahmana told Bhishma about Shamyaka's chant. What is unclear is whether Shamyaka himself told Bhishma this, or whether it was another brahmana who told Bhishma what Shamyaka had said. We have taken it as the former since that is simpler.

युधिष्ठिर उवाच

धनिनो वाधना ये च वर्तयन्ते स्वतन्त्रिण: ।
सुखदु:खागमस्तेषां क: कथं वा पितामह ॥ (1)

Yudhishthira asked, 'O Grandfather! The rich and the poor follow their own independent conduct. How, and from where, do they face happiness and unhappiness?'

भीष्म उवाच

अत्राप्युदाहरन्तीममितिहासं पुरातनम् ।
शम्याकेन विमुक्तेन गीतं शान्तिगतेन ह ॥ (2)

Bhishma replied, 'In this connection, an ancient history is recounted. Shamyaka, who was liberated and had obtained peace, sung a song.'

अब्रवीन्मां पुरा कश्चिद्ब्राह्मणस्त्यागमाश्रितः ।
क्लिश्यमानः कुदारेण कुचौलेन बुभुक्षया ॥ (3)

'"In ancient times, a brahmana who had renounced told me this. He was afflicted because of a bad wife, whose conduct was bad. He was also suffering from hunger."'

उत्पन्नमिह लोके वै जन्मप्रभृति मानवम् ।
विविधान्युपवर्तन्ते दुःखानि च सुखानि च ॥ (4)

'"Since the time a man is born in this world, many different kinds of joy and sorrow are faced by him."'

तयोरेकतरे मार्गे यद्येनमभिसंनयेत् ।
न सुखं प्राप्य संहृष्येन्न दुःखं प्राप्य संज्वरेत् ॥ (5)

'"If he is conveyed along either of these paths,[1] then he will not be delighted on obtaining joy or be anxious on obtaining sorrow."'

न वै चरसि यच्छ्रेय आत्मनो वा यदीहसे ।
अकामात्मापि हि सदा धुरमुद्यम्य चैव हि ॥ (6)

'"On this earth, you are not following what is best for yourself. Even though you have no desire, you are bearing a heavy burden."'

अकिंचनः परिपतन्सुखमास्वादयिष्यसि ।
अकिंचनः सुखं शेते समुत्तिष्ठति चैव हि ॥ (7)

'"If you roam around thinking all this to be insignificant, you will obtain happiness. A person with nothing sleeps and awakes in happiness."'

आकिंचन्यं सुखं लोके पथ्यं शिवमनामयम् ।
अनमित्रमथो ह्येतदुर्लभं सुलभं सताम् ॥ (8)

'"Not possessing anything is the medication for happiness in the world. This is healthy and auspicious. This path is extremely difficult

---

[1] Conveyed by an external force, destiny.

to achieve, even for those who have no enemies.[2] But it is easily obtained by those who are virtuous."'

अकिंचनस्य शुद्धस्य उपपन्नस्य सर्वशः ।
अवेक्षमाणस्त्रींल्लोकान् तुल्यमुपलक्षये ॥ (9)

"'Glancing at the three worlds, I do not find anyone with possessions who is equal to a pure person who possesses nothing.'"

आकिंचन्यं च राज्यं च तुलया समतोलयम् ।
अत्यरिच्यत दारिद्र्यं राज्यादपि गुणाधिकम् ॥ (10)

"'I weighed possessing nothing and possessing a kingdom on a balance and found that poverty surpassed the kingdom in qualities.'"

आकिंचन्ये च राज्ये च विशेषः सुमहानयम् ।
नित्योद्विग्नो हि धनवान्मृत्योरास्यगतो यथा ॥ (11)

"'Specifically, there is a great difference between possessing nothing and a kingdom. A prosperous person is always anxious, as if he is in the jaws of death.'"

नैवास्याग्निर्न चादित्यं न मृत्युर्न च दस्यवः ।
प्रभवन्ति धनज्यानिनिर्मुक्तस्य निराशिषः ॥ (12)

"'A fire, the sun, death and bandits have no power over a person who has freed himself from riches and is without hopes.'"

तं वै सदा कामचरमनुपस्तीर्णशायिनम् ।
बाहूपधानं शाम्यन्तं प्रशंसन्ति दिवौकसः ॥ (13)

"'He wanders around as he wills and lies down on the bare ground, using his arms as a pillow. He has obtained tranquillity and is praised by the residents of heaven.'"

धनवान्क्रोधलोभाभ्यामाविष्टो नष्टचेतनः ।
तिर्यगीक्षः शुष्कमुखः पापको भ्रुकुटीमुखः ॥ (14)

---

[2] But have desire.

"'A wealthy person is afflicted by both anger and avarice and loses his senses. He is wicked, casts sideways glances, has a frown on his face and his mouth is dry.'"

निर्दशंश्चाधरोष्ठं च क्रुद्धो दारुणभाषिता ।
कस्तमिच्छेत्परिद्रष्टुं दातुमिच्छति चेन्महीम् ॥ (15)

"'He bites his lower lips with his teeth. He is enraged and terrible in speech. Even if he desires to give the earth away, who will wish to look at him?'"

श्रिया ह्यभीक्ष्णं संवासो मोहयत्यविचक्षणम् ।
सा तस्य चित्तं हरति शारदाभ्रमिवानिल: ॥ (16)

"'Dwelling in continuous prosperity deludes a person who is not very discerning. It robs him of his senses, like the wind bearing away autumn clouds.'"

अथैनं रूपमानश्च धनमानश्च विन्दति ।
अभिजातोऽस्मि सिद्धोऽस्मि नास्मि केवलमानुष: ।
इत्येभि: कारणैस्तस्य त्रिभिश्चित्तं प्रसिच्यते ॥ (17)

"'He finds delight in, "I am handsome. I have wealth. I possess noble birth. I am successful. I am not an ordinary man." His consciousness is sprinkled with these three reasons.'"[3]

सा प्रसिक्तमना भोगान्विसृज्य पितृसंचितान् ।
परिक्षीण: परस्वानामादानं साधु मन्यते ॥ (18)

"'Thus sprinkled and attached to objects of pleasure, he is deprived of the riches his ancestors accumulated. When these have decayed, he thinks it is virtuous to appropriate the property of others.'"

तमतिक्रान्तमर्यादमाददानं ततस्तत: ।
प्रतिषेधन्ति राजानो लुब्धा मृगमिवेषुभि: ॥ (19)

---

[3]Probably beauty, wealth and nobility, considering success is not an independent reason.

'"He transgresses boundaries and seizes here and there. The kings then restrain the greedy person, like deer are with arrows."'

एवमेतानि दुःखानि तानि तानीह मानवम् ।
विविधान्युपवर्तन्ते गात्रसंस्पर्शजानि च ॥ (20)

'"These are the many different kinds of sorrows that then touch the man's body in this world."'

तेषां परमदुःखानां बुद्ध्या भैषज्यमाचरेत् ।
लोकधर्म समाज्ञाय ध्रुवाणामध्रुवैः सह ॥ (21)

'"Afflicted by these supreme miseries, he realizes that he needs medication and acts accordingly. He abandons the dharma of the world,[4] with everything that is temporary and permanent."'

नात्यक्त्वा सुखमाप्नोति नात्यक्त्वा विन्दते परम् ।
नात्यक्त्वा चाभयः शेते त्यक्त्वा सर्व सुखी भव ॥ (22)

'"Without renunciation, one cannot obtain happiness. Without renunciation, one cannot obtain the supreme. Without renunciation, one cannot sleep or obtain freedom from fear. Therefore, renounce and be happy in every way."'

इत्येतद्ध्रास्तिनपुरे ब्राह्मणेनोपवर्णितम् ।
शम्याकेन पुरा मह्यं तस्मात्त्यागः परो मतः ॥ (23)

'This is what the brahmana Shamyaka told me in earlier times in Hastinapura. Therefore, it is the view that renunciation is supreme.'

Thus ends the Shamyaka Gita.

---

[4] The pursuit of desire. Everything in the world is temporary and transient, even if it is seemingly permanent.

14

MANKI AND BODHYA GITAS

The Manki Gita is a single chapter with sixty-one shlokas in Moksha Dharma Parva of Shanti Parva, immediately following the Shamyaka Gita. Bhishma tells Yudhishthira the story of Manki and what Manki recited. After that bit is over, there is a shloka chanted by King Janaka, followed by five shlokas that constitute the Bodhya Gita, spoken by a rishi named Bodhya to King Nahusha.

युधिष्ठिर उवाच

ईहमानः समारम्भान्यदि नासादयेद्धनम् ।
धनतृष्णाभिभूतश्च किं कुर्वन्सुखमाप्नुयात् ॥ (1)

Yudhishthira said, 'If a person embarks on sacrifices and does not possess riches,[1] and the thirst for riches overcomes him, what can he possibly do to obtain happiness?'

भीष्म उवाच

सर्वसाम्यमनायासः सत्यवाक्यं च भारत ।
निर्वेदश्चाविवित्सा च यस्य स्यात्स सुखी नरः ॥ (2)

Bhishma replied, 'O Descendant of the Bharata Lineage! A person who looks on everything amiably, a person who does not make an

---

[1] Required for performing the sacrifices and rites.

effort,[2] a person who is truthful in speech, a person who disregards worldly objects and a person who pursues knowledge—such a man is indeed happy.'

एतान्येव पदान्याहुः पञ्च वृद्धाः प्रशान्तये ।
एष स्वर्गश्च धर्मश्च सुखं चानुत्तमं सताम् ॥ (3)

'The aged ones have said that these five are the steps towards tranquillity. This is heaven. This is dharma. This is happiness. This is supreme virtue.'

अत्राप्युदाहरन्तीममितिहासं पुरातनम् ।
निर्वेदान्मङ्किना गीतं तन्निबोध युधिष्ठिर ॥ (4)

'In this connection, an ancient history is recounted, about what Manki, who was indifferent to worldly possessions, had sung. O Yudhishthira! Listen to it.'

ईहमानो धनं मङ्किर्भग्नेहश्च पुनः पुनः ।
केनचिद्धनशेषेण क्रीतवान्दम्यगोयुगम् ॥ (5)

'Manki was repeatedly frustrated in his pursuit of riches. Finally, with some riches that were left, he bought two bulls and a yoke.'

सुसंबद्धौ तु तौ दम्यौ दमनायाभिनिःसृतौ ।
आसीनमुष्ट्रं मध्येन सहसैवाभ्यधावताम् ॥ (6)

'Once, he bound them to the yoke and took them out, so as to control them.[3] A camel was lying down in the middle and they suddenly rushed towards it.'

तयोः संप्राप्तयोरुष्ट्रः स्कन्धदेशममर्षणः ।
उत्थायोत्क्षिप्य तौ दम्यौ प्रससार महाजवः ॥ (7)

---

[2]For possessions and objects of desire.
[3]That is, to train them for domestication.

'They approached and fell down on the camel's neck. The enraged camel arose. It ran at great speed, dragging the two bulls with it.'

ह्रियमाणौ तु तौ दम्यौ तेनोष्ट्रेण प्रमाथिना ।
ह्रियमाणौ च संप्रेक्ष्य मङ्किस्तत्राब्रवीदिदम् ॥ (8)

'Dragged along by the camel, the two bulls were injured. On seeing that they were about to die, Manki spoke these words.'

न चैवाविहितं शक्यं दक्षेणापीहितुं धनम् ।
युक्तेन श्रद्धया सम्यगीहां समनुतिष्ठता ॥ (9)

'"If it has not been ordained, even an accomplished person is incapable of obtaining wealth, despite making every effort, faithfully and well."'

कृतस्य पूर्वं चानर्थैर्युक्तस्याप्यनुतिष्ठतः ।
इमं पश्यत संगत्या मम दैवमुपप्लवम् ॥ (10)

'"Earlier, I have tried many ways of obtaining riches. But behold the calamity that destiny has inflicted upon me."'

उद्यम्योद्यम्य मे दम्यौ विषमेणेव गच्छति ।
उत्क्षिप्य काकतालीयमुन्माथेनेव जम्बुकः ॥ (11)

'"My two bulls have been held aloft and are being dragged over uneven terrain. They are being raised up and flung down, as if a crow is tearing at palm fruit or rose apples."'[4]

मनी वोष्ट्रस्य लम्बेते प्रियौ वत्सतरौ मम ।
शुद्धं हि दैवमेवेदमतो नैवास्ति पौरुषम् ॥ (12)

---

[4]This shloka is not very clear and the translation is somewhat contrived. There is a nuance that the translation does not capture. The text uses the word '*kakataliya*', which means accident, and there is a story around this. A crow (*kaka*) sat on a palm tree and a ripe palm fruit (*tala*) fell down. The fruit fell down because it was ripe and had nothing to do with the crow. But this accidental or coincidental fall is mistakenly ascribed to the crow sitting on the tree.

'"My beloved calves are dangling from the camel's neck like jewels. This is purely because of destiny and I know that manliness[5] does not exist."'

यदि वाप्युपपद्येत पौरुषं नाम कर्हिचित् ।
अन्विष्यमाणं तदपि दैवमेवावतिष्ठते ॥ (13)

'"Even if something by the name of manliness exists, if one examines this, one will find that this, too, is based on destiny."'

तस्मान्निर्वेद एवेह गन्तव्यः सुखमीप्सता ।
सुखं स्वपिति निर्विण्णो निराशश्चार्थसाधने ॥ (14)

'"Therefore, someone who wishes to advance towards happiness must be indifferent. A person who shuns all hope of attaining riches and is non-attached sleeps happily."'

अहो सम्यक्शुकेनोक्तं सर्वतः परिमुच्यता ।
प्रतिष्ठता महारण्यं जनकस्य निवेशनात् ॥ (15)

'"When Shuka freed himself from everything and went to reside in the great forest, away from his father's residence, he spoke well."'[6]

यः कामान्प्राप्नुयात्सर्वान्यश्चैनान्केवलांस्त्यजेत् ।
प्रापनात्सर्वकामानां परित्यागो विशिष्यते ॥ (16)

'""Between a person who satisfies all his desires and a person who only renounces, the one who renounces is superior to the one who obtains all the objects of desire.""'[7]

नान्तं सर्वविवित्सानां गतपूर्वोऽस्ति कश्चन ।
शरीरे जीविते चैव तृष्णा मन्दस्य वर्धते ॥ (17)

---

[5] To be understood as vigour and enterprise, that is, human endeavour, not in the narrower sense of virility.
[6] The famous Shuka is Vedavyasa's son. The insertion of a quote ascribed to Shuka, therefore, suggests a later interpolation.
[7] The text does not indicate it clearly, but this seems to be the end of the Shuka quote and it is Manki speaking again.

'"There is no end to all desires and one can never attain a state where they belong to the past. As long as he is alive, a foolish person's thirst increases."'

निवर्तस्व विवित्साभ्यः शाम्य निर्विद्य मामक ।
असकृच्चासि निकृतो न च निर्विद्यसे तनो ॥ (18)

'"Withdraw from desire. Let tranquillity pervade me. Having been deceived by what should not be pursued, it should no longer pervade my body."'

यदि नाहं विनाश्यस्ते यद्येवं रमसे मया ।
मा मां योजय लोभेन वृथा त्वं वित्तकामुक ॥ (19)

'"O One Who Is Desirous of Riches![8] If I am not going to be destroyed and if you wish to take delight in me, then do not engage me in this futile path of greed."'

सञ्चितं सञ्चितं द्रव्यं नष्टं तव पुनः पुनः ।
कदा विमोक्ष्यसे मूढ धनेहां धनकामुक ॥ (20)

'"You have repeatedly accumulated riches, and they have repeatedly been destroyed. O Stupid One! O One Who Is Desirous of Riches! When will you free yourself from this desire for wealth?"'

अहो नु मम बालिश्यं योऽहं क्रीडनकस्तव ।
किं नैव जातु पुरुषः परेषां प्रेष्यतामियात् ॥ (21)

'"Shame on my folly. This has led me to becoming a puppet in your hands. It is in this way that men who are born become the servants of others."'

न पूर्वे नापरे जातु कामानामन्तमापुनुवन् ।
त्यक्त्वा सर्वसमारम्भान्प्रतिबुद्धोऽस्मि जागृमि ॥ (22)

'"No person born earlier has ever obtained an end to desire, nor will any person who is born later. Having abandoned all efforts, I have now understood and am awake."'

---

[8]Manki is addressing himself.

नूनं ते हृदयं काम वज्रसारमयं दृढम् ।
यदनर्थशताविष्टं शतधा न विदीर्यते ॥ (23)

'"O Desire! It is certain that your heart is as firm as a diamond. That is the reason why, though it is afflicted by one hundred calamities, it does not shatter into one hundred fragments."'

त्यजामि काम त्वां चैव यच्च किंचित्प्रियं तव ।
तवाहं सुखमन्विच्छन्नात्मन्युपलभे सुखम् ॥ (24)

'"O Desire! I will abandon you and everything that is agreeable to you. Severing what makes you feel happy, I will search out happiness."'

काम जानामि ते मूलं संकल्पात्किल जायसे ।
न त्वां संकल्पयिष्यामि समूलो न भविष्यसि ॥ (25)

'"O Desire! I know your foundation. You are certainly born from resolutions. If I do not have any resolutions, you will not have any foundations."'

ईहा धनस्य न सुखा लब्ध्वा चिन्ता च भूयसी ।
लब्धनाशो यथा मृत्युर्लब्धं भवति वा न वा ॥ (26)

'"Wealth does not yield happiness in this world. Then again, if obtained, it leads to a lot of anxiety. If it is destroyed after having been obtained, that is like death, irrespective of whether one has obtained it or not."'

परेत्य यो न लभते ततो दुःखतरं नु किम् ।
न च तुष्यति लब्धेन भूय एव च मार्गति ॥ (27)

'"Nor does one know whether it can be obtained later. There is nothing that is a greater misery than its going away after it has been obtained. One is not satisfied when it has been obtained. Instead, one looks for paths to enhance it."'

अनुतर्षुल एवार्थः स्वादु गाङ्गमिवोदकम् ।
मद्विलापनमेतत्तु प्रतिबुद्धोऽस्मि सन्त्यज ॥ (28)

'"Riches are like the tasty waters of the Ganga, since one keeps hankering for more. This is also the reason for my lamentation. I have now understood and will abandon it."'

य इमं मामकं देहं भूतग्रामः समाश्रितः ।
स यात्वितो यथाकामं वसतां वा यथासुखम् ॥ (29)

'"It[9] has sought refuge in the aggregation of elements in my body. As it wishes, let it dwell here, or wherever else it finds happiness."'[10]

न युष्मास्विह मे प्रीतिः कामलोभानुसारिषु ।
तस्मादुत्सृज्य सर्वान्वः सत्यमेवाश्रयाम्यहम् ॥ (30)

'"I have no affection for any of you[11] who follow desire and avarice. Therefore, I am abandoning all of you. I will seek refuge with truth alone."'

सर्वभूतान्यहं देहे पश्यन्मनसि चात्मनः ।
योगे बुद्धिं श्रुते सत्त्वं मनो ब्रह्मणि धारयन् ॥ (31)

'"My atman will behold all the elements in the body and my mind. I will base myself in yoga, intelligence, learning and spirit and uphold the brahman in my mind."'

विहरिष्याम्यनासक्तः सुखी लोकानिरामयः ।
यथा मा त्वं पुननैवं दुःखेषु प्रणिधास्यसि ॥ (32)

'"I will happily roam the worlds, without any attachment and without any disease, so that you can no longer try to immerse me in misery again."'[12]

त्वया हि मे प्रणुन्नस्य गतिरन्या न विद्यते ।
तृष्णाशोकश्रमाणां हि त्वं काम प्रभवः सदा ॥ (33)

---

[9]Desire.
[10]Since Manki has renounced desire, desire can do whatever it wants.
[11]Any other sentiments.
[12]Addressing himself. Alternatively, addressing desire.

"'I have been agitated by you and there is no other path left. O Desire! Thirst, sorrow and exertion have always been manifestations of your powers.'"

धननाशोऽधिकं दु:खं मन्ये सर्वमहत्तरम् ।
ज्ञातयो ह्यवमन्यन्ते मित्राणि च धनच्युतम् ॥ (34)

"'I think that the sorrow that results from the destruction of riches is the greatest of all miseries. Kin and friends disrespect a person who has been separated from his wealth.'"

अवज्ञानसहस्रैस्तु दोषा: कष्टतराधने ।
धने सुखकला या च सापि दु:खैर्विधीयते ॥ (35)

"'Other than disrespect, in the absence of riches, there are one thousand other taints that are more severe. However, even though riches provide a little bit of happiness, it is mingled with a great deal of unhappiness.'"

धनमस्येति पुरुषं पुरा निघ्नन्ति दस्यव: ।
क्लिश्यन्ति विविधैर्दण्डैर्नित्यमुद्वेजयन्ति च ॥ (36)

"'In everyone's sight, bandits slay the person who possesses riches. They torment him with many kinds of punishment and always cause him anxiety.'"

मन्दलोलुपता दु:खमिति बुद्धं चिरान्मया ।
यद्यदालम्बसे काम तत्तदेवानुरुध्यसे ॥ (37)

"'After a long period of time, I have realized the stupidity and misery that greed leads to. O Desire! You make me follow whatever you get addicted to.'"

अतत्त्वज्ञोऽसि बालश्च दुस्तोषोऽपूरणोऽनल: ।
नैव त्वं वेत्थ सुलभं नैव त्वं वेत्थ दुर्लभम् ॥ (38)

"'Thus, you do not know the truth. You are foolish. You are difficult to satisfy. You are never satiated. You are like a fire. You do not consider whether something is easy to obtain or difficult to obtain. You do not know.'"

पातालमिव दुष्पूरो मां दु:खैर्योक्तुमिच्छसि ।
नाहमद्य समावेष्टुं शक्य: काम पुनस्त्वया ॥ (39)

'"You are as difficult to fill as the nether regions. You wish to unite me with misery. O Desire! From today, I am incapable of residing with you again."'

निर्वेदमहमासाद्य द्रव्यनाशाद्यदृच्छया ।
निर्वृतिं परमां प्राप्य नाद्य कामान्विचिन्तये ॥ (40)

'"I am free from possessions now. As they will, let the objects be destroyed. I have obtained supreme non-attachment now. I no longer think about desire."'

अतिक्लेशान्सहामीह नाहं बुध्याम्यबुद्धिमान् ।
निकृतो धननाशेन शये सर्वाङ्गविज्वर: ॥ (41)

'"Because of you, I suffered greatly earlier. I now know myself to be intelligent. Because of the destruction of the riches, I have been deceived. But I can lie down now, without any fever in any of my limbs."'

परित्यजामि काम त्वां हित्वा सर्वमनोगती: ।
न त्वं मया पुन: काम नस्योतेनेव रंस्यते ॥ (42)

'"O Desire! I am casting you away and abandoning all my mental inclinations towards you. O Desire! You will not associate with me or find pleasure in me again."'

क्षमिष्येऽक्षममाणानां न हिंसिष्ये च हिंसित: ।
द्वेष्यमुक्त: प्रियं वक्ष्याम्यनादृत्य तदप्रियम् ॥ (43)

'"I will forgive even those who should not be forgiven. I will not cause violence, even if there is violence against me. I will speak pleasantly to those who hate me and ignore their disagreeable words."'

तृप्त: स्वस्थेन्द्रियो नित्यं यथालब्धेन वर्तयन् ।
न सकामं करिष्यामि त्वामहं शत्रुमात्मन: ॥ (44)

"'I will be satisfied and my senses will be at ease. I will always sustain myself on what has been obtained. You are an enemy of my atman and I will not satisfy your wishes.'"

निर्वेदं निर्वृतिं तृप्तिं शान्तिं सत्यं दमं क्षमाम् ।
सर्वभूतदयां चैव विद्धि मां शरणागतम् ॥ (45)

"'Know that lack of possessions, withdrawal, satisfaction, tranquillity, truth, self-control, forgiveness and compassion towards all beings have now sought refuge with me.'"

तस्मात्कामश्च लोभश्च तृष्णा कार्पण्यमेव च ।
त्यजन्तु मां प्रतिष्ठन्तं सत्त्वस्थो ह्यस्मि सांप्रतम् ॥ (46)

"'Therefore, desire, avarice, thirst and miserliness have been cast away. I have based myself on my spirit now.'"

प्रहाय कामं लोभं च क्रोधं पारुष्यमेव च ।
नाद्य लोभवशं प्राप्तो दुःखं प्राप्स्याम्यनात्मवान् ॥ (47)

"'I have abandoned desire, avarice, anger and harshness. Today, I will no longer come under the subjugation of greed and subject myself to misery.'"

यद्यत्यजति कामानां तत्सुखस्याभिपूर्यते ।
कामस्य वशगो नित्यं दुःखमेव प्रपद्यते ॥ (48)

"'Whoever casts aside desire is filled with happiness. Someone who is under the subjugation of desire is always confronted with misery.'"

कामान्व्युदस्य धुनुते यत्किंचित्पुरुषो रजः ।
कामक्रोधोद्भवं दुःखमहीररतिरेव च ॥ (49)

"'When a man casts aside the passions that result from desire, he abandons any rajas quality. Sorrow and other hardships always result from desire and anger.'"

एष ब्रह्मप्रविष्टोऽहं ग्रीष्मे शीतमिव ह्रदम् ।
शाम्यामि परिनिर्वामि सुखमासे च केवलम् ॥ (50)

'"I have now entered the brahman, like entering a cool lake during the summer. I have calmed myself. I have withdrawn myself. I only enjoy happiness."'

यच्च कामसुखं लोके यच्च दिव्यं महत्सुखम् ।
तृष्णाक्षयसुखस्यैते नार्हतः षोडशीं कलाम् ॥ (51)

'"The happiness one obtains in the world from the satisfaction of desire and the great happiness one enjoys in heaven are worth less than one-sixteenth of the happiness one obtains from the extinguishing of thirst."'

आत्मना सप्तमं कामं हत्वा शत्रुमिवोत्तमम् ।
प्राप्यावध्यं ब्रह्मपुरं राजेव स्यामहं सुखी ॥ (52)

'"I have slain supreme enemies of the atman, desire being the seventh.[13] I have attained Brahma's indestructible city. I will be happy there, like a king."'

एतां बुद्धिं समास्थाय मङ्किर्निर्वेदमागतः ।
सर्वान्कामान्परित्यज्य प्राप्य ब्रह्म महत्सुखम् ॥ (53)

'Resorting to this intelligence, Manki became free from all possessions. He abandoned all desire and obtained great bliss with the brahman.'

दम्यनाशकृते मङ्किरमरत्वं किलागमत् ।
अच्छिनत्कামमूलं स तेन प्राप महत्सुखम् ॥ (54)

'Because the bulls had been destroyed, Manki obtained immortality. Having severed the foundation of desire, he obtained great happiness.'

अत्राप्युदाहरन्तीममितिहासं पुरातनम् ।
गीतं विदेहराजेन जनकेन प्रशाम्यता ॥ (55)

---

[13] Usually, six enemies are mentioned, and kama is one of the six. Since desire has been mentioned as the seventh, the other six are probably the five senses and the mind.

'In this connection, an ancient history is recounted. This is a song sung by Janaka, the king of Videha, who obtained tranquillity.'

अनन्तं बत मे वित्तं यस्य मे नास्ति किंचन ।
मिथिलायां प्रदीप्तायां न मे दह्यति किंचन ॥ (56)

'"Though I possess nothing, my wealth is infinite. Even if Mithila[14] is set ablaze, nothing that belongs to me will be consumed."'

अत्रैवोदाहरन्तीमं बोध्यस्य पदसंचयम् ।
निर्वेदं प्रति विन्यस्तं प्रतिबोध युधिष्ठिर ॥ (57)

'In this connection, there are also the lines that Bodhya, who attained the supreme objective, uttered about lack of possessions. O Yudhishthira! Understand this.'

बोध्यं दान्तमृषिं राजा नहुषः पर्यपृच्छत ।
निर्वेदाच्छान्तिमापन्नं शान्तं प्रज्ञानतर्पितम् ॥ (58)
उपदेशं महाप्राज्ञ शमस्योपदिशस्व मे ।
कां बुद्धिं समनुध्याय शान्तश्चरसि निर्वृतः ॥ (59)

'The self-controlled Rishi Bodhya was asked by King Nahusha, "You are without possessions. You have obtained tranquillity. You are at peace. You are full of wisdom. O Immensely Wise One! Instruct me about how one can obtain tranquillity. What intelligence should one resort to, so that one can withdraw and roam around in peace?"'

बोध्य उवाच

उपदेशेन वर्तामि नानुशास्मीह कंचन ।
लक्षणं तस्य वक्ष्येऽहं तत्स्वयं प्रविमृश्यताम् ॥ (60)

'Bodhya replied, "I follow the instructions of others, but never instruct anyone. I will tell you about the signs. You can then yourself reflect on those."'

---

[14]Mithila was the capital of Videha. This King Janaka is different from the King Janaka who was Sita's father. There is a story about Mithila having been burnt down. This single shloka constitutes Janaka's song.

पिङ्गला कुररः सर्पः सारङ्गान्वेषणं वने ।
इषुकारः कुमारी च षडेते गुरवो मम॥ (61)

"'My six preceptors are Pingala, the osprey, the snake, the bee that is searching in the forest, the one who makes arrows and the maiden.'"[15]

Thus ends the Manki and Bodhya Gitas.

---

[15] By excising shlokas, the CE leaves this dangling. Pingala was a prostitute who turned to asceticism after being spurned by her lover. The Pingala Gita has been translated earlier in this book. If an osprey desires meat and finds it, other ospreys snatch that piece of meat away. However, there was an osprey that did not desire any meat and was happy. The preceptor is that osprey. A snake is happy and worthy of emulation because it does not try to make a house for itself but lives in someone else's house instead. The bee searching for honey in the forest does not harm anyone. There is a story about a person who made arrows. He was so busy in his work that he did not even notice that the king was passing. There is another story about a maiden who roamed alone. Since she did not consort with others, there was no scope of a quarrel. Quarrels require two people. Bodhya recommends learning from these examples to be free of possessions and at peace.

15

AJAGARA GITA

The Ajagara Gita, not to be confused with Ajagara sub-parva in Aranyaka Parva, which is about King Nahusha, continues where the Manki and Bodhya Gitas left off, with Bhishma instructing Yudhishthira in Moksha Dharma Parva of Shanti Parva. In this single chapter of thirty-seven shlokas, Bhishma tells Yudhishthira about the conversation between Prahrada and Sage Ajagara.

युधिष्ठिर उवाच

केन वृत्तेन वृत्तज्ञ वीतशोकश्चरेन्महीम् ।
किं च कुर्वन्नरो लोके प्राप्नोति परमां गतिम् ॥ (1)

Yudhishthira asked, 'O One Who Knows about Conduct! What is the conduct through which one can roam around on earth, with sorrow dispelled? What should a man do in this world, so as to attain the supreme objective?'

भीष्म उवाच

अत्राप्युदाहरन्तीममितिहासं पुरातनम् ।
प्रह्लादस्य च संवादं मुनेराजगरस्य च ॥ (2)

Bhishma replied, 'In this connection, an ancient history is recounted. This is a conversation between Prahrada and Sage Ajagara.'

चरन्तं ब्राह्मणं कंचित्कल्यचित्तमनामयम् ।
पप्रच्छ राजन्प्रह्लादो बुद्धिमान्प्राज्ञसंमतः ॥ (3)

'O King! There was a brahmana who was intelligent and was revered by the wise. His consciousness was unblemished. While he was roaming around, he was questioned by Prahrada.'

स्वस्थः शक्तो मृदुर्दान्तो निर्विवित्सोऽनसूयकः ।
सुवाग्बहुमतो लोके प्राज्ञश्चरति बालवत् ॥ (4)

'"You are at ease, capable, mild, self-controlled, without any desire, free from malice, extremely eloquent, extremely revered in the world and wise. You roam around like a child."'

नैव प्रार्थयसे लाभं नालाभेष्वनुशोचसि ।
नित्यतृप्त इव ब्रह्मन्किंचिदवमन्यसे ॥ (5)

'"There is nothing that you seek to obtain. You do not grieve over anything that has not been obtained. O Brahmana! It is as if you are always content. There is nothing that you think about."'

स्रोतसा ह्रियमाणासु प्रजास्वविमना इव ।
धर्मकामार्थकार्येषु कूटस्थ इव लक्ष्यसे ॥ (6)

'"The people seem to be distracted, as they are borne along on currents of deeds connected with dharma, kama and artha. But to you, these seem to be hidden."'

नानुतिष्ठसि धर्मार्थौ न कामे चापि वर्तसे ।
इन्द्रियार्थाननादृत्य मुक्तश्चरसि साक्षिवत् ॥ (7)

'"You do not practise dharma or artha, nor are you engaged in kama. You ignore the objects of the senses. You roam around free, like a witness."'

का नु प्रज्ञा श्रुतं वा किं वृत्तिर्वा का नु ते मुने ।
क्षिप्रमाचक्ष्व मे ब्रह्मञ्छ्रेयो यदिह मन्यसे ॥ (8)

"'O Sage! What is your wisdom? What is your learning? What is your conduct? How did you become like this? O Brahmana! If you think it is beneficial for me in this world, please tell me this quickly.'"

अनुयुक्त: स मेधावी लोकधर्मविधानवित् ।
उवाच श्लक्ष्णया वाचा प्रह्लादमनपार्थया ॥ (9)

'The intelligent one, who knew about dharma and the conduct of the worlds, was asked in this way. Asked by Prahrada, he gently spoke these words, which were full of import.'

पश्यन्प्रह्लाद भूतानामुत्पत्तिमनिमित्तत: ।
ह्रासं वृद्धिं विनाशं च न प्रहृष्ये न च व्यथे ॥ (10)

"'O Prahrada! Behold. The origin, decay, increase and destruction of beings have no evident reason. That is the reason I am neither delighted nor distressed.'"

स्वभावादेव संदृश्य वर्तमाना: प्रवृत्तय: ।
स्वभावनिरता: सर्वा: परितप्ये न केनचित् ॥ (11)

"'They are seen to be engaged in their own natural conduct. Everyone is engaged in natural conduct and there is nothing to be tormented about.'"

पश्यन्प्रह्लाद संयोगान्विप्रयोगपरायणान् ।
संचयांश्च विनाशान्तान् क्वचिद्दिदधे मन: ॥ (12)

"'O Prahrada! Behold. Every kind of union is subject to separation. All accumulation eventually ends in destruction. Hence, my mind has never turned to acquisition.'"

अन्तवन्ति च भूतानि गुणयुक्तानि पश्यत: ।
उत्पत्तिनिधनज्ञस्य किं कार्यमवशिष्यते ॥ (13)

"'As one looks on, every being that possesses qualities comes to an end. If one knows about origin and destruction, what tasks remain to be undertaken?'"

जलजानामपि ह्यन्तं पर्यायेणोपलक्षये ।
महतामपि कायानां सूक्ष्माणां च महोदधौ ॥ (14)

'"In due course, it is seen that everything that moves around in the water of this great ocean, be its form gigantic or subtle, confronts destruction."'

जङ्गमस्थावराणां च भूतानामसुराधिप ।
पार्थिवानामपि व्यक्तं मृत्युं पश्यामि सर्वशः ॥ (15)

'"O Lord of Asuras! I see it as evident that death comes to all beings on earth and to all mobile and immobile objects."'

अन्तरिक्षचराणां च दानवोत्तम पक्षिणाम् ।
उत्तिष्ठति यथाकालं मृत्युर्बलवतामपि ॥ (16)

'"O Supreme among Danavas! When the time comes, all the birds which rise up and roam around in the sky come under the power of death."'

दिवि संचरमाणानि ह्रस्वानि च महान्ति च ।
ज्योतींषि च यथाकालं पतमानानि लक्षये ॥ (17)

'"When the time is right, all the shining bodies that wander around in the firmament, whether they are small or large, are seen to fall down."'

इति भूतानि संपश्यन्ननुषक्तानि मृत्युना ।
सर्वसामान्यतो विद्वान्कृतकृत्यः सुखं स्वपे ॥ (18)

'"Thus, all beings are seen to be attracted by death. Knowing that everything has this general nature, I sleep happily, doing nothing, since there is nothing to be done."'

सुमहान्तमपि ग्रासं ग्रसे लब्धं यदृच्छया ।
शये पुनरभुञ्जानो दिवसानि बहून्यपि ॥ (19)

'"If, without trying for it, I obtain a great deal of food, I eat it. There are again many days when I lie down, without having had anything to eat."'

आस्रवत्यपि मामन्नं पुनर्बहुगुणं बहु ।
पुनरल्पगुणं स्तोकं पुननैंवोपपद्यते ॥ (20)

'"There are many who shower many different kinds of food on me, with many different qualities. However, sometimes I get little, with few qualities, and sometimes, nothing at all."'

कणान्कदाचित्खादामि पिण्याकमपि च ग्रसे ।
भक्षये शालिमांसानि भक्षांश्चोच्चावचान्पुनः ॥ (21)

'"There are times when I eat minute grains and food from which the oil has been squeezed out. There are also times when I eat the best of food, rice mixed with meat. I eat the superior, and then again, I eat the inferior."'

शये कदाचित्पर्यङ्के भूमावपि पुनः शये ।
प्रासादेऽपि मे शय्या कदाचिदुपपद्यते ॥ (22)

'"There are times when I sleep on beds and times when I sleep on the bare ground. There are also times when I get a bed inside a palace."'

धारयामि च चीराणि शाणीं क्षौमाजिनानि च ।
महार्हाणि च वासांसि धारयाम्यहमेकदा ॥ (23)

'"I am sometimes attired in rags, hemp, linen and hides. There was also a time when I was clad in extremely expensive garments."'

न संनिपतितं धर्म्यमुपभोगं यदृच्छया ।
प्रत्याचक्षे न चाप्येनमनुरुध्ये सुदुर्लभम् ॥ (24)

'"As I wish, I do not reject enjoying objects of pleasure that arrive, as long as they are in conformity with dharma, but I do not strive for things that are extremely difficult to obtain."'

अचलमनिधनं शिवं विशोकं शुचिमतुलं विदुषां मते निविष्टम् ।
अनभिमतमसेवितं च मूढैर्व्रतमिदमाजगरं शुचिश्चरामि ॥ (25)

"'I follow the pure vow that is known as ajagara.[1] I do not waver from this and have no possessions. This is auspicious and bereft of sorrow. This is infinitely sacred and I have immersed myself in this intelligence of the learned. Foolish ones do not follow it and show it disrespect.'"

अचलितमतिरच्युतः स्वधर्मात्परिमितसंसरणः परावरज्ञः ।
विगतभयकषायलोभमोहोव्रतमिदमाजगरं शुचिश्चरामि ॥ (26)

"'I follow the pure vow that is known as ajagara. My mind does not deviate from it. I have not been dislodged from my own dharma. I am restrained in everything and know everything about cause and effect. I am devoid of fear, stupidity, greed and confusion.'"

अनियतफलभक्ष्यभोज्यपेयं विधिपरिणामविभक्तदेशकालम् ।
हृदयसुखमसेवितं कदर्यैर्व्रतमिदमाजगरं सुचिश्चरामि ॥ (27)

"'I follow this pure vow that is known as ajagara. This has no rules about consequences, what should be eaten, what should be enjoyed and what should be drunk. Since everything depends on destiny, nothing is determined in accordance with the time and the place. This contributes to the happiness of my heart and those who are avaricious do not follow it.'"

इदमिदमिति तृष्णयाभिभूतंजनमनवाप्तधनं विषीदमानम् ।
निपुणमनुनिशाम्य तत्त्वबुद्ध्या व्रतमिदमाजगरं शुचिश्चरामि ॥ (28)

"'Listen. I follow this pure vow that is known as ajagara. Because they are overwhelmed by thirst, the minds of people pursue many kinds of riches. When they do not get them, they are distressed. I have used my accomplished intelligence to discern the truth.'"

बहुविधमनुदृश्य चार्थहेतोः कृपणमिहार्यमनार्यमाश्रयन्तम् ।
उपशमरुचिरात्मवान्प्रशान्तो व्रतमिदमाजगरं शुचिश्चरामि ॥ (29)

---

[1] The belief is that the python does not strive for food but eats whatever comes to it. If food does not come to a python, it starves.

"'I follow this pure vow that is known as ajagara. To obtain riches, I have seen miserable people seek refuge with both noble and ignoble men. However, I have been relieved of this for a long time and have found serenity in my atman.'"

सुखमसुखमनर्थमर्थलाभं रतिमरतिं मरणं च जीवितं च ।
विधिनियतमवेक्ष्य तत्त्वतोऽहं व्रतमिदमाजगरं शुचिश्चरामि ॥ (30)

"'I follow this pure vow that is known as ajagara. I have seen the truth—everything is ordained by destiny, happiness and unhappiness, the acquisition of riches and the loss of riches, love and hatred, death and life.'"

अपगतभयरागमोहदर्पोधृतिमतिबुद्धिसमन्वितः प्रशान्तः ।
उपगतफलभोगिनो निशाम्य व्रतमिदमाजगरं शुचिश्चरामि ॥ (31)

"'Listen. I follow this pure vow that is known as ajagara. I have overcome fear, attachment, delusion and insolence. I possess fortitude, wisdom and intelligence and am tranquil. I am content with enjoying the fruit that presents itself before me.'"[2]

अनियतशयनासनः प्रकृत्यादमनियमव्रतसत्यशौचयुक्तः ।
अपगतफलसंचयः प्रहृष्टो व्रतमिदमाजगरं शुचिश्चरामि ॥ (32)

"'I follow this pure vow that is known as ajagara. I have no restrictions on where I should sleep and what I should eat. I am naturally united with self-control, restraint, vows, truth and purity. I have transcended the need to accumulate any fruits and am happy.'"

अभिगतमसुखार्थमीहनार्थैरुपगतबुद्धिरवेक्ष्य चात्मसंस्थः ।
तृषितमनियतं मनो नियन्तुं व्रतमिदमाजगरं शुचिश्चरामि ॥ (33)

"'Having considered, I follow this pure vow that is known as ajagara. I have always controlled the thirst in my mind. Based on my atman, I look towards everything with my intelligence. I have transcended the unhappiness that comes from the pursuit of riches and the lack of riches.'"

---

[2]There is an imagery of a python in this shloka, with a play on words.

न हृदयमनुरुध्यते मनो वा प्रियसुखदुर्लभतामनित्यतां च ।
तदुभयमुपलक्षयन्निवाहं व्रतमिदमाजगरं शुचिश्चरामि ॥ (34)

'"I follow this pure vow that is known as ajagara. The heart and the mind strive for the agreeable and the pleasant. But these are difficult to obtain and are transient and I have noticed both these aspects. Therefore, I have overcome these."'

बहु कथितमिदं हि बुद्धिमद्भि: कविभिरपिप्रथयद्भिरात्मकीर्तिम् ।
इदमिदमिति तत्र तत्र तत्तत्स्वपरमतैर्गहनं प्रतर्कयद्भि: ॥ (35)

'"There are intelligent men who have spoken about this in many ways. Those wise ones have sought to describe and establish their own views. They have spoken about this and that and have censured the views of others, saying that what they say is true. But this is beyond debate."'

तदहमनुनिशाम्य विप्रयातं पृथगभिपन्नमिहाबुधैर्मनुष्यै: ।
अनवसितमनन्तदोषपारं नृषु विहरामि विनीतदोषतृष्ण: ॥ (36)

'"I have heard that there are many men who are not intelligent. Suffering from this, they have been led in separate directions. However, I dwell in the infinite that is beyond all these taints. Having controlled the taint of thirst, I humbly roam around among men."'

भीष्म उवाच

अजगरचरितं व्रतं महात्मा य इह नरोऽनुचरेद्विनीतराग: ।
अपगतभयमन्युलोभमोह: स खलु सुखी विहरेदिमं विहारम् ॥ (37)

Bhishma concluded, 'If there is a great-souled man who humbly follows the vow of ajagara in this world, having controlled attachment and having overcome fear, anger, avarice and delusion, he will certainly be happy. He will find delight in this pleasure.'

Thus ends the Ajagara Gita.

16

SRIGALA GITA

The Srigala Gita follows immediately after the Ajagara Gita in Moksha Dharma Parva of Shanti Parva. It consists of a single chapter with fifty-two shlokas. As is the pattern in Shanti Parva, it is a conversation between Bhishma and Yudhishthira. Within this, Indra, in the form of a jackal, instructs Sage Kashyapa. This Gita is named Srigala Gita because the word '*srigala*' means jackal. A jackal is usually written as शृगाल (shrigala). However, though rarer, it is also written as सृगाल (srigala). Since the CE uses the rarer form, we have listed this as the Srigala Gita.

युधिष्ठिर उवाच

बान्धवा: कर्म वित्तं वा प्रज्ञा वेह पितामह ।
नरस्य का प्रतिष्ठा स्यादेतत्पृष्टो वदस्व मे ॥ (1)

Yudhishthira asked, 'O Grandfather! Relatives, deeds, riches and wisdom—which of these actually establishes a man? I am asking you. Please tell me.'

भीष्म उवाच

प्रज्ञा प्रतिष्ठा भूतानां प्रज्ञा लाभ: परो मत: ।
प्रज्ञा नै:श्रेयसी लोके प्रज्ञा स्वर्गो मत: सताम् ॥ (2)

Bhishma replied, 'Wisdom is the foundation of beings. It is held that wisdom is the greatest of gains. Wisdom is the most beneficial in the world. The virtuous are of the view that wisdom leads to the attainment of heaven.'

प्रज्ञया प्रापितार्थो हि बलिरैश्वर्यसंक्षये ।
प्रह्लादो नमुचिर्मङ्किस्तस्याः किं विद्यते परम् ॥ (3)

'When their prosperity was destroyed, it is through wisdom that Bali, Prahrada, Namuchi and Manki attained their objectives. What can be greater than that?'

अत्राप्युदाहरन्तीममितिहासं पुरातनम् ।
इन्द्रकाश्यपसंवादं तन्निबोध युधिष्ठिर ॥ (4)

'In this connection, an ancient history is recounted about a conversation between Indra and Kashyapa. O Yudhishthira! Listen to this.'

वैश्यः कश्चिदृषिं तात काश्यपं संशितव्रतम् ।
रथेन पातयामास श्रीमान्दृप्तस्तपस्विनम् ॥ (5)

'O Son! There was a rishi named Kashyapa who was firm in his vows. There was a vaishya. Insolent because of his prosperity, he brought the ascetic down through his chariot.'[1]

आर्तः स पतितः क्रुद्धस्त्यक्त्वात्मानमथाब्रवीत् ।
मरिष्याम्यधनस्येह जीवितार्थो न विद्यते ॥ (6)

'He[2] fell down and was distressed and was about to give up his life. He angrily said, "I will die. There is no point to a person without riches seeking to remain alive."'

तथा मुमूर्षमासीनमकूजन्तमचेतसम् ।
इन्द्रः सृगालरूपेण बभाषे क्रुद्धमानसम् ॥ (7)

---

[1] Kashyapa is the name of a lineage of rishis rather than one specific individual. While we are not given details, it is clear this was not one of the more learned Kashyapas but a young person. While he was travelling along the road, an insolent vaishya on a chariot ran him down. This is not clearly stated, but can be inferred.
[2] Kashyapa.

'He was seated thus, about to die, and lamented, bereft of his senses. His mind was enraged. At that time, Indra appeared before him in the form of a jackal and spoke.'

मनुष्ययोनिमिच्छन्ति सर्वभूतानि सर्वशः ।
मनुष्यत्वे च विप्रत्वं सर्व एवाभिनन्दति ॥ (8)

'"All beings always desire to be born as humans. Among humans, the status of a brahmana causes delight to everyone."'

मनुष्यो ब्राह्मणश्चासि श्रोत्रियश्चासि काश्यप ।
सुदुर्लभमवाप्यैतददोषान्मर्तुमिच्छसि ॥ (9)

'"O Kashyapa! You are a human. You are a brahmana. You are learned. This is extremely difficult to obtain. Therefore, there is sin in wishing to die."'

सर्वे लाभाः साभिमाना इति सत्या बत श्रुतिः ।
संतोषणीयरूपोऽसि लोभाद्यदभिमन्यसे ॥ (10)

'"The Shrutis have truly said that all acquisitions give rise to pride. You are the form of contentment. But what you are thinking of is the outcome of greed."'

अहो सिद्धार्थता तेषां येषां सन्तीह पाणयः ।
पाणिमद्भ्यः स्पृहास्माकं यथा तव धनस्य वै ॥ (11)

'"The virtuous ones who possess hands accomplish their objectives. We desire hands, just as you desire riches."'

न पाणिलाभादधिको लाभः कश्चन विद्यते ।
अपाणित्वाद्वयं ब्रह्मन्कण्टकान्नोद्धरामहे ॥ (12)

'"There is no gain that is superior to the obtaining of hands. O Brahmana! Without hands, we cannot take out the thorns."'

अथ येषां पुनः पाणी देवदत्तौ दशाङ्गुली ।
उद्धरन्ति कृमीनङ्गाद्दशामानान्कषन्ति च ॥ (13)

"'For those who possess hands, devas have given them ten fingers. They can use these to scratch and uproot the insects that are biting their limbs.'"

हिमवर्षातपानां च परित्राणानि कुर्वते ।
चेलमन्नं सुखं शय्यां निवातं चोपभुञ्जते ॥ (14)

"'They can act so as to save themselves from the cold, the rains and the heat.[3] They can cheerfully obtain food and enjoy that in beds that are safe from the wind.'"

अधिष्ठाय च गां लोके भुञ्जते वाहयन्ति च ।
उपायैर्बहुभिश्चैव वश्यानात्मनि कुर्वते ॥ (15)

"'The world is established on cattle and they employ them to carry burdens. They use many other means to bring them under their subjugation.'"

ये खल्वजिह्वाः कृपणा अल्पप्राणा अपाणयः ।
सहन्ते तानि दुःखानि दिष्ट्या त्वं न तथा मुने ॥ (16)

"'Those without hands and those who grind with their tongues[4] do not live for a long time. They have to tolerate many hardships. O Sage! It is good fortune that you are not like them.'"

दिष्ट्या त्वं न सृगालो वै न कृर्मिर्न च मूषकः ।
न सर्पो न च मण्डूको न चान्यः पापयोनिजः ॥ (17)

"'It is good fortune that you are not a jackal, a worm, a rat, a snake, a frog or some other being born as a wicked species.'"

एतावतापि लाभेन तोष्टुमर्हसि काश्यप ।
किं पुनर्योऽसि सत्वानां सर्वेषां ब्राह्मणोत्तमः ॥ (18)

"'O Kashyapa! You should be content with your gain. Then again, among all living beings, you are a supreme brahmana.'"

---

[3] By constructing shelters.
[4] Lacking in teeth.

इमे मां कृमयोऽदन्ति येषामुद्धरणाय मे ।
नास्ति शक्तिरपाणित्वात्पश्यावस्थामिमां मम ॥ (19)

'"These worms are biting me and I cannot take them out. Look at my state. Because I lack hands, I lack the strength to do that."'

अकार्यमिति चौवेमं नात्मानं सन्त्यजाम्यहम् ।
नेत: पापीयसीं योनिं पतेयमपरामिति ॥ (20)

'"In spite of being unsuccessful in this, I do not wish to give up my life. If I performed this wicked deed, I would descend into an even more inferior species."'[5]

मध्ये वै पापयोनीनां सागाली यामहं गत: ।
पापीयस्यो बहुतरा इतोऽन्या: पापयोनय: ॥ (21)

'"I am in the state of a jackal, and this is medium among those of wicked species. There are many others who belong to even more wicked species and are more evil."'

जात्यैवैके सुखतरा: सन्त्यन्ये भृशदु:खिता: ।
नैकान्तसुखमेवेह क्वचित्पश्यामि कस्यचित् ॥ (22)

'"Through birth, some are happy and virtuous and others are extremely miserable. However, I do not see anyone who is only happy."'

मनुष्या ह्याढ्यतां प्राप्य राज्यमिच्छन्त्यनन्तरम् ।
राज्यादेवत्वमिच्छन्ति देवत्वादिन्द्रतामपि ॥ (23)

'"Having gained prosperity, humans next desire kingdoms. Having obtained kingdoms, they wish to become devas. Having become devas, they desire to become Indra."'

भवेस्त्वं यद्यपि त्वाढ्यो न राजा न च दैवतम् ।
देवत्वं प्राप्य चेन्द्रत्वं नैव तुष्येस्तथा सति ॥ (24)

---

[5] After rebirth.

"'Even if you obtain riches, you will never become a king or a deva.[6] Even if you become a deva, you will not be satisfied without becoming Indra.'"

न तृप्तिः प्रियलाभेऽस्ति तृष्णा नादिभः प्रशाम्यति ।
संप्रज्वलति सा भूयः समिद्भिरिव पावकः ॥ (25)

"'You will not be content after obtaining what is agreeable. The thirst will not be slaked. This is like a fire that blazes again because of the offering of kindling.'"

अस्त्येव त्वयि शोको वै हर्षश्चास्ति तथा त्वयि ।
सुखदुःखे तथा चोभे तत्र का परिदेवना ॥ (26)

"'There is sorrow in you. But there is also delight in you. Since there is both misery and joy, why should there be lamentation?'"

परिच्छिद्चैव कामानां सर्वेषां चैव कर्मणाम् ।
मूलं रून्धीन्द्रियग्रामं शकुन्तानिव पञ्जरे ॥ (27)

"'Like birds imprisoned in a cage, restrain the foundations of your aggregate senses and sever all your desires and your karma.'"

न खल्वप्यरसज्ञस्य कामः क्वचन जायते ।
संस्पर्शाद्दर्शनाद्वापि श्रवणाद्वापि जायते ॥ (28)

"'If a person does not taste something, there can be no desire on account of that, since it is generated from touch, sight and hearing.'"

न त्वं स्मरसि वारुण्या लट्वाकानां च पक्षिणाम् ।
ताभ्यां चाभ्यधिको भक्ष्यो न कश्चिद्विद्यते क्वचित् ॥ (29)

"'You do not remember *varuni* or the bird known as *latvaka*.[7] There is no food or drink that is superior to these two.'"

---

[6] This is because a brahmana cannot become a king, and the status of a brahmana is superior to that of a god.
[7] The liquor and the flesh of the bird, respectively. The brahmana has not tasted these.

यानि चान्यानि दूरेषु भक्ष्यभोज्यानि काश्यप ।
येषामभुक्तपूर्वं ते तेषामस्मृतिरेव ते ॥ (30)

"'O Kashyapa! There are many other distant objects of food and drink. Since you have not tasted these earlier, you do not remember them.'"

अप्राशनमसंस्पर्शमसंदर्शनमेव च ।
पुरुषस्यैष नियमो मन्ये श्रेयो न संशयः ॥ (31)

"'Not to eat, not to touch, not to see—I think that this is certainly the supreme rule for a man. There is no doubt about this.'"

पाणिमन्तो धनैर्युक्ता बलवन्तो न संशयः ।
मनुष्या मानुषैरेव दासत्वमुपपादिताः ॥ (32)

"'There is no doubt that those with hands obtain riches and are powerful. Men use these to reduce other men to a state of servitude.'"

वधबन्धपरिक्लेशैः क्लिश्यन्ते च पुनः पुनः ।
ते खल्वपि रमन्ते च मोदन्ते च हसन्ति च ॥ (33)

"'They repeatedly use these to torment, slay, bind and afflict. They take pleasure in deceit, and sport and laugh.'"

अपरे बाहुबलिनः कृतविद्या मनस्विनः ।
जुगुप्सितां सुकृपणां पापां वृत्तिमुपासते ॥ (34)

"'Accomplished in their learning, those spirited ones control others through the strength of their arms. They adopt reprehensible and extremely miserable conduct and follow wicked means of subsistence.'"

उत्सहन्ते च ते वृत्तिमन्यामप्युपसेवितुम् ।
स्वकर्मणा तु नियतं भवितव्यं तु तत्तथा ॥ (35)

"'They become interested in practising the conduct followed by others. They are controlled by their own karma, and this is the working of destiny.'"

न पुल्कसो न चण्डाल आत्मानं त्यक्तुमिच्छति ।
असंतुष्ट: स्वया योन्या मायां पश्यस्व यादृशीम् ॥ (36)

'"Even pulkasas and chandalas do not wish to give up their own lives.[8] Behold this *maya*[9] and consider others since you are dissatisfied with your own self."'

दृष्ट्वा कुणीन्पक्षहतान्मनुष्यानामयाविन: ।
सुसंपूर्ण: स्वया योन्या लब्धलाभोऽसि काश्यप ॥ (37)

'"Look towards the men who have withered arms. There are those who are not healthy. O Kashyapa! Looking towards the others, since you are complete in your limbs, you should think that you have gained."'

यदि ब्राह्मण देहस्ते निरातङ्को निरामय: ।
अङ्गानि च समग्राणि न च लोकेषु धिक्कृत: ॥ (38)

'"O Brahmana! You are without disease in your body and without fear. You possess all your limbs and are not shamed amongst people."'

न केनचित्प्रवादेन सत्येनैवापहारिणा ।
धर्मायोत्तिष्ठ विप्रर्षे नात्मानं त्यक्तुमर्हसि ॥ (39)

'"O Brahmana Rishi! Even if you are censured by someone, as long as your truth is not taken away and you are based on dharma, you should not give up your own life."'

यदि ब्रह्मञ्छृणोष्येतच्छ्रद्दधासि च मे वच: ।
वेदोक्तस्य च धर्मस्य फलं मुख्यमवाप्स्यसि ॥ (40)

'"O Brahmana! If you listen to my words faithfully, you will obtain the best of fruits, as stated in the dharma laid down in the Vedas."'

---

[8] These terms are often used as synonyms. Pedantically, a chandala is the son of a brahmana mother and a shudra father. A pulkasa (equivalently pukkasa) is the son of a *nishada* father and a shudra mother. Nishada refers to those who dwelt in mountainous regions and were often hunters.
[9] Illusion.

स्वाध्यायमग्निसंस्कारमप्रमत्तोऽनुपालय ।
सत्यं दमं च दानं च स्पर्धिष्ठा मा च केनचित् ॥ (41)

'"Study and without any distractions, maintain the sacrificial fire. Follow truth, self-control and generosity. Never seek to rival another."'

ये केचन स्वध्ययना: प्राप्ता यजनयाजनम् ।
कथं ते चानुशोचेयुर्ध्यायेयुर्वाऽप्यशोभनम् ॥ (42)

'"For those who study, sacrifice and perform sacrifices for others, how can there be any sorrow? They are ornaments among *adhvaryu*s."'[10]

इच्छन्तस्ते विहाराय सुखं महदवाप्नुयु: ।
उत जाता: सुनक्षत्रे सुतीर्था: सुमुहूर्तजा: ॥ (43)

'"They sport as they please and obtain great happiness. They are born under excellent nakshatras, during excellent muhurtas and at the best of tirthas."'

नक्षत्रेष्वासुरेष्वन्ये दुस्तीर्था दुर्मुहूर्तजा: ।
संपतन्त्यासुरीं योनिं यज्ञप्रसववर्जिताम् ॥ (44)

'"But there are also those who are born under nakshatras associated with asuras, during extremely bad muhurtas and at bad tirthas.[11] They descend into the wombs of asuras, and their birth deprives them of sacrifices."'

अहमासं पण्डितको हैतुको वेदनिन्दक: ।
आन्वीक्षिकीं तर्कविद्यामनुरक्तो निरर्थिकाम् ॥ (45)

---

[10]There are four types of officiating priests—*hotri* (one who recites from the Rig Veda), *udgatri* (one who recites from the Sama Veda), adhvaryu (one who recites from the Yajur Veda) and brahmana (one who recites from the Atharva Veda).

[11]A tirtha, that is, place of pilgrimage, cannot, by definition, be bad. Both in this shloka and in the preceding one, the text should probably read tithi (lunar day) and not tirtha, differentiating between good and bad tithis.

'"I used to be learned.[12] I sought out reasons and criticized the Vedas. My inclinations were argumentative and I was addicted to the art of pointless debating."'

हेतुवादान्प्रवदिता वक्ता संसत्सु हेतुमत् ।
आक्रोष्टा चातिवक्ता च ब्रह्मयज्ञेषु वै द्विजान् ॥ (46)

'"I was an exponent of arguments and reasoning and spoke about subtle differences. I disparagingly spoke excessively about the sacrifices performed by brahmanas to the brahman."'

नास्तिक: सर्वशङ्की च मूर्ख: पण्डितमानिक: ।
तस्येयं फलनिर्वृत्ति: सृगालत्वं मम द्विज ॥ (47)

'"I was a non-believer and was suspicious of everything. I was foolish and insolent about my learning. O Dvija! Because of that, after death, I have reaped the fruits of being born as a jackal."'

अपि जातु तथा तत्स्यादहोरात्रशतैरपि ।
यदहं मानुषीं योनिं सृगाल: प्राप्नुयां पुन: ॥ (48)

'"Though I have been born as a jackal, after hundreds of days and nights, I may again be born as a human."'

संतुष्टश्चाप्रमत्तश्च यज्ञदानतपोरति: ।
ज्ञेयज्ञाता भवेयं वै वर्ज्यवर्जयिता तथा ॥ (49)

'"I will then be satisfied and without being distracted, be devoted to sacrifices, donations and austerities. I will then know what should be known. I will then cast away what should be cast away."'

तत: स मुनिरूत्थाय काश्यपस्तमुवाच ह ।
अहो बतासि कुशलो बुद्धिमानिति विस्मित: ॥ (50)

'He spoke in this way and raised the sage up. Kashyapa said, "You are accomplished in your intelligence, and I marvel and am astounded at this."'

---

[12]In an earlier life.

समवैक्षत तं विप्रो ज्ञानदीर्घेण चक्षुषा ।
ददर्श चैनं देवानामिन्द्रं देवं शचीपतिम् ॥ (51)

'Because of his jnana, the brahmana was far-sighted in his vision. He looked and realized that it was actually Indra of the devas, the deva who was Shachi's consort.'

तत: संपूजयमास काश्यपो हरिवाहनम् ।
अनुज्ञातश्च तेनाथ प्रविवेश स्वमाश्रमम् ॥ (52)

'At this, Kashyapa worshipped the one with the tawny horses.[13] He took his permission and entered his own hermitage.'

Thus ends the Srigala Gita.

---

[13]Indra.

17

VICHAKHNU GITA

In continuance of the conversation between Bhishma and Yudhishthira in Moksha Dharma Parva of Shanti Parva, the Vichakhnu Gita is a brief Gita, consisting of a single chapter with thirteen shlokas. In the course of this, Bhishma tells Yudhishthira what King Vichakhnu said against violence.

भीष्म उवाच

अत्राप्युदाहरन्तीममितिहासं पुरातनम् ।
प्रजानामनुकम्पार्थं गीतं राज्ञा विचख्नुना ॥ (1)

Bhishma said, 'In this connection, an ancient history is recounted, about what King Vichakhnu sang, driven by compassion for subjects.'

छिन्नस्थूणं वृषं दृष्ट्वा विरावं च गवां भृशम् ।
गोग्रहे यज्ञवाटस्य प्रेक्षमाण: स पार्थिव: ॥ (2)

'He saw the mangled body of a bull and heard the extremely piteous cries of cattle. The lord of the earth saw a sacrificial enclosure where cows were being slaughtered.'

स्वस्ति गोभ्योऽस्तु लोकेषु ततो निर्वचनं कृतम् ।
हिंसायां हि प्रवृत्तायामाशीरेषानुकल्पिता ॥ (3)

'He said, "May there be safety to all the cattle in this world." When the violence had started, all these words of benediction were heard.'

अव्यवस्थितमर्यादैर्विमूढैर्नास्तिकैर्नरैः ।
संशयात्मभिरव्यक्तैर्हिंसा समनुकीर्तिता ॥ (4)

'Those who have deviated from the ordinances, those who are non-believers and foolish, those who have doubts within themselves, are the men who applaud violence.'

सर्वकर्मस्वहिंसा हि धर्मात्मा मनुरब्रवीत् ।
कामरागाद्विहिंसन्ति बहिर्वेद्यां पशून्नराः ॥ (5)

'Manu, with dharma in his atman, said that one should not engage in violence in all deeds. Driven by attachment to desire, men cause violence to animals outside the sacrificial enclosure.'[1]

तस्मात्प्रमाणतः कार्यो धर्मः सूक्ष्मो विजानता ।
अहिंसैव हि सर्वेभ्यो धर्मेभ्यो ज्यायसी मता ॥ (6)

'Therefore, one should follow the instructions and know the subtle nature of dharma. It has been held that non-violence is superior to all kinds of dharma.'

उपोष्य संशितो भूत्वा हित्वा वेदकृताः श्रुतीः ।
आचार इत्यनाचाराः कृपणाः फलहेतवः ॥ (7)

'They dwell near sacred places, but have abandoned the learning of the Vedas. These misers are driven by desire for the fruits and follow bad conduct, in the disguise of good conduct.'

यदि यज्ञांश्च वृक्षांश्च यूपांश्चोद्दिश्य मानवाः ।
वृथा मांसानि खादन्ति नैष धर्मः प्रशस्यते ॥ (8)

'Pointing to sacrifices, trees and sacrificial altars, men pointlessly eat flesh.[2] This kind of dharma is not praised.'

---

[1] They are slaughtered outside the enclosure.
[2] Implying that the flesh of animals killed at sacrifices is also not recommended. Often, there are no injunctions against eating flesh, provided the meat has been offered at sacrifices.

मांसं मधु सुरा मत्स्या आसवं कृसरौदनम् ।
धूर्तैः प्रवर्तितं ह्येतन्नैतद्वेदेषु कल्पितम् ॥ (9)

'Cunning people have brought about the practice of flesh, *madhu*, *sura*, fish, *asava* and *krisara*.³ They were not thought of in the Vedas.'

कामान्मोहाच्च लोभाच्च लौल्यमेतत्प्रवर्तितम् ।
विष्णुमेवाभिजानन्ति सर्वयज्ञेषु ब्राह्मणाः ।
पायसैः सुमनोभिश्च तस्यापि यजनं स्मृतम् ॥ (10)

'Desire, delusion and greed led to these temptations being introduced. The brahmanas know that Vishnu is present at all sacrifices. It has been said that offerings should consist of *payasam*⁴ and flowers.'

यज्ञियाश्चैव ये वृक्षा वेदेषु परिकल्पिताः ।
यच्चापि किंचित्कर्तव्यमन्यच्चोक्षैः सुसंस्कृतम् ।
महासत्त्वैः शुद्धभावैः सर्वं देवार्हमेव तत् ॥ (11)

'In the Vedas, trees have been thought of as sacrificial offerings. These are the kinds of things that should properly be offered, with pure sentiments and great enterprise. All these deserve to be offered to that divinity.'

युधिष्ठिर उवाच

शरीरमापद्श्चापि विवदन्त्यविहिंसतः ।
कथं यात्रा शरीरस्य निरारम्भस्य सेत्स्यति ॥ (12)

Yudhishthira asked, 'The body and various difficulties always quarrel and cause injury to each other. If one abstains from starting all work, how will it be possible to sustain the body?'

भीष्म उवाच

यथा शरीरं न ग्लायेन्नेयान्मृत्युवशं यथा ।
तथा कर्मसु वर्तेत समर्थो धर्ममाचरेत् ॥ (13)

---

³While madhu does mean honey, given the context, madhu, sura and asava are kinds of liquor. Krisara is made of wheat flour, rice and sesame.
⁴Payasam is rice cooked in milk and sugar.

Bhishma replied, 'One must act so that the body does not suffer and so that one does not come under the subjugation of death. According to capacity, one's karma should follow the norms of dharma.'

Thus ends the Vichakhnu Gita.

18

HARITA GITA

The Harita Gita is also a brief Gita, consisting of a single chapter with twenty shlokas. In Moksha Dharma Parva of Shanti Parva, Bhishma tells Yudhishthira what Sage Harita said about moksha dharma, with a focus on what a mendicant should do. There is no shloka that is directly uttered by Harita. Instead, everything is said by Bhishma, repeating Harita's words.

युधिष्ठिर उवाच

किंशील: किंसमाचार: किंविद्य: किंपरायण: ।
प्राप्नोति ब्रह्मण: स्थानं यत्परं प्रकृतेर्ध्रुवम् ॥ (1)

Yudhishthira asked, 'What kind of conduct, what kind of behaviour, what kind of knowledge and what kind of faith enable one to obtain the state of the brahman, which is permanent and is beyond nature?'

भीष्म उवाच

मोक्षधर्मेषु निरतो लघ्वाहारो जितेन्द्रिय: ।
प्राप्नोति परमं स्थानं यत्परं प्रकृतेर्ध्रुवम् ॥ (2)

Bhishma replied, 'A person who is devoted to the dharma of moksha must be restrained in diet and must conquer his senses. He will then obtain the supreme state, which is permanent and is beyond nature.'

स्वगृहादभिनि:सृत्य लाभालाभे समो मुनि: ।
समुपोढेषु कामेषु निरपेक्ष: परिव्रजेत् ॥ (3)

'A sage will depart from his home and regard gain and loss as equal. He will be indifferent to objects of desire, even when they present themselves. He will become a mendicant.'

न चक्षुषा न मनसा न वाचा दूषयेदपि ।
न प्रत्यक्षं परोक्षं वा दूषणं व्याहरेत्क्वचित् ॥ (4)

'He will not abuse anyone through sight, thoughts or words. He will not display any harsh conduct, whether the person is present or absent.'

न हिंस्यात्सर्वभूतानि मैत्रायणगतिश्चरेत् ।
नेदं जीवितमासाद्य वैरं कुर्वीत केनचित् ॥ (5)

'He will not cause violence to any being. He will roam around, following the course of the sun.[1] He should lead a life, so that he does not commit an act of enmity towards anyone.'

अतिवादांस्तितिक्षेत नाभिमन्येत्कथंचन ।
क्रोध्यमान: प्रियं ब्रूयादाक्रुष्ट: कुशलं वदेत् ॥ (6)

'He must tolerate harsh words and never be arrogant. Even when he is enraged, he will speak pleasant words. When he is censured, he will reply agreeably.'

प्रदक्षिणं प्रसव्यं च ग्राममध्ये न चाचरेत् ।
भैक्षचर्यामनापन्नो न गच्छेत्पूर्वकेतित: ॥ (7)

'When he is inside a village, he should not circumambulate it, either from the right or from the left. When begging for alms, he should not go to a house that he has visited earlier.'[2]

अविकीर्ण: सुगुप्तश्च न वाचा ह्यप्रियं वदेत् ।
मृदु: स्यादप्रतिक्रूरो विस्रब्ध: स्यादरोषण: ॥ (8)

'Even when he is reviled, he must protect himself well and not speak unpleasant words in reply. He must be mild and not injure

---

[1] This means that he will not reside in any fixed abode.
[2] He should not seek alms from the same house twice.

someone who has acted cruelly towards him. He must control fear and rage.'

विधूमे न्यस्तमुसले व्यङ्गारे भुक्तवज्जने ।
अतीते पात्रसञ्चारे भिक्षां लिप्सेत वै मुनिः ॥ (9)

'The sage should desire alms when the smoke has gone out, when the pestle has been laid down, when the fire has been extinguished, when food has been eaten and when the vessels are no longer laid out.'[3]

अनुयात्रिकमर्थस्य मात्रा लाभेष्वनादृतः ।
अलाभे न विहन्येत लाभश्चौनं न हर्षयेत् ॥ (10)

'He should only accept what is required for subsistence and ignore anything obtained in excess. He should not be distressed at not getting something, nor should he be delighted at getting something.'

लाभं साधारणं नेच्छेन्न भुञ्जीताभिपूजितः ।
अभिपूजितलाभं हि जुगुप्सेतैव तादृशः ॥ (11)

'He should not desire what ordinary people want. He should not eat when he is respectfully invited.[4] In a similar way, he should refuse anything that is offered as a mark of honour.'

न चान्नदोषानिन्देत न गुणानभिपूजयेत् ।
शय्यासने विविक्ते च नित्यमेवाभिपूजयेत् ॥ (12)

'He must not find fault with the food that has been offered, nor should he praise its qualities. He must always be indifferent to a bed or a seat offered as a mark of honour.'

शून्यागारं वृक्षमूलमरण्यमथ वा गुहाम् ।
अज्ञातचर्यां गत्वान्यां ततोऽन्यत्रैव संविशेत् ॥ (13)

---

[3] When the house is through with the meals.
[4] If he is invited to eat in a house, he should refuse it.

'He should reside in an empty house, at the foot of a tree, in a forest or in a cave. His conduct should not be known to others. If others come there, he should go somewhere else.'[5]

अनुरोधविरोधाभ्यां समः स्यादचलो ध्रुवः ।
सुकृतं दुष्कृतं चोभे नानुरुध्येत कर्मणि ॥ (14)

'He should treat requests and obstructions equally. He should be certain and fixed. He should not be obstructed by either good deeds or bad ones.'

वाचो वेगं मनसः क्रोधवेगं विवित्सावेगमुदरोपस्थवेगम् ।
एतान्वेगान्विनयेद्धै तपस्वी निन्दा चास्य हृदयं नोपहन्यात् ॥ (15)

'He should control the force of words, his mind and the force of anger. He should control the urge to search, and the force of the stomach and the penis. The ascetic should control these urges. No censure should be allowed to afflict his heart.'

मध्यस्थ एव तिष्ठेत प्रशंसानिन्दयोः समः ।
एतत्पवित्रं परमं परिव्राजक आश्रमे ॥ (16)

'He should be indifferent, regarding praise and censure as equal. This is the supremely sacred ashrama of a mendicant.'

महात्मा सुव्रतो दान्तः सर्वत्रैवानपाश्रितः ।
अपूर्वचारकः सौम्यो अनिकेतः समाहितः ॥ (17)

'He is great in atman and excellent in his vows. He is controlled and is detached in every way. He does not go to earlier places.[6] He is tranquil. He is without an abode. He is controlled.'

वानप्रस्थगृहस्थाभ्यां न संसृज्येत कर्हिचित् ।
अज्ञातलिप्सां लिप्सेत न चैनं हर्ष आविशेत् ॥ (18)

---

[5]This is also interpreted as retreating within his own self.
[6]Earlier places refer to his former life as a householder.

'He should not ever consort with those who are in vanaprastha or garhasthya stages. He should not unwittingly fall prey to desire, nor should he succumb to delight.'

विजानतां मोक्ष एष श्रम: स्यादविजानताम् ।
मोक्षयानमिदं कृत्स्नं विदुषां हारितोऽब्रवीत् ॥ (19)

'Know that this is the ashrama of moksha, known to those who are learned. Everything about moksha was spoken by the learned Harita.'

अभयं सर्वभूतेभ्यो दत्त्वा य: प्रव्रजेद्गृहात् ।
लोकास्तेजोमयास्तस्य तथानन्त्याय कल्पते ॥ (20)

'If a person departs from his house[7] and grants fearlessness to all beings, he obtains worlds that are full of energy, otherwise thought of as the infinite.'

Thus ends the Harita Gita.

---

[7] Becomes a mendicant.

19

VRITRA GITA

In Moksha Dharma Parva of Shanti Parva, the Vritra Gita has two chapters, amounting to 103 shlokas. As is the pattern throughout Shanti Parva, Bhishma is questioned by Yudhishthira. Having instructed Yudhishthira, Bhishma tells him about Vritra, the king of the daityas who was defeated and killed by Indra. That connection gives the Vritra Gita its name. Before Vritra died, a dialogue ensued between Vritra and Shukracharya (also known as Ushanas), the preceptor of the daityas. In the middle of this Gita, Sage Sanatkumara tells Vritra and Ushanas about Vishnu's greatness.

Chapter 1

युधिष्ठिर उवाच

धन्या धन्या इति जना: सर्वेऽस्मान्प्रवदन्त्युत ।
न दु:खिततर: कश्चित्पुमानस्माभिरस्ति ह ॥ (1)
लोकसम्भावितैर्दु:खं यत्प्राप्तं कुरुसत्तम ।
प्राप्य जातिं मनुष्येषु देवैरपि पितामह ॥ (2)
कदा वयं करिष्याम: संन्यासं दु:खसञ्ज्ञकम् ।
दु:खमेतच्छरीराणां धारणं कुरुसत्तम ॥ (3)
विमुक्ता: सप्तदशभिर्हेतुभूतैश्च पञ्चभि: ।
इन्द्रियार्थैर्गुणैश्चैव अस्टाभि: प्रपितामह ॥ (4)

न गच्छन्ति पुनर्भावं मुनयः संशितव्रताः ।
कदा वयं भविष्यामो राज्यं हित्वा परन्तप ॥ (5)

Yudhishthira said, 'All the people speak of us as being blessed and fortunate. However, there is no man who is more miserable than we are. O Supreme among the Kurus! O Grandfather! We have been born as humans, but have been born from devas. The worlds honour us, but we have obtained misery. When will we resort to sannyasa and destroy this sorrow? O Supreme among the Kurus! Bearing these bodies is a matter of sorrow. We will free ourselves of the seventeen attributes[1] and merge with the five elements. O Great Grandfather! We will also free ourselves from the eight objects of the senses and the gunas.[2] The sages who are firm in their vows depart and are not born again. O Scorcher of Enemies! When will we be in a position to give up the kingdom?'

भीष्म उवाच

नास्त्यनन्तं महाराज सर्वं संख्यानगोचरम् ।
पुनर्भावोऽपि संख्यातो नास्ति किंचिदिहाचलम् ॥ (6)

Bhishma replied, 'O Great King! Everything can be perceived through enumeration, and the number is not infinite. The number of rebirths can also be counted.[3] Nothing in this world is fixed.'

न चापि गम्यते राजन्नैष दोषः प्रसङ्गतः ।
उद्योगादेव धर्मज्ञ कालेनैव गमिष्यथ ॥ (7)

'O King! In connection with this progress, no sin has been attached to you. O One Who Knows about Dharma! Endeavour, and in the course of time, you will follow that path.'

ईशोऽयं सततं देही नृपते पुण्यपापयोः ।
तत एव समुत्थेन तमसा रुध्यतेऽपि च ॥ (8)

---

[1] The five senses, the five organs of action, the five kinds of breaths of life, mind and intelligence.
[2] The five objects of the senses and the qualities of sattva, rajas and tamas.
[3] There is an end to the cycle of death and rebirth.

'O Lord of Men! In this body, the atman is the lord of good and bad deeds. But the rising darkness obstructs the vision.'

यथाञ्जनमयो वायुः पुनर्मानःशिलं रजः ।
अनुप्रविश्य तद्वर्णो दृश्यते रञ्जयन्दिशः ॥ (9)

'The wind has no dust or colour in it. But when it is tinged with a pigment, that colour penetrates it and this is also seen to colour the directions.'

तथा कर्मफलैर्देही रञ्जितस्तमसावृतः ।
विवर्णो वर्णमाश्रित्य देहेषु परिवर्तते ॥ (10)

'In that way, because of the fruits of karma, the atman is tinged and enveloped in darkness. Though without complexion, it adopts that colour and circles around amidst bodies.'

ज्ञानेन हि यदा जन्तुरज्ञानप्रभवं तमः ।
व्यपोहति तदा ब्रह्म प्रकाशेत सनातनम् ॥ (11)

'In any creature, jnana destroys the ignorance that causes darkness. When that is dispelled, the eternal brahman manifests itself.'

अयत्नसाध्यं मुनयो वदन्ति ये चापि मुक्तास्त उपासितव्याः ।
त्वया च लोकेन च सामरेण तस्मान्न शाम्यन्ति महर्षिसङ्घाः ॥ (12)

'The sages say that this cannot be accomplished without care. Those who have been liberated should be worshipped, even by the worlds and the immortals. The large numbers of maharshis are also not at peace.'[4]

अस्मिन्नर्थे पुरा गीतं शृणुष्वैकमना नृप ।
यथा दैत्येन वृत्रेण भ्रष्टैश्वर्येण चेष्टितम् ॥ (13)

'In this connection, there is an ancient song. O King! Listen to it attentively. The daitya Vritra[5] was dislodged from his prosperity and sang this.'

---

[4] Without having attained the brahman.
[5] Vritra was defeated by Indra.

निर्जितेनासहायेन हृतराज्येन भारत ।
अशोचता शत्रुमध्ये बुद्धिमास्थाय केवलाम् ॥ (14)

'O Descendant of the Bharata Lineage! He was vanquished and was without aides. His kingdom was taken away. However, in spite of being in the midst of enemies, he resorted to his intelligence alone and did not grieve.'

भ्रष्टैश्वर्यं पुरा वृत्रमुशना वाक्यमब्रवीत् ।
कच्चित्पराजितस्याद्य न व्यथा तेऽस्ति दानव ॥ (15)

'In those ancient times, Vritra lost his riches and Ushanas spoke to him. "O Danava! Now that you have been defeated, are you distressed?"'

वृत्र उवाच

सत्येन तपसा चैव विदित्वा सक्षयं ह्यहम् ।
न शोचामि न हृष्यामि भूतानामागतिं गतिम् ॥ (16)

'Vritra said, "Because of truth and austerities, I know about destruction. I do not sorrow or rejoice at the creation and destruction of beings."'

कालसंचोदिता जीवा मज्जन्ति नरकेऽवशाः ।
परिदृष्टानि सर्वाणि दिव्यान्याहुर्मनीषिणः ॥ (17)

'"Goaded by destiny, beings are subjugated and submerged in hell. It has been seen that all the learned ones go to heaven."'

क्षपयित्वा तु तं कालं गणितं कालचोदिताः ।
सावशेषेण कालेन सम्भवन्ति पुनः पुनः ॥ (18)

'"Goaded by destiny, they spend the computed durations of time there. However, when that duration is over, they are born again and again."'

तिर्यग्योनिसहस्राणि गत्वा नरकमेव च ।
निर्गच्छन्त्यवशा जीवाः कालबन्धनबन्धनाः ॥ (19)

'"They are born thousands of times as inferior species and also go to hell. Bound by the nooses of destiny, beings are helpless and go there."'

एवं संसरमाणानि जीवान्यहमदृष्टवान् ।
यथा कर्म तथा लाभ इति शास्त्रनिदर्शनम् ॥ (20)

'"I have seen that creatures circle around in this way. The sacred texts have instructed that gains are commensurate with karma."'

तिर्यग्गच्छन्ति नरकं मानुष्यं दैवमेव च ।
सुखदुःखे प्रियद्वेष्ये चरित्वा पूर्वमेव च ॥ (21)

'"Creatures are born as inferior species, men and devas, and go to hell. After that unhappiness and happiness and love and hatred are over, they roam around, as was the case earlier."'[6]

कृतान्तविधिसंयुक्तं सर्वलोकः प्रपद्यते ।
गतं गच्छन्ति चाध्वानं सर्वभूतानि सर्वदा ॥ (22)

'"All the worlds are bound by the injunctions of the Destroyer.[7] All beings are always travellers along a path that has been travelled before."'

भीष्म उवाच

कालसंख्यानसंख्यातं सृष्टिस्थितिपरायणम् ।
तं भाषमाणं भगवानुशना प्रत्यभाषत ।
भीमान्दुष्टप्रलापांस्त्वं तात कस्मात्प्रभाषसे ॥ (23)

Bhishma said, 'He knew about time and its enumeration, about what cannot be enumerated and about creation and preservation. When he spoke in this way, the illustrious Ushanas replied, "O Son! Why are you speaking these terrible, wicked and crazy words?"'

---

[6]The cycle of death and rebirth.
[7]Yama.

वृत्र उवाच

प्रत्यक्षमेतद्भवतस्तथान्येषां मनीषिणाम् ।
मया यज्जयलुब्धेन पुरा तप्तं महत्तप: ॥ (24)

'Vritra said, "You and the other learned ones have directly seen the great austerities I tormented myself with in earlier times and the sacrifices that I performed out of greed."'

गन्धानादाय भूतानां रसांश्च विविधानपि ।
अवर्धं त्रीन्समाक्रम्य लोकान्वै स्वेन तेजसा ॥ (25)

'"I seized fragrances, beings and diverse kinds of scents. I grew in my energy and overcame the three worlds."'

ज्वालामालापरिक्षिप्तो वैहायसचरस्तथा ।
अजेय: सर्वभूतानामासं नित्यमपेतभी: ॥ (26)

'"I roamed through the air, scattering garlands of rays. I could not be defeated by any being and I was never frightened."'

ऐश्वर्यं तपसा प्राप्तं भ्रष्टं तच्च स्वकर्मभि: ।
धृतिमास्थाय भगवन्न् शोचामि ततस्त्वहम् ॥ (27)

'"However, the prosperity that I earned through my austerities was destroyed through my own karma. O Illustrious One! But resorting to my fortitude, I am not sorrowing over that."'

युयुत्सता महेन्द्रेण पुरा सार्धं महात्मना ।
ततो मे भगवान्दृष्टो हरिर्नारायण: प्रभु: ॥ (28)

'"In earlier times, when I was fighting with the great-souled and great Indra, I saw the illustrious lord, Hari Narayana."'

वैकुण्ठ: पुरुषो विष्णु: शुक्लोऽनन्त: सनातन: ।
मुञ्जकेशो हरिश्मश्रु: सर्वभूतपितामह: ॥ (29)

'"He is Vaikuntha, Purusha, Vishnu, Shukla, Ananta, Sanatana, Munjakesha, Harishmashru and the grandfather of all beings."'[8]

नूनं तु तस्य तपस: सावशेषं ममास्ति वै ।
यदहं प्रष्टुमिच्छामि भवन्तं कर्मण: फलम् ॥ (30)

'"There is no doubt that a little bit of those austerities are still left for me.[9] Therefore, I wish to ask you about the fruits of karma."'

ऐश्वर्यं वै महद्ब्रह्मन्कस्मिन्वर्णे प्रतिष्ठितम् ।
निवर्तते चापि पुन: कथमैश्वर्यमुत्तमम् ॥ (31)

'"O Brahmana! In which varna is the greatest prosperity established? How does one regain the excellent prosperity that has been lost?"'

कस्माद्भूतानि जीवन्ति प्रवर्तन्तेऽथ वा पुन: ।
किं वा फलं परं प्राप्य जीवस्तिष्ठति शाश्वत: ॥ (32)

'"How are beings created? How do they live? Who makes them act? What are the supreme fruits obtained by living for an eternity?"'

केन वा कर्मणा शक्यमथ ज्ञानेन केन वा ।
ब्रह्मर्षे तत्फलं प्राप्तुं तन्मे व्याख्यातुमर्हसि ॥ (33)

'"What can be achieved through karma and what can be achieved through jnana? What fruits are obtained? O Brahmana Rishi! You should explain this to me."'

इतीदमुक्त: स मुनिस्तदानीं प्रत्याह यत्तच्छृणु राजसिंह ।
मयोच्यमानं पुरुषर्षभ त्वमनन्यचित्त: सह सोदरीयै: ॥ (34)

Bhishma said, 'O Lion among Kings! Having been thus addressed at the time, the sage replied. O Bull among Men! Together with your brothers, listen attentively to what he said.'

---

[8] All of these are Vishnu's names. Vaikuntha is his name as well as that of his abode. Shukla means pure or white, Ananta means infinite and Sanatana means eternal. Munjakesha means one with yellow hair, while Harishmashru means one with a tawny beard.
[9] The original austerities as well as the rewards from seeing Hari. Since some of those fruits are still left, Vritra is entitled to ask Shukracharya about auspicious things.

Chapter 2

उशनोवाच

नमस्तस्मै भगवते देवाय प्रभविष्णवे ।
यस्य पृथ्वीतलं तात साकाशं बाहुगोचरम् ॥ (1)

'Ushanas said, "I prostrate myself before the illustrious and powerful divinity Vishnu. O Son! He holds up the surface of the earth and the sky in his hands."'

मूर्धा यस्य त्वनन्तं च स्थानं दानवसत्तम ।
तस्याहं ते प्रवक्ष्यामि विष्णोर्माहात्म्यमुत्तमम् ॥ (2)

'"O Excellent Danava! His head extends up to infinity. I will tell you about Vishnu's supreme greatness."'

भीष्म उवाच

तयो: संवदतोरेवमाजगाम महामुनि: ।
सनत्कुमारो धर्मात्मा संशयछेदनाय वै ॥ (3)

Bhishma said, 'While they were conversing in this way, the great sage Sanatkumara, with dharma in his atman, arrived there, to dispel their doubts.'

स पूजितोऽसुरेन्द्रेण मुनिनोशनसा तथा ।
निषसादासने राजन्महार्हे मुनिपुङ्गव: ॥ (4)

'The Indra among the asuras and Sage Ushanas worshipped him. O King! The bull among sages then sat down on an expensive seat.'

तमासीनं महाप्राज्ञमुशना वाक्यमब्रवीत् ।
ब्रूह्यस्मै दानवेन्द्राय विष्णोर्माहात्म्यमुत्तमम् ॥ (5)

'When the immensely wise one was seated, Ushanas spoke these words to him. "For the sake of the Indra among the danavas, please tell him about Vishnu's supreme greatness."'

सनत्कुमारस्तु ततः श्रुत्वा प्राह वचोऽर्थवत् ।
विष्णोर्माहात्म्यसंयुक्तं दानवेन्द्राय धीमते ॥ (6)

'On hearing this, Sanatkumara spoke words that were full of meaning. He told the intelligent Indra among the danavas about Vishnu's greatness.'

शृणु सर्वमिदं दैत्य विष्णोर्माहात्म्यमुत्तमम् ।
विष्णौ जगत्स्थितं सर्वमिति विद्धि परंतप ॥ (7)

'"O Daitya! Listen to everything about Vishnu's supreme greatness. O Scorcher of Enemies! Know that everything in the universe is established in Vishnu."'

सृजत्येष महाबाहो भूतग्रामं चराचरम् ।
एष चाक्षिपते काले काले विसृजते पुनः ।
अस्मिन्गच्छन्ति विलयमस्माच्च प्रभवन्त्युत ॥ (8)

'"O Mighty-Armed One! He is the one who creates the aggregate of all beings, mobile and immobile. In the course of time, it is he who withdraws them back and creates them again when the time arises. At the time of dissolution, everything enters into him. Everything is created from him."'

नैष दानवता शक्यस्तपसा नैव चेज्यया ।
संप्राप्तुमिन्द्रियाणां तु संयमेनैव शक्यते ॥ (9)

'"Danavas are incapable of obtaining him through austerities or through sacrifices. One is capable of obtaining him by controlling the senses."'

बाह्ये चाभ्यन्तरे चैव कर्मणा मनसि स्थितः ।
निर्मली कुरुते बुद्ध्या सोऽमुत्रानन्त्यमश्नुते ॥ (10)

'"Both internal and external acts must be based in the mind.[10] If they are purified through intelligence, one can obtain the eternal in this world."'

---

[10] External acts are sacrifices and rites. Internal acts are in the form of purification inside. Provided these are done well, they do help.

यथा हिरण्यकर्तां वै रूप्यमग्नौ विशोधयेत् ।
बहुशोऽतिप्रयत्नेन महतात्मकृतेन ह ॥ (11)

'"This is like a goldsmith purifying gold in the form of the fire. One can do that oneself, using a great deal of careful efforts."'

तद्व्रज्जातिशतैर्जीवः शुध्यतेऽल्पेन कर्मणा ।
यत्नेन महता चैवाप्येकजातौ विशुध्यते ॥ (12)

'"A being may purify himself through one hundred births. But through limited deeds and a great deal of effort, another being may purify himself in a single birth."'

लीलयाल्पं यथा गात्रात्प्रमृज्यादात्मनो रजः ।
बहु यत्नेन महता दोषनिर्हरणं तथा ॥ (13)

'"If the filth on the body is cleansed before it has become thick, it requires only a little bit of effort. In that way, one must make careful efforts to remove the taints."'

यथा चाल्पेन माल्येन वासितं तिलसर्षपम् ।
न मुञ्चति स्वकं गन्धं तद्वत्सूक्ष्मस्य दर्शनम् ॥ (14)

'"If a few garlands are mixed with sesame or mustard seeds, they do not shed their scent and become fragrant. This is the subtlety of insight."'

तदेव बहुभिर्माल्यैर्वास्यमानं पुनः पुनः ।
विमुञ्चति स्वकं गन्धं माल्यगन्धेऽवतिष्ठति ॥ (15)

'"In that way, a large number of garlands must repeatedly be mixed. Then the own scent[11] goes away and the fragrance of the garlands is established."'

एवं जातिशतैर्युक्तो गुणैरेव प्रसङ्गिषु ।
बुद्ध्या निवर्तते दोषो यत्नेनाभ्यासजेन वै ॥ (16)

---

[11] Of the sesame or mustard seeds.

'"In this way, through hundreds of lives, one must seek the qualities. One must use one's intelligence to control the taints and endeavour and practise."'

कर्मणा स्वेन रक्तानि विरक्तानि च दानव ।
यथा कर्मविशेषांश्च प्राप्नुवन्ति तथा शृणु ॥ (17)

'"O Danava! Listen to the reasons behind one's own karma, whereby creatures become addicted to, or detached from, the consequences of such specific karma."'

यथा च सप्रवर्तन्ते यस्मिंस्तिष्ठन्ति वा विभो ।
तत्तेऽनुपूर्व्या व्याख्यास्ये तदिहैकमनाः शृणु ॥ (18)

'"O Lord! Listen with single-minded attention. In due course, I will explain how creatures engage in action and refrain from it."'

अनादिनिधनं श्रीमान्हरिर्नारायणः प्रभुः ।
स वै सृजति भूतानि स्थावराणि चराणि च ॥ (19)

'"The illustrious lord Hari Narayana is without a beginning and without an end. He creates all the beings, mobile and immobile."'

एष सर्वेषु भूतेषु क्षरश्चाक्षर एव च ।
एकादश विकारात्मा जगत्पिबति रश्मिभिः ॥ (20)

'"He is in all beings that are mutable and immutable. He uses his rays to drink up the universe through his eleven transformations."'[12]

पादौ तस्य महीं विद्धि मूर्धानं दिवमेव च ।
बाहवस्तु दिशो दैत्य श्रोत्रमाकाशमेव च ॥ (21)

'"Know that his feet are the earth and the firmament is his head. O Daitya! His arms are the directions and his ears are the sky."'

तस्य तेजोमयः सूर्यो मनश्चन्द्रमसि स्थितम् ।
बुद्धिर्ज्ञानगता नित्यं रसस्त्वप्सु प्रवर्तते ॥ (22)

---

[12] The five senses of perception, the five organs of action and the mind.

"'His energy is the sun and his mind is established in the moon. His intelligence is always in jnana. and his juices are in the water.'"

भ्रुवोरन्तरास्तस्य ग्रहा दानवसत्तम ।
नक्षत्रचक्रं नेत्राभ्यां पादयोर्भूश्च दानव ॥ (23)

"'O Supreme among the Danavas! The planets are in the midst of his eyebrows. O Danava! The circle of nakshatras are his eyes and the earth constitutes his feet.'"

रजस्तमश्च सत्त्वं च विद्धि नारायणात्मकम् ।
सोऽऽश्रमाणां मुखं तात कर्मणस्तत्फलं विदु: ॥ (24)

"'Know that rajas, tamas and sattva are Narayana's atman. O Son! Know that the ashramas and the fruits of all karma are his face.'"

अकर्मण: फलं चैव स एव परमव्यय: ।
छन्दांसि तस्य रोमाणि अक्षरं च सरस्वती ॥ (25)

"'The supreme and undecaying one is also the fruit of not performing karma. The metres are his body hair and the syllables are his speech.'"

बह्वाश्रयो बहुमुखो धर्मो हृदि समाश्रित: ।
स ब्रह्मपरमो धर्मस्तपश्च सदसच्च स: ॥ (26)

"'The different kinds of external modes and the various aspects of dharma are based in his heart. He is the brahman. He is supreme dharma. He is austerities. He is cause and effect.'"

श्रुतिशास्त्रग्रहोपेत: षोडशर्त्विक्क्रतुश्च स: ।
पितामहश्च विष्णुश्च सोऽश्विनौ स पुरन्दर: ॥ (27)

"'He is the Shrutis and the sacred texts.[13] He constitutes the vessels used in sacrifices, sacrifices and the sixteen officiating priests.[14]

---

[13]Shrutis are sacred texts that are in the nature of revelation, but there are other sacred texts too.
[14]There were four categories of priests—hotri, adhvaryu, udgatri and brahmana. While each of these were associated with specifically one of the Vedas, in this case,

He is the grandfather. He is Vishnu. He is the two Ashvins. He is Purandara."'

मित्रश्च वरुणश्चैव यमोऽथ धनदस्तथा ।
ते पृथग्दर्शनास्तस्य संविदन्ति तथैकताम् ।
एकस्य विद्धि देवस्य सर्वं जगदिदं वशे ॥ (28)

'"He is Mitra.[15] He is Varuna. He is Yama. He is the lord of riches.[16] Though he is seen as separate, he is known as one. Know that this entire universe is under the control of that single divinity."'

नानाभूतस्य दैत्येन्द्र तस्यैकत्वं वदत्ययम् ।
जन्तुः पश्यति ज्ञानेन ततः सत्त्वं प्रकाशते ॥ (29)

'"O Indra among the Daityas! In all beings, he is spoken of as the single one. When a creature perceives this through his jnana, then truth is manifested before him."'

संहारविक्षेपसहस्रकोटीस्तिष्ठन्ति जीवाः प्रचरन्ति चान्ये ।
प्रजाविसर्गस्य च परिमाणं वापी सहस्राणि बहूनि दैत्य ॥ (30)

'"Between creation and destruction, beings exist for one thousand crores, and this is also true of the others.[17] O Daitya! The measure of the duration of the creation of beings is in terms of many thousands of lakes."'

वाप्यः पुनर्योजनविस्तृतास्ताः क्रोशं च गम्भीरतयावगाढाः ।
आयामतः पञ्चशताश्च सर्वाः प्रत्येकशो योजनतः प्रवृद्धाः ॥ (31)

'"Each lake is one *yojana* in width, one *krosha* in depth and five

---

the number four is probably being multiplied by the four Vedas.
[15]Divinity, one of the twelve adityas.
[16]Kubera or Dhanada.
[17]Meaning, years. The text uses the word '*koti*', naturally translated as crore. But this may very well be a mistranslation. A 'kalpa' or period of creation lasts for one thousand divine years. Koti also means highest point or eminent position. So perhaps, the shloka means to say one thousand divine years. The sense is that everyone exists for a limited duration of time.

hundred yojanas in length.[18] The distance between one lake and another is one yojana."'

वाप्या जलं क्षिप्यति वालकोट्या त्वहा सकृच्चाप्यथ न द्वितीयम् ।
तासां क्षये विद्धि कृतं विसर्गं संहारमेकं च तथा प्रजानाम् ॥ (32)

"'Let water be taken away from one of these lakes, using a single hair and not a second one, with this being done only once a day. Know that the time it takes for all the lakes to be dried up is the period of creation of beings, and destruction is of the same duration."'

षड्जीववर्णाः परमं प्रमाणं कृष्णो धूम्रो नीलमथास्य मध्यम् ।
रक्तं पुनः सह्यतरं सुखं तु हरिद्रवर्णं सुसुखं च शुक्लम् ॥ (33)

"'There is supreme evidence that creatures have six complexions—dark; smoky; blue in the middle; red, which is easier to tolerate; yellow, which is extremely pleasant; and white.'"[19]

परं तु शुक्लं विमलं विशोकं गतक्लमं सिध्यति दानवेन्द्र ।
गत्वा तु योनिप्रभवानि दैत्य सहस्रशः सिद्धिमुपैति जीवः ॥ (34)

"'White is supreme. O Indra among Danavas! It is unblemished and without sorrow. It is bereft of exhaustion and brings success. O Daitya! A creature goes through birth in thousands of wombs before it obtains success."'

गतिं च यां दर्शनमाह देवो गत्वा शुभं दर्शनमेव चाह ।
गतिः पुनर्वर्णकृता प्रजानां वर्णस्तथा कालकृतोऽसुरेन्द्र ॥ (35)

"'O Indra among Asuras! Devas considered all possible ends and what the sacred texts said about auspicious ends. They said that the ends of creatures were determined by their colour and that their colour was determined by destiny.'"

---

[18]Yojana is a measure of distance, roughly 13–14 km. There are four kroshas in a yojana.
[19]Implicitly, each succeeding colour is superior to the preceding one.

शतं सहस्राणि चतुर्दशेह परा गतिर्जीवगुणस्य दैत्य ।
आरोहणं तत्कृतमेव विद्धि स्थानं तथा निःसरणं च तेषाम् ॥ (36)

'"O Daitya! A being has to pass through fourteen hundred thousand existences,[20] and the ultimate number depends on the qualities.[21] Know that depending on deeds, a creature can ascend, stay in the same place or descend."'

कृष्णस्य वर्णस्य गतिर्निकृष्टा स मज्जते नरके पच्यमानः ।
स्थानं तथा दुर्गतिभिस्तु तस्य प्रजा विसर्गान्सुबहून्वदन्ति ॥ (37)

'"The end obtained by a dark complexion is the worst. Such a person is submerged in hell and is cooked there. It is said that the creature has to undergo hardships in that state for many thousands of cycles of creation."'

शतं सहस्राणि ततश्चरित्वा प्राप्नोति वर्णं हरितं तु पश्चात् ।
स चैव तस्मिन्निवसत्यनीशो युगक्षये तमसा संवृतात्मा ॥ (38)

'"After having been there for hundreds and thousands of years, the creature obtains a smoky complexion. The creature dwells there helplessly until the end of the yuga, with its atman enveloped in tamas."'

स वै यदा सत्त्वगुणेन युक्तस्तमो व्यपोहन्घटते स्वबुद्ध्या ।
स लोहितं वर्णमुपैति नीलो मनुष्यलोके परिवर्तते च ॥ (39)

'"But when the creature is united with the qualities of sattva, it uses its own intelligence to dispel the darkness. It may then obtain a red complexion. However, if it is stuck with blue, it circles around in the world of men."'[22]

---

[20]Lives.
[21]This has complicated interpretations and should not be interpreted in the straightforward sense of number of births. Five senses, five organs of action, mind, intelligence, ego and consciousness add up to fourteen. These have hundreds of thousands of variations, and a creature rises or falls depending on how these behave.
[22]The preceding colours signify birth as non-human species.

स तत्र संहारविसर्गमेव स्वकर्मजैर्बन्धनै: क्लिश्यमान: ।
तत: स हारिद्रमुपैति वर्णं संहारविक्षेपशते व्यतीते ॥ (40)

'"Bound by its own karma, it is then afflicted by death and rebirth. However, when it attains a yellow complexion, though it is beyond immediate destruction, it still has to return."'[23]

हारिद्रवर्णस्तु प्रजाविसर्गान्सहस्रशस्तिष्ठति सचरंन्वै ।
अविप्रमुक्तो निरये च दैत्य तत: सहस्राणि दशापराणि ॥ (41)

'"With that yellow complexion, it roams around for thousands of cycles of creation and destruction. O Daitya! But it has still not been emancipated and has to spend time in hell for a thousand and ten years."'

गती: सहस्राणि च पञ्च तस्य चत्वारि संवर्तकृतानि चैव ।
विमुक्तमेनं निरयाच्च विद्धि सर्वेषु चान्येषु च सम्भवेषु ॥ (42)

'"There are still ends determined by nineteen thousand cycles of deeds.[24] Know that one is freed from hell, and every other form of birth only through emancipation."'

स देवलोके विहरत्यभीक्ष्णं ततश्च्युतो मानुषतामुपैति ।
संहारविक्षेपशतानि चाष्टौ मर्त्येषु तिष्ठन्नमृतत्वमेति ॥ (43)

'"A creature may roam around in the world of devas. But when the merits decay, it is dislodged and becomes human again. After having remained a mortal for one hundred and eight cycles of creation and destruction, it can become immortal again."'

सोऽस्मादथ भ्रश्यति कालयोगात्कृष्णे तले तिष्ठति सर्वकष्टे ।
यथा त्वयं सिध्यति जीवलोकस्तत्तेऽभिधास्याम्यसुरप्रवीर ॥ (44)

---

[23]The yellow colour signifies the status of a god. However, divinity is not permanent either.
[24]To the earlier fourteen, the five breaths of life have been added to get nineteen. Devas are still subject to these nineteen and the thousands of consequences resulting from deeds undertaken by these nineteen. Therefore, they are still in hell.

'"However, if in that state,[25] it deviates because of destiny, it obtains the status of a dark complexion and suffers from every kind of hardship. O Supreme Asura! I will now tell you about how a creature in the world of the living can obtain success, if it so desires."'

दैवानि स व्यूहशतानि सप्त रक्तो हरिद्रोऽथ तथैव शुक्ल: ।
संश्रित्य सधांवति शुक्लमेतमष्टापरानर्च्यतमान्स लोकान् ॥ (45)

'"Through seven hundred different kinds of destiny, a creature progresses from red to yellow and white.[26] Having finally united with white, it obtains and roams around in the supreme eight worlds."'[27]

अष्टौ च षष्टिं च शतानि यानि मनो विरुद्धानि महाद्युतीनाम् ।
शुक्लस्य वर्णस्य परा गतिर्यात्रीण्येव रुद्धानि महानुभाव ॥ (46)

'"These eight, or sixty, or hundreds, are extremely radiant. But they are created by the mind.[28] The white complexion is the supreme objective, and its greatness is more than that of the other three."'[29]

संहारविक्षेपमनिष्टमेकं चत्वारि चान्यानि वसत्यनीश: ।
षष्टस्य वर्णस्य परा गतिर्यासिद्धा विशिष्टस्य गतक्लमस्य ॥ (47)

'"Even if one transcends the cycles of creation and destruction, one dwells cheerlessly in the eight worlds or in the other four.[30] The sixth

---

[25]Of a human.
[26]The five senses, the mind and the intelligence add up to seven. Each of these leads to hundreds of different kinds of acts.
[27]This probably means the worlds associated with the eight guardians of the worlds.
[28]That is, these regions of bliss are not permanent.
[29]These are sections that are extremely difficult to understand. The four states being referred to here are the states of being awake, in which turiya is superior to the other three. There are five elements, five senses, five attributes of the senses, five organs of action, mind, intelligence, ego, consciousness and the gross body. When ignorance, desire, karma, the atman and the jagrata state are added, it totals to thirty. For the svapna stage, one similarly has another thirty, adding up to sixty.
[30]Those other four worlds are those of maharloka, janaloka, tapoloka and satyaloka. These are not destroyed in the secondary cycles of creation and destruction.

complexion[31] attains the supreme objective. Such a distinguished person obtains success and is devoid of exhaustion."'

सप्तोत्तरं तेषु वसत्यनीशः संहारविक्षेपशतं सशेषम् ।
तस्मादुपावृत्य मनुष्यलोके ततो महान्मानुषताम् उपैति ॥ (48)

'"One can dwell cheerlessly in the seven superior worlds[32] for hundreds of cycles of creation and destruction. When this ends, one is born in the world of men, although one becomes a great human being."'

तस्मादुपावृत्य ततः क्रमेण सोऽग्रे स्म सतिंष्ठति भूतसर्गम् ।
स सप्तकृत्वश्च परैति लोकान्संहार विक्षेपकृतप्रवासः ॥ (49)

'"In due course of time, one transcends these and moves up in the hierarchy of creatures. For several cycles of creation and destruction, one dwells seven times in those superior worlds."'

सप्तैव संहारमुपप्लवानि संभाव्य सतिष्ठति सिद्धलोके ।
ततोऽव्ययं स्थानमनन्तमेति देवस्य विष्णोरथ ब्रह्मणश्च ।
शेषस्य चैवाथ नरस्य चैव देवस्य विष्णोः परमस्य चैव ॥ (50)

'"If one can escape from destruction and submergence there on seven occasions, it is possible that one might reach the world of the siddhas. Those regions are without decay and are infinite and belong to the divinity Vishnu, Brahma, Shesha, the divinity Nara and the supreme Vishnu."'

संहारकाले परिदग्धकाया ब्रह्माणमायान्ति सदा प्रजा हि ।
चेष्टात्मनो देवगणाश्च सर्वे ये ब्रह्मलोकादमराः स्म तेऽपि ॥ (51)

'"At the time of destruction, though their bodies are burnt, such subjects approach Brahma. All the various categories of devas also endeavour to obtain immortality in Brahma's world."'

---

[31]White.
[32]Bhuloka, bhuvarloka, svarloka, maharloka, janaloka, tapoloka and satyaloka.

प्रजाविसर्गं तु सशेषकालं स्थानानि स्वान्येव सरन्ति जीवाः ।
निःशेषाणां तत्पदं यान्ति चान्ते सर्वापदा ये सदृशा मनुष्याः ॥ (52)

'"When it is time for creation after the period of destruction is over, all beings move to their own designated regions. But once the fruits are over, those regions terminate. So do those ends, and they become like humans."'

ये तु च्युताः सिद्धलोकात्क्रमेण तेषां गतिं यान्ति तथानुपूर्व्या ।
जीवाः परे तद्बलवेषरूपा विधिं स्वकं यान्ति विपर्ययेण ॥ (53)

'"However, for those who are progressively dislodged from the world of the siddhas,[33] their end remains what it used to be earlier. When there is creation after destruction, all superior beings obtain forms that are in conformity with their own destinies."'

स यावदेवास्ति सशेषभुक्ते प्रजाश्च देव्यौ च तथैव शुक्ले ।
तावत्तदा तेषु विशुद्धभावः संयम्य पञ्चेन्द्रिय रूपमेतत् ॥ (54)

'"However, creatures who have obtained success retain their white complexion and both kinds of knowledge.[34] Their sentiments are pure and controlled, and they see everything as if with their own five senses."'[35]

शुद्धां गतिं तां परमां परैति शुद्धेन नित्यं मनसा विचिन्वन् ।
ततोऽव्ययं स्थानुमुपैति ब्रह्म दुष्प्रापमभ्येति स शाश्वतं वै ।
इत्येतदाख्यातमहीनसत्त्व नारायणस्येह बलं मया ते ॥ (55)

'"Their ends are pure. Their objectives are supreme. In their minds, they always think of what is auspicious. They obtain Brahma's world, which is without decay. It is eternal and is difficult to obtain. O Spirited One! I have thus recounted to you everything about Narayana's powers."'

---

[33]That is, those who have been emancipated. Because of their knowledge, they do not regress.
[34]*Para vidya*, knowledge about the self, and *apara vidya*, knowledge about the material world.
[35]Supreme knowledge is as evident as knowledge gained with one's own senses.

वृत्र उवाच

एवं गते मे न विषादोऽस्ति कश्चित्सम्यक्च पश्यामि वचस्तवैतत् ।
श्रुत्वा च ते वाचमदीनसत्त्वविकल्मषोऽस्म्यद्य तथा विपाप्मा ॥ (56)

'Vritra said, "Since this is the case, there is nothing for me to grieve. I can clearly see the truth in your words. O One with a Cheerful Spirit! On hearing your words, I have now become cleansed of all evil and sin."'

प्रवृत्तमेतद्भगवन्महर्षे महाद्युतेश्चक्रमनन्तवीर्यम् ।
विष्णोरनन्तस्य सनातनं तत्स्थानं सर्गा यत्र सर्वे प्रवृत्ताः ।
स वै महात्मा पुरुषोत्तमो वै तस्मिञ्जगत्सर्वमिदं प्रतिष्ठितम् ॥ (57)

'"O Illustrious One! O Maharshi! O Immensely Radiant One! The immensely energetic wheel[36] is moving. The infinite and eternal Vishnu is the spot from which all creation originates. He is the great-souled Purushottama. Everything in the universe is established in him."'

भीष्म उवाच

एवमुक्त्वा स कौन्तेय वृत्रः प्राणानवासृजत् ।
योजयित्वा तथात्मानं परं स्थानमवाप्तवान् ॥ (58)

Bhishma said, 'O Kounteya! Having said this, Vritra gave up his life. He united his atman and obtained the supreme region.'

युधिष्ठिर उवाच

अयं स भगवान्देवः पितामह जनार्दनः ।
सनत्कुमारो वृत्राय यत्तदाख्यातवान्पुरा ॥ (59)

Yudhishthira asked, 'O Grandfather! In ancient times, Sanatkumara spoke to Vritra about an illustrious divinity. Is this Janardana that same person?'

---

[36] Of time.

भीष्म उवाच

मूलस्थायी स भगवान्स्वेनानन्तेन तेजसा ।
तत्स्थः सृजति तान्भावान्नानारूपान्महातपाः ॥ (60)

Bhishma replied, 'In his own infinite energy, the illustrious one is the foundation. From there, the immensely ascetic one creates many kinds of beings.'

तुरीयार्धेन तस्येमं विद्धि केशवमच्युतम् ।
तुरीयार्धेन लोकांस्त्रीन्भावयत्येष बुद्धिमान् ॥ (61)

'Know that Keshava is not dislodged from his richness of turiya. The intelligent one creates the three worlds from his richness of turiya.'

अर्वाक्स्थितस्तु यः स्थायी कल्पान्ते परिवर्तते ।
स शेते भगवानप्सु योऽसावतिबलः प्रभुः ।
तान्विधाता प्रसन्नात्मा लोकांश्चरति शाश्वतान् ॥ (62)

'Stationed at one end, at the end of a kalpa, he transforms himself. The immensely strong and illustrious lord lies down on the water. From there, the creator, cheerful in his atman, roams around the eternal worlds.'

सर्वाण्यशून्यानि करोत्यनन्तः सनत्कुमारः संचरते च लोकान् ।
स चानिरुद्धः सृजते महात्मा तत्स्थं जगत्सर्वमिदं विचित्रम् ॥ (63)

'Ananta is the one who makes everything empty. In the form of Sanatkumara, he is the one who roams around in the worlds. The great-souled one is not obstructed in his creation. Everything in this wonderful universe is established in him.'

युधिष्ठिर उवाच

वृत्रेण परमार्थज्ञ दृष्टा मन्येऽऽत्मनो गतिः ।
शुभा तस्मात्सुखितो न शोचति पितामह ॥ (64)
शुक्लः शुक्लाभिजातीयः साध्यो नावर्ततेऽनघ ।
तिर्यग्गतेश्च निर्मुक्तो निरयाच्च पितामह ॥ (65)
हरिद्रवर्णे रक्ते वा वर्तमानस्तु पार्थिव ।

तिर्यग्गेवानुपश्येत कर्मभिस्तामसैर्वृतः ॥ (66)
वयं तु भृशमापन्ना रक्ताः कस्तमुखेऽसुखे ।
कां गतिं प्रतिपत्स्यामो नीलां कृष्णाधमामथ ॥ (67)

Yudhishthira said, 'O One Who Knows about the Supreme Truth! I think that Vritra knew his end was going to be auspicious. O Grandfather! That is the reason he was happy and did not grieve. O Unblemished One! A person who is white in complexion, a person who belongs to the white category and a person who is successful does not return.[37] O Grandfather! Such a person is freed from hell and from birth as inferior species. O Lord of the Earth! But a person who has a yellow or red complexion has karma that is enveloped by tamas and is seen to be born as inferior species. We are extremely afflicted. We are addicted to things that take us to the mouth of hardships and unhappiness. What ends will we obtain, blue or dark, the worst of them all?'

भीष्म उवाच

शुद्धाभिजनसम्पन्नाः पाण्डवाः संशितव्रताः ।
विहृत्य देवलोकेषु पुनर्मानुष्यमेष्यथ ॥ (68)
प्रजाविसर्गं च सुखेन काले प्रत्येत्य देवेषु सुखानि भुक्त्वा ।
सुखेन संयास्यथ सिद्धसङ्ख्यां मा वो भयं भूद्विमलाः स्थ सर्वे ॥ (69)

Bhishma replied, 'You are Pandavas and you have been born in a pure lineage. You are firm in your vows. Having obtained pleasure in the world of devas, you will again be born as men. Having enjoyed happiness as long as creation lasts, you will return as devas and enjoy bliss. In your joy, you will be counted among the siddhas. Do not entertain any fear on this account. All of you will be unblemished.'

Thus ends the Vritra Gita.

---

[37]There is no rebirth.

20

PARASHARA GITA

In Moksha Dharma Parva of Shanti Parva, Bhishma continues to speak to Yudhishthira. Within this, there are nine chapters with 286 shlokas. These constitute the Parashara Gita, so named because they comprise what Sage Parashara taught King Janaka, and the same was repeated by Bhishma to Yudhishthira.

Chapter 1

युधिष्ठिर उवाच

अत: परं महाबाहो यच्छ्रेयस्तद्वदस्व मे ।
न तृप्याम्यमृतस्येव वचसस्ते पितामह ॥ (1)
किं कर्म पुरुष: कृत्वा शुभं पुरुषसत्तम ।
श्रेय: परमवाप्नोति प्रेत्य चेह च तद्वद ॥ (2)

Yudhishthira said, 'O Mighty-Armed One! After this, tell me what is best for me. O Grandfather! I am not satisfied with your words, which are like amrita. O Supreme among Men! What are the auspicious acts a man can perform, so that he obtains supreme benefit in this world and in the world after death? Tell me that.'

भीष्म उवाच

अत्र ते वर्तयिष्यामि यथापूर्व महायशा: ।
पराशरं महात्मानं पप्रच्छ जनको नृप: ॥ (3)

किं श्रेयः सर्वभूतानामस्मिँल्लोके परत्र च ।
यद्भवेत्प्रतिपत्तव्यं तद्भवान्प्रब्रवीतु मे ॥ (4)

Bhishma replied, 'In this connection, I will tell you what the immensely illustrious King Janaka asked the great-souled Parashara in ancient times. "What is best for all beings here and in the hereafter, so that one can obtain prosperity? Please tell me about this."'

ततः स तपसा युक्तः सर्वधर्मविधानवित् ।
नृपायानुग्रह मना मुनिर्वाक्यमथाब्रवीत् ॥ (5)

'The sage was full of austerities and knew about the ordinances associated with all kinds of dharma. His inclination was to show favours to the king. So he spoke these words.'

धर्म एव कृतः श्रेयानिह लोके परत्र च ।
तस्माद्धि परमं नास्ति यथा प्राहुर्मनीषिणः ॥ (6)

'"Deeds of dharma bring benefit in this world and in the next. The learned ones have said that there is nothing that is superior to this."'

प्रतिपद्य नरो धर्मं स्वर्गलोके महीयते ।
धर्मात्मकः कर्म विधिर्देहिनां नृपसत्तम ।
तस्मिन्नाश्रमिणः सन्तः स्वकर्माणीह कुर्वते ॥ (7)

'"Through such dharma, a man obtains greatness in the world of heaven. O Supreme among Kings! For all embodied beings, the rites and ordinances that have been laid down represent the essence of dharma. That is the reason virtuous people perform their respective acts in their respective ashramas."'

चतुर्विधा हि लोकस्य यात्रा तात विधीयते ।
मर्त्या यत्रावतिष्ठन्ते सा च कामात्प्रवर्तते ॥ (8)

'"O Son! Four kinds of modes have been laid down for progress in this world.[1] When mortals follow these, they obtain what they desire."'

---

[1] This refers to the four varnas.

सुकृतासुकृतं कर्म निषेव्य विविधै: क्रमै: ।
दशार्ध प्रविभक्तानां भूतानां बहुधा गति: ॥ (9)

"'They perform many good and bad deeds and attain their respective ends. In different ways, creatures are divided into the five elements and have diverse ends.'"

सौवर्णं राजतं वापि यथा भान्दं निषिच्यते ।
तथा निषिच्यते जन्तु: पूर्वकर्मवशानुग: ॥ (10)

"'Just as a golden or silver vessel reflects the sheen of the metal, creatures are bound by the acts that they have performed earlier.'"

नाबीजाज्जायते किंचिन्नाकृत्वा सुखमेधते ।
सुकृती विन्दति सुखं प्राप्य देहक्षयं नर: ॥ (11)

"'Nothing is generated without a seed. Without acting for it, happiness cannot be obtained. When the body is destroyed, a man obtains happiness because of the good deeds he has performed.'"

दैवं तात न पश्यामि नास्ति दैवस्य साधनम् ।
स्वभावतो हि संसिद्धा देवगन्धर्वदानवा: ॥ (12)

"'O Son! I do not see any destiny in this, nor any attempt on the part of devas. Devas, gandharvas and danavas become what they are because of their natures.'"

प्रेत्य जातिकृतं कर्म न स्मरन्ति सदा जना: ।
ते वै तस्य फलप्राप्तौ कर्म चापि चतुर्विधम् ॥ (13)

"'After death, people never remember what they have done in their earlier lives. But they obtain the consequences of the four kinds of acts that they have performed.'"[2]

लोकयात्राश्रयश्चैव शब्दो वेदाश्रय: कृत: ।
शान्त्यर्थं मनसस्तात नैतद्बुद्ध्यानुशासनम् ॥ (14)

---

[2]Acts are divided into *nitya* (daily), *naimittika* (occasional), *kamya* (desirable) and *nishiddha* (prohibited).

"'For progress in the world, the words of the Vedas have described the deeds that one must resort to. O Son! That is what brings peace to the mind, not merely the instructions of the elders.'"

चक्षुषा मनसा वाचा कर्मणा च चतुर्विंधम् ।
कुरुते यादृशं कर्म तादृशं प्रतिपद्यते ॥ (15)

"'There are four kinds of action one can perform with the eye, the mind, words and deeds. Whatever the nature of the action, the consequence is like that.'"

निरन्तरं च मिश्रं च फलते कर्म पार्थिव ।
कल्याणं यदि वा पापं न तु नाशोऽस्य विद्यते ॥ (16)

"'O Lord of the Earth! Often, one obtains mixed consequences as a result of a deed. However, whether it is auspicious or wicked, deeds are never destroyed.'"

कदाचित्सुकृतं तात कूटस्थमिव तिष्ठति ।
मज्जमानस्य संसारे यावदु:खादिमुच्यते ॥ (17)

"'O Son! Sometimes, the consequences of good deeds remain concealed and submerged in samsara, and one is not freed from misery.'"

ततो दु:खक्षयं कृत्वा सुकृतं कर्म सेवते ।
सुकृतक्षयाद्दुष्कृतं च तद्विद्धि मनुजाधिप ॥ (18)

"'However, once the misery has been exhausted, the results of good deeds will become evident. O Lord of Men! Know that when good deeds have been exhausted, the results of bad deeds will become evident.'"

दम: क्षमा धृतिस्तेज: सन्तोष: सत्यवादिता ।
ह्रीरहिंसाव्यसनिता दाक्ष्यं चेति सुखावहा: ॥ (19)

"'Self-control, forgiveness, fortitude, energy, contentment, truthfulness in speech, modesty, lack of injury, not indulging in vices and skilfulness—these are the things that yield happiness.'"

दुष्कृते सुकृते वापि न जन्तुरयतो भवेत् ।
नित्यं मन:समाधाने प्रयतेत विचक्षण: ॥ (20)

'"For no creature are the effects of good deeds and bad deeds eternal. That is the reason a discriminating person always tries to fix his mind."

नायं परस्य सुकृतं दुष्कृतं वापि सेवते ।
करोति यादृशं कर्म तादृशं प्रतिपद्यते ॥ (21)

'"One does not face the consequences of the good or bad deeds performed by another person. The consequences one reaps are commensurate with the deeds that one has performed."

सुखदु:खे समाधाय पुमानन्येन गच्छति ।
अन्येनैव जन: सर्व: सङ्गतो यश्च पार्थिव ॥ (22)

'"Along one path,[3] a man can proceed, regardless of happiness and unhappiness. O Lord of the Earth! But along another path, there are other people who are always prone to attachment."

परेषां यदसूयेत न तत्कुर्यात्स्वयं नर: ।
यो ह्यसूयुस्तथायुक्त: सोऽवहासं नियच्छति ॥ (23)

'"A man must never undertake an act that he censures in someone else. If he does something that he has censured, he will be laughed at."'

भीरू राजन्यो ब्राह्मण: सर्वभक्षो वैश्योऽनीहावान्हीनवर्णोऽलसश्च ।
विद्वांश्चाशीलो वृत्तहीन: कुलीन: सत्याद्भ्रष्टो ब्राह्मण:
स्त्री च दुष्टा ॥ (24)
रागी मुक्त: पचमानोऽऽत्महेतोर्मूर्खों वक्ता नृपहीनं च राष्ट्रम् ।
एते सर्वे शोच्यतां यान्ति राजन्यश्चायुक्त: स्नेहहीन: प्रजासु ॥ (25)

---

[3]The path of knowledge. The word 'path' is not directly used in the text. We have added it to make the meaning clear.

'"A king who is a coward, a brahmana who eats everything, a vaishya without exertion, a person from an inferior varna[4] who is lazy, a learned person who lacks good conduct, a noble person who is without means of sustenance, a brahmana who has deviated from the truth, a wicked woman, a 'free' person who is still attached, a person who cooks only for himself,[5] a foolish person who is eloquent, a kingdom without a king and a king who has no affection for his subjects—all these are reasons for grief."'

Chapter 2

परशर उवाच

मनोरथरथं प्राप्य इन्द्रियार्थहयं नरः ।
रश्मिभिर्ज्ञानसम्भूतैर्यो गच्छति स बुद्धिमान् ॥ (1)

'Parashara said, "Having obtained a chariot[6] made up of wishes, if a man controls the horses that are the objects of the senses with the reins of jnana, he is intelligent."'

सेवाश्रितेन मनसा वृत्ति हीनस्य शस्यते ।
द्विजातिहस्तान्निर्वृत्ता न तु तुल्यात्परस्परम् ॥ (2)

'"A person who follows such conduct in his mind, even if he does not possess a means of sustenance, is praised. A dvija and a person who has withdrawn himself are not equal to each other."'[7]

आयुर्नसुलभं लब्ध्वा नावकर्षेद्दिशांपते ।
उत्कर्षार्थं प्रयतते नरः पुण्येन कर्मणा ॥ (3)

---

[4]Meaning a shudra.
[5]Without offering it to gods, guests and others.
[6]A metaphor for the body.
[7]The person who has refrained from action is superior. *Nivritti* has many shades of meaning but means withdrawal from action, that withdrawal being interpreted differently.

"'O Lord of the Earth! Having easily obtained a span of life, one should not diminish it. A man must strive for auspicious deeds, so that he can uplift himself.'"

वर्णेभ्योऽपि परिभ्रष्ट: स वै संमानमर्हति ।
न तु य: सत्क्रियां प्राप्य राजसं कर्म सेवते ॥ (4)

"'A person who has been dislodged from his varna does not deserve to be honoured. A person who has obtained the consequences of good deeds must not perform deeds associated with rajas.'"

वर्णोत्कर्षमवाप्नोति नर: पुण्येन कर्मणा ।
दुर्लभं तमलब्धा हि हन्यात्पापेन कर्मणा ॥ (5)

"'A man obtains a superior varna through auspicious deeds. However, having obtained what is difficult to obtain, one destroys it because one is overcome with tamas and performs wicked deeds.'"

अज्ञानाद्धि कृतं पापं तपसैवाभिनिर्णुदेत् ।
पापं हि कर्म फलति पापमेव स्वयं कृतम् ।
तस्मात्पापं न सेवेत कर्म दु:खफलोदयम् ॥ (6)

"'Wicked deeds perpetrated due to ignorance can be destroyed through the practice of austerities. But a wicked deed that is perpetrated knowingly leads to evil consequences. Therefore, one must never perform wicked deeds. They give rise to fruits of misery.'"

पापानुबन्धं यत्कर्म यद्यपि स्यान्महाफलम् ।
न तत्सेवेत मेधावी शुचि: कुसलिलं यथा ॥ (7)

"'An intelligent person will never be bound by wicked deeds, even if they lead to great fruits, just as an auspicious person will not touch water that has been tainted.'"

किंकृष्टमनुपश्यामि फलं पापस्य कर्मण: ।
प्रत्यापन्नस्य हि सतो नात्मा तावद्विरोचते ॥ (8)

'"As the fruits of wicked deeds, I see hardships. Though virtue and the atman are evident, one acts contrary to this."'

प्रत्यापत्तिश्च यस्येह बालिशस्य न जायते ।
तस्यापि सुमहांस्ताप: प्रस्थितस्योपजायते ॥ (9)

'"If a foolish person is not led to turn back, he is like a person who is dead and faces extremely great torments."'

विरक्तं शोध्यते वस्त्रं न तु कृष्णोपसंहितम् ।
प्रयत्नेन मनुष्येन्द्र पापमेवं निबोध मे ॥ (10)

'"A garment that is not dyed can be cleaned, but not one that has been dyed black. O Indra among Men! Listen to me. That is also the case with sinful efforts."'

स्वयं कृत्वा तु य: पापं शुभमेवानुतिष्ठति ।
प्रायश्चित्तं नर: कर्तुमुभयं सोऽश्नुते पृथक् ॥ (11)

'"If a man knowingly performs wicked deeds and then performs auspicious ones in *prayashchitta*, he will separately obtain the fruits of both."'[8]

अजानातु कृतां हिंसामहिंसा व्यपकर्षति ।
ब्राह्मणा: शास्त्रनिर्देशादित्याहुर्ब्रह्मवादिन: ॥ (12)

'"Brahmanas who know about the brahman mention the instructions of the sacred texts. If an act of injury is committed in ignorance, an act of non-injury can correct it."'

तथा कामकृतं चास्य विहिंसैवापकर्षति ।
इत्याहुर्धर्मशास्त्रज्ञा ब्राह्मणा वेदपारगा: ॥ (13)

'"However, if an act of violence is committed knowingly, brahmanas who are accomplished in the Vedas and versed in the sacred texts say that this is an act of adharma."'

---

[8]The good and the evil. Prayashchitta is a rite of atonement.

अहं तु तावत्पश्यामि कर्म यद्वर्तते कृतम् ।
गुणयुक्तं प्रकाशं च पापेनानुपसंहितम् ॥ (14)

"'I see that all the acts that are performed, good or evil ones, lead to manifestations of their qualities.'"

यथा सूक्ष्माणि कर्माणि फलन्तीह यथातथम् ।
बुद्धियुक्तानि तानीह कृतानि मनसा सह ॥ (15)

"'All deeds that are performed, using the intelligence and the mind, lead to corresponding fruits, gross or subtle.'"

भवत्यल्पफलं कर्म सेवितं नित्यमुल्बनम् ।
अबुद्धिपूर्वं धर्मज्ञ कृतमुग्रेण कर्मणा ॥ (16)

"'O One Who Knows about Dharma! But acts that are done involuntarily lead to smaller fruits. Fierce deeds performed knowingly always lead to strong consequences.'"

कृतानि यानि कर्माणि दैवतैर्मुनिभिस्तथा ।
नाचरेत्तानि धर्मात्मा श्रुत्वा चापि न कुत्सयेत् ॥ (17)

"'There may be acts that are performed by devas and sages.[9] If a person with dharma in his atman hears about these, he should not censure them. But nor should he practise them.'"

संचिन्त्य मनसा राजन्विदित्वा शक्तिमात्मनः ।
करोति यः शुभं कर्म स वै भद्राणि पश्यति ॥ (18)

"'O King! One should use one's mind to reflect on one's own capacity. A person who performs auspicious deeds looks at what is fortunate.'"

नवे कपाले सलिलं संन्यस्तं हीयते यथा ।
नवेतरे तथा भावं प्राप्नोति सुखभावितम् ॥ (19)

---

[9]That is, inappropriate acts.

"'If a vessel is new,[10] water placed into it gradually becomes less and less. But that is not the case if the vessel has been baked. One obtains happiness through such sentiments.'"

सतोयेऽन्यत्तु यत्तोयं तस्मिन्नेव प्रसिच्यते ।
वृद्धे वृद्धिमवाप्नोति सलिले सलिलं यथा ॥ (20)

"'When water is poured into a vessel that already has water, the quantity of the water is increased. Intelligence is also increased in that way.'"

एवं कर्माणि यानीह बुद्धियुक्तानि भूपते ।
नसमानीह हीनानि तानि पुण्यतमान्यपि ॥ (21)

"'O Lord of the Earth! That is the way one should perform deeds in this world, using one's intelligence. One's store of merits is then not diminished but added to.'"

राज्ञा जेतव्या: सायुधाश्चोन्ताश्च सम्यक्कर्तव्यं पालनं च प्रजानाम् ।
अग्निश्चेयो बहुभिश्चापि यज्ञैरन्ते मध्ये वा वनमाश्रित्य स्थेयम् ॥ (22)

"'A king's proper duty is to protect the subjects, raising his weapons to defeat those who are unruly. He must kindle many fires and perform sacrifices. Then, when he is middle aged, or at the end, he must resort to the forest.'"

दमान्वित: पुरुषो धर्मशीलो भूतानि चात्मानमिवानुपश्येत् ।
गरीयस: पूजयेदात्मशक्त्या सत्येन शीलेन सुखं नरेन्द्र ॥ (23)

"'Self-controlled and with dharma in conduct, a man must look upon all beings as one's own self. According to capacity, one must worship those who are superior. O Indra among Men! Through truthfulness and good conduct, one obtains happiness.'"

---

[10] An earthen vessel that has not been baked.

Chapter 3

पराशर उवाच

क: कस्य चोपकुरुते कश्च कस्मै प्रयच्छति ।
प्राणी करोत्ययं कर्म सर्वमात्मार्थमात्मना ॥ (1)

'Parashara said, "No one does a favour to another. No one gives anything to another. In every way, all creatures only act for their own selves."'

गौरवेण परित्यक्तं नि:स्नेहं परिवर्जयेत् ।
सोदर्यं भ्रातरमपि किमुतान्यं पृथग्जनम् ॥ (2)

'"When there is a lack of affection, one's own uterine brothers are proudly discarded. What should one say about unrelated people?"'

विशिष्टस्य विशिष्टाच्च तुल्यौ दानप्रतिग्रहौ ।
तयो: पुण्यतरं दानं तद्विजस्य प्रयच्छत: ॥ (3)

'"Giving gifts to superior people and receiving gifts from superior people are equal. But compared to these, the gift given to a brahmana is more sacred."'

न्यायागतं धनं वर्णैर्यायेनैव विवर्धितम् ।
संरक्ष्यं यत्नमास्थाय धर्मार्थमिति निश्चय: ॥ (4)

'"With the objectives of dharma and artha in mind, each of the varnas must endeavour to protect riches earned through fair means and increase them."'

न धर्मार्थी नृशंसेन कर्मणा धनमर्जयेत् ।
शक्तित: सर्वकार्याणि कुर्यान्नर्द्धिमनुस्मरेत् ॥ (5)

'"For the sake of dharma and artha, one should not undertake tasks that seek to obtain wealth through injurious means. One must remember the virtuous and perform all tasks according to one's capacity."'

अपो हि प्रयतः शीतास्तापिता ज्वलनेन वा ।
शक्तितोऽतिथये दत्त्वा क्षुधार्तायाश्नुते फलम् ॥ (6)

'"According to one's capacity, if one gives cool water or that heated through a fire to a guest, one obtains fruits that are like those got by giving food to someone suffering from hunger."'

रन्तिदेवेन लोकेष्टा सिद्धिः प्राप्ता महात्मना ।
फलपत्रैरथो मूलैर्मुनीनर्चितवानसौ ॥ (7)

'"The great-souled Rantideva obtained success in the world. But all he did was worship hermits with fruits, leaves and roots."'[11]

तैरेव फलपत्रैश्च स माठरमतोषयत् ।
तस्माल्लेभे परं स्थानं शैब्योऽपि पृथिवीपतिः ॥ (8)

'"Shaibya, lord of the earth, satisfied Mathara[12] with fruits and leaves and obtained a supreme region."'

देवतातिथिभृत्येभ्यः पितृभ्योऽथात्मनस्तथा ।
ऋणवाञ्जायते मर्त्यस्तस्मादनृणतां व्रजेत् ॥ (9)

'"Through being born, mortals incur debts to devas, guests, servants, ancestors and their own selves and one must act so as to repay these debts."'

स्वाध्यायेन महर्षिभ्यो देवेभ्यो यज्ञकर्मणा ।
पितृभ्यः श्राद्धदानेन नृणाम् अभ्यर्चनेन च ॥ (10)

'"There is studying for maharshis, sacrifices and rites for devas, funeral sacrifices and donations for ancestors and honouring for men."'[13]

वाचः शेषावहार्येण पालनेनात्मनोऽपि च ।
यथावद्त्यवर्गस्य चिकीर्षेद्धर्ममादितः ॥ (11)

---

[11] King Rantideva obtained success through his sacrifices.
[12] Shaibya was a famous king, and Mathara is one of the attendants of the Sun God, though this is a term also used for Vyasadeva.
[13] These are means of repaying those respective debts.

'"Debts to one's own self are repaid through words,[14] eating leftovers and protecting one's own self. If one is inclined towards following dharma, one should properly discharge debts due to the various categories of servants."'

प्रयत्नेन च संसिद्धा धनैरपि विवर्जिता: ।
सम्यग्घुत्वा हुतवहं मुनय: सिद्धिमागता: ॥ (12)

'"Even if one is devoid of riches, one can make efforts to obtain success. Sages offered oblations of clarified butter properly into the fire and obtained success."'

विश्वामित्रस्य पुत्रत्वमृचीकतनयोऽगमत् ।
ऋग्भि: स्तुत्वा महाभागो देवान्वै यज्ञभागिन: ॥ (13)

'"Vishvamitra's son went to Richika's son.[15] The immensely fortunate one praised devas, who have shares in sacrifices, with hymns from the Rig Veda."'

गत: शुक्रत्वमुशना देवदेव प्रसादनात् ।
देवीं स्तुत्वा तु गगने मोदते तेजसा वृत: ॥ (14)

'"Through the favours of the lord of devas,[16] Ushanas became Shukra. Through praising the goddess, he was surrounded by energy and found pleasure in the sky."'[17]

असितो देवलश्चैव तथा नारदपर्वतौ ।
कक्षीवाञ्जामदग्न्यश्च रामस्ताण्ड्यस्तथांशुमान् ॥ (15)
वसिष्ठो जमदग्निश्च विश्वामित्रोऽत्रिरेव च ।
भरद्वाजो हरिश्मश्रु: कुण्डधार: श्रुतश्रवा: ॥ (16)
एते महर्षय: स्तुत्वा विष्णुमृग्भि: समाहिता: ।
लेभिरे तपसा सिद्धिं प्रसादात्तस्य धीमत: ॥ (17)

---

[14]Probably the words of the sacred texts. Leftovers are food left after offering to gods, ancestors, guests, animals and birds.
[15]This is unclear in terms of who went to whom. Richika's son was Jamadagni. Vishvamitra's son was Koushika. So Koushika must have gone to Jamadagni.
[16]Shiva.
[17]As the planet Venus.

'"Asita-Devala, Narada and Parvata, Kakshivat, Jamadagni's son Rama, Tandya, Amshumat, Vasishtha, Jamadagni, Vishvamitra, Atri, Bharadvaja, Harishmashru, Kundadhara, Shrutashrava—these maharshis controlled themselves and praised Vishnu, using hymns from the Rig Veda. Through the favours of that intelligent one, they obtained success in their austerities."'

अनर्हाश्चार्हतां प्राप्ताः सन्तः स्तुत्वा तमेव ह ।
न तु वृद्धिमिहान्विच्छेत्कर्म कृत्वा जुगुप्सितम् ॥ (18)

'"By praising him, even those who are undeserving have become deserving and virtuous. One should not desire to perform acts that increase one's prosperity in this world."'

येऽर्था धर्मेण ते सत्या येऽधर्मेण धिगस्तु तान् ।
धर्म वै शाश्वतं लोके न जह्याद्धनकाङ्क्षया ॥ (19)

'"Riches obtained through dharma are true riches. Shame on those obtained through adharma. Dharma is eternal in this world and must not be abandoned for the sake of riches."'

आहिताग्निर्हि धर्मात्मा यः स पुण्यकृदुत्तमः ।
वेदा हि सर्वे राजेन्द्र स्थितास्त्रिष्वग्निषु प्रभो ॥ (20)

'"A person who has dharma in his atman and makes offerings to the fire is supreme among the performers of auspicious deeds. O Indra among Kings! O Lord! All the Vedas are established in the three fires."'[18]

स चाप्यग्न्याहितो विप्रः क्रिया यस्य न हीयते ।
श्रेयो ह्यनाहिताग्नित्वमग्निहोत्रं न निष्क्रियम् ॥ (21)

---

[18]*Dakshina*, *garhapatya* and *ahavaniya* fires. Dakshina fire is the fire that burns in a southern direction, for oblations to the ancestors, garhapatya fire is the fire that burns in a household, while ahavaniya fire is a fire into which oblations to the gods are offered. Though meanings depend a bit on the context, garhapatya fire burns constantly. Dakshina and ahavaniya fires are kindled from the garhapatya fire for a specific rite.

"'If a brahmana possesses the sacred fire, his deeds are never diminished. However, if one does not perform the rites of agnihotra, it is better to give up the sacred fire.'"

अग्निरात्मा च माता च पिता जनयिता तथा ।
गुरुश्च नरशार्दूल परिचर्या यथातथम् ॥ (22)

"'O Tiger among Men! The sacred fire, the mother, the father who has provided the seed and the guru must be served in the proper way.'"

मानं त्यक्त्वा यो नरो वृद्धसेवी विद्वान्क्लीबः पश्यति प्रीतियोगात् ।
दाक्ष्येणाहीनो धर्मयुक्तो नदान्तो लोकेऽस्मिन्वै पूज्यते सद्भिरार्यः ॥ (23)

"'If a man abandons pride and serves the aged, if he is learned, if he behaves as if he is impotent,[19] if he looks upon everything with affection and if he is accomplished—even if he does not possess wealth, he is worshipped in this world as a virtuous and noble person.'"

Chapter 4

पराशर उवाच

वृत्तिः सकाशाद्वर्णेभ्यस्त्रिभ्यो हीनस्य शोभना ।
प्रीत्योपनीता निर्दिष्टा धर्मिष्ठान्कुरुते सदा ॥ (1)

'Parashara said, "It is appropriate that the inferior varna[20] should earn a living by serving the other three. If this designated service is rendered affectionately, that person always remains devoted to dharma."'

वृत्तिश्चेन्नास्ति शूद्रस्य पितृपैतामही ध्रुवा ।
न वृत्तिं परतो मार्गेच्छुश्रूषां तु प्रयोजयेत् ॥ (2)

---

[19] If he has given up sexual desire.
[20] Shudra varna.

"'Even if the ancestors of the shudra were not engaged in such an occupation, it is certain that he should not engage himself in any other path of sustenance other than servitude.'"

सद्भिस्तु सह संसर्गः शोभते धर्मदर्शिभिः ।
नित्यं सर्वास्ववस्थासु नासद्भिरिति मे मतिः ॥ (3)

"'It is my view that under all circumstances, it is proper that they[21] should always associate with virtuous people who know about dharma, not with those who are wicked.'"

यथोदयगिरौ द्रव्यं सन्निकर्षेण दीप्यते ।
तथा सत्सन्निकर्षेण हीनवर्णोऽपि दीप्यते ॥ (4)

"'When they are close to Mount Udaya,[22] objects blaze. Similarly, an inferior varna blazes when it is associated with the virtuous.'"

यादृशेन हि वर्णेन भाव्यते शुक्लमम्बरम् ।
तादृशं कुरुते रूपमेतदेवमवैहि मे ॥ (5)

"'A white garment assumes the colour with which it is dyed. They assume their appearances in the same way.'"

तस्माद्गुणेषु रज्येथा मा दोषेषु कदाचन ।
अनित्यमिह मर्त्यानां जीवितं हि चलाचलम् ॥ (6)

"'Therefore, one should rejoice because of qualities and never because of taints. The lifespan of mortals, whether mobile or immobile, is temporary.'"

सुखे वा यदि वा दुःखे वर्तमानो विचक्षणः ।
यश्चिनोति शुभान्येव स भद्राणीह पश्यति ॥ (7)

"'If a person with discrimination only acts in accordance with auspicious policy, whether he faces joy or misery, he faces fortune in this world.'"

---

[21] This is specifically directed at shudras.
[22] The mountain behind which the sun rises.

धर्मादपेतं यत्कर्म यद्यपि स्यान्महाफलम् ।
न तत्सेवेत मेधावी न तद्धितमिहोच्यते ॥ (8)

'"It is said that in this world, an intelligent person should not deviate from dharma, even if that act of deviation from dharma yields great fruits."'

यो हत्वा गोसहस्राणि नृपो दद्यादरक्षिता ।
स शब्दमात्रफलभाग्राजा भवति तस्करः ॥ (9)

'"If a king steals thousands of unprotected cattle and then gives them away as a gift, he only obtains the fruits of the sound that action makes.[23] The king is actually a thief."'

स्वयम्भूरसृजच्चाग्रे धातारं लोकपूजितम् ।
धातासृजत्पुत्रमेकं प्रजानां धारणे रतम् ॥ (10)

'"Right at the beginning, Svayambhu created Dhatri, revered in the worlds. Dhatri created a single son who is engaged in sustaining beings."'[24]

तमर्चयित्वा वैश्यस्तु कुर्यादत्यर्थमृद्धिमत् ।
रक्षितव्यं तु राजन्यैरुपयोज्यं द्विजातिभिः ॥ (11)

'"It is through worshipping him that vaishyas earn wealth and prosperity. The kings must think of means to protect brahmanas."'

अजिह्मैरशठैरक्रोधैर्हव्यकव्यप्रयोक्तृभिः ।
शूद्रैर्निर्मार्जनं कार्यमेवं धर्मो न नश्यति ॥ (12)

'"Shudras should, honestly, without deceit or anger, clean the objects used to offer *havya* and *kavya*.[25] Through such acts, dharma is not destroyed."'

---

[23] There are no fruits obtained from that act of donation except the sound the king makes when he proclaims that he is donating.
[24] 'Dhatri' means the one who nurtures, and his son is regarded as the god of the clouds.
[25] 'Havya' is oblations offered to devas; 'kavya' is oblations offered to ancestors.

अप्रनष्टे ततो धर्मे भवन्ति सुखिता: प्रजा: ।
सुखेन तासां राजेन्द्र मोदन्ते दिवि देवता: ॥ (13)

"'If dharma is not destroyed, subjects are happy. O Indra among Kings! Through their happiness, devas in heaven are delighted.'"

तस्माद्यो रक्षति नृप: स धर्मेणाभिपूज्यते ।
अधीते चापि यो विप्रो वैश्यो यश्चार्जने रत: ॥ (14)
यश्च शुश्रूषते शूद्र: सततं नियतेन्द्रिय: ।
अतोऽन्यथा मनुष्येन्द्र स्वधर्मात्परिहीयते ॥ (15)

"'A king who follows dharma and protects is worshipped. So are brahmanas who study, vaishyas who are engaged in the welfare of people and shudras who serve, always in control of their senses. O Indra among Men! If they act in any other way, they deviate from their own dharma.'"

प्राणसंतापनिर्दिष्टा: काकिन्योऽपि महाफला: ।
न्यायेनोपार्जिता दत्ता: किमुतान्या: सहस्रश: ॥ (16)

"'Not to speak of thousands, even if a few *kakinis*[26] are earned lawfully and donated without causing torment to life, this leads to great fruits.'"

सत्कृत्य तु द्विजातिभ्यो यो ददाति नराधिप ।
यादृशं तादृशं नित्यमश्नाति फलमूर्जितम् ॥ (17)

"'If a lord of men honours brahmanas and donates to them, he earns fruits that are always commensurate.'"

अभिगम्य दत्तं तुष्ट्या यद्धन्यमाहुरभिष्टुतम् ।
याचितेन तु यद्दत्तं तदाहुर्मध्यमं बुधा: ॥ (18)

"'If one seeks out the donee and satisfies him, that is said to be the best. When one gives when asked, the learned say that this is medium.'"

---

[26]Cowrie shells used as money.

अवज्ञया दीयते यत्तथैवाश्रद्धयापि च ।
तदाहुरधमं दानं मुनयः सत्यवादिनः ॥ (19)

'"Sages who are truthful in speech say that gifts given negligently and disrespectfully are the worst donations."'

अतिक्रमे मज्जमानो विविधेन नरः सदा ।
तथा प्रयत्नं कुर्वीत यथा मुच्येत संशयात् ॥ (20)

'"Through transgressions, a man is always submerged in different ways. Therefore, one should make efforts, so that one is freed from one's doubts."'

दमेन शोभते विप्रः क्षत्रियो विजयेन तु ।
धनेन वैश्यः शूद्रस्तु नित्यं दाक्ष्येण शोभते ॥ (24)

'"A brahmana is always radiant through self-control, a kshatriya through victory, a vaishya through riches and a shudra through skill."'

Chapter 5

पराशर उवाच

प्रतिग्रहागता विप्रे क्षत्रिये शस्त्रनिर्जिताः ।
वैश्ये न्यायार्जिताश्चैव शूद्रे शुश्रूषयार्जिताः ।
स्वल्पाप्यर्थाः प्रशस्यन्ते धर्मस्यार्थे महाफलाः ॥ (1)

'Parashara said, "Whatever little riches a brahmana obtains through receiving gifts, a kshatriya through conquest by weapons, a vaishya through lawful means and a shudra through servitude, is praised. When spent for dharma, this yields great fruits."'

नित्यं त्रयाणां वर्णानां शूद्रः शुश्रूषुरुच्यते ।
क्षत्रधर्मा वैश्य धर्मा नावृत्तिः पतति द्विजः ।
शूद्रकर्मा यदा तु स्यात्तदा पतति वै द्विजः ॥ (2)

'"It is said that the shudra must always serve the three varnas. But if a brahmana does not have means of sustenance and follows the dharma of kshatriyas or the dharma of vaishyas, he suffers no downfall. However, if a brahmana follows the dharma of shudras, then he does face a downfall."'

वाणिज्यं पाशुपाल्यं च तथा शिल्पोपजीवनम् ।
शूद्रस्यापि विधीयन्ते यदा वृत्तिर्न जायते ॥ (3)

"'When a shudra does not possess a means of sustenance, then trade, animal husbandry and subsistence on the basis of artisanship are recommended for him."'

रङ्गावतरणं चैव तथारूपोपजीवनम् ।
मद्यमांसोपजीव्यं च विक्रयो लोहचर्मणो: ॥ (4)
अपूर्विणा न कर्तव्यं कर्म लोके विगर्हितम् ।
कृतपूर्विणस्तु त्यजतो महान्धर्म इति श्रुति: ॥ (5)

"'If a person has not engaged in such occupations earlier, then descending in an arena,[27] earning a living through one's beauty and earning a living through the sales of liquor, flesh, iron or leather is not recommended. These are censured in the world. It has been heard that if one has been engaged in such tasks earlier and has then given them up, this leads to great dharma."'

संसिद्ध: पुरुषो लोके यदाचरति पापकम् ।
मदेनाभिप्लुतमनास्तच्च नग्राह्ममुच्यते ॥ (6)

"'In this world, it is said that if a successful man is overcome by arrogance in his mind and acts wickedly, that cannot be accepted."'

श्रूयन्ते हि पुराणे वै प्रजा धिग्दण्डशासना: ।
दान्ता धर्मप्रधानाश्च न्यायधर्मानुवर्तका: ॥ (7)

"'It has been heard in the ancient accounts that subjects used to be self-controlled and placed dharma at the forefront, following the fair policy of dharma. Shaming them through words was sufficient chastisement."'

---

[27] Probably acting or dancing.

धर्म एव सदा नृणामिह राजन्प्रशस्यते ।
धर्मवृद्धा गुणानेव सेवन्ते हि नरा भुवि ॥ (8)

'"O King! At that time, dharma alone was praised among men. Men on earth served and enhanced the qualities of dharma."'

तं धर्ममसुरास्तात नामृष्यन्त जनाधिप ।
विवर्धमानाः क्रमशस्तत्र तेऽन्वाविशन्प्रजाः ॥ (9)

'"O Son! O Lord of Men! But the asuras could not tolerate this dharma. They multiplied themselves and gradually penetrated the subjects."'

तेषां दर्पः समभवत्प्रजानां धर्मनाशनः ।
दर्पात्मनां ततः क्रोधः पुनस्तेषामजायत ॥ (10)

'"Because of this, insolence was generated among subjects, and this destroyed dharma. Resulting from insolence, anger was again generated within them."'

ततः क्रोधाभिभूतानां वृत्तं लज्जासमन्वितम् ।
ह्रीश्चैवाप्यनशद्राजंस्ततो मोहो व्यजायत ॥ (11)

'"Having been overcome with anger, their conduct became shameful. O King! When they were overcome with lack of modesty, delusion was generated in them."'

ततो मोहपरीतास्ते नापश्यन्त यथा पुरा ।
परस्परावमर्देन वर्तयन्ति यथासुखम् ॥ (12)

'"Having become overwhelmed with delusion, they no longer looked at things the way they had done earlier. They conducted themselves as they willed and crushed each other."'

तान्प्राप्य तु स धिग्दण्डो नकारणमतोऽभवत् ।
ततोऽभ्यगच्छन्देवांश्च ब्राह्मणांश्चावमन्य ह ॥ (13)

'"Shaming them through words was no longer sufficient chastisement then. They tended to their pleasures and no longer showed respect towards devas and brahmanas."'

एतस्मिन्नेव काले तु देवा देववरं शिवम् ।
अगच्छञ्शरणं वीरं बहुरूपं गणाधिपम् ॥ (14)

"'At this time, devas sought refuge with Shiva, supreme among the gods, the brave one with many forms and the lord of the *ganas*.'"[28]

तेन स्म ते गगनगाः सपुराः पातिताः क्षितौ ।
तिस्रोऽप्येकेन बानेन देवाप्यायिततेजसा ॥ (15)

"'With the combined energy of devas, with a single arrow, he brought down the three cities from the sky onto the ground.'"[29]

तेषामधिपतिस्त्वासीद्भीमो भीमपराक्रमः ।
देवतानां भयकरः स हतः शूलपाणिना ॥ (16)

"'Their lord was terrible and fearsome in valour, frightful to devas. But he was slain by the wielder of the trident.'"

तस्मिन्हतेऽथ स्वं भावं प्रत्यपद्यन्त मानवाः ।
प्रावर्तन्त च वेदा वै शास्त्राणि च यथा पुरा ॥ (17)

"'When he was slain, men regained their own nature. As was the case earlier, the Vedas and the sacred texts were revived.'"

ततोऽभ्यसिञ्चन्राज्येन देवानां दिवि वासवम् ।
सप्तर्षयश्चान्वयुञ्जन्नराणां दण्डधारणे ॥ (18)

"'The saptarshis instated Vasava in the kingdom of devas in heaven, and he was given the task of wielding the staff of chastisement over men.'"[30]

सप्तर्षीणामथोर्ध्वं च विपृथुर्नाम पार्थिवः ।
राजानः क्षत्रियाश्चैव मण्डलेषु पृथक्पृथक् ॥ (19)

---

[28] Ganas are Shiva's companions and attendants.
[29] This is the story of Tripura, the three cities of the asuras in the sky, destroyed by Shiva. However, this is sometimes interpreted in metaphorical fashion, where the three cities stand for desire, anger and greed.
[30] The list of saptarshis varies, but the standard one is Marichi, Atri, Angira, Pulastya, Pulaha, Kratu and Vasishtha. Vasava is Indra.

"'After the saptarshis, there was the king named Viprithu and several other kshatriyas who became kings over separate dominions.'"

महाकुलेषु ये जाता वृत्ताः पूर्वतराश्च ये ।
तेषामथासुरो भावो हृदयान्नापसर्पति ॥ (20)

"'However, even when they were born in great lineages, there were some who continued to follow the earlier conduct. Sentiments like those of the asuras swirled around in their hearts.'"

तस्मात्तेनैव भावेन सानुषङ्गेन पार्थिवाः ।
आसुराण्येव कर्माणि न्यषेवन्भीमविक्रमाः ॥ (21)

"'Because of those sentiments, those kings, terrible in valour, continued to be attached to deeds that were like those of the asuras.'"

प्रत्यतिष्ठंश्च तेष्वेव तान्येव स्थापयन्ति च ।
भजन्ते तानि चाद्यापि ये बालिशतमा नराः ॥ (22)

"'Men who are exceedingly foolish continue to be devoted to such acts, worship them and establish them.'"

तस्मादहं ब्रवीमि त्वां राजन्सञ्चिन्त्य शास्त्रतः ।
संसिद्धाधिगमं कुर्यात्कर्म हिंसात्मकं त्यजेत् ॥ (23)

"'O King! That is the reason I am telling you that you must reflect about the sacred texts. You must discard all notions of violence within you and act so as to obtain success.'"

न सकरेण द्रविणं विचिन्वीत विचक्षणः ।
धर्मार्थं न्यायमुत्सृज्य न तत्कल्याणमुच्यते ॥ (24)

"'A discriminating person does not think of obtaining riches by mixing up the means. For the sake of dharma or artha, he does not abandon what is right. That is not said to be the way towards welfare.'"

स त्वमेवंविधो दान्तः क्षत्रियः प्रियबान्धवः ।
प्रजा भृत्यांश्च पुत्रांश्च स्वधर्मेणानुपालय ॥ (25)

'"Thus, it is recommended that a kshatriya should be self-controlled and affectionate towards relatives, and he must protect subjects, servants and sons in accordance with his own dharma."

इष्टानिष्टसमायोगो वैरं सौहार्दमेव च ।
अथ जातिसहस्राणि बहूनि परिवर्तते ॥ (26)

'"Because of prosperity and adversity, there can be enmity and affection. One is born and circles around in thousands of lives."

तस्माद्गुणेषु रज्येथा मा दोषेषु कदाचन ।
निर्गुणो यो हि दुर्बुद्धिरात्मनः सोऽरिरुच्यते ॥ (27)

'"Therefore, find delight in the qualities and never in sins. If a person is evil-minded and devoid of qualities, he is said to be an enemy."

मानुषेषु महाराज धर्माधर्मौ प्रवर्ततः ।
न तथान्येषु भूतेषु मनुष्यरहितेष्विह ॥ (28)

'"O Great King! Dharma and adharma are prevalent among men. In this world, other than men, these notions are not seen to exist in other creatures."

धर्मशीलो नरो विद्वानीहकोऽनीहकोऽपि वा ।
आत्मभूतः सदा लोके चरेद्भूतान्यहिंसयन् ॥ (29)

'"Whether a man is concerned with this world or is not concerned with this world, he must be learned and must follow dharma in conduct. He must not cause injury and must always act towards everyone, like towards his own self."

यदा व्यपेतद्धृल्लेखं मनो भवति तस्य वै ।
नानृतं चैव भवति तदा कल्याणमृच्छति ॥ (30)

'"When there is no longer any desire etched in the mind, there is no longer any falsehood and one desires what is beneficial."

Chapter 6

पराशर उवाच

एष धर्मविधिस्तात गृहस्थस्य प्रकीर्तित: ।
तपोविधिं तु वक्ष्यामि तन्मे निगदत: शृणु ॥ (1)

'Parashara said, "O Son! I have told you about the dharma that is recommended for householders. I will now tell you about the techniques for austerities. Listen attentively."'

प्रायेण हि गृहस्थस्य ममत्वं नाम जायते ।
सङ्गागतं नरश्रेष्ठ भावैस्तामसराजसै: ॥ (2)

'"O Best among Men! It is often seen that because of being overcome with tamas and rajas, householders suffer from attachment and have a sense of ownership."'

गृहाण्याश्रित्य गावश्च क्षेत्राणि च धनानि च ।
दारा: पुत्राश्च भृत्याश्च भवन्तीह नरस्य वै ॥ (3)

'"In this world, having become a householder, a man resorts to houses and acquires cattle, fields, riches, wives, sons and servants."'

एवं तस्य प्रवृत्तस्य नित्यमेवानुपश्यत: ।
रागद्वेषौ विवर्धेते ह्यनित्यत्वमपश्यत: ॥ (4)

'"Hence, in his conduct, he is always seen to look towards these. His attachment and aversion are always seen to increase."'

रागद्वेषाभिभूतं च नरं द्रव्यवशानुगम् ।
मोहजाता रतिर्नाम समुपैति नराधिप ॥ (5)

'"Overcome by attachment and aversion, a man comes under the control of material objects. O Lord of Men! When delusion has been generated, the object known as desire is the result."'

कृतार्थो भोगतो भूत्वा स वै रतिपरायण: ।
लाभं ग्राम्यसुखादन्यं रतितो नानुपश्यति ॥ (6)

'"Seeking to obtain objects of pleasure, he becomes addicted to desire. He does not see anything beyond the gains from *gramya* and desire."'[31]

ततो लोभाभिभूतात्मा सङ्गाद्वर्धयते जनम् ।
पुष्ट्यर्थं चैव तस्येह जनस्यार्थं चिकीर्षति ॥ (7)

'"Having become overwhelmed by greed, attachment increases in people. Men become interested in sustaining these objects."'

स जानन्नपि चाकार्यमर्थार्थं सेवते नरः ।
बालस्नेहपरीतात्मा तत्क्षयाच्चानुतप्यते ॥ (8)

'"Even if he knows, a man performs acts that should not be undertaken, for the sake of objects. Because he is overcome with childish affection, he is tormented at the prospect of these[32] being destroyed."'

ततो मानेन सम्पन्नो रक्षन्नात्मपराजयम् ।
करोति येन भोगी स्यामिति तस्माद्विनश्यति ॥ (9)

'"He is full of pride and seeks to protect himself against all defeat. He acts so as to enjoy pleasure and is thereby destroyed."'

तपो हि बुद्धियुक्तानां शाश्वतं ब्रह्मदर्शनम् ।
अनिच्छतां शुभं कर्म नराणां त्यजतां सुखम् ॥ (10)

'"It is known that those who have seen the brahman are full of intelligence and engage in austerities. Such men seek auspicious deeds and give up happiness."'[33]

स्नेहायतननाशाच्च धननाशाच्च पार्थिव ।
आधिव्याधिप्रतापाच्च निर्वेदमुपगच्छति ॥ (11)

'"O Lord of the Earth! They attain indifference towards loss of affection and riches and torment from physical and mental ailments."'

---

[31]Gramya signifies ordinary, material, vulgar and carnal pleasures.
[32]The objects.
[33]Happiness that results from desire for material objects.

निर्वेदादात्मसंबोध: संबोधाच्छास्त्रदर्शनम् ।
शास्त्रार्थदर्शनाद्राजंस्तप एवानुपश्यति ॥ (12)

'"That indifference leads to knowledge of the atman and knowledge of what the sacred texts have said. O King! Having understood the purport of the sacred texts, they see the importance of austerities."'

दुर्लभो हि मनुष्येन्द्र नर: प्रत्यवमर्शवान् ।
यो वै प्रियसुखे क्षीणे तप: कर्तुं व्यवस्यति ॥ (13)

'"O Indra among Men! A man who realizes what is essential and what is damaging is extremely rare. Realizing that all beloved happiness decays, he resorts to austerities."'

तप: सर्वगतं तात हीनस्यापि विधीयते ।
जितेन्द्रियस्य दान्तस्य स्वर्गमार्गप्रदेशकम् ॥ (14)

'"O Son! Austerities take you everywhere. They are recommended even for those who are inferior. A person who has conquered his senses and is self-controlled is on the road to heaven."'

प्रजापति: प्रजा: पूर्वमसृजत्तपसा विभु: ।
क्वचित्क्वचिद्व्रतपरो व्रतान्यास्थाय पार्थिव ॥ (15)

'"O King! Earlier, Lord Prajapati[34] created subjects through austerities, sometimes resorting to different kinds of vows."'

आदित्या वसवो रुद्रास्तथैवाग्न्यश्विवमारुता: ।
विश्वेदेवास्तथा साध्या: पितरोऽथ मरुद्गणा: ॥ (16)
यक्षराक्षसगन्धर्वा: सिद्धाश्चान्ये दिवौकस: ।
संसिद्धास्तपसा तात ये चान्ये स्वर्गवासिन: ॥ (17)

'"O Son! The adityas, the vasus, the rudras, Agni, the ashvins, the maruts, the vishvadevas, the sadhyas, the ancestors, the large numbers of maruts,[35] the yakshas, the rakshasas, the gandharvas, the siddhas, the other residents of heaven and all other celestial ones obtained success through austerities."'

---

[34] Brahma.
[35] Maruts are mentioned twice.

ये चादौ ब्रह्मणा सृष्टा ब्राह्मणास्तपसा पुरा ।
ते भावयन्त: पृथिवीं विचरन्ति दिवं तथा ॥ (18)

'"In the beginning, Brahma created brahmanas. Earlier, through their austerities, they made the earth prosper and also roamed around in heaven."'

मर्त्यलोके च राजानो ये चान्ये गृहमेधिन: ।
महाकुलेषु दृश्यन्ते तत्सर्वं तपस: फलम् ॥ (19)

'"In the world of mortals, kings and other householders who are seen to have been born in great lineages have all obtained the fruits of their austerities."'[36]

कौशिकानि च वस्त्राणि शुभान्याभरणानि च ।
वाहनासनयानानि सर्वं तत्तपस: फलम् ॥ (20)

'"The silken garments, the radiant ornaments, the mounts, the seats and the vehicles—all these are the fruits of austerities."'

मनोऽनुकूला: प्रमदा रूपवत्य: सहस्रश: ।
वास: प्रासादपृष्ठे च तत्सर्वं तपस: फलम् ॥ (21)

'"Thousands of agreeable and beautiful women who follow them and the dwellings in palaces—all these are the fruits of austerities."'

शयनानि च मुख्यानि भोज्यानि विविधानि च ।
अभिप्रेतानि सर्वाणि भवन्ति कृतकर्मणाम् ॥ (22)

'"The best of beds, many kinds of food and all that is desired—these are the consequences of past deeds."'

नाप्राप्यं तपसा किंचित्त्रैलोक्येऽस्मिन्परन्तप ।
उपभोगपरित्याग: फलान्यकृतकर्मणाम् ॥ (23)

'"O Scorcher of Enemies! There is nothing in the three worlds that cannot be obtained through austerities. The renunciation of objects of pleasure also represents the fruits of earlier deeds."'

---

[36]Austerities performed in earlier lives.

सुखितो दु:खितो वापि नरो लोभं परित्यजेत् ।
अवेक्ष्य मनसा शास्त्रं बुद्ध्या च नृपसत्तम ॥ (24)

'"Whether he is happy or miserable, a man must abandon greed. O Supreme among Kings! He must use his mind and intelligence to look towards the sacred texts."'

असन्तोषोऽसुखायैव लोभादिन्द्रियविभ्रम: ।
ततोऽस्य नश्यति प्रज्ञा विद्येवाभ्यासवर्जिता ॥ (25)

'"Discontent leads to misery. Greed leads to confusion of the senses. Wisdom is then destroyed and knowledge is not accompanied by practice."'

नष्टप्रज्ञो यदा भवति तदा न्यायं न पश्यति ।
तस्मात्सुखक्षये प्राप्ते पुमानुग्रं तपश्चरेत् ॥ (26)

'"When wisdom is destroyed, one does not see what is proper policy. Therefore, even when happiness has been destroyed, a man must resort to fierce austerities."'

यदिष्टं तत्सुखं प्राहुर्द्वेष्यं दु:खमिहोच्यते ।
कृताकृतस्य तपस: फलं पश्यस्व यादृशम् ॥ (27)

'"Whatever is beneficial represents happiness. Whatever is hated is said to represent misery. Behold. These are the fruits of austerities that have been performed and have not been performed."'

नित्यं भद्राणि पश्यन्ति विषयांश्चोपभुञ्जते ।
प्राकाश्यं चैव गच्छन्ति कृत्वा निष्कल्मषं तप: ॥ (28)

'"If one performs unblemished austerities,[37] one goes to what is best. One always beholds the fortunate and enjoys the objects of pleasure."'

अप्रियाण्यवमानांश्च दु:खं बहुविधात्मकम् ।
फलार्थी तत्पथत्यक्त: प्राप्नोति विषयात्मकम् ॥ (29)

---

[37] Unblemished austerities are those that are performed without any desire for the fruits.

"'However, a person who gives up the virtuous path and goes after the fruits obtains the unpleasant and faces many kinds of misery, despite obtaining objects of pleasure.'"

धर्मे तपसि दाने च विचिकित्सास्य जायते ।
स कृत्वा पापकान्येव निरयं प्रतिपद्यते ॥ (30)

"'Dharma, austerities and donations are desirable. But because desire is generated, one performs wicked deeds and obtains hell.'"

सुखे तु वर्तमानो वै दुःखे वापि नरोत्तम ।
स्ववृत्ताद्यो न चलति शास्त्रचक्षुः स मानवः ॥ (31)

"'O Supreme among Men! But whether he faces joy or misery, if a man does not deviate from his own conduct, he possesses the insight of the sacred texts.'"

इषुप्रपातमात्रं हि स्पर्शयोगे रतिः स्मृता ।
रसने दर्शने घ्राणे श्रवणे च विशां पते ॥ (32)

"'O Lord of the Earth! It is said that the pleasure from touch, taste, sight, scent and hearing only lasts for as long as it takes for an arrow to fall down on the ground.'"

ततोऽस्य जायते तीव्रा वेदना तत्क्षयात्पुनः ।
बुधा येन प्रशंसन्ति मोक्षं सुखमनुत्तमम् ॥ (33)

"'When these are over, a fierce pain again takes over. That is the reason the learned praise emancipation, productive of supreme bliss.'"

ततः फलार्थं चरति भवन्ति ज्यायसो गुणाः ।
धर्मवृत्त्या च सततं कामार्थाभ्यां न हीयते ॥ (34)

"'Those who pursue such fruits obtain superior qualities. Those who always have a conduct in accordance with dharma, kama and artha do not diminish them.'"

अप्रयत्नागताः सेव्या गृहस्थैर्विषयाः सदा ।
प्रयत्नेनोपगम्यश्च स्वधर्म इति मे मतिः ॥ (35)

'"Householders must never make efforts to serve objects of pleasure. But it is my view that they must always make efforts to follow their own dharma."'

मानिनां कुलजातानां नित्यं शास्त्रार्थचक्षुषाम् ।
धर्मक्रियावियुक्तानामशक्त्या संवृतात्मनाम् ॥ (36)

'"Those who are revered and have been born in noble families always have the insight of the sacred texts. However, those who have separated themselves from acts of dharma are incapable of controlling their atmans."'

क्रियमाणं यदा कर्म नाशं गच्छति मानुषम् ।
तेषां नान्यदृते लोके तपसः कर्म विद्यते ॥ (37)

'"All other deeds that are performed by men are destroyed. These should be ignored in this world and nothing other than deeds of austerities followed."'

सर्वात्मना तु कुर्वीत गृहस्थः कर्मनिश्चयम् ।
दाक्ष्येण हव्यकव्यार्थं स्वधर्मं विचरेन्नृप ॥ (38)

'"However, there may be householders who have made up their minds to perform deeds. O King! They should skilfully follow their own dharma and offer havya and kavya."'

यथा नदीनदाः सर्वे सागरे यान्ति संस्थितम् ।
एवमाश्रमिणः सर्वे गृहस्थे यान्ति संस्थितम् ॥ (39)

'"All the large and small rivers proceed to the ocean and find their refuge there. In that way, all the other ashramas are based on that of the householder."'

Chapter 7

जनक उवाच

वर्णो विशेषवर्णानां महर्षे केन जायते ।
एतदिच्छाम्यहं श्रोतुं तद्ब्रूहि वदतां वर ॥ (1)
यदेतज्जायतेऽपत्यं स एवायमिति श्रुतिः ।
कथं ब्राह्मणतो जातो विशेषग्रहणं गतः ॥ (2)

'Janaka asked, "O Maharshi! How were the different complexions generated among the varnas? O Supreme among Eloquent Ones! I wish to hear about this. Tell me. The sacred texts say that one's offspring are nothing but one's own self. In particular, having been generated from brahmanas, how has there been decay?"'

पराशर उवाच

एवमेतन्महाराज येन जातः स एव सः ।
तपसस्त्वपकर्षेण जातिग्रहणतां गतः ॥ (3)

'Parashara replied, "O Great King! It is indeed that way. The offspring are generated from one's own self. But because of the deviation from austerities, this decay into *jati*s has set in."'[38]

सुक्षेत्राच्च सुबीजाच्च पुण्यो भवति सम्भवः ।
अतोऽन्यतरतो हीनादवरो नाम जायते ॥ (4)

'"When the field is good and the seed is good, an auspicious crop results. However, if these are inferior, an inferior crop results."'

वक्त्राद्भुजाभ्यामूरुभ्यां पद्भ्यां चैवाथ जज्ञिरे ।
सृजतः प्रजापतेर्लोकानिति धर्मविदो विदुः ॥ (5)

'"Those who are learned about dharma know that when Prajapati created the worlds, some were created from his mouth, some from his arms, some from his thighs and some from his feet."'

---

[38] The jati or class one is born into is not the same as varna.

मुखजा ब्राह्मणास्तात बाहुजाः क्षत्रबन्धवः ।
ऊरुजा धनिनो राजन्पादजाः परिचारकाः ॥ (6)

'"O Son! The brahmanas were born from the mouth and the kshatriyas and *kshatra-bandhu*[39] from the arms. O King! The rich ones[40] were born from the thighs. The attendants[41] were born from the feet."'

चतुर्णामेव वर्णानामागमः पुरुषर्षभ ।
अतोऽन्ये त्वतिरिक्ता ये ते वै सङ्करजाः स्मृताः ॥ (7)

'"O Bull among Men! These were the only four varnas that were created. The Smritis say that all other others that were created, over and above these, were the result of a mixture."'

क्षत्रजातिरथाम्बस्था उग्रा वैदेहकास्तथा ।
श्वपाकाः पुल्कसाः स्तेना निषादाः सूतमागधाः ॥ (8)
आयोगाः करण व्रात्याश्चन्डालाश्च नराधिप ।
एते चतुर्भ्यों वर्णेभ्यो जायन्ते वै परस्परम् ॥ (9)

'"Among those that resulted from the kshatriya jati were atirathas, ambashthas, ugras, vaidehakas, shvapakas, pulkasas, stenas, nishadas, sutas and magadhas. O Lord of Men! The ayogas, karanas, vratyas and chandalas were born from an intermingling between the four varnas."'

जनक उवाच

ब्राह्मणैकेन जातानां नानात्वं गोत्रतः कथम् ।
बहूनीह हि लोके वै गोत्राणि मुनिसत्तम ॥ (10)
यत्र तत्र कथं जाताः स्वयोनिं मुनयो गताः ।
शूद्रयोनौ समुत्पन्ना वियोनौ च तथापरे ॥ (11)

'Janaka asked, "How did brahmanas with different gotras result? O Supreme among Sages! There are many gotras in the world. How

---

[39] This often stands for inferior kshatriyas.
[40] The vaishyas.
[41] The shudras.

can those born from different wombs, those born from shudra wombs and those born from inferior wombs become sages?"'

पराशर उवाच

राजन्नेतद्भवेद्ब्राह्ममपकृष्टेन जन्मना ।
महात्मानं समुत्पत्तिस्तपसा भावितात्मनाम् ॥ (12)

'Parashara replied, "O King! Though these are not brahmanas by virtue of their inferior birth, these great-souled ones can resort to austerities and cleanse their atmans."'

उत्पाद्य पुत्रान्मुनयो नृपतौ यत्र तत्र ह ।
स्वेनैव तपसा तेषामृषित्वं विदधुः पुनः ॥ (13)

'"O King! Here and there, the sages had sons. However, because of their[42] own austerities, they again succeeded in becoming rishis."'

पितामहश्च मे पूर्वमृश्यशृङ्गश्च काश्यप: ।
वटस्ताण्ड्यः कृपश्चैव कक्षीवान्कमठादयः ॥ (14)
यवक्रीतश्च नृपते द्रोणश्च वदतां वरः ।
आयुर्मतङ्गो दत्तश्च द्रुपदो मत्स्य एव च ॥ (15)
एते स्वां प्रकृतिं प्राप्ता वैदेह तपसोऽऽश्रयात् ।
प्रतिष्ठिता वेदविदो दमे तपसि चैव हि ॥ (16)

'"O Lord of Men! O Ruler of Videha! Earlier, my grandfather[43]; Rishyashringa; Kashyapa; Vata; Tandya; Kripa; Kakshivat; Kamatha and the others; Yavakrita; Drona, supreme among eloquent ones; Ayu; Matanga; Datta; Drupada; and Matysa obtained their own natural states by resorting to austerities. They were knowledgable about the Vedas and were established in self-control and austerities."'

मूलगोत्राणि चत्वारि समुत्पन्नानि पार्थिव ।
अङ्गिराः कश्यपश्चैव वसिष्ठो भृगुरेव च ॥ (17)

---

[42]Referring to the offspring.
[43]Parashara's grandfather was Vasishtha.

"'O Lord of the Earth! Initially, only four gotras originated—Angiras, Kashyapa, Vasishtha and Bhrigu.'"

कर्मतोऽन्यानि गोत्राणि समुत्पन्नानि पार्थिव ।
नामधेयानि तपसा तानि च ग्रहणं सताम् ॥ (18)

"'O Lord of the Earth! But because of their deeds, other gotras were generated. Their names resulted from the austerities that those virtuous ones resorted to.'"

जनक उवाच

विशेषधर्मान्वर्णानां प्रब्रूहि भगवन्मम ।
तथा सामान्य धर्मांश्च सर्वत्र कुशलो ह्यसि ॥ (19)

'Janaka asked, "O Illustrious One! Tell me about the specific dharma of different varnas. What is the general template of dharma that leads to welfare everywhere?"'

पराशर उवाच

प्रतिग्रहो याजनं च तथैवाध्यापनं नृप ।
विशेषधर्मो विप्राणां रक्षा क्षत्रस्य शोभना ॥ (20)

'Parashara replied, "O King! Receiving gifts, officiating at sacrifices and studying represent the specific dharma for brahmanas. Kshatriyas are radiant when they protect."'

कृषिश्च पाशुपाल्यं च वाणिज्यं च विशामपि ।
द्विजानां परिचर्या च शूद्रकर्म नराधिप ॥ (21)

"'The vaishyas must engage in agriculture, animal husbandry and trade. O Lord of Men! The task of shudras is to serve the other three varnas.'"[44]

विशेषधर्मा नृपते वर्णानां परिकीर्तिताः ।
धर्मान्साधारणांस्तात विस्तरेण शृणुष्व मे ॥ (22)

---

[44] The word used is dvija, which means twice born.

"'O King! I have described to you the specific dharma of the varnas. O Son! Now listen to the details about general dharma.'"

आनृशंस्यमहिंसा चाप्रमादः संविभागिता ।
श्राद्धकर्मातिथेयं च सत्यमक्रोध एव च ॥ (23)
स्वेषु दारेषु सन्तोषः शौचं नित्यानसूयता ।
आत्मज्ञानं तितिक्षा च धर्माः साधारणा नृप ॥ (24)

"'O King! Non-violence, lack of injury, lack of distraction, giving proper shares, performing funeral rites, attending to guests, truthfulness, lack of anger, contentment with one's own wife, purity, constant lack of malice, knowledge of the atman and endurance—these represent general dharma.'"

ब्राह्मणाः क्षत्रिया वैश्यास्त्रयो वर्णा द्विजातयः ।
अत्र तेषामधीकारो धर्मेषु द्विपदां वर ॥ (25)

"'Brahmanas, kshatriyas and vaishyas are the three varnas that are dvijas. O Supreme among Bipeds! These are the ones who have rights to such dharma.'"

विकर्मावस्थिता वर्णाः पतन्ति नृपते त्रयः ।
उन्नमन्ति यथा सन्तमाश्रित्येह स्वकर्मसु ॥ (26)

"'O King! If these three varnas resort to perverse deeds, then that leads to their downfall. They are elevated if they stick to their own deeds, just as the virtuous ones do.'"

न चापि शूद्रः पततीति निश्चयो न चापि संस्कारमिहार्हतीति वा ।
श्रुतिप्रवृत्तं न च धर्ममाप्नुते न चास्य धर्मे प्रतिषेधनं कृतम् ॥ (27)

"'No downfall has been determined for a shudra, nor is there any means of his cleansing himself from such a downfall. He cannot follow the conduct of dharma laid down in the Shrutis. However, he should not act against such dharma.'"

वैदेहकं शूद्रमुदाहरन्ति द्विजा महाराज श्रुतोपपन्नाः ।
अहं हि पश्यामि नरेन्द्र देवं विश्वस्य विष्णुं जगतः प्रधानम् ॥ (28)

'"O Ruler of Videha! O Great King! Learned ones say that shudras are like dvijas. O Indra among Men! I see such a person as the god Vishnu, the foremost one in the universe."'[45]

सतां वृत्तमनुष्ठाय निहीना उज्जिहीर्षव: ।
मन्त्रवर्जं न दुष्यन्ति कुर्वाणा: पौष्टिकी: क्रिया: ॥ (29)

'"Even an inferior person can desire to uplift himself by resorting to the conduct of the virtuous. They are not censured if they perform any of the rites that lead to nourishment. But they must avoid mantras."'

यथा यथा हि सद्वृत्तमालम्बन्तीतरे जना: ।
तथा तथा सुखं प्राप्य प्रेत्य चेह च शेरते ॥ (30)

'"Whenever inferior people resort to the conduct of the virtuous, they obtain happiness, both in this world and in the hereafter."'

जनक उवाच

किं कर्म दूषयत्येनमथ जातिर्महामुने ।
सन्देहो मे समुत्पन्नस्तन्मे व्याख्यातुमर्हसि ॥ (31)

'Janaka asked, "O Great Sage! What taints a person? Is it his deeds or his jati? A doubt has arisen in my mind. You should explain this to me."'

पराशर उवाच

असंशयं महाराज उभयं दोषकारकम् ।
कर्म चैव हि जातिश्च विशेषं तु निशामय ॥ (32)

'Parashara replied, "O Great King! There is no doubt that both can give rise to taints. But listen specifically to how both deeds and jati can be countered."'

---

[45]This is cryptic and requires interpretation. Brahma is equated with brahmanas and Vishnu with kshatriyas. The preceding sentence seems to say that shudras can become brahmanas in their next lives. But Parashara thinks that they can only become kshatriyas in their next lives.

जात्या च कर्मणा चौव दुष्टं कर्म निषेवते ।
जात्या दुष्टश्च य: पापं न करोति स पूरुष: ॥ (33)

'"Regardless of birth and deeds,⁴⁶ a person may perform wicked acts. However, even if the birth is tainted, if a person does not act wickedly, he is truly a man."'

जात्या प्रधानं पुरुषं कुर्वाणं कर्म धिक्कृतम् ।
कर्म तद्दूषयत्येनं तस्मात्कर्म नशोभनम् ॥ (34)

'"If a man of superior birth performs wicked deeds, he is censured. Those acts taint him. Therefore, such deeds are not appropriate."'

जनक उवाच

कानि कर्माणि धर्म्याणि लोकेऽस्मिन्द्विजसत्तम ।
न हिंसन्तीह भूतानि क्रियमाणानि सर्वदा ॥ (35)

'Janaka asked, "O Supreme among Dvijas! In this world, which are the acts of dharma? Which are the acts that never lead to injury to beings?"'

पराशर उवाच

शृणु मेऽत्र महाराज यन्मां त्वं परिपृच्छसि ।
यानि कर्माण्यहिंस्राणि नरं त्रायन्ति सर्वदा ॥ (36)

'Parashara replied, "O Great King! Listen to what you have asked me. These are acts of non-injury that always save a man."'

संन्यस्याग्नीनुपासीना: पश्यन्ति विगतज्वरा: ।
नै:श्रेयसं धर्मपथं समारुह्य यथाक्रमम् ॥ (37)

'"Those who renounce and worship the fire can see that their anxiety is dispelled. They are the ones who resort to the beneficial path of dharma and ascend progressively."'

---

⁴⁶Presumably deeds in earlier lives.

प्रश्रिता विनयोपेता दमनित्या: सुसंशिता: ।
प्रयान्ति स्थानमजरं सर्वकर्म विवर्जिता: ॥ (38)

'"They are devoted and humble. They are always self-controlled and restrained. They abandon all kinds of action and go to the spot that is without decay."'

सर्वे वर्णा धर्मकार्याणि सम्यक्कृत्वा राजन्सत्यवाक्यानि चोक्त्वा ।
त्यक्त्वाधर्म दारुणं जीवलोके यान्ति स्वर्गं नात्र कार्यो विचार: ॥ (39)

'"O King! All the varnas should perform the tasks of dharma properly and speak truthful words. In the world of the living, they must give up terrible adharma. They will go to heaven. There is no need to reflect on this."'

Chapter 8

पराशर उवाच

पिता सखायो गुरव: स्त्रियश्च न निर्गुणा नाम भवन्ति लोके ।
अनन्यभक्ता: प्रियवादिनश्च हिताश्च वश्याश्च तथैव राजन् ॥ (1)

'Parashara said, "In this world, fathers, friends, gurus and women are never devoid of qualities. O King! Therefore, one must be devoted to them, speak pleasantly to them, ensure their welfare and serve them."'

पिता परं दैवतं मानवानां मातुर्विशिष्टं पितरं वदन्ति ।
ज्ञानस्य लाभं परमं वदन्ति जितेन्द्रियार्थ: परमाप्नुवन्ति ॥ (2)

'"For men, the father is the supreme divinity. The father is said to be superior to the mother. Jnana is said to be the supreme gain. By conquering the objects of the senses, one obtains the supreme."'

रणाजिरे यत्र शराग्निसंस्तरे नृपात्मजो घातमवाप्य दह्यते ।
प्रयाति लोकानमरै: सुदुर्लभान्निषेवते स्वर्गफलं यथासुखम् ॥ (3)

"'If the son of a king faces the flames of arrows in the field of battle and is consumed by them and killed, he goes to the immortal worlds that are extremely difficult to obtain. Full of joy, he obtains the fruits of heaven there.'"

श्रान्तं भीतं भ्रष्टशस्त्रं रुदन्तं पराङ्मुखं परिबर्हैश्च हीनम् ।
अनुद्यतं रोगिणं याचमानं न वै हिंस्याद्बालवृद्धौ च राजन् ॥ (4)

"'O King! One should not cause injury to the exhausted, the terrified, those who have lost their weapons, the weeping, those who are not willing to fight, those who have been deprived of their mounts, those who are not exerting themselves, those who are ill, those who are seeking refuge, those who are very young and those who are aged.'"

परिबर्हैः सुसंपन्नमुद्यतं तुल्यतां गतम् ।
अतिक्रमेत नृपतिः सङ्ग्रामे क्षत्रियात्मजम् ॥ (5)

"'One should fight someone who is mounted, properly equipped, ready to fight and one's equal. In a battle, a king should engage with the son of a kshatriya.'"

तुल्यादिह वधः श्रेयान्विशिष्टाच्चेति निश्चयः ।
निहीनात्कातराच्चैव नृपाणां गर्हितो वधः ॥ (6)

"'It has been determined that it is best to be killed by someone who is an equal or superior. Kings who are slain by inferiors and cowards are censured.'"

पापात्पापसमाचारान्निहीनाच्च नराधिप ।
पाप एव वधः प्रोक्तो नरकायेति निश्चयः ॥ (7)

"'O Lord of Men! It is said that if one is slain by a wicked person who resorts to evil conduct or is inferior, that is wicked and certainly leads to hell.'"

न कश्चित्त्राति वै राजन्दिष्टान्तवशमागतम् ।
सावशेषायुषं चापि कश्चिद्देवापकर्षति ॥ (8)

'"O King! If a person's fortune is over and he has come under subjugation,[47] then no one can save him. But if the lifespan is left, no one can assail him."'

स्निग्धैश्च क्रियमाणानि कर्माणीह निवर्तयेत् ।
हिंसात्मकानि कर्माणि नायुरिच्छेत्परायुषा ॥ (9)

'"If a person has attained his lifespan or is senior in age, one must gently restrain him from performing any injurious acts."'

गृहस्थानां तु सर्वेषां विनाशमभिकाङ्क्षताम् ।
निधनं शोभनं तात पुलिनेषु क्रियावताम् ॥ (10)

'"O Son! When a householder suspects that his end is near, he should desire that his death should take place near the bank of a river or at a sacred place."'

आयुषि क्षयमापन्ने पञ्चत्वमुपगच्छति ।
नाकारणात्तद्भवति कारणैरुपपादितम् ॥ (11)

'"When the lifespan is over, one merges into the five elements. This can happen without reason and can also occur with reason."'[48]

तथा शरीरं भवति देहाद्येनोपपादितम् ।
अध्वानं गतकश्चायं प्राप्तश्चायं गृहाद्गृहम् ॥ (12)

'"Having obtained a body, if a person gives it up in a mishap, after losing the body, he follows the same kind of course.[49] This is like a man going from one house to another house."'

द्वितीयं कारणं तत्र नान्यत्किंचन विद्यते ।
तदेहं देहिनां युक्तं मोक्षभूतेषु वर्तते ॥ (13)

---

[47] This means if one's life is over.
[48] Accidental and natural deaths, respectively. Death, merging into the five elements is represented by the word '*panchatva*'.
[49] That is, obtains a similar kind of body. This seems to mean accidents and suicides.

'"There is no second reason for an embodied being to obtain a similar kind of body. That is the way a creature pursues the goal of emancipation."'

सिरास्नाय्वस्थिसङ्घातं बीभत्सामेध्यसकुलम् ।
भूतानामिन्द्रियाणां च गुणानां च समागमम् ॥ (14)

'"The body consists of a mass of arteries, sinews and bones. It is terrible and impure. It is a mixture of the elements, the senses and the qualities."'

त्वगन्तं देहमित्याहुर्विद्वांसोऽध्यात्मचिन्तका: ।
गुणैरपि परिक्षीणं शरीरं मर्त्यतां गतम् ॥ (15)

'"This body is then covered by a skin. Learned ones who have thought about the adhyatma say this. When the qualities decay, the body becomes mortal."'

शरीरिणा परित्यक्तं निश्चेष्टं गतचेतनम् ।
भूतै: प्रकृतिमापन्नैस्ततो भूमौ निमज्जति ॥ (16)

'"The body is abandoned and becomes immobile and senseless. The elements return to their natural states and the body merges with earth."'

भावितं कर्मयोगेन जायते तत्र तत्र ह ।
इदं शरीरं वैदेह म्रियते यत्र तत्र ह ।
तत्स्वभावोऽपरो दृष्टो विसर्ग: कर्मणस्तथा ॥ (17)

'"Driven by the urge to act, the body is born, here and there. O Ruler of Videha! Whatever be the state in which the body dies, driven by the karma it has performed, its next birth is seen to be determined by that nature."'

न जायते तु नृपते कंचित्कालमयं पुन: ।
परिभ्रमति भूतात्मा द्यामिवाम्बुधरो महान् ॥ (18)

'"O Lord of Men! But the atman in the creature is not born again immediately. Like a giant cloud, it roams around in the sky."'

स पुनर्जायते राजन्प्राप्येहायतनं नृप ।
मनसः परमो ह्यात्मा इन्द्रियेभ्यः परं मनः ॥ (19)

'"O King! It is born again only after it has obtained a new receptacle. O Lord of Men! The atman is superior to the mind. The mind is superior to the senses."'

द्विविधानां च भूतानां जङ्गमाः परमा नृप ।
जङ्गमानामपि तथा द्विपदाः परमा मताः ।
द्विपदानामपि तथा द्विजा वै परमाः स्मृताः ॥ (20)

'"O Lord of Men! Of the two kinds of creations, the mobile are superior.[50] It is held that bipeds are supreme among mobile ones. Among bipeds, dvijas are held to be superior."'

द्विजानामपि राजेन्द्र प्रज्ञावन्तः परा मताः ।
प्राज्ञानामात्मसंबुद्धाः संबुद्धानाममानिनः ॥ (21)

'"O Indra among Kings! Among dvijas, the wise are held to be superior. Among the wise, those who know about the atman are superior and among those who know about the atman, the ones who are humble."'

जातमन्वेति मरणं नॄणामिति विनिश्चयः ।
अन्तवन्ति हि कर्माणि सेवन्ते गुणतः प्रजाः ॥ (22)

'"It is certain that men who are born must die. Because of the qualities,[51] people undertake karma that also comes to an end."'

आपन्ने तूत्तरां काष्ठां सूर्ये यो निधनं व्रजेत् ।
नक्षत्रे च मुहूर्ते च पुण्ये राजन्स पुण्यकृत् ॥ (23)

'"O King! A man who dies when the sun is in its *kashtha*[52] and when the nakshatras and muhurtas are auspicious, is a person who has performed auspicious deeds."'

---

[50]Compared to the immobile.
[51]Sattva, rajas and tamas. The fruits of deeds are not eternal.
[52]Kashtha has more than one meaning. Northern solstice fits best, though it might also mean when the sun is in one of the northern cardinal directions.

अयोजयित्वा क्लेशेन जनं प्लाव्य च दुष्कृतम् ।
मृत्युनाप्राकृतेनेह कर्म कृत्वात्मशक्तित: ॥ (24)

'"A person must undertake karma to the best of his capacity. He must cleanse himself of all wicked deeds and without causing hardship to people, face the natural course of death."'

विषमुद्बन्धनं दाहो दस्युहस्तात्तथा वध: ।
दंष्ट्रिभ्यश्च पशुभ्यश्च प्राकृतो वध उच्यते ॥ (25)

'"Poison, hanging, burning, being slain by bandits and being bitten to death by animals are said to be inferior kinds of death."'

न चौभि: पुण्यकर्माणो युज्यन्ते नाभिसंधिजै: ।
एवंविधैश्च बहुभिरपरै: प्राकृतैरपि ॥ (26)

'"Those who are the performers of auspicious deeds do not confront these and many other inferior kinds of death."'

ऊर्ध्वं हित्वा प्रतिष्ठन्ते प्राणा: पुण्यकृतां नृप ।
मध्यतो मध्यपुण्यानामधो दुष्कृतकर्मणाम् ॥ (27)

'"O Lord of Men! When it leaves, the breath of life of virtuous ones ascends upwards, that of those who are middling in merit remains towards the middle and that of the perpetrators of wicked deeds heads downwards."'

एक: शत्रुर्न द्वितीयोऽस्ति शत्रुरज्ञानतुल्य: पुरुषस्य राजन् ।
येनावृत: कुरुते संप्रयुक्तो घोराणि कर्माणि सुदारुणानि ॥ (28)

'"O King! For any man, there is only one foe and no second enemy, and that happens to be ignorance. If he is enveloped by this, he is goaded to perform extremely terrible and loathsome deeds."'

प्रबोधनार्थं श्रुतिधर्मयुक्तं वृद्धानुपास्यं च भवेत यस्य ।
प्रयत्नसाध्यो हि स राजपुत्र प्रज्ञाशरेणोन्मथित: पैति ॥ (29)

'"For the sake of understanding, one must serve the elders and follow the dharma of the Shrutis. O Prince! One must make efforts for success. That enemy can only be brought down through the arrow of wisdom.'"

अधीत्य वेदांस्तपसा ब्रह्मचारी यज्ञाञ्छक्त्या संनिसृज्येह पञ्च ।
वनं गच्छेत्पुरुषो धर्मकामः श्रेयश्चित्वा स्थापयित्वा स्ववंशम् ॥ (30)

'"One must study the Vedas, observe austerities and perform the five sacrifices.[53] Having established his own lineage, with a desire to obtain dharma, a man must then go to the forest. He must control himself, practise brahmacharya and seek out what is best."'

उपभोगैरपि त्यक्तं नात्मानमवसादयेत् ।
चण्डालत्वेऽपि मानुष्यं सर्वथा तात दुर्लभम् ॥ (31)

'"However, he must not emaciate himself by giving up all material objects. O Son! Birth as a human is extremely difficult to obtain, even as a chandala."'[54]

इयं हि योनिः प्रथमा यां प्राप्य जगतीपते ।
आत्मा वै शक्यते त्रातुं कर्मभिः शुभलक्षणैः ॥ (32)

'"O Lord of the Earth! This is the first kind of birth, because one can seek to save the atman by undertaking karma that has auspicious traits."'

कथं न विप्रणश्येम योनितोऽस्या इति प्रभो ।
कुर्वन्ति धर्म मनुजाः श्रुतिप्रामाण्यदर्शनात् ॥ (33)

'"O Lord! Who will destroy such a life once it has been obtained? Using the norms of Shrutis as a yardstick, men undertake acts of dharma."'

यो दुर्लभतरं प्राप्य मानुष्यमिह वै नरः ।
धर्मावमन्ता कामात्मा भवेत्स खलु वञ्च्यते ॥ (34)

---

[53]Brahma yajna, deva yajna, pitri yajna, manushya yajna and *bhuta* yajna. These are the five essential sacrifices for a householder—studying, offering sacrifices to gods and oblations to ancestors, and offering hospitality to men and other creatures.
[54]Therefore, that life must be preserved.

"'But though a status as a human may be very difficult to obtain in this world, there may be a man who ignores dharma. He is overcome by desire and thereby deceives himself.'"

यस्तु प्रीतिपुरोगेण चक्षुषा तात पश्यति ।
दीपोपमानि भूतानि यावदर्चिर्न नश्यति ॥ (35)

"'O Son! A person who looks at all beings with eyes of affection is not destroyed, like the flames of a lamp that have been protected.'"

सान्त्वेनानुप्रदानेन प्रियवादेन चाप्युत ।
समदुःखसुखो भूत्वा स परत्र महीयते ॥ (36)

"'He comforts everyone and speaks pleasantly to them. He is impartial towards delight and misery. He obtains greatness in the world hereafter.'"

दानं त्यागः शोभना मूर्तिरद्भ्यो भूयः प्लाव्यं तपसा वै शरीरम् ।
सरस्वतीनैमिषपुष्करेषु ये चाप्यन्ये पुण्यदेशाः पृथिव्याम् ॥ (37)

"'Donations, renunciation, making the appearance pleasant and amiable, repeated purification of the body through bathing and austerities—these must be undertaken near the Sarasvati,[55] in Naimisha, in Pushkara, or in other sacred spots on earth.'"

गृहेषु येषामसवः पतन्ति तेषामथो निर्हरनं प्रशस्तम् ।
यानेन वै प्रापणं च श्मशाने शौचेन नूनं विधिना चैव दाहः ॥ (38)

"'For those who die in houses, it is recommended that their dead bodies should be taken out from there and taken to cremation grounds in vehicles. Cremation must be performed in accordance with the rites of purification.'"

इष्टिः पुष्टिर्यजनं याजनं च दानं पुण्यानां कर्मणां च प्रयोगः ।
शक्त्या पित्र्यं यच्च किं चित्प्रशस्तं सर्वाण्यात्मार्थे मानवो यः
करोति ॥ (39)

---

[55] A reference to the river.

'"Rites, beneficial sacrifices, officiating at sacrifices, donations and efforts to undertake auspicious deeds according to one's capacity—these have been recommended for the sake of the departed ancestors. A man also undertakes these for his own self."'

धर्मशास्त्राणि वेदाश्च षडङ्गानि नराधिप ।
श्रेयसोऽर्थं विधीयन्ते नरस्याक्लिष्ट कर्मणः ॥ (40)

'"O Lord of Men! The texts of dharma, the Vedas and the six Vedangas have been laid down for the benefit of a man who performs unblemished deeds."'

भीष्म उवाच

एवद्वै सर्वमाख्यातं मुनिना सुमहात्मना ।
विदेहराजाय पुरा श्रेयसोऽर्थं नराधिप ॥ (41)

Bhishma said, 'O Lord of Men! In this way, the extremely great-souled sage related all this and in those ancient times, spoke to the king of Videha for his benefit.'

Chapter 9

भीष्म उवाच

पुनरेव तु पप्रच्छ जनको मिथिलाधिपः ।
पराशरं महात्मानं धर्मे परमनिश्चयम् ॥ (1)
किं श्रेयः का गतिर्ब्रह्मन्किं कृतं न विनश्यति ।
क्व गतो न निवर्तेत तन्मे ब्रूहि महामुने ॥ (2)

Bhishma said, 'For the sake of determining supreme dharma, Janaka, the lord of Mithila, again asked the great-souled Parashara. "O Brahmana! What is the beneficial objective? Which deeds are never destroyed? Which is the spot from which one does not have to return, once one has reached it? O Great Sage! Please tell me that."'

पराशर उवाच

असङ्गः श्रेयसो मूलं ज्ञानं ज्ञानगतिः पुरा ।
चीर्णं तपो न प्रनश्येद्वाप्यः क्षेत्रे न नश्यति ॥ (3)

'Parashara replied, "Non-attachment is the best foundation of jnana. Jnana represents the ancient path. Austerities are never destroyed. Seeds sown in a field are not destroyed."'

छित्त्वाधर्ममयं पाशं यदा धर्मेऽभिरज्यते ।
दत्त्वाभयकृतं दानं तदा सिद्धिमवाप्नुयात् ॥ (4)

'"If a person severs the noose of adharma and takes pleasure in dharma, if he grants the gift of fearlessness, then he obtains success."'

यो ददाति सहस्राणि गवामश्वशतानि च ।
अभयं सर्वभूतेभ्यस्तद्दानमतिवर्तते ॥ (5)

'"A person who gives away thousands of cattle and hundreds of horses is surpassed by the donations of one who grants fearlessness to all beings."'

वसन्विषयमध्येऽपि न वसत्येव बुद्धिमान् ।
संवसत्येव दुर्बुद्धिरसत्सु विषयेष्वपि ॥ (6)

'"One may dwell in the midst of material objects. However, if one is intelligent, one does not really dwell amidst them. It is only the evil-minded person who dwells amidst trifling material objects."'

नाधर्मः श्लिष्यते प्राज्ञमापः पुष्करपर्णवत् ।
अप्राज्ञमधिकं पापं श्लिष्यते जतु काष्ठवत् ॥ (7)

'"Like water on the leaf of a lotus, a wise person is not touched by adharma. Sin attaches more to an ignorant person, just as lac and wood attach to each other."'

नाधर्मः कारणापेक्षी कर्तारमभिमुञ्चति ।
कर्ता खलु यथाकालं तत्सर्वमभिपद्यते ।
न भिद्यन्ते कृतात्मान आत्मप्रत्ययदर्शिनः ॥ (8)

'"Adharma can only be extinguished after the fruits have been felt and do not let go of the doer. At the right time, the doer will have to endure all of these. But they do not afflict those who have clean atmans and have seen the atman."'

बुद्धिकर्मेन्द्रियाणां हि प्रमत्तो यो न बुध्यते ।
शुभाशुभेषु सक्तात्मा प्राप्नोति सुमहद्भयम् ॥ (9)

'"An ignorant person is distracted by his intelligence and the organs of action and does not understand. Attached to good and bad deeds, he suffers from extremely great fear."'

वीतरागो जितक्रोध: सम्यग्भवति य: सदा ।
विषये वर्तमानोऽपि न स पापेन युज्यते ॥ (10)

'"Even when he is in the midst of material objects, a person who is devoid of attachment and has properly conquered his anger is never united with sin."'

मर्यादायां धर्मसेतुर्निबद्धो नैव सीदति ।
पुष्टस्रोत इवायत्त: स्फीतो भवति सञ्चय: ॥ (11)

'"When there is a dam, one does not suffer even if the store of water swells up. In that way, someone with the dam of dharma does not suffer."'

यथा भानुगतं तेजो मणि: शुद्ध: समाधिना ।
आदत्ते राजशार्दूल तथा योग: प्रवर्तते ॥ (12)

'"The gem purifies itself by attracting the rays of the sun.[56] O Tiger among Kings! A person who practises yoga receives in that way."'

यथा तिलानामिह पुष्पसंश्रयात्पृथक्पृथग्याति गुणोऽतिसौम्यताम् ।
तथा नराणां भुवि भावितात्मनां यथाश्रयं सत्त्वगुण: प्रवर्तते ॥ (13)

---

[56]This is the *suryakanta* jewel, the sun stone, not quite a crystal. It possessed the property of absorbing the sun's rays and radiating heat. In the process, it purified itself.

'"When sesame seeds are separately mingled with flowers, they separately imbibe those pleasant qualities. By resorting to the quality of sattva, men on earth can improve themselves by associating with those who have cleansed their atmans."'

जहाति दारानिहते न सम्पदः सदश्वयानं विविधाश्च याः क्रियाः ।
त्रिविष्टपे जातमतिर्यदा नरस्तदास्य बुद्धिर्विषयेषु भिद्यते ॥ (14)

'"When a man makes up his mind about heaven, he abandons his wife, destroys his riches, his excellent horses, his vehicles and all kinds of rites. His intelligence is then delinked from material objects."'

प्रसक्तबुद्धिर्विषयेषु यो नरो यो बुध्यते ह्यात्महितं कदाचन ।
स सर्वभावानुगतेन चेतसा नृपामिषेणेव झषो विकृष्यते ॥ (15)

'"If a man's intelligence is addicted to material objects, he can never comprehend what brings welfare to his atman. O King! His consciousness is attracted by all these sentiments, like fish after the bait of meat."'

सघांतवान्मर्त्यलोकः परस्परमपाश्रितः ।
कदलीगर्भनिःसारो नौरिवाप्सु निमज्जति ॥ (16)

'"All mortal beings in this world encounter each other and depend on each other. But like a plantain tree, this lacks substance. They sink, like a boat in the ocean."'

न धर्मकालः पुरुषस्य निश्चितो न चापि मृत्युः पुरुषं प्रतीक्षते ।
क्रिया हि धर्मस्य सदैव शोभना यदा नरो मृत्युमुखेऽभिवर्तते ॥ (17)

'"No time has been designated for a man to follow dharma. Death does not wait for any man. It is appropriate that one should always practise the rites of dharma, since a man is always headed towards the jaws of death."'

यथान्धः स्वगृहे युक्तो ह्यभ्यासादेव गच्छति ।
तथायुक्तेन मनसा प्राज्ञो गच्छति तां गतिम् ॥ (18)

'"Through practice, a blind man can roam around in his own house. In that way, by concentrating the mind, a wise person can proceed along the desired path."'

मरणं जन्मनि प्रोक्तं जन्म वै मरणाश्रितम् ।
अविद्वान्मोक्षधर्मेषु बद्धो भ्रमति चक्रवत् ॥ (19)

'"It has been said that everything that is born must die. Birth is associated with death. A person who is ignorant about the dharma of moksha is bound and is whirled around, like on a wheel."'

यथा मृणालोऽनुगतमाशु मुञ्चति कर्दमम् ।
तथात्मा पुरुषस्येह मनसा परिमुच्यते ।
मन: प्रणयतेऽऽत्मानं स एनमभियुञ्जति ॥ (20)

'"The stalk of a lotus can swiftly free itself from the mire. In that way, a man's atman can free itself of the mind. It is the mind that conveys the atman towards union."'

परार्थे वर्तमानस्तु स्वकार्यं योऽभिमन्यते ।
इन्द्रियार्थेषु सक्त: सन्स्वकार्यात्परिहीयते ॥ (21)

'"Engaged in one's own acts, one tends to ignore the supreme objective. By being addicted to the objects of the senses, one falls away from one's true tasks."'

अधस्तिर्यग्गतिं चैव स्वर्गे चैव परां गतिम् ।
प्राप्नोति स्वकृतैरात्मा प्राज्ञस्येहेतरस्य च ॥ (22)

'"Though heaven is the supreme objective, one heads downwards and obtains birth as inferior species. Through his own deeds, a wise person's atman obtains the supreme benefit."'

मृन्मये भाजने पक्वे यथा वै न्यस्यते द्रव: ।
तथा शरीरं तपसा तप्तं विषयमश्नुते ॥ (23)

'"When an earthen vessel has been baked, the liquid kept there does not escape and diminish. Even if one is in the midst of material objects, it is the same with a person who has tormented his body through austerities."'

विषयानश्नुते यस्तु न स भोक्ष्यत्यसंशयम् ।
यस्तु भोगांस्त्यजेदात्मा स वै भोक्तुं व्यवस्यति ॥ (24)

'"There is no doubt that a person who discards material objects can attain moksha, delinking his atman from objects of pleasure. But there are others who base themselves on objects of pleasure."'

नीहारेण हि संवीतः शिश्नोदरपरायणः ।
जात्यन्ध इव पन्थानमावृतात्मा न बुध्यते ॥ (25)

'"A person attached to his penis and stomach is shrouded in mist. His atman is enveloped, like a person who has been born blind, and he does not understand."'

वणिग्यथा समुद्राद्धै यथार्थं लभते धनम् ।
तथा मर्त्यार्णवे जन्तोः कर्मविज्ञानतो गतिम् ॥ (26)

'"Merchants who go out to sea obtain riches that are proportionate to the capital invested. Like that, one should know that in the ocean of mortality, creatures obtain ends that are proportionate to their karma."'

अहोरात्रमये लोके जरारूपेण सचरन् ।
मृत्युर्ग्रसति भूतानि पवनं पन्नगो यथा ॥ (27)

'"In this world, made up of days and nights, death roams around in the form of old age and devours creatures, like a serpent devouring the air."'[57]

स्वयं कृतानि कर्माणि जातो जन्तुः प्रपद्यते ।
नाकृतं लभते कश्चित्किंचिदत्र प्रियाप्रियम् ॥ (28)

'"A creature obtains a birth that is determined by the karma that he has himself performed. There is nothing, pleasant or unpleasant, that is obtained but is not dependent on earlier acts."'

---

[57]Some serpents were believed to subsist on air.

शयानं यान्तमासीनं प्रवृत्तं विषयेषु च ।
शुभाशुभानि कर्माणि प्रपद्यन्ते नरं सदा ॥ (29)

'"Whether he is lying down, moving around or is seated, or is in the midst of material objects, a man always obtains the fruits of good and bad deeds."'

न ह्यन्यत्तीरमासाद्य पुनस्तर्तुं व्यवस्यति ।
दुर्लभो दृश्यते ह्यस्य विनिपातो महार्णवे ॥ (30)

'"But it is seen that someone who has obtained the furthest shore,[58] which is so difficult to reach in this great ocean, does not return again."'

यथा भारावसक्ता हि नौर्महाम्भसि तन्तुना ।
तथा मनोऽभियोगाद्धै शरीरं प्रतिकर्षति ॥ (31)

'"When a burden has to be carried, boats are lowered into the great ocean through ropes.[59] That is the way the mind uses yoga to uplift the body."'

यथा समुद्रमभितः संस्यूताः सरितोऽपराः ।
तथाद्या प्रकृतियोगादभिसंस्यूयते सदा ॥ (32)

'"Rivers head towards the ocean and unite with it. In that way, yoga always makes one unite with one's original nature."'

स्नेहपाशैर्बहुविधैरासक्तमनसो नराः ।
प्रकृतिस्था विषीदन्ति जले सैकतवेश्मवत् ॥ (33)

'"The minds of men are attached to many kinds of bonds of affection. Their nature is destroyed, like houses made of sand by the water."'

शरीरगृहसंस्थस्य शौचतीर्थस्य देहिनः ।
बुद्धिमार्गप्रयातस्य सुखं त्विह परत्र च ॥ (34)

---

[58] Has been emancipated by crossing the ocean of samsara, so that there is no rebirth.
[59] If boats are not being used, they are not left in the water for fear of damage. When they are needed, ropes are used to lower them into the water.

"'The embodied being must realize that the body is like a house and that it has to be purified, like through the waters of a tirtha. If one advances along the path of intelligence, one obtains happiness in this world and in the next world.'"

विस्तरः क्लेशसंयुक्ताः सक्षेपास्तु सुखावहाः ।
परार्थं विस्तराः सर्वे त्यागमात्महितं विदुः ॥ (35)

"'There are many things that lead to hardship, but there are only a few that bring happiness. The learned say that among the many things that lead to benefit in the hereafter, renunciation is the best.'"

सकंल्पजो मित्रवर्गो ज्ञातयः कारणात्मकाः ।
भार्या दासाश्च पुत्राश्च स्वमर्थमनुयुञ्जते ॥ (36)

"'There are large numbers of friends who have their own intentions. There are relatives who follow their own reasons. There are wives, servants and sons. All of them wish to enjoy one's riches for their own reasons.'"

न माता न पिता किंचित्कस्यचित्प्रतिपद्यते ।
दानपथ्योदनो जन्तुः स्वकर्मफलमश्नुते ॥ (37)

"'A mother or a father cannot bring about anything in the hereafter. Donations are the medication, and a being reaps the fruits of his own karma.'"

माता पुत्रः पिता भ्राता भार्या मित्र जनस्तथा ।
अष्टापदपदस्थाने त्वक्षमुद्रेव न्यस्यते ॥ (38)

"'Mothers, sons, fathers, brothers, wives and friends are only like *ashtapada* against the real stuff.'"[60]

सर्वाणि कर्माणि पुरा कृतानि शुभाशुभान्यात्मनो यान्ति जन्तोः ।
उपस्थितं कर्मफलं विदित्वा बुद्धिं तथा चोदयतेऽन्तरात्मा ॥ (39)

---

[60]Ashtapada is a measure of gold. The shloka indicates that relatives are like etchings—they are not real gold.

"'All the karma that has been done earlier, good and bad, follows a creature's atman. Knowing that the fruits of karma present themselves, one should turn one's intelligence towards the inner atman.'"

व्यवसायं समाश्रित्य सहायान्योऽधिगच्छति ।
न तस्य कश्चिदारम्भः कदाचिदवसीदति ॥ (40)

"'One should resort to one's conduct, using others as aides. One who has begun his acts in this way never suffers.'"

अद्वैधमनसं युक्तं शूरं धीरं विपश्चितम् ।
न श्रीः सन्त्यजते नित्यमादित्यमिव रश्मयः ॥ (41)

"'One must have no doubt in one's mind. One must be brave, patient and learned. Prosperity will never abandon such a person, just as the rays don't leave the sun.'"

आस्तिक्यव्यवसायाभ्यामुपायाद्विस्मयाद्धिया ।
यमारभत्यनिन्द्यात्मा न सोऽर्थः परिसीदति ॥ (42)

"'If a person believes and uses means to engage in such conduct, without any wonder and without any doubt, and if he controls himself, then his atman does not suffer and he does not deviate from the objective.'"

सर्वैः स्वानि शुभाशुभानि नियतं कर्माणि जन्तुः स्वयं
गर्भात्सम्प्रतिपद्यते तदुभयं यत्तेन पूर्वं कृतम् ।
मृत्युश्चापरिहारवान्समगतिः कालेन विच्छेदिता
दारोश्चूर्णमिवाश्मसारविहितं कर्मान्तिकं प्रापयेत् ॥ (43)

"'All the karma that a creature has himself performed, good and bad, controls him from the moment he obtains a womb. Both types of earlier deeds restrain him. Death cannot be countered and time severs everything, like a saw scattering dust from wood. In the end, the fruits of karma are obtained.'"

स्वरूपतामात्मकृतं च विस्तरं कुलान्वयं द्रव्यसमृद्धिसंचयम् ।
नरो हि सर्वो लभते यथाकृतं शुभाशुभेनात्मकृतेन कर्मणा ॥ (44)

'"Through the karma that he has himself performed earlier, good and bad, a man obtains everything—his own appearance, nobility of birth, material objects, prosperity and other stores."'

भीष्म उवाच

इत्युक्तो जनको राजन्यथातथ्यं मनीषिणा ।
श्रुत्वा धर्मविदां श्रेष्ठ: परां मुदमवाप ह ॥ (45)

Bhishma said, 'O King! The learned one thus spoke about the truth to Janaka. Having heard, the best among those who were knowledgable about dharma, obtained great delight.'

Thus ends the Parashara Gita.

21

HAMSA GITA

Towards the end of Moksha Dharma Parva in Shanti Parva, after being questioned by Yudhishthira, Bhishma tells him about a conversation between the sadhyas, who are minor divinities, and a *hamsa* (swan). This single chapter with forty-five shlokas constitutes the Hamsa Gita and is named after the swan. A swan is believed to be able to drink up the milk from a mixture of milk and water. Therefore, the imagery of someone who is able to discern is associated with a swan.

युधिष्ठिर उवाच

सत्यं दमं क्षमां प्रज्ञां प्रशंसन्ति पितामह ।
विद्वांसो मनुजा लोके कथमेतन्मतं तव ॥ (1)

Yudhishthira asked, 'O Grandfather! Learned men in this world praise truthfulness, self-control, forgiveness and wisdom. What is your view?'

भीष्म उवाच

अत्र ते वर्तयिष्येऽहमितिहासं पुरातनम् ।
साध्यानामिह संवादं हंसस्य च युधिष्ठिर ॥ (2)

Bhishma replied, 'O Yudhishthira! In this connection, there is an ancient history about a conversation that took place between the sadhyas and a swan.'

हंसो भूत्वाथ सौवर्णस्त्वजो नित्यः प्रजापतिः ।
स वै पर्येति लोकांस्त्रीनथ साध्यानुपागमत् ॥ (3)

'Once upon a time, the eternal Prajapati assumed the form of a golden swan. In this form, he travelled through the three worlds and came upon the sadhyas.'

साध्या ऊचुः

शकुने वयं स्म देवा वै साध्यास्त्वामनुयुञ्ज्महे ।
पृच्छामस्त्वां मोक्षधर्मं भवांश्च किल मोक्षवित् ॥ (4)

'The sadhyas said, "O Bird! We are devas who are known as the sadhyas. You are indeed the one who truly knows about moksha, and we wish to ask you about moksha dharma."

श्रुतोऽसि नः पण्डितो धीरवादी साधुशब्दः पतते ते पतत्रिन् ।
किं मन्यसे श्रेष्ठतमं द्विज त्वं कस्मिन्मनस्ते रमते महात्मन् ॥ (5)

'"We have heard that you are learned, patient and eloquent. O Bird! Virtuous words are heard from you. O Dvija![1] What do you think is best? O Great-Souled One! Where does your mind find delight?"'

तन्नः कार्यं पक्षिवर प्रशाधि यत्कार्याणां मन्यसे श्रेष्ठमेकम् ।
यत्कृत्वा वै पुरुषः सर्वबन्धैर्विमुच्यते विहगेन्द्रेह शीघ्रम् ॥ (6)

'"O Supreme among Birds! Therefore, it should be your task to instruct us. O Indra among Birds! What do you think is the single task, best among deeds, so that a man can be swiftly emancipated?"'

हंस उवाच

इदं कार्यममृताशाः शृणोमि तपो दमः सत्यमात्माभिगुप्तिः ।
ग्रन्थीन्विमुच्य हृदयस्य सर्वान्द्रियाप्रिये स्वं वशमानयीत ॥ (7)

---

[1] The word 'dvija' means someone who is born twice. Therefore, for humans, it is used for any of the first three varnas, who go through the sacred thread ceremony. However, it also means a bird, since a bird is born twice, once when the egg is laid and the second time when the egg is hatched.

'The swan replied, "O Ones Who Have Fed on Amrita! I have heard that one must resort to these tasks: austerities, self-control, truthfulness and the protection of the atman. With all the strands of the heart loosened, the pleasant and the unpleasant must be brought under one's control."'

नारुन्तुद: स्यान्न नृशंसवादी न हीनत: परमभ्याददीत ।
ययास्य वाचा पर उद्विजेत न तां वदेदुशतीं पापलोक्याम् ॥ (8)

'"One must not make others suffer or be harsh in speech. One must not receive anything supreme from those who are inferior. One must not agitate others through speech. One must not speak words that make them go to wicked worlds."'

वाक्सायका वदनान्निष्पतन्ति यैराहत: शोचति रात्र्यहानि ।
परस्य नामर्मसु ते पतन्ति तान्पण्डितो नावसृजेत्परेषु ॥ (9)

'"Spoken words descend like arrows. Struck by spoken words, one grieves day and night. A learned person will not release them and make them descend towards the vital organs of others."'

परश्चेदेनमति वादबानैर्भृशं विध्येच्छम एवेह कार्य: ।
संरोष्यमाण: प्रतिमृष्यते य: स आदत्ते सुकृतं वै परस्य ॥ (10)

'"If another person is severely struck with arrows of excessive words, it is his task to pacify himself. If a person replies angrily, all his good merits for the hereafter are taken away by the other."'

क्षेपाभिमानादभिषङ्गव्यलीकं निगृह्णाति ज्वलितं यश्च मन्युम् ।
अदुष्टचेता मुदितोऽनसूयु: स आदत्ते सुकृतं वै परेषाम् ॥ (11)

'"A person should control his blazing anger, pacify his pride and negate the futile humiliation. He should be cheerful and free from malice. He then takes away the good merits that the evil-minded person has earned in the hereafter."'

आक्रुश्यमानो न वदामि किंचित्क्षाम्यहं ताड्यमानश्च नित्यम् ।
श्रेष्ठं ह्येतत्क्षमामाहुरार्या: सत्यं तथैवार्जवमानृशंस्यम् ॥ (12)

"'I do not say anything when I am censured. Even when I am incessantly assailed, I forgive it. Noble ones say that forgiveness, truthfulness, uprightness and non-violence are the best.'"

वेदस्योपनिषत्सत्यं सत्यस्योपनिषद्दम: ।
दमस्योपनिषन्मोक्ष एतत्सर्वानुशासनम् ॥ (13)

"'Truth is the seat for the Vedas. Self-control is the seat for the truth. Moksha is the seat for self-control. These are all the various instructions.'"

वाचो वेगं मनस: क्रोधवेगं विवित्सावेगमुदरोपस्थवेगम् ।
एतान्वेगान्यो विषहेद्दीनांस्तं मन्येऽहं ब्राह्मणं वै मुनिं च ॥ (14)

"'I think that a person who can control the force of words, the force of anger in the mind, the force of desire to know, the force of the stomach and the force of the genitals and all the other poisons that consume and destroy is a brahmana and a sage.'"

अक्रोधन: क्रुध्यतां वै विशिष्टस्तथा तितिक्षुरतितिक्षोर्विशिष्ट: ।
अमानुषान्मानुषो वै विशिष्टस्तथा ज्ञानाज्ज्ञानवान्वै प्रधान: ॥ (15)

"'Lack of anger is superior to anger. Patience is superior to the lack of patience. A human is superior to those who are not human. In that way, jnana is superior to the lack of jnana.'"

आक्रुश्यमानो नाक्रोशेन्मन्युरेव तितिक्षत: ।
आक्रोष्टारं निर्दहति सुकृतं चास्य विन्दति ॥ (16)

"'One who is not enraged is superior to one who is angered. One must be patient when one is raged against. In that event, the assailant is burnt[2] and one obtains all his good merits.'"

यो नात्युक्त: प्राह रूक्षं प्रियं वा यो वा हतो न प्रतिहन्ति धैर्यात् ।
पापं च यो नेच्छति तस्य हन्तुस्तस्मै देवा: स्पृहयन्ते सदैव ॥ (17)

---

[2] The person who has assailed is scorched through remorse.

'"When struck, if a person does not say anything harsh or pleasant in reply; when struck, if a person is patient and does not strike back; when assailed, if a person does not desire to do anything wicked in retaliation—such a person is always desired by devas."'

पापीयस: क्षमेतैव श्रेयस: सदृशस्य च ।
विमानितो हतोऽऽक्रुष्ट एवं सिद्धिं गमिष्यति ॥ (18)

'"A wicked person must be forgiven as if he is equal to a superior person, even if one has been dishonoured, assailed and censured. That is the way to progress towards siddhi."'

सदाहमार्यान्निभृतोऽप्युपासे न मे विवित्सा न च मेऽस्ति रोष: ।
न चाप्यहं लिप्समान: परैमि न चैव किंचिद्दिषमेण यामि ॥ (19)

'"I no longer seek to obtain anything, nor is there any rage in me. In private, I always serve noble ones. I do not desire anything that belongs to others and I do not seek any of their possessions."'

नाहं शप्त: प्रतिशपामि किंचिदमं द्वारं ह्यमृतस्येह वेद्मि ।
गुह्यं ब्रह्म तदिदं वो ब्रवीमि न मानुषाच्छ्रेष्ठतरं हि किंचित् ॥ (20)

'"When I am cursed, I do not curse anything back. I know that this is the door towards immortality. I am telling you the secret of the brahman. There is nothing superior for men."'

विमुच्यमान: पापेभ्यो घनेभ्य इव चन्द्रमा: ।
विरजा: कालमाकाङ्क्षन्धीरो धैर्येण सिध्यति ॥ (21)

'"They will then be freed from sin, like the moon from the clouds. Such a patient person will obtain success through his patience and be radiant, while he waits for the right time to come."'[3]

य: सर्वेषां भवति ह्यर्चनीय उत्सेचने स्तम्भ इवाभिजात: ।
यस्मै वाचं सुप्रशस्तां वदन्ति स वै देवानगच्छति संयतात्मा ॥ (22)

---

[3]The right time for death.

'"He deserves to be worshipped by everyone and is like a noble pillar that holds everything up. Words of great praise are spoken about him. Such a person has control over his atman and goes to the devas."'

न तथा वक्तुमिच्छन्ति कल्याणान्पुरुषे गुणान् ।
यथैषां वक्तुमिच्छन्ति नैर्गुण्यमनुयुञ्जकाः ॥ (23)

'"Revilers who are full of anger and speak about lack of qualities cannot speak in that way about such a man's auspicious qualities."'

यस्य वाङ्मनसी गुप्ते सम्यक्प्रणिहिते सदा ।
वेदास्तपश्च त्यागश्च स इदं सर्वमाप्नुयात् ॥ (24)

'"His words and mind are always protected and controlled in the appropriate way. Through the Vedas, austerities and renunciation, he obtains everything."'

आक्रोशनावमानाभ्यामबुधाद्दर्धते बुधः ।
तस्मान् वर्धयेदन्यं न चात्मानं विहिंसयेत् ॥ (25)

'"Such a learned person does not react to the censure and disrespect shown by people who do not know, nor does he cause injury to his own self by extolling others."'[4]

अमृतस्येव संतृप्येदवमानस्य वै द्विजः ।
सुखं ह्यवमतः शेते योऽवमन्ता स नश्यति ॥ (26)

'"Like one who is content with amrita, he ignores this. Such a person is a dvija. He sleeps happily and disrespect does not destroy him."'

यत्क्रोधनो यजते यद्ददाति तद्वा तपस्तप्यति यज्जुहोति ।
वैवस्वतस्तद्धरतेऽस्य सर्वं मोघः श्रमो भवति क्रोधनस्य ॥ (27)

'"If there is rage when sacrifices are performed, gifts given, austerities performed or oblations offered, Vaivasvata[5] takes all these away. The efforts of a person who is enraged are futile."'

---

[4]Extolling those who praise him. He is beyond both praise and censure.
[5]Yama.

चत्वारि यस्य द्वाराणि सुगुप्तान्यमरोत्तमाः ।
उपस्थमुदरं हस्तौ वाक्चतुर्थी स धर्मवित् ॥ (28)

'"O Supreme among the Immortals! If a person protects the four gates well—the genitals, the stomach, the hands and speech as the fourth—he knows about dharma."'

सत्यं दमं ह्यार्जवमानृशंस्यं धृतिं तितिक्षामभिसेवमानः ।
स्वाध्यायनित्योऽस्पृहयन्परेषामेकान्तशील्यूर्ध्वगतिर्भवेत्सः ॥ (29)

'"Truthfulness, self-control, modesty, uprightness, non-violence, fortitude, patience, renunciation, constant studying, lack of desire towards the possessions of others—if a person has the good conduct to practise these single-mindedly, he will rise upwards."'

सर्वानेताननुचरन्वत्सवच्चतुरः स्तनान् ।
न पावनतमं किंचित्सत्यादध्यगमं क्वचित् ॥ (30)

'"Like a calf sucking at the four udders of the cow, these are all the things that one should follow. There is nothing that is purer than the truth."'

आचक्षेऽहं मनुष्येभ्यो देवेभ्यः प्रतिसंचरन् ।
सत्यं स्वर्गस्य सोपानं पारावारस्य नौरिव ॥ (31)

'"I have seen men and have travelled around among devas. Truth represents the stairs to heaven, like a boat helps to cross on an ocean."'

यादृशैः संनिवसति यादृशांश्चोपसेवते ।
यादृगिच्छेच्च भवितुं तादृग्भवति पूरुषः ॥ (32)

'"One becomes like the people one dwells and associates with. Whoever a man advances towards, he becomes like him."'

यदि सन्तं सेवति यद्यसन्तं तपस्विनं यदि वा स्तेनमेव ।
वासो यथा रङ्गवशं प्रयाति तथा स तेषां वशमभ्युपैति ॥ (33)

"'If one associates with the virtuous, one becomes virtuous. The same is the case with ascetics or thieves. This is like a garment being dyed with the colour [it has been immersed in]. In that way, one comes under their subjugation.'"

सदा देवाः साधुभिः संवदन्ते न मानुषं विषयं यान्ति द्रष्टुम् ।
नेन्दुः समः स्यादसमो हि वायुरूच्चावचं विषयं यः स वेद ॥ (34)

"'Devas always converse with the virtuous. They are not seen to be interested in human objects. A person should know that material objects come and go, like the moon and the wind.'"[6]

अदुष्टं वर्तमाने तु हृदयान्तरपूरुषे ।
तेनैव देवाः प्रीयन्ते सतां मार्गस्थितेन वै ॥ (35)

"'If the being inside the heart has not been stained and walks along the path of the virtuous, devas are pleased with the person.'"

शिश्नोदरे येऽभिरताः सदैव स्तेना नरा वाक्परुषाश्च नित्यम् ।
अपेतदोषानिति तान्विदित्वा दूराद्देवाः संपरिवर्जयन्ति ॥ (36)

"'From a distance, devas avoid those who are always addicted to their penis and stomach, men who are thieves and always harsh in speech, even if one knows that they have tried to atone for those sins.'"

न वै देवा हीनसत्त्वेन तोष्याः सर्वाशिना दुष्कृतकर्मणा वा ।
सत्यव्रता ये तु नराः कृतज्ञा धर्मे रतास्तैः सह संभजन्ते ॥ (37)

"'Devas are not satisfied with those who are inferior in spirit, those who eat everything and those who are perpetrators of wicked deeds. They honour men who are truthful in their vows, grateful and devoted to dharma.'"

अव्याहतं व्याहताच्छ्रेय आहुः सत्यं वदेद्व्याहतं तद्द्वितीयम् ।
धर्मं वदेद्व्याहतं तत्तृतीयं प्रियंवदेद्व्याहतं तच्चतुर्थम् ॥ (38)

---

[6] The moon waxes and wanes and the wind comes and goes.

'"It is said that silence is superior to speech. The second course is that of speaking the truth. The third course is to speak words of dharma. The fourth course is to speak pleasant words."'[7]

साध्या ऊचु:

केनायमावृतो लोक: केन वा न प्रकाशते ।
केन त्यजति मित्राणि केन स्वर्गं न गच्छति ॥ (39)

'The sadhyas asked, "What is the world covered by? When does it not shine? Why are friends cast away? Why does one not reach heaven?"'

हंस उवाच

अज्ञानेनावृतो लोको मात्सर्यान्न प्रकाशते ।
लोभात्त्यजति मित्राणि सङ्गात्स्वर्गं न गच्छति ॥ (40)

'The swan replied, "The world is enveloped in ignorance. Malice leads to a lack of shining. Friends are abandoned because of greed. Because of attachment, one does not go to heaven."'

साध्या ऊचु:

क: स्विदेको रमते ब्राह्मणानां क: स्विदेको बहुभिर्जोषमास्ते ।
क: स्विदेको बलवान् दुर्बलोऽपि क: स्विदेषां कलहं नान्ववैति ॥ (41)

'The sadhyas asked, "Among brahmanas, who is the single one who is always happy? Who is the single one who is silent amidst the many? Who is the single one who, though weak, is strong? Who is the single one who does not quarrel?"'

हंस उवाच

प्राज्ञ एको रमते ब्राह्मणानां प्राज्ञ एको बहुभिर्जोषमास्ते ।
प्राज्ञ एको बलवान्दुर्बलोऽपि प्राज्ञ एषां कलहं नान्ववैति ॥ (42)

---

[7]This is a hierarchy of different kinds of speech in terms of desirability.

'The swan replied, "Among brahmanas, the wise one is the single one who is always delighted. The wise one is the single one who is silent amidst many. The wise one is the single one who is strong though weak. The wise one is the one who does not quarrel."'

साध्या ऊचु:

किं ब्राह्मणानां देवत्वं किं च साधुत्वमुच्यते ।
असाधुत्वं च किं तेषां किमेषां मानुषं मतम् ॥ (43)

'The sadhyas asked, "What is divinity among brahmanas? What is said to be their virtue? What is wicked among them? What is held to constitute their humanity?"'

हंस उवाच

स्वाध्याय एषां देवत्वं व्रतं साधुत्वमुच्यते ।
असाधुत्वं परीवादो मृत्युर्मानुष्यमुच्यते ॥ (44)

'The swan replied, "Studying represents their divinity. Vows are said to be their virtue. Censuring others is their wickedness. Mortality constitutes their humanity."'

भीष्म उवाच

संवाद इत्ययं श्रेष्ठ: साध्यानां परिकीर्तित: ।
क्षेत्रं वै कर्मणां योनि: सद्भाव: सत्यमुच्यते ॥ (45)

Bhishma concluded, 'I have recounted the excellent conversation concerning the sadhyas. The body is the womb for karma and a virtuous existence is said to be the truth.'

Thus ends the Hamsa Gita.

22

YAJNAVALKYA GITA

The Yajnavalkya Gita is one of the most important Gitas in the Mahabharata, and reading it greatly facilitates comprehension of the Bhagavat Gita. It occurs right towards the end of Moksha Dharma Parva of Shanti Parva. As is the case throughout Shanti Parva, Bhishma is speaking to Yudhishthira. In the course of this, he relates what Sage Yajnavalkya told King Janaka, and the Yajnavalkya Gita is named after the sage. The Yajnavalkya Gita has 283 shlokas, spread over nine chapters. Many sections can be subject to diverse interpretations and it is not an easy Gita to understand or translate, especially when those sections are about samkhya. Samkhya is one of the six darshanas, founded by Sage Kapila and his disciples. It is based on the direct enumeration of principles. While samkhya texts differ, all of them emphasize the three gunas and the twenty-five *tattva*s (principles), leading up to Prakriti and Purusha. Prakriti is the active principle, while Purusha is inactive. When there is equilibrium between the three gunas, Prakriti is not manifested. However, when Prakriti comes into contact with Purusha, there is disequilibrium, and Prakriti is manifested. Among other things, creation results from this.

Chapter 1

युधिष्ठिर उवाच

धर्माधर्मविमुक्तं यद्विमुक्तं सर्वसंश्रयात् ।
जन्ममृत्युविमुक्तं च विमुक्तं पुण्यपापयोः ॥ (1)

Yudhishthira said, 'It[1] bestows freedom from adharma and dharma, freedom from all foundations, freedom from birth and death and also freedom from good and evil.'[2]

यच्छिवं नित्यमभयं नित्यं चाक्षरमव्ययम् ।
शुचि नित्यमनायासं तद्भवान्वक्तुमर्हति ॥ (2)

'It is always auspicious and bestows freedom from fear. It is always eternal and without decay. It is pure and always brings comfort. You should speak to me about this.'

भीष्म उवाच

अत्र ते वर्तयिष्येऽहमितिहासं पुरातनम् ।
याज्ञवल्क्यस्य संवादं जनकस्य च भारत ॥ (3)

Bhishma replied, 'O Descendant of the Bharata Lineage! In this connection, there is the ancient history of a conversation between Yajnavalkya and Janaka.'

याज्ञवल्क्यमृषिश्रेष्ठं दैवरातिर्महायशाः ।
पप्रच्छ जनको राजा प्रश्नं प्रश्नविदां वरः ॥ (4)

'Yajnavalkya was the best among rishis and was supreme among those who knew the answers to all questions. The immensely illustrious King Daivarati, from Janaka's lineage, asked him this question.'

---

[1] The unmanifest. The meaning will become clear later.
[2] This is a direct translation. Yudhishthira is asking a question about what it is that does all this.

कतीन्द्रियाणि विप्रर्षे कति प्रकृतयः स्मृताः ।
किमव्यक्तं परं ब्रह्म तस्माच्च परतस्तु किम् ॥ (5)

'"O Brahmana Rishi! How many senses are there? How many kinds of Prakriti are there said to be? What is the unmanifest and supreme brahman? What is superior to even that?"'

प्रभवं चाप्ययं चैव कालसंख्यां तथैव च ।
वक्तुमर्हसि विप्रेन्द्र त्वदनुग्रहकाङ्क्षिणः ॥ (6)

'"What is creation and destruction? What is the measurement of time? O Indra among Brahmanas! You should tell me about this. I desire to obtain your favours."'

अज्ञानात्परिपृच्छामि त्वं हि ज्ञानमयो निधिः ।
तदहं श्रोतुमिच्छामि सर्वमेतदसंशयम् ॥ (7)

'"You are a store of jnana. I am ignorant and am asking you. On all these doubts, I wish to hear from you."'

याज्ञवल्क्य उवाच

श्रूयतामवनीपाल यदेतदनुपृच्छसि ।
योगानां परमं ज्ञानं सांख्यानां च विशेषतः ॥ (8)

'Yajnavalkya replied, "O Protector of the Earth! Listen to what you have asked. This is the supreme jnana of yoga and, in particular, that of samkhya."'

न तवाविदितं किंचिन्मां तु जिज्ञासते भवान् ।
पृष्टेन चापि वक्तव्यमेष धर्मः सनातनः ॥ (9)

'"None of this is unknown to you. Nevertheless, you have asked me. It is eternal dharma that one must answer when one has been asked."'

अष्टौ प्रकृतयः प्रोक्ता विकाराश्चापि षोडश ।
अथ सप्त तु व्यक्तानि प्राहुरध्यात्मचिन्तकाः ॥ (10)

'"It is said that there are eight kinds of Prakriti and sixteen kinds of transformations. Those who have thought about the adhyatma have said that there are seven kinds of the manifest."'

अव्यक्तं च महांश्चैव तथाहंकार एव च ।
पृथिवी वायुराकाशमापो ज्योतिश्च पञ्चमम् ॥ (11)

'"There are the unmanifest, mahat, ahamkara, earth, wind, space, water and light as the fifth."'[3]

एता: प्रकृतयस्त्वष्टौ विकारानपि मे शृणु ।
श्रोत्रं त्वक्चैव चक्षुश्च जिह्वा घ्राणं च पञ्चमम् ॥ (12)
शब्दस्पर्शौ च रूपं च रसो गन्धस्तथैव च ।
वाक्च हस्तौ च पादौ च पायुर्मेंढ्रं तथैव च ॥ (13)

'"These eight are Prakriti. Hear from me about the *vikara*s.[4] These are the ear, the skin, the eye, the tongue, the nose as the fifth, sound, touch, form, taste, scent, speech, the two hands, the two feet, the anus and the penis."'[5]

एते विशेषा राजेन्द्र महाभूतेषु पञ्चसु ।
बुद्धीन्द्रियाण्यथैतानि सविशेषाणि मैथिल ॥ (14)

'"O Indra among Kings! O One from Mithila! Those that originate in the five great elements[6] are known as *vishesha* and the senses of intelligence are known as *savishesha*."'

मन: षोडशकं प्राहुर्ध्यात्मगतिचिन्तका: ।
त्वं चैवान्ये च विद्वांसस्तत्त्वबुद्धिविशारदा: ॥ (15)

'"Those who have thought about the adhyatma say that the mind is

---

[3] Here, the unmanifest means Prakriti. The other seven are manifest.
[4] The word 'vikara' means transformation, modification, change. The context determines the meaning. In samkhya, when the equilibrium of the gunas is disturbed, these are derived from Prakriti.
[5] The two hands are counted as one and the two feet are also counted as one. When one adds the mind, which has been mentioned in a later shloka, one gets the sixteen transformations.
[6] The organs of action and the objects of the senses.

the sixteenth. You, and other intelligent ones who know the truth, accomplished in intelligence, also believe that.'"

अव्यक्ताच्च महानात्मा समुत्पद्यति पार्थिव ।
प्रथमं सर्गमित्येतदाहुः प्राधानिकं बुधाः ॥ (16)

"'O Lord of the Earth! The mahat atman is generated from the unmanifest. The learned say that this is the first and most important creation.'"

महतश्चाप्यहंकार उत्पद्यति नराधिप ।
द्वितीयं सर्गमित्याहुरेतद्बुद्ध्यात्मकं स्मृतम् ॥ (17)

"'O Lord of Men! Ahamkara is created from mahat. Those who know about the adhyatma say that this second creation is that of intelligence.'"

अहंकाराच्च संभूतं मनो भूतगुणात्मकम् ।
तृतीयः सर्ग इत्येष आहंकारिक उच्यते ॥ (18)

"'The mind is generated from ahamkara, and this creates qualities in beings. This is said to be the third creation, which results from ahamkara.'"

मनसस्तु समुद्भूता महाभूता नराधिप ।
चतुर्थं सर्गमित्येतन्मानसं परिचक्षते ॥ (19)

"'O Lord of Men! The five great elements are generated from the mind. It is said that this fourth creation is from the mind.'"

शब्दः स्पर्शश्च रूपं च रसो गन्धस्तथैव च ।
पञ्चमं सर्गमित्याहुभौतिकं भूतचिन्तकाः ॥ (20)

"'Those who have thought about the elements say that sound, touch, form, taste and scent are the fifth creation and concern the elements.'"

श्रोत्रं त्वक्चैव चक्षुश्च जिह्वा घ्राणं च पञ्चमम् ।
सर्गं तु षष्ठमित्याहुर्बहुचिन्तात्मकं स्मृतम् ॥ (21)

'"The ear, the skin, the eye, the tongue and the nose as the fifth are said to be the sixth creation by those who have thought a lot about the atman."'

अधः श्रोत्रेन्द्रियग्राम उत्पद्यति नराधिप ।
सप्तमं सर्गमित्याहुरेतदैन्द्रियकं स्मृतम् ॥ (22)

'"O Lord of Men! Those that are created below the aggregate of the senses, the ear and others are said to be the seventh creation, concerning the senses."'[7]

ऊर्ध्वस्रोतस्तथा तिर्यगुत्पद्यति नराधिप ।
अष्टमं सर्गमित्याहुरेतदार्जवकं बुधाः ॥ (23)

'"O Lord of Men! There are the flows that rise upwards and move diagonally and the learned know these as the eighth and straight creation."'[8]

तिर्यक्स्रोतस्त्वधःस्रोत उत्पद्यति नराधिप ।
नवमं सर्गमित्याहुरेतदार्जवकं बुधाः ॥ (24)

'"O Lord of Men! There are also flows that move directly and diagonally downwards. The learned call these the ninth and straight creation."'

एतानि नव सर्गाणि तत्त्वानि च नराधिप ।
चतुर्विंशतिरुक्तानि यथाश्रुतिनिदर्शनात् ॥ (25)

'"O Lord of Men! This is the truth about the nine different kinds of creation. The Shrutis speak of these as possessing twenty-four signs."'[9]

अत ऊर्ध्वं महाराज गुणस्यैतस्य तत्त्वतः ।
महात्मभिरनुप्रोक्तां कालसङ्ख्यां निबोध मे ॥ (26)

---

[7]This is not very clear but probably refers to the organs of action.
[8]This refers to the various breaths of life, some of which rise upwards, while there are others that move diagonally.
[9]Five organs of perception, five organs of action, five gross elements, five subtle elements, mind, ahamkara, intelligence and jivatman.

"'O Great King! After this truth about the qualities, the great-souled ones have spoken about the measurement of time. Listen to me.'"

Chapter 2

याज्ञवल्क्य उवाच
अव्यक्तस्य नरश्रेष्ठ कालसंख्यां निबोध मे ।
पञ्च कल्पसहस्राणि द्विगुणान्यहरुच्यते ॥ (1)

'Yajnavalkya said, "O Best among Men! I will tell you about the measurement of time for the unmanifest. Ten thousand kalpas are said to make up a single day for him."'[10]

रात्रिरेतावती चास्य प्रतिबुद्धो नराधिप ।
सृजत्योषधिमेवाग्रे जीवनं सर्वदेहिनाम् ॥ (2)

"'O Lord of Men! His night is said to be of the same duration. When that is over, he awakes and first creates the herbs, which provide sustenance to all embodied beings.'"

ततो ब्रह्माणमसृजद्धैरण्याण्डसमुद्भवम् ।
सा मूर्तिः सर्वभूतानामित्येवमनुशुश्रुम ॥ (3)

"'He then creates Brahma, who arises from the golden egg. It has been heard by us that his form is there in all living beings.'"

संवत्सरमुषित्वाण्डे निष्क्रम्य च महामुनिः ।
संदधेऽर्धं महीं कृत्स्नां दिवमर्धं प्रजापतिः ॥ (4)

"'Having dwelt for one year inside the egg, the great sage Prajapati emerged and created the entire earth, heaven above it, and all that is below.'"

द्यावापृथिव्योरित्येष राजन्वेदेषु पठ्यते ।
तयोः शकलयोर्मध्यमाकाशमकरोत्प्रभुः ॥ (5)

---

[10]This is Purusha, which is, of course, infused with Prakriti's principles.

"'O King! Those who have studied the Vedas know that the sky is between earth and heaven. The lord created a fragment of the sky to lie between them.'"

एतस्यापि च संख्यानं वेदवेदाङ्गपारगैः ।
दश कल्पसहस्राणि पादोनान्यहरुच्यते ।
रात्रिमेतावतीं चास्य प्राहुरध्यात्मचिन्तकाः ॥ (6)

"'Those who are accomplished in the Vedas and the Vedangas say that the duration of his day is ten thousand and a quarter kalpas.[11] Those who have thought about the adhyatma say that his night is of an equal duration.'"

सृजत्यहंकारमृषिर्भूतं दिव्यात्मकं तथा ।
चतुरश्चापरान्पुत्रान्देहात्पूर्वं महानृषिः ।
ते वै पितृभ्यः पितरः श्रूयन्ते राजसत्तम ॥ (7)

"'From his divine form as a rishi, he created ahamkara. Before creating any other beings, the great rishi created four sons.[12] O Excellent King! We have heard that these were the fathers of the ancestors.'"

देवाः पितृणां च सुता देवैर्लोकाः समावृताः ।
चराचरा नरश्रेष्ठ इत्येवमनुशुश्रुम ॥ (8)

"'O Best among Men! We have heard that devas, ancestors, all those who surround the world of devas, and mobile and immobile objects were their sons.'"

परमेष्ठी त्वहंकारोऽसृजद्भूतानि पञ्चधा ।
पृथिवी वायुराकाशमापो ज्योतिश्च पञ्चमम् ॥ (9)

---

[11] This refers to another 250 (a quarter of a thousand) kalpas. The 'ten thousand' is an approximation.
[12] Through his mental powers, Brahma created four sons—Sanaka, Sanatana, Sananda and Sanatkumara. However, this is also interpreted as mind, intelligence, consciousness and super-consciousness.

'"Parameshthi, the ahamkara, then created the five elements—earth, wind, sky, water and light as the fifth."'

एतस्यापि निशामाहुस्तृतीयमिह कुर्वत: ।
पञ्च कल्पसहस्राणि तावदेवाहरुच्यते ॥ (10)

'"For the one who created the third creation, night is said to have five thousand kalpas and day is said to possess an equal duration."'

शब्द: स्पर्शश्च रूपं च रसो गन्धश्च पञ्चम: ।
एते विशेषा राजेन्द्र महाभूतेषु पञ्चसु ।
यैराविष्टानि भूतानि अहन्यहनि पार्थिव ॥ (11)

'"O Indra among Kings! O Lord of the Earth! Sound, touch, form, taste and scent as the fifth are known as vishesha. From one day to another day, these adhere to the five great elements in beings."'

अन्योन्यं स्पृहयन्त्येते अन्योन्यस्य हिते रता: ।
अन्योन्यमभिमन्यन्ते अन्योन्यस्पर्धिनस्तथा ॥ (12)

'"Because of these, beings desire each other and are engaged in each other's welfare. They respect each other, but also rival each other."'

ते वध्यमाना अन्योन्यं गुणैर्हारिभिरव्यया: ।
इहैव परिवर्तन्ते तिर्यग्योनिप्रवेशिन: ॥ (13)

'"Overcome by these undecaying qualities, they slaughter each other. They whirl around in this world and are born as inferior species."'

त्रीणि कल्पसहस्राणि एतेषामहरुच्यते ।
रात्रिरेतावती चैव मनसश्च नराधिप ॥ (14)

'"O Lord of Men! Their[13] day is said to last for three thousand kalpas. Their night is of the same duration and this is also the case with the mind."'

---

[13] Of the great elements.

मनश्चरति राजेन्द्र चरितं सर्वमिन्द्रियैः ।
न चेन्द्रियाणि पश्यन्ति मन एवात्र पश्यति ॥ (15)

'"O Indra among Kings! The mind wanders around in all the senses. The senses do not see anything. It is the mind that sees."'

चक्षुः पश्यति रूपाणि मनसा तु न चक्षुषा ।
मनसि व्याकुले चक्षुः पश्यन्नपि न पश्यति ।
तथेन्द्रियाणि सर्वाणि पश्यन्तीत्यभिचक्षते ॥ (16)

'"The eye perceives form. But the eye does not do this—it is done by the mind. When the mind is agitated, the eye may seem to see, but does not actually see. In that way, it is said that all the senses perceive."'

मनस्युपरते राजन्निन्द्रियोपरमो भवेत् ।
न चेन्द्रियव्युपरमे मनस्युपरमो भवेत् ।
एवं मनःप्रधानानि इन्द्रियाणि विभावयेत् ॥ (17)

'"O King! When the mind does not act, the senses do not act either. The mind does not cease to act because the senses cease to act. The mind is the foremost and influences them."'

इन्द्रियाणां हि सर्वेषामीश्वरं मन उच्यते ।
एतद्विशन्ति भूतानि सर्वाणीह महायशाः ॥ (18)

'"The mind is said to be the lord of all the senses. O Immensely Illustrious One! These penetrate all beings."'

Chapter 3

याज्ञवल्क्य उवाच

तत्त्वानां सर्गसंख्या च कालसंख्या तथैव च ।
मया प्रोक्तानुपूर्व्येण संहारमपि मे शृणु ॥ (1)

'Yajnavalkya said, "I have enumerated the nature of the different types of creation and the measurement of time too. I have progressively spoken about them. Now hear from me about destruction."'

यथा संहरते जन्तून्ससर्ज च पुन: पुन: ।
अनादिनिधनो ब्रह्मा नित्यश्चाक्षर एव च ॥ (2)

"'Beings are repeatedly created and destroyed. Brahma is eternal and undecaying, without a beginning and without an end.'"

अह:क्षयमथो बुद्ध्वा निशि स्वप्नमनास्तथा ।
चोदयामास भगवानव्यक्तोऽहंकृतं नरम् ॥ (3)

"'When day is over and he realizes that it is night, he makes up his mind to sleep. The illustrious and unmanifest one urges the creation of a being from his ahamkara.'"

तत: शतसहस्रांशुरव्यक्तेनाभिचोदित: ।
कृत्वा द्वादशधात्मानमादित्यो ज्वलदग्निवत् ॥ (4)

"'Urged, he manifests himself as a sun with a hundred thousand rays. He then divides himself into twelve suns that blaze like fire.'"

चतुर्विधं प्रजाजालं निर्दहत्याशु तेजसा ।
जराय्वण्डस्वेदजातमुद्भिज्जं च नराधिप ॥ (5)

"'O Lord of Men! With this blazing energy, the four kinds of beings are swiftly burnt up—those born from wombs, those born from eggs, those born from sweat[14] and plants.'"

एतदुन्मेषमात्रेण विनष्टं स्थाणुजङ्गमम् ।
कूर्मपृष्ठसमा भूमिर्भवत्यथ समन्तत: ॥ (6)

"'In a *nimesha*,[15] all mobile and immobile objects are destroyed and, in every direction, the earth becomes as plain as the back of a tortoise.'"

जगद्दग्ध्वामितबल: केवलं जगतीं तत: ।
अम्भसा बलिना क्षिप्रमापूर्यत समन्तत: ॥ (7)

---

[14] Worms and insects.
[15] Nimesha is the duration of the blink of an eye.

"'When everything in the universe has been destroyed with this great force, in every direction, it is swiftly filled up with the great force of water.'"

ततः कालाग्निमासाद्य तदम्भो याति संक्षयम् ।
विनस्तेऽम्भसि राजेन्द्र जाज्वलीत्यनलो महा ॥ (8)

"'At this, the fire of destruction dries up the water. O Indra among Kings! When the water has been destroyed, a great fire begins to blaze.'"

तमप्रमेयोऽतिबलं ज्वलमानं विभावसुम् ।
ऊष्माणं सर्वभूतानां सप्तार्चिषमथाञ्जसा ॥ (9)

"'An immeasurable and extremely powerful fire continues to blaze. The energy of those seven flames is infused with the heat from all creatures.'"

भक्षयामास बलवान्वायुरष्टात्मको बली ।
विचरन्नमितप्राणस्तिर्यगूर्ध्वमधस्तथा ॥ (10)

"'But it is devoured by an extremely powerful wind that blows strongly from the eight directions. Unlimited in strength, this courses upwards, downwards and diagonally.'"

तमप्रतिबलं भीममाकाशं ग्रसतेऽत्ममना ।
आकाशमप्यतिनदन्मनो ग्रसति चारिकम् ॥ (11)

"'However, that infinitely strong and terrible wind is devoured by space. But mind cheerfully and swiftly swallows up space.'"

मनो ग्रसति सर्वात्मा सोऽहंकारः प्रजापतिः ।
अहंकारं महानात्मा भूतभव्यभविष्यवित् ॥ (12)

"'Ahamkara, Prajapati and the atman of everything devour mind. Ahamkara is devoured by the atman of mahat, who knows about the past, the present and the future.'"

तमप्यनुपमात्मानं विश्वं शंभुः प्रजापतिः ।
अनिमा लघिमा प्राप्तिरीशानो ज्योतिरव्ययः ॥ (13)

'"The unmatched atman, Shambhu Prajapati, swallows up mahat. This is the radiant and undecaying Ishana, with the properties of *anima, laghima* and *prapti*."'[16]

सर्वत:पाणिपादान्त: सर्वतोक्षिशिरोमुख: ।
सर्वत:श्रुतिमाँल्लोके सर्वमावृत्य तिष्ठति ॥ (14)

'"His hands and feet extend towards every extremity. His eyes, heads and faces are everywhere. His ears are everywhere. He is established, enveloping all the worlds."'

हृदयं सर्वभूतानां पर्वणोऽङ्गुष्ठमात्रक: ।
अनुग्रसत्यनन्तं हि महात्मा विश्वमीश्वर: ॥ (15)

'"He is in the heart of all creatures and his size is only that of a thumb. The infinite and great-souled lord of the universe devours."'

तत:समभवत्सर्वमक्षयाव्ययमव्रणम् ।
भूतभव्यमनुष्याणां स्रष्टारमनघं तथा ॥ (16)

'"With everything devoured, what is left is the immutable and the undecaying. This is the unblemished one, the creator of the past and the future of humans."'

एषोऽप्ययस्ते राजेन्द्र यथावत्परिभाषित: ।
अध्यात्মमधिभूतं च अधिदैवं च श्रूयताम् ॥ (17)

'"O Indra among Kings! I have thus described all this to you accurately. Now hear about adhyatma, *adhibhuta* and *adhidaiva*."'[17]

---

[16] The eight major siddhis or powers are anima (becoming as small as one desires), mahima (as large as one desires), laghima (as light as one wants), garima (as heavy as one wants), prapti (obtaining what one wants), prakamya (travelling where one wants), vashitvam (powers to control creatures) and ishitvam (obtaining divine powers).

[17] Adhibhuta relates to the elements, nature. Adhidaiva is the divine agent, destiny. Adhyatma is the self, relation between the jivatman and the paramatman.

Chapter 4

याज्ञवल्क्य उवाच
पादावध्यात्ममित्याहुर्ब्राह्मणास्तत्त्वदर्शिनः ।
गन्तव्यमधिभूतं च विष्णुस्तत्राधिदैवतम् ॥ (1)

'Yajnavalkya said, "Brahmanas who have seen the truth speak of the two feet as adhyatma, the act of motion as adhibhuta and Vishnu as adhidaiva."

पायुरध्यात्ममित्याहुर्यथातत्त्वार्थदर्शिनः ।
विसर्गमधिभूतं च मित्रस्तत्राधिदैवतम् ॥ (2)

'"Those who have accurately seen the truth say that the anus is adhyatma, the releasing is adhibhuta and Mitra is adhidaiva."'[18]

उपस्थोऽध्यात्ममित्याहुर्यथायोगनिदर्शनम् ।
अधिभूतं तथानन्दो दैवतं च प्रजापतिः ॥ (3)

'"Those who know the examples of yoga accurately say that the penis is adhyatma, its pleasure is adhibhuta and Prajapati is adhidaiva."'

हस्तावध्यात्ममित्याहुर्यथासांख्यनिदर्शनम् ।
कर्तव्यमधिभूतं तु इन्द्रस्तत्राधिदैवतम् ॥ (4)

'"Those who know the examples of samkhya accurately say that the hands are adhyatma, tasks are adhibhuta and Indra is adhidaiva there."'

वागध्यात्ममिति प्राहुर्यथाश्रुतिनिदर्शनम् ।
वक्तव्यमधिभूतं तु वह्निस्तत्राधिदैवतम् ॥ (5)

'"Those who know the examples of the Shrutis accurately say that speech is adhyatma, what is spoken is adhibhuta, and Vahni[19] is adhidaiva there."'

---

[18]Mitra is sometimes equated with Surya, and Mitra is adhidaiva for this organ.
[19]Agni.

चक्षुरध्यात्ममित्याहुर्यथाश्रुतिनिदर्शनम् ।
रूपमत्राधिभूतं तु सूर्यस्तत्राधिदैवतम् ॥ (6)

'"Those who know the examples of the Shrutis accurately say that the eyes are adhyatma, form is adhibhuta and Surya is adhidaiva there."'

श्रोत्रमध्यात्ममित्याहुर्यथाश्रुतिनिदर्शनम् ।
शब्दस्तत्राधिभूतं तु दिशास्तत्राधिदैवतम् ॥ (7)

'"Those who know the examples of the Shrutis accurately say that the ears are adhyatma, sound is adhibhuta and the directions are adhidaiva there."'

जिह्वामध्यात्ममित्याहुर्यथातत्त्वनिदर्शनम् ।
रस एवाधिभूतं तु आपस्तत्राधिदैवतम् ॥ (8)

'"Those who know the truth accurately say that the tongue is adhyatma, taste is adhibhuta and water is adhidaiva there."'

घ्राणमध्यात्ममित्याहुर्यथाश्रुतिनिदर्शनम् ।
गन्ध एवाधिभूतं तु पृथिवी चाधिदैवतम् ॥ (9)

'"Those who know the examples of the Shrutis accurately say that the nose is adhyatma, smell is adhibhuta and the earth is adhidaiva there."'

त्वगध्यात्ममिति प्राहुस्तत्त्वबुद्धिविशारदाः ।
स्पर्श एवाधिभूतं तु पवनश्चाधिदैवतम् ॥ (10)

'"Those who are accomplished in their intelligence and know the truth say that the skin is adhyatma, touch is adhibhuta and the wind is adhidaiva."'

मनोऽध्यात्ममिति प्राहुर्यथाश्रुतिनिदर्शनम् ।
मन्तव्यमधिभूतं तु चन्द्रमाश्चाधिदैवतम् ॥ (11)

'"Those who know the examples of the Shrutis accurately say that the mind is adhyatma, the object of the mind is adhibhuta and the moon is adhidaiva."'

अहंकारिकमध्यात्ममाहुस्तत्त्वनिदर्शनम् ।
अभिमानोऽधिभूतं तु भवस्तत्राधिदैवतम् ॥ (12)

'"Those who know the true indications say that ahamkara is adhyatma, pride is adhibhuta and *bhava*[20] is adhidaiva there."'

बुद्धिरध्यात्ममित्याहुर्यथावेदनिदर्शनम् ।
बोद्धव्यमधिभूतं तु क्षेत्रज्ञोऽत्राधिदैवतम् ॥ (13)

'"Those who know the examples of the Vedas accurately say that intelligence is adhyatma, what is understood is adhibhuta and kshetrajna is adhidaiva."'

एषा ते व्यक्ततो राजन्विभूतिरनुवर्णिता ।
आदौ मध्ये तथा चान्ते यथातत्त्वेन तत्त्ववित् ॥ (14)

'"O King! O One Who Knows about the Truth! I have thus described to you the power of the manifest and the truth about the beginning, the middle and the end."'

प्रकृतिर्गुणान्विकुरुते स्वच्छन्देनात्मकाम्यया ।
क्रीडार्थं तु महाराज शतशोऽथ सहस्रशः ॥ (15)

'"O Great King! As if in sport and easily according to desire, Prakriti brings about hundreds and thousands of transformations in qualities."'

यथा दीपसहस्राणि दीपान्मर्त्याः प्रकुर्वते ।
प्रकृतिस्तथा विकुरुते पुरुषस्य गुणान्बहून् ॥ (16)

'"It is like mortals lighting thousands of lamps from a single lamp. In that way, Prakriti creates many qualities in Purusha."'

सत्त्वमानन्द उद्रेकः प्रीतिः प्राकाश्यमेव च ।
सुखं शुद्धित्वमारोग्यं सन्तोषः श्रद्धानता ॥ (17)
अकार्पण्यमसंरम्भः क्षमा धृतिरहिंसता ।
समता सत्यमानृण्यं मार्दवं ह्रीरचापलम् ॥ (18)

---

[20]State of existence.

शौचमार्जवमाचारमलौल्यं हृद्यसंभ्रम: ।
इष्टानिष्टवियोगानां कृतानामविकत्थनम् ॥ (19)
दानेन चानुग्रहणमस्पृहार्थे परार्थता ।
सर्वभूतदया चैव सत्त्वस्यैते गुणा: स्मृता: ॥ (20)

"'Spirit, joy, abundance, affection, radiance, happiness, purity, lack of disease, satisfaction, devotion, lack of miserliness, lack of hatred, forgiveness, fortitude, lack of injury, equanimity, truthfulness, repayment of debts, mildness, humility, lack of fickleness, cleanliness, uprightness, observance of conduct, lack of passion, lack of fear in the heart, indifference at separation from good and bad, lack of boasting about acts performed, receptivity when shown favours, lack of desire for riches, welfare of others and compassion towards all beings—these are said to be the qualities of sattva.'"

रजोगुणानां संघातो रूपमैश्वर्यविग्रहे ।
अत्याशित्वमकारुण्यं सुखदु:खोपसेवनम् ॥ (21)
परापवादेषु रतिर्विवादानां च सेवनम् ।
अहंकारस्त्वसत्कारश्चिन्ता वैरोपसेवनम् ॥ (22)
परितापोऽपहरणं हीनाशोऽनार्जवं तथा ।
भेद: परुषता चैव कामक्रोधौ मदस्तथा ।
दर्पो द्वेषोऽतिवादश्च एते प्रोक्ता रजोगुणा: ॥ (23)

"'The accumulation of qualities of rajas is manifested in conflicts over beauty and prosperity, lack of generosity, lack of compassion, the enjoyment of happiness and unhappiness, attachment towards speaking ill of others, fondness for disputes, ego, thoughts that show no respect, practice of enmity, repentance, seizing the property of others, lack of humility, lack of uprightness, dissension, harshness, desire, anger, intoxication, insolence, hatred and excessive speech. These are said to be the qualities of rajas.'"

तामसानां तु संघातं प्रवक्ष्याम्युपधार्यताम् ।
मोहोऽप्रकाशस्तामिस्रमन्धतामिस्रसंज्ञितम् ॥ (24)
मरणं चान्धतामिस्रं तामिस्रं क्रोध उच्यते ।
तमसो लक्षणानीह भक्षाणामभिरोचनम् ॥ (25)

भोजनानानपर्याप्तिस्तथा पेयेष्वतृप्तता ।
गन्धवासो विहारेषु शयनेष्वासनेषु च ॥ (26)
दिवास्वप्ने विवादे च प्रमादेषु च वै रति: ।
नृत्यवादित्रगीतानामज्ञानाच्छृद्धानता ।
द्वेषो धर्मविशेषाणामेते वै तामसा गुणा: ॥ (27)

'"I will now tell you about the accumulations that tamas leads to—delusion, lack of radiance, darkness, and darkness with the characteristic of making one blind. This should be understood. Darkness is said to be anger, and darkness that makes one blind is death. In this world, the signs of tamas are gluttony in eating; lack of satisfaction even though one has enough and many kinds of things to eat and drink; attachment towards fragrances, garments, pleasure, beds and seats; sleeping during the day; quarrels and distraction; taking pleasure in singing, music and dancing; ignorance; lack of faith; and hatred of dharma. In particular, these are the qualities of tamas."'

Chapter 5

याज्ञवल्क्य उवाच

एते प्रधानस्य गुणास्त्रय: पुरुषसत्तम ।
कृत्स्नस्य चैव जगतस्तिष्ठन्त्यनपगा: सदा ॥ (1)

'Yajnavalkya said, "O Supreme among Men! These are the signs of the three gunas of Pradhana.[21] They always attach themselves to everything in the universe and are established there."'

शतधा सहस्रधा चैव तथा शतसहस्रधा ।
कोटिशश्च करोत्येष प्रत्यगात्मानमात्मना ॥ (2)

---

[21]Pradhana means the principal entity. In samkhya, Pradhana is an expression for Prakriti.

"'He[22] divides himself into hundreds, thousands, hundreds of thousands and crores of different selves.'"

सात्त्विकस्योत्तमं स्थानं राजसस्येह मध्यमम् ।
तामसस्याधमं स्थानं प्राहुरध्यात्मचिन्तकाः ॥ (3)

"'Those who have thought about the adhyatma say that sattva has a superior place, rajas a medium one and tamas an inferior one.'"

केवलेनेह पुण्येन गतिमूर्ध्वामवाप्नुयात् ।
पुण्यपापेन मानुष्यमधर्मेणाप्यधोगतिम् ॥ (4)

"'One heads towards an upwards destination through auspicious deeds alone. As a result of good and wicked deeds, one becomes human. Through adharma, one obtains a destination that is downwards.'"[23]

द्वन्द्वमेषां त्रयाणां तु संनिपातं च तत्त्वतः ।
सत्त्वस्य रजसश्चैव तमसश्च शृणुष्व मे ॥ (5)

"'There is also the truth about what happens if two or three of the gunas are mixed. Sattva may exist with rajas or tamas. Listen to me.'"

सत्त्वस्य तु रजो दृष्टं रजसश्च तमस्तथा ।
तमसश्च तथा सत्त्वं सत्त्वस्याव्यक्तमेव च ॥ (6)

"'Sattva can be seen with rajas and rajas with tamas. Sattva can exist with tamas and sattva may exist with the unmanifest.'"[24]

अव्यक्तसत्त्वसंयुक्तो देवलोकमवाप्नुयात् ।
रजःसत्त्वसमायुक्तो मनुष्येषूपपद्यते ॥ (7)

"'When sattva is united with the unmanifest, one obtains the world of devas. When rajas is united with sattva, one becomes human.'"

---

[22]Pradhana.
[23]Tamas leads to birth as inferior species, rajas as humans and sattva as devas.
[24]Prakriti.

रजस्तमोभ्यां संयुक्तस्तिर्यग्योनिषु जायते ।
रजस्तामससत्त्वैश्च युक्तो मानुष्यमाप्नुयात् ॥ (8)

"When rajas is united with tamas, one is born as inferior species. When rajas, tamas and sattva are united, one becomes human."

पुण्यपापवियुक्तानां स्थानमाहुर्मनीषिणाम् ।
शाश्वतं चाव्ययं चैव अक्षरं चाभयं च यत् ॥ (9)

"It is said that learned ones obtain a region that is separated from both good deeds and wicked ones. It is eternal and immutable. It is without decay and there is no fear there."

ज्ञानिनां संभवं श्रेष्ठं स्थानमव्रणमच्युतम् ।
अतीन्द्रियमबीजं च जन्ममृत्युतमोनुदम् ॥ (10)

"Those with jnana obtain births in that best of places, without blemishes and without decay. They go beyond the senses. That does not have any seed of generation and is beyond the darkness of birth and death."

अव्यक्तस्थं परं यत्तत्पृष्टस्तेऽहं नराधिप ।
स एष प्रकृतिस्थो हि तस्थुरित्यभिधीयते ॥ (11)

"O Lord of Men! You asked me about the supreme[25] and the unmanifest. It is said that he is established in his own nature."

अचेतनश्चैष मतः प्रकृतिस्थश्च पार्थिव ।
एतेनाधिष्ठितश्चैव सृजते संहरत्यपि ॥ (12)

"O Lord of the Earth! It is the view that he resides in Prakriti, without any consciousness. She can create and destroy only when she is presided over by him."

जनक उवाच

अनादिनिधनावेतावुभावेव महामुने ।
अमूर्तिमन्तावचलावप्रकम्प्यौ च निर्व्रणौ ॥ (13)

---

[25]Purusha.

'Janaka replied, "O Great Sage! Both of them are without beginning and without end. They are without form and without movement. They do not waver and are without blemish."'

अग्राह्यावृषिशार्दूल कथमेको ह्यचेतनः ।
चेतनावांस्तथा चौकः क्षेत्रज्ञ इति भाषितः ॥ (14)

'"O Tiger among Rishis! They cannot be comprehended. How can one of them be without consciousness? How can one have consciousness? Why is one spoken of as kshetrajna?"'

त्वं हि विप्रेन्द्र कात्स्न्येन मोक्षधर्ममुपाससे ।
साकल्यं मोक्षधर्मस्य श्रोतुमिच्छामि तत्त्वतः ॥ (15)

अस्तित्वं केवलत्वं च विनाभावं तथैव च ।
तथैवोत्क्रमणस्थानं देहिनोऽपि वियुज्यतः ॥ (16)

'"O Indra among Brahmanas! You are the one who has practised everything about the dharma of moksha. It is my resolution that I wish to hear the truth about moksha dharma, about the existence of the absolute and about lack of existence, about the regions that embodied beings progressively go to and about their separation from those."'

कालेन यद्धि प्राप्नोति स्थानं तद्ब्रूहि मे द्विज ।
सांख्यज्ञानं च तत्त्वेन पृथग्योगं तथैव च ॥ (17)

'"With the progress of time, what regions do they obtain? O Dvija! Tell me this. Tell me the truth about the knowledge of samkhya and separately about yoga."'

अरिष्टानि च तत्त्वेन वक्तुमर्हसि सत्तम ।
विदितं सर्वमेतत्ते पाणावामलकं यथा ॥ (18)

'"O Excellent One! You should also tell me the truth about misfortune. You know everything about these, like a myrobalan[26] that is held in your hand."'

---

[26] Amalaka tree.

Chapter 6[27]

याज्ञवल्क्य उवाच
न शक्यो निर्गुणस्तात गुणी कर्तुं विशां पते ।
गुणवांश्चाप्यगुणवान्यथातत्त्वं निबोध मे ॥ (1)

'Yajnavalkya said, "O Son! O Lord of the Earth! One cannot describe something without qualities by ascribing qualities to it. I will tell you the truth about what possesses qualities and what does not possess qualities. Listen to me."'

गुणैर्हि गुणवानेव निर्गुणश्चागुणस्तथा ।
प्राहुरेवं महात्मानो मुनयस्तत्त्वदर्शिनः ॥ (2)

'"The great-souled sages who have seen the truth have spoken about the qualities obtained by the one with qualities and the qualities not obtained by the one without qualities."'

गुणस्वभावस्त्वव्यक्तो गुणानेवाभिवर्तते ।
उपयुङ्क्ते च तानेव स चैवाज्ञः स्वभावतः ॥ (3)

'"The unmanifest one[28] naturally has qualities and cannot surpass those qualities. Because it is united with those, it naturally lacks knowledge."'

अव्यक्तस्तु न जानीते पुरूषो ज्ञः स्वभावतः ।
न मत्तः परमस्तीति नित्यमेवाभिमन्यते ॥ (4)

'"The unmanifest Purusha is the one who naturally knows and always thinks, 'There is nothing superior to me.'"'

अनेन कारणेनैतदव्यक्तं स्यादचेतनम् ।
नित्यत्वादक्षरत्वाच्च क्षराणां तत्त्वतोऽन्यथा ॥ (5)

---

[27]Some of the shlokas in this chapter are extremely difficult to understand, and liberties have been taken, so that the intended meaning becomes clear. Inevitably, there is some subjectivity.
[28]Prakriti.

'"It is because of this reason that this unmanifest one is without consciousness. It is always spoken of as indestructible. But it is also true that it combines with the destructible."'[29]

यदज्ञानेन कुर्वीत गणुसर्गं पुनः पुनः ।
यदात्मानं न जानीते तदाव्यक्तमिहोच्यते ॥ (6)

'"It is because of repeated association with various categories of gunas that one acts without jnana. When one does not know the atman, it is spoken of as unmanifest."'

कर्तृत्वाच्चापि तत्त्वानां तत्त्वधर्मी तथोच्यते ।
कर्तृत्वाच्चैव योनीनां योनिधर्मी तथोच्यते ॥ (7)

'"When it[30] assumes lordship over those principles,[31] it is said to follow the dharma of those principles. Because it has lordship over wombs, it is said to follow the dharma of wombs."'

कर्तृत्वाप्रकृतीनां तु तथा प्रकृतिधर्मिता ।
कर्तृत्वाच्चापि बीजानां बीजधर्मी तथोच्यते ॥ (8)

'"Because it has lordship over Prakriti, it is said to follow the dharma of Prakriti. Because it has lordship over seeds, it is said to follow the dharma of seeds."'

गुणानां प्रसवत्वाच्च तथा प्रसवधर्मवान् ।
कर्तृत्वाप्रलयानां च तथा प्रलयधर्मिता ॥ (9)

'"Because it is associated with birth, it observes the dharma of birth.[32] Because it has lordship over dissolution, it follows the dharma of dissolution."'

बीजत्वात्प्रकृतित्वच्चा प्रलयत्वात्तथवै च ।
उपेक्षकत्वादन्यत्वादभिमानाच्च केवलम् ॥ (10)

---

[29]Prakriti.
[30]The atman.
[31]Prakriti.
[32]Here, birth is used in the sense of creation.

'"Because of association with Prakriti, it follows creation and destruction. This is despite the absolute knowledge that it is indifferent and distinct."'

मन्यते यतयः शुद्धा अध्यात्मविगतज्वराः ।
अनित्यं नित्यमव्यक्तमेवमेतद्धि शुश्रुम ॥ (11)

'"Ascetics who are pure, devoid of anxiety and knowledgeable about the adhyatma think of it in this way. We have heard of it as permanent and unmanifest, but also as impermanent."'[33]

अव्यक्तैकत्वमित्याहुर्नानात्वं पुरूषस्तथा ।
सर्वभूतदयावन्तः केवलं ज्ञानमास्थिताः ॥ (12)

'"However, those who depend only on jnana and are compassionate towards all beings say that the unmanifest is one and Purusha is many."'[34]

अन्यः स पुरूषोऽव्यक्तस्त्वध्रुवो ध्रुवसंज्ञकः ।
यथा मुञ्ज इषीकायास्तथैवैतद्धि जायते ॥ (13)

'"There is another who holds that the unmanifest Purusha, even though apparently impermanent, has all the signs of permanence. It is distinct, just as a blade of grass is different from the sheath from which it is generated."'

अन्यं च मशकं विद्यादन्यच्चोदुम्बरं तथा ।
न चोदुम्बरसंयोगैर्मशकस्तत्र लिप्यते ॥ (14)

'"Another holds that the gnat that is inside a fig should be known as distinct. In spite of being associated with the fig, the gnat doesn't get attached to it."'

अन्य एव तथा मत्स्यस्तथान्यदुदकं स्मृतम् ।
न चोदकस्य स्पर्शेन मत्स्यो लिप्यति सर्वशः ॥ (15)

---

[33] Because of the association with Prakriti.
[34] Prakriti is one and Purusha is many. But clearly, the suggestion is that this is not a valid point of view.

"'Like that, another holds that the fish is said to be different from the water it is in. Though the fish is touched by the water, it isn't in any way attached to it.'"

अन्यो ह्याग्निरुखाप्यन्या नित्यमेवमवैहि भोः ।
न चोपलिप्यते सोऽग्निरुखासंस्पर्शनेन वै ॥ (16)

"'Another holds that the fire in a boiler is always known to be distinct. Though the fire touches the boiler, it is not attached to it.'"

पुष्करं त्वन्यदेवात्र तथान्यदुदकं स्मृतम् ।
न चोदकस्य स्पर्शेन लिप्यते तत्र पुष्करम् ॥ (17)

"'Another holds that a lotus is said to be different from the water. Though it touches the water, the lotus is not attached to it.'"

एतेषां सह संवासं विवासं चैव नित्यशः ।
यथा तथैनं पश्यन्ति न नित्यं प्राकृता जनाः ॥ (18)

"'In this way, there is always separation, even when one resides together. This can never be seen in this way by people who are always ordinary.'"

ये त्वन्यथैव पश्यन्ति न सम्यक्तेषु दर्शनम् ।
ते व्यक्तं निरयं घोरं प्रविशन्ति पुनः पुनः ॥ (19)

"'Those who cannot see it in this way do not see properly. It is evident that they will repeatedly enter a terrible hell.'"

सांख्यदर्शनमेतत्ते परिसंख्यातमुत्तमम् ।
एवं हि परिसंख्याय सांख्याः केवलतां गताः ॥ (20)

"'I have enumerated this excellent insight of samkhya. Enumerating it in this way, those who follow samkhya obtain the absolute.'"

ये त्वन्ये तत्त्वकुशलास्तेषामेतन्निदर्शनम् ।
अतः परं प्रवक्ष्यामि योगानामपि दर्शनम् ॥ (21)

'"I have also told you about the others who are accomplished and know the truth about the examples. I will next tell you about the insight of yoga."'

Chapter 7

याज्ञवल्क्य उवाच

सांख्यज्ञानं मया प्रोक्तं योगज्ञानं निबोध मे ।
यथाश्रुतं यथादृष्टं तत्त्वेन नृपसत्तम ॥ (1)

'Yajnavalkya said, "I have already spoken to you about the jnana of samkhya. Now hear about the jnana of yoga. O Excellent King! This is the truth about what I have heard and what I have seen."'

नास्ति सांख्यसमं ज्ञानं नास्ति योगसमं बलम् ।
तावुभावेकचर्यौ तु उभावनिधनौ स्मृतौ ॥ (2)

'"There is no jnana that is equal to samkhya. There is no strength that is equal to yoga. They prescribe similar practices and both are said to lead to the destruction of hardships."'

पृथक्पृथक्तु पश्यन्ति येऽल्पबुद्धिरता नराः ।
वयं तु राजन्पश्याम एकमेव तु निश्चयात् ॥ (3)

'"Men who possess limited intelligence perceive them as distinct. O King! However, we see them as one and have arrived at this determination."'

यदेव योगाः पश्यन्ति तत्सांख्यैरपि दृश्यते ।
एकं सांख्यं च योगं यः पश्यति स तत्त्ववित् ॥ (4)

'"Whatever is seen through yoga is exactly the same as whatever is seen through samkhya. A person who sees yoga and samkhya as the same actually sees the truth."'

रुद्रप्रधानानपरान्विद्धि योगान्परंतप ।
तेनैव चाथ देहेन विचरन्ति दिशो दश ॥ (5)

"O Scorcher of Enemies! Know that restraining the breath[35] is the foremost and supreme aspect of yoga. Through this, they roam around in the ten directions in their bodies."[36]

यावद्धि प्रलयस्तात् सूक्ष्मेणाष्टगुणेन वै ।
योगेन लोकान्विचरन्सुखं संन्यस्य चानघ ॥ (6)

"O Son! O Unblemished One! When the body is dissolved, one cheerfully abandons it and in subtle form, uses the eight qualities of yoga[37] to roam around in the worlds."

वेदेषु चाष्टगुणितं योगमाहुर्मनीषिणः ।
सूक्ष्ममष्टगुणं प्राहुर्नेतरं नृपसत्तम ॥ (7)

"Those who are learned about yoga speak of these eight qualities. O Supreme among Kings! They also speak about the eight other subtle qualities."[38]

द्विगुणं योगकृत्यं तु योगानां प्राहुरुत्तमम् ।
सगुणं निर्गुणं चैव यथाशास्त्रनिदर्शनम् ॥ (8)

"The practice of yoga has been said to be excellent and these are the two kinds of qualities that are practised in yoga. The sacred texts have given indications about how this is to be done, with qualities and without qualities."[39]

धारणा चैव मनसः प्राणायामश्च पार्थिव ।
प्राणायामो हि सगुणो निर्गुणं धारणं मनः ॥ (9)

---

[35] The text uses the word *'rudra'*, a rare term for prana.
[36] Yogis roam around in their subtle bodies.
[37] There are eight steps in yoga. But this probably refers to eight major siddhis or powers.
[38] This probably means the eight steps of asana, pranayama, yama, niyama, pratyahara, dhyana, dharana and samadhi.
[39] Pranayama with qualities is when a mantra is simultaneously chanted, recommended for early stages. When a mantra is no longer necessary, that is pranayama without qualities.

"'O Lord of the Earth! Together with pranayama, there has to be dharana in the mind. Pranayama can be with qualities. Without qualities, dharana occurs in the mind.'"

यत्र दृश्येत मुञ्चन्वै प्राणान्मैथिलसत्तम ।
वाताधिक्यं भवत्येव तस्माद्धि न समाचरेत् ॥ (10)

"'O Supreme among Those from Mithila! Prana is seen to be released. However, one should not act so as to have an excess of the breath.'"[40]

निशायाः प्रथमे यामे चोदना द्वादश स्मृताः ।
मध्ये सुप्त्वा परे यामे द्वादशैव तु चोदनाः ॥ (11)

"'In the first yama of the night,[41] twelve principles of breathing have been prescribed. Having slept in the middle, in the last quarter of the night, there are another twelve principles of breathing.'"

तदेवमुपशान्तेन दान्तेनैकान्तशीलना ।
आत्मारामेण बुद्धेन योक्तव्योऽऽत्मा न संशयः ॥ (12)

"'One must practise these, self-controlled and satisfied within one's own self. One must turn one's intelligence towards finding pleasure within one's own atman. There is no doubt that one must unite with the atman.'"[42]

पञ्चानामिन्द्रियाणां तु दोषानाक्षिप्य पञ्चधा ।
शब्दं स्पर्शं तथा रूपं रसं गन्धं तथैव च ॥ (13)

"'The five taints associated with the five senses—sound, touch, form, taste and scent—must be flung away.'"

प्रतिभामपवर्गं च प्रतिसंहृत्य मैथिल ।
इन्द्रियग्राममखिलं मनस्यभिनिवेश्य ह ॥ (14)

---

[40]Inhalation, holding breath and exhalation are for a prescribed period of time. This duration is gradually increased. The purport seems to be that in the initial stages, this duration should not be excessively great.
[41]Yama means a period of three hours.
[42]Paramatman.

"'O One from Mithila! One must withdraw from thoughts of what can be obtained as fruits of acts. All the objects of the senses must be immersed in the mind.'"

मनस्तथैवाहंकारे प्रतिष्ठाप्य नराधिप ।
अहंकारं तथा बुद्धौ बुद्धिं च प्रकृतावपि ॥ (15)

"'O Lord of Men! The mind must be established in ahamkara, ahamkara in intelligence and intelligence in Prakriti.'"

एवं हि परिसंख्याय ततो ध्यायेत केवलम् ।
विरजस्कमलं नित्यमनन्तं शुद्धमव्रणम् ॥ (16)

"'Having merged in this way, one must meditate on the absolute. He is radiant and without blemish. He is eternal and infinite. He is pure and without decay.'"

तस्थुषं पुरुषं सत्त्वमभेद्यमजरामरम् ।
शाश्वतं चाव्ययं चैव ईशानं ब्रह्म चाव्ययम् ॥ (17)

"'He is the Purusha of sattva, beyond division, old age and mortality. He is eternal and unmanifest. He is Ishana and the unmanifest Brahma.'"

युक्तस्य तु महाराज लक्षणान्युपधारयेत् ।
लक्षणं तु प्रसादस्य यथा तृप्तः सुखं स्वपेत् ॥ (18)

"'O Great King! Understand the signs of someone who has been united in this fashion. The signs are satisfaction, contentment and cheerful sleep.'"

निवाते तु यथा दीपो ज्वलेत्स्नेहसमन्वितः ।
निश्चलोर्ध्वशिखस्तद्वद्युक्तमाहुर्मनीषिणः ॥ (19)

"'He is like a lamp ignited with oil, but burning in a place where there is no wind, with straight flames rising upwards. The learned speak about it in this way.'"

पाषाण इव मेघोत्थैर्यथा बिन्दुभिराहतः ।
नालं चालयितुं शक्यस्तथा युक्तस्य लक्षणम् ॥ (20)

'"He is like a rock that does not move, even when it has been struck by drops from the clouds. He is incapable of being moved in any way. These are the signs of a person who is united."'

शङ्खदुन्दुभिनिर्घोषैर्विविधैर्गीतवादितैः ।
क्रियमाणैर्न कम्पेत युक्तस्यैतन्निदर्शनम् ॥ (21)

'"The sounds of conch shells, drums and diverse kinds of singing and the playing of musical instruments do not make him tremble. These are the signs of a person who is united."'

तैलपात्रं यथा पूर्णं कराभ्यां गृह्य पूरुषः ।
सोपानमारुहेद्भीतस्तर्ज्यमानोऽसिपाणिभिः ॥ (22)

'"This is like a man who climbs a flight of steps with a full vessel of oil in his hand, not scared even if people threaten him with swords in their hands."'

संयतात्मा भयात्तेषां न पात्रादि्बन्दुमुत्सृजेत् ।
तथैवोत्तरमाणस्य एकाग्रमनसस्तथा ॥ (23)

'"A person who has controlled his atman is like that, not scared of them and not spilling a drop from the vessel. He ascends, single-minded."'

स्थिरत्वादिन्द्रियाणां तु निश्चलत्वात्तथैव च ।
एवं युक्तस्य तु मुनेर्लक्षणान्युपधारयेत् ॥ (24)

'"He steadies his senses and seems to be immobile. These should be understood as the signs of a sage who has been united in this way."'

स युक्तः पश्यति ब्रह्म यत्तत्परममव्ययम् ।
महतस्तमसो मध्ये स्थितं ज्वलनसंनिभम् ॥ (25)

'"Having been united in this way, he sees the supreme and unmanifest brahman, blazing, as if located in the midst of a great darkness."'

एतेन केवलं याति त्यक्त्वा देहमसाक्षिकम् ।
कालेन महता राजञ्श्रुतिरेषा सनातनी ॥ (26)

'"O King! The eternal Shrutis say that after a long period of time, he is like a witness and abandons this body, advancing to the absolute."'

एतद्धि योगं योगानां किमन्यद्योगलक्षणम् ।
विज्ञाय तद्धि मन्यन्ते कृतकृत्या मनीषिण: ॥ (27)

'"This is the yoga of yogis. What other signs can there be of yoga? Knowing this, the learned ones think themselves to have been successful."'

Chapter 8

याज्ञवल्क्य उवाच

तथैवोत्क्रममाणं तु शृणुष्वावहितो नृप ।
पद्भ्यामुत्क्रममाणस्य वैष्णवं स्थानमुच्यते ॥ (1)

'Yajnavalkya said, "O King! Now listen attentively to the places that they go to. If it[43] emerges through the feet, the person is said to go to Vishnu's region."'

जङ्घाभ्यां तु वसून्देवानाप्नुयादिति न श्रुतम् ।
जानुभ्यां च महाभागान्देवान्साध्यानवाप्नुयात् ॥ (2)

'"If it emerges through the calves, we have heard that he obtains devas known as vasus. If it emerges through the knees, he obtains the immensely fortunate devas known as sadhyas."'

पायुनोत्क्रममाणस्तु मैत्रं स्थानमवाप्नुयात् ।
पृथिवीं जघनेनाथ ऊरुभ्यां तु प्रजापतिम् ॥ (3)

'"If it emerges through the anus, he obtains Mitra's region. If it emerges through the loins, it is the earth's region.[44] If it is through the thighs, it is Prajapati's."'

---

[43]This is after death. The reference is to that part of the anatomy from where the jivatman emerges at the time of death.
[44]This is probably not meant to signify being born on earth but is a reference to Prithivi's (earth's) region, meaning, belonging to Prithivi.

पार्श्वाभ्यां मरुतो देवान्नासाभ्यामिन्दुमेव च ।
बाहुभ्यामिन्द्रमित्याहुरुरसा रुद्रमेव च ॥ (4)

'"Through the flanks, it is the devas known as maruts. Through the nose, it is the region of the moon. Through the arms, it is Indra's. Through the chest, it is rudras'."'

ग्रीवायास्तमृषिश्रेष्ठं नरमाप्नोत्यनुत्तमम् ।
विश्वेदेवान्मुखेनाथ दिश: श्रोत्रेण चाप्नुयात् ॥ (5)

'"Through the neck, he obtains the supreme region of the best of rishis, Nara. Through the mouth, he obtains the vishvadevas and through the ears, the directions."'

घ्राणेन गन्धवहनं नेत्राभ्यां सूर्यमेव च ।
भ्रूभ्यां चौवाश्विनौ देवौ ललाटेन पितृनथ ॥ (6)

'"Through the nose, he obtains the bearer of smell[45] and through the eyes, Surya. Through the brows, it is the region of the devas, ashvins. Through the forehead, it is the ancestors."'

ब्रह्माणमाप्नोति विभुं मूर्ध्ना देवाग्रजं तथा ।
एतान्युत्क्रमणस्थानान्युक्तानि मिथिलेश्वर ॥ (7)

'"Through the crown of the head, it is the region of Lord Brahma, the foremost among devas. O Lord of Mithila! I have thus told you about the different places that can be obtained through emerging."'

अरिष्टानि तु वक्ष्यामि विहितानि मनीषीभि: ।
संवत्सरवियोगस्य संभवेयु: शरीरिण: ॥ (8)

'"I will now tell you about the signs described by learned ones, signifying that an embodied being only has one year of lifespan left before separation occurs."'

---

[45] The wind god is the one who bears smells. The nose has figured in a preceding shloka too, with two different words for the nose being used. In this case, the word used for nose highlights the nose's function in inhaling smells.

योऽरुन्धतीं न पश्येत दृष्टपूर्वां कदाचन ।
तथैव ध्रुवमित्याहुः पूर्णेन्दुं दीपमेव च ।
खण्डाभासं दक्षिणतस्तेऽपि संवत्सरायुषः ॥ (9)

"'If a person fails to see Arundhati, although he has seen it earlier, or if it is the same with Dhruva, or if the full moon appears like a lamp, with the radiance broken towards the south, it is said that there is only one year of lifespan left.'"[46]

परचक्षुषि चात्मानं ये न पश्यन्ति पार्थिव ।
आत्मच्छायाकृती भूतं तेऽपि संवत्सरायुषः ॥ (10)

"'O Lord of the Earth! Those who can no longer see their own selves reflected in the eyes of others only have one year of lifespan left.'"

अतिद्युतिरतिप्रज्ञा अप्रज्ञा चाद्युतिस्तथा ।
प्रकृतेर्विक्रियापत्तिः षण्मासान्मृत्युलक्षणम् ॥ (11)

"'If a person has been extremely radiant, but loses that radiance, or if a person has been extremely wise, but loses that wisdom, or if there are changes that are contrary to his nature, those are signs that he will die within six months.'"

दैवतान्यवजानाति ब्राह्मणैश्च विरुध्यते ।
कृष्णश्यावच्छविच्छायः षण्मासान्मृत्युलक्षणम् ॥ (12)

"'If a person disrespects the devas, if he acts against brahmanas, if his dark complexion turns pale—those are signs that he will die within six months.'"

शीर्णनाभिः यथा चक्रं छिद्रं सोमं प्रपश्यति ।
तथैव च सहस्रांशुं सप्तरात्रेण मृत्युभाक् ॥ (13)

"'If the lunar disc is seen to have holes, like a spider's web, or if this is the case with the one with one thousand rays[47]—such a

---

[46] Arundhati is the wife of Sage Vasishtha. She is also the fainter of the two stars in the double star in Ursa Major. Mizar is Vasishtha and Arundhati is Alcor. Dhruva is the Pole Star.
[47] Of the sun.

person will confront death within seven nights.'"

शवगन्धमुपाघ्राति सुरभिं प्राप्य यो नर: ।
देवतायतनस्थस्तु षड्रात्रेण मृत्युभाक् ॥ (14)

'"If the fragrant scents in temples of devas appear to a man to be like the putrid scent from corpses, he will confront death within six nights."'

कर्णनासावनमनं दन्तदृष्टिविरागिता ।
संज्ञालोपो निरूष्मत्वं सद्योमृत्युनिदर्शनम् ॥ (15)

'"A depression in the ears or the nose, a discolouring of the teeth or the eye, the loss of consciousness and the loss of heat from the body—these are the signs of imminent death."'

अकस्माच्च स्रवेद्यस्य वाममक्षि नराधिप ।
मूर्धतश्चोत्पतेद्धूम: सद्योमृत्युनिदर्शनम् ॥ (16)

'"O Lord of Men! If there is a sudden flow of tears from the left eye or if vapour rises from the crown of the head—these are the signs of imminent death."'

एतावन्ति त्वरिष्टानि विदित्वा मानवोऽऽत्मवान् ।
निशि चाहनि चात्मानं योजयेत्परमात्मनि ॥ (17)

'"Knowing these signs, a man with a cleansed atman should spend day and night in uniting the atman with the paramatman."'

प्रतीक्षमाणस्तत्कालं यत्कालं प्रति तद्भवेत् ।
अथास्य नेष्टं मरणं स्थातुमिच्छेदिमां क्रियाम् ॥ (18)

'"That is the way one should spend his time, until the time for setting arrives. Even if one doesn't wish to die, one should establish oneself in all the rites."'

सर्वगन्धान्रसांश्चैव धारयेत समाहित: ।
तथा हि मृत्युं जयति तत्परेणान्तरात्मना ॥ (19)

'"One should control oneself and discard all fragrances and tastes. By fixing one's atman on the supreme, one can conquer death."'

ससांख्यधारणं चैव विदित्वा मनुजर्षभ ।
जयेच्च मृत्युं योगेन तत्परेणान्तरात्मना ॥ (20)

'"O Bull among Men! Such a person knows the practice of those who follow samkhya. By using yoga to fix his atman on the supreme, he conquers death."'

गच्छेत्राप्याक्षयं कृत्स्नमजन्म शिवमव्ययम् ।
शाश्वतं स्थानमचलं दुष्प्रापमकृतात्मभिः ॥ (21)

'"He goes to the place that is completely indestructible, without birth and death. It is auspicious and without decay. It is the eternal and immutable region, difficult for those with unclean atmans to obtain."'

Chapter 9

याज्ञवल्क्य उवाच

अव्यक्तस्थं परं यत्तत्पृष्टस्तेऽहं नराधिप ।
परं गुह्यमिमं प्रश्नं शृणुष्वावहितो नृप ॥ (1)

'Yajnavalkya said, "O Lord of Men! You asked me about the supreme, established in the unmanifest. This question is about a great secret. O King! Listen attentively."'

यथार्षेणेह विधिना चरतावमतेन ह ।
मयादित्यादवाप्तानि यजूंषि मिथिलाधिप ॥ (2)

'"O Lord of Mithila! Having conducted myself in accordance with the precepts of the rishis, I obtained the *yajus* from Aditya."'[48]

---

[48] We have deliberately retained this as yajus, meaning sacrificial formulae. The mantras were compiled into the Yajur Veda Samhita. There are two versions of the Yajur Veda Samhita, Shukla and Krishna. Yajnavalkya compiled the Shukla Yajur Veda.

महता तपसा देवस्तपिष्ठः सेवितो मया ।
प्रीतेन चाहं विभुना सूर्येणोक्तस्तदानघ ॥ (3)

'"I served the deva who heats through great austerities. O Unblemished One! Pleased with me, Lord Surya spoke to me."'

वरं वृणीष्व विप्रर्षे यदिष्टं ते सुदुर्लभम् ।
तत्ते दास्यामि प्रीतात्मा मत्प्रसादो हि दुर्लभः ॥ (4)

'"O Brahmana Rishi! Ask for the boon you desire, even if it is very difficult to obtain. I am pleased and will give it to you. It is extremely difficult to obtain my favours."'

ततः प्रणम्य शिरसा मयोक्तस्तपतां वरः ।
यजूंसि नोपयुक्तानि क्षिप्रमिच्छामि वेदितुम् ॥ (5)

'"At this, I bowed my head down before that supreme of heat-givers and said, 'I do not know the yajus. I wish to know them quickly.'"'

ततो मां भगवानाह वितरिष्यामि ते द्विज ।
सरस्वतीह वाग्भूता शरीरं ते प्रवेक्ष्यति ॥ (6)

'"The illustrious one replied, 'O Dvija! I will give it to you. Sarasvati, speech personified, will enter your body.'"'

ततो मामाह भगवानास्यं स्वं विवृतं कुरु ।
विवृतं च ततो मेऽऽस्यं प्रविष्टा च सरस्वती ॥ (7)

'"The illustrious one then asked me to open my mouth. When I opened my mouth, Sarasvati entered through the mouth."'

ततो विदह्यमानोऽहं प्रविष्टोऽम्भस्तदानघ ।
अविज्ञानादमर्षाच्च भास्करस्य महात्मनः ॥ (8)

'"O Unblemished One! When she entered, I began to burn and plunged into the water. Not understanding what the great-souled Bhaskara[49] intended, I became angry."'

---

[49]Bhaskara, Ravi and Vibhavasu are names of the sun god.

ततो विदह्यमानं मामुवाच भगवान्रविः ।
मुहूर्तं सह्यतां दाहस्तत: शीतीभविष्यसि ॥ (9)

'"However, while I was burning, the illustrious Ravi told me, 'Tolerate this burning for a muhurta. You will be cooled down.'"'

शीतीभूतं च मां दृष्ट्वा भगवानाह भास्करः ।
प्रतिष्ठास्यति ते वेदः सोत्तरः सखिलो द्विज ॥ (10)
कृत्स्नं शतपथं चैव प्रणेष्यसि द्विजर्षभ ।
तस्यान्ते चापुनर्भवे बुद्धिस्तव भविष्यति ॥ (11)
प्राप्स्यसे च यदिष्टं तत्सांख्ययोगेप्सितं पदम् ।
एतावदुक्त्वा भगवानस्तमेवाभ्यवर्तत ॥ (12)

'"When he saw that I had cooled down, the illustrious Bhaskara said, 'O Dvija! All the Vedas and the subsequent texts will be established in you. O Bull among Dvijas! You will compile all the Shatapathas.[50] When that has been done, your intelligence will turn towards the question of rebirth. You will obtain the objective desired by those who practise samkhya and yoga.' Having said this, the illustrious one disappeared."'

ततोऽनुव्याहृतं श्रुत्वा गते देवे विभावसौ ।
गृहमागत्य संहृष्टोऽचिन्तयं वै सरस्वतीम् ॥ (13)

'"On hearing these words and on seeing that Deva Vibhavasu had departed, I happily returned home and thought of Sarasvati."'

ततः प्रवृत्तातिशुभा स्वरव्यञ्जनभूषिता ।
ओंकारमादितः कृत्वा मम देवी सरस्वती ॥ (14)

'"The auspicious devi Sarasvati instantly appeared. She was adorned with the vowels and the consonants and she gave me the syllable 'OUM'."'

ततोऽहमर्घ्यं विधिवत्सरस्वत्यै न्यवेदयम् ।
तपतां च वरिष्ठाय निषण्णस्तत्परायणः ॥ (15)

---

[50]The Shatapatha Brahmana is associated with the Shukla Yajur Veda.

'"As is prescribed, I offered Sarasvati an arghya and another to the best of heat-givers,[51] the refuge of the distressed."'

ततः शतपथं कृत्स्नं सहरस्यं ससंग्रहम् ।
चक्रे सपरिशेषं च हर्षेण परमेण ह ॥ (16)

'"To my great delight, all the Shatapathas, with their mysteries, compilations and appendices, appeared before me."'

कृत्वा चाध्ययनं तेषां शिष्याणां शतमुत्तमम् ।
विप्रियार्थं सशिष्यस्य मातुलस्य महात्मनः ॥ (17)

'"I taught them to one hundred excellent disciples and caused displeasure to my great-souled maternal uncle and his disciples."'[52]

ततः सशिष्येण मया सूर्येणेव गभस्तिभिः ।
व्याप्तो यज्ञो महाराज पितुस्तव महात्मनः ॥ (18)

'"O Great King! With my disciples, like the sun with its rays, I was engaged in performing a sacrifice for your great-souled father."'

मिषतो देवलस्यापि ततोऽर्धं हृतवानहम् ।
स्ववेदद्दक्षिणायाथ विमर्दें मातुलेन ह ॥ (19)

'"There was a dispute about who should get the dakshina. In Devala's presence, I took half of the dakshina and gave the other half to my maternal uncle."'

सुमन्तुनाथ पैलेन तथ जैमिनिना च वै ।
पित्रा ते मुनिभिश्चैव ततोऽहमनुमानितः ॥ (20)

'"Sumantu, Paila, Jaimini, your father and the other sages honoured what I had done."'

---

[51] The sun god.
[52] Vaishampayana was Vedavyasa's disciple and used to teach the Krishna Yajur Veda. He was also Yajnavalkya's maternal uncle and teacher. There is a story of a dispute between Vaishampayana and Yajnavalkya. When Yajnavalkya subsequently began to teach the Shukla Yajur Veda, Vaishampayana was understandably unhappy.

दश पञ्च च प्राप्तानि यजूंस्यकर्मयानघ ।
तथैव लोमहर्षाच्च पुराणमवधारितम् ॥ (21)

'"O Unblemished One! I thus obtained fifty yajus. I then studied the Puranas from Lomaharshana."'[53]

बीजमेतत्पुरस्कृत्य देवीं चैव सरस्वतीम् ।
सूर्यस्य चानुभावेन प्रवृत्तोऽहं नराधिप ॥ (22)
कर्तुं शतपथं वेदमपूर्वं कारितं च मे ।
यथाभिलषितं मार्गं तथा तच्चोपपादितम् ॥ (23)

'"O Lord of Men! Placing the original mantra[54] and Goddess Sarasvati at the forefront, and with the power obtained from Surya, I comprehended and compiled the Shatapatha, not done by anyone earlier. I thus accomplished the path I wished to follow."'

शिष्याणामखिलं कृत्स्नमनुज्ञातं ससंग्रहम् ।
सर्वे च शिष्याः शुचयो गताः परमहर्षिताः ॥ (24)

'"I instructed that entire and complete compilation to my disciples. All those disciples were purified and became supremely delighted."'

शाखाः पञ्चदशेमास्तु विद्या भास्करदर्शिताः ।
प्रतिष्ठाप्य यथाकामं वेद्यं तदनुचिन्तयम् ॥ (25)

'"The knowledge instructed by Bhaskara had fifty branches[55] and I established it. As I desired, I then began to think about knowledge."'

किमत्र ब्रह्मण्यमृतं किं च वेद्यमनुत्तमम् ।
चिन्तये तत्र चागत्य गन्धर्वो मामपृच्छत ॥ (26)
विश्वावसुस्ततो राजन्वेदान्तज्ञानकोविदः ।

---

[53]Lomaharshana (alternatively Romaharshana) was Vedavyasa's disciple, and Vedavyasa taught him the Puranas.
[54]The text uses the word *bija* (seed), which is not quite 'original'. 'Bija' is the mystical syllable that exists in any mantra, and is used to express a mantra in cryptic form.
[55]The word '*shakha*' means branch, but is usually applied to recension. Two shakhas of the Shukla Yajur Veda are now known.

चतुर्विंशतिकान्प्रश्नान्पृष्ट्वा वेदस्य पार्थिव ।
पञ्चविंशतिमं प्रश्नं पप्रच्छान्विक्षिकीं तथा ॥ (27)

'"O King! The gandharva Vishvavasu was accomplished in jnana about vedanta. While I was contemplating, he came there and asked me, 'What is the immortal brahman? What is excellent knowledge?' O Lord of the Earth! He thus asked me twenty-four questions about knowledge. He then asked me a twenty-fifth question about metaphysics."'

विश्वाविश्वं तथाश्वाश्वं मित्रं वरुणमेव च ।
ज्ञानं ज्ञेयं तथाज्ञो ज्ञ: कस्तपा अतपास्तथा ।
सूर्यादः सूर्य इति च विद्याविद्ये तथैव च ॥ (28)

'""What is the universe? What is the negation of the universe? What is ashva and what is the negation of ashva?[56] What is Mitra? What is Varuna? What is jnana? What is the object of jnana? Who is ignorant? Who is not ignorant? Who possesses heat? Who is without heat? Who devours Surya? Who is Surya? What is knowledge? What is ignorance?"'

वेद्यावेद्यं तथा राजन्नचलं चलमेव च ।
अपूर्वमक्षयं क्षय्यमेतत्प्रश्नमनुत्तमम् ॥ (29)

'"O King! 'What can be known? What cannot be known? What is mobile? What is immobile? What has no beginning? What is without destruction? What can be destroyed?' These were the excellent questions."'

अथोक्तश्च मया राजन्राजा गन्धर्वसत्तम: ।
पृष्टवाननुपूर्वेण प्रश्नमुत्तममर्थवत् ॥ (30)

'"O King! These were the questions that the supreme king of the gandharvas asked me. One after another, he asked me these questions, which were full of meaning."'

---

[56]'Ashva' usually (not always) means horse, or something related to a horse. The answer that follows suggests that there might be a typo here. Perhaps it should read *'asva'*, meaning, without properties.

मुहूर्तं मृष्यतां तावद्यावदेनं विचिन्तये ।
बाढमित्येव कृत्वा स तूष्णीं गन्धर्व आस्थित: ॥ (31)

"'I told him to wait for an instant, while I thought about it. The gandharva agreed. He was silent and remained there.'"

ततोऽन्वचिन्तयमहं भूयो देवीं सरस्वतीम् ।
मनसा स च मे प्रश्नो दद्ध्नो घृतमिवोद्धृतम् ॥ (32)

"'I thought again about Goddess Sarasvati and the answers to the questions arose in my mind, like clarified butter from curds.'"

तत्रोपनिषदं चैव परिशेषं च पार्थिव ।
मथ्नामि मनसा तात दृष्ट्वा चान्वीक्षिकीं पराम् ॥ (33)

"'O Lord of the Earth! O Son! I churned the Upanishads and their annexes in my mind and saw the supreme objective of metaphysics.'"

चतुर्थी राजशार्दूल विद्यैषा सांपरायिकी ।
उदीरिता मया तुभ्यं पञ्चविंशेऽधि धिष्ठिता ॥ (34)

"'O Tiger among Kings! This is the fourth kind of knowledge, concerning the next world.[57] I have already spoken to you about this, which is based on the twenty-fifth.'"

अथोक्तस्तु मया राजन्राजा विश्वावसुस्तदा ।
श्रूयतां यद्भवानस्मान्प्रश्नं संपृष्टवानिह ॥ (35)

"'O King! I spoke about it to King Vishvavasu[58] then. I told him, 'Listen. I have heard the questions that you asked me.'"

विश्वाविश्वेति यदिदं गन्धर्वेन्द्रानुपृच्छसि ।
विश्वाव्यक्तं परं विद्याद्भूतभव्यभयंकरम् ॥ (36)

"'O Gandharva! You asked me—what is the universe and what is the negation of the universe? Know that the supreme and unmanifest

---

[57] Fourth because it is about moksha, not about dharma, artha and kama.
[58] He was the king of the gandharvas.

one[59] is the universe. She has the terrible aspects of creation and destruction.'"

त्रिगुणं गुणकर्तृत्वादशिश्वो निष्कलस्तथा ।
अश्वस्तथैव मिथुनमेवमेवानुदृश्यते ॥ (37)

'"'She possesses the three gunas and invests everything with these. The one without these is said to be the negation of the universe.[60] In that way, ashva and the negation of ashva are seen to be the couple.'"'[61]

अव्यक्तं प्रकृतिं प्राहु: पुरुषेति च निर्गुणम् ।
तथैव मित्रं पुरुषं वरुणं प्रकृतिं तथा ॥ (38)

'"'The unmanifest is said to be Prakriti and the one without gunas is Purusha. In that way, Mitra is Purusha and Varuna is Prakriti.'"'

ज्ञानं तु प्रकृतिं प्राहुर्ज्ञेयं निष्कलमेव च ।
अज्ञश्च ज्ञश्च पुरुषस्तस्मान्निष्कल उच्यते ॥ (39)

'"'Jnana is said to be Prakriti, and the object of knowledge is the unblemished one.[62] The ignorant and the not ignorant are said to be Purusha, since both are without blemishes.'"'

कस्तपा अतपा: प्रोक्ता: कोऽसौ पुरुष उच्यते ।
तपा: प्रकृतिरित्याहुरतपा निष्कल: स्मृत: ॥ (40)

'"'Who is the one with heat and who is the one without heat? Who is said to be Purusha? The one with heat is Prakriti and the one without heat is said to be the one without blemishes.'"'

तथैवावेद्यमव्यक्तं वेद्यं पुरुष उच्यते ।
चलाचलमिति प्रोक्तं त्वया तदपि मे शृणु ॥ (41)

---

[59] Prakriti.
[60] Purusha.
[61] If this is asva, it will correspond to Purusha and the negation of asva will be Prakriti.
[62] Purusha.

"'In that way, ignorance is the unmanifest one[63] and knowledge is said to be Purusha. You asked me about the mobile and the immobile. Listen to me.'"

चलां तु प्रकृतिं प्राहुः कारणं क्षेपसर्गयोः ।
अक्षेपसर्गयोः कर्ता निश्चलः पुरुषः स्मृतः ॥ (42)

"'Prakriti is said to be mobile. It undertakes transformations and is the reason behind creation and destruction. The immobile one, who has lordship, but does not undertake transformations for creation and destruction, is said to be Purusha.'"

अजावुभावप्रजौ च अक्षयौ चाप्युभावपि ।
अजौ नित्यावुभौ प्राहुरध्यात्मगतिनिश्चयाः ॥ (43)

"'Those who have determined the nature of adhyatma speak of both of them as without beginning, without sentiments, without offspring, without destruction, without decay, without creation and eternal.'"[64]

अक्षयत्वात्प्रजनने अजमत्राहुरव्ययम् ।
अक्षयं पुरुषं प्राहुः क्षयो ह्यास्य न विद्यते ॥ (44)

"'Though she[65] leads to creation, she is said to be without decay, without beginning and without change. Purusha is said to be without destruction. There is no decay in him.'"

गुणक्षयत्वात्प्रकृतिः कर्तृत्वादक्षयं बुधाः ।
एषा तेऽन्वीक्षिकी विद्या चतुर्थी सांपरायिकी ॥ (45)

"'The learned say that the gunas created by Prakriti are destructible, but not she herself. This is the fourth knowledge of metaphysics, that concerning the next world.'"

---

[63]Prakriti.
[64]There seems to be an inconsistency with what has been said about Prakriti earlier. That is probably because there were different schools and types of belief.
[65]Prakriti.

विद्योपेतं धनं कृत्वा कर्मणा नित्यकर्मणि ।
एकान्तदर्शना वेदाः सर्वे विश्वावसो स्मृताः ॥ (46)

"'"O Vishvavasu! It has been said that one's karma is to obtain riches through knowledge and always perform nitya karma, studying all the Vedas with single-minded insight."'"

जायन्ते च म्रियन्ते च यस्मिन्नेते यतश्च्युताः ।
वेदार्थं ये न जानन्ति वेद्यं गन्धर्वसत्तम ॥ (47)

"'"O Supreme among Gandharvas! This[66] is not dislodged. Everything is born from it and merges into it after death. Those who do not understand this purport of the Vedas do not know."'"

साङ्गोपाङ्गानपि यदि पञ्च वेदानधीयते ।
वेदवेद्यं न जानीते वेदभारवहो हि सः ॥ (48)

"'"Even if they study the five Vedas,[67] with the Vedangas and the subsequent branches, they do not understand the knowledge of the Vedas. Such a person only bears the weight of the Vedas."'"

यो घृतार्थी खरीक्षीरं मथेद्गन्धर्वसत्तम ।
विष्ठां तत्रानुपश्येत न मण्डं नापि वा घृतम् ॥ (49)

"'"O Supreme among Gandharvas! This is like a person who desires ghee churning the milk of a she-ass. He only sees the excrement there. There is no cream from the milk, nor any clarified butter."'"

तथा वेद्यमवेद्यं च वेदविद्यो न विन्दति ।
स केवलं मूढमतिर्ज्ञानभारवहः स्मृतः ॥ (50)

"'"In that way, despite studying what should be learnt of the Vedas, one does not obtain the knowledge in the Vedas. Such a person is said to be foolish in his intelligence and only bears the burden of jnana."'"

---

[66] The brahman.
[67] The Itihasa Purana and other Puranas are known as the fifth Veda.

द्रष्टव्यौ नित्यमेवैतौ तत्परेणान्तरात्मना ।
यथास्य जन्मनिधने न भवेतां पुनः पुनः ॥ (51)

'"'In one's atman, one must always single-mindedly look for the supreme objective, so that one does not have to repeatedly go through birth and death.'"'

अजस्रं जन्मनिधनं चिन्तयित्वा त्रयीमिमाम् ।
परित्यज्य क्षयमिह अक्षयं धर्ममास्थितः ॥ (52)

'"'If one thinks about these three,[68] there are innumerable births and deaths in this world. One must abandon what is indestructible in this world and resort to the dharma of the indestructible.'"'

यदा तु पश्यतेऽत्यन्तमहन्यहनि काश्यप ।
तदा स केवलीभूतः षड्विंशमनुपश्यति ॥ (53)

'"'O Kashyapa![69] Day and night, if one only contemplates the absolute, then one sees oneself as united only with the absolute and the twenty-sixth.'"'[70]

अन्यश्च शश्वदव्यक्तस्तथान्यः पञ्चविंशकः ।
तस्य द्वावनुपश्येत तमेकमिति साधवः ॥ (54)

'"'There are those who know the eternal and the unmanifest and those who know the twenty-five. Some practitioners see the two[71] as distinct, others as one.'"'

तेनैतन्नाभिजानन्ति पञ्चविंशकमच्युतम् ।
जन्ममृत्युभयाद्योगाः सांख्याश्च परमैषिणः ॥ (55)

---

[68]Probably the three gunas, or the past, the present and the future.
[69]The gandharvas were also descended from Sage Kashyapa. They are Kashyapa's descendants.
[70]The brahman. In samkhya philosophy, the lower twenty-four tattvas are the five senses of perception, five organs of action, five gross elements, five subtle elements, mind, intelligence, ahamkara and mahat. Prakriti and Purusha make it twenty-five and twenty-six. Sometimes, mahat is not added and Prakriti becomes the twenty-fourth, with Vishnu (Achyuta) regarded as the twenty-fifth.
[71]Purusha and Prakriti.

"'They get to know the undecaying nature of the twenty-fifth. Desiring the supreme, those practitioners of samkhya are beyond birth, death, fear and enterprise.'"

विश्वावसुरुवाच

पञ्चविंशं यदेतत्ते प्रोक्तं ब्राह्मणसत्तम ।
तथा तन्न तथा वेति तद्भवान्वक्तुमर्हति ॥ (56)

"'Vishvavasu replied, 'O Excellent Brahmana! You have spoken about the twenty-fifth. But this is not always known in this way. Therefore, you should explain it.'"

जैगीषव्यस्यासितस्य देवलस्य च मे श्रुतम् ।
पराशरस्य विप्रर्षेर्वार्षगण्यस्य धीमतः ॥ (57)
भिक्षोः पञ्चशिखस्याथ कपिलस्य शुकस्य च ।
गौतमस्यार्ष्टिषेणस्य गर्गस्य च महात्मनः ॥ (58)
नारदस्यासुरेश्चैव पुलस्त्यस्य च धीमतः ।
सनत्कुमारस्य ततः शुक्रस्य च महात्मनः ॥ (59)
कश्यपस्य पितुश्चैव पूर्वमेव मया श्रुतम् ।
तदनन्तरं च रुद्रस्य विश्वरूपस्य धीमतः ॥ (60)
दैवतेभ्यः पितृभ्यश्च दैत्येभ्यश्च ततस्ततः ।
प्राप्तमेतन्मया कृत्स्नं वेद्यं नित्यं वदन्त्युत ॥ (61)

"'I have heard about this earlier from Jaigishavya, Asita-Devala, the brahmana rishi Parashara, the intelligent Varshaganya, Bhikshu, Panchashikha, Kapila, Shuka, Goutama, Arshtishena, the great-souled Garga, Narada, Asuri, the intelligent Pulastya, Sanatkumara and the great-souled Shukra. I have also heard this from my father, Kashyapa. Later, I heard about this from Rudra and the intelligent Vishvarupa, and also devas, ancestors and daityas. I have obtained all the knowledge that they always speak about.'"

तस्मात्त्वद्भवद्बुद्ध्या श्रोतुमिच्छामि ब्राह्मण ।
भवान्प्रवरः शास्त्राणां प्रगल्भश्चातिबुद्धिमान् ॥ (62)

"'O Brahmana! However, through your intelligence, I wish to hear about this from you. You are foremost among those who know the sacred texts. You are eloquent and extremely intelligent."'

न तवाविदितं किंचिद्भवाञ्छ्रुतिनिधिः स्मृतः ।
कथ्यते देवलोके च पितृलोके च ब्राह्मण ॥ (63)

'"There is nothing that is not known to you. O Brahmana! In the world of devas and in the world of ancestors, you are said to be an ocean of learning about Shrutis."'

ब्रह्मलोकगताश्चैव कथयन्ति महर्षयः ।
पतिश्च तपतां शश्वदादित्यस्तव भाषते ॥ (64)

'"The maharshis who have gone to Brahma's abode say that Aditya, the eternal lord of all those who provide heat, speaks to you about this."'

सांख्यज्ञानं त्वया ब्रह्मन्नवाप्तं कृत्स्नमेव च ।
तथैव योगज्ञानं च याज्ञवल्क्य विशेषतः ॥ (65)

'"O Brahmana! O Yajnavalkya! You have obtained the entire jnana of samkhya and, in particular, the jnana of yoga."'

निःसंदिग्धं प्रबुद्धस्त्वं बुध्यमानश्चराचरम् ।
श्रोतुमिच्छामि तज्ज्ञानं घृतं मण्डमयं यथा ॥ (66)

'"It is certainly the case that you have understood and know about the mobile and the immobile. I wish to hear about that jnana, which is like clarified butter inside cream."'

याज्ञवल्क्य उवाच

कृत्स्नधारिणमेव त्वां मन्ये गन्धर्ववसत्तम ।
जिज्ञाससि च मां राजंस्तन्निबोध यथाश्रुतम् ॥ (67)

'Yajnavalkya said, "O Supreme among Gandharvas! I think that you are capable of bearing all of it. O King! You have asked me. Listen to what I have learned."'[72]

---

[72]Here, Bhishma is repeating the conversation between Yajnavalkya and Vishvavasu.

अबुध्यमानां प्रकृतिं बुध्यते पञ्चविंशकः ।
न तु बुध्यति गन्धर्व प्रकृतिः पञ्चविंशकम् ॥ (68)

'"Prakriti cannot be comprehended, but can be realized by the twenty-fifth.[73] O Gandharva! But the twenty-fifth cannot be comprehended by Prakriti."'

अनेनाप्रतिबोधेन प्रधानं प्रवदन्ति तम् ।
सांख्ययोगाश्च तत्त्वज्ञा यथा श्रुतिनिदर्शनात् ॥ (69)

'"Because it cannot be understood in this way, those who know the truth about samkhya and yoga and about the instructions of the Shrutis speak of it as Pradhana."'

पश्यंस्तथैवापश्यंश्च पश्यत्यन्यस्तथानघ ।
षड्विंशः पञ्चविंशं च चतुर्विंशं च पश्यति ।
न तु पश्यति पश्यंस्तु यश्चैनमनुपश्यति ॥ (70)

'"O Unblemished One! But though it cannot be seen, it can see itself and can see others. It can see the twenty-fourth, the twenty-fifth and the twenty-sixth.[74] Even when it does not see,[75] it thinks that it is capable of seeing and sees."'

पञ्चविंशोऽभिमन्येत नान्योऽस्ति परमो मम ।
न चतुर्विंशकोऽग्राह्यो मनुजैर्ज्ञानदर्शिभिः ॥ (71)

'"The twenty-fifth thinks that there is nothing superior to itself. The twenty-fourth is incapable of being grasped by a man who does not possess the insight of jnana."'

---

[73]This brings in the notion of Pradhana, an inferred entity. This is primordial nature, distinct from Prakriti. Samkhya interpretations vary on whether Pradhana exists as an independent entity, as opposed to Purusha and Prakriti.
[74]Here, the simplest interpretation is that the twenty-fourth is Prakriti, the twenty-fifth is the jivatman and the twenty-sixth is the paramatman. In a state of knowledge, the jivatman can comprehend the paramatman.
[75]That is, Pradhana is in a state of ignorance.

मत्स्येवोदकमन्वेति प्रवर्तति प्रवर्तनात् ।
यथैव बुध्यते मत्स्यस्तथैषोऽप्यनुबुध्यते ।
सस्नेहः सहवासाच्च साभिमानश्च नित्यशः ॥ (७२)

'"The fish dwells in water. But though they are together, they are distinct. Like the fish, those who are learned understand that it is different.[76] There is always a misconception due to the attachment that results from residing together."'

स निमज्जति कालस्य यदैकत्वं न बुध्यते ।
उन्मज्जति हि कालस्य ममत्वेनाभिसंवृतः ॥ (७३)

'"However, those who do not understand the unity[77] are submerged in time. Enveloped by a sense of ownership, they are immersed in destiny."'

यदा तु मन्यतेऽन्योऽहमन्य एष इति द्विजः ।
तदा स केवलीभूतः षड्विंशमनुपश्यति ॥ (७४)

'"When a person thinks that he is no different from the other one, he is a true dvija. He becomes one with the absolute and sees the twenty-sixth."'

अन्यश्च राजन्नवरस्तथान्यः पञ्चविंशकः ।
तत्स्थत्वादनुपश्यन्ति एक एवेति साधवः ॥ (७५)

'"O King! There may be those who perceive the supreme other one and the twenty-fifth to be distinct. But those who see them as one are virtuous."'

तेनैतन्नाभिनन्दन्ति पञ्चविंशकमच्युतम् ।
जन्ममृत्युभयाद्भीता योगाः सांख्याश्च काश्यप ।
षड्विंशमनुपश्यन्ति शुचयस्तत्परायणाः ॥ (७६)

'"They do not find delight in the undecaying twenty-fifth alone. O Kashyapa! Those practitioners of samkhya and yoga are not terrified

---

[76]Prakriti is different from jivatman.
[77]Of the jivatman and the paramatman.

because of their fear of birth and death. They are devoted to purity and see the twenty-sixth."'

यदा स केवलीभूतः षड्विंशमनुपश्यति ।
तदा स सर्वविद्विद्वान् पुनर्जन्म विन्दति ॥ (77)

'"United with the absolute, such a person sees the twenty-sixth. He is learned in every way and does not enjoy rebirth."'

एवमप्रतिबुद्धश्च बुध्यमानश्च तेऽनघ ।
बुद्धश्चोक्तो यथातत्त्वं मया श्रुतिनिदर्शनात् ॥ (78)

'"O Unblemished One! Having understood, I have thus told you about what is to be known. Following the indications of the Shrutis, I have spoken to you about true knowledge."'

पश्यापश्यं योऽनुपश्येत्क्षेमं तत्त्वं च काश्यप ।
केवलाकेवलं चाद्यं पञ्चविंशात्परं च यत् ॥ (79)

'"O Kashyapa! I have told you about what is seen and what is not seen, about seeing what is indestructible, about what is absolute and what is not absolute and about what is superior to the twenty-fifth."'

विश्वावसुरुवाच

तथ्यं शुभं चैतदुक्तं त्वया भोः सम्यक्क्षेमं देवताद्यं यथावत् ।
स्वस्त्यक्षयं भवतश्चास्तु नित्यं बुद्ध्या सदा बुधियुक्तं नमस्ते ॥ (80)

'Vishvavasu replied, "You have spoken auspicious words to me and told me properly about what is indestructible and what the origin of divinity is. May you always be fortunate and without decay. I bow down before you. May you always be vested with intelligence and use your intelligence."'

याज्ञवल्क्य उवाच

एवमुक्त्वा संप्रयातो दिवं स विभ्राजन्वै श्रीमता दर्शनेन ।
तुष्टश्च तुष्ट्या पर्याभिनन्द्य प्रदक्षिणं मम कृत्वा महात्मा ॥ (81)

'Yajnavalkya said, "Having said this, he left for heaven, radiant in his handsome appearance. Having been satisfied, the great-souled one circumambulated me first and I was exceedingly pleased with him."'[78]

ब्रह्मादीनां खेचराणां क्षितौ च ये चाधस्तात्संवसन्ते नरेन्द्र ।
तत्रैव तद्दर्शनं दर्शयन्वै सम्यक्क्षेम्यं ये पथं संश्रिता वै ॥ (82)

'"O Indra among Men! He passed on the insight that he obtained from me to those who live in Brahma's world and those who dwell in the sky and below and they appropriately chose the path that leads to the indestructible."'

सांख्या: सर्वे सांख्यधर्मे रताश्च तद्धद्योगा योगधर्मे रताश्च ।
ये चाप्यन्ये मोक्षकामा मनुष्यास्तेषामेतद्दर्शनं ज्ञानदृष्टम् ॥ (83)

'"Those who follow samkhya are devoted to the dharma of samkhya. Those who follow yoga are devoted to the dharma of yoga. There are other humans who desire moksha. All those who are instructed by this jnana attain insight."'

ज्ञानान्मोक्षो जायते पूरुषाणां नास्त्यज्ञानादेवमाहुनरेन्द्र ।
तस्माज्ज्ञानं तत्त्वतोऽन्वेषितव्यं येनात्मानं मोक्षयेज्जन्ममृत्यो: ॥ (84)

'"Among men, moksha results from jnana. O Indra among Men! It is said that it cannot be obtained through lack of jnana. Therefore, one must search for the truth about jnana, so that one can free oneself from birth and death."'

प्राप्य ज्ञानं ब्राह्मणात्क्षत्रियाद्वावैश्याच्छूद्रादपि नीचादभीक्ष्णम् ।
श्रद्धातव्यं श्रद्दधानेन नित्यं न श्रद्दधिनं जन्ममृत्यू विशेताम् ॥ (85)

'"With faith and devotion, one must always obtain jnana from a brahmana, a kshatriya, a vaishya or even a shudra who is of low birth. Because of his devotion, a person who has faith is never assailed by birth and death, but not a person who lacks faith."'

---

[78]Yajnavalkya is now speaking to Janaka.

सर्वे वर्णा ब्राह्मणा ब्रह्मजाश्च सर्वे नित्यं व्याहरन्ते च ब्रह्म ।
तत्त्वं शास्त्रं ब्रह्मबुद्ध्या ब्रवीमि सर्वं विश्वं ब्रह्म चैतत्समस्तम् ॥ (86)

'"Since they are born from Brahma, all the varnas are brahmanas. All of them always speak about the brahman. I have spoken to you the truth about the sacred texts and about intelligence about the brahman. The entire universe is completely pervaded by the brahman."'

ब्रह्मास्यतो ब्राह्मणाः संप्रसूता बाहुभ्यां वै क्षत्रियाः संप्रसूताः ।
नाभ्यां वैश्याः पादतश्चापि शूद्राः सर्वे वर्णा नान्यथा वेदितव्याः ॥ (87)

'"Brahmanas were generated from Brahma's mouth. Kshatriyas were generated from his arms. Vaishyas were generated from his navel and shudras from his feet. All the varnas should not be thought of in any other way."'

अज्ञानतः कर्मयोनिं भजन्ते तां तां राजंस्ते यथा यान्त्यभावम् ।
तथा वर्णा ज्ञानहीनाः पतन्ते घोरादज्ञानात्प्राकृतं योनिजालम् ॥ (88)

'"O King! It is because of the lack of jnana that one suffers from birth and karma and the pangs of existence. Devoid of jnana, all the varnas fall down in this way. They are immersed in terrible ignorance and enveloped in Prakriti's net of birth."'

तस्माज्ज्ञानं सर्वतो मार्गितव्यं सर्वत्रस्थं चैतदुक्तं मया ते ।
तस्थौ ब्रह्मा तस्थिवांश्चापरो यस्तस्मै नित्यं मोक्षमाहुर्द्विजेन्द्राः ॥ (89)

'"Therefore, one must seek every means to stick to the path of jnana. I have spoken to you about this. Those who are established in the supreme brahman are always said to obtain moksha and are Indras among brahmanas."'

यत्ते पृष्टं तन्मया चोपदिष्टं याथातथ्यं तद्विशोको भवस्व ।
राजन्गच्छस्वैतदर्थस्य पारं सम्यक्प्रोक्तं स्वस्ति तेऽस्त्वत्र नित्यम् ॥ (90)

'"I have instructed you about what you had asked me. I have told you the truth. Be bereft of grief. O King! Cross over to the other side. You have spoken properly. May you always be fortunate."'

भीष्म उवाच

स एवमनुशास्तस्तु याज्ञवल्क्येन धीमता ।
प्रीतिमानभवद्राजा मिथिलाधिपतिस्तदा ॥ (91)

Bhishma concluded, 'Then, having been thus instructed by the intelligent Yajnavalkya, the king, the lord of Mithila, was delighted.'

गते मुनिवरे तस्मिन्कृते चापि प्रदक्षिणे ।
दैवरातिर्नरपतिरासीनस्तत्र मोक्षवित् ॥ (92)
गोकोटिं स्पर्शयामास हिरण्यस्य तथैव च ।
रत्नाञ्जलिमथैकं च ब्राह्मणेभ्यो ददौ तदा ॥ (93)

'He did pradakshina of the supreme among sages and departed. Daivarati, the lord of men, obtained knowledge about moksha. He seated himself and, touching one crore cattle, gold and an accumulation of jewels, gave them away to brahmanas.'

विदेहराज्यं च तथा प्रतिष्ठाप्य सुतस्य वै ।
यतिधर्ममुपासंश्चाप्यवसन्मिथिलाधिप: ॥ (94)

'He instated his son in the kingdom of Videha. The lord of Mithila then resorted to the dharma of mendicants.'

सांख्यज्ञानमधीयानो योगशास्त्रं च कृत्स्नश: ।
धर्माधर्मौ च राजेन्द्र प्राकृतं परिगर्हयन् ॥ (95)

'He studied the entire knowledge of samkhya and the sacred texts of yoga. O Indra among Kings! He abandoned the ordinary practices of dharma and adharma.'

अनन्तमिति कृत्वा स नित्यं केवलमेव च ।
धर्माधर्मौ पुण्यपापे सत्यासत्ये तथैव च ॥ (96)

'He always thought of himself as the infinite and the absolute. He thought of dharma, adharma, good, bad, truth and false in that way.'

जन्ममृत्यू च राजेन्द्र प्राकृतं तदचिन्तयत् ।
ब्रह्माव्यक्तस्य कर्मेदमिति नित्यं नराधिप ॥ (97)

'O Indra among Kings! O Lord of Men! He no longer thought of ordinary things like birth and death, but always devoted himself to karma associated with the unmanifest brahman.'

पश्यन्ति योगाः सांख्याश्च स्वशास्त्रकृतलक्षणाः ।
इष्टानिष्टवियुक्तं हि तस्थौ ब्रह्म परात्परम् ।
नित्यं तमाहुर्विद्वांसः शुचिस्तस्माच्छुचिर्भव ॥ (98)

'The practitioners of yoga and samkhya, accomplished about the indications of their own sacred texts, see that the brahman is supreme of the supreme and is delinked from good and evil. Those learned ones always speak of it as pure. You should also become pure.'

दीयते यच्च लभते दत्तं यच्चानुमन्यते ।
ददाति च नरश्रेष्ठ प्रतिगृह्णाति यच्च ह ।
ददात्यव्यक्तमेवैतत्प्रतिगृह्णाति तच्च वै ॥ (99)

'O Best among Men! The giver, the receiver, what is intended as a gift, what is given, what is received, what is instructed to be given, what is instructed to be received—all these are aspects of the unmanifest.'

आत्मा ह्येवात्मनो ह्येकः कोऽन्यस्त्वत्तोऽधिको भवेत् ।
एवं मन्यस्व सततमन्यथा मा विचिन्तय ॥ (100)

'The atman is the only thing that belongs to the atman and there is nothing that is superior to this. Always regard it in this way and do not think otherwise.'

यस्याव्यक्तं न विदितं सगुणं निर्गुणं पुनः ।
तेन तीर्थानि यज्ञाश्च सेवितव्याविपश्चिता ॥ (101)

'A person who does not know the unmanifest, with gunas and without gunas,[79] always goes to tirthas and performs sacrifices. He is not learned.'

---

[79] Prakriti and Purusha, respectively.

न स्वाध्यायैस्तपोभिर्वा यज्ञैर्वा कुरुनन्दन ।
लभतेऽव्यक्तसंस्थानं ज्ञात्वाव्यक्तं महीपते ॥ (102)

'O Descendant of the Kuru Lineage! One cannot realize the state of the unmanifest through studying, austerities or sacrifices. O Lord of the Earth! The unmanifest must be comprehended in this way.'

तथैव महत: स्थानमाहंकारिकमेव च ।
अहंकारात्परं चापि स्थानानि समवाप्नुयात् ॥ (103)

'It is the same with the state of mahat and ahamkara. One must obtain the state that is superior to that of ahamkara.'

ये त्वव्यक्तात्परं नित्यं जानते शास्त्रतत्परा: ।
जन्ममृत्युवियुक्तं च वियुक्तं सदसच्च यत् ॥ (104)

'Those who are devoted to the sacred texts always know about the supreme and the unmanifest. They are disassociated from birth and death and are disassociated from existence and non-existence.'[80]

एतन्मयाप्तं जनकात्पुरस्तात्तेनापि चाप्तं नृप याज्ञवल्क्यात् ।
ज्ञानं विशिष्टं न तथा हि यज्ञा ज्ञानेन दुर्गं तरते न यज्ञै: ॥ (105)

'O King! In ancient times, I obtained this from Janaka, and he obtained it from Yajnavalkya. This special jnana is superior to sacrifices. It is through jnana that one can traverse what is difficult to cross, not through sacrifices.'

दुर्गं जन्म निधनं चापि राजन्न भूतिकं ज्ञानविदो वदन्ति ।
यज्ञैस्तपोभिर्नियमैर्व्रतैश्च दिवं समासाद्य पतन्ति भूमौ ॥ (106)

'O King! Those who possess jnana say that birth, death and hardships are difficult to traverse through sacrifices, austerities, rituals and vows. Even if one obtains heaven, one falls down on the ground.'

---

[80] Alternatively, cause and effect.

तस्मादुपासस्व परं महच्छुचि शिवं विमोक्षं विमलं पवित्रम् ।
क्षेत्रज्ञवित्पार्थिव ज्ञानयज्ञमुपास्य वै तत्त्वमृषिर्भविष्यसि ॥ (107)

'Therefore, you should worship the supreme, great and pure one, auspicious, without blemish and sacred, the path to moksha. O Lord of the Earth! As the kshetrajna, perform the sacrifice of jnana. That is what the rishi spoke about. You will obtain the truth.'

उपनिषदमुपाकरोत्तदा वै जनक नृपस्य पुरा हि याज्ञवल्क्य:।
यदुपगणितशाश्वताव्ययं तच्छुभममृतत्त्वमशोकमृच्छतीति ॥ (108)

'This has been spoken about in the Upanishads, and in ancient times, Yajnavalkya told King Janaka about this. This is the eternal and the undecaying, and he enumerated the auspicious and the immortal. He[81] then obtained the one who is beyond sorrow.'

Thus ends the Yajnavalkya Gita.

---

[81]Janaka.

23

KAMA GITA

Ashva means a horse and '*medha*' means a sacrifice. Thus, Ashvamedhika Parva or Ashvamedha Parva is about a horse sacrifice. In the eighteen-Parva classification of the epic, Ashvamedhika Parva is the fourteen, and has ninety-six chapters. It doesn't have any sub-parvas. The Kama Gita consists of a single chapter in this parva, with twenty-one shlokas. The word 'kama' means desire and attachment, and the Kama Gita is named after this. Krishna speaks about desire and non-attachment to Yudhishthira and, in the course of the conversation, describes what Kama himself said about desire.

वासुदेव उवाच ।
न बाह्यं द्रव्यमुत्सृज्य सिद्धिर्भवति भारत ।
शारीरं द्रव्यमुत्सृज्य सिद्धिर्भवति वा न वा ॥ (1)

Vasudeva said, 'O Descendant of the Bharata Lineage! One does not obtain success by giving up external objects. Success may or may not be obtained by giving up physical objects.'

बाह्यद्रव्यविमुक्तस्य शारीरेषु च गृध्यतः ।
यो धर्मो यत्सुखं चैव द्विषतामस्तु तत्तथा ॥ (2)

'Even if one is freed from external objects, one may still hanker after the body. Let the dharma and happiness that result from this be the lot of the enemy.'

द्व्यक्षरस्तु भवेन्मृत्युस्त्र्यक्षरं ब्रह्म शाश्वतम् ।
ममेति द्व्यक्षरो मृत्युर्न ममेति च शाश्वतम् ॥ (3)

'The word *"mrityu"* has two syllables.[1] The eternal brahman has three syllables.[2] A sense of ownership has two syllables and represents death.[3] A lack of ownership is eternal.'

ब्रह्म मृत्युश्च तौ राजन्नात्मन्येव व्यवस्थितौ ।
अदृश्यमानौ भूतानि योधयेतामसंशयम् ॥ (4)

'O King! Both mrityu and the brahman are inside all creatures, though they are invisible. There is no doubt that they are fighting with each other.'

अविनाशोऽस्य सत्त्वस्य नियतो यदि भारत ।
भित्त्वा शरीरं भूतानामहिंसां प्रतिपद्यते ॥ (5)

'O Descendant of the Bharata Lineage! If it is true that the atman is indestructible and eternal, then no injury results if one strikes the physical bodies of creatures.'

लब्ध्वापि पृथिवीं कृत्स्नां सहस्थावरजङ्गमाम् ।
ममत्वं यस्य नैव स्यात्किं तया स करिष्यति ॥ (6)

'Even after having obtained the earth with all its mobile and immobile objects, if a person has no sense of ownership, there is nothing else left for him to do.'

अथ वा वसतः पार्थ वने वन्येन जीवतः ।
ममता यस्य द्रव्येषु मृत्योरास्ये स वर्तते ॥ (7)

---

[1] We have translated '*akshara*' as syllable. Mrityu means death and consists of the syllables 'mrit' and 'yu'.
[2] '*Shasvata*' means eternal and consists of the syllables 'shas', 'va' and 'ta'.
[3] '*Mama*' means mine and has the two syllables 'ma' and 'ma'. *Namama* is lack of ownership and has the three syllables, 'na', 'ma' and 'ma'. The implication is that three syllables, and entities with three syllables, are superior to those with two.

'O Partha! But there may be a person who dwells in the forest, surviving on forest fare. If he still possesses a sense of ownership in objects, he is in the jaws of death.'

ब्राह्यान्तराणां शत्रूणां स्वभावं पश्य भारत ।
यन्न पश्यति तद्भूतं मुच्यते स महाभयात् ॥ (8)

'O Descendant of the Bharata Lineage! Behold the nature of external and internal enemies. If a person does not see these in creatures, he is freed from great fear.'

कामात्मानं न प्रशंसन्ति लोके न चाकामात्काचिदस्ति प्रवृत्ति: ।
दानं हि वेदाध्ययनं तपश्च कामेन कर्माणि च वैदिकानि ॥ (9)

'In this world, those with desire in the atman are not praised. But without desire, there can be no inclination towards action. It is because of desire that one often undertakes the rites of the Vedas, donations, studying the Vedas and austerities.'

व्रतं यज्ञानियमान्ध्यानयोगान्कामेन यो नारभते विदित्वा ।
यद्द्वयं कामयते स धर्मो न यो धर्मो नियमस्तस्य मूलम् ॥ (10)

'It should be known that vows, sacrifices, rules, meditation and yoga, started without any desire, and anything not undertaken because of desire, is dharma. Something with rules as the foundation does not constitute dharma.'

अत्र गाथा: कामगीता: कीर्तयन्ति पुराविद: ।
शृणु संकीर्त्यमानास्ता निखिलेन युधिष्ठिर ॥ (11)

'Those who know about the ancient accounts have chanted the Kama Gita in this connection.[4] O Yudhishthira! Listen to that being recounted in its entirety.'

---

[4] The Kama Gita is something recited by kama (desire) personified. The text does not have the quotes. We have inserted them in the appropriate place. This is not an easy translation, but the sense is that desire cannot be conquered without non-attachment.

नाहं शक्योऽनुपायेन हन्तुं भूतेन केनचित् ।
यो मां प्रयतते हन्तुं ज्ञात्वा प्रहरणे बलम् ।
तस्य तस्मिन्प्रहरणे पुनः प्रादुर्भवाम्यहम् ॥ (12)

'"No creature is capable of destroying me without using the proper methods. If someone knows my strength and tries to destroy me using weapons, I destroy him using those same weapons and manifest myself again."'

यो मां प्रयतते हन्तुं यज्ञैर्विविधदक्षिणैः ।
जङ्गमेष्विव कर्मात्मा पुनः प्रादुर्भवाम्यहम् ॥ (13)

'"If he tries to destroy me through sacrifices that involve many kinds of dakshina, I become those mobile objects and the atman of that karma, thus manifesting myself again."'

यो मां प्रयतते हन्तुं वेदैर्वेदान्तसाधनैः ।
स्थावरेष्विव शान्तात्मा तस्य प्रादुर्भवाम्यहम् ॥ (14)

'"If he tries to destroy me through the rites of the Vedas and vedanta, I become the tranquil atman in those immobile objects and manifest myself again."'

यो मां प्रयतते हन्तुं धृत्या सत्यपराक्रमः ।
भावो भवामि तस्याहं स च मां नावबुध्यते ॥ (15)

'"If someone tries to destroy me through fortitude and the valour of truth, I become those sentiments and he is not able to comprehend me."'

यो मां प्रयतते हन्तुं तपसा संशितव्रतः ।
ततस्तपसि तस्याथ पुनः प्रादुर्भवाम्यहम् ॥ (16)

'"If someone tries to destroy me through austerities and strictness in vows, I base myself on those austerities of his and manifest myself again."'

यो मां प्रयतते हन्तुं मोक्षमास्थाय पण्डितः ।
तस्य मोक्षरतिस्थस्य नृत्यामि च हसामि च ।
अवध्यः सर्वभूतानामहमेकः सनातनः ॥ (17)

'"If a learned man tries to destroy me by resorting to moksha, I base myself on his love for that state of moksha and laugh and dance. Among all creatures, I alone cannot be slain and am eternal."'

तस्मात्त्वमपि तं कामं यज्ञैर्विविधदक्षिणैः ।
धर्मे कुरु महाराज तत्र मे स भविष्यति ॥ (18)

'Therefore, you should desire to perform a sacrifice with many kinds of dakshina. O Great King! Act in accordance with dharma, and kama will also be served by that.'

यजस्व वाजिमेधेन विधिवद्दक्षिणावता ।
अन्यैश्च विविधैर्यज्ञैः समृद्धैयैराप्तदक्षिणैः ॥ (19)

'Perform a horse sacrifice with the prescribed kinds of dakshina. Perform the other different sacrifices, prosperous with offerings of dakshina.'

मा ते व्यथास्तु निहतान्बन्धून्वीक्ष्य पुनः पुनः ।
न शक्यास्ते पुनर्द्रष्टुं ये हतास्मिन्रणाजिरे ॥ (20)

'Do not look towards your slain relatives and be repeatedly distressed. You are incapable of again seeing those who have been killed in this field of battle.'

स त्वमिष्ट्वा महायज्ञैः समृद्धैराप्तदक्षिणैः ।
लोके कीर्तिं परां प्राप्य गतिमग्र्यां गमिष्यसि ॥ (21)

'Perform great sacrifices, rich with offerings of copious quantities of dakshina. You will then obtain fame in this world and go to the supreme destination after death.'

Thus ends the Kama Gita.

24

ANU GITA

As has been mentioned previously, Ashvamedha means a horse sacrifice, and the Parva is so named because Vedavyasa and Krishna ask Yudhishthira to undertake a horse sacrifice. The Kurukshetra War has emptied the treasury, and the horse sacrifice is undertaken to build it up again. At that time, when Krishna is about to leave for Dvaraka, Arjuna asks Krishna to remind him about the lessons of the Bhagavat Gita since he has forgotten everything.

The Anu Gita consists of thirty-five chapters from Ashvamedhika Parva, with 996 shlokas. There are three different parts in the Anu Gita, all repeated by Krishna to Arjuna: a conversation between a siddha brahmana and Kashyapa (the first four chapters; this briefer version is sometimes called the Anu Gita), followed by a conversation between a brahmana and a *brahmani* (the next fifteen chapters, sometimes called the Brahmana Gita) and a conversation between Brahma and the rishis (the last sixteen chapters).

If one excludes the Bhagavat Gita, the Anu Gita is undoubtedly the most translated of all Mahabharata Gitas, though not normally in English. As far as I am aware, the first unabridged translation in English was done by Kashinath Trimbak Telang in 1882.[1]

---

[1] *The Bhagavadgita, with the Sanatsugatiya and the Anu Gita*, K.T. Telang (trans.), *Sacred Books of the East*, Vol. 8, F. Max Muller (ed.), second edition, Clarendon Press, Oxford, 1898. Since we have followed BORI, there are some minor differences between Telang's manuscript and our Sanskrit text. Telang's follows an academic style, with a lot of cross-referencing. We have avoided such

Chapter 1

जनमेजय उवाच

सभायां वसतोस्तस्यां निहत्यारीन्महात्मनो: ।
केशवार्जुनयो: का नु कथा समभवद्द्विज ॥ (1)

Janamejaya asked, 'O Dvija! When the enemies were slain, those great-souled ones, Keshava and Arjuna, were in the assembly hall. What was the conversation between them?'

वैशम्पायन उवाच

कृष्णेन सहित: पार्थ: स्वराज्यं प्राप्य केवलम् ।
तस्यां सभायां रम्यायां विजहार मुदा युत: ॥ (2)

Vaishampayana replied, 'Having regained his own kingdom, Partha was in that beautiful assembly hall with Krishna and sported, filled with delight.'

तत: कं चित्सभोद्देशं स्वर्गोद्देशसमं नृप ।
यदृच्छया तौ मुदितौ जग्मतु: स्वजनावृतौ ॥ (3)

'O King! That region was like a spot in heaven. Surrounded by their relatives, they cheerfully roamed around, as they willed.'

तत: प्रतीत: कृष्णेन सहित: पाण्डवोऽर्जुन: ।
निरीक्ष्य तां सभां रम्यामिदं वचनमब्रवीत् ॥ (4)

'Content, with Krishna, Pandava Arjuna looked at that beautiful assembly hall and spoke these words.'

विदितं ते महाबाहो संग्रामे समुपस्थिते ।
माहात्म्यं देवकीमातस्तच्च ते रूपमैश्वरम् ॥ (5)

"'O Mighty-Armed One! O One Whose Mother Is Devaki! When the battle presented itself, I got to know about your greatness, the truth about your lordship and your form.'"

यतु तद्भवता प्रोक्तं तदा केशव सौहृदात् ।
तत्सर्वं पुरुषव्याघ्र नष्टं मे नष्टचेतसः ॥ (6)

"'O Keshava! Out of affection towards me, you spoke to me then. O Tiger among Men! However, my intelligence has been destroyed and I have forgotten everything.'"

मम कौतूहलं त्वस्ति तेष्वर्थेषु पुनः प्रभो ।
भवांश्च द्वारकां गन्ता नचिरादिव माधव ॥ (7)

"'O Lord! However, my curiosity about that truth has again been ignited. O Madhava! You will soon go away to Dvaraka.'"

एवमुक्तस्ततः कृष्णः फल्गुनं प्रत्यभाषत ।
परिष्वज्य महातेजा वचनं वदतां वरः ॥ (8)

Vaishampayana said, 'Having been thus addressed, the greatly energetic Krishna, supreme among eloquent ones, embraced Phalguna[2] and replied in these words.'

श्रावितस्त्वं मया गुह्यं ज्ञापितश्च सनातनम् ।
धर्मं स्वरूपिणं पार्थ सर्वलोकांश्च शाश्वतान् ॥ (9)

"'I made you listen to something that is secret and told you about the eternal. O Partha! This was about the true nature of eternal dharma for all the worlds.'"

अबुद्ध्वा यन्न गृह्णीथास्तन्मे सुमहदप्रियम् ।
नूनमश्रद्दधानोऽसि दुर्मेधाश्चासि पाण्डव ॥ (10)

"'I am greatly displeased that you have ignorantly not grasped what I told you. O Pandava! It is evident that you have not been faithful, or your intelligence is not adequate.'"

---

[2]Arjuna.

स हि धर्मः सुपर्याप्तो ब्रह्मणः पदवेदने ।
न शक्यं तन्मया भूयस्तथा वक्तुमशेषतः ॥ (11)

'"That dharma is extremely adequate to obtain the state of the brahman. However, I am incapable of telling you everything in detail again."'

परं हि ब्रह्म कथितं योगयुक्तेन तन्मया ।
इतिहासं तु वक्ष्यामि तस्मिन्नर्थे पुरातनम् ॥ (12)

'"I immersed myself in yoga and told you about the supreme brahman.[3] But I will tell you about an ancient history with the same purport."'

यथा तां बुद्धिमास्थाय गतिमग्र्यां गमिष्यसि ।
शृणु धर्मभृतां श्रेष्ठ गदतः सर्वमेव मे ॥ (13)

'"Using that, if you use your intelligence, you will go to the ultimate destination. O Best among Those Who Uphold Dharma! Hear everything attentively."'

आगच्छद्ब्राह्मणः कश्चित्स्वर्गलोकादरिंदम ।
ब्रह्मलोकाच्च दुर्धर्षः सोऽस्माभिः पूजितोऽभवत् ॥ (14)

'"O Scorcher of Enemies! On one occasion, a brahmana came from the world of heaven. He was unassailable and arrived from Brahma's world. He was worshipped by us."[4]

अस्माभिः परिपृष्टश्च यदाह भरतर्षभ ।
दिव्येन विधिना पार्थ तच्छृणुष्वाविचारयन् ॥ (15)

'"O Bull of the Bharata Lineage! When he was asked by us, following the divine rites, he answered. Without any hesitation, listen to that."'

---

[3] This is a reference to the Bhagavat Gita.
[4] Krishna and all the others in the world of mortals.

ब्राह्मण उवाच

मोक्षधर्मं समाश्रित्य कृष्ण यन्मानुपृच्छसि ।
भूतानामनुकम्पार्थं यन्मोहच्छेदनं प्रभो ॥ (16)

'"The brahmana said, 'O Krishna! What you have asked me concerns the adoption of the dharma of moksha. O Lord! This is driven by compassion for creatures and is meant to sever delusion.'"

तत्तेऽहं संप्रवक्ष्यामि यथावन्मधुसूदन ।
शृणुष्वावहितो भूत्वा गदतो मम माधव ॥ (17)

'"'O Madhusudana! I will tell you about its nature accurately. O Madhava! Concentrate and listen attentively to me.'"

कश्चिद्द्विप्रस्तपोयुक्तः काश्यपो धर्मवित्तमः ।
आससाद द्विजं कं चिद्धर्माणामागतागमम् ॥ (18)

'"'There was a brahmana named Kashyapa. He was full of austerities and rich in dharma. He went to another brahmana who knew everything about the coming and going of dharma.'"

गतागते सुबहुशो ज्ञानविज्ञानपारगम् ।
लोकतत्त्वार्थकुशलं ज्ञातारं सुखदुःखयोः ॥ (19)

'"'He[5] was accomplished in jnana and vijnana and knew the past and the future in great detail. He was skilled in the truth about the worlds and knew about misery and joy.'"

जातिमरणतत्त्वज्ञं कोविदं पुण्यपापयोः ।
द्रष्टारमुच्चनीचानां कर्मभिर्देहिनां गतिम् ॥ (20)

'"'He knew the truth about birth and death. He was learned about virtue and sin. He could see the superior and inferior ends that embodied beings obtained, depending on their karma.'"

चरन्तं मुक्तवत्सिद्धं प्रशान्तं संयतेन्द्रियम् ।
दीप्यमानं श्रिया ब्राह्म्या क्रममाणं च सर्वशः ॥ (21)

---

[5]The second brahmana.

"'He roamed around emancipated and was a siddha. He was tranquil and in control of his senses. He blazed in the prosperity of the brahman and could go everywhere.'"

अन्तर्धानगतिज्ञं च श्रुत्वा तत्त्वेन काश्यपः ।
तथैवान्तर्हितैः सिद्धैर्यान्तं चक्रधरैः सह ॥ (22)

"'Kashyapa had heard that he knew the truth about how to disappear. Thus, he[6] would vanish with the siddhas and the lords of the world.'"

सम्भाषमाणमेकान्ते समासीनं च तैः सह ।
यदृच्छया च गच्छन्तमसक्तं पवनं यथा ॥ (23)

"'He would sit down with them in private and converse with them. He would roam around as he willed, unattached, like the wind.'"

तं समासाद्य मेधावी स तदा द्विजसत्तमः ।
चरणौ धर्मकामो वै तपस्वी सुसमाहितः ।
प्रतिपेदे यथान्यायं भक्त्या परमया युतः ॥ (24)

"'The intelligent and excellent dvija approached him. Desiring dharma, he controlled himself well and prostrated himself at the feet of the ascetic. He met him in the appropriate way, filled with great devotion.'"

विस्मितश्चाद्भुतं दृष्ट्वा काश्यपस्तं द्विजोत्तमम् ।
परिचारेण महता गुरुं वैद्यमतोषयत् ॥ (25)

"'Kashyapa was astounded on seeing that extraordinary person, who was supreme among brahmanas. To satisfy him and obtain learning, he served his guru with great devotion.'"

प्रीतात्मा चोपपन्नश्च श्रुतचारित्रसंयुतः ।
भावेन तोषयच्चैनं गुरुवृत्त्या परंतपः ॥ (26)

---

[6] The sage.

""""The scorcher of enemies possessed learning and character. By following the conduct and sentiments due to a guru, he satisfied him and obtained his pleasure.""""

तस्मै तुष्टः स शिष्याय प्रसन्नोऽथाब्रवीद्गुरुः ।
सिद्धिं परामभिप्रेक्ष्य शृणु तन्मे जनार्दन ॥ (27)

""""Having been satisfied with the shishya, the guru realized that he desired supreme success. Pleased, he spoke. O Janardana! Listen to those words from me.""""

विविधैः कर्मभिस्तात पुण्ययोगैश्च केवलैः ।
गच्छन्तीह गतिं मर्त्या देवलोकेऽपि च स्थितिम् ॥ (28)

""""O Son! Through different kinds of karma and only by resorting to auspicious yoga, those who are mortal can come to this world, or go to the world of the devas and find a sojourn there.""""

न क्वचित्सुखमत्यन्तं न क्वचिच्छाश्वती स्थितिः ।
स्थानाच्च महतो भ्रंशो दुःखलब्ध्यात्पुनः पुनः ॥ (29)

""""However, there is no happiness that is ultimate. There is no sojourn that is eternal. When one is dislodged from a great position, one has to face misery again and again.""""

अशुभा गतयः प्राप्ताः कष्टा मे पापसेवनात् ।
काममन्युपरीतेन तृष्णया मोहितेन च ॥ (30)

""""Because I practised sin, I obtained inauspicious ends and suffered misery. I was overcome by desire, anger, thirst and delusion.""""

पुनः पुनश्च मरणं जन्म चैव पुनः पुनः ।
आहारा विविधा भुक्ताः पीता नानाविधाः स्तनाः ॥ (31)

""""I have gone through deaths again and again. I have gone through births again and again. I have eaten many kinds of food. I have suckled at many kinds of breasts.""""

मातरो विविधा दृष्टाः पितरश्च पृथग्विधाः ।
सुखानि च विचित्राणि दुःखानि च मयानघ ॥ (32)

"'I have seen many kinds of mothers and fathers who are different from each other. O Unblemished One! I have faced diverse kinds of happiness and unhappiness.'"

प्रियैर्विर्विवासो बहुशः संवासश्चाप्रियैः सह ।
धननाशश्च सम्प्राप्तो लब्ध्वा दुःखेन तद्धनम् ॥ (33)

"'There are many occasions when I have been separated from what I love and united with what I do not love. I have confronted the destruction of riches. I have faced misery on account of those riches.'"

अवमानाः सुकष्टाश्च परतः स्वजनात्तथा ।
शारीरा मानसाश्चापि वेदना भृशदारुणाः ॥ (34)

"'I have suffered disrespect and great hardships on account of relatives and those who are not related. I have suffered from extreme and terrible physical and mental pain.'"

प्राप्ता विमाननाश्चोग्रा वधबन्धाश्च दारुणाः ।
पतनं निरये चैव यातनाश्च यमक्षये ॥ (35)

"'I have faced extreme dishonour and the terrible death of my relatives. I have descended into hell and endured hardships in Yama's abode.'"

जरा रोगाश्च सततं वासनानि च भूरिशः ।
लोकेऽस्मिन्ननुभूतानि द्वंद्वजानि भृशं मया ॥ (36)

"'There has always been old age, disease and many kinds of hardship. In this world, I have experienced extreme opposite sentiments.'"[7]

ततः कदाचिन्निर्वेदान्निकारान्निकृतेन च ।
लोकतन्त्रं परित्यक्तं दुःखार्तेन भृशं मया ।
ततः सिद्धिरियं प्राप्ता प्रसादादात्मनो मया ॥ (37)

"'After a time, I became indifferent, was beyond the opposites and without a desire to do anything. Afflicted by great grief, I abandoned this world. Through satisfaction in the atman, I then obtained this siddhi.'"

---

[7]Like joy and misery, heat and cold.

नाहं पुनरिहागन्ता लोकानालोकयाम्यहम् ।
आ सिद्धेरा प्रजासर्गादात्मनो मे गति: शुभा ॥ (38)

'"'I will not come to this world again, nor will I go to any other world. Amidst this creation of subjects, through this siddhi, my atman has obtained an auspicious end.'"'

उपलब्धा द्विजश्रेष्ठ तथेयं सिद्धिरुत्तमा ।
इत: परं गमिष्यामि तत: परतरं पुन: ।
ब्रह्मण: पदमव्यग्रं मा ते भूदत्र संशय: ॥ (39)

'"'O Best among Dvijas! That is the reason I have experienced excellent success. From here, I will go to the supreme. From there, I will go to what is superior still. There is no doubt that I will obtain the foremost state of being merged with the brahman.'"'

नाहं पुनरिहागन्ता मर्त्यलोके परन्तप ।
प्रीतोऽस्मि ते महाप्राज्ञ ब्रूहि किं करवाणि ते ॥ (40)

'"'O Scorcher of Enemies! I will not return to the mortal world again. O Immensely Wise One! I am pleased with you. Tell me what I can do for you.'"'

यदीप्सुरुपपन्नस्त्वं तस्य कालोऽयमागत: ।
अभिजाने च तदहं यदर्थं मा त्वमागत: ।
अचिरात्तु गमिष्यामि येनाहं त्वामचूचुदम् ॥ (41)

'"'The time for your desires to be satisfied has arrived. Indeed, I know the reason why you have come here. I will soon leave this place. That is the reason I have told you this.'"'

भृशं प्रीतोऽस्मि भवतश्चारित्रेण विचक्षण ।
परिपृच्छ यावद्भवते भाषेयं यत्तवेप्सितम् ॥ (42)

'"'O One with a Sense of Discrimination! I am extremely pleased with you, at your character. Ask what you want and I will tell you what you wish to hear.'"'

बहु मन्ये च ते बुद्धिं भृशं संपूजयामि च ।
येनाहं भवता बुद्धो मेधावी ह्यसि काश्यप ॥ (43)

"'I think that your intelligence is great. I honour you greatly. O Kashyapa! Since you have understood,[8] you clearly possess intelligence.'"

Chapter 2

वासुदेव उवाच

ततस्तस्योपसंगृह्य पादौ प्रश्नान्सुदुर्वचान् ।
पप्रच्छ तांश्च सर्वान्स प्राह धर्मभृतां वरः ॥ (1)

'Vasudeva said, "Touching his feet, he[9] asked some questions that were extremely difficult to answer. The supreme among upholders of dharma answered all the questions that he was asked."'

काश्यप उवाच

कथं शरीरं च्यवते कथं चैवोपपद्यते ।
कथं कष्टाच्च संसारात्संसरन्परिमुच्यते ॥ (2)

"'Kashyapa asked, How does the body go away and how does one get another again? How is one freed from the hardships of roaming around in this cycle of samsara?'"

आत्मानं वा कथं युक्त्वा तच्छरीरं विमुञ्चति ।
शरीरतश्च निर्मुक्तः कथमन्यत्प्रपद्यते ॥ (3)

"'Having freed oneself from the body, how is one united with the atman? Having been freed from this body, how does one obtain the other one?'"[10]

---

[8]Kashyapa was able to identify the siddha, though the siddha was disguised. Hence, he was intelligent.
[9]Kashyapa.
[10]'The other one' is the brahman.

कथं शुभाशुभे चायं कर्मणी स्वकृते नरः ।
उपभुङ्क्ते क्व वा कर्म विदेहस्योपतिष्ठति ॥ (4)

'"'How does a man enjoy the fruits of the good and bad karma done by him? If one is freed from the body, what about the karma that one enjoys?'"'

ब्राह्मण उवाच

एवं सञ्चोदितः सिद्धः प्रश्नांस्तान्प्रत्यभाषत ।
आनुपूर्व्येण वार्ष्णेय यथा तन्मे वचः शृणु ॥ (5)

'"'The brahmana said, 'Thus asked, the siddha replied to the questions, one after another. O Varshneya![11] Listen to my words.'"'

सिद्ध उवाच

आयुःकीर्तिकराणीह यानि कर्माणि सेवते ।
शरीरग्रहणेऽन्यस्मिंस्तेषु क्षीणेषु सर्वशः ॥ (6)

'"'The siddha replied, A body is adopted to undertake karma that increases the lifespan and brings fame. Everything else eventually decays.'"'

आयुःक्षयपरीतात्मा विपरीतानि सेवते ।
बुद्धिर्व्यावर्तते चास्य विनाशे प्रत्युपस्थिते ॥ (7)

'"'When the lifespan has been exhausted, the jivatman acts in a contrary way.[12] When destruction presents itself, the intelligence is whirled around.'"'

सत्त्वं बलं च कालं चाप्यविदित्वात्मनस्तथा ।
अतिवेलमुपाश्नाति तैर्विरुद्धान्यनात्मवान् ॥ (8)

'"'The jivatman knows his spirit, strength and the time. Yet, though this acts against the jivatman, he eats excessively and not what is appropriate for the time.'"'[13]

---

[11]Descendant of the Vrishni lineage, i.e., Krishna.

[12]In a different body, deeds can be perverse.

[13]Food has to be appropriate for age and season. The jivatman knows, but the

यदायमतिकष्टानि सर्वाण्युपनिषेवते ।
अत्यर्थमपि वा भुङ्क्ते न वा भुङ्क्ते कदाचन ॥ (9)

'"'He practises everything that causes greater difficulties for him. He eats too much or does not eat at all.'"'

दुष्टान्नं विषमान्नं च सोऽन्योन्येन विरोधि च ।
गुरु वापि समं भुङ्क्ते नातिजीर्णेऽपि वा पुनः ॥ (10)

'"'He eats rotten food and tainted food and other kinds that are contrary. He eats more food than he should. Or, even if the amount is right, he eats before the earlier food has been digested.'"'

व्यायाममतिमात्रं वा व्यवायं चोपसेवते ।
सततं कर्म लोभाद्वा प्राप्तं वेगविधारणम् ॥ (11)

'"'He indulges in excessive exercise or sexual intercourse. Though his speed has diminished, driven by greed, he always engages in tasks.'"'

रसातियुक्तमन्नं वा दिवा स्वप्नं निषेवते ।
अपक्वानागते काले स्वयं दोषान्प्रकोपयन् ॥ (12)

'"'He eats food that is too juicy. Or he sleeps during the day. Even when the time has not come, these taints cause agitation that are brought on by the person himself.'"'[14]

स्वदोषकोपनाद्रोगं लभते मरणान्तिकम् ।
अथ चोद्बन्धनादीनि परीतानि व्यवस्यति ॥ (13)

'"'Because of one's own sins and rage, there is disease as a person approaches death. Sometimes, one resorts to hanging and other methods.'"'[15]

तस्य तैः कारणैर्जन्तोः शरीराच्च्यवते यथा ।
जीवितं प्रोच्यमानं तद्यथावदुपधारय ॥ (14)

---

body does not act accordingly.
[14] Improper diet leads to imbalance in wind, bile and phlegm and premature death.
[15] To kill oneself.

"'Because of such reasons, the physical body of a creature decays, despite the person being spoken of as alive. Understand this correctly.'"

ऊष्मा प्रकुपितः काये तीव्रवायुसमीरितः ।
शरीरमनुपर्येति सर्वान्प्राणान्‌रुणद्धि वै ॥ (15)

"'When the wind in the body is fierce and begins to blow violently, heat is generated. This reaches all parts of the body and constricts the breath of life.'"

अत्यर्थं बलवानूष्मा शरीरे परिकोपितः ।
भिनत्ति जीवस्थानानि तानि मर्माणि विद्धि च ॥ (16)

"'Know that when the heat in the body becomes excessive, strong and violent, it pierces the inner organs and the place where the breath of life resides.'"

ततः सवेदनः सद्यो जीवः प्रच्यवते क्षरन्‌ ।
शरीरं त्यजते जन्तुश्छिद्यमानेषु मर्मसु ।
वेदनाभिः परीतात्मा तद्विद्धि द्विजसत्तम ॥ (17)

"'In great pain, the physical body of the jivatman instantly melts away. The inner organs are pierced and the creature gives up the physical body. O Excellent Dvija! Know that the jivatman suffers great pain.'"

जातीमरणसंविग्नाः सततं सर्वजन्तवः ।
दृश्यन्ते सन्त्यजन्तश्च शरीराणि द्विजर्षभ ॥ (18)

"'All creatures are always extremely anxious about birth and death. O Bull among Dvijas! They are seen to abandon the physical bodies.'"

गर्भसंक्रमणे चापि मर्मणामतिसर्पणे ।
तादृशीमेव लभते वेदनां मानवः पुनः ॥ (19)

"'A human being experiences a similar kind of pain when he enters a womb or emerges from the inner organs.'"[16]

---

[16] Birth and death, respectively.

भिन्नसंधिरथ क्लेदमद्भि: स लभते नर: ।
यथा पञ्चसु भूतेषु संश्रितत्वं निगच्छति ।
शैत्यात्प्रकुपित: काये तीव्रवायुसमीरित: ॥ (20)

"""A man's joints are shattered and he suffers in the moistness.[17] When the wind in the body is fierce and is agitated, cold is also generated. Then, the body seeks refuge in the five elements."""

य: स पञ्चसु भूतेषु प्राणापाने व्यवस्थित: ।
स गच्छत्यूर्ध्वगो वायु: कृच्छ्रान्मुक्त्वा शरीरिणम् ॥ (21)

"""The five elements are established in prana and apana. This breath of life ascends upwards and, causing hardship, frees itself from the body."""

शरीरं च जहात्येव निरुच्छ्वासश्च दृश्यते ।
निरूष्मा स निरुच्छ्वासो नि:श्रीको गतचेतन: ॥ (22)

"""When it leaves the body, there is no longer any breath of life to be seen. There is no heat. There is no breath. There is no beauty and the consciousness has left."""

ब्रह्मणा संपरित्यक्तो मृत इत्युच्यते नर: ।
स्रोतोभिर्यैर्विजानाति इन्द्रियार्थाञ्शरीरभृत् ।
तैरेव न विजानाति प्राणमाहारसंभवम् ॥ (23)

"""When the brahman[18] abandons the body, a man is said to be dead. There are ducts[19] through which a person with a body perceives the objects of the senses. However, the prana, which is sustained through food, can no longer comprehend them."""

तत्रैव कुरुते काये य: स जीव: सनातन: ।
तेषां यद्भवेद्युक्तं संनिपाते क्वचित्क्वचित् ।
तत्तन्मर्म विजानीहि शास्त्रदृष्टं हि तत्तथा ॥ (24)

---

[17] After the reference to fire comes a reference to the element of water.
[18] The jivatman.
[19] A reference to the senses.

"'The eternal jivatman makes those ducts in the body work. These are sometimes combined together and sometimes they collapse. Know that the sacred texts have stated these to be the inner organs.'"

तेषु मर्मसु भिन्नेषु ततः स समुदीरयन् ।
आविश्य हृदयं जन्तोः सत्त्वं चाशु रुणद्धि वै ।
ततो स चेतनो जन्तुर्नाभिजानाति किंचन ॥ (25)

"'When those inner organs are shattered, the jivatman rises up and enters the heart, thereby swiftly curtailing all spirit. In such a situation, despite being conscious, a creature cannot discern anything.'"

तमसा संवृतज्ञानः संवृतेष्वथ मर्मसु ।
स जीवो निरधिष्ठानश्चाव्यते मातरिश्वना ॥ (26)

"'The inner organs are overwhelmed and jnana is enveloped in darkness. The jivatman no longer has a place to reside and is agitated by the wind.'"

ततः स तं महोच्छ्वासं भृशमुच्छ्वस्य दारुणम् ।
निष्क्रामन्कम्पयत्याशु तच्छरीरमचेतनम् ॥ (27)

"'At such a time, the being sighs deeply and breathes extremely painfully. The jivatman emerges swiftly, causing trembling. The body is bereft of sensation.'"

स जीवः प्रच्युतः कायात्कर्मभिः स्वैः समावृतः ।
अङ्कितः स्वैः शुभैः पुण्यैः पापैर्वाप्युपपद्यते ॥ (28)

"'The jivatman discards the body, but is still enveloped by its own karma. It is marked by all its sacred and auspicious acts and also by all its wicked deeds.'"

ब्राह्मणा ज्ञानसम्पन्ना यथावच्छ्रुतनिश्चयाः ।
इतरं कृतपुण्यं वा तं विजानन्ति लक्षणैः ॥ (29)

"'There are brahmanas who are accomplished in jnana and also possess the determination of the sacred texts. Through the signs, they can discern whether good or bad deeds have been committed.'"

यथान्धकारे खद्योतं लीयमानं ततस्ततः ।
चक्षुष्मन्तः प्रपश्यन्ति तथा तं ज्ञानचक्षुषः ॥ (३०)

"'"Even when it is dark, those with eyes can see fireflies here and there. In that way, those who possess the sight of jnana can see."'"

पश्यन्त्येवंविधाः सिद्धा जीवं दिव्येन चक्षुषा ।
च्यवन्तं जायमानं च योनिं चानुप्रवेशितम् ॥ (३१)

"'"Similarly, siddhas with divine sight can see the act of a creature abandoning the body and being born again, as it enters a womb."'"

तस्य स्थानानि दृष्टानि त्रिविधानीह शास्त्रतः ।
कर्मभूमिरियं भूमिर्यत्र तिष्ठन्ति जन्तवः ॥ (३२)

"'"According to the sacred texts, creatures are seen to occupy three places.[20] There is **karmabhumi**, *this earth, where they can be.*"'"

ततः शुभाशुभं कृत्वा लभन्ते सर्वदेहिनः ।
इहैवोच्चावचान्भोगान्प्राप्नुवन्ति स्वकर्मभिः ॥ (३३)

"'"All those with bodies reap the fruits of their good and bad deeds here. Depending on the karma they have themselves performed in this world, they enjoy the fruits, superior and inferior."'"

इहैवाशुभकर्मा तु कर्मभिर्निरयं गतः ।
अवाक्स् निरये पापो मानवः पच्यते भृशम् ।
तस्मात्सुदुर्लभो मोक्ष आत्मा रक्ष्यो भृशं ततः ॥ (३४)

"'"Those with wicked deeds in this world go to hell because of that karma. A wicked man is severely roasted and cooked in hell. Since it is extremely difficult for the atman to be freed from such a state, one must do one's utmost to protect oneself against this."'"

ऊर्ध्वं तु जन्तवो गत्वा येषु स्थानेष्ववस्थिताः ।
कीर्त्यमानानि तानीह तत्त्वतः सन्निबोध मे ।
तच्छ्रुत्वा नैष्ठिकीं बुद्धिं बुध्येथाः कर्मनिश्चयात् ॥ (३५)

---

[20] This world, the next world and the womb.

"'"There are states obtained by creatures who ascend upwards. I will recount the truth about these. Listen to me. Having heard, you will obtain faith and intelligence. Using that intelligence, you will be able to determine the course of action."'"

तारा रूपाणि सर्वाणि यच्चैतच्चन्द्रमण्डलम् ।
यच्च विभ्राजते लोके स्वभासा सूर्यमण्डलम् ।
स्थानान्येतानि जानीहि नराणां पुण्यकर्मणाम् ॥ (36)

"'"There are stars of many forms along the solar and lunar orbits. There are worlds that illuminate the solar orbit through their own radiance. Know that these places, and others, are meant for men who are performers of auspicious karma."'"

कर्मक्षयाच्च ते सर्वे च्यवन्ते वै पुनः पुनः ।
तत्रापि च विशेषोऽस्ति दिवि नीचोच्चमध्यमः ॥ (37)

"'"However, when that karma has been exhausted, they are repeatedly dislodged from there. Heaven is also special. But even there, the superior, the medium and the inferior exist."'"

न तत्राप्यस्ति सन्तोषो दृष्ट्वा दीप्ततरां श्रियम् ।
इत्येता गतयः सर्वाः पृथक्त्वे समुदीरिताः ॥ (38)

"'"However, there is no contentment even there,[21] whenever one sees prosperity that is more resplendent than one's own. These are all the separate destinations that have been recounted."'"

उपपत्तिं तु गर्भस्य वक्ष्याम्यहमतः परम् ।
यथावत्तां निगदतः शृणुष्वावहितो द्विज ॥ (39)

"'"I will now tell you about conception in the womb. O Dvija! When I recount this accurately, listen attentively."'"

---

[21] In heaven.

Chapter 3

ब्राह्मण उवाच

शुभानामशुभानां च नेह नाशोऽस्ति कर्मणाम् ।
प्राप्य प्राप्य तु पच्यन्ते क्षेत्रं क्षेत्रं तथा तथा ॥ (1)

'"'The brahmana said, *Good and bad karma performed in this world is never destroyed. The fruits are cooked as one moves from one kshetra to another kshetra.*"'[22]

यथा प्रसूयमानस्तु फली दद्यात्फलं बहु ।
तथा स्याद्विपुलं पुण्यं शुद्धेन मनसा कृतम् ॥ (2)

'"'*A high-yielding fruit tree produces large quantities of fruit. In that way, deeds performed with an auspicious and pure mind yield a great deal.*"'

पापं चापि तथैव स्यात्पापेन मनसा कृतम् ।
पुरोधाय मनो हीह कर्मण्यात्मा प्रवर्तते ॥ (3)

'"'*This is also true of wicked deeds perpetrated with an evil mind. In this world, the atman places the mind at the forefront and then undertakes karma.*"'

यथा कर्मसमादिष्टं काममन्युसमावृतः ।
नरो गर्भं प्रविशति तच्चापि शृणु चोत्तरम् ॥ (4)

'"'*After this, listen to how a man enters a womb, when karma is determined, overwhelmed by desire and anger.*"'

शुक्रं शोणितसंसृष्टं स्त्रिया गर्भाशयं गतम् ।
क्षेत्रं कर्मजमाप्नोति शुभं वा यदि वाशुभम् ॥ (5)

'"'*Inside a woman's womb, the kshetra is derived from a mixture of semen and blood and from karma, a function of good and bad acts.*"'

---

[22]Kshetra here stands for the physical body.

सौक्ष्म्यादव्यक्तभावाच्च न स क्वचन सज्जते ।
संप्राप्य ब्रह्मण: कायं तस्मात्तद्ब्रह्म शाश्वतम् ।
तद्बीजं सर्वभूतानां तेन जीवन्ति जन्तव: ॥ (6)

'"'The brahman[23] is subtle and unmanifest in nature. The brahman resorts to the body but is not attached to anything. That is the reason it is the eternal brahman. This is the seed of all beings and it is because of this that all creatures are alive.'"'

स जीव: सर्वगात्राणि गर्भस्याविश्य भागश: ।
दधाति चेतसा सद्य: प्राणस्थानेष्ववस्थित: ।
तत: स्पन्दयतेऽङ्गानि स गर्भश्चेतनान्वित: ॥ (7)

'"'Having entered the womb, the jivatman penetrates all the different limbs in the body. Basing itself on the place meant for the breath of life, it instantly imparts consciousness. The limbs begin to move and the foetus has consciousness.'"'

यथा हि लोहनिष्यन्दो निषिक्तो बिम्बविग्रहम् ।
उपैति तद्वज्जानीहि गर्भे जीवप्रवेशनम् ॥ (8)

'"'When liquid iron is drained and poured into a mould, it assumes the form of an image. Know that this is the way the jivatman approaches and penetrates a foetus.'"'

लोहपिण्डं यथा वह्नि: प्रविशत्यभितापयन् ।
तथा त्वमपि जानीहि गर्भे जीवोपपादनम् ॥ (9)

'"'When fire enters a lump of iron, it heats it up. Know that this is the way the jivatman approaches and penetrates a foetus.'"'

यथा च दीप: शरणं दीप्यमान: प्रकाशयेत् ।
एवमेव शरीराणि प्रकाशयति चेतना ॥ (10)

'"'When one resorts to a lamp, the light illuminates everything. In that way, consciousness illuminates different parts of the body.'"'

---

[23]That is, the jivatman.

यद्यच्च कुरुते कर्म शुभं वा यदि वाशुभम् ।
पूर्वदेहकृतं सर्वमवश्यमुपभुज्यते ॥ (11)

'"Whatever karma has been committed, good or bad, in an earlier body, all of it must certainly be enjoyed."'

ततस्तत्क्षीयते चैव पुनश्चान्यत्प्रचीयते ।
यावत्तन्मोक्षयोगस्थं धर्म नैवाववबुध्यते ॥ (12)

'"These are thus extinguished and others are gathered together again. This continues as long as one does not understand the dharma that leads to moksha yoga."'

तत्र धर्मं प्रवक्ष्यामि सुखी भवति येन वै ।
आवर्तमानो जातीषु तथान्योन्यासु सत्तम ॥ (13)

'"O Excellent One! When one is born and is repeatedly circling around, I will tell you about the dharma that ensures happiness."'

दानं व्रतं ब्रह्मचर्यं यथोक्तव्रतधारणम् ।
दम: प्रशान्तता चैव भूतानां चानुकम्पनम् ॥ (14)
संयमश्चानृशंस्यं च परस्वादानवर्जनम् ।
व्यलीकानामकरणं भूतानां यत्र सा भुवि ॥ (15)
मातापित्रोश्च शुश्रूषा देवतातिथिपूजनम् ।
गुरु पूजा घृणा शौचं नित्यमिन्द्रियसंयम: ॥ (16)
प्रवर्तनं शुभानां च तत्सतां वृत्तमुच्यते ।
ततो धर्म: प्रभवति य: प्रजा: पाति शाश्वती: ॥ (17)

'"Donations, vows, brahmacharya, sustaining the prescribed rites, self-restraint, tranquillity, compassion towards all beings, self-control, lack of injury, not appropriating the possessions of others, uprightness, abstention from futile censure of all creatures on earth, serving the mother and the father, worshipping devas and guests, honouring seniors, tenderness, purity, constant restraint of the senses and ensuring what is auspicious—these are said to be virtuous conduct. Dharma flows from this and protects subjects eternally."'

एवं सत्सु सदा पश्येत्तत्र ह्येषा ध्रुवा स्थितिः ।
आचारो धर्ममाचष्टे यस्मिन्सन्तो व्यवस्थिताः ॥ (18)

"'This conduct is always seen among the virtuous and they obtain a state that is permanent. Conduct in conformity with dharma is said to be that which is resorted to by those who are virtuous.'"

तेषु तद्धर्ममनिक्षिप्तं यः स धर्मः सनातनः ।
यस्तं समभिपद्येत न स दुर्गतिमाप्नुयात् ॥ (19)

"'They are immersed in dharma, and this is the dharma that is eternal. If one resorts to this, one never has to confront extreme hardship.'"

अतो नियम्यते लोकः प्रमुह्य धर्मवर्त्मसु ।
यस्तु योगी च मुक्तश्च स एतेभ्यो विशिष्यते ॥ (20)

"'When the world is deluded, it is through such rules that it is brought back to the path of dharma. Yogis and those who are emancipated are superior to these.'"[24]

वर्तमानस्य धर्मेण पुरुषस्य यथातथा ।
संसारतारणं ह्यस्य कालेन महता भवेत् ॥ (21)

"'If a man follows the appropriate dharma, he is freed from samsara after a long period of time and crosses over.'"

एवं पूर्वकृतं कर्म सर्वो जन्तुर्निषेवते ।
सर्वं तत्कारणं येन निकृतोऽयमिहागतः ॥ (22)

"'In this way, all creatures have to follow the karma they have undertaken earlier. All the wicked deeds are the reason why one has arrived in this world.'"

शरीरग्रहणं चास्य केन पूर्वं प्रकल्पितम् ।
इत्येवं संशयो लोके तच्च वक्ष्याम्यतः परम् ॥ (23)

---

[24]Virtuous people.

"'"Who first determined the acceptance of a body?[25] There is a doubt in the world about this. I will tell you about this next."'"

शरीरमात्मनः कृत्वा सर्वभूतपितामहः ।
त्रैलोक्यमसृजद्ब्रह्मा कृत्स्नं स्थावरजङ्गमम् ॥ (24)

"'"The grandfather of all creatures[26] first created his own body. Brahma then created the three worlds and all the mobile and immobile objects."'"

ततः प्रधानमसृजच्चेतना सा शरीरिणाम् ।
यया सर्वमिदं व्याप्तं यां लोके परमां विदुः ॥ (25)

"'"Having created consciousness in that body, he created Pradhana.[27] A learned person knows this pervades all the worlds and is supreme."'"

इह तत्क्षरमित्युक्तं परं त्वमृतमक्षरम् ।
त्रयाणां मिथुनं सर्वमेकैकस्य पृथक्पृथक् ॥ (26)

"'"This world is said to be kshara. The other one is immortal and Akshara. There are couples formed of these three. They all exist together, but they also exist separately."'"[28]

असृजत्सर्वभूतानि पूर्वसृष्टं प्रजापतिः ।
स्थावराणि च भूतानि इत्येषा पौर्विकी श्रुतिः ॥ (27)

"'"In his first creation, Prajapati created all the creatures and the immobile objects. This is what the sacred texts say about that first creation."'"

---

[25] The adoption of a body is determined by the deeds committed in earlier lives. But what determined the adoption of the first body?
[26] Brahma.
[27] Pradhana has different interpretations in samkhya. For our purposes, Pradhana is the cause of the material world.
[28] Kshara is destructible, Akshara is indestructible. The body is destructible, but the atman is indestructible. The second part of the shloka is difficult to understand. The three possibly mean the physical body, the jivatman and the paramatman. These exist together and also exist separately. One can form different pairs out of these three.

तस्य कालपरीमाणमकरोत्स पितामहः ।
भूतेषु परिवृत्तिं च पुनरावृत्तिमेव च ॥ (28)

"'"Thereafter, the grandfather determined the measurement of time and decreed the going and coming of creatures."'"[29]

यथात्र कश्चिन्मेधावी दृष्टात्मा पूर्वजन्मनि ।
यत्प्रवक्ष्यामि तत्सर्वं यथावदुपपद्यते ॥ (29)

"'"There may be an intelligent person who has seen his atman in his earlier birth. I will accurately tell you everything that such a person experiences here."'"

सुखदुःखे सदा सम्यगनित्ये यः प्रपश्यति ।
कायं चामेध्यसङ्घातं विनाशं कर्मसंहितम् ॥ (30)

"'"Such a person always looks upon happiness and unhappiness as transitory. He regards the body as a vigorous arena for conflicting karma, certain to decay."'"

यच्च किंचित्सुखं तच्च सर्वं दुःखमिति स्मरन् ।
संसारसागरं घोरं तरिष्यति सुदुस्तरम् ॥ (31)

"'"Whenever there is the slightest bit of happiness, he remembers all the unhappiness. Such a person is able to cross this terrible ocean that is samsara and which is so very difficult to traverse."'"

जातीमरणरोगैश्च समाविष्टः प्रधानवित् ।
चेतनावत्सु चौतन्यं समं भूतेषु पश्यति ॥ (32)

"'"Immersed in birth, death and disease, he knows about Pradhana. Basing his consciousness on that universal consciousness, he looks upon all creatures impartially."'"

निर्विद्यते ततः कृत्स्नं मार्गमाणः परं पदम् ।
तस्योपदेशं वक्ष्यामि याथातथ्येन सत्तम ॥ (33)

---

[29]Death and rebirth, respectively, and a lifespan for each species.

"'He is indifferent towards everything and seeks the supreme path and destination. O Excellent One! I will tell you and instruct you about the true nature of that.'"

शाश्वतस्याव्ययस्याथ पदस्य ज्ञानमुत्तमम् ।
प्रोच्यमानं मया विप्र निबोधेदमशेषत: ॥ (34)

"'That is the eternal state, without any decay. That is supreme jnana. O Brahmana! I will tell you about it in detail. Hear about everything.'"

Chapter 4

ब्राह्मण उवाच

य: स्यादेकायने लीनस्तूष्णीं किंचिदचिन्तयन् ।
पूर्वं पूर्वं परित्यज्य स निरारम्भको भवेत् ॥ (1)

"'The brahmana said,[30] A person who silently submerges himself in that receptacle,[31] not thinking about anything, not even thinking about his own identity, progressively casting off the layers, is freed from all bonds.'"[32]

सर्वमित्र: सर्वसह: समरक्तो जितेन्द्रिय: ।
व्यपेतभयमन्युश्च कामहा मुच्यते नर: ॥ (2)

"'He is a friend to everyone. He endures everything. He loves everything equally. He has conquered his senses. He has overcome fear and anger. He has killed desire. Such a man is emancipated.'"

आत्मवत्सर्वभूतेषु यश्चरेन्नियत: शुचि: ।
अमानी निरभीमान: सर्वतो मुक्त एव स: ॥ (3)

---

[30] This is the brahmana who spoke to Kashyapa. It is also the brahmana who spoke to Krishna. As will be evident later, both individuals are the same brahmana.
[31] The brahman.
[32] The shloka is cryptic and some liberties have been taken. The progressive casting away of layers is a reference to the different steps of yoga.

'"He looks towards all beings as he does towards his own self. He roams around, controlled and pure. He is without insolence and without ego. It is as if such a man is emancipated in every way."'

जीवितं मरणं चोभे सुखदुःखे तथैव च ।
लाभालाभे प्रियद्वेष्ये यः समः स च मुच्यते ॥ (4)

'"He is impartial towards both life and death, happiness and unhappiness, gain and loss and the pleasant and the unpleasant. Such a man is emancipated."'

न कस्यचित्स्पृहयते नावजानाति किंचन ।
निर्द्वन्द्वो वीतरागात्मा सर्वतो मुक्त एव सः ॥ (5)

'"He does not desire anyone. He does not show disrespect towards anyone. He is beyond the opposite pairs of sentiments and is devoid of attachment. Such a man is emancipated in every way."'

अनमित्रोऽथ निर्बन्धुरनपत्यश्च यः क्वचित् ।
त्यक्तधर्मार्थकामश्च निराकाङ्क्षी स मुच्यते ॥ (6)

'"He has no enemy. He has no relative. He has no offspring. He has abandoned dharma, artha and kama. He does not hope for anything. Such a person is emancipated."'

नैव धर्मी न चाधर्मी पूर्वोपचितहा च यः ।
धातुक्षयप्रशान्तात्मा निर्द्वन्द्वः स विमुच्यते ॥ (7)

'"He has neither dharma nor adharma. He has cast aside everything accumulated from earlier.[33] When the elements waste away,[34] he is tranquil in his atman. He is without the opposite pairs of sentiments. Such a man is emancipated."'

अकर्मा चाविकाङ्क्षश्च पश्यञ्जगदशाश्वतम् ।
अस्वस्थमवशं नित्यं जन्मसंसारमोहितम् ॥ (8)

---

[33] From earlier births.
[34] The elements in the body.

"'He has no karma. He has no hope and only looks at the eternal universe, which is always submerged helplessly in ill health, delusion, birth and samsara.'"

वैराग्यबुद्धि: सततं तापदोषव्यपेक्षक: ।
आत्मबन्धविनिर्मोक्षं स करोत्यचिरादिव ॥ (9)

"'His intelligence is always focussed on non-attachment. He is indifferent towards any type of torment. In a short while, he is able to free his atman from bonds.'"

अगन्धरसमस्पर्शमशब्दमपरिग्रहम् ।
अरूपमनभिज्ञेयं दृष्ट्वात्मानं विमुच्यते ॥ (10)

"'He sees his own atman, which does not experience smell, taste, touch, sound and ownership and is without form. It is difficult to comprehend. Such a person is emancipated.'"

पञ्चभूतगुणैर्हीनममूर्तिमदलेपकम् ।
अगुणं गुणभोक्तारं य: पश्यति स मुच्यते ॥ (11)

"'It[35] is independent of the five elements. It is without form and without cause. Though it enjoys the gunas, it is devoid of gunas. A person who sees it in this way is emancipated.'"

विहाय सर्वसंकल्पान्बुद्ध्या शारीरमानसान् ।
शनैर्निर्वाणमाप्नोति निरिन्धन इवानल: ॥ (12)

"'He uses his intelligence to cast aside all resolutions of the body and of the mind. Like a fire that is without kindling, such a person gradually obtains nirvana.'"[36]

विमुक्त: सर्वसंस्कारैस्ततो ब्रह्म सनातनम् ।
परमाप्नोति संशान्तमचलं दिव्यमक्षरम् ॥ (13)

---

[35] The atman.
[36] Emancipation, literally, to be extinguished.

"'He is freed from all samskaras[37] and obtains the eternal brahman. He obtains the supreme, which is tranquil and stable. This is the divine Akshara.'"

अतः परं प्रवक्ष्यामि योगशास्त्रमनुत्तमम् ।
यज्ज्ञात्वा सिद्धमात्मानं लोके पश्यन्ति योगिनः ॥ (14)

"'Thereafter, I will tell you about the supreme and sacred texts of yoga. Knowing this, in this world, yogis become siddhas and see their own atmans.'"

तस्योपदेशं पश्यामि यथावत्तन्निबोध मे ।
यैर्द्वारैश्चारयन्नित्यं पश्यत्यात्मानमात्मनि ॥ (15)

"'I will convey the instructions accurately, as I see them. Listen to me. By always following this conduct, one passes through those doors and sees the paramatman within the jivatman.'"[38]

इन्द्रियाणि तु संहृत्य मन आत्मनि धारयेत् ।
तीव्रं तप्त्वा तपः पूर्वं ततो योक्तुमुपक्रमेत् ॥ (16)

"'The senses must be restrained. The mind must be fixed on the atman. Having first tormented oneself through terrible austerities, one must then undertake this yoga.'"

तपस्वी त्यक्तसंकल्पो दम्भाहंकारवर्जितः ।
मनीषी मनसा विप्रः पश्यत्यात्मानमात्मनि ॥ (17)

"'An ascetic abandons all resolution. He is devoid of pride and ahamkara. A learned brahmana uses his mind to see the paramatman within his jivatman.'"

---

[37]There are thirteen samskaras or sacraments. The list varies a bit. But one list comprises *vivaha* (marriage), *garbhalambhana* (conception), *pumshavana* (engendering a male child), *simantonnayana* (parting the hair, performed in the fourth month of pregnancy), *jatakarma* (birth rites), *namakarana* (naming), *chudakarma* (tonsure), *annaprashana* (first solid food), *keshanta* (first shaving of the head), *upanayana* (sacred thread), *vidyarambha* (commencement of studies), *samavartana* (graduation) and *antyeshti* (funeral rites).
[38]Alternatively, sees the atman within one's own self.

स चेच्छक्नोत्ययं साधुर्योक्तुमात्मानमात्मनि ।
तत एकान्तशील: स पश्यत्यात्मानमात्मनि ॥ (18)

"'Such a virtuous person is capable of seeing the paramatman within his jivatman. Devoted to good conduct alone, he sees the paramatman within his jivatman.'"

संयत: सततं युक्त आत्मवान्विजितेन्द्रिय: ।
तथायमात्मनात्मानं साधु युक्त: प्रपश्यति ॥ (19)

"'He is always full of restraint. He is united with his atman. He conquers his senses. Such a virtuous person, engaged in yoga, sees the paramatman within his jivatman.'"

यथा हि पुरुष: स्वप्ने दृष्ट्वा पश्यत्यसाविति ।
तथारूपमिवात्मानं साधु युक्त: प्रपश्यति ॥ (20)

"'In a dream, a man may see someone and, recognizing him on waking up, exclaim, This is he. In that way, a virtuous person engaged in yoga sees the form of the atman.'"[39]

इषीकां वा यथा मुञ्जात्कश्चिन्निर्हृत्य दर्शयेत् ।
योगी निष्कृष्टमात्मानं यथा सम्पश्यते तनौ ॥ (21)

"'When the outer case is extracted from munja grass, the strand inside can be seen. In that way, taking away the body, the yogi sees the atman.'"

मुञ्जं शरीरं तस्याहुरिषीकामात्मनि श्रिताम् ।
एतन्निदर्शनं प्रोक्तं योगविद्भिरनुत्तमम् ॥ (22)

"'The outer case of the munja grass is like the body. The inner strand is the beautiful atman. Those who know about the excellent texts of yoga cite this as an example.'"

यदा हि युक्तमात्मानं सम्यक्पश्यति देहभृत् ।
तदास्य नेशते कश्चित्त्रैलोक्यस्यापि य: प्रभु: ॥ (23)

---

[39] There is a metaphor of a yogi waking up after samadhi.

"'"When a person with a body is united with yoga and sees the atman properly, there is no one who can bring him down. He is like a lord of the three worlds."'"

अन्योन्याश्चैव तनवो यथेष्टं प्रतिपद्यते ।
विनिवृत्य जरामृत्यू न हृष्यति न शोचति ॥ (24)

"'"As he wishes, he moves from one body to another one. Without any joy and without any grief, he withdraws himself from the phenomena of old age and death."'"

देवानामपि देवत्वं युक्त: कारयते वशी ।
ब्रह्म चाव्ययमाप्नोति हित्वा देहमशाश्वतम् ॥ (25)

"'"Such a person, engaged in yoga, can obtain the status of a deva over all devas. Casting aside this temporary body, he obtains the undecaying brahman."'"

विनश्यत्स्वपि लोकेषु न भयं तस्य जायते ।
क्लिश्यमानेषु भूतेषु न स क्लिश्यति केनचित् ॥ (26)

"'"Even if all the worlds are destroyed, no fear is generated in him. Even if all creatures are afflicted, he is not afflicted in the least bit."'"

दु:खशोकमयैर्घोरै: सङ्गस्नेहसमुद्भवै: ।
न विचाल्येत युक्तात्मा निस्पृह: शान्तमानस: ॥ (27)

"'"A person who uses yoga to unite with his atman is without desire and is tranquil in his mind. He is not disturbed by sorrow, misery, fear, terror or the affection that flows from attachment."'"

नैनं शस्त्राणि विध्यन्ते न मृत्युश्चास्य विद्यते ।
नात: सुखतरं किंचिल्लोके क्वचन विद्यते ॥ (28)

"'"Weapons do not pierce him. There is no death for him. There is no one in the world who is happier than him."'"

सम्यग्युक्त्वा यदात्मानमात्मन्येव प्रपश्यति ।
तदैव न स्पृहयते साक्षादपि शतक्रतो: ॥ (29)

"'Having properly engaged himself in yoga, he looks at his atman. Shatakratu[40] himself wishes to be like him.'"

निर्वेदस्तु न गन्तव्यो युञ्जानेन कथंचन ।
योगमेकान्तशीलस्तु यथा युञ्जीत तच्छृणु ॥ (30)

"'If one has engaged in yoga, one obtains a state of indifference and there is nowhere else to go to. This requires single-minded devotion to yoga alone. Listen to how one must embark on yoga.'"

दृष्टपूर्वां दिशं चिन्त्य यस्मिन्संनिवसेत्पुरे ।
पुरस्याभ्यन्तरे तस्य मनश्चार्यं न बाह्यतः ॥ (31)

"'Whichever city one resides in, one must first think of a direction one has seen before.[41] The mind should be fixed inside the city, not outside.'"

पुरस्याभ्यन्तरे तिष्ठन्यस्मिन्नावस्थे वसेत् ।
तस्मिन्नावस्थे धार्यं स बाह्याभ्यन्तरं मनः ॥ (32)

"'Whichever city he resides in, he must faithfully reside within it. In that abode, the mind must be taken away from external and internal distractions and fixed on that habitation.'"

प्रचिन्त्यावसथं कृत्स्नं यस्मिन्काये ऽवतिष्ठते ।
तस्मिन्काये मनश्चार्यं न कथंचन बाह्यतः ॥ (33)

"'All the thoughts must then be withdrawn and fixed on the body one inhabits. The mind must be fixed on the body, never on anything outside it.'"

संनियम्येन्द्रियग्रामं निर्घोषे निर्जने वने ।
कायमभ्यन्तरं कृत्स्नमेकाग्रः परिचिन्तयेत् ॥ (34)

---

[40]Indra.

[41]The city stands for the body. A direction probably refers to the part of the body one is focussing on, such as a *chakra* within the body. Chakras are focal points of energy and, usually, seven are mentioned.

"'"One can control all of one's senses in a silent and desolate forest.[42] One must single-mindedly fix all of one's thoughts inside the body.'"'

दन्तांस्तालु च जिह्वां च गलं ग्रीवां तथैव च ।
हृदयं चिन्तयेच्चापि तथा हृदयबन्धनम् ॥ (35)

"'"One must meditate on the teeth, the palate, the tongue, the throat, the neck, the heart and the arteries and veins inside the heart.'"'

इत्युक्तः स मया शिष्यो मेधावी मधुसूदन ।
पप्रच्छ पुनरेवेमं मोक्षधर्मं सुदुर्वचम् ॥ (36)

"'"O Madhusudana![43] Thus addressed by me, the intelligent disciple again asked me about moksha dharma, which is extremely difficult to explain.'"'

भुक्तं भुक्तं कथमिदमन्नं कोष्ठे विपच्यते ।
कथं रसत्वं व्रजति शोणितं जायते कथम् ।
तथा मांसं च मेदश्च स्नाय्वस्थीनि च पोषति ॥ (37)

"'"How is the food, eaten every once in a while, digested in the stomach? How does it become juices? How is blood generated from that? How does this sustain flesh, marrow, sinews and bones?'"'

कथमेतानि सर्वाणि शरीराणि शरीरिणाम् ।
वर्धन्ते वर्धमानस्य वर्धते च कथं बलम् ।
निरोजसां निष्क्रमणं मलानां च पृथक्पृथक् ॥ (38)

"'"How do all the limbs of embodied creatures grow? As one keeps growing, how does the strength increase? How is waste that is without substance separately excreted?'"'

कुतो वायं प्रश्वसिति उच्छ्वसित्यपि वा पुनः ।
कं च देशमधिष्ठाय तिष्ठत्यात्मायमात्मनि ॥ (39)

---

[42]These shlokas are somewhat terse.
[43]Here, the brahmana talking to Krishna abruptly tells us that he is the same brahmana who had the conversation with Kashyapa. This is where we realize that this brahmana and the siddha brahmana are the same person, though there was nothing to suggest this earlier.

"'From where does one inhale and exhale? Within one's own self, which part of the body is inhabited by the atman?'"

जीव: कायं वहति चेच्चेष्टयान: कलेवरम् ।
किं वर्णं कीदृशं चैव निवेशयति वै मन: ।
याथातथ्येन भगवन्वक्तुमर्हसि मेऽनघ ॥ (40)

"'How does the jivatman exert itself and move the body around? What is the complexion of the mind and where does it dwell? O Illustrious One! O Unblemished One! You should describe this to me accurately.'"

इति संपरिपृष्टोऽहं तेन विप्रेण माधव ।
प्रत्यब्रुवं महाबाहो यथा श्रुतमरिन्दम ॥ (41)

"'O Madhava![44] I was asked this by that brahmana. O Mighty-Armed One! O Scorcher of Enemies! Based on what I had heard, I replied.'"

यथा स्वकोष्ठे प्रक्षिप्य कोष्ठं भाण्डमना भवेत् ।
तथा स्वकाये प्रक्षिप्य मनो द्वारैरनिश्चलै: ।
आत्मानं तत्र मार्गेत प्रमादं परिवर्जयेत् ॥ (42)

"'If one has a vessel full of riches, one places it in a room and uses one's mind to guard it. In that way, the mind should unwaveringly be used to guard against the gates within one's own body. One must fix it on the path that leads to the atman and discard all carelessness.'"

एवं सततमुद्युक्त: प्रीतात्मा नचिरादिव ।
आसादयति तद्ब्रह्म यद्दृष्ट्वा स्यात्प्रधानवित् ॥ (43)

"'If one always exerts in this way, one will soon find delight in the atman. One will see and obtain the brahman and become knowledgeable about Pradhana.'"

न त्वसौ चक्षुषा ग्राह्यो न च सर्वैरपीन्द्रियै: ।
मनसैव प्रदीपेन महानात्मनि दृश्यते ॥ (44)

---

[44] Krishna.

"'It cannot be grasped with the eyes, or with all the other senses. The great atman[45] can be seen with the lamp of the mind.'"

सर्वतःपाणिपादं तं सर्वतोऽक्षिशिरोमुखम् ।
जीवो निष्क्रान्तमात्मानं शरीरात्संप्रपश्यति ॥ (45)

"'His hands and feet are in all the directions. His eyes, head and faces are in all the directions. The creature sees the atman, extracted from the body.'"

स तदुत्सृज्य देहं स्वं धारयन्ब्रह्म केवलम् ।
आत्मानमालोकयति मनसा प्रहसन्निव ॥ (46)

"'Having abandoned the body, he is sustained only by the brahman. As if smiling in delight, he sees the atman with the help of his mind.'"

इदं सर्वरहस्यं ते मयोक्तं द्विजसत्तम ।
आपृच्छे साधयिष्यामि गच्छ शिष्ययथासुखम् ॥ (47)

"'O Supreme among Dvijas![46] I have now told you about all the mysteries. O Disciple! I grant you permission. Cheerfully, go wherever you wish to.'"

इत्युक्तः स तदा कृष्ण मया शिष्यो महातपाः ।
अगच्छत यथाकामं ब्राह्मणश्छिन्नसंशयः ॥ (48)

"'O Krishna! Having been thus addressed, my immensely ascetic disciple, the brahmana, went away as he desired, his doubts having been dispelled.'"

वासुदेव उवाच

इत्युक्त्वा स तदा वाक्यं मां पार्थ द्विजपुंगवः ।
मोक्षधर्माश्रितः सम्यक्तत्रैवान्तरधीयत ॥ (49)

---

[45]Brahman.
[46]There is a minor overlap because the siddha brahmana is speaking to Krishna here. However, later in the shloka, he is repeating what he told Kashyapa.

'Vasudeva said, "O Partha! These are the words the bull among dvijas spoke to me at that time. These were appropriate words for those who wish to resort to moksha dharma. He then disappeared."'

कच्चिदेतत्त्वया पार्थ श्रुतमेकाग्रचेतसा ।
तदापि हि रथस्थस्त्वं श्रुतवानेतदेव हि ॥ (50)

'"O Partha! Have you heard this truth with single-minded attention? This is exactly what you heard when you were on your chariot."'[47]

नैतत्पार्थं सुविज्ञेयं व्यामिश्रेणेति मे मतिः ।
नरेणाकृत संज्ञेन विदग्धेनाकृतात्मना ॥ (51)

'"O Partha! It is my view that a man who is not accomplished in consciousness is not learned and has not cleansed his atman, will be confused about this and will find it extremely difficult to grasp it."'

सुरहस्यमिदं प्रोक्तं देवानां भरतर्षभ ।
कच्चिन्नेदं श्रुतं पार्थ मर्त्येनान्येन केनचित् ॥ (52)

'"O Bull of the Bharata Lineage! This is a great secret even among devas. O Partha! It is rare for any other mortal to have heard it, anywhere."'

न ह्येतच्छ्रोतुमर्होऽन्यो मनुष्यस्त्वामृतेऽनघ ।
नैतद्द्य सुविज्ञेयं व्यामिश्रेणान्तरात्मना ॥ (53)

'"O Unblemished One! No human other than you deserves to hear it. A person whose atman is confused will not be able to comprehend it easily."'

क्रियावद्भिर्हि कौन्तेय देवलोकः समावृतः ।
न चौतदिष्टं देवानां मर्त्यै रूपनिवर्तनम् ॥ (54)

'"O Kounteya! The world of devas is full of those who observe rites. For those who have mortal forms, devas disapprove of withdrawal from sacrifices."'[48]

---

[47] A reference to the Bhagavat Gita.
[48] In such an event, devas will not get their share and humans will also become like devas.

परा हि सा गतिः पार्थ यत्तद्ब्रह्म सनातनम् ।
यत्रामृतत्वं प्राप्नोति त्यक्त्वा दुःखं सदा सुखी ॥ (55)

"'O Partha! The eternal brahman is the supreme destination. One obtains immortality there, abandoning misery. One is always happy.'"

एवं हि धर्ममास्थाय योऽपि स्युः पापयोनयः ।
स्त्रियो वैश्यास्तथा शूद्रास्तेऽपि यान्ति परां गतिम् ॥ (56)
किं पुनर्ब्राह्मणाः पार्थ क्षत्रिया वा बहुश्रुताः ।
स्वधर्मरतयो नित्यं ब्रह्मलोकपरायणाः ॥ (57)

"'O Partha! If they resort to this dharma, those with evil births, women, vaishyas and shudras also go to the supreme destination, not to speak of extremely learned brahmanas and kshatriyas, who are always devoted to their own dharma and to the object of obtaining Brahma's world.'"

हेतुमच्चैतदुद्दिष्टमुपायाश्चास्य साधने ।
सिद्धेः फलं च मोक्षश्च दुःखस्य च विनिर्णयः ।
अतः परं सुखं त्वन्यत्किं नु स्यादभरतर्षभ ॥ (58)

"'This has been indicated in the reasons and means for that pursuit. There are determinations about misery and the successful obtaining of the fruits of moksha. O Bull of the Bharata Lineage! There is no bliss that is superior to this.'"

श्रुतवाञ्श्रद्दधानश्च पराक्रान्तश्च पाण्डव ।
यः परित्यजते मर्त्यो लोकतन्त्रमसारवत् ।
एतैरुपायैः स क्षिप्रं परां गतिमवाप्नुयात् ॥ (59)

"'O Pandava! A man who is learned, faithful and brave, one who abandons the insubstantial practices of the mortal world, can use these means to quickly obtain the supreme destination.'"

एतावदेव वक्तव्यं नातो भूयोऽस्ति किंचन ।
षण्मासान्नित्ययुक्तस्य योगः पार्थ प्रवर्तते ॥ (60)

'"This is all that needs to be said and there is nothing more. O Partha! This becomes evident if one steadily practises yoga for six months."'

Chapter 5

वासुदेव उवाच

अत्राप्युदाहरन्तीममितिहासं पुरातनम् ।
दम्पत्यो: पार्थ संवादमभयं नाम नामत: ॥ (1)

'Vasudeva said, "O Partha! In this connection, an ancient history is recounted, one that is known as the conversation between a couple."'

ब्राह्मणी ब्राह्मणं कंचिज्ज्ञानविज्ञानपारगम् ।
दृष्ट्वा विविक्त आसीनं भार्या भर्तारमब्रवीत् ॥ (2)

'"There was a brahmana who was accomplished in jnana and vijnana. On seeing that he was seated alone, the brahmani, the wife, spoke to her husband."'

कं नु लोकं गमिष्यामि त्वामहं पतिमाश्रिता ।
न्यस्तकर्माणमासीनं कीनाशमविचक्षणम् ॥ (3)

'"'I am devoted to my husband. What world will I go to? You are seated here, having abandoned all rites. You do not discern that I have no hope.'"'

भार्या: पतिकृतांल्लोकानाप्नुवन्तीति न: श्रुतम् ।
त्वामहं पतिमासाद्य कां गमिष्यामि वै गतिम् ॥ (4)

'"'We have heard that a wife goes to the world obtained by her husband. Having got you as a husband, what is the destination I will obtain?'"'

एवमुक्तः स शान्तात्मा तामुवाच हसन्निव ।
सुभगे नाभ्यसूयामि वाक्यस्यास्य तवानघे ॥ (5)

'"The one who was tranquil in his atman was addressed in this way. He smiled and replied, 'O Fortunate One! O Unblemished One! I have not taken umbrage at your words.'"'

ग्राह्यं दृश्यं च श्राव्यं च यदिदं कर्म विद्यते ।
एतदेव व्यवस्यन्ति कर्म कर्मेति कर्मिणः ॥ (6)

'"There is karma that is accepted,[49] seen and heard. Those who are devoted to karma practise this karma and follow this karma.'"'

मोहमेव नियच्छन्ति कर्मणा ज्ञानवर्जिताः ।
नैष्कर्म्यं न च लोकेऽस्मिन्मौर्तमित्युपलभ्यते ॥ (7)

'"Those who are constrained by karma are confused and bereft of jnana. In this mortal world, freedom from karma can never be obtained.'"'

कर्मणा मनसा वाचा शुभं वा यदि वाशुभम् ।
जन्मादिमूर्तिभेदानां कर्म भूतेषु वर्तते ॥ (8)

'"Whatever is committed, good or bad, in deeds, thoughts and speech, leads to differences in birth and form among creatures.'"'

रक्षोभिर्वध्यमानेषु दृश्यद्रव्येषु कर्मसु ।
आत्मस्थमात्मना तेन दृष्टमायतनं मया ॥ (9)

'"Karma is always vested in creatures. Material objects used in rites are seen to be destroyed by rakshasas.[50] Having seen the seat of the atman inside, I have based myself there.'"'

यत्र तद्ब्रह्म निर्द्वन्द्वं यत्र सोमः सहाग्निना ।
व्यवायं कुरुते नित्यं धीरो भूतानि धारयन् ॥ (10)

---

[49] These acts are practised by others.
[50] The material objects are like oblations. There is the nuance that visible rites are destroyed by rakshasas.

'"'The brahman, devoid of opposite sentiments, is there. So are Soma and Agni. Vayu always courses there, sustaining creatures with fortitude.'"'⁵¹

यत्र ब्रह्मादयो युक्तास्तदक्षरमुपासते ।
विद्वांस: सुव्रता यत्र शान्तात्मानो जितेन्द्रिया: ॥ (11)

'"'That is the reason Brahma and the others practise yoga and worship Akshara. This is also sought by those who are learned, excellent in their vows, tranquil in their atmans and in control of their senses.'"'

घ्राणेन न तदाघ्रेयं न तदाद्यं जिह्वया ।
स्पर्शेन च न तत्स्पृश्यं मनसा त्वेव गम्यते ॥ (12)

'"'The nose cannot smell it. The tongue cannot taste it. The organ of touch cannot touch it. It can only be reached through the mind.'"'

चक्षुषा न विषह्यं च यत्किंचिच्छ्रवणात्परम् ।
अगन्धमरसस्पर्शमरूपाशब्दमव्ययम् ॥ (13)

'"'The eye cannot see it. It is beyond any sense of hearing. It is without smell, without taste, without touch, without form and without sound. It is without decay.'"'

यत: प्रवर्तते तन्त्रं यत्र च प्रतितिष्ठति ।
प्राणोऽपान: समानश्च व्यानश्चोदान एव च ॥ (14)

'"'Everything flows from it and everything is established in it—prana, apana, samana, vyana and udana.'"'

तत एव प्रवर्तन्ते तमेव प्रविशन्ति च ।
समानव्यानयोर्मध्ये प्राणापानौ विचेरतु: ॥ (15)

---

⁵¹There is a yoga-oriented interpretation of this. The seat of the atman is between the eyebrows. Soma is *ida*, Agni is *pingala* and the seat of the brahman is where ida and pingala meet. Ida is the channel of energy on the left of the body, pingala is to the right. *Sushumna* is the channel of energy in the centre.

"'They flow from it and merge into it again. Prana and apana course around between samana and vyana.'"

तस्मिन्सुप्ते प्रलीयेते समानो व्यान एव च ।
अपानप्राणयोर्मध्ये उदानो व्याप्य तिष्ठति ।
तस्माच्छयानं पुरुषं प्राणापानौ न मुञ्चतः ॥ (16)

"'When one sleeps, samana and vyana remain absorbed. Udana remains pervaded in the space between apana and prana. Thus, even when a man sleeps, prana and apana do not abandon him.'"

प्राणानायम्यते येन तदुदानं प्रचक्षते ।
तस्मात्तपो व्यवस्यन्ति तद्भवं ब्रह्मवादिनः ॥ (17)

"'The one which controls all the breaths of life is known as udana. Therefore, those who know about the brahman and resort to austerities try to control it.'"

तेषामन्योन्यभक्षाणां सर्वेषां देहचारिणाम् ।
अग्निर्वैश्वानरो मध्ये सप्तधा विहितोऽन्तरा ॥ (18)

"'For those who roam around in bodies, all these different breaths of life seek to devour each other. The fire known as Vaishvanara[52] courses in the space between them and it has seven flames.'"

घ्राणं जिह्वा च चक्षुश्च त्वक्च श्रोत्रं च पञ्चमम् ।
मनो बुद्धिश्च सप्तैता जिह्वा वैश्वानरार्चिषः ॥ (19)

"'The nose, the tongue, the eyes, the skin, the ears as the fifth, the mind and intelligence as the seventh—these are the seven tongues and flames of Vaishvanara.'"

घ्रेयं पेयं च दृश्यं च स्पृश्यं श्रव्यं तथैव च ।
मन्तव्यमथ बोद्धव्यं ताः सप्त समिधो मम ॥ (20)

"'That which is smelt, that which is drunk, that which is touched, that which is heard, that which is thought and that which is understood—for me, these are the seven kinds of kindling.'"

---

[52] An image for the jivatman.

घ्राता भक्षयिता द्रष्टा स्प्रष्टा श्रोता च पञ्चमः ।
मन्ता बोद्धा च सप्तैते भवन्ति परमर्त्विजः ॥ (21)

"'"The one who smells, the one who eats, the one who sees, the one who touches, the one who hears as the fifth, the one who thinks and the one who understands—these are the seven supreme officiating priests."'"[53]

घ्रेये पेये च देश्ये च स्पृश्ये श्रव्ये तथैव च ।
हवींष्यग्निषु होतारः सप्तधा सप्त सप्तसु ।
सम्यक्प्रक्षिप्य विद्वांसो जनयन्ति स्वयोनिषु ॥ (22)

"'"In smelling, drinking, seeing, touching and hearing, there are seven kinds of oblations, seven kinds of fires and seven kinds of officiating priests. Learned ones who know about the respective wombs from which these are generated offer the oblations properly."'"

पृथिवी वायुराकाशमापो ज्योतिश्च पञ्चमम् ।
मनो बुद्धिश्च सप्तैत योनिरित्येव शब्दिताः ॥ (23)

"'"The earth, the wind, space, water, light as the fifth, the mind and intelligence—these are said to be the seven wombs."'"

हविर्भूता गुणाः सर्वे प्रविशन्त्यग्निजं मुखम् ।
अन्तर्वासमुषित्वा च जायन्ते स्वासु योनिषु ।
तत्रैव च निरुध्यन्ते प्रलये भूतभावने ॥ (24)

"'"All the qualities in the oblations enter into the mouth of what results from the fire. Having spent time inside, they are again reborn in their respective wombs. They are the origin of creatures.[54] However, at the time of dissolution, they remain restrained."'"

ततः संजायते गन्धस्ततः संजायते रसः ।
ततः संजायते रूपं ततः स्पर्शोऽभिजायते ॥ (25)

---

[53] The divinities presiding over these.
[54] The seven wombs.

'"'Smell is born from that.⁵⁵ Taste is born from that. Form is born from that. Touch is born from that.'"'

तत: संजायते शब्द: संशयस्तत्र जायते ।
तत: संजायते निष्ठा जन्मैतत्सप्तधा विदु: ॥ (26)

'"'Sound is born from that. Doubt is born from that. Faith is born from that. The learned know that these are the seven kinds of birth.'"'

अनेनैव प्रकारेण प्रगृहीतं पुरातनै: ।
पूर्णाहुतिभिरापूर्णास्तेऽभिपूर्यन्ति तेजसा ॥ (27)

'"'These were the methods that were grasped by the ancient ones. The complete offering of oblations makes them full and also fills them with energy.'"'

Chapter 6

ब्राह्मण उवाच

अत्राप्युदाहरन्तीममितिहासं पुरातनम् ।
निबोध दशहोतॄणां विधानमिह यादृशम् ॥ (1)

'"The brahmana said, 'In this connection, there is an ancient history. Listen to what the ordinances for the ten hotris are like.'"⁵⁶

सर्वमेवात्र विज्ञेयं चित्तं ज्ञानमवेक्षते ।
रेत: शरीरभृत्काये विज्ञाता तु शरीरभृत् ॥ (2)

'"'Know everything about this. Reflect on the consciousness with the tool of jnana. Know that all those who bear bodies sustain their bodily forms with the aid of semen.'"'

---

⁵⁵At the time of creation.
⁵⁶The CE excises some shlokas here. The missing shlokas tell us that the ten chief priests are ears, eyes, tongue, nose, feet, hands, the genital organs and the anus. If ears and eyes are counted in the singular but feet and hands in the plural, this gives a total of ten.

शरीरभृद्गार्हपत्यस्तस्मादन्य: प्रणीयते ।
ततश्चाहवनीयस्तु तस्मिन्सङ्क्षिप्यते हवि: ॥ (3)

'"'The garhapatya fire is said to be the one who sustains an entity who bears a body. The ahavaniya fire is the one into which oblations are offered.'"'[57]

ततो वाचस्पतिर्जज्ञे समान: पर्यवेक्षते ।
रूपं भवति वै व्यक्तं तदनुद्रवते मन: ॥ (4)

'"'The lord of speech originated from that and when he glanced towards measurement, form manifested itself from that and began to follow the mind.'"'

ब्राह्मण्युवाच

कस्माद्वागभवत्पूर्वं कस्मात्पश्चान्मनोऽभवत् ।
मनसा चिन्तितं वाक्यं यदा समभिपद्यते ॥ (5)

'"'The brahmani asked, 'How did the word originate first and why was the mind created afterwards? Words are seen to be pronounced after they have been thought of by the mind.'"'

केन विज्ञानयोगेन मतिश्चित्तं समास्थिता ।
समुन्नीता नाध्यगच्छत्को वैनां प्रतिषेधति ॥ (6)

'"'Through what vijnana and what yoga can one say that intelligence is based on consciousness? When it is raised up, why is it incapable of following? What restrains it?'"'[58]

ब्राह्मण उवाच

तामपान: पतिर्भूत्वा तस्मात्प्रेष्यत्यपानताम् ।
तां मतिं मनस: प्राहुर्मनस्तस्मादवेक्षते ॥ (7)

---

[57]These expressions are metaphors.
[58]This is cryptic and requires explanation. When one is asleep, the mind does not seem to exist. But the breath of life still continues to be raised. If it is distinct from the mind, why can it not be used to sense things? What restrains it?

"'The brahmana replied, 'Apana is the lord. Therefore, it is the one that despatches everything. It is said to control the mind and the mind controls intelligence.'"

प्रश्नं तुवाङ्मनसोर्मा यस्मात्त्वमनुपृच्छसि ।
तस्मात्ते वर्तयिष्यामि तयोरेव समाह्वयम् ॥ (8)

"'"However, you have asked me a question about the word and the mind. Therefore, I will recount to you a rivalry that took place between them.'"

उभे वान्मनसी गत्वा भूतात्मानमपृच्छताम् ।
आवयो: श्रेष्ठमाचक्ष्व छिन्धि नौ संशयं विभो ॥ (9)

"'"Both word and mind went to the jivatman of a being and asked a question. *O Lord! Dispel a doubt that exists in our minds. Which among us is superior? Tell us.*'"

मन इत्येव भगवांस्तदा प्राह सरस्वतीम् ।
अहं वै कामधुक्तुभ्यमिति तं प्राह वागथ ॥ (10)

"'"The illustrious one told Sarasvati,[59] *The mind is superior*. However, word responded, *I am the one who leads to the accomplishment of your desires.*'"

स्थावरं जङ्गमं चैव विद्ध्युभे मनसी मम ।
स्थावरं मत्सकाशे वै जङ्गमं विषये तव ॥ (11)

"'"*Know that I have two kinds of minds, mobile and immobile.*[60] *The immobile is with me and the mobile is your dominion.*'"

यस्तु ते विषयं गच्छेन्मन्त्रो वर्ण: स्वरोऽपि वा ।
तन्मनो जङ्गमं नाम तस्मादसि गरीयसी ॥ (12)

"'"*That in your dominion depends on mantras, vowels and sound. Therefore, the mind that is immobile is superior.*'"[61]

---

[59]The goddess of speech, equated with the word
[60]The brahmana is repeating the jivatman's response.
[61]This is extremely cryptic and requires interpretation. The immobile mind is

यस्मादसि च मा वोच: स्वयमभ्येत्य शोभने ।
तस्मादुच्छ्वासमासाद्य न वक्ष्यसि सरस्वति ॥ (13)

"'"O Beautiful One!⁶² However, you came to me of your own accord and spoke to me. O Sarasvati! Therefore, I will not pronounce your name."'"⁶³

प्राणापानान्तरे देवी वाग्वै नित्यं स्म तिष्ठति ।
प्रेर्यमाणा महाभागे विना प्राणमपानती ।
प्रजापतिमुपाधावत्प्रसीद भगवन्निति ॥ (14)

"'"O Goddess! You are always based in speech, in the space between prana and apana. O Immensely Fortunate One! However, in prana's absence, you rushed towards Prajapati and asked the illustrious one to show his favours and rescue you."'"

तत: प्राण: प्रादुर्भूद्वाचमाप्याययन्मुन: ।
तमादुच्छ्वासमासाद्य न वाग्वदति कर्हिचित् ॥ (15)

"'"At this, prana manifested itself and the word appeared again. That is the reason why, when there is inhalation alone, no words can ever be pronounced."'"

घोषिणी जातनिर्घोषा नित्यमेव प्रवर्तते ।
तयोरपि च घोषिण्योर्निर्घोषैव गरीयसी ॥ (16)

"'"Letters⁶⁴ are always either aspirated or unaspirated. Among these two, the unaspirated ones are superior to the aspirated ones."'"

गौरिव प्रस्रवत्येषा रसमुत्तमशालिनी ।
सततं स्यन्दते ह्येषा शाश्वतं ब्रह्मवादिनी ॥ (17)

"'"O One Who Speaks about the Eternal Brahman! You are always excellent, like a cow that yields a large quantity of milk."'"

---

internal. The mobile mind means the external world, which is subject to perception by the senses. This mobile mind is inferior to the immobile mind.
⁶²This is being addressed to the goddess of speech.
⁶³Sarasvati's name will not be articulated.
⁶⁴Of the alphabet.

दिव्यादिव्यप्रभावेन भारती गौ: शुचिस्मिते ।
एतयोरन्तरं पश्य सूक्ष्मयो: स्यन्दमानयो: ॥ (18)

"'"O Bharati![65] O One with a Beautiful Smile! You are like a cow. You are both divine and not divine in your powers.[66] Behold the subtle difference between these two.'"

अनुत्पन्नेषु वाक्येषु चोद्यमाना सिसृक्षया ।
किं नु पूर्वं ततो देवी व्याजहार सरस्वती ॥ (19)

"'"Earlier, when she wished to speak, but words did not come out, what did the goddess Sarasvati say?"'"[67]

प्राणेन या संभवते शरीरे प्राणादपानं प्रतिपद्यते च ।
उदानभूता च विसृज्य देहं व्यानेन सर्वं दिवमावृणोति ॥ (20)

"'"The body results from prana. Apana follows from prana. It then becomes udana and is released from the body. It then envelopes all the directions with vyana."'"[68]

तत: समाने प्रतितिष्ठतीह इत्येव पूर्वं प्रजजल्प चापि ।
तस्मान्मन: स्थावरत्वाद्विशिष्टं तथा देवी जङ्गमत्वाद्विशिष्टा ॥ (21)

"'"After that, it remains established in samana. This has been stated earlier. Thus, the immobile mind is superior. And the goddess is superior to the mobile mind."'"

Chapter 7

ब्राह्मण उवाच

अत्राप्युदाहरन्तीममितिहासं पुरातनम् ।
सुभगे सप्त होतृणां विधानमिह यादृशम् ॥ (1)

---

[65] Sarasvati.
[66] This probably means speech that is divine and speech that is human.
[67] The brahmani asks this.
[68] The brahmana responds to the brahmani's question.

'"The brahmana said, 'O Extremely Fortunate One! In this connection, there is an ancient history about the ordinances for the seven hotris.'"'

घ्राणं चक्षुश्च जिह्वा च त्वक्श्रोत्रं चैव पञ्चमम् ।
मनो बुद्धिश्च सप्तैते होतार: पृथगाश्रिता: ॥ (2)

'"The nose, the eyes, the tongue, the skin, the ears as the fifth, the mind and intelligence—these are the seven separate hotris.'"'

सूक्ष्मेऽवकाशे सन्तस्ते न पश्यन्तीतरेतरम् ।
एतान्वै सप्त होतृंस्त्वं स्वभावाद्विद्धि शोभने ॥ (3)

'"These exist in the subtle intervening space and do not perceive each other. O Beautiful One! Given this, know the natures of the seven hotris.'"'

ब्राह्मणी उवाच

सूक्ष्मेऽवकाशे सन्तस्ते कथं नान्योन्यदर्शिन: ।
कथं स्वभावा भगवन्नेतदाचक्ष्व मे विभो ॥ (4)

'"The brahmani asked, 'When they exist in the subtle intervening space, why can't they see each other? O Illustrious One! O Lord! What is their nature? Please tell me.'"'

ब्राह्मण उवाच

गुणाज्ञानमविज्ञानं गुणिज्ञानमभिज्ञता ।
परस्परगुणानेते न विजानन्ति कर्हिचित् ॥ (5)

'"The brahmana replied, 'Not knowing about the qualities is the absence of jnana. Knowing about the qualities is said to be jnana. They can never know each other's qualities.'"'

जिह्वा चक्षुस्तथा श्रोत्रं त्वङ्मनो बुद्धिरेव च ।
न गन्धानधिगच्छन्ति घ्राणस्तानधिगच्छति ॥ (6)

'"The tongue, the eyes, the ears, the skin and intelligence do not experience smell. It is the nose alone that can experience it.'"'

घ्राणं चक्षुस्तथा श्रोत्रं त्वङ्मनो बुद्धिरेव च ।
न रसानधिगच्छन्ति जिह्वा तानदिगच्छति ॥ (7)

'"'The nose, the eyes, the ears, the skin and intelligence do not experience taste. It is the tongue alone that can experience it.'"'

घ्राणं जिह्वा तथा श्रोत्रं त्वङ्मनो बुद्धिरेव च ।
न रूपाण्यधिगच्छन्ति चक्षुस्तान्यधिगच्छति ॥ (8)

'"'The nose, the tongue, the ears, the skin and intelligence cannot experience form. It is the eyes alone that can experience it.'"'

घ्राणं जिह्वा च चक्षुश्च श्रोत्रं बुद्धिर्मनस्तथा ।
न स्पर्शानधिगच्छन्ति त्वक्च तानधिगच्छति ॥ (9)

'"'The nose, the tongue, the eyes, the ears, intelligence and the mind cannot experience touch. It is the skin alone that can experience it.'"'

घ्राणं जिह्वा च चक्षुश्च त्वङ्मनो बुद्धिरेव च ।
न शब्दानधिगच्छन्ति श्रोत्रं तानधिगच्छति ॥ (10)

'"'The nose, the tongue, the ears, the skin and intelligence cannot experience sound. It is the ears alone that can experience it.'"'

घ्राणं जिह्वा च चक्षुश्च त्वक्श्रोत्रं बुद्धिरेव च ।
संशयान्नाधिगच्छन्ति मनस्तानधिगच्छति ॥ (11)

'"'The nose, the tongue, the eyes, the skin, the ears and intelligence cannot experience doubt. It is the mind alone that can experience it.'"'

घ्राणं जिह्वा च चक्षुश्च त्वक्श्रोत्रं मन एव च ।
न निष्ठामधिगच्छन्ति बुद्धिस्तामधिगच्छति ॥ (12)

'"'The nose, the tongue, the eyes, the skin, the ears and the mind cannot experience devotion. It is intelligence alone that can experience it.'"'

अत्राप्युदाहरन्तीममितिहासं पुरातनम् ।
इन्द्रियाणां च संवादं मनसश्चैव भामिनि ॥ (13)

"''O Beautiful One! In this connection, there is an ancient history about a conversation between the senses and the mind.'''"

मन उवाच

न जिघ्राति मामृते घ्राणं रसं जिह्वा न बुध्यते ।
रूपं चक्षुर्न गृह्णाति त्वक्स्पर्शं नावबुध्यते ॥ (14)

"''The mind said, *Without me, the nose cannot smell and the tongue does not comprehend taste. The eyes cannot grasp form and the skin does not comprehend touch.*'''"

न श्रोत्रं बुध्यते शब्दं मया हीनं कथंचन ।
प्रवरं सर्वभूतानामहमस्मि सनातनम् ॥ (15)

"''*In my absence, the ears can never comprehend sound. I am supreme and eternal among all the elements.*'''"

अगाराणीव शून्यानि शान्तार्चिष इवाग्नयः ।
इन्द्रियाणि न भासन्ते मया हीनानि नित्यशः ॥ (16)

"''*In my absence, the senses can never illuminate. They are like an empty house where the flames of the sacrificial fire have been doused.*'''"

काष्ठानीवार्द्रशुष्काणि यतमानैरपीन्द्रियैः ।
गुणार्थान्नाधिगच्छन्ति मामृते सर्वजन्तवः ॥ (17)

"''*In my absence, all the creatures cannot understand the purport of the gunas. Even when they try, the senses are like fuelwood that is wet and is not dry.*'''"

इन्द्रियाण्यूचुः

एवमेतद्भवेत्सत्यं यथैतन्मन्यते भवान् ।
ऋतेऽस्मानस्मदर्थांस्तु भोगान्भुङ्क्ते भवान्यदि ॥ (18)

"''The senses responded, *What you think is not true. Without us or our objects, you cannot enjoy any objects of pleasure.*'''"

यद्यस्मासु प्रलीनेषु तर्पणं प्राणधारणम् ।
भोगान्भुङ्क्ते रसान्भुङ्क्ते यथैतन्मन्यते तथा ॥ (19)

"'You think that when we are destroyed, you will be content, able to sustain life, able to enjoy objects of pleasure and able to taste.'"

अथ वास्मासु लीनेषु तिष्ठत्सु विषयेषु च ।
यदि संकल्पमात्रेण भुङ्क्ते भोगान्यथार्थवत् ॥ (20)

"'You think that when we are destroyed, your resolution alone will enable you to remain in those objects and enjoy the objects of pleasure, as they should be enjoyed.'"

अथ चेन्मन्यसे सिद्धिमस्मदर्थेषु नित्यदा ।
घ्राणेन रूपमादत्स्व रसमादत्स्व चक्षुषा ॥ (21)
श्रोत्रेण गन्धमादत्स्व निष्ठामादत्स्व जिह्वया ।
त्वचा च शब्दमादत्स्व बुद्ध्या स्पर्शमथापि च ॥ (22)

"'You think that you will be successful in enjoying the objects of the senses as you always have, perhaps form through the nose, taste through the eyes, smell through the ears, faith through the tongue, sound through the skin and touch through intelligence.'"

बलवन्तो ह्यनियमा नियमा दुर्बलीयसाम् ।
भोगान्पूर्वानादत्स्व नोच्छिष्टं भोक्तुमर्हसि ॥ (23)

"'Those who are strong do not follow any rules. Rules are for the weak. Do not experience what you have enjoyed earlier. You should experience what you have not enjoyed earlier.'"[69]

यथा हि शिष्यः शास्तारं श्रुत्यर्थमभिधावति ।
ततः श्रुतमुपादाय श्रुतार्थमुपतिष्ठति ॥ (24)

"'To understand the meaning of the sacred texts, a disciple rushes to an instructor. Even after having obtained the sacred texts, he serves the teacher to understand the meaning of the sacred texts.'"

---

[69] Since you are strong, break the rules and experience touch through intelligence and so on.

विषयानेवमस्माभिर्दर्शितानभिमन्यसे ।
अनागतानतीतांश्च स्वप्ने जागरणे तथा ॥ (25)

"'"You think that we have not shown you what exists in the objects, whether it is in sleep or when in a state of waking, whether it is in the past or in the future."'"

वैमनस्यं गतानां च जन्तूनामल्पचेतसाम् ।
अस्मदर्थे कृते कार्ये दृश्यते प्राणधारणम् ॥ (26)

"'"There are creatures who are limited in intelligence and who, therefore, seem to have lost their minds. However, it is seen that for sustaining their lives, it is we who discharge their tasks for them."'"

बहूनपि हि संकल्पान्मत्वा स्वप्नानुपास्य च ।
बुभुक्षया पीड्यमानो विषयानेव धावसि ॥ (27)

"'"There are many kinds of resolutions that are formed in dreams. However, when afflicted by hunger, one runs after material objects."'"[70]

अगारमद्वारमिव प्रविश्य संकल्पभोगो विषयानविन्दन् ।
प्राणक्षये शान्तिमुपैति नित्यं दारुक्षयेऽग्निर्ज्वलितो यथैव ॥ (28)

"'"If one avoids material objects and seeks to enjoy resolutions alone, that is like entering a house without any doors. In that case, one always obtains the peace that comes from the extinguishing of life, like a blazing fire when all the wood has been exhausted."'"

कामं तु नः स्वेषु गुणेषु सङ्गः कामं च नान्योन्यगुणोपलब्धिः ।
अस्मानृते नास्ति तवोपलब्धिस्त्वामप्यृतेऽस्मान् भजेत हर्षः ॥ (29)

"'"We desire to be attached to our own respective qualities. We do not desire to be attached to the qualities of another sense. But nothing is experienced without us. Without us, you will not experience any delight."'"

---

[70]Resolutions and dreams fail to satisfy cravings. That requires the senses.

Chapter 8

ब्राह्मण उवाच

अत्राप्युदाहरन्तीममितिहासं पुरातनम् ।
सुभगे पञ्चहोतॄणां विधानमिह यादृशम् ॥ (1)

'"The brahmana said, 'O Extremely Fortunate One! In this connection, there is an ancient history about the ordinances followed by the five hotris.'"'

प्राणापानावुदानश्च समानो व्यान एव च ।
पञ्चहोतॄनथैतान्वै परं भावं विदुर्बुधाः ॥ (2)

'"Those who are learned about the supreme know that the five hotris are prana, apana, udana, samana and vyana.'"'

ब्राह्मण्युवाच

स्वभावात्सप्त होतार इति ते पूर्विका मतिः ।
यथा वै पञ्च होतारः परो भावस्तथोच्यताम् ॥ (3)

'"The brahmani said, 'Earlier, it was my view that there are seven natural hotris. But tell me about the supreme belief, whereby there are five hotris.'"'

ब्राह्मण उवाच

प्राणेन संभृतो वायुरपानो जायते ततः ।
अपाने संभृतो वायुस्ततो व्यानः प्रवर्तते ॥ (4)

'"The brahmana replied, 'The breath of life is nurtured by prana, and apana originates from that. The breath of life is nurtured by apana and makes this vyana flow.'"'

व्यानेन संभृतो वायुस्तदोदानः प्रवर्तते ।
उदाने संभृतो वायुः समानः संप्रवर्तते ॥ (5)

'"The breath of life is nurtured by vyana and makes udana flow. The breath of life is nurtured by udana and makes samana flow.'"'

तेऽपृच्छन्त पुरा गत्वा पूर्वजातं प्रजापतिम् ।
यो नो ज्येष्ठस्तमाचक्ष्व स नः श्रेष्ठो भविष्यति ॥ (6)

"'In earlier times, they went to Prajapati, who was born first, and asked, *Please tell us who is the eldest among us. He is the one who will be the foremost among us.*'"

ब्रह्मोवाच

यस्मिन्प्रलीने प्रलयं व्रजन्ति सर्वे प्राणाः प्राणभृतां शरीरे ।
यस्मिन्प्रचीर्णे च पुनश्चरन्ति स वै श्रेष्ठो गच्छत यत्र कामः ॥ (7)

"'Brahma responded, *In all creatures that have bodies and sustain life, there is a breath of life. When that is destroyed, the creature is destroyed. When it is revived, the creature moves again. That is the best among you. Now go wherever you wish.*'"

प्राण उवाच

मयि प्रलीने प्रलयं व्रजन्ति सर्वे प्राणाः प्राणभृतां शरीरे ।
मयि प्रचीर्णे च पुनश्चरन्ति श्रेष्ठो ह्यहं पश्यत मां प्रलीनम् ॥ (8)

"'Prana said, *When I am destroyed, the creature who has a body and sustains life also heads towards destruction. When I am revived, the creature moves again. Therefore, among all the breaths, I am foremost. Behold my destruction.*'"

ब्राह्मण उवाच

प्राणः प्रलीयत ततः पुनश्च प्रचचार ह ।
समानश्चाप्युदानश्च वचोऽब्रूतां ततः शुभे ॥ (9)

"'The brahmana continued, 'Prana was destroyed. But the creature continued to move. O Auspicious One! At this, samana and udana spoke these words.'"

न त्वं सर्वमिदं व्याप्य तिष्ठसीह यथा वयम् ।
न त्वं श्रेष्ठोऽसि नः प्राण अपानो हि वशे तव ।
प्रचचार पुनः प्राणस्तमपानोऽभ्यभाषत ॥ (10)

""'You do not pervade everything. You are not established like us. O Prana! You are not the foremost. Apana alone is under your control. Prana began to move around again and apana spoke.'""

मयि प्रलीने प्रलयं व्रजन्ति सर्वे प्राणाः प्राणभृतां शरीरे ।
मयि प्रचीर्णे च पुनश्चरन्ति श्रेष्ठो ह्यहं पश्यत मां प्रलीनम् ॥ (11)

""'When I am destroyed, the creature who has a body and sustains life also heads towards destruction. When I am revived, the creature moves again. Therefore, among all the breaths, I am foremost. Behold my destruction.'""

व्यानश्च तमुदानश्च भाषमाणमथोचतुः ।
अपान न त्वं श्रेष्ठोऽसि प्राणो हि वशगस्तव ॥ (12)

""'Vyana and udana spoke these words: *O Apana! You are not the foremost. Only prana is under your control.*'""

अपानः प्रचचाराथ व्यानस्तं पुनरब्रवीत् ।
श्रेष्ठोऽहमस्मि सर्वेषां श्रूयतां येन हेतुना ॥ (13)

""'Apana began to move again and vyana now said, *I am the foremost among all of us. Listen to the reason.*'""

मयि प्रलीने प्रलयं व्रजन्ति सर्वे प्राणाः प्राणभृतां शरीरे ।
मयि प्रचीर्णे च पुनश्चरन्ति श्रेष्ठो ह्यहं पश्यत मां प्रलीनम् ॥ (14)

""'When I am destroyed, the creature who has a body and sustains life also heads towards destruction. When I am revived, the creature moves again. Therefore, among all the breaths, I am foremost. Behold my destruction.'""

प्रालीयत ततो व्यानः पुनश्च प्रचचार ह ।
प्राणापानावुदानश्च समानश् च तमब्रुवन् ।
न त्वं श्रेष्ठोऽसि नो व्यान समानो हि वशे तव ॥ (15)

""'Vyana was destroyed. But the creature continued to move. Prana, apana, udana and samana said, *O Vyana! You are not the foremost. Samana alone is under your control.*'""

प्रचचार पुनर्व्यान: समान: पुनरब्रवीत् ।
श्रेष्ठोऽहमस्मि सर्वेषां श्रूयतां येन हेतुना ॥ (16)

'"Vyana began to move again, and samana said, *I am the foremost among all of us. Listen to the reason.*"'

मयि प्रलीने प्रलयं व्रजन्ति सर्वे प्राणा: प्राणभृतां शरीरे ।
मयि प्रचीर्णे च पुनश्चरन्ति श्रेष्ठो ह्यहं पश्यत मां प्रलीनम् ॥ (17)

'"When I am destroyed, the creature who has a body and sustains life also heads towards destruction. When I am revived, the creature moves again. Therefore, among all the breaths, I am foremost. Behold my destruction.*"'

तत: समान: प्रालिल्ये पुनश्च प्रचचार ह ।
प्राणापानावुदानश्च व्यानश्चैव तमब्रूवन् ।
समानन त्वं श्रेष्ठोऽसि व्यान एव वशे तव ॥ (18)

'"Samana was destroyed. But the creature continued to move. At this, prana, apana, udana and vyana said, *O Samana! You are not the foremost. Vyana alone is under your control.*"'

समान: प्रचचाराथ उदानस्तमुवाच ह ।
श्रेष्ठोऽहमस्मि सर्वेषां श्रूयतां येन हेतुना ॥ (19)

'"Samana began to move again and udana said, *I am the foremost among all of us. Listen to the reason.*"'

मयि प्रलीने प्रलयं व्रजन्ति सर्वे प्राणा: प्राणभृतां शरीरे ।
मयि प्रचीर्णे च पुनश्चरन्ति श्रेष्ठो ह्यहं पश्यत मां प्रलीनम् ॥ (20)

'"When I am destroyed, the creature who has a body and sustains life also heads towards destruction. When I am revived, the creature moves again. Therefore, among all the breaths, I am foremost. Behold my destruction.*"'

तत: प्रालीयतोदान: पुनश्च प्रचचार ह ।
प्राणापानौ समानश्च व्यानश्चैव तमब्रूवन् ।
उदान न त्वं श्रेष्ठोऽसि व्यान एव वशे तव ॥ (21)

"'"Udana was destroyed. But the creature continued to move. Prana, apana, samana and vyana said, *O Udana! You are not the foremost. Vyana alone is under your control.*"'"

ततस्तानब्रवीद्ब्रह्मा समवेतान्प्रजापतिः ।
सर्वे श्रेष्ठा न वा श्रेष्ठाः सर्वे चान्योन्यधर्मिणः ।
सर्वे स्वविषये श्रेष्ठाः सर्वे चान्योन्य रक्षिणः ॥ (22)

"'"At this, Brahma Prajapati spoke to the assembled ones: *All of you are foremost. Yet, not a single one is foremost. All of you follow different kinds of dharma. All of you are foremost in your own area. All of you are protected by each other.*"'"

एकः स्थिरश्चास्थिरश्च विशेषात्पञ्च वायवः ।
एक एव ममैवात्मा बहुधाप्युपचीयते ॥ (23)

"'"There are five special breaths of life. They are both mobile and immobile. My atman is one, but is experienced in many different forms.'"'"

परस्परस्य सुहृदो भावयन्तः परस्परम् ।
स्वस्ति व्रजत भद्रं वो धारयध्वं परस्परम् ॥ (24)

"'"*Be affectionate towards each other and make each other prosper. O Fortunate Ones! Depart in peace. Sustain each other.*"'"

Chapter 9

ब्राह्मण उवाच

अत्राप्युदाहरन्तीममितिहासं पुरातनम् ।
नारदस्य च संवादमृषेर्देवमतस्य च ॥ (1)

"'The brahmana said, 'In this connection, an ancient history is recounted, about a conversation between Narada and Rishi Devamata.'"'

देवमत उवाच

जन्तो: संजायमानस्य किं नु पूर्वं प्रवर्तते ।
प्राणोऽपान: समानो वा व्यानो वोदान एव च ॥ (2)

"'Devamata asked, *When a creature is born, which comes first—prana, apana, samana, vyana or udana?*'"

नारद उवाच

येनायं सृज्यते जन्तुस्ततोऽन्य: पूर्वमेति तम् ।
प्राणद्वन्द्वं च विज्ञेयं तिर्यगं चोर्ध्वगं च यत् ॥ (3)

"'Narada replied, *When a being is created, it is the other one that comes first.*[71] *Know that the breath of life has two components—one that moves diagonally and one that moves upwards.*'"

देवमत उवाच

केनायं सृज्यते जन्तु: कश्चान्य: पूर्वमेति तम् ।
प्राणद्वन्द्वं च मे ब्रूहि तिर्यगूर्ध्वं च निश्चयात् ॥ (4)

"'Devamata asked, *When a being is created, who creates the other one that comes first? Who determines the two breaths of life, one that moves diagonally and one that moves upwards? Please tell me clearly.*'"

नारद उवाच

संकल्पाज्जायते हर्ष: शब्दादपि च जायते ।
रसात्संजायते चापि रूपादपि च जायते ॥ (5)

"'Narada replied, *Delight is generated from resolution. It is also generated from sound. It is also generated from taste. It is also generated from form.*'"

स्पर्शात्संजायते चापि गन्धादपि च जायते ।
एतद्रूपमुदानस्य हर्षो मिथुन संभव: ॥ (6)

---

[71]This probably means that the breath of life comes before the physical body.

"'It is also generated from touch. It is also generated from smell. These are the forms that result from udana. Delight results from physical intercourse.'"

कामात्संजायते शुक्रं कामात्संजायते रसः ।
समानव्यानजनिते सामान्ये शुक्रशोणिते ॥ (7)

"'Semen results from desire. Juices flow from desire.[72] Generally, the mixture of semen and blood results from the union of samana and vyana.'"

शुक्राच्छोणितसंसृष्टात्पूर्वं प्राणः प्रवर्तते ।
प्राणेन विकृते शुक्रे ततोऽपानः प्रवर्तते ॥ (8)

"'When semen and blood are mixed, the first outcome is that of prana flowing. When the semen is transformed by prana, apana results.'"

प्राणापानाविदं द्वन्द्वमवाक्चोर्ध्वं च गच्छतः ।
व्यानः समानश्चैवोभौ तिर्यग्द्वंद्वत्वमुच्यते ॥ (9)

"'The pair of prana and apana are said to move upwards. The pair of vyana and samana are said to move diagonally.'"

अग्निर्वै देवताः सर्वा इति वेदस्य शासनम् ।
संजायते ब्राह्मणेषु ज्ञानं बुद्धिसमन्वितम् ॥ (10)

"'Agni represents all devas. This is the instruction of the Vedas. This knowledge generates jnana in brahmanas and confers them with intelligence.'"

तस्य धूमस्तमोरूपं रजो भस्म सुरेतसः ।
सत्त्वं संजायते तस्य यत्र प्रक्षिप्यते हविः ॥ (11)

"'Smoke is its terrible tamas form, the potent ashes represent rajas. Sattva is generated from it when oblations are offered into it.'"

---

[72] This is a reference to the menstrual flow.

आधारौ समानो व्यानश्च इति यज्ञविदो विदुः ।
प्राणापानावाज्यभागौ तयोर्मध्ये हुताशनः ।
एतद्रूपमुदानस्य परमं ब्राह्मणा विदुः ॥ (12)

"'Those who are learned and knowledgeable about sacrifices say that samana and vyana form the foundation. Prana and apana are the offerings of clarified butter and the fire is between them. Brahmanas know that this is the supreme form of udana.'"

निर्द्वंद्वमिति यत्त्वेतत्तन्मे निगदतः शृणु ॥ (13)

"'I will also tell you about the pairs and what is separate from them. Listen attentively.'"[73]

अहोरात्रमिदं द्वंद्वं तयोर्मध्ये हुताशनः ।
एतद्रूपमुदानस्य परमं ब्राह्मणा विदुः ॥ (14)

"'Day and night are a pair and the fire is between them. Brahmanas know that this is the supreme form of udana.'"

उभे चैवायने द्वंद्वं तयोर्मध्ये हुताशनः ।
एतद्रूपमुदानस्य परमं ब्राह्मणा विदुः ॥ (15)

"'The two ayanas[74] constitute a pair and the fire is between them. Brahmanas know that this is the supreme form of udana.'"

उभे सत्यानृते द्वंद्वं तयोर्मध्ये हुताशनः ।
एतद्रूपमुदानस्य परमं ब्राह्मणा विदुः ॥ (16)

"'Truth and falsehood constitute a pair and the fire is between them. Brahmanas know that this is the supreme form of udana.'"

उभे शुभाशुभे द्वंद्वं तयोर्मध्ये हुताशनः ।
एतद्रूपमुदानस्य परमं ब्राह्मणा विदुः ॥ (17)

---

[73]For emancipation. The idea is to transcend these pairs.
[74]*Uttarayana* and *dakshinayana*. Uttarayana is the northern movement of the sun, from winter solstice to summer solstice. Dakshinayana is the southern movement, from summer solstice to winter solstice.

'"Good and bad constitute a pair and the fire is between them. Brahmanas know that this is the supreme form of udana."'

सच्चासच्चैव तद्द्वन्द्वं तयोर्मध्ये हुताशनः ।
एतद्रूपमुदानस्य परमं ब्राह्मणा विदुः ॥ (18)

'"Existence and non-existence constitute a pair and the fire is between them. Brahmanas know that this is the supreme form of udana."'

प्रथमं समानो व्यानो व्यस्यते कर्म तेन तत् ।
तृतीयं तु समानेन पुनरेव व्यवस्यते ॥ (19)

'"Samana comes first and the pervasive vyana undertakes its task. The third is the pervasive samana, which acts next."'[75]

शान्त्यर्थं वामदेवं च शान्तिर्ब्रह्म सनातनम् ।
एतद्रूपमुदानस्य परमं ब्राह्मणा विदुः ॥ (20)

'"Vamadeva is for the sake of tranquillity. Tranquillity is the eternal brahman. Brahmanas know that this is the supreme form of udana."'

Chapter 10

ब्राह्मण उवाच

अत्राप्युदाहरन्तीममितिहासं पुरातनम् ।
चातुर्होत्र विधानस्य विधानमिह यादृशम् ॥ (1)

'"The brahmana said, 'In this connection, there is an ancient history about the ordinances for *chaturhotra*,[76] explaining why the rites are like that.'"

---

[75]*Savana* is the act of drinking soma juice and drinking it thrice a day. These shlokas are difficult to understand and are interpreted as a reference to the three savanas. The reference to samana means the first savana, while the reference to vyana means the second savana. The reference to Vamadeva, in the next shloka, is a reference to a mantra chanted in the course of the third savana.
[76]Sacrifice with four officiating priests.

तस्य सर्वस्य विधिवद्विधानमुपदेक्ष्यते ।
शृणु मे गदतो भद्रे रहस्यमिदमुत्तमम् ॥ (2)

"'All those ordinances and rites are now being recounted to you. O Fortunate One! I will tell you. Listen to this supreme mystery.'"

करणं कर्म कर्ता च मोक्ष इत्येव भामिनि ।
चत्वार एते होतारो यैरिदं जगदावृतम् ॥ (3)

"'O Beautiful One! The agent, the action, the instrument and emancipation—these are the four hotris that envelope the universe.'"

होतॄणां साधनं चैव शृणु सर्वमशेषत: ।
घ्राणं जिह्वा च चक्षुश्च त्वक्व श्रोत्रं च पञ्चमम् ।
मनो बुद्धिश्च सप्तैते विज्ञेया गुणहेतव: ॥ (4)

"'Listen to the means that are used by all these hotris. The nose, the tongue, the eyes, the skin, the ears as the fifth, the mind and intelligence—these seven are used by the agent to perceive qualities.'"

गन्धो रसश्च रूपं च शब्द: स्पर्शश्च पञ्चम: ।
मन्तव्यमथ बोद्धव्यं सप्तैते कर्महेतव: ॥ (5)

"'Smell, taste, form, sound, touch as the fifth, what is thought and what is understood—these seven are the causes behind action.'"

घ्राता भक्षयिता द्रष्टा स्प्रष्टा श्रोता च पञ्चम: ।
मन्ता बोद्धा च सप्तैते विज्ञेया: कर्तृहेतव: ॥ (6)

"'The one who smells, the one who eats, the one who sees, the one who touches, the one who hears as the fifth, the one who thinks and the one who understands—these seven are known as the causes behind the agent.'"

स्वगुणं भक्षयन्त्येते गुणवन्त: शुभाशुभम् ।
अहं च निर्गुणोऽत्रेति सप्तैते मोक्षहेतव: ॥ (7)

'"'They possess qualities, good or bad, and consume their own respective qualities. A person who knows himself to be beyond the seven and devoid of qualities has reason for emancipation.'"'

विदुषां बुध्यमानानां स्वं स्वस्थानं यथाविधि ।
गुणास्ते देवताभूताः सततं भुञ्जते हविः ॥ (8)

'"'Learned ones understand that these qualities occupy their respective places. They are like forms of devas and always enjoy the oblations.'"'

अदन्द्यविद्वानन्नानि ममत्वेनोपपद्यते ।
आत्मार्थं पाचयन्नित्यं ममत्वेनोपहन्यते ॥ (9)

'"'An ignorant person eats and develops a sense of ownership.[77] Such a person only cooks for himself and is always destroyed by this sense of ownership.'"'

अभक्ष्यभक्षणं चैव मद्यपानं च हन्ति तम् ।
स चान्नं हन्ति तच्चान्नं स हत्वा हन्यते बुधः ॥ (10)

'"'He eats what he should not eat and he is also destroyed by the drinking of liquor. He destroys the food he has eaten. Having destroyed the food, he also destroys his sense of knowledge.'"'

अत्ता ह्यन्नमिदं विद्वान्पुनर्जनयतीश्वरः ।
स चान्नाज्जायते तस्मिन्सूक्ष्मो नाम व्यतिक्रमः ॥ (11)

'"'However, a learned lord eats the food and destroys it, generating it again. Because of the food he has eaten, there is not the slightest bit of transgression in him.'"'[78]

मनसा गम्यते यच्च यच्च वाचा निरुध्यते ।
श्रोत्रेण श्रूयते यच्च चक्षुषा यच्च दृश्यते ॥ (12)
स्पर्शेन स्पृश्यते यच्च घ्राणेन घ्रायते च यत् ।
मनःषष्ठानि संयम्य हवींष्येतानि सर्वशः ॥ (13)

---

[77] The senses consume, not the atman. Learned ones know the difference between the senses and the atman.
[78] Even if he has destroyed living beings in the process.

"'"What is thought by the mind, what is spoken in words, what is heard by the ears, what is seen by the eyes, what is touched by the skin, what is smelt by the ears—all these six are like oblations and must be controlled by the mind."'"

गुणवत्पावको मह्यं दीप्यते हव्यवाहनः ।
योगयज्ञः प्रवृत्तो मे ज्ञानब्रह्ममनोद्भवः ।
प्राणस्तोत्रोऽपानशस्त्रः सर्वत्यागसुदक्षिणः ॥ (14)

"'"These qualities must be offered to the blazing fire that rages inside the body.[79] This is the sacrifice of yoga that I am engaged in. This jnana about the brahman emanates from the mind. Prana is the hymn for that sacrifice and apana is the weapon that is used. Renouncing everything is the excellent dakshina."'"

कर्मानुमन्ता ब्रह्मा मे कर्ताध्वर्युः कृतस्तुतिः ।
कृतप्रशास्ता तच्छास्त्रमपवर्गोऽस्य दक्षिणा ॥ (15)

"'"The action and ahamkara are both adhvaryus, with which I praise the beloved brahman. I praise him with the rules of the sacred texts and offer dakshina."'"

ऋचश्चाप्यत्र शंसन्ति नारायणविदो जनाः ।
नारायणाय देवाय यदबध्नन्पशूनुरा ॥ (16)

"'"Those who know about Narayana praise him with a hymn from the Rig Veda—*In ancient times, animals were slaughtered in the name of the divinity Narayana.*"'"

तत्र सामानि गायन्ति तानि चाहुर्निदर्शनम् ।
देवं नारायणं भीरु सर्वात्मानं निबोध मे ॥ (17)

"'"Hymns chanted from the Sama Veda are also cited as an example. O Timid One! Listen to me. The god Narayana is the atman of everything."'"

---

[79] The atman is being compared to a fire.

Chapter 11

ब्राह्मण उवाच

एक: शास्ता न द्वितीयोऽस्ति शास्ता यथा नियुक्तोऽस्मि तथा चरामि ।
हृद्येष तिष्ठन्पुरुष: शास्ति शास्ता तेनैव युक्त: प्रवणादिवोदकम् ॥ (1)

'"The brahmana said, 'There is one ruler. There is no second ruler. Wherever I am engaged, that is where I roam around. The ruler is the being who is lodged in the heart and he rules from there. I am moved by him, like water down a slope.'"

एको गुरुर्नास्ति ततो द्वितीयो यो हृच्छयस्तमहमनुब्रवीमि ।
तेनानुशिष्टा गुरुणा सदैव पराभूता दानवा: सर्व एव ॥ (2)

'"There is one guru. There is no second one. He is in the heart and I will speak about him. I am always instructed by that guru and all the danavas are defeated because of that.'"

एको बन्धुर्नास्ति ततो द्वितीयो यो हृच्छयस्तमहमनुब्रवीमि ।
तेनानुशिष्टा बान्धवा बन्धुमन्त: सप्तर्षय: सप्त दिवि प्रभान्ति ॥ (3)

'"There is one relative. There is no second one. He is in the heart and I will speak about him. It is because of his instructions that relatives behave like relatives and the saptarshis blaze in the seven firmaments.'"

एक: श्रोता नास्ति ततो द्वितीयो यो हृच्छयस्तमहमनुब्रवीमि ।
तस्मिन्गुरौ गुरुवासं निरुष्य शक्रो गत: सर्वलोकामरत्वम् ॥ (4)

'"There is one person who hears. There is no second one. He is in the heart and I will speak about him. Having resided with that guru in the guru's house, Shakra obtained immortality in all the worlds.'"

एको द्रष्टा नास्ति ततो द्वितीयो यो हृच्छयस्तमहमनुब्रवीमि ।
तेनानुशिष्टा गुरुणा सदैव लोकदृष्टा: पन्नगा: सर्व एव ॥ (5)

"'"There is one enemy. There is no second one. Having always been instructed by that guru, the pannagas[80] are hated by all the worlds."'"

अत्राप्युदाहरन्तीममितिहासं पुरातनम् ।
प्रजापतौ पन्नगानां देवर्षीणां च संविदम् ॥ (6)

"'"In this connection, an ancient history is recounted about what Prajapati told the pannagas, devas and rishis."'"

देवर्षयश्च नागाश्च असुराश्च प्रजापतिम् ।
पर्यपृच्छन्नुपासीना: श्रेयो न: प्रोच्यताम् इति ॥ (7)

"'"Approaching Prajapati, the devas, rishis, nagas and asuras asked, What is best for us? Please tell us."'"

तेषां प्रोवाच भगवाञ्श्रेय: समनुपृच्छताम् ।
ओमित्येकाक्षरं ब्रह्म ते श्रुत्वा प्राद्रवन्दिश: ॥ (8)

"'"Asked about their welfare, the illustrious Brahma only uttered the akshara of *OUM*. Hearing this, they fled in different directions."'"

तेषां प्राद्रवमाणानामुपदेशार्थमात्मन: ।
सर्पाणां दशने भाव: प्रवृत्त: पूर्वमेव तु ॥ (9)

"'"Having received what was meant to be an instruction to their own selves, they fled. The attribute of an inclination to bite first emerged among snakes."'"

असुराणां प्रवृत्तस्तु दम्भभाव: स्वभावज: ।
दानं देवा व्यवसिता दममेव महर्षय: ॥ (10)

"'"Asuras developed natural insolence in their conduct. Devas were engaged in giving and maharshis in self-control."'"

एकं शास्तारमासाद्य शब्देनैकेन संस्कृता: ।
नाना व्यवसिता: सर्वे सर्पदेवर्षिदानवा: ॥ (11)

---

[80]Serpents, uraga and naga are synonyms for pannaga.

'"They received the single refined word from the same instructor. However, all the snakes, devas, rishis and danavas followed different pursuits."'

शृणोत्ययं प्रोच्यमानं गृह्णाति च यथातथम् ।
पृच्छतस्तावतो भूयो गुरुरन्योऽनुमन्यते ॥ (12)

'"One hears what is spoken only when one receives it in the proper way. This is true even if one asks again. No other guru can be thought of."'[81]

तस्य चानुमते कर्म तत: पश्चात्प्रवर्तते ।
गुरुर्बोद्धा च शत्रुश्च द्वेष्टा च हृदि संश्रित: ॥ (13)

'"An act is thought of first. It is undertaken subsequently. The guru, the one who understands, the enemy and the one who hates are all lodged inside the heart."'

पापेन विचरँल्लोके पापचारी भवत्ययम् ।
शुभेन विचरँल्लोके शुभचारी भवत्युत ॥ (14)

'"By undertaking wicked acts in the world, one becomes an evil-doer. By undertaking good acts in the world, one becomes a doer of good deeds."'

कामचारी तु कामेन य इन्द्रियसुखे रत: ।
व्रतचारी सदैवैष य इन्द्रियजये रत: ॥ (15)

'"If a person is addicted to the pleasure that comes from gratifying the senses, he is driven by desire and his conduct follows desire. A person who follows vows is always engaged in conquering the senses."'

अपेतव्रतकर्मा तु केवलं ब्रह्मणि श्रित: ।
ब्रह्मभूतश्चरँल्लोके ब्रह्म चारी भवत्ययम् ॥ (16)

---

[81] In understanding a preceptor's words, the true preceptor is one's own self.

"'"There may be a person who abandons all vows and deeds and bases himself on the brahman alone. Immersing himself in the brahman, he roams around in this world and becomes a brahmachari."'"

ब्रह्मैव समिधस्तस्य ब्रह्माग्निर्ब्रह्मसंस्तर: ।
आपो ब्रह्म गुरुर्ब्रह्म स ब्रह्मणि समाहित: ॥ (17)

"'"The brahman is the kindling. The brahman is the fire. The brahman is the origin. The brahman is the water. The brahman is the guru. He is submerged in the brahman."'"

एतदेतादृशं सूक्ष्मं ब्रह्मचर्यं विदुर्बुधा: ।
विदित्वा चान्वपद्यन्त क्षेत्रज्ञेनानुदर्शिन: ॥ (18)

"'"This is the subtle nature of brahmacharya, understood by those who are learned. Having understood it and being instructed by kshetrajna,[82] they follow this."'"

Chapter 12

ब्राह्मण उवाच

संकल्पदंशमशकं शोकहर्षहिमातपम् ।
मोहान्धकारतिमिरं लोभव्याल सरीसृपम् ॥ (1)
विषयैकात्ययाध्वानं कामक्रोधविरोधकम् ।
तदतीत्य महादुर्गं प्रविष्टोऽस्मि महद्वनम् ॥ (2)

"'The brahmana said, 'I have entered this great forest, having crossed the terrain that is extremely difficult to traverse.[83] It has grief, joy, cold and heat, and resolutions are like gnats and mosquitoes. It is enveloped in the blinding darkness of confusion, and greed is like predators and reptiles. Possessions are hardships and desire and anger are obstructions along the road.'"

---

[82]Meaning, either their own jivatmanas or the paramatman.
[83]The brahman is being compared to a great forest and the material world to the terrain.

ब्राह्मण्युवाच

क्व तद्वनं महाप्राज्ञ के वृक्षाः सरितश्च काः ।
गिरयः पर्वताश्चैव कियत्यध्वनि तद्वनम् ॥ (3)

'"The brahmani asked, 'O Immensely Wise One! Where is that forest? What are its trees and rivers? What are its hills and mountains? How far away is the forest?'"

न तदस्ति पृथग्भावे किं चिदन्यत्ततः समम् ।
न तदस्त्यपृथग्भावे किंचिद्दूरतरं ततः ॥ (4)

'"The brahmana replied, 'There is nothing that is distinct from it. There is nothing that is equal to it. Since there is nothing that is distinct from it, there is nothing further than it.'"

तस्मादह्रस्वतरं नास्ति न ततोऽस्ति बृहत्तरम् ।
नास्ति तस्माद्दुःखतरं नास्त्यन्यत्तत्समं सुखम् ॥ (5)

'""There is nothing smaller than it. There is nothing larger than it. There is nothing that is more miserable than it. There is nothing that is its equal in happiness.'"

न तत्प्रविश्य शोचन्ति न प्रहृष्यन्ति च द्विजाः ।
न च बिभ्यति केषांचित्तेभ्यो बिभ्यति के च न ॥ (6)

'""Once dvijas enter it, they no longer have any reason to grieve or rejoice. They are not frightened of anyone, nor does anyone have reason to be frightened of them.'"

तस्मिन्वने सप्त महाद्रुमाश्च फलानि सप्तातिथयश्च सप्त ।
सप्ताश्रमाः सप्त समाधयश्च दीक्षाश्च सप्तैतदरण्यरूपम् ॥ (7)

'""There are seven large trees in that forest, seven fruits, seven guests, seven hermitages, seven kinds of meditation and seven different types of initiation.[84] Such is the nature of that forest.'"

---

[84] The seven trees are the five senses, the mind and intelligence. The seven fruits are what are experienced by these, the seven guests being the qualities that lead to this experience. These seven guests seek recourse with the seven trees, which

पञ्चवर्णानि दिव्यानि पुष्पाणि च फलानि च ।
सृजन्त: पादपास्तत्र व्याप्य तिष्ठन्ति तद्वनम् ॥ (8)

"'"The trees that exist in that forest and pervade it yield divine flowers and fruits of five colours."'"[85]

सुवर्णानि द्विवर्णानि पुष्पाणि च फलानि च ।
सृजन्त: पादपास्तत्र व्याप्य तिष्ठन्ति तद्वनम् ॥ (9)

"'"The trees that exist in that forest and pervade it yield golden flowers and fruits of two colours."'"

चतुर्वर्णानि दिव्यानि पुष्पाणि च फलानि च ।
सृजन्त: पादपास्तत्र व्याप्य तिष्ठन्ति तद्वनम् ॥ (10)

"'"The trees that exist in that forest and pervade it yield divine flowers and fruits of four colours."'"

शंकराणित्रि वर्णानि पुष्पाणि च फलानि च ।
सृजन्त: पादपास्तत्र व्याप्य तिष्ठन्ति तद्वनम् ॥ (11)

"'"The trees that exist in that forest and pervade it yield divine flowers and fruits of three colours and mixed colours."'"

सुरभीण्येकवर्णानि पुष्पाणि च फलानिच ।
सृजन्त: पादपास्तत्र व्याप्य तिष्ठन्ति तद्वनम् ॥ (12)

"'"The trees that exist in that forest and pervade it are fragrant and yield flowers and fruits of a single colour."'"

बहून्यव्यक्तवर्णानि पुष्पाणि च फलानि च ।
विसृजन्तौ महावृक्षौ तद्वनं व्याप्य तिष्ठत: ॥ (13)

---

are thus also like seven hermitages. The seven kinds of meditation and initiation are meant to progressively extinguish the seven trees.

[85]The imagery is not easy to understand. The trees are the *tanmatra*s (subtle elements) and lead to the five qualities of sound, touch, form, taste and smell. In samkhya, they progressively originate from one another and are also progressively dissolved.

"'"The large trees that exist in that forest and pervade it yield flowers and fruits that have many colours and those with colours not manifest."'"[86]

एको ह्यग्नि: सुमना ब्राह्मणोऽत्र पञ्चेन्द्रियाणि समिधश्चात्र सन्ति ।
तेभ्यो मोक्ष: सप्त भवन्ति दीक्षा गुणा: फलान्यतिथय: फलाशा: ॥ (14)

"'"For a brahmana with an excellent mind, there is a single fire there.[87] The five senses are the kindling. For the sake of moksha, there are seven kinds of initiation. The qualities are the fruits and the guests survive on those fruits."'"

आतिथ्यं प्रतिगृह्णन्ति तत्र सप्त महर्षय: ।
अर्चितेषु प्रलीनेषु तेष्वन्यद्रोचते वनम् ॥ (15)

"'"The seven maharshis accept the hospitality there. When they have been honoured and disappear,[88] another beautiful forest manifests itself."'"

प्रतिज्ञावृक्षमफलं शान्तिच्छायासमन्वितम् ।
ज्ञानाश्रयं तृप्तितोयमन्त:क्षेत्रज्ञभास्करम् ॥ (16)

"'"Resolution is the tree and tranquillity is the fruit, full of shade. Jnana is the refuge and contentment is the water. Beyond this, the kshetrajna is the sun."'"

येऽधिगच्छन्ति तत्सन्तस्तेषां नास्ति भयं पुन: ।
ऊर्ध्वं चावाक्च तिर्यक्च तस्य नान्तोऽधिगम्यते ॥ (17)

"'"Virtuous ones who go there never have to suffer from fear again. Whether upwards, diagonally or downwards, the extremities[89] cannot be discerned."'"

---

[86]The colours refer to the five senses, those without colours refer to the mind and the intelligence.
[87]The jivatman.
[88]When the five senses, the mind and the intelligence have been absorbed into the jivatman.
[89]Of the tree.

सप्त स्त्रियस्तत्र वसन्ति सद्यो अवाङ्मुखा भानुमत्यो जनित्र्य: ।
ऊर्ध्वं रसानां ददते प्रजाभ्य: सर्वान्यथा सर्वमनित्यतां च ॥ (18)

'"Seven women always dwell there. Their visages face downwards and they are radiant mothers. From above, they provide juices to the subjects. In every other way, they are all transient."'[90]

तत्रैव प्रतितिष्ठन्ति पुनस्तत्रोदयन्ति च ।
सप्त सप्तर्षय: सिद्धा वसिष्ठप्रमुखा: सह ॥ (19)

'"The seven siddha saptarshis, with Vasishtha as the foremost, are established there and repeatedly emerge from there."'[91]

यशो वर्चो भगश्चैव विजय: सिद्धितेजसी ।
एवमेवानुवर्तन्ते सप्त ज्योतींषि भास्करम् ॥ (20)

'"Fame, radiance, greatness, victory, success and energy—these always follow them, who are like the seven radiant rays of the sun."'

गिरय: पर्वताश्चैव सन्ति तत्र समासत: ।
नद्यश्च सरितो वारिवहन्त्यो ब्रह्मसंभवम् ॥ (21)

'"Collected together, there are hills and mountains there. There are rivers and streams that bear water, all originating with the brahman."'

नदीनां संगमस्तत्र वैतान: समुपह्वरे ।
स्वात्मतृप्ता यतो यान्ति साक्षाद्दान्ता: पितामहम् ॥ (22)

'"There is a sacred sacrificial ground[92] at the confluence of the rivers. There, those who are content in their own atmans advance towards the grandfather[93] himself."'

---

[90]These seven are the five tanmatras, mahat and ahamkara; they are all transient. They face downwards, towards the material world, and not upwards, towards emancipation.
[91]From the brahman. The saptarshis are a metaphor for the five senses, the mind and intelligence.
[92]Inside the heart.
[93]Brahma.

कृशाशा: सुव्रताशाश्च तपसा दग्धकिल्बिषा: ।
आत्मन्यात्मानमावेश्य ब्रह्माणं समुपासते ॥ (23)

'"'Their desires have been extinguished. They are excellent in their vows. They have burnt their sins through austerities. They enter the atman in their own selves and worship the brahman.'"'

ऋचमप्यत्र शंसन्ति विद्यारण्यविदो जना: ।
तदरण्यमभिप्रेत्य यथा धीरमजायत ॥ (24)

'"'People who know about that forest of knowledge praise it with hymns from the Rig Veda. For those who desire that forest, patience is generated.'"'

एतदेतादृशं दिव्यमरण्यं ब्राह्मणा विदु: ।
विदित्वा चान्वतिष्ठन्त क्षेत्रज्ञेनानुदर्शितम् ॥ (25)

'"'Learned brahmanas instruct us about that divine forest in this way. Having obtained the knowledge, they follow the instructions of the kshetrajna.'"'

Chapter 13

ब्राह्मण उवाच

गन्धान्न जिघ्रामि रसान्न वेद्मि रूपं न पश्यामि न च स्पृशामि ।
न चापि शब्दान्विविधाञ्श्रृणोमि न चापि संकल्पमुपैमि किंचित् ॥ (1)

'"The brahmana said, 'I do not smell scents. I do not know taste. I do not see form. I do not touch. I do not hear different kinds of sound. I do not entertain the slightest bit of resolution.'"'

अर्थानिष्टान्कामयते स्वभाव: सर्वान्द्वेष्यान्प्रद्विषते स्वभाव: ।
कामद्वेषावुद्भवत: स्वभावात्प्राणापानौ जन्तु देहान्निवेश्य ॥ (2)

'"'It is nature that desires agreeable objects. It is nature that dislikes disagreeable objects. Like prana and apana when they enter the bodies of living creatures, it is nature that experiences desire and hatred.'"'

तेभ्यश्चान्यांस्तेष्वनित्यांश्च भावान्भूतात्मानं लक्षयेयं शरीरे ।
तस्मिंस्तिष्ठन्नासि शक्य: कर्थंचित्कामक्रोधाभ्यां जरया मृत्युना च ॥ (3)

"""There is another sentiment that is permanent. The atman in creatures cannot be discerned through the body. When I am based there,[94] how am I capable of being distracted by desire, anger, old age and death?""

अकामयानस्य च सर्वकामानविद्विषाणस्य च सर्वदोषान् ।
न मे स्वभावेषु भवन्ति लेपास्तोयस्य बिन्दोरिव पुष्करेषु ॥ (4)

"""I do not desire any of the objects of desire. I do not hate all the sins. There is no taint in my nature, like a drop of water is not left on lotuses.""

नित्यस्य चैतस्य भवन्ति नित्या निरीक्षमाणस्य बहून्स्वभावान् ।
न सज्जते कर्मसु भोगजालं दिवीव सूर्यस्य मयूखजालम् ॥ (5)

"""The eternal, with transient attributes, glances at these many kinds of nature. The net of enjoyment is no longer attached to deeds, just as the blazing rays of the sun are not attached to the firmament.""

अत्राप्युदाहरन्तीममितिहासं पुरातनम् ।
अध्वर्युयतिसंवादं तं निबोध यशस्विनि ॥ (6)

"""In this connection, there is an ancient history about a conversation between an adhvaryu and a mendicant. O Illustrious One! Listen to it.""

प्रोक्ष्यमाणं पशुं दृष्ट्वा यज्ञकर्मण्यथाब्रवीत् ।
यतिरध्वर्युमासीनो हिंसेयमिति कुत्सयन् ॥ (7)

"""On seeing an animal sprinkled with water for a sacrificial rite, a mendicant censured the violence and spoke to an adhvaryu who was seated there.""

---

[94] In the atman.

तमध्वर्युः प्रत्युवाच नायं छागो विनश्यति ।
श्रेयसा योक्ष्यते जन्तुर्यदि श्रुतिरियं तथा ॥ (8)

'"'The adhvaryu replied, *This goat will not be destroyed. The sacred texts say that this animal will obtain great benefit.*'"'

यो ह्यस्य पार्थिवो भागः पृथिवीं स गमिष्यति ।
यदस्य वारिजं किंचिदपस्तत्प्रतिपद्यते ॥ (9)

'"'*This part, constituted of earth, will enter the earth. This part, constituted of water, will enter the water.*'"'

सूर्यं चक्षुर्दिशः श्रोत्रे प्राणोऽस्य दिवमेव च ।
आगमे वर्तमानस्य न मे दोषोऽस्ति कश्चन ॥ (10)

'"'*The eyes will enter the sun. The ears will enter the directions. The breath of life will enter the firmament. I follow the agama texts*[95] *and there is no sin in this.*'"'

यतिरुवाच

प्राणैर्वियोगे छागस्य यदि श्रेयः प्रपश्यसि ।
छागार्थे वर्तते यज्ञो भवतः किं प्रयोजनम् ॥ (11)

'"'The mendicant said, *If you perceive a benefit from the goat giving up its life, then the sacrifice is for the sake of the goat. Why do you need the sacrifice?*'"'

अनु त्वा मन्यतां माता पिता भ्राता सखापि च ।
मन्त्रयस्वैनमुन्नीय परवन्तं विशेषतः ॥ (12)

'"'*Take the permission of the goat's mother, father, brother and friends and let them pronounce the mantras. In particular, the goat depends on them.*'"'

य एवमनुमन्येरंस्तान्भवान्प्रष्टुमर्हति ।
तेषामनुमतं श्रुत्वा शक्या कर्तुं विचारणा ॥ (13)

---

[95]Agamas are texts other than the Vedas, such as the tantra texts.

"'You should ask them and obtain their consent. It is only after their permission has been obtained that one can think about what should be done.'"

प्राणा अप्यस्य छागस्य प्रापितास्ते स्वयोनिषु ।
शरीरं केवलं शिष्टं निश्चेष्टमिति मे मति: ॥ (14)

"'The life-breath of the goat has left[96] and returned to its own origin. It is my view that only the immobile body is left.'"

इन्धनस्य तु तुल्येन शरीरेण विचेतसा ।
हिंसा निर्वेष्टुकामानामिन्धनं पशुसंज्ञितम् ॥ (15)

"'This body, bereft of consciousness, is like kindling. Those whose desires are addicted to violence have described this as an animal and have reduced it to kindling.'"

अहिंसा सर्वधर्माणामिति वृद्धानुशासनम् ।
यदहिंस्रं भवेत्कर्म तत्कार्यमिति विद्महे ॥ (16)

"'Non-violence is the instruction of the elders in all dharmas. I know that a rite is indeed a rite if it does not involve any violence.'"

अहिंसेति प्रतिज्ञेयं यदि वक्ष्याम्यत: परम् ।
शक्यं बहुविधं वक्तुं भवत: कार्यदूषणम् ॥ (17)

"'One should have a pledge of non-violence. If I wish to say anything beyond this, I can find faults with what you have done in many different ways.'"

अहिंसा सर्वभूतानां नित्यमस्मासु रोचते ।
प्रत्यक्षत: साधयामो न परोक्षमुपास्महे ॥ (18)

"'All of us always find delight in non-violence towards all beings. We seek to achieve this through what is directly manifest, not through what is indirectly manifest.'"

---

[96]The goat has already been sacrificed.

अध्वर्युरुवाच

भूमेर्गन्धगुणान्भुङ्क्ष्वे पिबस्यापोमयान्रसान् ।
ज्योतिषां पश्यसे रूपं स्पृशस्यनिलजान्गुणान् ॥ (19)

'"'The adhvaryu replied, *You enjoy the qualities of smell that belong to the earth. You drink and taste the quality of the water. You see form, the quality of fire. You touch the quality of the wind.*'"'

शृणोष्याकाशजं शब्दं मनसा मन्यसे मतिम् ।
सर्वाण्येतानि भूतानि प्राणा इति च मन्यसे ॥ (20)

'"'*You hear sound, which originates in space. You use your mind to mentally think of different things. You think that all these elements have life.*'"'

प्राणादाने च नित्योऽसि हिंसायां वर्तते भवान् ।
नास्ति चेष्टा विना हिंसां किं वा त्वं मन्यसे द्विज ॥ (21)

'"'*You are always engaged in taking away life. You are engaged in violence. There is no endeavour without violence. O Dvija! What do you think?*'"'

यतिरुवाच

अक्षरं च क्षरं चैव द्वैधी भावोऽयमात्मनः ।
अक्षरं तत्र सद्भावः स्वभावः क्षर उच्यते ॥ (22)

'"'The mendicant said, *The indestructible and the destructible are the two opposite aspects of the atman. The indestructible has existence. The destructible is said to be non-existent nature.*'"'

प्राणो जिह्वा मनः सत्त्वं स्वभावो रजसा सह ।
भावैरेतैर्विमुक्तस्य निर्द्वन्द्वस्य निराशिषः ॥ (23)

'"'*Life, the tongue, the mind, the spirit, sattva and rajas are expressions of nature. When one has been freed from the opposite pairs of sentiments, one is without wishes.*'"'

समस्य सर्वभूतेषु निर्ममस्य जितात्मनः ।
समन्तात्परिमुक्तस्य न भयं विद्यते क्वचित् ॥ (24)

'"Such a person looks upon all creatures impartially. He has no sense of ownership and has conquered his atman. When one has been freed in every possible way, there no longer is any fear."'

अध्वर्युरुवाच

सद्भिरेवेह संवासः कार्यो मतिमतां वर ।
भवतो हि मतं श्रुत्वा प्रतिभाति मतिर्मम ॥ (25)

'"The adhvaryu replied, O Supreme among Intelligent Ones! One should always reside with those who are virtuous. Hearing your views, my intelligence has been illuminated."'

भगवन्भगवद्बुद्ध्या प्रतिबुद्धो ब्रवीम्यहम् ।
मतं मन्तुं क्रतुं कर्तुं नापराधोऽस्ति मे द्विज ॥ (26)

'"O Illustrious One! Realizing that you were an enlightened and illustrious person, I spoke to you in this way. O Dvija! I honoured the customs in performing this sacrifice. No crime attaches to me because of this sacrifice."'[97]

ब्राह्मण उवाच

उपपत्त्या यतिस्तूष्णीं वर्तमानस्ततः परम् ।
अध्वर्युरपि निर्मोहः प्रचचार महामखे ॥ (27)

'"The brahmana continued, 'When this was said, the mendicant remained silent. The adhvaryu was freed from his delusion and continued with the rites of the great sacrifice.'"

एवमेतादृशं मोक्षं सुसूक्ष्मं ब्राह्मणा विदुः ।
विदित्वा चानुतिष्ठन्ति क्षेत्रज्ञेनानुदर्शिना ॥ (28)

---

[97] I followed the customs. Having been enlightened, I will henceforth desist.

"'"In this way, learned brahmanas know about the extremely subtle nature of moksha. They know and follow the instructions of kshetrajna.'"'

Chapter 14

ब्राह्मण उवाच

अत्राप्युदाहरन्तीममितिहासं पुरातनम् ।
कार्तवीर्यस्य संवादं समुद्रस्य च भामिनि ॥ (1)

"'"The brahmana said, 'O Beautiful One! In this connection, there is an ancient history about a conversation between Kartavirya and the ocean.'"'

कार्तवीर्यार्जुनो नाम राजा बाहुसहस्रवान् ।
येन सागरपर्यन्ता धनुषा निर्जिता मही ॥ (2)

"'"There was a king named Kartavirya Arjuna, and he possessed one thousand arms. Using his bow, he conquered the earth, up to the frontiers of the ocean.'"'

स कदाचित्समुद्रान्ते विचरन्बलदर्पितः ।
अवाकिरच्छरशतैः समुद्रमिति नः श्रुतम् ॥ (3)

"'"We have heard that, on one occasion, intoxicated with his strength, on the shores of the ocean, he enveloped the ocean with hundreds of arrows.'"'

तं समुद्रो नमस्कृत्य कृताञ्जलिरुवाच ह ।
मा मुञ्च वीर नाराचान्ब्रूहि किं करवाणि ते ॥ (4)

"'"The ocean joined its hands in salutation and bowed down before him. *O Brave One! Do not shoot* narachas[98] *at me. What can I do for you?*"'"

---

[98] A naracha is an iron arrow.

मदाश्रयाणि भूतानि त्वद्विसृष्टैर्महेषुभिः ।
वध्यन्ते राजशार्दूल तेभ्यो देह्यभयं विभो ॥ (5)

'"'O Tiger among Kings! The creatures that have sought refuge in me are being slaughtered by the great arrows you have released. O Lord! Grant them freedom from fear.'"'

अर्जुन उवाच

मत्समो यदि संग्रामे शरासनधरः क्वचित् ।
विद्यते तं ममाचक्ष्व यः समासीत मां मृधे ॥ (6)

'"'Arjuna replied, If there is any archer who is equal to me in battle, tell me about him, so that he can face me in an encounter.'"'

समुद्र उवाच

महर्षिर्जमदग्निस्ते यदि राजन्परिश्रुतः ।
तस्य पुत्रस्तवातिथ्यं यथावत्कर्तुमर्हति ॥ (7)

'"'The ocean said, O King! You may have heard of Maharshi Jamadagni. His son is capable of receiving you as a guest.'"'[99]

ततः स राजा प्रययौ क्रोधेन महता वृतः ।
स तमाश्रममागम्य राममेवान्वपद्यत ॥ (8)

'"'At this, the king was suffused with great rage. He left for the hermitage and confronted Rama.'"'

स रामप्रतिकूलानि चकार सह बन्धुभिः ।
आयासं जनयामास रामस्य च महात्मनः ॥ (9)

'"'With his relatives, he engaged in hostilities against Rama, and this caused stress to the great-souled Rama.'"'

ततस्तेजः प्रजज्वाल राजस्यामिततेजसः ।
प्रदहद्रिपुसैन्यानि तदा कमललोचने ॥ (10)

---

[99]Jamadagni's son was Parashurama. 'Guest' is an indirect way of saying that Parashurama would accept Kartavirya Arjuna's challenge in a battle. Jamadagni was Richika's son and was killed by Kartavirya Arjuna.

"'"O Lotus-Eyed One! The infinitely energetic Rama's energy blazed forth and he burnt down the enemy soldiers.'"'

ततः परशुमादाय स तं बाहुसहस्रिणम् ।
चिच्छेद सहसा रामो बाहुशाखमिव द्रुमम् ॥ (11)

"'"Rama violently grasped a battleaxe and sliced down the thousand arms, like lopping off the branches from a tree.'"'

तं हतं पतितं दृष्ट्वा समेताः सर्वबान्धवाः ।
असीनादाय शक्तीश्च भार्गवं पर्यवारयन् ॥ (12)

"'"When they saw that he[100] had been slain, all the relatives assembled together. They surrounded Bhargava[101] and attacked him with swords and spears.'"'

रामोऽपि धनुरादाय रथमारुह्य सत्वरः ।
विसृजञ्शरवर्षाणि व्यधमत्पार्थिवं बलम् ॥ (13)

"'"Rama seized his bow and swiftly ascended a chariot. He released a shower of arrows and pierced the king's soldiers.'"'

ततस्तु क्षत्रियाः केचिज्जमदग्निं निहत्य च ।
विविशुर्गिरिदुर्गाणि मृगाः सिंहार्दिता इव ॥ (14)

"'"Some of the kshatriyas were slain by Jamadagni's son. Others entered fortifications in the mountains, like deer afflicted by a lion.'"'

तेषां स्वविहितं कर्म तद्भयान्नानुतिष्ठताम् ।
प्रजा वृषलतां प्राप्ता ब्राह्मणानामदर्शनात् ॥ (15)

"'"Because of their fear, some of them could not see any brahmanas and could not engage in their own rites. Their offspring became vrishalas.'"'[102]

---

[100]Kartavirya Arjuna.
[101]Bhrigu's descendant, Parashurama.
[102]Kshatriyas require brahmanas for the performance of rites. This shloka means to indicate that there were no kings left to protect the virtuous and punish the wicked.

त एते द्रमिडाः काशाः पुण्ड्राश्च शबरैः सह ।
वृषलत्वं परिगता व्युत्थानात्क्षत्रधर्मतः ॥ (16)

'"'In this way, Dramidas, Kashas, Pundras and Shabaras were uprooted from the dharma of kshatriyas and became vrishalas.'"'

ततस्तु हतवीरासु क्षत्रियासु पुनः पुनः ।
द्विजैरुत्पादितं क्षत्रं जामदग्न्यो न्यकृन्तत ॥ (17)

'"'When the brave ones were slain, the brahmanas obtained sons through the kshatriya women.[103] However, Jamadagni's son repeatedly killed these kshatriyas too.'"'

एव विंशतिमेधान्ते रामं वागशरीरिणी ।
दिव्या प्रोवाच मधुरा सर्वलोकपरिश्रुता ॥ (18)

'"'When this had happened twenty-one times, an invisible and divine voice spoke gentle words and these were heard by all the worlds.'"'

राम राम निवर्तस्व कं गुणं तात पश्यसि ।
क्षत्रबन्धूनिमान्प्राणैर्विप्रयोज्य पुनः पुनः ॥ (19)

'"'*O Rama! Desist. O Son! O Rama! What gain do you see in this? Why are you repeatedly depriving the kshatra-bandhus of their lives?*'"'[104]

तथैव तं महात्मानमृचीकप्रमुखास्तदा ।
पितामहा महाभाग निवर्तस्वेत्यथाब्रुवन् ॥ (20)

'"'His great-souled ancestors, with Richika at the forefront, asked the immensely fortunate one to desist.'"'

पितुर्वधममृष्यंस्तु रामः प्रोवाच तानृषीन् ।
नार्हन्तीह भवन्तो मां निवारयितुमित्युत ॥ (21)

'"'However, unable to tolerate his father's death, Rama told those rishis, *You should not restrain me in this way.*'"'

---

[103]Since the male kshatriyas were killed.
[104]Parashurama's ancestors spoke.

पितर ऊचु:

नाहसे क्षत्रबन्धूंस्त्वं निहन्तुं जयतां वर ।
न हि युक्तं त्वया हन्तुं ब्राह्मणेन सता नृपान् ॥ (22)

'"The ancestors replied, *O Supreme among Victorious Ones! You should not kill the kshatra-bandhus in this way. You are a brahmana. You should not kill these kings.*"'

Chapter 15

पितर ऊचु:

अत्राप्युदाहरन्तीममितिहासं पुरातनम् ।
श्रुत्वा च तत्तथा कार्यं भवता द्विजसत्तम ॥ (1)

'"The ancestors said, *In this connection, an ancient history is recounted. O Supreme among Dvijas! Having heard the truth about this, decide on your course of action.*"'

अलर्को नाम राजर्षिरभवत्सुमहातपा: ।
धर्मज्ञ: सत्यसन्धश्च महात्मा सुमहाव्रत: ॥ (2)

'"*There was a rajarshi[105] named Alarka and he was extremely great in his austerities. He was knowledgeable about dharma and devoted to the truth.*"'

स सागरान्तां धनुषा विनिर्जित्य महीमिमाम् ।
कृत्वा सुदुष्करं कर्म मन: सूक्ष्मे समादधे ॥ (3)

'"*He was great-souled and extremely great in his vows. Seizing his bow, he conquered the earth, up to the frontiers of the ocean. Having performed this extremely difficult task, his mind turned towards what was subtle.*"'

---

[105]Royal sage.

स्थितस्य वृक्षमूलेऽथ तस्य चिन्ता बभूव ह ।
उत्सृज्य सुमहद्राज्यं सूक्ष्मं प्रति महामते ॥ (4)

'"*He sat down at the foot of a tree. O Immensely Intelligent One! Forgetting that extremely large kingdom, his thoughts turned towards what was subtle.*"'

अलर्क उवाच

मनसो मे बलं जातं मनो जित्वा ध्रुवो जय: ।
अन्यत्र बाणानस्यामि शत्रुभि: परिवारित: ॥ (5)

'"*Alarka said, Strength has been generated in my mind. When one conquers the mind, victory is certain. I will shoot my arrows at other enemies who surround me.*"'[106]

यदिदं चापलान्मूर्ते: सर्वमेतच्चिकीर्षति ।
मन: प्रति सुतीक्ष्णाग्राणहं मोक्ष्यामि सायकान् ॥ (6)

'"*If my mind assumes a fickle form and tries to distract me towards everything else, I will unleash extremely sharp-pointed arrows towards it.*"'

मन उवाच

नेमे बाणास्तरिष्यन्ति मामलर्क कथंचन ।
तवैव मर्म भेत्स्यन्ति भिन्नमर्मा मरिष्यसि ॥ (7)

'"*The mind replied, O Alarka! Those arrows will never be able to pierce me. They will pierce your inner organs instead. With your inner organs pierced, you will die.*"'

अन्यान्बाणान्समीक्षस्व यैस्त्वं मां सूदयिष्यसि ।
तच्छ्रुत्वा स विचिन्त्याथ ततो वचनमब्रवीत् ॥ (8)

'"*Consider other arrows with which you can strike at me. Hearing these words, he thought and spoke these words.*"'

---

[106]Internal ones and not external ones.

अलर्क उवाच

आघ्राय सुबहून्गन्धांस्तानेव प्रतिगृध्यति ।
तस्माद्घ्राणं प्रति शरान्प्रतिमोक्ष्याम्यहं शितान् ॥ (9)

'"*Alarka said*, I inhale many kinds of smells and desire them. Therefore, I will release sharp arrows towards my nose."'

घ्राण उवाच

नेमे बाणास्तरिष्यन्ति मामलर्क कथंचन ।
तवैव मर्म भेत्स्यन्ति भिन्नमर्मा मरिष्यसि ॥ (10)

'"*The nose replied*, O Alarka! Those arrows will never be able to pierce me. They will pierce your inner organs instead. With your inner organs pierced, you will die."'

अन्यान्बाणान्समीक्षस्व यैस्त्वं मां सूदयिष्यसि ।
तच्छ्रुत्वा स विचिन्त्याथ ततो वचनमब्रवीत् ॥ (11)

'"*Consider other arrows with which you can strike at me. Hearing these words, he thought and spoke these words.*"'

अलर्क उवाच

इयं स्वादून्रसान्भुक्त्वा तानेव प्रतिगृध्यति ।
तस्माज्जिह्वां प्रति शरान्प्रतिमोक्ष्याम्यहं शितान् ॥ (12)

'"*Alarka said*, I enjoy many kinds of succulent tastes and desire them. Therefore, I will release sharp arrows towards my tongue."'

जिह्वा उवाच

नेमे बाणास्तरिष्यन्ति मामलर्क कथंचन ।
तवैव मर्म भेत्स्यन्ति भिन्नमर्मा मरिष्यसि ॥ (13)

'"*The tongue replied*, O Alarka! Those arrows will never be able to pierce me. They will pierce your inner organs instead. With your inner organs pierced, you will die."'

अन्यान्बाणान्समीक्षस्व यैस्त्वं मां सूदयिष्यसि ।
तच्छ्रुत्वा स विचिन्त्याथ ततो वचनमब्रवीत् ॥ (14)

""'Consider other arrows with which you can strike at me. *Hearing these words, he thought and spoke these words.*"'

अलर्क उवाच

स्पृष्ट्वा त्वग्विविधान्स्पर्शांस्तानेव प्रतिगृध्यति ।
तस्मात्त्वचं पाटयिष्ये विविधै: कङ्कपत्रभि: ॥ (15)

""'*Alarka said*, I touch with my skin and desire the sensation of touch. Therefore, I will bring the skin down with many arrows shafted with the feathers of herons.'"'

त्वगुवाच

नेमे बाणास्तरिष्यन्ति मामलर्क कथंचन ।
तवैव मर्म भेत्स्यन्ति भिन्नमर्मा मरिष्यसि ॥ (16)

""'*The skin replied*, O Alarka! Those arrows will never be able to pierce me. They will pierce your inner organs instead. With your inner organs pierced, you will die.'"'

अन्यान्बाणान्समीक्षस्व यैस्त्वं मां सूदयिष्यसि ।
तच्छ्रुत्वा स विचिन्त्याथ ततो वचनमब्रवीत् ॥ (17)

""'Consider other arrows with which you can strike at me. *Hearing these words, he thought and spoke these words.*"'

अलर्क उवाच

श्रुत्वा वै विविधाञ्शब्दांस्तानेव प्रतिगृध्यति ।
तस्माच्छ्रोत्रं प्रति शरान्प्रतिमोक्ष्याम्यहं शितान् ॥ (18)

""'*Alarka said*, I hear many kinds of sound and desire them. Therefore, I will release sharp arrows towards my ears.'"'

श्रोत्रमुवाच

नेमे बाणास्तरिष्यन्ति मामलर्क कथंचन ।
तवैव मर्म भेत्स्यन्ति ततो हास्यसि जीवितम् ॥ (19)

"'The ear replied, O Alarka! Those arrows will never be able to pierce me. They will pierce your inner organs instead. With your inner organs pierced, you will no longer live.'"

अन्यान्बाणान्समीक्षस्व यैस्त्वं मां सूदयिष्यसि ।
तच्छ्रुत्वा स विचिन्त्याथ ततो वचनमब्रवीत् ॥ (20)

"'Consider other arrows with which you can strike at me. *Hearing these words, he thought and spoke these words.*'"

अलर्क उवाच

दृष्ट्वा वै विविधान्भावांस्तानेव प्रतिगृध्यति ।
तस्माच्चक्षुः प्रति शरान्प्रतिमोक्ष्याम्यहं शितान् ॥ (21)

"'*Alarka said*, I see many kinds of attributes and desire them. Therefore, I will release sharp arrows towards my eyes.'"

चक्षुरुवाच

नेमे बाणास्तरिष्यन्ति मामालर्क कथंचन ।
तवैव मर्म भेत्स्यन्ति भिन्नमर्मा मरिष्यसि ॥ (22)

"'*The eye replied*, O Alarka! Those arrows will never be able to pierce me. They will pierce your inner organs instead. With your inner organs pierced, you will die.'"

अन्यान्बाणान्समीक्षस्व यैस्त्वं मां सूदयिष्यति ।
तच्छ्रुत्वा स विचिन्त्याथ ततो वचनमब्रवीत् ॥ (23)

"'Consider other arrows with which you can strike at me. *Hearing these words, he thought and spoke these words.*'"

अलर्क उवाच

इयं निष्ठा बहुविधा प्रज्ञया त्वध्यवस्यति ।
तस्माद्बुद्धिं प्रति शरान्प्रतिमोक्ष्याम्यहं शितान् ॥ (24)

"'*Alarka said*, There are many kinds of devotion, but wisdom constrains them. Therefore, I will release sharp arrows towards my intelligence.'"

बुद्धिरुवाच

नेमे बाणास्तरिष्यन्ति मामलर्क कथंचन ।
तवैव मर्म भेत्स्यन्ति भिन्नमर्मा मरिष्यसि ॥ (25)

"*The intelligence replied*, O Alarka! Those arrows will never be able to pierce me. They will pierce your inner organs instead. With your inner organs pierced, you will die.""

पितर ऊचुः

ततोऽलर्कस्तपो घोरमास्थायाथ सुदुष्करम् ।
नाध्यगच्छत्परं शक्त्या बाणमेतेषु सप्तसु ।
सुसमाहित चित्तास्तु ततोऽचिन्तयत प्रभुः ॥ (26)

"*The ancestors continued*, At this, Alarka engaged in terrible, supreme and extremely difficult austerities. However, he was unable to touch those seven[107] with his arrows. The lord controlled his senses and began to think.""

स विचिन्त्य चिरं कालमलर्को द्विजसत्तम ।
नाध्यगच्छत्परं श्रेयो योगान्मतिमतां वरः ॥ (27)

""O Supreme among Dvijas! Alarka thought for a long time. The supreme among intelligent ones could not think of anything that was better than, and superior to, yoga.""

स एकाग्रं मनः कृत्वा निश्चलो योगमास्थितः ।
इन्द्रियाणि जघानाशु बाणेनैकेन वीर्यवान् ।
योगेनात्मानमाविश्य संसिद्धिं परमां ययौ ॥ (28)

""*Single-minded and without moving, he resorted to yoga. Using a single arrow, the valiant one quickly slew his senses. Immersing his atman in yoga, he obtained supreme siddhi.*""

विस्मितश्चापि राजर्षिरिमां गाथां जगाद ह ।
अहो कष्टं यदस्माभिः पूर्वं राज्यमनुष्ठितम् ।
इति पश्चान्मया ज्ञातं योगान्नास्ति परं सुखम् ॥ (29)

---

[107] The five senses, the mind and intelligence.

"'"Astounded, the rajarshi chanted this song. Alas! It was a hardship that I formerly served the kingdom. I only got to know later that yoga brings supreme bliss."'"

इति त्वमपि जानीहि राम मा क्षत्रियाञ्जहि ।
तपो घोरमुपातिष्ठ ततः श्रेयोऽभिपत्स्यसे ॥ (30)

"'"O Rama! You should also know this. Do not kill the kshatriyas. Engage in terrible austerities and you will obtain what is best for you."'"

ब्राह्मण उवाच

इत्युक्तः स तपो घोरं जामदग्न्यः पितामहैः ।
आस्थितः सुमहाभागो ययौ सिद्धिं च दुर्गमाम् ॥ (31)

"'The brahmana continued, 'Having been thus addressed by his ancestors, Jamadagni's son engaged in terrible austerities. Having resorted to those, the immensely fortunate one obtained siddhi that is extremely difficult to obtain.'"

Chapter 16

ब्राह्मण उवाच

त्रयो वै रिपवो लोके नव वै गुणतः स्मृताः ।
हर्षः स्तम्भोऽभिमानश्च त्रयस्ते सात्त्विका गुणाः ॥ (1)

"'The brahmana said, 'There are said to be three enemies and nine qualities in the world. Delight, stupefaction and pride—these are the qualities of sattva.'"[108]

शोकः क्रोधोऽतिसंरम्भो राजसास्ते गुणाः स्मृताः ।
स्वप्नस्तन्द्री च मोहश्च त्रयस्ते तामसा गुणाः ॥ (2)

"'"Sorrow, anger and extreme intolerance—these are said to be the qualities of rajas. Sleep, lassitude and delusion—these are the qualities of tamas."'"

---

[108] Three gunas multiplied by three attributes gives nine. Interpretations are convoluted.

एतान्निकृत्य धृतिमान्बाणसंघैरतन्द्रित: ।
जेतुं परानुत्सहते प्रशान्तात्मा जितेन्द्रिय: ॥ (3)

"'An intelligent person does not waver and cuts these off with large numbers of arrows. He is tranquil in his atman and conquers his senses. He is interested in vanquishing the enemy.'"[109]

अत्र गाथा: कीर्तयन्ति पुराकल्पविदो जना: ।
अम्बरीषेण या गीता राज्ञा राज्यं प्रशासता ॥ (4)

"'Those who know about the ancient accounts recite a chant in this connection. When he ruled the kingdom, this was sung by King Ambarisha.'"

समुदीर्णेषु दोषेषु वध्यमानेषु साधुषु ।
जग्राह तरसा राज्यमम्बरीष इति श्रुति: ॥ (5)

"'It has been heard that Ambarisha swiftly seized the kingdom, after using virtue to slay the rising tide of vices.'"

स निगृह्य महादोषान्साधून्समभिपूज्य च ।
जगाम महतीं सिद्धिं गाथां चेमां जगाद ह ॥ (6)

"'He subdued the great vices and honoured the virtuous. He obtained great siddhi and chanted this song.'"

भूयिष्ठं मे जिता दोषा निहता: सर्वशत्रव: ।
एको दोषोऽवशिष्टस्तु वध्य: स न हतो मया ॥ (7)

"'I have conquered many vices. I have slain all the enemies.[110] However, there is one vice that should have been killed, but still remains. I have not been able to slay it.'"

येन युक्तो जन्तुरयं वैतृष्ण्यं नाधिगच्छति ।
तृष्णार्त इव निम्नानि धावमानो न बुध्यते ॥ (8)

---

[109] The senses, the mind and the intelligence.
[110] The internal enemies.

"'As long as a creature is afflicted by this, one does not obtain freedom from desire. Driven by desire, one dashes downwards and does not understand.'"

अकार्यमपि येनेह प्रयुक्तः सेवते नरः ।
तं लोभमसिभिस्तीक्ष्णैर्निकृन्तन्तं निकृन्तत ॥ (9)

"'Because a man is addicted to this, he commits acts that should not be undertaken in this world. Greed must be severed with an extremely sharp sword. It should be sliced off.'"

लोभाद्धि जायते तृष्णा ततश्चिन्ता प्रसृज्यते ।
स लिप्समानो लभते भूयिष्ठं राजसान्गुणान् ॥ (10)

"'Desire results from greed and that gives rise to anxiety. A person who desires obtains many qualities that are associated with rajas.'"

स तैर्गुणैः संहतदेहबन्धनः पुनः पुनर्जायति कर्म चेहते ।
जन्मक्षये भिन्नविकीर्ण देहः पुनर्मृत्युं गच्छति जन्मनि स्वे ॥ (11)

"'Because of these qualities, he is tied down to the bondage of the body. He is repeatedly born to perform karma in this world. When life is over and the body is mangled and scattered, he again confronts death because of the act of being reborn.'"

तस्मादेनं सम्यगवेक्ष्य लोभं निगृह्य धृत्यात्मनि राज्यमिच्छेत् ।
एतद्राज्यं नान्यदस्तीति विद्याद्यस्त्वत्र राजा विजितो ममैकः ॥ (12)

"'Therefore, one must look towards greed properly. If one desires true sovereignty, one must restrain it with the fortitude of the atman. This is the true kingdom. A king should know that this alone is what needs to be conquered.'"

इति राज्ञाम्बरीषेण गाथा गीता यशस्विना ।
आधिराज्यं पुरस्कृत्य लोभमेकं निकृन्तता ॥ (13)

"'The illustrious King Ambarisha sung this chant. Having severed greed, he placed this sovereignty at the forefront.'"

Chapter 17

ब्राह्मण उवाच

अत्राप्युदाहरन्तीममितिहासं पुरातनम् ।
ब्राह्मणस्य च संवादं जनकस्य च भामिनि ॥ (1)

"'The brahmana said, 'O Beautiful One! In this connection, an ancient history is recounted about a conversation between a brahmana and Janaka.'"

ब्राह्मणं जनको राजा सन्नं कस्मिंश्चिदागमे ।
विषये मे न वस्तव्यमिति शिष्ट्यर्थमब्रवीत् ॥ (2)

"'A brahmana committed a crime. Wishing to punish him, King Janaka said, *You will not reside in my kingdom.*'"

इत्युक्तः प्रत्युवाचाथ ब्राह्मणो राजसत्तमम् ।
आचक्ष्व विषयं राजन्यावांस्तव वशे स्थितः ॥ (3)

"'Thus addressed, the brahmana replied to the best of kings. *O King! Please tell me. Which is the kingdom that is under your subjugation?*'"

सोऽन्यस्य विषये राज्ञो वस्तुमिच्छाम्यहं विभो ।
वचस्ते कर्तुमिच्छामि यथाशास्त्रं महीपते ॥ (4)

"'*O Lord! I wish to dwell in the territory of another king. O Lord of the Earth! I wish to act in accordance with the words of the sacred texts.*'"

इत्युक्तः स तदा राजा ब्राह्मणेन यशस्विना ।
मुहुरुष्णं च निःश्वस्य न स तं प्रत्यभाषत ॥ (5)

"'Thus addressed by the illustrious brahmana, the king sighed repeatedly and did not say anything in reply.'"

तमासीनं ध्यायमानं राजानममितौजसम् ।
कश्मलं सहसागच्छद्भानुमन्तमिव ग्रहः ॥ (6)

"'The infinitely energetic king sat down and thought. He was suddenly immersed in great lassitude, like the sun devoured by a planet.'"[111]

समाश्वास्य ततो राजा व्यपेते कश्मले तदा ।
ततो मुहूर्तादिव तं ब्राह्मणं वाक्यमब्रवीत् ॥ (7)

"'After a muhurta,[112] the king reassured himself and overcame that lassitude. He spoke these words to the brahmana.'"

पितृपैतामहे राज्ये वश्ये जनपदे सति ।
विषयं नाधिगच्छामि विचिन्वन्पृथिवीमिमाम् ॥ (8)

"'This is the kingdom of my fathers and grandfathers and is ruled by me. But in the habitations, and indeed when I searched the entire earth, I could not find a single place that is my dominion.'"

नाध्यगच्छं यदा पृथ्व्यां मिथिला मार्गिता मया ।
नाध्यगच्छं यदा तस्यां स्वप्रजा मार्गिता मया ॥ (9)

"'When I could not find such a place on earth, I searched for such a place in Mithila. When I could not find such a place there, I searched for it among my own offspring.'"

नाध्यगच्छं यदा तासु तदा मे कश्मलोऽभवत् ।
ततो मे कश्मलस्यान्ते मतिः पुनरुपस्थिता ॥ (10)

"'When I could not find such a place even there, I was overcome by lassitude. With that lassitude over, my intelligence has been aroused again.'"

तया न विषयं मन्ये सर्वो वा विषयो मम ।
आत्मापि चायं न मम सर्वा वा पृथिवी मम ।
उष्यतां यावदुत्साहो भुज्यतां यावदिष्यते ॥ (11)

"'I think that nothing is under my subjugation and everything is under my subjugation. My atman is not my own. Yet, this entire

---
[111] By Rahu during an eclipse.
[112] The sense here is after some time.

earth belongs to me. Dwell here as long as you want. Enjoy it as long as you wish.'"

ब्राह्मण उवाच

पितृपैतामहे राज्ये वश्ये जनपदे सति ।
ब्रूहि कां बुद्धिमास्थाय ममत्वं वर्जितं त्वया ॥ (12)

'"The brahmana replied, *This kingdom of your father and grandfathers and these habitations are under your subjugation. But please tell me this. Have you resorted to your intelligence and given up a sense of ownership?*'"

कां वा बुद्धिं विनिश्चित्य सर्वो वै विषयस्तव ।
नावैषि विषयं येन सर्वो वा विषयस्तव ॥ (13)

'"*On the basis of what intelligence have you determined that everything is your dominion? Why is nothing your dominion? And why is everything your dominion?*'"

जनक उवाच

अन्तवन्त इहारम्भा विदिता सर्वकर्मसु ।
नाध्यगच्छमहं यस्मान्ममेदमिति यद्भवेत् ॥ (14)

'"Janaka said, *I have realized that all the deeds that are started in this world come to an end. Therefore, I could not think of anything that belongs to me.*'"

कस्येदमिति कस्य स्वमिति वेदवचस्तथा ।
नाध्यगच्छमहं बुद्ध्या ममेदमिति यद्भवेत् ॥ (15)

'"*Who does this belong to? Who is the owner? These are the words of the Vedas. Using my intelligence, I could not understand what belongs to me.*'"

एतां बुद्धिं विनिश्चित्य ममत्वं वर्जितं मया ।
शृणु बुद्धिं तु यां ज्ञात्वा सर्वत्र विषयो मम ॥ (16)

"'Having resorted to this intelligence, I gave up all sense of ownership. Listen to the intelligence whereby I decided that every dominion belongs to me.'"

नाहमात्मार्थमिच्छामि गन्धान्घ्राणगतानपि ।
तस्मान्मे निर्जिता भूमिर्वशे तिष्ठति नित्यदा ॥ (17)

"'For my own sake, I do not desire the scents that are received by my nose. It has been conquered by me and, therefore, the earth is always under my subjugation.'"[113]

नाहमात्मार्थमिच्छामि रसानास्येऽपि वर्तत: ।
आपो मे निर्जितास्तस्माद्वशे तिष्ठन्ति नित्यदा ॥ (18)

"'For my own sake, I do not desire what is savoured by my tongue. It has been conquered by me and, therefore, the water is always under my subjugation.'"

नाहमात्मार्थमिच्छामि रूपं ज्योतिश्च चक्षुषा ।
तस्मान्मे निर्जितं ज्योतिर्वशे तिष्ठति नित्यदा ॥ (19)

"'For my own sake, I do not desire the form and light received by my eyes. It has been conquered by me and, therefore, the fire is always under my subjugation.'"

नाहमात्मार्थमिच्छामि स्पर्शांस्त्वचि गताश्च ये ।
तस्मान्मे निर्जितो वायुर्वशे तिष्ठति नित्यदा ॥ (20)

"'For my own sake, I do not desire what is touched by my skin. It has been conquered by me and, therefore, the wind is always under my subjugation.'"

नाहमात्मार्थमिच्छामि शब्दाञ्श्रोत्रगतानपि ।
तस्मान्मे निर्जिता: शब्दा वशे तिष्ठन्ति नित्यदा ॥ (21)

---

[113]Smell is an attribute of the earth. Since that has been conquered, the earth has also been conquered and so on for the other senses. The atman has nothing to do with the senses.

'"'For my own sake, I do not desire the sound that is received by my ears. It has been conquered by me and therefore, sound is always under my subjugation.'"'

नाहमात्मार्थमिच्छामि मनो नित्यं मनोन्तरे ।
मनो मे निर्जितं तस्माद्वशे तिष्ठति नित्यदा ॥ (22)

'"'For my own sake, I never desire my mind or what is in my mind. It has been conquered by me and therefore, the mind is always under my subjugation.'"'

देवेभ्यश्च पितृभ्यश्च भूतेभ्योऽतिथिभिः सह ।
इत्यर्थं सर्व एवेमे समारम्भा भवन्ति वै ॥ (23)

'"'Therefore, all the acts that I start are for devas, ancestors, creatures and guests.'"'

ततः प्रहस्य जनकं ब्राह्मणः पुनरब्रवीत् ।
त्वज्जिज्ञासार्थमद्येह विद्धि मां धर्ममागतम् ॥ (24)

'"'At this, the brahmana smiled and spoke to Janaka again. *Know me to be Dharma. I have come here now to test you*.'"'

त्वमस्य ब्रह्म नाभस्य बुद्ध्यारस्यानिवर्तिनः ।
सत्त्वनेमि निरुद्धस्य चक्रस्यैकः प्रवर्तकः ॥ (25)

'"'Once set in motion, the wheel does not return. Its circumference, which checks it, is sattva. The brahman is the nave and intelligence constitutes the spokes.'"'

Chapter 18

ब्राह्मण उवाच

नाहं तथा भीरु चरामि लोके तथा त्वं मां तर्कयसे स्वबुद्ध्या ।
विप्रोऽस्मि मुक्तोऽस्मि वनेचरोऽस्मि गृहस्थधर्मा ब्रह्मचारी तथास्मि ॥ (1)

'"The brahmana said, 'O Timid One! You have censured me according to your own intelligence. But I am not that. I do not roam around in the world in that way. I am a brahmana. I am free. I roam in the forest. In spite of resorting to the dharma of being a householder, I am a brahmachari.'"

नाहमस्मि यथा मां त्वं पश्यसे चक्षुषा शुभे ।
मया व्याप्तमिदं सर्वं यत्किंचिज्जगतीगतम् ॥ (2)

'"'O Beautiful One! I am not what you see with your eyes. Everything in this universe, mobile and immobile, is pervaded by me.'"

ये केचिज्जन्तवो लोके जङ्गमाः स्थावराश्च ह ।
तेषां मामन्तकं विद्धि दारूणामिव पावकम् ॥ (3)

'"'Know me to be the one that destroys every object in this world, mobile and immobile, like fire consuming wood.'"

राज्यं पृथिव्यां सर्वस्यामथ वापि त्रिविष्टपे ।
तथा बुद्धिरियं वेत्ति बुद्धिरेव धनं मम ॥ (4)

'"'I know that this intelligence is superior to sovereignty over everything on earth and even that in heaven. That intelligence is my wealth.'"[114]

एकः पन्था ब्राह्मणानां येन गच्छन्ति तद्विदः ।
गृहेषु वनवासेषु गुरु वासेषु भिक्षुषु ।
लिङ्गैर्बहुभिरव्यग्रैरेका बुद्धिरुपास्यते ॥ (5)

'"'This is the single path that is traversed by all brahmanas. Whether they reside in houses or in forests, dwell in the houses of their gurus or are mendicants, irrespective of the many kinds of signs they display, they use their intelligence to worship only this.'"

नाना लिङ्गाश्रमस्थानां येषां बुद्धिः शमात्मिका ।
ते भावमेकमायान्ति सरितः सागरं यथा ॥ (6)

---

[114]The intelligence of being one with the brahman.

"'"They may resort to many kinds of signs and ashramas, but the intelligence is based on tranquillity in the atman. The destination is a single one, like that of rivers heading to the ocean."'"

बुद्ध्यायं गम्यते मार्ग: शरीरेण न गम्यते ।
आद्यन्तवन्ति कर्माणि शरीरं कर्मबन्धनम् ॥ (7)

"'"That path is traversed using the intelligence. It is not a path that is traversed by the body. All karma has a beginning and an end, and the body is bound by karma."'"

तस्मात्ते सुभगे नास्ति परलोककृतं भयम् ।
मद्भावभावनिरता ममैवात्मानमेष्यसि ॥ (8)

"'"O Extremely Beautiful One! Therefore, because of what you have done, you should not entertain any fear about the world hereafter. Be devoted to me,[115] and it is into me that your atman will merge."'"

Chapter 19

ब्राह्मण्युवाच

नेदमल्पात्मना शक्यं वेदितुं नाकृतात्मना ।
बहु चाल्पं च संक्षिप्तं विप्लुतं च मतं मम ॥ (1)

"'The brahmani said, 'A person who is limited in his intelligence or has not cleansed his atman is incapable of comprehending this. My intelligence is extremely fickle, limited and confused.'"

उपायं तु मम ब्रूहि येनैषा लभ्यते मति: ।
तन्मन्ये कारणतमं यत एषा प्रवर्तते ॥ (2)

"'"Please tell me a means whereby I can obtain intelligence. I wish to learn from you the source from which this knowledge emanates.'"

---

[115] As the brahman.

ब्राह्मण उवाच

अरणीं ब्राह्मणीं विद्धि गुरुरस्योत्तरारणिः ।
तपः श्रुतेऽभिमथ्नीतो ज्ञानाग्निर्जायते ततः ॥ (3)

'"The brahmana said, 'Know that the brahman is the lower arani and the guru is the upper arani. Austerities and the sacred texts provide the friction and this leads to the fire of jnana being generated.'"

ब्राह्मण्युवाच

यदिदं ब्रह्मणो लिङ्गं क्षेत्रज्ञमिति संज्ञितम् ।
ग्रहीतुं येन तच्छक्यं लक्षणं तस्य तत्त्व नु ॥ (4)

'"The brahmani asked, 'Kshetrajna is said to be a sign of the brahman. What are its signs? How is one capable of grasping it?'"

ब्राह्मण उवाच

अलिङ्गो निर्गुणश्चैव कारणं नास्य विद्यते ।
उपायमेव वक्ष्यामि येन गृह्येत वा न वा ॥ (5)

'"The brahmana said, 'It[116] is without signs and without qualities. There is nothing that is his origin. I will tell you about the methods whereby he can be grasped, or not be grasped.'"

सम्यगप्युपदिष्टश्च भ्रमरैरिव लक्ष्यते ।
कर्म बुद्धिरबुद्धित्वाज्ज्ञानलिङ्गैरिवाश्रितम् ॥ (6)

'""I will instruct you about a proper method, like the one that is seen in bees.[117] The signs are that intelligence must determine karma, and jnana must determine intelligence.'"

इदं कार्यमिदं नेति न मोक्षेषूपदिश्यते ।
पश्यतः शृण्वतो बुद्धिरात्मनो येषु जायते ॥ (7)

---

[116] The brahman. The text is gender neutral.
[117] The way bees determine where a flower is.

'"In instructions about moksha, it is not said that this must be done or that must not be done. Through hearing and sight, intelligence is generated in the atman."'[118]

यावन्त इह शक्येरंस्तावतोंऽशान्प्रकल्पयेत् ।
व्यक्तानव्यक्तरूपांश्च शतशोऽथ सहस्रशः ॥ (8)

'"As long as one is capable of doing this, one must contemplate hundreds and thousands of manifest and unmanifest forms."'

सर्वान्नानात्वयुक्तांश्च सर्वान्प्रत्यक्षहेतुकान् ।
यतः परं न विद्येत ततोऽभ्यासे भविष्यति ॥ (9)

'"There are many kinds of yoga, and all of these directly provide the means. Through practice, one obtains the supreme, beyond which nothing exists."'

वासुदेव उवाच

ततस्तु तस्या ब्राह्मण्या मतिः क्षेत्रज्ञसंक्षये ।
क्षेत्रज्ञादेव परतः क्षेत्रज्ञोऽन्यः प्रवर्तते ॥ (10)

'Vasudeva said, "At this, the brahmani's intelligence became such that the kshetrajna was destroyed.[119] Having obtained what is beyond kshetrajna, it became other than the kshetrajna."'

अर्जुन उवाच

क्व नु सा ब्राह्मणी कृष्ण क्व चासौ ब्राह्मणर्षभः ।
याभ्यां सिद्धिरियं प्राप्ता तावुभौ वद मेऽच्युत ॥ (11)

---

[118]Hearing through the preceptor and sight through inner contemplation. It is easier to contemplate on direct and manifest objects first—ones that can be perceived. Once this has been mastered, one moves on to contemplate the unmanifest—that which is beyond perception.

[119]'Kshetrajna' is being used in the sense of the jivatman. Here, kshetrajna was destroyed in the sense of the jivatman merging with the paramatman.

'Arjuna asked, "O Krishna! Where is that brahmani and where is that bull among brahmanas? They obtained siddhi. O Achutya! Please tell me about them."'

वासुदेव उवाच

मनो मे ब्राह्मणं विद्धि बुद्धिं मे विद्धि ब्राह्मणीम् ।
क्षेत्रज्ञ इति यश्चोक्तः सोऽहमेव धनंजय ॥ (12)

'Vasudeva replied, "Know that my mind is that brahmana. Know that my intelligence is that brahmani. O Dhananjaya! I am the one who has been spoken of as kshetrajna."'

Chapter 20

अर्जुन उवाच

ब्रह्म यत्परमं वेद्यं तन्मे व्याख्यातुमर्हसि ।
भवतो हि प्रसादेन सूक्ष्मे मे रमते मतिः ॥ (1)

'Arjuna said, "The brahman is the supreme object of knowledge, and you should explain this to me. Through your favours, my mind finds pleasure in these subtle subjects."'

वासुदेव उवाच

अत्राप्युदाहरन्तीममितिहासं पुरातनम् ।
संवादं मोक्षसंयुक्तं शिष्यस्य गुरूणा सह ॥ (2)

'Vasudeva replied, "In this connection, an ancient history is cited about a conversation between a shishya and a guru on the question of moksha."'

कश्चिद्ब्राह्मणमासीनमाचार्यं संशितव्रतम् ।
शिष्यः पप्रच्छ मेधावी किंस्विच्छ्रेयः परंतप ॥ (3)

'"O Scorcher of Enemies! There was a brahmana preceptor who was firm in his vows. While he was seated, his intelligent disciple asked him, 'What is supremely beneficial?'"'

भगवन्तं प्रपन्नोऽहं निःश्रेयसपरायणः ।
याचे त्वां शिरसा विप्र यद्ब्रूयां तद्विबचक्ष्व मे ॥ (4)

"'O Illustrious One! Desiring supreme benefit, I have sought refuge with you. O Brahmana! I have bowed down my head and am soliciting you. Please tell me and instruct me.'"

तमेवंवादिनं पार्थ शिष्यं गुरुरुवाच ह ।
कथयस्व प्रवक्ष्यामि यत्र ते संशयो द्विज ॥ (5)

"'O Partha! The guru told the shishya, 'O Dvija! I will explain whatever you have doubts about.'"

इत्युक्तः स कुरुश्रेष्ठ गुरुणा गुरुवत्सलः ।
प्राञ्जलिः परिपप्रच्छ यत्तच्छृणु महामते ॥ (6)

"'O Best among the Kuru Lineage! The one who was devoted to his guru was thus addressed by the guru. He joined his hands in salutation and asked. O Immensely Intelligent One! Listen to this.'"

शिष्य उवाच

कुतश्चाहं कुतश्च त्वं तत्सत्यं ब्रूहि यत्परम् ।
कुतो जातानि भूतानि स्थावराणि चराणि च ॥ (7)

"'The disciple asked, 'Where have I come from? Where have you come from? Tell me about the supreme truth. From where do mobile and immobile creatures originate?'"

केन जीवन्ति भूतानि तेषामायुः किमात्मकम् ।
किं सत्यं किं तपो विप्र के गुणाः सद्भिरीरिताः ।
के पन्थानः शिवाः सन्ति किं सुखं किं च दुष्कृतम् ॥ (8)

"'How do creatures remain alive? What is their lifespan? O Brahmana! What is truth? What are austerities? What are the qualities of those who are virtuous? What are auspicious paths? What is happiness? What are wicked deeds?'"

एतान्मे भगवन्प्रश्नान्याथातथ्येन सत्तम ।
वक्तुमर्हसि विप्रर्षे यथावदिह तत्त्वतः ॥ (9)

'"O Illustrious One! O Excellent One! O Brahmana Rishi! There is no one other than you who knows the truth about these questions and you should tell me accurately."'

वासुदेव उवाच

तस्मै संप्रतिपन्नाय यथावत्परिपृच्छते ।
शिष्याय गुणयुक्ताय शान्ताय गुरुवर्तिने ।
छायाभूताय दान्ताय यतये ब्रह्मचारिणे ॥ (10)

'Vasudeva continued, "The disciple asked humbly, in the proper way. He was tranquil and possessed the qualities. He followed his guru like a shadow. He was a self-controlled mendicant who observed brahmacharya."'

तान्प्रश्नानब्रवीत्पार्थ मेधावी स धृतव्रतः ।
गुरुः कुरुकुलश्रेष्ठ सम्यक्सर्वानरिंदम ॥ (11)

'"O Partha! He asked these questions. O Best among Those of the Kuru Lineage! O Scorcher of Enemies! The guru, who was intelligent and firm in his vows, answered them properly."'

ब्रह्मप्रोक्तमिदं धर्ममृषिप्रवरसेवितम् ।
वेदविद्यासमावाप्यं तत्त्वभूतार्थभावनम् ॥ (12)

'"This was stated by Brahma and is practised by the best of rishis who are devoted to dharma. This constitutes knowledge of the Vedas. It is the truth behind the reason why beings were created."'

भूतभव्यभविष्यादिधर्मकामार्थनिश्चयम् ।
सिद्धसंघपरिज्ञातं पुराकल्पं सनातनम् ॥ (13)

'"It is a determination about the past, the present and the future and about dharma, kama and artha. This is known to the large number of siddhas. It is eternal and was thought of in ancient times."'

प्रवक्ष्येऽहं महाप्राज्ञ पदमुत्तममद्य ते ।
बुद्ध्वा यदिह संसिद्धा भवन्तीह मनीषिणः ॥ (14)

"'O Immensely Wise One! Using excellent words, I will now tell you about it. Learned ones who possess this intelligence obtain siddhi in this world.'"

उपगम्यर्षय: पूर्वं जिज्ञासन्त: परस्परम् ।
बृहस्पतिभरद्वाजौ गौतमो भार्गवस्तथा ॥ (15)
वसिष्ठ: काश्यपश्चैव विश्वामित्रोऽत्रिरेव च ।
मार्गान्सर्वान्परिक्रम्य परिश्रान्ता: स्वकर्मभि: ॥ (16)

"'In earlier times, the rishis wished to ask each other and assembled together—Brihaspati, Bharadvaja, Goutama, Bhargava, Vasishtha, Kashyapa, Vishvamitra and Atri. All of them had traversed along various paths, performing their own karma, and were exhausted.'"

ऋषिमाङ्गिरसं वृद्धं पुरस्कृत्य तु ते द्विजा: ।
ददृशुर्ब्रह्मभवने ब्रह्माणं वीतकल्मषम् ॥ (17)

"'With the aged Angiras leading them, they went to Brahma's abode and saw Brahma, cleansed of sin.'"

तं प्रणम्य महात्मानं सुखासीनं महर्षय: ।
पप्रच्छुर्विनयोपेता नि:श्रेयसमिदं परम् ॥ (18)

"'He was seated happily, and the maharshis bowed down before the great-souled one. They humbly asked him about the supreme benefit.'"

कथं कर्म क्रियात्साधु कथं मुच्येत किल्बिषात् ।
के नो मार्गा: शिवाश्च स्यु: किं सत्यं किं च दुष्कृतम् ॥ (19)

"'How should virtuous karma be undertaken? How is one freed from sin? What are auspicious paths for us? What is truth? What is extremely wicked?'"

केनोभौ कर्मपन्थानौ महत्त्वं केन विन्दति ।
प्रलयं चापवर्गं च भूतानां प्रभवाप्ययौ ॥ (20)

"'Which are the two paths of karma?[120] How does one obtain greatness? What is the dissolution of beings? What is their origin? What is their creation and destruction?'"[121]

इत्युक्तः स मुनिश्रेष्ठैर्यदाह प्रपितामहः ।
तत्तेऽहं संप्रवक्ष्यामि शृणु शिष्य यथागमम् ॥ (21)1

"'The best among sages spoke in this way to the great-grandfather. I will tell you what he said. O Disciple! Listen to what the sacred texts have to say.'"

ब्रह्मोवाच

सत्याद्भूतानि जातानि स्थावराणि चराणि च ।
तपसा तानि जीवन्ति इति तद्विद्ध सुव्रताः ॥ (22)

"'Brahma said, *All mobile and immobile objects are born from the truth. O Ones Who Are Firm in Your Vows! They live through austerities.*'"

स्वां योनिं पुनरागम्य वर्तन्ते स्वेन कर्मणा ।
सत्यं हि गुणसंयुक्तं नियतं पञ्चलक्षणम् ॥ (23)

"'*It is because of their own karma that they are again born in their own species. Truth is always united with the gunas and has five manifestations.*'"[122]

ब्रह्म सत्यं तपः सत्यं सत्यं चैव प्रजापतिः ।
सत्याद्भूतानि जातानि भूतं सत्यमयं महत् ॥ (24)

"'*The brahman is truth. Austerities are truth. Prajapati is truth. Creatures are born from truth. The elements are full of the greatness of truth.*'"

---

[120]Pitriyana and devayana.
[121]There is no repetition. The primary creation and dissolution refers to the end of Brahma's lifespan and rebirth, while the secondary creation and destruction refers to the end of Brahma's day and night.
[122]The five elements.

तस्मात्सत्याश्रया विप्रा नित्यं योगपरायणाः ।
अतीतक्रोधसंतापा नियता धर्मसेतवः ॥ (25)

'"'That is the reason brahmanas resort to truth and are always devoted to yoga. They overcome anger and repentance and are the bridges of dharma.'"'

अन्योन्यनियतान्वैद्यान्-धर्मसेतुप्रवर्तकान् ।
तानहं संप्रवक्ष्यामि शाश्वतान्लोकभावनान् ॥ (26)

'"'There are other learned brahmanas who have laid down the ordinances of dharma. I will tell you about them, the eternal ones who have created people.'"'

चातुर्विद्यं तथा वर्णांश्चतुरश्चाश्रमान्पृथक् ।
धर्ममेकं चतुष्पादं नित्यमाहुर्मनीषिणः ॥ (27)

'"'There are four branches of knowledge, four separate varnas and four separate ashramas. Dharma is one. But the learned have always said that it has four parts.'"'

पन्थानं वः प्रवक्ष्यामि शिवं क्षेमकरं द्विजाः ।
नियतं ब्रह्मभावाय यातं पूर्वं मनीषिभिः ॥ (28)

'"'O Dvijas! I will tell you about the path that is auspicious and brings benefit. Earlier, learned ones who have immersed themselves in the brahman have always traversed along this.'"'

गदतस्तं ममाद्येह पन्थानं दुर्विदं परम् ।
निबोधत महाभागा निखिलेन परं पदम् ॥ (29)

'"'Listen to me now. This supreme path is difficult to comprehend. O Immensely Fortunate Ones! Listen to everything about that supreme destination.'"'

ब्रह्मचारिकमेवाहुराश्रमं प्रथमं पदम् ।
गार्हस्थ्यं तु द्वितीयं स्याद्वानप्रस्थमतः परम् ।
ततः परं तु विज्ञेयमध्यात्मं परमं पदम् ॥ (30)

"'"The first step is said to be the ashrama of brahmacharya. Garhasthya is the second and vanaprastha comes after that. After this, it is known as the supreme step of adhyatma.'"'[123]

ज्योतिराकाशमादित्यो वायुरिन्द्र: प्रजापति: ।
नोपैति यावदध्यात्मं तावदेतान् पश्यति ।
तस्योपायं प्रवक्ष्यामि पुरस्तात्तं निबोधत ॥ (31)

"'"Light, space, Aditya, Vayu, Indra and Prajapati—these can only be seen as long as one has not attained the state of adhyatma. Understand next the means of obtaining that state. I will tell you.'"'

फलमूलानिलभुजां मुनीनां वसतां वने ।
वानप्रस्थं द्विजातीनां त्रयाणामुपदिश्यते ॥ (32)

"'"Sages reside in the forest and subsist on fruits, roots and air. This stage of vanaprastha has been laid down for the first three categories of dvijas.'"'

सर्वेषामेव वर्णानां गार्हस्थ्यं तद्विधीयते ।
श्रद्धालक्षणमित्येवं धर्मं धीरा: प्रचक्षते ॥ (33)

"'"Garhasthya is recommended for all the varnas. In this stage, it has been said that patience and faith are the signs of dharma.'"'

इत्येते देवयाना व: पन्थान: परिकीर्तिता: ।
सद्भिरध्यासिता धीरै: कर्मभिर्धर्मसेतव: ॥ (34)

"'"I have thus described to you the paths known as devayana. The virtuous and the patient use this karma as the bridge of dharma.'"'

एतेषां पृथगध्यास्ते यो धर्मं संशितव्रत: ।
कालात्पश्यति भूतानां सदैव प्रभवाप्ययौ ॥ (35)

"'"Other than this, there is another kind of dharma for those who are firm in their vows. Such people can always visualize the creation and destruction of beings.'"'

---

[123]That is, sannyasa.

अतस्तत्त्वानि वक्ष्यामि याथातथ्येन हेतुना ।
विषयस्थानि सर्वाणि वर्तमानानि भागशः ॥ (36)

"I will now accurately tell you the truth and the reasons as to why different essences exist separately in objects."

महानात्मा तथाव्यक्तमहंकारस्तथैव च ।
इन्द्रियाणि दशैकं च महाभूतानि पञ्च च ॥ (37)

"'There is mahat. There is the one who is not manifest.[124] There is ahamkara. There are eleven senses[125] and the five great elements.'"

विशेषः पञ्चभूतानामित्येषा वैदिकी श्रुतिः ।
चतुर्विंशतिरेषा वस्तत्त्वानां संप्रकीर्तिता ॥ (38)

"'The Shrutis of the Vedas have mentioned the specific qualities of the five elements.[126] The attributes are said to be twenty-four.'"[127]

तत्त्वानामथ यो वेद सर्वेषां प्रभवाप्ययौ ।
स धीरः सर्वभूतेषु न मोहमधिगच्छति ॥ (39)

"'One who understands the truth about this is patient and knows the truth about the creation and destruction of all beings. He is not overcome by delusion.'"

तत्त्वानि यो वेदयते यथातथं गुणांश्च सर्वानखिलाश्च देवताः ।
विधूतपाप्मा प्रविमुच्य बन्धनं स सर्वलोकानमलान्समश्नुते ॥ (40)

"'A person who knows the exact truth about the attributes and the qualities and everything about devas is cleansed of all sin and is freed from his bonds. He obtains all the unblemished worlds.'"

---

[124]Prakriti.
[125]The five senses of perception, five organs of action and the mind.
[126]Smell, sound and so on.
[127]Following samkhya—five senses of perception, five objects of the senses, five organs of action, five great elements, the mind, intelligence (mahat), ego (ahamkara) and Prakriti.

Chapter 21

ब्रह्मोवाच

तदव्यक्तमनुद्रिक्तं सर्वव्यापि ध्रुवं स्थिरम् ।
नवद्वारं पुरं विद्यात्त्रिगुणं पञ्चधातुकम् ॥ (1)

'"Brahma said, *That is unmanifest. It cannot be identified. It pervades everything. It is permanent and does not move. It is known as a city with nine gates, with three gunas and five constituents.*"'[128]

एकादशपरिक्षेपं मनो व्याकरणात्मकम् ।
बुद्धिस्वामिकमित्येतत्परमेकादशं भवेत् ॥ (2)

'"*The mind discriminates inside and pervades the eleven.*[129] *Intelligence is the supreme lord over these eleven.*"'

त्रीणि स्रोतांसि यान्यस्मिन्नाप्यायन्ते पुनः पुनः ।
प्रणाड्यस्तिस्र एवैताः प्रवर्तन्ते गुणात्मिकाः ॥ (3)
तमो रजस्तथा सत्त्वं गुणानेतान्प्रचक्षते ।
अन्योन्यमिथुनाः सर्वे तथान्योन्यानुजीविनः ॥ (4)

'"*This is repeatedly nurtured by three flows. These are the nadis*[130] *and the gunas flow along these, known as the gunas of tamas, rajas and sattva. All of these are joined to each other in pairs and obtain support from each other.*"'

अन्योन्यापाश्रयाश्चैव तथान्योन्यानुवर्तिनः ।
अन्योन्यव्यतिषक्ताश्च त्रिगुणाः पञ्च धातवः ॥ (5)

---

[128]The nine gates of the body are two eyes, two ears, two nostrils, the mouth, the anus and the genital organ. The three gunas are sattva, rajas and tamas. The five constituents are the five gross elements.

[129]Three gunas, five elements, intelligence, ahamkara and the senses are being counted as a single entity.

[130]Ida, pingala and sushumna are the three most important of nadis (channels of energy or the breath of life). Those who pass through this reach the brahman. Those who pass through the passage known as pingala reach devas. Those who pass through the passage known as ida reach the ancestors.

'"'They find refuge with each other and also follow each other. The three gunas are attached to each other and also to the five elements.'"'

तमसो मिथुनं सत्त्वं सत्त्वस्य मिथुनं रज: ।
रजसश्चापि सत्त्वं स्यात्सत्त्वस्य मिथुनं तम: ॥ (6)

'"'Tamas is paired with sattva. Sattva is paired with rajas. Other than rajas being paired with sattva, sattva is also paired with tamas.'"'

नियम्यते तमो यत्र रजस्तत्र प्रवर्तते ।
नियम्यते रजो यत्र सत्त्वं तत्र प्रवर्तते ॥ (7)

'"'When tamas is restrained, rajas flows there. When rajas is restrained, sattva flows there.'"'

नैशात्मकं तमो विद्यात्त्रिगुणं मोहसंज्ञितम् ।
अधर्मलक्षणं चैव नियतं पापकर्मसु ॥ (8)

'"'Tamas should be known as the night, since it has signs of delusion and its three characteristics.[131] It has the attributes of adharma and is always associated with wicked deeds.'"'

प्रवृत्त्यात्मकमेवाहू रज: पर्यायकारकम् ।
प्रवृत्तं सर्वभूतेषु दृश्यतोत्पत्तिलक्षणम् ॥ (9)

'"'Rajas is said to progressively stimulate enterprise and action. In all beings, when it flows, its signs are generation.'"'

प्रकाशं सर्वभूतेषु लाघवं श्रद्दधानता ।
सात्त्विकं रूपमेवं तु लाघवं साधुसंमितम् ॥ (10)

'"'Radiance, dexterity and faith—in all beings, these are seen to be the forms of sattva and dexterity is respected by the virtuous.'"'

एतेषां गुणतत्त्वं हि वक्ष्यते हेत्वहेतुभि: ।
समासव्यासयुक्तानि तत्त्वतस्तानि वित्त मे ॥ (11)

---

[131]Ignorance, delusion and wickedness.

"'I will now tell you about the nature of these gunas and their reasons. Understand from me the truth about these qualities, individually and collectively.'"

संमोहोऽज्ञानमत्याग: कर्मणामविनिर्णय: ।
स्वप्न: स्तम्भो भयं लोभ: शोक: सुकृतदूषणम् ॥ (12)
अस्मृतिश्चाविपाकश्च नास्तिक्यं भिन्नवृत्तिता ।
निर्विशेषत्वमन्धत्वं जघन्यगुणवृत्तिता ॥ (13)
अकृते कृतमानित्वमज्ञाने ज्ञानमानिता ।
अमैत्री विकृतो भावो अश्रद्धा मूढभावना ॥ (14)
अनार्जवमसंज्ञत्वं कर्म पापमचेतना ।
गुरुत्वं सन्नभावत्वमसितत्त्वमवाग्गति: ॥ (15)
सर्व एते गुणा विप्रास्तामसा: संप्रकीर्तिता: ।
ये चान्ये नियता भावा लोकेऽस्मिन्मोहसंज्ञिता: ॥ (16)

"'Delusion, ignorance, absence of renouncement, inability to take a decision about action, sleep, insolence, fear, greed, sorrow, censure of good acts, lack of memory, lack of intelligence, non-belief, perverse conduct, lack of discrimination, blindness, vileness in conduct, boasting about action even when no action has been performed, pride in knowledge despite being ignorant, lack of friendliness, contrary action, lack of faith, stupidity in beliefs, crookedness, lack of sense, wicked sentiments in action, heaviness, lassitude, darkness and degradation—brahmanas recount these as the qualities of tamas. There are other sentiments that constrain one in this world, laced with signs of delusion.'"

तत्र तत्र नियम्यन्ते सर्वे ते तामसा गुणा: ।
परिवादकथा नित्यं देवब्राह्मणवैदिका: ॥ (17)

"'Wherever these constraints are caused, those are the qualities of tamas. Such people always censure devas, brahmanas and the Vedas.'"

अत्यागश्चाभिमानश्च मोहो मन्युस्तथाक्षमा ।
मत्सरश्चैव भूतेषु तामसं वृत्तमिष्यते ॥ (18)

"'Not renouncing, insolence, delusion, anger, lack of forgiveness and malice towards creatures—such conduct has the attributes of tamas.'"

वृथारम्भाश्च ये केचिद्वृथादानानि यानि च ।
वृथाभक्षणमित्येतत्तामसं वृत्तमिष्यते ॥ (19)

"'Beginning futile tasks, donating in vain and eating in vain—such conduct has the attributes of tamas.'"

अतिवादोऽतितितिक्षा च मात्सर्यमतिमानिता ।
अश्रद्दधानता चैव तामसं वृत्तमिष्यते ॥ (20)

"'Slandering others, lack of patience, jealousy, excessive pride and lack of faith—such conduct has the attributes of tamas.'"

एवंविधास्तु ये केचिल्लोकेऽस्मिन्पापकर्मिणः ।
मनुष्या भिन्नमर्यादाः सर्वे ते तामसा जनाः ॥ (21)

"'There are men in this world who perpetrate such wicked deeds. They break the ordinances. All such people are tamas.'"

तेषां योनिं प्रवक्ष्यामि नियतां पापकर्मणाम् ।
अवाङ्निरयभावाय तिर्यङ्निरयगामिनः ॥ (22)

"'I will speak about the wombs those constant performers of evil deeds are destined for. Their sentiments lead them downwards and they go to hell and are born as inferior species.'"

स्थावराणि च भूतानि पशवो वाहनानि च ।
क्रव्यादा दन्दशूकाश्च कृमिकीटविहंगमाः ॥ (23)
अण्डजा जन्तवो ये च सर्वे चापि चतुष्पदाः ।
उन्मत्ता बधिरा मूका ये चान्ये पापरोगिणः ॥ (24)
मग्नास्तमसि दुर्वृत्ताः स्वकर्मकृतलक्षणाः ।
अवाक्स्रोतस इत्येते मग्नास्तमसि तामसाः ॥ (25)

"[They become] immobile objects, animals, beasts of burden, predatory beasts, snakes, worms, insects, birds, creatures born from eggs, all the other kinds of quadrupeds, or those who are mad, deaf and dumb, or those who suffer from other vile diseases. Because of the consequences of their own karma, these evil-doers are immersed in tamas. Their course is downwards. From one kind of tamas, they sink into greater tamas."'

तेषामुत्कर्षमुद्रेकं वक्ष्याम्यहमतः परम् ।
यथा ते सुकृतॉल्लोकॉल्लभन्ते पुण्यकर्मिणः ॥ (26)

"'I will next tell you what can be done for benefit. Through such means, they become the performers of auspicious deeds and can obtain worlds meant for the virtuous.'"

अन्यथा प्रतिपन्नास्तु विवृद्धा ये च कर्मसु ।
स्वकर्मनिरतानां च ब्राह्मणानां शुभैषिणाम् ॥ (27)

"'Countering their own deeds, they can enhance their karma, engaging brahmanas who are kindly disposed in the performance of their own karma.'"[132]

संस्कारेणोर्ध्वमायान्ति यतमानाः सलोकताम् ।
स्वर्गं गच्छन्ति देवानामित्येषा वैदिकी श्रुतिः ॥ (28)

"'If one endeavours to ensure this process of cleansing, one ascends to superior worlds. It is even possible to be with the devas in heaven. This is what is said in the Shrutis of the Vedas.'"

अन्यथा प्रतिपन्नास्तु विवृद्धाः स्वेषु कर्मसु ।
पुनरावृत्तिधर्माणस्ते भवन्तीह मानुषाः ॥ (29)

"'Otherwise, the store of contrary karma increases. They become humans, subject to the dharma of returning again.'"[133]

पापयोनिं समापन्नाश्चण्डाला मूकचूचुकाः ।
वर्णान्पर्यायशश्चापि प्राप्नुवन्त्युत्तरोत्तरम् ॥ (30)

---

[132]Liberty has been taken to translate this. Else, the meaning would not have been clear. Even if one is born as inferior species, if one engages in rites, officiated by brahmanas, one is capable of uplifting one's own self.
[133]Dying and being reborn.

"'They obtain wicked births, like those of chandalas, or they are dumb, or stammer. However, progressively, they obtain better and better varnas.'"

शूद्रयोनिमतिक्रम्य ये चान्ये तामसा गुणाः ।
स्रोतोमध्ये समागम्य वर्तन्ते तामसे गुणे ॥ (31)

"'They transcend birth as a shudra and other qualities of tamas. But those who indulge in the qualities of tamas continue to remain submerged in that flow.'"

अभिषङ्गस्तु कामेषु महामोह इति स्मृतः ।
ऋषयो मुनयो देवा मुह्यन्त्यत्र सुखेप्सवः ॥ (32)

"'The attachment to desire is said to be a great delusion. Desiring happiness, even rishis, sages and devas become confused.'"

तमो मोहो महामोहस्तामिस्रः क्रोधसंज्ञितः ।
मरणं त्वन्धतामिस्रं तामिस्रं क्रोध उच्यते ॥ (33)

"'Darkness, delusion, great delusion, the darkness known as anger, death and blinding ignorance—of these, the darkness of rage is said to be the worst.'"

भावतो गुणतश्चैव योनितश्चैव तत्त्वतः ।
सर्वमेतत्तमो विप्राः कीर्तितं वो यथाविधि ॥ (34)

"'O Brahmanas! I have recounted to you the truth about different kinds of birth, the sentiments and the qualities. I have also accurately told you everything about tamas.'"

को न्वेतद्बुध्यते साधु को न्वेतत्साधु पश्यति ।
अतत्त्वे तत्त्वदर्शी यस्तमसस्तत्त्वलक्षणम् ॥ (35)

"'Who is the virtuous one who understands it? Who is the virtuous one who sees it? Taking falsehood to be the truth is indeed a characteristic of tamas.'"

तमोगुणा वो बहुधा प्रकीर्तिता यथावदुक्तं च तमः परावरम् ।
नरो हि यो वेद गुणानिमान्सदा स तामसैः सर्वगुणैः प्रमुच्यते ॥ (36)

"'"The qualities of tamas have been recounted to you in many ways. I have also told you about the superior and inferior forms of tamas. A man who knows these qualities will always be freed from all the qualities of tamas."'"

Chapter 22

ब्रह्मोवाच

रजोऽहं व: प्रवक्ष्यामि याथातथ्येन सत्तमा: ।
निबोधत महाभागा गुणवृत्तं च सर्वश: ॥ (1)

"'"Brahma said, O Excellent Ones! I will tell you the truth about rajas. O Immensely Fortunate Ones! Listen to everything about the qualities in this kind of conduct."'"

संघातो रूपमायास: सुखदु:खे हिमातपौ ।
ऐश्वर्यं विग्रह: संधिर्हेतुवादोऽरति: क्षमा ॥ (2)
बलं शौर्यं मदो रोषो व्यायामकलहावपि ।
ईर्ष्येप्सा पैशुनं युद्धं ममत्वं परिपालनम् ॥ (3)
वधबन्धपरिक्लेशा: क्रयो विक्रय एव च ।
निकृन्त छिन्धि भिन्धीति परमर्मावकर्तनम् ॥ (4)
उग्रं दारुणमाक्रोश: परवित्तानुशासनम् ।
लोकचिन्ता विचिन्ता च मत्सर: परिभाषणम् ॥ (5)
मृषावादो मृषादानं विकल्प: परिभाषणम् ।
निन्दा स्तुति: प्रशंसा च प्रताप: परितर्पणम् ॥ (6)
परिचर्या च शुश्रूषा सेवा तृष्णा व्यपाश्रय: ।
व्यूहोऽनय: प्रमादश्च परिताप: परिग्रह: ॥ (7)
संस्कारा ये च लोकेऽस्मिन्प्रवर्तन्ते पृथक्पृथक् ।
नृषु नारीषु भूतेषु द्रव्येषु शरणेषु च ॥ (8)
संतापोऽप्रत्ययश्चैव व्रतानि नियमाश्च ये ।
प्रदानमाशीर्युक्तं च सततं मे भवन्त्विति ॥ (9)
स्वधाकारो नमस्कार: स्वाहाकारो वषट्क्रिया ।
याजनाध्यापने चोभे तथैवाहु: परिग्रहम् ॥ (10)
इदं मे स्यादिदं मे स्यात्स्नेहो गुणसमुद्भव: ।

अभिद्रोहस्तथा माया निकृतिर्मान एव च ॥ (11)
स्तैन्यं हिंसा परीवाद: परिताप: प्रजागर: ।
स्तम्भो दम्भोऽथ रागश्च भक्ति: प्रीति: प्रमोदनम् ॥ (12)
द्यूतं च जनवादश्च संबन्धा: स्त्रीकृताश्च ये ।
नृत्तवादित्रगीतानि प्रसङ्गा ये च केचन ।
सर्व एते गुणा विप्रा राजसा: संप्रकीर्तिता: ॥ (13)

"'*O Brahmanas! Harming the beauty of others, exertion, happiness, unhappiness, cold, heat, prosperity, conflict, peace, debates, discontent, forgiveness, strength, valour, intoxication, anger, physical exertion, quarrels, jealousy, calumny, battles, a sense of ownership, preservation, slaughter, imprisonment, hardships, buying, selling, slicing off, piercing, severing, mangling, fierceness, terror, violence, earning a living through the wealth of others, thinking of worldly affairs, anxiety, intolerance in speech, false speech, false gifts, hesitation in speech, censure, worship, praise, influence, contentment, being served, serving, obedience, thirst, being self-centred, separation, bad policy, distraction, repentance, receiving, the separate samskaras that are prescribed in the world for men, women, animals, objects and houses, torment, lack of confidence, rites, rituals, incessant gifts for benedictions on one's own self, svadha, namaskara, svaha, vashatkara,[134] performing sacrifices, studying, receiving gifts, attachment that is generated for various qualities, treachery, deception, dishonour, honour, theft, injury, delusion, dishonouring one's own self, robbery, wakefulness, vanity, insolence, attachment, devotion, joy, delight, gambling, scandal, alliances with women, attachment to dancing, musical instruments and singing—these are said to be the qualities associated with rajas.*'"

भूतभव्यभविष्याणां भावानां भुवि भावना: ।
त्रिवर्गनिरता नित्यं धर्मोऽर्थ: काम इत्यपि ॥ (14)

"'*There are those who think about the past, the present and the future.*

---

[134] Vashatkara is a general exclamation (the sound of *vashat*) when oblations are offered; svaha is the exclamation when oblations are offered to gods; svadha that when oblations are offered to ancestors; and namaskara is the act of prostration, bowing down.

They are always devoted to the three objectives of dharma, artha and kama.'"

कामवृत्ताः प्रमोदन्ते सर्वकामसमृद्धिभिः ।
अर्वाक्स्रोतस इत्येते तैजसा रजसावृताः ॥ (15)

"'They act because they find delight in desire and in the successful obtaining of all the objects of desire. Since their energy is enveloped in rajas, they have a downward flow.'"

अस्मिँल्लोके प्रमोदन्ते जायमानाः पुनः पुनः ।
प्रेत्यभाविकमीहन्त इह लौकिकमेव च ।
ददति प्रतिगृह्णन्ति जपन्त्यथ च जुह्वति ॥ (16)

"'They find pleasure in this world and are repeatedly born again. They desire what can be obtained in this world and in the world after death. They give and they receive. They perform japa and offer oblations.'"

रजोगुणा वो बहुधानुकीर्तिता यथावदुक्तं गुणवृत्तमेव च ।
नरो हि यो वेद गुणानिमान्सदा स राजसैः सर्वगुणैर्विमुच्यते ॥ (17)

"'The qualities of rajas have been recounted to you in many ways. The conduct that follows this quality has also been described accurately. A man who always understands these qualities is freed from all the qualities that are associated with rajas.'"

Chapter 23

ब्रह्मोवाच

अतः परं प्रवक्ष्यामि तृतीयं गुणमुत्तमम् ।
सर्वभूतहितं लोके सतां धर्ममनिन्दितम् ॥ (1)

"'Brahma said, After this, I will tell you about the third and supreme guna. This is beneficial for all creatures in this world. This is the unblemished dharma followed by the virtuous.'"

आनन्द: प्रीतिरुद्रेक: प्राकाश्यं सुखमेव च ।
अकार्पण्यमसंरम्भ: संतोष: श्रद्दधानता ॥ (2)
क्षमा धृतिरहिंसा च समता सत्यमार्जवम् ।
अक्रोधश्चानसूया च शौचं दाक्ष्यं पराक्रम: ॥ (3)
मुधा ज्ञानं मुधा वृत्तं मुधा सेवा मुधा श्रम: ।
एवं यो युक्तधर्म: स्यात्सोऽमुत्रानन्त्यमश्नुते ॥ (4)

"'"Joy, happiness, not causing anxiety, enlightenment, bliss, lack of niggardliness, lack of insolence, contentment, devotion, forgiveness, fortitude, lack of violence, impartiality, truthfulness, uprightness, lack of anger, lack of malice, purity, skill, valour and realization that jnana, conduct, service and toil are futile[135]—a person who follows these in the practice of dharma, obtains the infinite in the world hereafter.'"

निर्ममो निरहंकारो निराशी: सर्वत: सम: ।
अकामहत इत्येष सतां धर्म: सनातन: ॥ (5)

"'"He has no sense of ownership. He is without ahamkara and without wishes. He looks upon everyone equally. He is free from desire. This is the eternal dharma followed by the virtuous."'"

विश्रम्भो ह्रीस्तितिक्षा च त्याग: शौचमतन्द्रिता ।
आनृशंस्यमसंमोहो दया भूतेष्वपैशुनम् ॥ (6)
हर्षस्तुष्टिर्विस्मयश्च विनय: साधुवृत्तता ।
शान्तिकर्म विशुद्धिश्च शुभा बुद्धिर्विमोचनम् ॥ (7)
उपेक्षा ब्रह्मचर्यं च परित्यागश्च सर्वश: ।
निर्ममत्वमनाशीस्त्वमपरिक्रीतधर्मता ॥ (8)

"'"Confidence, modesty, patience, renunciation, purity, constancy, lack of violence, lack of delusion, compassion towards all creatures, absence of calumny, joy, contentment, wonder, humility, good conduct, tranquillity and purity in deeds, auspicious intelligence, liberation, indifference, brahmacharya, detachment in every way, lack of ownership, lack of wishes and being surrounded by dharma.'"

---

[135]These are futile when pursued for fruits.

मुधा दानं मुधा यज्ञो मुधाधीतं मुधा व्रतम् ।
मुधा प्रतिग्रहश्चैव मुधा धर्मो मुधा तपः ॥ (9)

'"'Donations are futile. Sacrifices are futile. Studying is futile. Vows are futile. Receiving of gifts is futile. Dharma is futile. Austerities are futile.'"'[136]

एवंवृत्तास्तु ये केचिल्लोकेऽस्मिन्सत्त्वसंश्रयाः ।
ब्राह्मणा ब्रह्मयोनिस्थास्ते धीराः साधुदर्शिनः ॥ (10)

'"'There are some people who seek refuge in sattva and follow this kind of conduct. These brahmanas are patient, virtuous in their insight and are located in the seat of the brahman.'"'

हित्वा सर्वाणि पापानि निःशोका ह्यजरामराः ।
दिवं प्राप्य तु ते धीराः कुर्वते वै ततस्ततः ॥ (11)

'"'They abandon all kinds of sin. They are without grief. They are beyond old age. They are immortal. The patient ones create and obtain heaven, here and there.'"'[137]

ईशित्वं च वशित्वं च लघुत्वं मनसश्च ते ।
विकुर्वते महात्मानो देवास्त्रिदिवगा इव ॥ (12)

'"'Through their minds, they possess the powers of lordship, subjugation and lightness. Those great-souled ones behave like devas in heaven.'"'[138]

ऊर्ध्वस्रोतस इत्येते देवा वैकारिकाः स्मृताः ।
विकुर्वते प्रकृत्या वै दिवं प्राप्तास्ततस्ततः ।
यद्यदिच्छन्ति तत्सर्वं भजन्ते विभजन्ति च ॥ (13)

'"'They are said to move upwards and, like devas, can create. Having reached heaven, they can use their natures to modify everything. They obtain everything that they desire and distribute these.'"'

---

[136]These are futile because people with sattva transcend narrow forms of these that are performed with a desire for fruits.
[137]They can create their own worlds.
[138]Yoga leads to eight major siddhis or powers.

इत्येतत्सात्त्विकं वृत्तं कथितं वो द्विजर्षभा: ।
एतद्विज्ञाय विधिवल्लभते यद्यदिच्छति ॥ (14)

"'O Bulls among Dvijas! I have thus told you about sattva conduct. If one understands this in the proper way, one can obtain whatever one wishes.'"

प्रकीर्तिता: सत्त्वगुणा विशेषतो यथावदुक्तं गुणवृत्तमेव च ।
नरस्तु यो वेद गुणानिमान्सदा गुणान्स
भुङ्क्ते न गुणै: स भुज्यते ॥ (15)

"'The qualities of sattva have specially been recounted. The conduct associated with this guna has also been described. A man who always knows these qualities enjoys these qualities. But the qualities do not enjoy him.'"[139]

Chapter 24

ब्रह्मोवाच

नैव शक्या गुणा वक्तुं पृथक्त्वेनेह सर्वश: ।
अविच्छिन्नानि दृश्यन्ते रज: सत्त्वं तमस्तथा ॥ (1)

"'Brahma said, One is incapable of speaking about all the gunas separately. Rajas, sattva and tamas are seen to be together.'"

अन्योन्यमनुषज्जन्ते अन्योन्यं चानुजीविन: ।
अन्योन्यापाश्रया: सर्वे तथान्योन्यानुवर्तिन: ॥ (2)

"'They are attached to each other and depend on each other. All of them seek refuge with each other and follow each other.'"

यावत्सत्त्वं तमस्तावद्वर्तते नात्र संशय: ।
यावत्तमश्च सत्त्वं च रजस्तावदिहोच्यते ॥ (3)

---

[139] He remains unattached.

"'There is no doubt that where there is sattva, tamas also proliferates. It is said that as long as tamas and sattva exist, rajas also coexists.'"

संहत्य कुर्वते यात्रां सहिताः संघचारिणः ।
संघातवृत्तयो ह्येते वर्तन्ते हेत्वहेतुभिः ॥ (4)

"'They progress together along the path. They combine and adhere to each other. Their conduct is also collective, sometimes with reason, sometimes without reason.'"

उद्रेकव्यतिरेकाणां तेषामन्योन्यवर्तिनाम् ।
वर्तते तद्यथान्यूनं व्यतिरिक्तं च सर्वशः ॥ (5)

"'However, even when they follow each other, the outcomes may be different. Collectively, they can progress in a superior way and also in an inferior way.'"

व्यतिरिक्तं तमो यत्र तिर्यग्भावगतं भवेत् ।
अल्पं तत्र रजो ज्ञेयं सत्त्वं चाल्पतरं ततः ॥ (6)

"'When there is an excess of tamas, the progress is downwards. A little bit of rajas will be discerned there and sattva will be lesser still.'"

उद्रिक्तं च रजो यत्र मध्यस्रोतोगतं भवेत् ।
अल्पं तत्र तमो ज्ञेयं सत्त्वं चाल्पतरं ततः ॥ (7)

"'When there is an excess of rajas, the progress is then middling. A little bit of tamas will be discerned there and sattva will be lesser still.'"

उद्रिक्तं च यदा सत्त्वमूर्ध्वस्रोतोगतं भवेत् ।
अल्पं तत्र रजो ज्ञेयं तमश्चाल्पतरं ततः ॥ (8)

"'When there is an excess of sattva, the progress is upwards. A little bit of rajas will be discerned there and tamas will be lesser still.'"

सत्त्वं वैकारिकं योनिरिन्द्रियाणां प्रकाशिका ।
न हि सत्त्वात्परो भावः कश्चिदन्यो विधीयते ॥ (9)

"'Sattva is the origin for any transformation and illumination of the senses. There is no other attribute that is superior to sattva.'"

ऊर्ध्वं गच्छन्ति सत्त्वस्था मध्ये तिष्ठन्ति राजसाः ।
जघन्यगुणसंयुक्ता यान्त्यधस्तामसा जनाः ॥ (10)

"'"The progress of sattva is upwards, that of rajas is middling. People who have tamas possess inferior qualities and progress downwards."'"

तमः शूद्रे रजः क्षत्रे ब्राह्मणे सत्त्वमुत्तमम् ।
इत्येवं त्रिषु वर्णेषु विवर्तन्ते गुणास्त्रयः ॥ (11)

"'"The three gunas course in the three varnas—tamas in shudras, rajas in kshatriyas and the excellent sattva in brahmanas."'"

दूरादपि हि दृश्यन्ते सहिताः संघचारिणः ।
तमः सत्त्वं रजश्चैव पृथक्त्वं नानुशुश्रुम ॥ (12)

"'"Even from a distance,[140] they are seen to exist together and collectively. We have not heard of tamas, sattva or rajas existing separately."'"

दृष्ट्वा चादित्यमुद्यन्तं कुचोराणां भयं भवेत् ।
अध्वगाः परितप्येरंस्तृष्णार्ता दुःखभागिनः ॥ (13)

"'"When they see the sun rising, wicked thieves suffer from fear. Travellers are tormented [by the heat]. They are afflicted by thirst and suffer from hardships."'"

आदित्यः सत्त्वमुद्दिष्टं कुचोरास्तु यथा तमः ।
परितापोऽध्वगानां च राजसो गुण उच्यते ॥ (14)

"'"The rising sun is like sattva. Wicked thieves are tamas. The heat that torments travellers is said to be the quality of rajas."'"

प्राकाश्यं सत्त्वमादित्ये संतापो राजसो गुणः ।
उपप्लवस्तु विज्ञेयस्तामसस्तस्य पर्वसु ॥ (15)

"'"The radiance in the sun is sattva. The torment is the quality of rajas. The invasion on a parva day is known as the quality of tamas."'"[141]

---

[140]That is, from a cursory examination.
[141]When the sun is invaded by Rahu, causing an eclipse.

एवं ज्योतिःषु सर्वेषु विवर्तन्ते गुणास्त्रयः ।
पर्यायेण च वर्तन्ते तत्र तत्र तथा तथा ॥ (16)

'"'In this way, all three qualities exist in luminous bodies. In due course, they manifest themselves, here and there.'"'

स्थावरेषु च भूतेषु तिर्यग्भावगतं तमः ।
राजसास्तु विवर्तन्ते स्नेहभावास्तु सात्त्विकः ॥ (17)

'"'Even in immobile objects, tamas leads to an inferior state. Rajas exists in the variations[142] and sattva in oleaginous substances.'"'

अहस्त्रिधा तु विज्ञेयं त्रिधा रात्रिर्विधीयते ।
मासार्धमासवर्षाणि ऋतवः संधयस्तथा ॥ (18)

'"'Know that the day has three parts. The night has also been divided into three parts. Months, fortnights, years, seasons and sandhyas[143] are also like that.'"'

त्रिधा दानानि दीयन्ते त्रिधा यज्ञः प्रवर्तते ।
त्रिधा लोकास्त्रिधा वेदास्त्रिधा विद्यास्त्रिधा गतिः ॥ (19)

'"'Three kinds of gifts can be given. Three kinds of sacrifices can be undertaken. There are three worlds. There are three Vedas. There are three kinds of knowledge. There are three destinations.'"'

भूतं भव्यं भविष्यच्च धर्मोऽर्थः काम इत्यपि ।
प्राणापानावुदानश्चाप्येत एव त्रयो गुणाः ॥ (20)

'"'There is the past, the present and the future. There is dharma, artha and kama. The three gunas are also there in prana, apana and udana.'"'

यत्किंचिदिह वै लोके सर्वमेष्वेव तत्त्रिषु ।
त्रयो गुणाः प्रवर्तन्ते अव्यक्ता नित्यमेव तु ।
सत्त्वं रजस्तमश्चैव गुणसर्गः सनातनः ॥ (21)

---

[142] As they pass through different forms of existence.
[143] The two points where night and day meet, morning and evening.

"'"Everything that exists in the world has three components. The three gunas always exist in a form that is not manifest. The creation of the three gunas, sattva, rajas and tamas, is eternal."'"

तमोऽव्यक्तं शिवं नित्यमजं योनि: सनातन: ।
प्रकृतिर्विकार: प्रलय: प्रधानं प्रभवाप्ययौ ॥ (22)
अनुद्रिक्तमनूनं च ह्यकम्पमचलं ध्रुवम् ।
सदसच्चैव तत्सर्वमव्यक्तं त्रिगुणं स्मृतम् ।
ज्ञेयानि नामधेयानि नैरध्यात्मचिन्तकै: ॥ (23)

"'"Darkness, the unmanifest, the auspicious, the constant, the one without birth, the womb, the eternal, Prakriti, transformation, dissolution, Pradhana, creation, destruction, the minute, the large, the certain, the unwavering, the immutable, the existent and the non-existent—everything is said to possess the three gunas. A man who thinks about adhyatma must know these names and meditate about them."'"

अव्यक्तनामानि गुणांश्च तत्त्वतो यो वेद सर्वाणि गतीश्च केवला: ।
विमुक्तदेह: प्रविभागतत्त्ववित्स मुच्यते सर्वगुणैर्निरामय: ॥ (24)

"'"If a person knows the names and the truth about the gunas of the unmanifest, he will not only know about all the destinations. He will know the truth about different distinctions and will be freed from his body. He will be liberated from all the gunas and be without disease."'"

Chapter 25

ब्रह्मोवाच

अव्यक्तात्पूर्वमुत्पन्नो महानात्मा महामति: ।
आदिगुणानां सर्वेषां प्रथम: सर्ग उच्यते ॥ (1)

"'"Brahma said, From the unmanifest, the great intelligence, mahat, was generated first. This is the origin of all the gunas and is known as the first creation."'"

महानात्मा मतिर्विष्णुर्विश्वः शंभुश्च वीर्यवान् ।
बुद्धिः प्रज्ञोपलब्धिश्च तथा ख्यातिर्धृतिः स्मृतिः ॥ (2)

'"'Mahat is known as the great atman, intelligence, Vishnu, Vishva, Shambhu, the valiant one, understanding, wisdom, realization, fame, fortitude and memory.'"'

पर्यायवाचकैः शब्दैर्महानात्मा विभाव्यते ।
तं जानन्ब्राह्मणो विद्वान् प्रमोहं निगच्छति ॥ (3)

'"'Progressively, mahat is thought of in these different words. A learned brahmana who knows this is not immersed in delusion.'"'

सर्वतःपाणिपादश्च सर्वतोक्षिशिरोमुखः ।
सर्वतःश्रुतिमाँल्लोके सर्वं व्याप्य स तिष्ठति ॥ (4)

'"'His arms and feet are in every direction. His eyes, heads and faces are in every direction. His ears are everywhere in the worlds. He is established, pervading everything.'"'

महाप्रभार्चिः पुरुषः सर्वस्य हृदि निश्रितः ।
अणिमा लघिमा प्राप्तिरीशानो ज्योतिरव्ययः ॥ (5)

'"'With the attributes of greatness, power and radiance, Purusha is based in the heart of everything. He is the lord of being minute, being light and obtaining everything. He is resplendent and without decay.'"'[144]

तत्र बुद्धिमतां लोकाः संन्यासनिरताश्च ये ।
ध्यानिनो नित्ययोगाश्च सत्यसंधा जितेन्द्रियाः ॥ (6)

'"'There are intelligent people in the world who are devoted to renunciation. They meditate and always immerse themselves in yoga. They are devoted to the truth and conquer their senses.'"'

ज्ञानवन्तश्च ये केचिदलुब्धा जितमन्यवः ।
प्रसन्नमनसो धीरा निर्ममा निरहंकृताः ।
विमुक्ताः सर्व एवैते महत्त्वमुपयान्ति वै ॥ (7)

---

[144] This describes him as possessing the siddhis.

"'Some are learned, without greed and have conquered their anger. They are patient and cheerful in their minds. They are without a sense of ownership and without a sense of ego. They are free in every possible way and obtain greatness.'"

आत्मनो महतो वेद यः पुण्यां गतिमुत्तमाम् ।
स धीरः सर्वलोकेषु न मोहमधिगच्छति ।
विष्णुरेवादिसर्गेषु स्वयंभूर्भवति प्रभुः ॥ (8)

"'Those who perceive mahat in their own atmans go to the supreme and auspicious destination. Among all the people, they are patient and are not submerged in delusion. Svayambhu Vishnu is himself the lord of that first creation.'"

एवं हि यो वेद गुहाशयं प्रभुं नरः पुराणं पुरुषं विश्वरूपम् ।
हिरण्मयं बुद्धिमतां परां गतिं स बुद्धिमान्बुद्धिमतीत्य तिष्ठति ॥ (9)

"'This is the ancient lord, Purusha. He is hidden in a cave[145] and the universe is his form. He is golden and is the supreme destination for those who are intelligent. A person who knows him is intelligent and obtains an understanding that is greater than all kinds of intelligence.'"

Chapter 26

ब्रह्मोवाच

य उत्पन्नो महान्पूर्वमहंकारः स उच्यते ।
अहमित्येव संभूतो द्वितीयः सर्ग उच्यते ॥ (1)

"'Brahma said, mahat originated first and then came what is known as ahamkara. The sense of I am originated and is known as the second creation.'"

---

[145] The understanding in the heart. In texts, it is quite common for the heart to be compared to a cave or cavity.

अहंकारश्च भूतादिवैकारिक इति स्मृतः ।
तेजसश्चेतना धातुः प्रजासर्गः प्रजापतिः ॥ (२)

"*"It is said that ahamkara is the reason behind the creation of beings. Prajapati has the substance of energy and consciousness and is responsible for the creation of subjects."*"

देवानां प्रभवो देवो मनसश्च त्रिलोककृत् ।
अहमित्येव तत्सर्वमभिमन्ता स उच्यते ॥ (३)

"*"He is the divinity who is the creator of devas through his mental powers. He is the creator of the three worlds. This is said to be the sense of ego—I am all this."*"

अध्यात्मज्ञाननित्यानां मुनीनां भावितात्मनाम् ।
स्वाध्यायक्रतुसिद्धानामेष लोकः सनातनः ॥ (४)

"*"There are sages who have cleansed their atmans and are always devoted to jnana about the adhyatma. They have obtained siddhi and the eternal worlds through studying and sacrifices."*"

अहंकारेणाहृतो गुणानिमान्भूतादिरेवं सृजते स भूतकृत् ।
वैकारिकः सर्वमिदं विचेष्टते स्वतेजसा रञ्जयते जगत्तथा ॥ (५)

"*"The gunas are attached to the sense of ahamkara. It is in this way that the creator of beings creates all creatures. It is this that causes all the transformations and all movement. It is through his own energy that he delights the universe."*"

Chapter 27

ब्रह्मोवाच

अहंकारात्प्रसूतानि महाभूतानि पञ्च वै ।
पृथिवी वायुराकाशमापो ज्योतिश्च पञ्चमम् ॥ (१)

"*"Brahma said, *The five great elements were generated from ahamkara—earth, air, space, water and light as the fifth.*"*"

तेषु भूतानि मुह्यन्ते महाभूतेषु पञ्चसु ।
शब्दस्पर्शनरूपेषु रसगन्धक्रियासु च ॥ (2)

"'All beings are deluded because of these five great elements, through the action of sound, touch, form, taste and smell.'"

महाभूतविनाशान्ते प्रलये प्रत्युपस्थिते ।
सर्वप्राणभृतां धीरा महदुत्पद्यते भयम् ॥ (3)

"'When the five great elements are destroyed, there is universal dissolution. O Patient Ones! There is great fear to all those who possess life.'"

यद्यस्माज्जायते भूतं तत्र तत्प्रविलीयते ।
लीयन्ते प्रतिलोमानि जायन्ते चोत्तरोत्तरम् ॥ (4)

"'Every entity is dissolved into its source of origin. That dissolution occurs in an order that is the reverse of the progress of creation.'"

ततः प्रलीने सर्वस्मिन्भूते स्थावरजङ्गमे ।
स्मृतिमन्तस्तदा धीरा न लीयन्ते कदाचन ॥ (5)

"'All mobile and immobile objects face destruction. However, those who are patient and possess memory are never destroyed.'"

शब्दः स्पर्शस्तथा रूपं रसो गन्धश्च पञ्चमः ।
क्रियाकारणयुक्ताः स्युरनित्या मोहसंज्ञिताः ॥ (6)

"'Sound, touch, form, taste and smell as the fifth are the effects. Because of being tinged with delusion, they are thought of as the causes.'"

लोभप्रजनसंयुक्ता निर्विशेषा ह्यकिंचनाः ।
मांसशोणितसंघाता अन्योन्यस्योपजीविनः ॥ (7)

"'They are not different from each other. But they are insignificant and are created in that way because of greed. In the mixture of flesh and blood, they draw sustenance from each other.'"

बहिरात्मान इत्येते दीना: कृपणवृत्तय: ।
प्राणापानावुदानश्च समानो व्यान एव च ॥ (8)

"'They are external to the atman. They cause distress and miserable conduct. Prana, apana, udana, samana and vyana are also like that.'"

अन्तरात्मेति चाप्येते नियता: पञ्च वायव: ।
वाङ्मनोबुद्धिरित्येभि: सार्धमष्टात्मकं जगत् ॥ (9)

"'These five kinds of breaths of life are always attached to the inner atman. Together with speech, mind and intelligence, these eight are the atman of the universe.'"

त्वग्घ्राणश्रोत्रचक्षूंषि रसनं वाक्च संयता ।
विशुद्धं च मनो यस्य बुद्धिश्चाव्यभिचारिणी ॥ (10)

"'There may be a person who has controlled his skin, nose, ears, eyes, tongue and speech. His mind is pure and his intelligence does not stray from the course.'"

अष्टौ यस्याग्नयो ह्येते न दहन्ते मन: सदा ।
स तद्ब्रह्म शुभं याति यस्मादभूयो न विद्यते ॥ (11)

"'His mind is never consumed by these eight fires. Such a person obtains the auspicious brahman and nothing is superior to that.'"

एकादश च यान्याहुरिन्द्रियाणि विशेषत: ।
अहंकारप्रसूतानि तानि वक्ष्याम्यहं द्विजा: ॥ (12)

"'In particular, there are said to be eleven senses. These originate in ahamkara. O Dvijas! I will speak about these.'"

श्रोत्रं त्वक्चक्षुषी जिह्वा नासिका चैव पञ्चमी ।
पादौ पायुरुपस्थं च हस्तौ वाग्दशमी भवेत् ॥ (13)

"'These are the ears, the skin, the eyes, the tongue, the nose as the fifth, the feet, the anus, the genital organ, the hands and speech as the tenth.'"

इन्द्रियग्राम इत्येष मन एकादशं भवेत् ।
एतं ग्रामं जयेत्पूर्वं ततो ब्रह्म प्रकाशते ॥ (14)

'"'In this aggregate of senses, the mind is the eleventh. When this aggregate is conquered, it is only then that the brahman is manifested.'"'

बुद्धीन्द्रियाणि पञ्चाहु: पञ्च कर्मेन्द्रियाणि च ।
श्रोत्रादीन्यपि पञ्चाहुर्बुद्धियुक्तानि तत्त्वत: ॥ (15)

'"'Five of these are said to be organs of perception and five are organs of action. It is the truth that the five that begin with the ears are said to be the organs of perception.'"'

अविशेषाणि चान्यानि कर्मयुक्तानि तानि तु ।
उभयत्र मनो ज्ञेयं बुद्धिर्द्वादशमी भवेत् ॥ (16)

'"'The remaining ones are the organs of action. The mind should be known as both.[146] Intelligence is the twelfth.'"'

इत्युक्तानीन्द्रियाणीमान्येकादश मया क्रमात् ।
मन्यन्ते कृतमित्येव विदित्वैतानि पण्डिता: ॥ (17)

'"'In due order, I have thus recounted the eleven organs of sense. Learned ones who know this think that they have become successful.'"'

त्रीणि स्थानानि भूतानां चतुर्थं नोपपद्यते ।
स्थलमापस्तथाकाशं जन्म चापि चतुर्विधम् ॥ (18)
अण्डजोद्भिज्जसंस्वेदजरायुजमथापि च ।
चतुर्धा जन्म इत्येतद्भूतग्रामस्य लक्ष्यते ॥ (19)

'"'There are three places for beings—land, water and sky. There is no fourth location. There are four kinds of birth—from eggs, upwards,[147] from sweat and from wombs. In all categories of creatures, these four kinds of birth are seen.'"'

---

[146] An organ of perception and an organ of action. In this case, intelligence is the twelfth, as mind is being counted twice.
[147] Plants, trees and herbs, which germinate upwards from seeds.

अचराण्यपि भूतानि खेचराणि तथैव च ।
अण्डजानि विजानीयात्सर्वांश्चैव सरीसृपान् ॥ (20)

"'"There are immobile creatures too. Among the ones that roam in the sky, know that all these are born from eggs, or are reptiles."'"

संस्वेदाः कृमयः प्रोक्ता जन्तवश्च तथाविधाः ।
जन्म द्वितीयमित्येतज्जघन्यतरमुच्यते ॥ (21)

"'"Worms are born from sweat and there are other creatures like that. This is said to be the second kind of birth, one that is inferior."'"

भित्त्वा तु पृथिवीं यानि जायन्ते कालपर्ययात् ।
उद्भिज्जानीति तान्याहुर्भूतानि द्विजसत्तमाः ॥ (22)

"'"O Supreme among Dvijas! After some time, there are some who are born after sprouting through the earth. These are known as plants and trees."'"

द्विपादबहुपादानि तिर्यग्गतिमतीनि च ।
जरायुजानि भूतानि वित्त तान्यपि सत्तमाः ॥ (23)

"'"O Excellent Ones! Now learn about the creatures that are born from wombs. Some have two feet. Some have many feet. Some move diagonally."'"

द्विविधापीह विज्ञेया ब्रह्मयोनिः सनातना ।
तपः कर्म च यत्पुण्यमित्येष विदुषां नयः ॥ (24)

"'"Know that Brahma's eternal womb is the outcome of two things—austerities and auspicious karma. This is the view held by the learned."'"[148]

द्विविधं कर्म विज्ञेयमिज्या दानं च यन्मखे ।
जातस्याध्ययनं पुण्यमिति वृद्धानुशासनम् ॥ (25)

---

[148]This is not clear and the meaning has to be deduced. Brahma's eternal womb probably means birth as a brahmana, and the intention is to convey that among humans, one is born as a brahmana because of austerities and good deeds.

"'Know that there are two kinds of auspicious karma for those who have been born—sacrifices and donations at sacrifices and studying. This is the instruction of the ancients.'"

एतद्यो वेद विधिवत्स मुक्त: स्याद्द्विजर्षभा: ।
विमुक्त: सर्वपापेभ्य इति चैव निबोधत ॥ (26)

"'O Bulls among Dvijas! A person who knows this in the proper way becomes liberated. Listen. In this way, he is freed from all sins.'"

आकाशं प्रथमं भूतं श्रोत्रमध्यात्ममुच्यते ।
अधिभूतं तथा शब्दो दिशस्तत्राधिदैवतम् ॥ (27)

"'Space is the first element, and it is connected with the atman through the ear. It is connected with objects as sound and the directions are its divinity.'"

द्वितीयं मारुतो भूतं त्वगध्यात्मं च विश्रुतम् ।
स्प्रष्टव्यमधिभूतं च विद्युत्तत्राधिदैवतम् ॥ (28)

"'Wind is the second element, and it is connected with the atman through the skin. It is connected with objects as touch, and lightning is its divinity.'"

तृतीयं ज्योतिरित्याहुश्चक्षुरध्यात्ममुच्यते ।
अधिभूतं ततो रूपं सूर्यस्तत्राधिदैवतम् ॥ (29)

"'Light is the third element and is said to be connected with the atman through the eyes. It is connected with objects as form and its divinity is said to be the sun.'"

चतुर्थमापो विज्ञेयं जिह्वा चाध्यात्ममिष्यते ।
अधिभूतं रसश्चात्र सोमस्तत्राधिदैवतम् ॥ (30)

"'Know that water is the fourth and is connected with the atman through the tongue. It is connected with objects as taste and its divinity is the moon.'"

पृथिवी पञ्चमं भूतं घ्राणश्चाध्यात्ममिष्यते ।
अधिभूतं तथा गन्धो वायुस्तत्राधिदैवतम् ॥ (31)

'"'Earth is the fifth element and is connected with the atman through the nose. It is connected with objects as smell and the wind is its divinity.'"'

एष पञ्चसु भूतेषु चतुष्टयविधिः स्मृतः ।
अतः परं प्रवक्ष्यामि सर्वं त्रिविधमिन्द्रियम् ॥ (32)

'"'These five elements are said to be progressively divided into four categories.[149] I will next relate how all the senses are divided into three categories.'"'

पादावध्यात्ममित्याहुर्ब्राह्मणास्तत्त्वदर्शिनः ।
अधिभूतं तु गन्तव्यं विष्णुस्तत्राधिदैवतम् ॥ (33)

'"'Brahmanas who have seen the truth have said that the feet are connected with the atman. They are connected with objects as movement, and Vishnu is their divinity.'"'

अवाग्गतिरपानश्च पायुरध्यात्ममिष्यते ।
अधिभूतं विसर्गश्च मित्रस्तत्राधिदैवतम् ॥ (34)

'"'When apana moves downwards, it is connected with the atman through the anus. It is connected with objects as excrement, and Mitra is its divinity.'"'

प्रजनः सर्वभूतानामुपस्थोऽध्यात्ममुच्यते ।
अधिभूतं तथा शुक्रं दैवतं च प्रजापतिः ॥ (35)

'"'In the act of procreation of all beings, the genital organ is connected with the atman. It is connected with objects as semen, and Prajapati is its divinity.'"'

हस्तावध्यात्ममित्याहुरध्यात्मविदुषो जनाः ।
अधिभूतं तु कर्माणि शक्रस्तत्राधिदैवतम् ॥ (36)

'"'Those who are learned about adhyatma say that the hands are connected with the atman. They are connected with objects as action, and Shakra is the divinity.'"'

---

[149]This probably means the four kinds of birth—from wombs, from eggs, from sweat (worms and insects) and vegetation (through sprouting).

वैश्वदेवी मन:पूर्वा वागध्यात्ममिहोच्यते ।
वक्तव्यमधिभूतं च वह्निस्तत्राधिदैवतम् ॥ (37)

'"The goddess of speech comes before the mind and is said to be connected with the atman through the tongue. She is connected with objects as speech, and the divinity is Agni."'

अध्यात्मं मन इत्याहु: पञ्चभूतानुचारकम् ।
अधिभूतं च मन्तव्यं चन्द्रमाश्चाधिदैवतम् ॥ (38)

'"In adhyatma, the mind is said to urge the five senses and is connected with objects through inference. Its divinity is the moon."'

अध्यात्मं बुद्धिरित्याहु: षडिन्द्रियविचारिणी ।
अधिभूतं तु विज्ञेयं ब्रह्मा तत्राधिदैवतम् ॥ (39)

'"In adhyatma, intelligence is said to be that which moves the six senses.[150] It is connected with objects in the form of what there is to be known, and its divinity is Brahma."'

यथावदध्यात्मविधिरेष व: कीर्तितो मया ।
ज्ञानमस्य हि धर्मज्ञा: प्राप्तं बुद्धिमतामिह ॥ (40)

'"I have recounted the rules of the adhyatma in the proper way. O Ones Who Know about Dharma! A person who possesses this knowledge is said to have obtained intelligence."'

इन्द्रियाणीन्द्रियार्थाश्च महाभूतानि पञ्च च ।
सर्वाण्येतानि संधाय मनसा संप्रधारयेत् ॥ (41)

'"The senses, the objects of the senses and the five great elements—all these should be collected and absorbed in the mind."'

क्षीणे मनसि सर्वस्मिन् जन्मसुखमिष्यते ।
ज्ञानसंपन्नसत्त्वानां तत्सुखं विदुषां मतम् ॥ (42)

---

[150] The five senses and the mind.

"'"When the mind manages to reduce the importance of all these, there is no longer any happiness from birth. It is the view that learned beings who possess this jnana experience bliss."'"

अतः परं प्रवक्ष्यामि सूक्ष्मभावकरीं शिवाम् ।
निवृत्तिं सर्वभूतेषु मृदुना दारुणेन वा ॥ (43)

"'"I will next tell you about what is subtle in sentiment and auspicious. This is about strong and weak renunciation in all beings."'"

गुणागुणमनासङ्गमेकचर्यमनन्तरम् ।
एतद्ब्राह्मणतो वृत्तमाहुरेकपदं सुखम् ॥ (44)

"'"A brahmana who is no longer attached to differences between the existence and non-existence of qualities and follows the conduct of being alone obtains bliss."'"

विद्वान्कूर्म इवाङ्गानि कामान्संहृत्य सर्वशः ।
विरजः सर्वतो मुक्तो यो नरः स सुखी सदा ॥ (45)

"'"Such a learned person withdraws all desire, like a tortoise drawing in its limbs. Such a liberated man is bereft of rajas in every way and is always happy."'"

कामानात्मनि संयम्य क्षीणतृष्णः समाहितः ।
सर्वभूतसुहृन्मैत्रो ब्रह्मभूयं स गच्छति ॥ (46)

"'"He controls desire in his atman. He is restrained and his thirst has been exhausted. He has friendly sentiments of affection towards all creatures. He becomes merged in the brahman."'"

इन्द्रियाणां निरोधेन सर्वेषां विषयैषिणाम् ।
मुनेर्जनपदत्यागादध्यात्माग्निः समिध्यते ॥ (47)

"'"He restrains all the senses that hanker after material objects. Such a sage abandons habitations and uses the fire of adhyatma as kindling."'"

यथाग्निरिन्धनैरिद्धो महाज्योतिः प्रकाशते ।
तथेन्द्रियनिरोधेन महानात्मा प्रकाशते ॥ (48)

'"'When kindling is offered into the fire, it blazes forth in great radiance. Through the restraint of the senses, the great atman is illuminated in that way."'

यदा पश्यति भूतानि प्रसन्नात्मनो हृदि ।
स्वयंयोनिस्तदा सूक्ष्मात्सूक्ष्ममाप्नोत्यनुत्तमम् ॥ (49)

'"'With a tranquil atman, he considers all the elements in his heart. Originating within himself, he obtains what is supreme, subtler than the most subtle."'

अग्नी रूपं पयः स्रोतो वायुः स्पर्शनमेव च ।
मही पङ्कधरं घोरमाकाशं श्रवणं तथा ॥ (50)

'"'Fire is the form.[151] Water is the flow of liquids. Wind is touch. The earth is the terrible mire.[152] Space is in the ears."'

रागशोकसमाविष्टं पञ्चस्रोतःसमावृतम् ।
पञ्चभूतसमायुक्तं नवद्वारं द्विदैवतम् ॥ (51)

'"'It is enveloped by these five kinds of flows and is overwhelmed with attachment and grief. It is made up of the five elements. It has nine gates. It has two divinities."'[153]

रजस्वलमथादृश्यं त्रिगुणं च त्रिधातुकम् ।
संसर्गाभिरतं मूढं शरीरमिति धारणा ॥ (52)

'"'It is full of rajas and does not deserve to be seen. It has three gunas and three attributes.[154] Foolishly, one assumes a body and is delighted with attachment."'

दुश्चरं जीवलोकेऽस्मिन्सत्त्वं प्रति समाश्रितम् ।
एतदेव हि लोकेऽस्मिन्कालचक्रं प्रवर्तते ॥ (53)

---

[151] All these refer to the physical body.
[152] Flesh and blood.
[153] The jivatman and the paramatman.
[154] Wind, bile and phlegm.

"'Those who have sought refuge with the real essence find it difficult to roam around in this world of the living. It is in this way that the wheel of time revolves in this world.'"

एतन्महार्णवं घोरमगाधं मोहसंज्ञितम् ।
विसृजेत्संक्षिपेच्चैव बोधयेत्सामरं जगत् ॥ (54)

"'This is a terrible, fathomless and great ocean. It is full of delusion. It[155] extends and contracts the universe, including the immortals. This should be understood.'"

कामक्रोधौ भयं मोहमभिद्रोहमथानृतम् ।
इन्द्रियाणां निरोधेन स तांस्त्यजति दुस्त्यजान् ॥ (55)

"'Desire, anger, fear, delusion, hatred and falsehood are extremely difficult to cast away. They can be abandoned through the restraint of the senses.'"

यस्यैते निर्जिता लोके त्रिगुणाः पञ्च धातवः ।
व्योम्नि तस्य परं स्थानमनन्तमथ लक्ष्यते ॥ (56)

"'If a person conquers the world, with its three gunas and five elements, it is seen that he obtains an infinite status, beyond the sky.'"

कामकूलामपारान्तां मनःस्रोतोभयावहाम् ।
नदीं दुर्गहदां तीर्णः कामक्रोधावुभौ जयेत् ॥ (57)

"'He crosses the river that has desire as its banks and the mind as the fearful current. He crosses the river and the lakes that are so difficult to traverse and vanquishes both desire and anger.'"

स सर्वदोषनिर्मुक्तस्ततः पश्यति यत्परम् ।
मनो मनसि संधाय पश्यत्यात्मानमात्मनि ॥ (58)

"'He is freed from all taints and beholds the ultimate. By using his mind to control his mind, he sees his atman within his own self.'"

---

[155]Time.

सर्ववित्सर्वभूतेषु वीक्षत्यात्मानमात्मनि ।
एकधा बहुधा चैव विकुर्वाणस्ततस्ततः ॥ (59)

'"'He knows everything. He sees the atman within his own self and sees himself in all beings, in one form and in many forms.'"'

ध्रुवं पश्यति रूपाणि दीपाद्दीपशतं यथा ।
स वै विष्णुश्च मित्रश्च वरुणोऽग्निः प्रजापतिः ॥ (60)
स हि धाता विधाता च स प्रभुः सर्वतोमुखः ।
हृदयं सर्वभूतानां महानात्मा प्रकाशते ॥ (61)

'"'There is no doubt that he sees all those forms, like a hundred lamps lit from a single lamp. He is Vishnu, Mitra, Varuna, Agni, Prajapati, Dhatri and Vidhatri. He is the lord with a face in every direction. The great atman is illuminated in the hearts of all beings.'"'

तं विप्रसंघाश्च सुरासुराश्च यक्षाः पिशाचाः पितरो वयांसि ।
रक्षोगणा भूतगणाश्च सर्वे महर्षयश्चैव सदा स्तुवन्ति ॥ (62)

'"'He is the one who is always praised by large numbers of brahmanas, gods, asuras, yakshas, pishachas, ancestors, birds and all the large numbers of rakshasas and bhutas and maharshis.'"'[156]

Chapter 28

ब्रह्मोवाच

मनुष्याणां तु राजन्यः क्षत्रियो मध्यमो गुणः ।
कुञ्जरो वाहनानां च सिंहश्चारण्यवासिनाम् ॥ (1)

'"'Brahma said, Among men, royal kshatriyas possess medium qualities.[157] Among mounts, elephants are like that. Among residents of the forest, lions are like that.'"'

---

[156] The word 'bhuta' has several meanings. Any being is a bhuta. Shiva's attendants are bhutas. However, 'bhuta' also means a malevolent being.
[157] That is, rajas.

अविः पशूनां सर्वेषामाखुश्च बिलवासिनाम् ।
गवां गोवृषभश्चैव स्त्रीणां पुरुष एव च ॥ (2)

'"'Among all animals, it is sheep.[158] Among those that live in holes, it is the rat. Among cattle, it is the bull. Amidst females, it is the male.'"'

न्यग्रोधो जम्बुवृक्षश्च पिप्पलः शाल्मलिस्तथा ।
शिंशपा मेषशृङ्गश्च तथा कीचकवेणवः ।
एते द्रुमाणां राजानो लोकेऽस्मिन्नात्र संशयः ॥ (3)

'"'There is no doubt that in this world that the kings of trees are the Indian fig tree, the rose apple tree, the holy fig tree, the silk cotton tree, the Indian rosewood tree, the Indian paintbrush, the hollow bamboo and cane.'"'[159]

हिमवान्पारियात्रश्च सह्यो विन्ध्यस्त्रिकूटवान् ।
श्वेतो नीलश्च भासश्च काष्ठवांश्चैव पर्वतः ॥ (4)
शुभस्कन्धो महेन्द्रश्च माल्यवान्पर्वतस्तथा ।
एते पर्वतराजानो गणानां मरुतस्तथा ॥ (5)

'"'Like the maruts among the ganas, the kings of mountains are the Himalayas, Pariyatra, Sahya, Vindhya, Trikuta, Shveta, Nila, Bhasa, Mount Kashthavat, Shubhaskandha, Mahendra and Mount Malyavat.'"'

सूर्यो ग्रहाणामधिपो नक्षत्राणां च चन्द्रमाः ।
यमः पितृणामधिपः सरितामथ सागरः ॥ (6)

'"'The sun is the lord of the planets and the moon of the nakshatras. Yama is the lord of the ancestors and the ocean of the rivers.'"'

अम्भसां वरुणो राजा सत्त्वानां मित्र उच्यते ।
अर्कोऽधिपतिरुष्णानां ज्योतिषामिन्दुरुच्यते ॥ (7)

---

[158] This means among sacrificial animals.
[159] The names of trees in Sanskrit are *nyagrodha, jambuvriksha, pippala, shalmali, shimshapa, meshashringa, kichaka* and *venu*, respectively.

"'Varuna is said to be the king of the waters and Mitra of all those with life. The sun is said to the lord of all hot bodies and the moon of bodies that shine.'"[160]

अग्निर्भूतपतिर्नित्यं ब्राह्मणानां बृहस्पतिः ।
ओषधीनां पतिः सोमो विष्णुर्बलवतां वरः ॥ (8)

"'Agni is the eternal lord of the elements and Brihaspati of brahmanas. The moon is the lord of herbs and Vishnu of those who are supremely strong.'"

त्वष्टाधिराजो रूपाणां पशूनामीश्वरः शिवः ।
दक्षिणानां तथा यज्ञो वेदानामृषयस्तथा ॥ (9)

"'Tvashtri is the sovereign of those with form and Shiva is the lord of animals. A sacrifice is the lord of dakshina and the rishis of the Vedas.'"

दिशामुदीची विप्राणां सोमो राजा प्रतापवान् ।
कुबेरः सर्वयक्षाणां देवतानां पुरंदरः ।
एष भूतादिकः सर्गः प्रजानां च प्रजापतिः ॥ (10)

"'The north is the king of the directions and the powerful moon of brahmanas. Kubera is the lord of all the yakshas and Purandara of the devas. Among people, it is Prajapati. This represents the various categories in which beings were created.'"

सर्वेषामेव भूतानामहं ब्रह्ममयो महान् ।
भूतं परतरं मत्तो विष्णोर्वापि न विद्यते ॥ (11)

"'Among all beings who are immersed in the brahman, I am the greatest. There is no other being who is superior to me or Vishnu.'"

राजाधिराजः सर्वासां विष्णुर्ब्रह्ममयो महान् ।
ईश्वरं तं विजानीमः स विभुः स प्रजापतिः ॥ (12)

---

[160] The text has this repetition about the sun and the moon. There is some repetition subsequently as well.

"'"The great Vishnu is immersed in the brahman, and he is sovereign over all kings. He should be known as Ishvara, Vibhu and Prajapati.'"'

नरकिंनरयक्षाणां गन्धर्वोरगरक्षसाम् ।
देवदानवनागानां सर्वेषामीश्वरो हि स: ॥ (13)

"'"He is the lord over all men, kinnaras, yakshas, gandharvas, uragas, rakshasas, devas, danavas and nagas.'"'

भगदेवानुयातानां सर्वासां वामलोचना ।
माहेश्वरी महादेवी प्रोच्यते पार्वतीति या ॥ (14)

"'"Among the fortunate ones who follow the divinity, there is the one with beautiful eyes. She is spoken of as Maheshvari, Mahadevi and Parvati.'"'

उमां देवीं विजानीत नारीणामुत्तमां शुभाम् ।
रतीनां वसुमत्यस्तु स्त्रीणामप्सरसस्तथा ॥ (15)

"'"Know her as Goddess Uma, supremely auspicious among women. Among women who provide pleasure, the radiant apsaras are the foremost.'"'

धर्मकामाश्च राजानो ब्राह्मणा धर्मलक्षणा: ।
तस्माद्राजा द्विजातीनां प्रयतेतेह रक्षणे ॥ (16)

"'"Kings desire dharma and brahmanas possess the signs of dharma. Therefore, kings must make efforts to protect brahmanas.'"'

राज्ञां हि विषये येषामवसीदन्ति साधव: ।
हीनास्ते स्वगुणै: सर्वै: प्रेत्यावाङ्मार्गगामिन: ॥ (17)

"'"If virtuous people suffer in a king's kingdom, then they take away all his own qualities. After death, he moves downwards.'"'

राज्ञां तु विषये येषां साधव: परिरक्षिता: ।
तेऽस्मँल्लोके प्रमोदन्ते प्रेत्य चानन्त्यमेव च ।
प्राप्नुवन्ति महात्मान इति वित्त द्विजर्षभा: ॥ (18)

"'O Bulls among Dvijas! Understand this. But if virtuous people are protected in a kingdom, then those great-souled kings find delight in this world and, after death, obtain the infinite.'"

अत ऊर्ध्वं प्रवक्ष्यामि नियतं धर्मलक्षणम् ।
अहिंसालक्षणो धर्मो हिंसा चाधर्मलक्षणा ॥ (19)

"'After this, I will tell you about how those who possess attributes of dharma always move upwards. Non-violence is a sign of dharma. Violence is a sign of adharma.'"

प्रकाशलक्षणा देवा मनुष्याः कर्मलक्षणाः ।
शब्दलक्षणमाकाशं वायुस्तु स्पर्शलक्षणः ॥ (20)

"'Illumination is the sign of devas. Karma constitutes the sign of men. Sound is the sign of space. Touch is the sign of the wind.'"

ज्योतिषां लक्षणं रूपमापश्च रसलक्षणाः ।
धरणी सर्वभूतानां पृथिवी गन्धलक्षणा ॥ (21)

"'Form is the sign of light. Taste is the sign of water. The earth holds up all creatures and its sign is smell.'"

स्वरव्यञ्जनसंस्कारा भारती सत्यलक्षणा ।
मनसो लक्षणं चिन्ता तथोक्ता बुद्धिरन्वयात् ॥ (22)

"'Words are the true characteristics of speech, refined through vowels and consonants. Thoughts constitute the attribute of the mind. These are also said to be an attribute of intelligence.'"

मनसा चिन्तयानोऽर्थान्बुद्ध्या चैव व्यवस्यति ।
बुद्धिर्हि व्यवसायेन लक्ष्यते नात्र संशयः ॥ (23)

"'Intelligence imparts meaning to the thoughts in the mind. There is no doubt that it is intelligence that provides discernment.'"

लक्षणं महतो ध्यानमव्यक्तं साधुलक्षणम् ।
प्रवृत्तिलक्षणो योगो ज्ञानं संन्यासलक्षणम् ॥ (24)

"'A great attribute is meditation. The attribute of a virtuous person is to remain undetected.[161] Pravritti is the attribute of yoga.[162] Jnana is the attribute of sannyasa.'"

तस्माज्ज्ञानं पुरस्कृत्य संन्यसेदिह बुद्धिमान् ।
संन्यासी ज्ञानसंयुक्तः प्राप्नोति परमां गतिम् ।
अतीतोऽद्वंद्वमभ्येति तमोमृत्युजरातिगम् ॥ (25)

"'Therefore, in this world, an intelligent person should place jnana at the forefront and practise sannyasa. United with knowledge and renunciation, he obtains the supreme objective. Such a person overcomes opposite sentiments and darkness, death and old age, attaining the unmatched.'"

धर्मलक्षणसंयुक्तमुक्तं वो विधिवन्मया ।
गुणानां ग्रहणं सम्यग्वक्ष्याम्यहमतः परम् ॥ (26)

"'I have accurately told you about the signs of dharma. After this, I will properly tell you my view about how the gunas should be received.'"

पार्थिवो यस्तु गन्धो वै घ्राणेनेह स गृह्यते ।
घ्राणस्थश्च तथा वायुर्गन्धज्ञाने विधीयते ॥ (27)

"'Smell is the quality of the earth and is received by the nose. The wind that is in the nose has been ordained to obtain knowledge of smell.'"

अपां धातुरसो नित्यं जिह्वया स तु गृह्यते ।
जिह्वास्थश्च तथा सोमो रसज्ञाने विधीयते ॥ (28)

"'Taste is the quality of water and is always received by the tongue. Soma resides in the tongue and has been ordained to obtain knowledge of taste.'"

---

[161] By others.
[162] Implying karma yoga. In this context, 'pravritti' means inclination towards action.

ज्योतिषश्च गुणो रूपं चक्षुषा तच्च गृह्यते ।
चक्षु:स्थश्च तथादित्यो रूपज्ञाने विधीयते ॥ (29)

"'Form is the quality of light and is received by the eyes. Aditya[163] resides in the eyes and has been ordained to obtain knowledge of form.'"

वायव्यस्तु तथा स्पर्शस्त्वचा प्रज्ञायते च स: ।
त्वक्स्थश्चैव तथा वायु: स्पर्शज्ञाने विधीयते ॥ (30)

"'Touch is the quality of the wind, and this is comprehended through the skin. The wind that resides in the skin has been ordained to obtain knowledge of touch.'"

आकाशस्य गुणो घोष: श्रोत्रेण स तु गृह्यते ।
श्रोत्रस्थाश्च दिश: सर्वा: शब्दज्ञाने प्रकीर्तिता: ॥ (31)

"'Sound is the quality of space and this is received by the ears. All the directions reside in the ears and are cited by those who know about sound.'"

मनसस्तु गुणश्चिन्ता प्रज्ञया स तु गृह्यते ।
हृदिस्थचेतनाधातुर्मनोज्ञाने विधीयते ॥ (32)

"'Thought is the quality of the mind and this is received by wisdom. The attribute of consciousness resides in the heart and has been ordained to obtain the mind's knowledge.'"

बुद्धिरध्यवसायेन ध्यानेन च महांस्तथा ।
निश्चित्य ग्रहणं नित्यमव्यक्तं नात्र संशय: ॥ (33)

"'Through endeavour in the use of intelligence and great meditation, one can receive intelligence. Thus, there is no doubt that one can always comprehend the unmanifest.'"

अलिङ्गग्रहणो नित्य: क्षेत्रज्ञो निर्गुणात्मक: ।
तस्मादलिङ्ग: क्षेत्रज्ञ: केवलं ज्ञानलक्षण: ॥ (34)

---

[163] The sun.

"'Kshetrajna possesses no gunas. It is eternal and is incapable of being grasped through signs. Since kshetrajna has no manifestations, its only attribute is jnana.'"

अव्यक्तं क्षेत्रमुद्दिष्टं गुणानां प्रभवाप्ययम् ।
सदा पश्याम्यहं लीनं विजानामि शृणोमि च ॥ (35)

"'The unmanifest resides in the body, and it is through this that gunas are created and destroyed. I always see, know and hear how it is latent.'"

पुरुषस्तद्विजानीते तस्मात्क्षेत्रज्ञ उच्यते ।
गुणवृत्तं तथा कृत्स्नं क्षेत्रज्ञः परिपश्यति ॥ (36)

"'Purusha knows this and that is the reason it is known as kshetrajna. Kshetrajna sees everything about the progress of the gunas.'"

आदिमध्यावसानान्तं सृज्यमानमचेतनम् ।
न गुणा विदुरात्मानं सृज्यमानं पुनः पुनः ॥ (37)

"'The gunas do not know themselves, since they lack consciousness. After the beginning, middle and end,[164] they are created again and again.'"

न सत्यं वेद वै कश्चित्क्षेत्रज्ञस्त्वेव विन्दति ।
गुणानां गुणभूतानां यत्परं परतो महत् ॥ (38)

"'No one other than kshetrajna can know, or obtain, the truth, which is beyond gunas produced by the gunas, and is supreme and great.'"

तस्माद्गुणांश्च तत्त्वं च परित्यज्येह तत्त्ववित् ।
क्षीणदोषो गुणान्हित्वा क्षेत्रज्ञं प्रविशत्यथ ॥ (39)

"'Therefore, a person who knows about the truth casts aside the gunas and everything based on them. When the taints are destroyed and gunas cast aside, one enters into kshetrajna.'"

---

[164] Meaning creation, preservation and destruction.

निर्द्वंद्वो निर्नमस्कारो निःस्वधाकार एव च ।
अचलश्चानिकेतश्च क्षेत्रज्ञः स परो विभुः ॥ (40)

'"'Such a person is beyond opposite pairs of sentiments. Such a person does not bow down before anyone and has no need for svadha. He does not move and he has no abode. He is actually kshetrajna and the supreme lord.'"'

Chapter 29

ब्रह्मोवाच

यदादिमध्यपर्यन्तं ग्रहणोपायमेव च ।
नामलक्षणसंयुक्तं सर्वं वक्ष्यामि तत्त्वतः ॥ (1)

'"'Brahma said, I will tell you the entire truth about comprehending the beginning, the middle and the end and about the names and signs that are associated with this.'"'

अहः पूर्वं ततो रात्रिर्मासाः शुक्लादयः स्मृताः ।
श्रविष्ठादीनि ऋक्षाणि ऋतवः शिशिरादयः ॥ (2)

'"'It has been said that day was the first. Night came after that. Within months, Shuklapaksha[165] comes first. Among nakshatras, Shravishtha is the first.[166] Among seasons, winter is the first.'"'

भूमिरादिस्तु गन्धानां रसानामाप एव च ।
रूपाणां ज्योतिरादिस्तु स्पर्शादिर्वायुरुच्यते ।
शब्दस्यादिस्तथाकाशमेष भूतकृतो गुणः ॥ (3)

---

[165]The bright lunar fortnight when the moon waxes.
[166]The text uses the word 'riksha' instead of 'nakshatra', which mean the same thing. There is no nakshatra called Shravishtha. Instead, there are Shravana and Dhanishtha. Either Shravishtha is to be taken as Shravana, or is shorthand for Shravana and Dhanishtha taken together. In the standard listing of nakshatras, Shravana is twenty-third and Dhanishtha is twenty-fourth. Therefore, 'first' should be interpreted in some other sense. Alternatively, this is a reflection of precession of the equinoxes.

"'"Earth is the source of all smells and water of all tastes. Light is the source of all forms and the wind of all sensations of touch. Space is the source of all sound. These are qualities created by the elements.'"'

अत: परं प्रवक्ष्यामि भूतानामादिमुत्तमम् ।
आदित्यो ज्योतिषामादिरग्निर्भूतादिरिष्यते ॥ (4)

"'"After this, I will tell you about what is supreme and first among all entities. Aditya is the first among all luminous bodies and Agni is the first among all elements.'"'

सावित्री सर्वविद्यानां देवतानां प्रजापति: ।
ओंकार: सर्ववेदानां वचसां प्राण एव च ।
यद्यस्मिन्नियतं लोके सर्वं सावित्रमुच्यते ॥ (5)

"'"Savitri[167] among all kinds of knowledge and Prajapati among all devas. Omkara[168] among all the Vedas and prana among all kinds of speech. Everything that restrains this world is known as Savitri.'"'

गायत्री छन्दसामादि: पशूनामज उच्यते ।
गावश्चतुष्पदामादिर्मनुष्याणां द्विजातय: ॥ (6)

"'"Gayatri among all sama metres and, among all animals, it is said to be the goat.[169] The cow among all quadrupeds and dvijas among all men.'"'

श्येन: पतत्रिणामादिर्यज्ञानां हुतमुत्तमम् ।
परिसर्पिणां तु सर्वेषां ज्येष्ठ: सर्पो द्विजोत्तम: ॥ (7)

"'"The hawk among all birds. Among all sacrifices, the pouring of oblations is supreme. O Best among Dvijas! Among all the things that creep along the ground, it is the snake.'"'

कृतमादिर्युगानां च सर्वेषां नात्र संशय: ।
हिरण्यं सर्वरत्नानामोषधीनां यवास्तथा ॥ (8)

---

[167] The Savitri Mantra. However, here it is being used in a general sense of all mantras.
[168] OUM.
[169] That is, sacrificial animals.

"'"There is no doubt that among all the yugas, it is krita which is the first. Gold among all jewels and barley among all plants."'"

सर्वेषां भक्ष्यभोज्यानामन्नं परममुच्यते ।
द्रवाणां चैव सर्वेषां पेयानामाप उत्तमाः ॥ (9)

"'"Food is said to be supreme among all things that are eaten or swallowed. Water is supreme among all liquid objects that are drunk."'"

स्थावराणां च भूतानां सर्वेषामविशेषतः ।
ब्रह्मक्षेत्रं सदा पुण्यं प्लक्षः प्रथमजः स्मृतः ॥ (10)

"'"Without any exception, among all the immobile regions, plaksha is always said to be the first. This is the sacred region of Brahmakshetra."'"[170]

अहं प्रजापतीनां च सर्वेषां नात्र संशयः ।
मम विष्णुरचिन्त्यात्मा स्वयंभूरिति स स्मृतः ॥ (11)

"'"There is no doubt that among all Prajapatis, it is I. Vishnu, whose atman is incomprehensible, is the same as me. He is known as Svayambhu."'"

पर्वतानां महामेरुः सर्वेषामग्रजः स्मृतः ।
दिशां च प्रदिशां चोर्ध्वा दिग्जाता प्रथमं तथा ॥ (12)

"'"The great Meru is said to be the first among all mountains. Among the directions and the subdirections, the northern direction[171] is the one that was born first."'"

तथा त्रिपथगा गङ्गा नदीनामग्रजा स्मृता ।
तथा सरोदपानानां सर्वेषां सागरोऽग्रजः ॥ (13)

---

[170]This could refer to Plakshadvipa out of the seven *dvipa*s (continents). However, Brahmakshetra often refers to Kurukshetra. This might simply mean that plaksha (the fig tree) grew in Kurukshetra.
[171]Literally, the upward direction.

"'Like that, Ganga, with its three flows,[172] is said to be the first among rivers. The ocean is the first among all lakes and water bodies.'"

देवदानवभूतानां पिशाचोरगरक्षसाम् ।
नरकिंनरयक्षाणां सर्वेषामीश्वर: प्रभु: ॥ (14)

"'Ishvara[173] is the lord of all devas, danavas, bhutas, pishachas, uragas, rakshasas, men, kinnaras and yakshas.'"

आदिर्विश्वस्य जगतो विष्णुर्ब्रह्ममयो महान् ।
भूतं परतरं तस्मात्त्रैलोक्ये नेह विद्यते ॥ (15)

"'The great Vishnu, immersed in the brahman, is the origin of the world and the universe. In the three worlds, there is no entity which is superior to him.'"

आश्रमाणां च गार्हस्थ्यं सर्वेषां नात्र संशय: ।
लोकानामादिरव्यक्तं सर्वस्यान्तस्तदेव च ॥ (16)

"'There is no doubt that garhasthya is foremost among ashramas. The unmanifest is the origin of all the worlds and is also their end.'"

अहान्यस्तमयान्तानि उदयान्ता च शर्वरी ।
सुखस्यान्त: सदा दु:खं दु:खस्यान्त: सदा सुखम् ॥ (17)

"'A day ends when the sun sets. A night ends when the sun rises. Happiness always ends with unhappiness. Unhappiness always ends with happiness.'"

सर्वे क्षयान्ता निचया: पतनान्ता: समुच्छ्रया: ।
संयोगा विप्रयोगान्ता मरणान्तं हि जीवितम् ॥ (18)

"'All accumulations have an end. All ascent ends in descent. Association ends in disassociation. Life ends in death.'"

सर्वं कृतं विनाशान्तं जातस्य मरणं ध्रुवम् ।
अशाश्वतं हि लोकेऽस्मिन्सर्वं स्थावरजङ्गमम् ॥ (19)

---

[172]Ganga has three flows—in heaven, earth and the netherworld.
[173]Shiva.

"'"All action is destroyed. Everything that is born is certain to die. Everything in this world, mobile and immobile, is transient."'"

इष्टं दत्तं तपोऽधीतं व्रतानि नियमाश्च ये ।
सर्वमेतद्विनाशान्तं ज्ञानस्यान्तो न विद्यते ॥ (20)

"'"Sacrifices, donations, austerities, studies, vows and rituals—all this ends in destruction. However, jnana has no destruction."'"

तस्माज्ज्ञानेन शुद्धेन प्रसन्नात्मा समाहितः ।
निर्ममो निरहंकारो मुच्यते सर्वपाप्मभिः ॥ (21)

"'"Therefore, if a person is tranquil in his atman, is restrained and is without a sense of ownership and devoid of ego, he can use pure jnana to be free from all his sins."'"

Chapter 30

ब्रह्मोवाच

बुद्धिसारं मनस्तम्भमिन्द्रियग्रामबन्धनम् ।
महाभूतारविष्कम्भं निमेषपरिवेष्टनम् ॥ (1)

"'"Brahma said, Intelligence is the essence. The mind is the pole.[174] The aggregate of senses constitute the spokes. The great elements are the circumference and nimesha sets the boundaries."'"

जराशोकसमाविष्टं व्याधिव्यसनसंचरम् ।
देशकालविचारीदं श्रमव्यायामनिस्वनम् ॥ (2)

"'"It[175] is overwhelmed by old age and sorrow. It moves in the midst of disease and hardship. Depending on the time and the place, there is the sound of toil and endeavour."'"

अहोरात्रपरिक्षेपं शीतोष्णपरिमण्डलम् ।
सुखदुःखान्तसंक्लेशं क्षुत्पिपासावकीलनम् ॥ (3)

---

[174]There is the imagery of a wheel of life.
[175]The physical body.

"'"Day and night constitute the rotations. Hot and cold set the limits. Both happiness and unhappiness end in hardships. Hunger and thirst are like nails."'"

छायातपविलेखं च निमेषोन्मेषविह्वलम् ।
घोरमोहजनाकीर्णं वर्तमानमचेतनम् ॥ (4)

"'"Shade and heat leave marks along the path. Even the opening and closing of an eye can cause distraction. It is full of people who are terribly confused and lack consciousness, being dragged along."'"

मासार्धमासगणितं विषमं लोकसंचरम् ।
तमोनिचयपङ्कं च रजोवेगप्रवर्तकम् ॥ (5)

"'"Measured in months and fortnights, it moves unevenly in this world. The store of tamas is the mud. Rajas provides the impulse for movement."'"

सत्त्वालंकारदीप्तं च गुणसंघातमण्डलम् ।
स्वरविग्रहनाभीकं शोकसंघातवर्तनम् ॥ (6)

"'"The ornament of sattva provides illumination. The wheel is made out of the clash of gunas. Sounds of not having obtained what one wants are like the nave and increase grief as it revolves."'"

क्रियाकारणसंयुक्तं रागविस्तारमायतम् ।
लोभेप्सापरिसंख्यातं विविक्तज्ञानसंभवम् ॥ (7)

"'"It has action and instruments of action. Attachment increases its size.[176] Greed and ignorance are clearly responsible for making it unsteady."'"

भयमोहपरीवारं भूतसंमोहकारकम् ।
आनन्दप्रीतिधारं च कामक्रोधपरिग्रहम् ॥ (8)

"'"Fear and confusion become possessions and cause delusion among creatures. One hopes to obtain what brings joy and pleasure and is seized by desire and anger."'"

---

[176] Increases the size of the wheel.

महदादिविशेषान्तमसक्तप्रभवाव्ययम् ।
मनोजवनमश्रान्तं कालचक्रं प्रवर्तते ॥ (9)

'"'Though it is specially brought into existence by mahat and the others, it is destroyed because of the influence of an attachment to tamas. Without tiring, the wheel of time[177] moves on, with the speed of thought.'"'

एतद्द्वंद्वसमायुक्तं कालचक्रमचेतनम् ।
विसृजेत्संक्षिपेच्चापि बोधयेत्सामरं जगत् ॥ (10)

'"'This wheel of time is devoid of consciousness and is united with opposite pairs of sentiments. The entire universe, with the immortals, is awakened,[178] extended and then contracted again.'"'

कालचक्रप्रवृत्तिं च निवृत्तिं चैव तत्त्वत: ।
यस्तु वेद नरो नित्यं न स भूतेषु मुह्यति ॥ (11)

'"'Among all creatures, a man who always knows about the pravritti associated with the wheel of time and the truth about nivritti is never confused.'"'[179]

विमुक्त: सर्वसंक्लेशै: सर्वद्वंद्वातिगो मुनि: ।
विमुक्त: सर्वपापेभ्य: प्राप्नोति परमां गतिम् ॥ (12)

'"'He is liberated from all kinds of hardships. Such a sage overcomes all kinds of opposite sentiments. He is freed from all sins and obtains the supreme objective.'"'

गृहस्थो ब्रह्मचारी च वानप्रस्थोऽथ भिक्षुक: ।
चत्वार आश्रमा: प्रोक्ता: सर्वे गार्हस्थ्यमूलका: ॥ (13)

---

[177]There is a wheel of time, and the being moves around in the wheel of life, that is, samsara.
[178]Created.
[179]Pravritti is attachment to action and the fruits, nivritti is withdrawal from action and its fruits.

"'"Among all the four ashramas, garhasthya, brahmacharya, vanaprastha and the state of being a mendicant,[180] garhasthya is said to be the foundation."'"

यः कश्चिदिह लोके च ह्यागमः संप्रकीर्तितः ।
तस्यान्तगमनं श्रेयः कीर्तिरेषा सनातनी ॥ (14)

"'"It has eternally been stated that the following ordinances of the agama texts bring benefit and fame."'"

संस्कारैः संस्कृतः पूर्वं यथावच्चरितव्रतः ।
जातौ गुणविशिष्टायां समावर्तेत वेदवित् ॥ (15)

"'"A person who is born in a family with special qualities should first observe the vows, follow the samskaras and cleanse himself. Having got to know the Vedas, he should return."'"[181]

स्वदारनिरतो दान्तः शिष्टाचारो जितेन्द्रियः ।
पञ्चभिश्च महायज्ञैः श्रद्दधानो यजेत ह ॥ (16)

"'"He must always be devoted to his own wife. He must be controlled and good in conduct. He must conquer his senses. He must faithfully perform the five great sacrifices."'"[182]

देवतातिथिशिष्टाशी निरतो वेदकर्मसु ।
इज्याप्रदानयुक्तश्च यथाशक्ति यथाविधि ॥ (17)

"'"Always engaged in the rites mentioned in the Vedas, he must eat what is left after serving the devas and guests. According to capacity and following the prescribed ordinances, he must donate at sacrifices."'"

न पाणिपादचपलो न नेत्रचपलो मुनिः ।
न च वागङ्गचपल इति शिष्टस्य गोचरः ॥ (18)

---

[180] Sannyasa.
[181] This is a reference to residing in the house of the preceptor and studying there. Having completed the studies, the student graduates and returns to his own house.
[182] A householder's sacrifices meant for gods, ancestors, sages, humans and animals.

"'A sage will not use his hands or feet excessively, nor will he excessively use his eyes. He will not be excessive in speech. He will then be recognized as someone virtuous.'"

नित्ययज्ञोपवीती स्याच्छुक्लवासाः शुचिव्रतः ।
नियतो दमदानाभ्यां सदा शिष्टैश्च संविशेत् ॥ (19)

"'He will always wear the sacred thread. He will wear clean and white clothes. He will be pure in his vows. He will always be controlled, restrained and generous. He will associate with those who are good.'"

जितशिश्नोदरो मैत्रः शिष्टाचारसमाहितः ।
वैणवीं धारयेद्यष्टिं सोदकं च कमण्डलुम् ॥ (20)

"'He will conquer his penis and his stomach. He will be friendly, good in conduct and calm. He will sport a staff made out of bamboo and hold a water-pot filled with water.'"

अधीत्याध्यापनं कुर्यात्तथा यजनयाजने ।
दानं प्रतिग्रहं चैव षड्गुणां वृत्तिमाचरेत् ॥ (21)

"'Having studied, he will teach.[183] He will perform sacrifices and officiate at sacrifices. He will give and receive. He will follow these six attributes of conduct.'"[184]

त्रीणि कर्माणि यानीह ब्राह्मणानां तु जीविका ।
याजनाध्यापने चोभे शुद्धाच्चापि प्रतिग्रहः ॥ (22)

"'In this world, there are three tasks brahmanas can use for earning a living. Studying, teaching and performing sacrifices are only for purification.'"[185]

अवशेषाणि चान्यानि त्रीणि कर्माणि यानि तु ।
दानमध्ययनं यज्ञो धर्मयुक्तानि तानि तु ॥ (23)

---

[183]All this is meant for brahmanas.
[184]Studying, teaching, performing sacrifices, officiating at sacrifices, receiving gifts and giving gifts.
[185]Thus, officiating at sacrifices, receiving gifts and giving gifts are for the purpose of livelihood.

""'The other three tasks, studying, teaching and the performance of sacrifices, are for purposes of dharma.'"

तेष्वप्रमादं कुर्वीत त्रिषु कर्मसु धर्मवित् ।
दान्तो मैत्र: क्षमायुक्त: सर्वभूतसमो मुनि: ॥ (24)

""'A person who knows about dharma will therefore perform these three tasks without any distraction. A sage is controlled, friendly and full of forgiveness. He looks upon all creatures impartially.'"

सर्वमेतद्यथाशक्ति विप्रो निर्वर्तयञ्शुचि: ।
एवं युक्तो जयेत्स्वर्गं गृहस्थ: संशितव्रत: ॥ (25)

""'A householder brahmana, who does all this to the best of his capacity, is firm in his vows and is controlled and pure conquers heaven.'"

Chapter 31

ब्रह्मोवाच
एवमेतेन मार्गेण पूर्वोक्तेन यथाविधि ।
अधीतवान्यथाशक्ति तथैव ब्रह्मचर्यवान् ॥ (1)

""'Brahma said, One must properly follow the path mentioned earlier. One must study to the best of one's capacity and observe brahmacharya.'"

स्वधर्मनिरतो विद्वान्सर्वेन्द्रिययतो मुनि: ।
गुरो: प्रियहिते युक्त: सत्यधर्मपर: शुचि: ॥ (2)

""'A sage will be engaged in his own dharma. He will be learned and will control all his senses. He will be engaged in what brings pleasure to his guru. He will be pure and devoted to the dharma of truth.'"

गुरुणा समनुज्ञातो भुञ्जीतान्नमकुत्सयन् ।
हविष्यभैक्ष्यभुक्चापि स्थानासनविहारवान् ॥ (3)

"'"Having taken the guru's permission, he will eat the food without criticizing it. He will eat havishya[186] obtained through begging for alms. He will sit, stand, or roam around.'"'[187]

द्विकालमग्निं जुह्वानः शुचिर्भूत्वा समाहितः ।
धारयीत सदा दण्डं बैल्वं पालाशमेव वा ॥ (4)

"'"Pure and controlled, he will offer oblations into the fire twice a day. He will always wield a staff made out of bilva[188] or palasha.'"'

क्षौमं कार्पासिकं वापि मृगाजिनमथापि वा ।
सर्वं काषायरक्तं स्याद्वासो वापि द्विजस्य ह ॥ (5)

"'"A dvija must wear linen or cotton clothes, or deer skin, or garments that are dyed reddish brown.'"'

मेखला च भवेन्मौञ्जी जटी नित्योदकस्तथा ।
यज्ञोपवीती स्वाध्यायी अलुप्तनियतव्रतः ॥ (6)

"'"There can be a girdle made out of munja grass. His hair must be matted and he must always have water with him. He must wear the sacred thread. He must study. Without any greed, he must always observe the vows.'"'

पूताभिश्च तथैवाद्भिः सदा दैवततर्पणम् ।
भावेन नियतः कुर्वन्ब्रह्मचारी प्रशस्यते ॥ (7)

"'"He must always offer pure water to the devas. A brahmachari who controls his mind in this way is praised.'"'

एवं युक्तो जयेत्स्वर्गमूध्वरेताः समाहितः ।
न संसरति जातीषु परमं स्थानमाश्रितः ॥ (8)

---

[186]'Havishya' means food that is fit to be offered as an oblation. This means that it is vegetarian and free from oil and spices, cooked in a single vessel.
[187]As instructed by the preceptor.
[188]Wood apple.

"'He is self-restrained and controls his seed. Such a person conquers heaven. Having obtained the best kind of birth,[189] he is not dislodged to a different kind of birth.'"

संस्कृतः सर्वसंस्कारैस्तथैव ब्रह्मचर्यवान् ।
ग्रामान्निष्क्रम्य चारण्यं मुनिः प्रव्रजितो वसेत् ॥ (9)

"'He must cleanse himself and observe all the samskaras in the stage of brahmacharya. After that, he can leave the village and dwell in the forest as a mendicant sage.'"[190]

चर्मवल्कलसंवीतः स्वयं प्रातरुपस्पृशेत् ।
अरण्यगोचरो नित्यं न ग्रामं प्रविशेत्पुनः ॥ (10)

"'He will be clad in hides and bark and have his bath in the morning. He will always roam around in the forest and never return to the village again.'"

अर्चयन्नतिथीन्काले दद्याच्चापि प्रतिश्रयम् ।
फलपत्रावरैर्मूलैः श्यामाकेन च वर्तयन् ॥ (11)

"'When guests arrive, he will honour them and offer them refuge. He will subsist on fruits, leaves, ordinary roots and dark millet.'"[191]

प्रवृत्तमुदकं वायुं सर्वं वानेयमा तृणात् ।
प्राश्नीयादानुपूर्व्येण यथादीक्षमतन्द्रितः ॥ (12)

"'He will subsist on water and air and everything else that is obtained from the forest, even grass. Single-mindedly and in due progression, he will eat according to his initiation.'"[192]

आमूलफलभिक्षाभिरर्चेदतिथिमागतम् ।
यद्भक्षः स्यात्ततो दद्यादिभक्षां नित्यमतन्द्रितः ॥ (13)

---

[189]As a brahmana.
[190]As opposed to becoming a householder.
[191]Not cultivated.
[192]The initiation into vanaprastha prescribes the diet. This progression refers to first surviving on roots and fruits, then leaves, then water, and finally only air.

"'If a guest arrives, he will honour him with roots and fruits as alms. He must always, single-mindedly, offer as alms whatever food there is available.'"

देवतातिथिपूर्वं च सदा भुञ्जीत वाग्यतः ।
अस्कन्दितमनाश्चैव लघ्वाशी देवताश्रयः ॥ (14)

"'He must always control his speech and eat after the devas and guests have eaten. His mind should not be fickle. He must eat whatever he gets and seek refuge with devas.'"

दान्तो मैत्रः क्षमायुक्तः केशश्मश्रु च धारयन् ।
जुह्वन्स्वाध्यायशीलश्च सत्यधर्मपरायणः ॥ (15)

"'He must be self-controlled, friendly and forgiving. He must wear his hair and beard long. He must be engaged in offering oblations and studying. He must be devoted to the dharma of truth.'"

त्यक्तदेहः सदा दक्षो वननित्यः समाहितः ।
एवं युक्तो जयेत्स्वर्गं वानप्रस्थो जितेन्द्रियः ॥ (16)

"'He must abandon all attachment to the body. In the forest, he must be accomplished and always controlled. He must conquer his senses. A person in the vanaprastha stage who acts in this way conquers heaven.'"

गृहस्थो ब्रह्मचारी च वानप्रस्थोऽथ वा पुनः ।
य इच्छेन्मोक्षमास्थातुमुत्तमां वृत्तिमाश्रयेत् ॥ (17)

"'After having followed garhasthya, brahmacharya and vanaprastha, a person who desires moksha can resort to the supreme conduct.'"[193]

अभयं सर्वभूतेभ्यो दत्त्वा नैष्कर्म्यमाचरेत् ।
सर्वभूतहितो मैत्रः सर्वेन्द्रिययतो मुनिः ॥ (18)

"'He grants fearlessness to all creatures and no longer undertakes any karma. He is engaged in the welfare of all beings. He is friendly. Such a sage controls all his senses.'"

---

[193] Sannyasa.

अयाचितमसंकॢप्तमुपपन्नं यदृच्छया ।
जोषयेत् सदा भोज्यं ग्रासमागतमस्पृहः ॥ (19)

"'As he wishes, he eats food that has not been solicited or has not been prepared, but has just presented itself. He must approve of whatever food has presented itself and must desire to eat only a mouthful.'"

यात्रामात्रं च भुञ्जीत केवलं प्राणयात्रिकम् ।
धर्मलब्धं तथाश्नीयान् काममनुवर्तयेत् ॥ (20)

"'He must eat only to survive on this journey of life and only for the sake of sustaining life. He will eat whatever has been obtained through dharma and not to satisfy desire.'"

ग्रासादाच्छादनाच्चान्यन्न गृह्णीयात्कथंचन ।
यावदाहारयेत्तावत्प्रतिगृह्णीत नान्यथा ॥ (21)

"'He will accept only a mouthful of food and garments and nothing more than that. He will accept what he can eat and never more than that.'"

परेभ्यो न प्रतिग्राह्यं न च देयं कदाचन ।
दैन्यभावाच्च भूतानां संविभज्य सदा बुधः ॥ (22)

"'He will not accept gifts from others, nor will he ever give to them. Because of the helplessness of beings, a learned person will always share with them.'"

नाददीत परस्वानि न गृह्णीयादयाचितम् ।
न किंचिद्विषयं भुक्त्वा स्पृहयेत्तस्य वै पुनः ॥ (23)

"'He will not seize the possessions of others, nor will he receive without having been asked to. Having enjoyed some object, he will not desire it again.'"

मृदमापस्तथाश्मानं पत्रपुष्पफलानि च ।
असंवृतानि गृह्णीयात्प्रवृत्तानीह कार्यवान् ॥ (24)

"'He will only use earth, water, stones, leaves, flowers and fruits that are lying around.[194] His action will not be driven by desire.'"

न शिल्पजीविकां जीवेद्द्विवरन्नं नोत कामयेत् ।
न द्वेष्टा नोपदेष्टा च भवेत् निरुपस्कृतः ।
श्रद्धापूतानि भुञ्जीत निमित्तानि विवर्जयेत् ॥ (25)

"'He will not earn a living as an artisan. He will not desire gold. He will not hate, nor will he teach. He will not own any possessions. He will only eat what has been purified through devotion. He will stay away from arguments.'"

मुधावृत्तिरसक्तश्च सर्वभूतैरसंविदम् ।
कृत्वा वह्निं चरेद्भैक्ष्यं विधूमे भुक्तवज्जने ॥ (26)

"'He will not be addicted to futile occupations. He will not have any associations with any creatures. Having ignited a fire, he will roam around for alms. However, he will only seek these from a house where the fire has been put out and the residents have eaten.'"[195]

वृत्ते शरावसंपाते भैक्ष्यं लिप्सेत मोक्षवित् ।
लाभे न च प्रहृष्येत नालाभे विमना भवेत् ॥ (27)

"'A person who knows about moksha will only wish to beg after the kitchen vessels have been washed. He will not rejoice at having obtained something, nor will he be distressed if he does not obtain something.'"

मात्राशी कालमाकाङ्क्षंश्चरेद्भैक्ष्यं समाहितः ।
लाभं साधारणं नेच्छेन्न भुञ्जीताभिपूजितः ।
अभिपूजितलाभाद्धि विजुगुप्सेत भिक्षुकः ॥ (28)

"'When he wishes to beg, he will be controlled and will only seek what is sufficient for the moment. He will not seek gains that ordinary people want, nor will he eat when he has been honoured. A mendicant will hide himself, so that he is not given things as a mark of respect.'"

---

[194] Not owned by anybody.
[195] He will beg only when the fire for cooking has been put out and the householders have eaten.

शुक्तान्यम्लानि तिक्तानि कषायकटुकानि च ।
नास्वादयीत भुञ्जानो रसांश्च मधुरांस्तथा ।
यात्रामात्रं च भुञ्जीत केवलं प्राणयात्रिकम् ॥ (29)

"'"He will not eat food that is putrid, acidic, bitter, astringent, pungent, succulent, sweet, or not fit to be tasted. He will only eat enough to sustain life, enough to remain alive on this journey."'"

असंरोधेन भूतानां वृत्तिं लिप्सेत मोक्षवित् ।
न चान्यमनुभिक्षेत भिक्षमाण: कथंचन ॥ (30)

"'"A person who knows about moksha will not desire to earn sustenance through conduct that causes conflict with other creatures. When he seeks alms, he should never follow another person who is also begging."'"

न संनिकाशयेद्धर्मं विविक्ते विरजाश्चरेत् ।
शून्यागारमरण्यं वा वृक्षमूलं नदीं तथा ।
प्रतिश्रयार्थं सेवेत पार्वतीं वा पुनर्गुहाम् ॥ (31)

"'"He should never reveal the dharma he practises. He should be pure and roam around alone. He should seek refuge in an empty house, in the forest, under a tree, near a river or in a mountainous cavern."'"

ग्रामैकरात्रिको ग्रीष्मे वर्षास्वेकत्र वा वसेत् ।
अध्वा सूर्येण निर्दिष्ट: कीटवच्च चरेन्महीम् ॥ (32)

"'"During the summer, he can spend a night in a village. During the monsoon, it can be more than one night. With his progress determined by the movement of the sun, he should roam around the earth like a worm."'"

दयार्थं चैव भूतानां समीक्ष्य पृथिवीं चरेत् ।
संचयांश्च न कुर्वीत स्नेहवासं च वर्जयेत् ॥ (33)

"'"He should roam around on earth with an eye of compassion towards all beings. He should not accumulate anything and should not become attached to where he resides."'"

पूतेन चाम्भसा नित्यं कार्यं कुर्वीत मोक्षवित् ।
उपस्पृशेदुद्धृताभिरद्भिश्च पुरुषः सदा ॥ (34)

"'A person who knows about moksha will always perform his rites with pure water. Such a man will always perform his ablutions with water that has been taken.'"[196]

अहिंसा ब्रह्मचर्यं च सत्यमार्जवमेव च ।
अक्रोधश्चानसूया च दमो नित्यमपैशुनम् ॥ (35)

"'He will always practise non-violence, brahmacharya, truth, uprightness, lack of anger, lack of jealousy, self-control and lack of calumny.'"

अष्टास्वेतेषु युक्तः स्याद्व्रतेषु नियतेन्द्रियः ।
अपापमशठं वृत्तमजिह्मं नित्यमाचरेत् ॥ (36)

"'He will possess these eight attributes and control his senses in following the vows. He will always have a conduct that is without sin, without deceit and without falsehood.'"

आशीर्युक्तानि कर्माणि हिंसायुक्तानि यानि च ।
लोकसंग्रहधर्मं च नैव कुर्यान्न कारयेत् ॥ (37)

"'He will never perform tasks for the sake of obtaining benedictions or those that are associated with violence, nor will he follow the dharma of accumulation followed in the world.'"

सर्वभावानतिक्रम्य लघुमात्रः परिव्रजेत् ।
समः सर्वेषु भूतेषु स्थावरेषु चरेषु च ॥ (38)

"'He will overcome all the sentiments and wander around, satisfied with only a little. He will be impartial towards all creatures, mobile and immobile.'"

परं नोद्वेजयेत्कंचिन्न च कस्यचिदुद्विजेत् ।
विश्वास्यः सर्वभूतानामग्र्यो मोक्षविदुच्यते ॥ (39)

---

[196]The sense seems to be that one should bathe by taking water from rivers, ponds and lakes and not plunge into these.

"'"He will not seek to defeat another person, nor will he be defeated by another. A person who is trusted by all creatures is said to be someone who knows about moksha."'"

अनागतं च न ध्यायेन्नातीतमनुचिन्तयेत् ।
वर्तमानमुपेक्षेत कालाकाङ्क्षी समाहित: ॥ (40)

"'"He will not reflect on the future, nor will he think about the past. He will be indifferent towards the present. He will be controlled and wait for the time."'"[197]

न चक्षुषा न मनसा न वाचा दूषयेत्क्वचित् ।
न प्रत्यक्षं परोक्षं वा किंचिद्दुष्टं समाचरेत् ॥ (41)

"'"He will not soil anything through sight, thoughts and words. Directly or indirectly, he will not do anything that is a sin."'"

इन्द्रियाण्युपसंहृत्य कूर्मोऽङ्गानीव सर्वशः ।
क्षीणेन्द्रियमनोबुद्धिर्निरीक्षेत निरिन्द्रिय: ॥ (42)

"'"He will withdraw his senses, like a tortoise draws in all its limbs. He will make the senses decay. Devoid of the senses, he will look towards his mind and his intelligence."'"

निर्द्वन्द्वो निर्नमस्कारो नि:स्वाहाकार एव च ।
निर्ममो निरहंकारो निर्योगक्षेम एव च ॥ (43)

"'"He will be without the opposite pairs of sentiments. He will be devoid of any bowing down. He will be without sounds of svaha.[198] He will be without a sense of ownership. He will be without ahamkara. He will be without yoga and kshema."'"[199]

निराशी: सर्वभूतेषु निरासङ्गो निराश्रय: ।
सर्वज्ञ: सर्वतो मुक्तो मुच्यते नात्र संशय: ॥ (44)

---

[197]For death.
[198]There will no longer be a need for such oblations.
[199]Kshema is protecting what one already possesses, in contrast with yoga, which is acquiring what one does not possess.

"'He will be without wishes. He will be unattached towards all creatures. He will be without refuge. He will know everything. He will be free in every way. There is no doubt that he will be emancipated.'"

अपाणिपादपृष्ठं तमशिरस्कमनूदरम् ।
प्रहीणगुणकर्माणं केवलं विमलं स्थिरम् ॥ (45)

"'He will only base himself on the sparkling one.[200] It is without hands, feet and back. It is without a head and without a stomach. It is free from the gunas and karma.'"

अगन्धरसमस्पर्शमरूपाशब्दमेव च ।
अत्वगस्थ्यथ वामज्जममांसमपि चैव ह ॥ (46)

"'It is without smell, without taste, without touch, without form and without sound. It is without skin, without marrow and without flesh. It is the objective.'"

निश्चिन्तमव्ययं नित्यं हृदिस्थमपि नित्यदा ।
सर्वभूतस्थमात्मानं ये पश्यन्ति न ते मृताः ॥ (47)

"'It is without anxiety and without decay. It is eternal and is always based in the heart. Those who see the atman in all creatures do not die.'"[201]

न तत्र क्रमते बुद्धीन्द्रियाणि न देवताः ।
वेदा यज्ञाश्च लोकाश्च न तपो न पराक्रमः ।
यत्र ज्ञानवतां प्राप्तिरलिङ्गग्रहणा स्मृता ॥ (48)

"'Intelligence cannot reach it, nor can the senses, devas, the Vedas, sacrifices, the worlds, austerities or valour. It cannot be comprehended through signs. It is said that those who possess jnana obtain it.'"

तस्मादलिङ्गो धर्मज्ञो धर्मव्रतमनुव्रतः ।
गूढधर्माश्रितो विद्वानज्ञातचरितं चरेत् ॥ (49)

---

[200] The atman.
[201] They are freed from the cycle of birth and death.

"'Therefore, a person who knows about dharma and follows the vows of dharma does not show signs. A learned man knows the nature of true conduct and follows this hidden dharma.'"

अमूढो मूढरूपेण चरेद्धर्ममदूषयन् ।
यथैनमवमन्येरन्परे सततमेव हि ॥ (50)

"'He may not be foolish. However, he does not censure dharma[202] and follows it as if he is foolish. He always does this, even if others disrespect him.'"

तथावृत्तश्चरेद्धर्मं सतां वर्त्माविदूषयन् ।
यो ह्येवं वृत्तसंपन्नः स मुनिः श्रेष्ठ उच्यते ॥ (51)

"'He does not condemn the practice of dharma by the virtuous. A person who possesses this kind of conduct is said to the best among sages.'"

इन्द्रियाणीन्द्रियार्थांश्च महाभूतानि पञ्च च ।
मनोबुद्धिरथात्मानमव्यक्तं पुरुषं तथा ॥ (52)
सर्वमेतत्प्रसंख्याय सम्यक्सन्त्यज्य निर्मलः ।
ततः स्वर्गमवाप्नोति विमुक्तः सर्वबन्धनैः ॥ (53)

"'He accurately understands the senses, the objects of the senses, the five great elements, the mind, the intelligence, the atman, the unmanifest,[203] Purusha and everything else that is enumerated. However, he abandons all this for the sake of what is sparkling. Such a person is freed from all his bonds and obtains heaven.'"

एतदेवान्तवेलायां परिसंख्याय तत्त्ववित् ।
ध्यायेदेकान्तमास्थाय मुच्यतेऽथ निराश्रयः ॥ (54)

"'A person who knows the truth understands all these enumerations at the time of his death. He meditates single-mindedly, without any refuge, and is emancipated.'"

---

[202] The ordinary rites of dharma.
[203] Prakriti.

निर्मुक्त: सर्वसङ्गेभ्यो वायुराकाशगो यथा ।
क्षीणकोशो निरातङ्क: प्राप्नोति परमं पदम् ॥ (55)

'"'He is free from all attachments, like the wind in the sky. Even when everything that he has accumulated is destroyed, he is without terror. He obtains the supreme destination.'"' .

Chapter 32

ब्रह्मोवाच

संन्यासं तप इत्याहुर्वृद्धा निश्चितदर्शिन: ।
ब्राह्मणा ब्रह्मयोनिस्था ज्ञानं ब्रह्म परं विदु: ॥ (1)

'"'Brahma said, The ancient ones who are certain in their determinations say that sannyasa is an austerity. Learned brahmanas who are immersed in the brahman know that jnana is the supreme brahman.'"'

अविदूरात्परं ब्रह्म वेदविद्याव्यपाश्रयम् ।
निर्द्वन्द्वं निर्गुणं नित्यमचिन्त्यं गुह्यमुत्तमम् ॥ (2)

'"'Knowledge of the supreme brahman is a long distance away. But the knowledge of the Vedas provides the support. It is without the opposite pairs of sentiments. It is without gunas. It is eternal. It cannot be thought of. It is the supreme secret.'"'

ज्ञानेन तपसा चैव धीरा: पश्यन्ति तत्पदम् ।
निर्णिक्ततमस: पूता व्युत्क्रान्तरजसोऽमला: ॥ (3)

'"'Those who have fortitude see that objective through jnana and austerities. These are the purified and sparkling ones, who have transcended tamas and rajas and have been cleansed.'"'

तपसा क्षेममध्वानं गच्छन्ति परमैषिण: ।
संन्यासनिरता नित्यं ये ब्रह्मविदुषो जना: ॥ (4)

"'Cheerfully, those who resort to austerities proceed along the path towards the supreme objective. People who know about the brahman are always devoted to sannyasa.'"

तपः प्रदीप इत्याहुराचारो धर्मसाधकः ।
ज्ञानं त्वेव परं विद्व संन्यासस्तप उत्तमम् ॥ (5)

"'Those who follow the pursuit of dharma say that austerities are like a lamp. They know that jnana is supreme and that sannyasa is the best form of austerities.'"

यस्तु वेद निराबाधं ज्ञानं तत्त्वविनिश्चयात् ।
सर्वभूतस्थमात्मानं स सर्वगतिरिष्यते ॥ (6)

"'A person who has determined the truth and knows it, using his unobstructed jnana, succeeds in going everywhere and knows the atman inside all creatures.'"

यो विद्वान्सहवासं च विवासं चैव पश्यति ।
तथैवैकत्वनानात्वे स दुःखात्परिमुच्यते ॥ (7)

"'Such a learned person can see association and also disassociation. He sees the unity between the two and is freed from all misery.'"

यो न कामयते किंचिन्न किंचिदवमन्यते ।
इहलोकस्थ एवैष ब्रह्मभूयाय कल्पते ॥ (8)

"'He does not desire anything. He does not disrespect anything. Even when he is in this world, he is worthy of being immersed in the brahman.'"

प्रधानगुणतत्त्वज्ञः सर्वभूतविधानवित् ।
निर्ममो निरहंकारो मुच्यते नात्र संशयः ॥ (9)

"'He knows the true qualities of Pradhana, the one who has ordained all creatures. He is without a sense of ownership. He is without ahamkara. There is no doubt that he is freed.'"

निर्द्वंद्वो निर्नमस्कारो निःस्वधाकार एव च ।
निर्गुणं नित्यमद्वंद्वं प्रशमेनैव गच्छति ॥ (10)

"'"One is beyond the opposite sentiments. One does not bow down before anyone. One is devoid of sounds of svadha.[204] One is devoid of gunas and is always without any conflict. One advances towards tranquillity."'"

हित्वा गुणमयं सर्वं कर्म जन्तुः शुभाशुभम् ।
उभे सत्यानृते हित्वा मुच्यते नात्र संशयः ॥ (11)

"'"Such a being gives up everything associated with gunas and all karma, good or bad. One gives up both truth and falsehood. There is no doubt that such an entity is emancipated."'"

अव्यक्तबीजप्रभवो बुद्धिस्कन्धमयो महान् ।
महाहंकारविटप इन्द्रियान्तरकोटरः ॥ (12)

"'"The unmanifest is the seed of creation. Intelligence is the gigantic trunk. Great ahamkara represents the branches and the sense are the hollows inside them."'"

महाभूतविशाखश्च विशेषप्रतिशाखवान् ।
सदापर्णः सदापुष्पः शुभाशुभफलोदयः ।
आजीवः सर्वभूतानां ब्रह्मवृक्षः सनातनः ॥ (13)

"'"The giant elements are the smaller branches and the smaller branches the objects of the senses. This tree results from the eternal brahman. It is always full of leaves and flowers. It yields fruits that are good and bad. It provides sustenance to all beings."'"

एतच्छित्त्वा च भित्त्वा च ज्ञानेन परमासिना ।
हित्वा चामरतां प्राप्य जह्याद्द्वै मृत्युजन्मनी ।
निर्ममो निरहंकारो मुच्यते नात्र संशयः ॥ (14)

"'"Through the supreme sword of jnana, one can cut and pierce this tree. One then abandons the association with death and birth and obtains immortality. Such a person is without a sense of ownership and without a sense of ahamkara. There is no doubt that he is liberated."'"

---

[204] There will no longer be any need for such oblations.

द्वावेतौ पक्षिणौ नित्यौ सखायौ चाप्यचेतनौ ।
एताभ्यां तु परो यस्य चेतनावानिति स्मृतः ॥ (15)

'"'There are always two birds that are friends.²⁰⁵ Of these, one is said to be unconscious and the other is said to be conscious.'"'

अचेतनः सत्त्वसंघातयुक्तः सत्त्वात्परं चेतयतेऽन्तरात्मा ।
स क्षेत्रज्ञः सत्त्वसंघातबुद्धिर्गुणातिगो मुच्यते मृत्युपाशात् ॥ (16)

'"'The unconscious spirit is full of conflict. The other intelligent spirit is inside the atman. The kshetrajna uses intelligence to understand the conflict of the spirits. It overcomes the gunas and is freed from the noose of death.'"'

Chapter 33

ब्रह्मोवाच

केचिद्ब्रह्ममयं वृक्षं केचिद्ब्रह्ममयं महत् ।
केचित्पुरुषमव्यक्तं केचित्परमनामयम् ।
मन्यन्ते सर्वमप्येतदव्यक्तप्रभवाव्ययम् ॥ (1)

'"'Brahma said, *Some say that the tree is full of the brahman. Some say that mahat is full of the brahman. Some say that Purusha is unmanifest. Some say that it is supreme and is free from disease. Some think that everything is created from the unmanifest and also dissolves into it.*'"'

उच्छ्वासमात्रमपि चेद्योऽन्तकाले समो भवेत् ।
आत्मानमुपसंगम्य सोऽमृतत्वाय कल्पते ॥ (2)

'"'*If a person is equable and breathes without agitation when the time for his death arrives, he obtains his atman and deserves to be immortal.*'"'

---

²⁰⁵The two birds are the jivatman and the paramatman. In the absence of true knowledge, the jivatman is unconscious.

निमेषमात्रमपि चेत्संयम्यात्मानमात्मनि ।
गच्छत्यात्मप्रसादेन विदुषां प्राप्तिमव्ययाम् ॥ (3)

'"'Even if he controls himself with his atman for a nimesha, through the favours of the atman, he obtains an end that is without decay, meant for the learned.'"'

प्राणायामैरथ प्राणान्संयम्य स पुन: पुन: ।
दशद्वादशभिर्वापि चतुर्विंशात्परं तत: ॥ (4)

'"'Such a person uses pranayama to control the breath of life again and again. He does this for ten times, twelve times, twenty-four times and beyond that.'"'[206]

एवं पूर्वं प्रसन्नात्मा लभते यद्यदिच्छति ।
अव्यक्तात्सत्त्वमुद्रिक्तममृतत्वाय कल्पते ॥ (5)

'"'Having thus made the atman tranquil, one obtains everything that one wants. When the quality of sattva arises from the unmanifest, such a person deserves to be immortal.'"'

सत्त्वात्परतरं नान्यत्प्रशंसन्तीह तद्विद: ।
अनुमानाद्विजानीम: पुरुषं सत्त्वसंश्रयम् ।
न शक्यमन्यथा गन्तुं पुरुषं तमथो द्विजा: ॥ (6)

'"'Those who know about sattva praise it, since there is nothing that is superior to this. The learned have deduced that one can obtain Purusha by resorting to sattva. O Dvijas! One is incapable of reaching Purusha through any other means.'"'

क्षमा धृतिरहिंसा च समता सत्यमार्जवम् ।
ज्ञानं त्यागोऽथ संन्यास: सात्त्विकं वृत्तमिष्यते ॥ (7)

---

[206]These numbers relate to the cycle of pranayama. The technical term is *'matra'* and concerns the duration for which the breath is inhaled, retained or exhaled. When this is for twelve matras, this is an inferior kind of pranayama. An average kind of pranayama has twenty-four matras and a superior type has thirty-two matras.

"'Forgiveness, fortitude, non-violence, impartiality, truth, uprightness, knowledge, renunciation and giving up—these are said to be the conduct that is associated with sattva.'"

एतेनैवानुमानेन मन्यन्तेऽथ मनीषिण: ।
सत्त्वं च पुरुषश्चैकस्तत्र नास्ति विचारणा ॥ (8)

"'It is through such deductions that learned people think that sattva and Purusha are one and the same. There is no need for any further reflection on this.'"

आहुरेके च विद्वांसो ये ज्ञाने सुप्रतिष्ठिता: ।
क्षेत्रज्ञसत्त्वयोरैक्यमित्येतन्नोपपद्यते ॥ (9)

"'Some learned people who have based themselves well on jnana have said that kshetrajna and nature are identical and there is no difference between them.'"[207]

पृथग्भूतस्ततो नित्यमित्येतदविचारितम् ।
पृथग्भावश्च विज्ञेय: सहजश्चापि तत्त्वत: ॥ (10)

"'However, without reflection, there are those who say these are always different.[208] One should understand the truth about the natural difference.'"

तथैवैकत्वनानात्वमिष्यते विदुषां नय: ।
मशकोदुम्बरे त्वैक्यं पृथक्त्वमपि दृश्यते ॥ (11)

"'Those who are learned about policy have determined the difference between unity and disassociation. It is evident that a gnat and a fig tree are together, but are also different.'"

मत्स्यो यथान्य: स्यादप्सु संप्रयोगस्तथानयो: ।
संबन्धस्तोयबिन्दूनां पर्णे कोकनदस्य च ॥ (12)

---

[207] In which case, nature will adhere to the atman, even if the entity is emancipated.
[208] In which case, karma will devolve on the atman and karma cannot be destroyed without the atman being destroyed.

"'Though a fish and water may be together, they are actually different. A drop of water may be united with the leaf of a lotus, but they are different.'"[209]

गुरुरुवाच

इत्युक्तवन्तं ते विप्रास्तदा लोकपितामहम् ।
पुनः संशयमापन्नाः पप्रच्छुर्द्विजसत्तमाः ॥ (13)

"'The preceptor said, 'The brahmanas were thus addressed by the grandfather of the worlds. However, overcome by doubts, the excellent brahmanas asked again.'"

ऋषय ऊचुः

किं स्विदेवेह धर्माणामनुष्ठेयतमं स्मृतम् ।
व्याहतामिव पश्यामो धर्मस्य विविधां गतिम् ॥ (14)

"'The rishis asked, Which of the many kinds of dharma is said to be the best? We see that the progress of different kinds of dharma is often contradictory.'"

ऊर्ध्वं देहाद्भदन्त्येके नैतदस्तीति चापरे ।
केचित्संशयितं सर्वं निःसंशयमथापरे ॥ (15)

"'When the body is destroyed, some say nothing remains. Others say something is left and have no doubts about this. Still others have doubts about everything.'"

अनित्यं नित्यमित्येके नास्त्यस्तीत्यपि चापरे ।
एकरूपं द्विधेत्येके व्यामिश्रमिति चापरे ।
एकमेके पृथक्वान्ये बहुत्वमिति चापरे ॥ (16)

---

[209] Some parts are left implicit and have to be deduced. The discussion seems to be about Purusha and Prakriti. Prakriti is associated with qualities, including sattva. However, Purusha is independent of qualities and is distinct from Prakriti. In these sections, the word sattva is being used as a synonym for Prakriti.

"'Some say that the eternal is not truly eternal. Others say that it is non-existent, others that it does exist.[210] Some say that it has a single form. Others say that it has two parts. And still others say that it is mixed. Some say that it is one and the same. Others that they are distinct. Still others say it is many.'"

मन्यन्ते ब्राह्मणा एवं प्राज्ञास्तत्त्वार्थदर्शिनः ।
जटाजिनधराश्चान्ये मुण्डाः केचिदसंवृताः ॥ (17)

"'In this way, there are brahmanas who are wise and think they have seen the truth. They think in this way. There are others who have matted hair, clad in deer skin. Others have shaved heads. Some are naked.'"

अस्नानं केचिदिच्छन्ति स्नानमित्यपि चापरे ।
आहारं केचिदिच्छन्ति केचिच्चानशने रताः ॥ (18)

"'Some do not wish to bathe. Others are devoted to bathing. Some desire to eat. Others are devoted to fasting.'"

कर्म केचित्प्रशंसन्ति प्रशान्तिमपि चापरे ।
देशकालावुभौ केचिन्नैतदस्तीति चापरे ।
केचिन्मोक्षं प्रशंसन्ति केचिद्भोगान्पृथग्विधान् ॥ (19)

"'Some praise karma, others tranquillity. Some extol the time and the place, others not so. Some praise moksha. Others praise different kinds of enjoyment.'"

धनानि केचिदिच्छन्ति निर्धनत्वं तथापरे ।
उपास्यसाधनं त्वेके नैतदस्तीति चापरे ॥ (20)

"'Some desire riches, others penury. Some highlight the means used. Others say these are unimportant.'"

अहिंसानिरताश्चान्ये केचिद्धिंसापरायणाः ।
पुण्येन यशसेत्येके नैतदस्तीति चापरे ॥ (21)

---

[210] These statements in this shloka are references to the atman. The subsequent statements are references to the jivatman and the paramatman.

"'Some are devoted to non-violence, others to violence. Some praise sacred deeds and fame. Others say these are unimportant.'"

सद्भावनिरताश्चान्ये केचित्संशयिते स्थिताः ।
दुःखाद्न्ये सुखाद्न्ये ध्यानमित्यपरे स्थिताः ॥ (22)

"'Some are devoted to good sentiments. Others are immersed in doubt. Some follow misery. Others follow joy. Still others are engaged in dhyana.'"

यज्ञमित्यपरे धीराः प्रदानमिति चापरे ।
सर्वमेके प्रशंसन्ति न सर्वमिति चापरे ॥ (23)

"'Some patient ones are engaged in sacrifices. Others follow the practice of giving. Some praise all the modes, others do not praise everything.'"

तपस्त्वन्ये प्रशंसन्ति स्वाध्यायमपरे जनाः ।
ज्ञानं संन्यासमित्येके स्वभावं भूतचिन्तकाः ॥ (24)

"'Some praise austerities. Others are devoted to studying. Some speak of jnana and sannyasa. Others think of nature and the elements.'"

एवं व्युत्थापिते धर्मे बहुधा विप्रधावति ।
निश्चयं नाधिगच्छामः संमूढाः सुरसत्तम ॥ (25)

"'In this way, many kinds of dharma present themselves and brahmanas follow them. O Supreme among the Gods! We are confused and undecided. We cannot understand.'"

इदं श्रेय इदं श्रेय इत्येवं प्रस्थितो जनः ।
यो हि यस्मिन्रतो धर्मे स तं पूजयते सदा ॥ (26)

"'People present themselves and say, This is best. That is best. Everyone always worships the dharma that he practises.'"

तत्र नो विहता प्रज्ञा मनश्च बहुलीकृतम् ।
एतदाख्यातुमिच्छामः श्रेयः किमिति सत्तम ॥ (27)

'"'Consequently, our wisdom is destroyed and our minds are dragged in different directions. O Excellent One! Hence, we desire that you should tell us what is beneficial.'"'

अतः परं च यद्गुह्यं तद्भवान्वक्तुमर्हति ।
सत्त्वक्षेत्रज्ञयोश्चैव संबन्धः केन हेतुना ॥ (28)

'"'Thereafter, you should tell us what is supremely secret. What is the connection between nature and kshetrajna and what is the cause of this?'"'

एवमुक्तः स तैर्विप्रैर्भगवाँल्लोकभावनः ।
तेभ्यः शशंस धर्मात्मा याथातथ्येन बुद्धिमान् ॥ (29)

'Vasudeva said, "The illustrious one, the creator of the worlds, was addressed by the brahmanas in this way. The intelligent one, with dharma in his atman, instructed them accurately."'

Chapter 34

ब्रह्मोवाच

हन्त वः संप्रवक्ष्यामि यन्मां पृच्छथ सत्तमाः ।
समस्तमिह तच्छ्रुत्वा सम्यगेवावधार्यताम् ॥ (1)

'"'Brahma said, O Excellent Ones! I will now tell you what you have asked. Listen to everything properly and think about it properly.'"'

अहिंसा सर्वभूतानामेतत्कृत्यतमं मतम् ।
एतत्पदमनुद्विग्नं वरिष्ठं धर्मलक्षणम् ॥ (2)

'"'It is the view that non-violence towards all creatures is the supreme task. That is the highest state and is free of anxiety. It is the best sign of dharma.'"'

ज्ञानं निःश्रेय इत्याहुर्वृद्धा निश्चयदर्शिनः ।
तस्माज्ज्ञानेन शुद्धेन मुच्यते सर्वपातकैः ॥ (3)

""'The ancient ones, certain in their insight, have said that jnana is the best. Therefore, through pure jnana, one is freed from all sins.'"

हिंसापराश्च ये लोके ये च नास्तिकवृत्तय: ।
लोभमोहसमायुक्तास्ते वै निरयगामिन: ॥ (4)

""'Those who are violent in conduct towards other people and are non-believers are immersed in greed and confusion. They go to hell.'"

आशीर्युक्तानि कर्माणि कुर्वते ये त्वतन्द्रिता: ।
तेऽस्मिँल्लोके प्रमोदन्ते जायमाना: पुन: पुन: ॥ (5)

""'Those who single-mindedly pursue beneficial acts are born again and again and find delight in this world.'"

कुर्वते ये तु कर्माणि श्रद्दधाना विपश्चित: ।
अनाशीर्योगसंयुक्तास्ते धीरा: साधुदर्शिन: ॥ (6)

""'A learned person faithfully performs his karma. He does not desire anything. He is patient and virtuous in his insight.'"

अत: परं प्रवक्ष्यामि सत्त्वक्षेत्रज्ञयोर्यथा ।
संयोगो विप्रयोगश्च तन्निबोधत सत्तमा: ॥ (7)

""'After this, I will tell you about the association between nature and kshetrajna. O Excellent Ones! Listen to the association between them and to the disassociation.'"

विषयो विषयित्वं च संबन्धोऽयमिहोच्यते ।
विषयी पुरुषो नित्यं सत्त्वं च विषय: स्मृत: ॥ (8)

""'This is said to be the connection between the subject and the object. Purusha is always the subject and nature is said to be the object.'"

व्याख्यातं पूर्वकल्पेन मशकोदुम्बरं यथा ।
भुज्यमानं न जानीते नित्यं सत्त्वमचेतनम् ।
यस्त्वेव तु विजानीते यो भुङ्क्ते यश्च भुज्यते ॥ (9)

""'In an earlier section, this has been explained as the difference between a gnat and a fig tree. Nature is always unconscious. It is enjoyed, but does not know. The one who enjoys[211] and the one who is enjoyed is what needs to be known.'"

अनित्यं द्वंद्वसंयुक्तं सत्त्वमाहुर्गुणात्मकम् ।
निर्द्वंद्वो निष्कलो नित्यः क्षेत्रज्ञो निर्गुणात्मकः ॥ (10)

'"Nature is said to be associated with the gunas. It is transient and is associated with opposite sentiments. Kshetrajna has the attribute of being without gunas. It is eternal and without opposite sentiments. It has no parts.'"

समः संज्ञागतस्त्वेवं यदा सर्वत्र दृश्यते ।
उपभुङ्क्ते सदा सत्त्वमापः पुष्करपर्णवत् ॥ (11)

'"It can be seen equally everywhere, identified with knowledge. It always enjoys nature, like the leaf of a lotus enjoys the water on it.'"

सर्वैरपि गुणैर्विद्वान्व्यतिषक्तो न लिप्यते ।
जलबिन्दुर्यथा लोलः पद्मिनीपत्रसंस्थितः ।
एवमेवाप्यसंसक्तः पुरुषः स्यान्न संशयः ॥ (12)

'"It knows all the gunas. In spite of being associated with them, it is not attached. It is like a drop of water that moves on the leaf of a lotus. There is no doubt that Purusha is unattached in that way.'"

द्रव्यमात्रमभूत्सत्त्वं पुरुषस्येति निश्चयः ।
यथा द्रव्यं च कर्ता च संयोगोऽप्यनयोस्तथा ॥ (13)

'"It has been determined that matter originates with nature, which is in turn owned by Purusha. The connection between the two is like that between matter and its creator.'"

यथा प्रदीपमादाय कश्चित्तमसि गच्छति ।
तथा सत्त्वप्रदीपेन गच्छन्ति परमैषिणः ॥ (14)

'"When one is in a place that is dark, one advances with the help of a lamp. In that way, if one desires the supreme, one advances with the lamp of nature.'"

---

[211] Purusha.

यावद्द्रव्यगुणस्तावत्प्रदीपः संप्रकाशते ।
क्षीणद्रव्यगुणं ज्योतिरन्तर्धानाय गच्छति ॥ (15)

"'That lamp shines as long as matter and its qualities exist.[212] When matter and its qualities are destroyed, the light is also extinguished.'"

व्यक्तः सत्त्वगुणस्त्वेवं पुरुषोऽव्यक्त इष्यते ।
एतद्विप्रा विजानीत हन्त भूयो ब्रवीमि वः ॥ (16)

"'The manifest is said to be the quality of nature, while Purusha is unmanifest. O Brahmanas! Know this. I will tell you more.'"

सहस्रेणापि दुर्मेधा न वृद्धिमधिगच्छति ।
चतुर्थेनाप्यथांशेन बुद्धिमान्सुखमेधते ॥ (17)

"'Even if there is a thousand, it is difficult to comprehend and one doesn't attain intelligence.[213] However, even with one-fourth of that,[214] if one possesses intelligence, one can obtain happiness.'"

एवं धर्मस्य विज्ञेयं संसाधनमुपायतः ।
उपायज्ञो हि मेधावी सुखमत्यन्तमश्नुते ॥ (18)

"'Know that the attainment of dharma depends on the means. A person who knows the means is intelligent and obtains extreme happiness.'"

यथाध्वानमपाथेयः प्रपन्नो मानवः क्वचित् ।
क्लेशेन याति महता विनश्यत्यन्तरापि वा ॥ (19)

"'There may be a man who is travelling without the requisite provisions. He suffers from great hardships and may even die before he reaches his destination.'"

तथा कर्मसु विज्ञेयं फलं भवति वा न वा ।
पुरुषस्यात्मनिःश्रेयः शुभाशुभनिदर्शनम् ॥ (20)

---

[212]Interpreted as the oil and the wick.
[213]Even if one tries to explain it in one thousand different ways.
[214]One-fourth of the explanations.

"'In that way, one should know that actions may, or may not, yield fruits.²¹⁵ By resorting to his own atman, a man can determine what is auspicious and what is inauspicious.'"

यथा च दीर्घमध्वानं पद्भ्यामेव प्रपद्यते ।
अदृष्टपूर्वं सहसा तत्त्वदर्शनवर्जितः ॥ (21)

"'If a person proceeds without knowledge of the truth, this is like a man rashly advancing on foot along a long road that he has not seen before.'"

तमेव च यथाध्वानं रथेनेहाशुगामिना ।
यायादश्वप्रयुक्तेन तथा बुद्धिमतां गतिः ॥ (22)

"'However, when an intelligent person advances along that same road, it is like swiftly advancing on a chariot yoked to horses.'"

उच्चं पर्वतमारुह्य नान्ववेक्षेत भूगतम् ।
रथेन रथिनं पश्येत्क्लिश्यमानमचेतनम् ॥ (23)

"'When one has ascended a tall mountain, one should not look down at the ground.²¹⁶ However, even if a charioteer is mounted on a chariot, he can be seen to be afflicted and lacking in consciousness.'"

यावद्रथपथस्तावद्रथेन स तु गच्छति ।
क्षीणे रथपथे प्राज्ञो रथमुत्सृज्य गच्छति ॥ (24)

"'Therefore, one should advance on a chariot as long as there is a road for the chariot. When a track for the chariot no longer exists, a wise person abandons the chariot and proceeds.'"

एवं गच्छति मेधावी तत्त्वयोगविधानवित् ।
समाज्ञाय महाबुद्धिरुत्तरादुत्तरोत्तरम् ॥ (25)

---

²¹⁵Action without intelligence is like travelling without provisions.
²¹⁶The sense seems to be the following: once one has obtained lofty intelligence and knowledge, one is no longer concerned with more mundane tasks and rites. But a person on a chariot is still tied to the chariot.

"'An intelligent person who knows the truth about the ordinances of yoga advances in that way. He uses his great intelligence to progressively move from one stage to the next.'"

यथा महार्णवं घोरमप्लव: संप्रगाहते ।
बाहुभ्यामेव संमोहाद्ध्रुवं चच्छेत्यसंशयम् ॥ (26)

"'If a person plunges into a great and terrible ocean without a boat and tries to cross using his arms, there is no doubt that the delusion will lead to his destruction.'"

नावा चापि यथा प्राज्ञो विभागज्ञस्तरित्रया ।
अक्लान्त: सलिलं गाहेत्क्षिप्रं संतरति ध्रुवम् ॥ (27)

"'However, a wise person knows about the different distinctions and uses a boat. There is no doubt that using oars, he is not exhausted and, immersing himself in the water, swiftly crosses over.'"

तीर्णो गच्छेत्परं पारं नावमुत्सृज्य निर्मम: ।
व्याख्यातं पूर्वकल्पेन यथा रथिपदातिनौ ॥ (28)

"'Having crossed over to the other side, he no longer possesses any sense of ownership and abandons the boat. For the person on a chariot and on foot, this has already been explained earlier.'"

स्नेहात्संमोहमापन्नो नावि दाशो यथा तथा ।
ममत्वेनाभिभूत: स तत्रैव परिवर्तते ॥ (29)

"'If a person is overwhelmed by attachment and delusion, he is like a fisherman attached by a sense of ownership to his boat. He is whirled around.'"

नावं न शक्यमारुह्य स्थले विपरिवर्तितुम् ।
तथैव रथमारुह्य नाप्सु चर्या विधीयते ॥ (30)

"'One cannot climb onto a boat and roam around on land. In that way, it is not recommended that one should ascend a chariot and travel on water.'"

एवं कर्म कृतं चित्रं विषयस्थं पृथक्पृथक् ।
यथा कर्म कृतं लोके तथा तदुपपद्यते ॥ (31)

"'In different kinds of terrain, one accordingly has different kinds of karma. Depending on the karma that is performed in this world, one obtains the fruits.'"

यन्नैव गन्धिनो रस्यं न रूपस्पर्शशब्दवत् ।
मन्यन्ते मुनयो बुद्ध्या तत्प्रधानं प्रचक्षते ॥ (32)

"'There is an entity that has no smell, taste, form, touch or sound. Using their intelligence, sages think about this. This is said to be Pradhana.'"

तत्र प्रधानमव्यक्तमव्यक्तस्य गुणो महान् ।
महत: प्रधानभूतस्य गुणोऽहंकार एव च ॥ (33)

"'Pradhana is unmanifest and one of the aspects of the unmanifest is mahat. An attribute of mahat, generated from Pradhana, is ahamkara.'"

अहंकारप्रधानस्य महाभूतकृतो गुण: ।
पृथक्त्वेन हि भूतानां विषया वै गुणा: स्मृता: ॥ (34)

"'Through Pradhana, the attribute of the great elements originates from ahamkara. The qualities of objects are said to be different from the elements.'"

बीजधर्म यथाव्यक्तं तथैव प्रसवात्मकम् ।
बीजधर्मा महानात्मा प्रसवश्चेति न: श्रुतम् ॥ (35)

"'The unmanifest follows the dharma of a seed and creates from its own self. We have also heard that mahat follows the dharma of a seed and has also been created.'"

बीजधर्मा त्वहंकार: प्रसवश्च पुन: पुन: ।
बीजप्रसवधर्माणि महाभूतानि पञ्च वै ॥ (36)

"'Ahamkara follows the dharma of a seed and has also been created again and again. The five great elements follow the dharma of being a seed and have also been created.'"

बीजधर्मिण इत्याहुः प्रसवं च न कुर्वते ।
विशेषाः पञ्चभूतानां तेषां वित्तं विशेषणम् ॥ (37)

'"'Those that possess the dharma of seeds are usually said to be ones that do not create. However, the five elements are special in this way and possess a distinctive property.'"'

तत्रैकगुणमाकाशं द्विगुणो वायुरुच्यते ।
त्रिगुणं ज्योतिरित्याहुरापश्चापि चतुर्गुणाः ॥ (38)

'"'Space has only one quality, and wind is said to possess two qualities. Light is said to possess three qualities, and water has four qualities.'"'

पृथ्वी पञ्चगुणा ज्ञेया त्रसस्थावरसंकुला ।
सर्वभूतकरी देवी शुभाशुभनिदर्शना ॥ (39)

'"'Know that Goddess Earth, full of mobile and immobile objects, has five qualities. She is the creator of all beings and has agreeable and disagreeable aspects.'"'

शब्दः स्पर्शस्तथा रूपं रसो गन्धश्च पञ्चमः ।
एते पञ्च गुणा भूमेर्विज्ञेया द्विजसत्तमाः ॥ (40)

'"'O Supreme among Dvijas! Sound, touch, form, taste and smell as the fifth—know that these are the five qualities associated with the earth.'"'

पार्थिवश्च सदा गन्धो गन्धश्च बहुधा स्मृतः ।
तस्य गन्धस्य वक्ष्यामि विस्तरेण बहून्गुणान् ॥ (41)

'"'Smell is always associated with the earth and smell is said to have many different types. Therefore, I will tell you in detail about the many qualities of smell.'"'

इष्टश्चानिष्टगन्धश्च मधुरोऽम्लः कटुस्तथा ।
निहारी संहतः स्निग्धो रूक्षो विशद एव च ।
एवं दशविधो ज्ञेयः पार्थिवो गन्ध इत्युत ॥ (42)

'"'Agreeable, disagreeable, sweet, sour, pungent, pervasive, concentrated, oily, dry and clear—know that these are the ten kinds of qualities associated with the earth.'"'

शब्द: स्पर्शस्तथा रूपं रसश्चापां गुणा: स्मृता: ।
रसज्ञानं तु वक्ष्यामि रसस्तु बहुधा स्मृत: ॥ (43)

"'"Sound, touch, form and taste are said to be the qualities of water. I will tell you about the many kinds of taste that have been spoken about."'"

मधुरोऽम्ल: कटुस्तिक्त: कषायो लवणस्तथा ।
एवं षड्विधविस्तारो रसो वारिमय: स्मृत: ॥ (44)

"'"Sweet, sour, pungent, bitter, astringent and saline—in detail, these are the six kinds of taste that are said to be associated with water."'"

शब्द: स्पर्शस्तथा रूपं त्रिगुणं ज्योतिरुच्यते ।
ज्योतिषश्च गुणो रूपं रूपं च बहुधा स्मृतम् ॥ (45)

"'"Sound, touch and form—these are said to be the three qualities associated with light. Form is said to be the quality of light and form is of many different types."'"

शुक्लं कृष्णं तथा रक्तं नीलं पीतारुणं तथा ।
ह्रस्वं दीर्घं तथा स्थूलं चतुरस्राणु वृत्तकम् ॥ (46)
एवं द्वादशविस्तारं तेजसो रूपमुच्यते ।
विज्ञेयं ब्राह्मणैर्नित्यं धर्मज्ञै: सत्यवादिभि: ॥ (47)

"'"White, dark, red, blue, yellow, orange, short, long, broad, narrow, square and circular—in detail, these are the twelve qualities associated with form. Brahmanas who know about dharma and are truthful in speech should always know this."'"

शब्दस्पर्शौ च विज्ञेयौ द्विगुणो वायुरुच्यते ।
वायोश्चापि गुण: स्पर्श: स्पर्शश्च बहुधा स्मृत: ॥ (48)

"'"Sound and touch—it should be known that these are the two qualities associated with the wind. Touch is a quality of the wind and there are said to be many kinds of touch."'"

उष्ण: शीत: सुखो दु:ख: स्निग्धो विशद एव च ।
कठिनश्चिक्कण: श्लक्ष्ण: पिच्छिलो दारुणो मृदु: ॥ (49)

एवं द्वादशविस्तारो वायव्यो गुण उच्यते ।
विधिवद्ब्रह्मणै: सिद्धैर्धर्मज्ञैस्तत्त्वदर्शिभि: ॥ (50)

'"'Hot, cold, agreeable, disagreeable, gentle, extensive, hard, oily, smooth, slippery, rough, soft—in detail, these are said to the twelve qualities associated with the wind. Brahmanas who know dharma, have insight about the truth and are siddhas know this.'"'

तत्रैकगुणमाकाशं शब्द इत्येव च स्मृत: ।
तस्य शब्दस्य वक्ष्यामि विस्तरेण बहुगुणान् ॥ (51)

'"'It has been said that space has the single quality of sound. In detail, I will recount the many different qualities of sound.'"'

षड्जर्षभौ च गान्धारो मध्यम: पञ्चमस्तथा ।
अत: परं तु विज्ञेयो निषादो धैवतस्तथा ॥ (52)

'"'These should be understood as *shadaja, rishabha, gandhara, madhyama, panchama and, after that, nishada and dhaivata.*'"'[217]

इष्टोऽनिष्टश्च शब्दस्तु संहत: प्रविभागवान् ।
एवं बहुविधो ज्ञेय: शब्द आकाशसंभव: ॥ (53)

'"'It should be known that there are agreeable and disagreeable sounds, combined together and separately. In this way, sound is generated from space and has many different types.'"'

आकाशमुत्तमं भूतमहंकारस्तत: परम् ।
अहंकारात्परा बुद्धिर्बुद्धेरात्मा तत: पर: ॥ (54)

'"'Space is supreme among the elements and ahamkara is superior to it. Intelligence is superior to ahamkara and the atman is superior to intelligence.'"'

तस्मातु परमव्यक्तमव्यक्तात्पुरुष: पर: ।
परावरज्ञो भूतानां यं प्राप्यानन्त्यमश्नुते ॥ (55)

---

[217] The seven primary musical notes.

"'The unmanifest[218] is superior to the atman and Purusha is superior to the unmanifest. A person who knows the difference between superior and inferior obtains the infinite.'"

Chapter 35

ब्रह्मोवाच

भूतानामथ पञ्चानां यथैषामीश्वरं मनः ।
नियमे च विसर्गे च भूतात्मा मन एव च ॥ (1)

"'"Brahma said, The mind is the lord of the five elements. In restraining them and releasing them, the mind is like the atman of the elements."'"

अधिष्ठाता मनो नित्यं भूतानां महतां तथा ।
बुद्धिरैश्वर्यमाचष्टे क्षेत्रज्ञः सर्व उच्यते ॥ (2)

"'"The mind always rules over the great elements. Intelligence possesses the power over everything and is said to be kshetrajna."'"

इन्द्रियाणि मनो युङ्क्ते सदश्वानिव सारथिः ।
इन्द्रियाणि मनो बुद्धिं क्षेत्रज्ञो युञ्जते सदा ॥ (3)

"'"The mind controls the senses, like a charioteer controls well-trained horses. The senses, the mind and intelligence are always associated with kshetrajna."'"

महाभूतसमायुक्तं बुद्धिसंयमनं रथम् ।
तमारुह्य स भूतात्मा समन्तात्परिधावति ॥ (4)

"'"The atman that is in beings ascends the chariot and drives it around on all sides. The great elements are yoked to it and intelligence constitutes the reins."'"

इन्द्रियग्रामसंयुक्तो मनःसारथिरेव च ।
बुद्धिसंयमनो नित्यं महान्ब्रह्ममयो रथः ॥ (5)

---

[218]Prakriti.

"'The aggregate of senses are yoked[219] and the mind is the charioteer. Intelligence is always like the reins and the chariot is immersed in the great brahman.'"

एवं यो वेत्ति विद्वान्वै सदा ब्रह्ममयं रथम् ।
स धीरः सर्वलोकेषु न मोहमधिगच्छति ॥ (6)

"'A learned person always knows that the chariot is immersed in the brahman. Among all the people, such a person is patient and is never overcome by delusion.'"

अव्यक्तादि विशेषान्तं त्रसस्थावरसंकुलम् ।
चन्द्रसूर्यप्रभालोकं ग्रहनक्षत्रमण्डितम् ॥ (7)

"'The unmanifest, with all these mobile and immobile objects, has a specific end. The moon and the sun provide illumination to the worlds, adorned by the planets and the nakshatras.'"

नदीपर्वतजालैश्च सर्वतः परिभूषितम् ।
विविधाभिस्तथादिभश्च सततं समलंकृतम् ॥ (8)

"'On every side, it is decorated by nets of rivers and mountains. There are many kinds of ornaments of water in every direction.'"

आजीवः सर्वभूतानां सर्वप्राणभृतां गतिः ।
एतद्ब्रह्मवनं नित्यं यस्मिंश्चरति क्षेत्रवित् ॥ (9)

"'This provides sustenance to all creatures and it is also the objective of all those who possess life. A person who knows about the kshetra[220] always roams around in the forest that is the brahman.'"

लोकेऽस्मिन्यानि भूतानि स्थावराणि चराणि च ।
तान्येवाग्रे प्रलीयन्ते पश्चाद्भूतकृता गुणाः ।
गुणेभ्यः पञ्चभूतानि एष भूतसमुच्छ्रयः ॥ (10)
देवा मनुष्या गन्धर्वाः पिशाचासुरराक्षसाः ।
सर्वे स्वभावतः सृष्टा न क्रियाभ्यो न कारणात् ॥ (11)

---

[219]Like horses.
[220]That is, the kshetrajna.

'"'There are many creatures, mobile and immobile, in this world. Those are the first to be destroyed. The gunas that result from the elements are destroyed later. Depending on their qualities, many different kinds of beings have progressively originated from the five elements—devas, men, gandharvas, pishachas, asuras and rakshasas. All of them have been created from nature, not from deeds and not from any other cause.'"'

एते विश्वकृतो विप्रा जायन्ते ह पुनः पुनः ।
तेभ्यः प्रसूतास्तेष्वेव महाभूतेषु पञ्चसु ।
प्रलीयन्ते यथाकालमूर्मयः सागरे यथा ॥ (12)

'"'The brahmanas[221] are the creators of the universe and are born again and again. When the time arrives, everything generated from them is dissolved into the five great elements, like waves in the ocean.'"'

विश्वसृग्भ्यस्तु भूतेभ्यो महाभूतानि गच्छति ।
भूतेभ्यश्चापि पञ्चभ्यो मुक्तो गच्छेत्प्रजापतिम् ॥ (13)

'"'Then, the elements that create the universe merge into the great elements. These five elements are freed and merge into Prajapati.'"'

प्रजापतिरिदं सर्वं तपसैवासृजत्प्रभुः ।
तथैव वेदानृषयस्तपसा प्रतिपेदिरे ॥ (14)

'"'Through his austerities,[222] Prajapati is the lord who created everything. In that way, the rishis know him through their austerities.'"'

तपसश्चानुपूर्व्येण फलमूलाशिनस्तथा ।
त्रैलोक्यं तपसा सिद्धाः पश्यन्तीह समाहिताः ॥ (15)

'"'In due order, they undertake austerities, surviving on fruits and roots. They control themselves. Having become siddhas through their austerities, they can see the three worlds.'"'

---

[221]Not ordinary brahmanas, but Marichi, Kashyapa and so on, Prajapatis—the special brahmanas.
[222]In this case, mental meditation.

ओषधान्यगदादीनि नानाविद्याश्च सर्वशः ।
तपसैव प्रसिध्यन्ति तपोमूलं हि साधनम् ॥ (16)

"'"Herbs, medicines and every kind of knowledge is obtained through austerities. Austerities are the foundations for the means."'"

यद्दुरापं दुराम्नायं दुराधर्षं दुरन्वयम् ।
तत्सर्वं तपसा साध्यं तपो हि दुरतिक्रमम् ॥ (17)

"'"There are things that are difficult to obtain, difficult to name, difficult to conquer and difficult to learn. Austerities ensure success in all this. Austerities are difficult to surpass."'"

सुरापो ब्रह्महा स्तेयी भ्रूणहा गुरुतल्पगः ।
तपसैव सुतप्तेन मुच्यन्ते किल्बिषात्ततः ॥ (18)

"'"A person who drinks liquor, kills a brahmana, steals, kills a foetus or violates his guru's bed can torment himself well through austerities and be freed from his sins."'"

मनुष्याः पितरो देवाः पशवो मृगपक्षिणः ।
यानि चान्यानि भूतानि त्रसानि स्थावराणि च ॥ (19)
तपःपरायणा नित्यं सिध्यन्ते तपसा सदा ।
तथैव तपसा देवा महाभागा दिवं गताः ॥ (20)

"'"If men, ancestors, devas, animals,[223] animals, birds and all other mobile and immobile objects are constantly devoted to austerities, they can always obtain success through austerities. It is through austerities that the immensely fortunate devas went to heaven."'"

आशीर्युक्तानि कर्माणि कुर्वते ये त्वतन्द्रिताः ।
अहंकारसमायुक्तास्ते सकाशे प्रजापतेः ॥ (21)

"'"If a person single-mindedly performs beneficial acts, even if these are tinged with ahamkara, he approaches Prajapati."'"

---

[223] This means sacrificial animals. The subsequent mention of animals refers to other animals.

ध्यानयोगेन शुद्धेन निर्मेमा निरहंकृताः ।
प्राप्नुवन्ति महात्मानो महान्तं लोकमुत्तमम् ॥ (22)

'"'However, there are pure ones without a sense of ownership and without ahamkara. They are devoted to the yoga of dhyana. Those great-souled ones obtain supreme and great worlds.'"'

ध्यानयोगादुपागम्य प्रसन्नमतयः सदा ।
सुखोपचयमव्यक्तं प्रविशन्त्यात्मवत्तया ॥ (23)

'"'They are devoted to the yoga of dhyana and are always tranquil. Their atmans enter the unmanifest and obtain an accumulation of bliss there.'"'

ध्यानयोगादुपागम्य निर्मेमा निरहंकृताः ।
अव्यक्तं प्रविशन्तीह महान्तं लोकमुत्तमम् ॥ (24)

'"'There are those without a sense of ownership and without ahamkara. They are devoted to the yoga of dhyana. They enter the unmanifest and obtain supreme and great worlds.'"'

अव्यक्तादेव संभूतः समयज्ञो गतः पुनः ।
तमोरजोभ्यां निर्मुक्तः सत्त्वमास्थाय केवलम् ॥ (25)

'"'[Such a person] is generated from the unmanifest and merges into it again. He is freed from tamas and rajas and resorts to sattva alone.'"'

विमुक्तः सर्वपापेभ्यः सर्वं त्यजति निष्कलः ।
क्षेत्रज्ञ इति तं विद्याद्यस्तं वेद स वेदवित् ॥ (26)

'"'He is freed from all sins and liberated from all divisions. He should be known as kshetrajna. He knows what there is to be known.'"'

चित्तं चित्तादुपागम्य मुनिरासीत संयतः ।
यच्चित्तस्तन्मना भूत्वा गुह्यमेतत्सनातनम् ॥ (27)

'"'A sage must always be controlled and resort to consciousness alone. The mind must be fixed on the consciousness and on the eternal mystery.'"'

अव्यक्तादि विशेषान्तमविद्यालक्षणं स्मृतम् ।
निबोधत यथा हीदं गुणैर्लक्षणमित्युत ॥ (28)

"'The unmanifest has objects as a manifestation. But a focus on these is said to be a sign of ignorance. Understand what is beyond all signs associated with the gunas.'"

द्व्यक्षरस्तु भवेन्मृत्युस्त्र्यक्षरं ब्रह्म शाश्वतम् ।
ममेति च भवेन्मृत्युर्न ममेति च शाश्वतम् ॥ (29)

"'The word mrityu has two syllables. Akshara, the eternal brahman, has three syllables. Mama is mrityu and namama is eternal.'"

कर्म केचित्प्रशंसन्ति मन्दबुद्धितरा नराः ।
ये तु बुद्धा महात्मानो न प्रशंसन्ति कर्म ते ॥ (30)

"'There are some evil-minded men who praise karma. The great-souled ones who know do not praise karma.'"

कर्मणा जायते जन्तुर्मूर्तिमान्षोडशात्मकः ।
पुरुषं सृजतेऽविद्या अग्राह्यममृताशिनम् ॥ (31)

"'Karma leads to birth as a creature, characterized by the sixteen.[224] A man is the creation of ignorance. Those who are after immortality refuse to accept it.'"

तस्मात्कर्मसु निःस्नेहा ये केचित्पारदर्शिनः ।
विद्यामयोऽयं पुरुषो न तु कर्ममयः स्मृतः ॥ (32)

"'Therefore, those who are accomplished are not attached to karma. It is said that Purusha is full of knowledge and karma.'"

अपूर्वममृतं नित्यं य एनमविचारिणम् ।
य एनं विन्दतेऽऽत्मानमग्राह्यममृताशिनम् ॥ (33)

---

[224] The five senses, the five organs of action, the five objects of the senses and the mind. Alternatively, the five objects of the senses can be replaced by the five great elements.

"""It is without something that has come before. It is immortal. It is eternal. It is immutable. A person who realizes it within his atman refuses to accept something that does not lead to immortality."''

अग्राह्योऽमृतो भवति य एभिः कारणैर्ध्रुवः ।
अपोह्य सर्वसंकल्पान्संयम्यात्मानमात्मनि ।
स तद्ब्रह्म शुभं वेत्ति यस्मादभूयो न विद्यते ॥ (34)

"""It is because of this certain reason that he refuses to accept something that is not immortal. He casts aside all resolution and controls his atman through his own self. He knows the auspicious brahman and there is no return after that.""'

प्रसादेनैव सत्त्वस्य प्रसादं समवाप्नुयात् ।
लक्षणं हि प्रसादस्य यथा स्यात्स्वप्नदर्शनम् ॥ (35)

"""Because of sattva, he obtains tranquillity. The sign of this tranquillity is that everything is seen as if in a dream."'"[225]

गतिरेषा तु मुक्तानां ये ज्ञानपरिनिष्ठिताः ।
प्रवृत्तयश्च याः सर्वाः पश्यन्ति परिणामजाः ॥ (36)

"""This is the destination of liberated ones who are devoted to jnana. They can see all the consequences of action."'"

एषा गतिरसक्तानामेष धर्मः सनातनः ।
एषा ज्ञानवतां प्राप्तिरेतद्वृत्तमनिन्दितम् ॥ (37)

"""They are not addicted to these outcomes. This is eternal dharma. Those who possess jnana obtain this. This is unblemished conduct.""'

समेन सर्वभूतेषु निःस्पृहेण निराशिषा ।
शक्या गतिरियं गन्तुं सर्वत्र समदर्शिना ॥ (38)

"""A person who is impartial towards all creatures, without desire and without hope and always indifferent towards what he sees, is capable of progressing to that destination."'"

---

[225]Everything seems unreal.

एतद्व: सर्वमाख्यातं मया विप्रर्षिसत्तमा: ।
एवमाचरत क्षिप्रं तत: सिद्धिमवाप्स्यथ ॥ (39)

'"'O Supreme among Brahmana Rishis! I have thus told you everything. Act swiftly in this way and you will obtain siddhi.'"'

गुरुरुवाच

इत्युक्तास्ते तु मुनयो ब्रह्मणा गुरुणा तथा ।
कृतवन्तो महात्मानस्ततो लोकानवाप्नुवन् ॥ (40)

'"The guru said, 'Thus addressed Guru Brahma, the great-souled sages acted in this way and obtained the worlds.'"'

त्वमप्येतन्महाभाग यथोक्तं ब्रह्मणो वच: ।
सम्यगाचर शुद्धात्मंस्तत: सिद्धिमवाप्स्यसि ॥ (41)

'"'O Immensely Fortunate One! You should also act in accordance with Brahma's words. If you purify yourself and act properly in that way, you will obtain siddhi.'"'

वासुदेव उवाच

इत्युक्त: स तदा शिष्यो गुरुणा धर्ममुत्तमम् ।
चकार सर्वं कौन्तेय ततो मोक्षमवाप्तवान् ॥ (42)

'Vasudeva continued, "The guru thus spoke to the shishya about supreme dharma. O Kounteya! He acted in that way and obtained moksha."'

कृतकृत्यश्च स तदा शिष्य: कुरुकुलोद्वह ।
तत्पदं समनुप्राप्तो यत्र गत्वा न शोचति ॥ (43)

'"O Extender of the Kuru Lineage! Having accomplished what he was meant to do, the shishya obtained that state. Having obtained it, one does not grieve."'

अर्जुन उवाच

को न्वसौ ब्राह्मण: कृष्ण कश्च शिष्यो जनार्दन ।
श्रोतव्यं चेन्मयैतद्वै तत्त्वमाचक्ष्व मे विभो ॥ (44)

'Arjuna asked, "O Krishna! O Janardana! Who was that brahmana and who was the shishya? O Lord! If I can hear the truth about this, please tell me."'

वासुदेव उवाच

अहं गुरुर्महाबाहो मन: शिष्यं च विद्धि मे ।
त्वत्प्रीत्या गुह्यमेतच्च कथितं मे धनंजय ॥ (45)

'Vasudeva replied, "O Mighty-Armed One! Know me. I am the guru and the mind is the shishya. O Dhananjaya! It is because of my affection towards you that I have revealed this secret to you."'

मयि चेदस्ति ते प्रीतिर्नित्यं कुरुकुलोद्वह ।
अध्यात्ममेतच्छ्रुत्वा त्वं सम्यगाचर सुव्रत ॥ (46)

'"O Extender of the Kuru Lineage! O One Who Is Excellent in Vows! If you love me, having heard about the adhyatma, act properly."'

ततस्त्वं सम्यगाचीर्णे धर्मेऽस्मिन्कुरुनन्दन ।
सर्वपापविशुद्धात्मा मोक्षं प्राप्स्यसि केवलम् ॥ (47)

'"If you practise this dharma properly, your atman will be cleansed of all sins and you will obtain moksha alone."'

पूर्वमप्येतदेवोक्तं युद्धकाल उपस्थिते ।
मया तव महाबाहो तस्मादत्र मन: कुरु ॥ (48)

'"I told you this earlier, when the time for battle had presented itself. O Mighty-Armed One! Therefore, make up your mind to follow this."'

मया तु भरतश्रेष्ठ चिरदृष्ट: पिता विभो ।
तमहं द्रष्टुमिच्छामि संमते तव फल्गुन ॥ (49)

'"O Foremost among the Bharata Lineage! O Lord! It has been a long time since I have seen my father. O Phalguna! With your permission, I wish to see him."'

वैशंपायन उवाच

इत्युक्तवचनं कृष्णं प्रत्युवाच धनंजय: ।
गच्छावो नगरं कृष्ण गजसाह्वयमद्य वै ॥ (50)
समेत्य तत्र राजानं धर्मात्मानं युधिष्ठिरम् ।
समनुज्ञाप्य दुर्धर्षं स्वां पुरीं यातुमर्हसि ॥ (51)

Vaishampayana said, 'Addressed by Krishna in such words, Dhananjaya replied, "O Krishna! Today, we will go to the city of Gajasahvya.[226] We will meet King Yudhishthira, who has dharma in his atman. Take his permission and then go to your own unassailable city."'

Thus ends the Anu Gita.

---

[226]Hastinapura.

25

PANDAVA GITA

There is a case for including the Pandava Gita in a book on the Mahabharata Gitas, but it is only half-convincing. This text is not a part of the Mahabharata. But it has characters from the Mahabharata singing chants about Bhagavan's greatness. It is permeated with *bhakti*.[1] Therefore, though not a part of the epic, it has strong links with the Mahabharata.

Among the characters, the most important are the Pandavas. Hence, it is known as the Pandava Gita, though it is really about what the Pandavas and others chanted. The word '*prapanna*' means to seek refuge in, as in Bhagavat Gita 2.7. Since this is about seeking refuge with Bhagavan, it is also known as the Prapanna Gita.

The compilation has a single chapter with eighty-three shlokas. The most famous of these shlokas is undoubtedly the one spoken by Duryodhana (58) or perhaps Gandhari (28). There is, of course, the concluding verse of the Bhagavat Gita, attributed in this case to Vaishampayana and not Sanjaya (65). Some of the shlokas are indeed from the Mahabharata, others from various Puranas. The name of the compiler of this popular text is unknown. Nevertheless, it is a popular and Mahabharata-related Gita. Thus, there is that half a case for its inclusion. Since the text is not part of the Mahabharata, the CE or otherwise,

---

[1] Devotion and faith, complete surrender.

one cannot use BORI as a source for the text. We have used the version published by Khemraj Publishers in 1901.²

Chapter 1

बेंचजमत 1

प्रह्लादनारदपराशरपुंडरीकव्यासाम्बरीषशुकशौनकभीष्मकाद्याः ।
रुक्माङ्गदार्जुनवसिष्ठविभीषणाद्या एतान्हं परमभागवतान्नमामि ॥ (1)

I prostrate myself before the supreme devotees of Bhagavan—Prahlada (same as Prahrada),³ Narada, Parashara, Pundarika,⁴ Vyasa, Ambarisha,⁵ Shuka,⁶ Shounaka,⁷ Bhishmaka,⁸ Rukmangada,⁹ Arjuna, Vasishtha, Vibhishana and others.¹⁰

लोमहर्षण उवाच

धर्मो विवर्धति युधिष्ठिरकीर्तनेन पापं प्रणश्यति वृकोदरकीर्तनेन ।
शत्रुर्विनश्यति धनंजयकीर्तनेन माद्रीसुतौ कथ्यतां न भवन्ति रोगाः ॥ (2)

Lomaharshana said, 'Dharma is enhanced by chanting about Yudhishthira. Sin is destroyed by chanting about Vrikodara. Enemies are destroyed by chanting about Dhananjaya. If the two sons of Madri are spoken about, there is no disease.'

---

²*Pandava Gita*, Keshvaprasad Sharma Dvivedi (ed. and trans.), Khemraj Publishers, Mumbai, 1901.
³Also written as Prahrada.
⁴Probably Pundarika (Pundalika), the Vishnu devotee who worshipped Vishnu in the form of Vithoba.
⁵The famous king who was Vishnu's devotee.
⁶Vyasadeva's son.
⁷The sage who recited the Mahabharata and the Puranas to the assembled sages in the Naimisha forest.
⁸Rukmini's father.
⁹The king who was Vishnu's devotee. Rukmangada's story involves the apsara Mohini.
¹⁰This shloka is a general address by the devotee who is reciting Pandava Gita.

ब्रह्मोवाच

ये मानवा विगतरागपराऽपरज्ञा नारायणं सुरगुरुं सततं स्मरन्ति ।
ध्यानेन तेन हतकिल्बिषचेतनास्ते मातुः पयोधररसं न पुनः पिबन्ति ॥ (3)

Brahma said, 'There are men who know about the supreme and are devoid of attachment. They always remember Narayana, the guru of the gods. Through this dhyana, they destroy all sins in their minds. They do not drink the mother's milk again.'[11]

इन्द्र उवाच

नारायणो नाम नरो नराणां प्रसिद्धचौरः कथितः पृथिव्याम् ।
अनेकजन्मार्जितपापसंचयं हरत्यशेषं स्मृतमात्र एव यः ॥ (4)

Indra said, 'The man named Narayana is famously spoken about among men on earth as a thief. As soon as he is remembered, he steals away all the accumulated sins earned over many births.'

युधिष्ठिर उवाच

मेघश्यामं पीतकौशेयवासं श्रीवत्सांकं कौस्तुभोद्भासिताङ्गम् ।
पुण्योपेतं पुण्डरीकायताक्षं विष्णुं वन्दे सर्वलोकैकनाथम् ॥ (5)

Yudhishthira said, 'His complexion is like that of a dark cloud. He is attired in a yellow silken garment. Because of Koustubha, his body is radiant. He associates with the virtuous. His large eyes resemble a lotus. I worship Vishnu, who is alone the lord of all the worlds.'

भीमसेन उवाच

जलौघमग्ना सचराऽचरा धराविषाणकोट्याऽखिलविश्वमूर्तिना ।
समुद्धृता येन वराहरूपिणा स मे स्वयम्भूर्भगवान् प्रसीदतु ॥ (6)

Bhimasena said, 'The earth, with all its mobile and immobile objects, was submerged in the flood of water and the one whose form is the universe assumed the form of a *varaha*[12] to raise her up on his snout. May that illustrious Svayambhu show me his favours.'

---

[11] They are not born again.
[12] A reference to Vishnu's incarnation in the form of a boar.

अर्जुन उवाच

अचिन्त्यमव्यक्तमनन्तमव्ययंविभुं प्रभुं भावितविश्वभावनम् ।
त्रैलोक्यविस्तारविचारकारकं हरिं प्रपन्नोऽस्मि गतिं महात्मनाम् ॥ (7)

Arjuna said, 'I seek refuge with Hari, the destination for great-souled ones. He cannot be thought of. He is not manifest. He is infinite. He is the lord without decay. He is the lord who thinks of the creation of the universe. He is the one who thinks about the extension of the three worlds.'

नकुल उवाच

यदि गमनमधस्तात् कालपाशानुबंधाद्यदि च कुलविहीने जायते पक्षिकीटे ।
कृमिशतमपि गत्वा ध्यायते चान्तरात्मा मम भवतु हृदिस्था केशवे
भक्तिरेका ॥ (8)

Nakula said, 'Bound by the noose of destiny, if I descend downwards,[13] or am born in an ignoble lineage or as a bird or insect, or have hundreds of births as a worm, let my inner atman meditate on Keshava. Let him be in my heart and let me have single-minded devotion towards him alone.'

सहदेव उवाच

तस्य यज्ञवराहस्य विष्णोरतुलतेजसः ।
प्रणामं ये प्रकुर्वन्ति तेषामपि नमो नमः ॥ (9)

Sahadeva said, 'There are those who prostrate themselves before the infinitely energetic Vishnu, in the form of a Yajna Varaha.[14] I bow down before them repeatedly.'

कुन्ती उवाच

स्वकर्मफलनिर्दिष्टां यां यां योनिं व्रजाम्यहम् ।
तस्यां तस्यां हृषीकेश त्वयि भक्तिर्दृढाऽस्तु मे ॥ (10)

---

[13]Into hell.
[14]Vishnu's form in the varaha incarnation, also identified as the presiding divinity of a sacrifice.

Kunti said, 'O Hrishikesha! Determined by the fruits of my own karma, whichever birth I proceed towards, in that form, let my devotion towards you be firm.'

मादी उवाच

कृष्णे रताः कृष्णमनुस्मरन्ति रात्रौ च कृष्णं पुनरुत्थिता ये ।
ते भिन्नदेहाः प्रविशन्ति कृष्णे हविर्यथा मन्त्रहुतं हुताशे ॥ (11)

Madri said, 'There are those who are devoted to Krishna. They remember Krishna in the night and also remember Krishna when they wake up. Like oblations aided by mantras enter the fire, in other bodies, they enter Krishna.'

द्रौपदी उवाच

कीटेषु पक्षिषु मृगेषु सरीसृपेषु रक्षःपिशाचमनुजेष्वपि यत्र यत्र ।
जातस्य मे भवतु केशव त्वत्प्रसादात्त्वय्येव भक्तिरचलाऽव्यभिचारिणी च ॥ (12)

Droupadi said, 'O Keshava! Wherever I am born, as an insect, bird, animal, reptile, rakshasa, pishacha or as a human, through your favours, let me behave in such a way that my devotion towards you does not waver.'

सुभद्रा उवाच

एकोऽपि कृष्णस्य कृतः प्रणामो दशाश्वमेधावभृथेन तुल्यः ।
दशाश्वमेधी पुनरेति जन्म कृष्णप्रणामी न पुनर्भवाय ॥ (13)

Subhadra said, 'Prostrating oneself before Krishna alone is equal to performing *avabhritha*[15] after ten horse sacrifices. However, there is rebirth after ten horse sacrifices. After prostrating oneself before Krishna, there is no rebirth.'

---

[15] Avabhritha is the most important final component of a sacrifice, characterized by taking a bath.

अभिमन्युरुवाच

गोविन्द गोविन्द हरे मुरारे गोविन्द गोविन्द मुकुन्द कृष्ण ।
गोविन्द गोविन्द रथाङ्गपाणे गोविन्द गोविन्द नमामि नित्यम् ॥ (14)

Abhimanyu said, 'O Govinda! O Govinda! O Hari! O Murari! O Govinda! O Govinda! O Mukunda! O Krishna! O Govinda! O Govinda! O One with Part of a Chariot in Your Hand![16] O Govinda! O Govinda! I always prostrate myself before you.'

धृष्टद्युम्न उवाच

श्रीराम नारायण वासुदेव गोविन्द वैकुण्ठ मुकुन्द कृष्ण ।
श्रीकेशवानन्त नृसिंह विष्णो मां त्राहि संसारभुजङ्गदष्टम् ॥ (15)

Dhristadhyumna[17] said, 'O Shri Rama! O Narayana! O Vasudeva! O Govinda! O Vaikuntha! O Mukunda! O Krishna! O Shri Keshava! O Ananta! O Nrisimha! O Vishnu! Please save me. I have been bitten by the serpent of samsara.'

सात्यकिरुवाच

अप्रमेय हरे विष्णो कृष्ण दामोदराच्युत ।
गोविन्दानन्त सर्वेश वासुदेव नमोऽस्तु ते ॥ (16)

Satyaki[18] said, 'O Immeasurable One! O Hari! O Vishnu! O Krishna! O Damodara! O Achyuta! O Govinda! O Ananta! O Lord of Everything! O Vasudeva! I prostrate myself before you.'

उद्धव उवाच

वासुदेवं परित्यज्य योऽन्यदेवमुपासते ।
तृषितो जाह्नवीतीरे कूपं खनति दुर्मतिः ॥ (17)

---

[16] The part (*anga*) of a chariot (*ratha*) means the wheel (*chakra*). Thus, this stands for the chakra in Krishna's hand.

[17] Drupada's son, Droupadi's brother, commander of Pandava forces.

[18] A great Yadava warrior, also known as Yuyudhana, Arjuna's disciple.

Uddhava[19] said, 'If a person forsakes Vasudeva and worships another deva, he is like an evil-minded and thirsty man who digs a well along the banks of the Jahnavi.'[20]

धौम्य उवाच

अपां समीपे शयनासनस्थिते दिवा च रात्रौ च यथाधिगच्छताम् ।
यद्यस्ति किञ्चित् सुकृतं कृतं मया जनार्दनस्तेन कृतेन तुष्यतु ॥ (18)

Dhoumya[21] said, 'There may be good deeds I have performed near the water, while lying down, while seated, during the day, or at night. Let Janardana be satisfied with what I have done.'

संजय उवाच

आर्ता विषण्णाः शिथिलाश्च भीता घोरेषु व्याघ्रादिषु वर्तमानाः ।
सङ्कीर्त्य नारायणशब्दमात्रं विमुक्तदुःखाः सुखिनो भवन्ति ॥ (19)

Sanjaya said, 'There are those who are afflicted, distressed, limp and scared, with terrors like tigers and other things present. As soon as they chant Narayana's name, from that very sound, they are freed from their miseries and become happy.'

अक्रूर उवाच

अहं तु नारायणदास दासदासस्य दासस्य च दासदासः ।
अन्यो न हीशो जगतो नराणां तस्मादहं धन्यतरोऽस्मि लोके ॥ (20)

Akrura[22] said, 'I am Narayana's servant, the servant of his servant, the servant of the servant of his servant. Indeed, in this world, there is no other lord for men. Therefore, I am the most blessed in this world.'

---

[19]Yadava, Krishna's friend and devotee.
[20]Ganga.
[21]The family priest of the Pandavas.
[22]A Yadava prince.

विराट उवाच

वासुदेवस्य ये भक्ताः शान्तास्तद्गतचेतसः ।
तेषां दासस्य दासोऽहं भवेयं जन्मजन्मनि ॥ (21)

Virata said, 'There are those who are Vasudeva's devotees, serene, with their minds only on him. From one birth to another birth, let me be the servant of their servants.'

भीष्म उवाच

विपरीतेषु कालेषु परिक्षीणेषु बन्धुषु ।
त्राहि मां कृपया कृष्ण शरणागतवत्सल ॥ (22)

Bhishma said, 'O Krishna! O One Who Is Affectionate towards Those Who Seek Refuge! When destiny is adverse and relatives dwindle away, please show your compassion and save me.'

द्रोण उवाच

ये ये हताश्चक्रधरेण दैत्यास्त्रैलोक्यनाथेन जनार्दनेन ।
ते ते गता विष्णुपुरीं नरेन्द्रक्रोधोऽपि देवस्य वरेण तुल्यः ॥ (23)

Drona said, 'Janardana is the lord of the three worlds. The wielder of the chakra has killed daityas and lords among men. But they have gone to Vishnu's city. Therefore, the divinity's rage is equal to a boon.'

कृपाचार्य उवाच

मज्जन्मनः फलमिदं मधुकैटभारे मत्प्रार्थनीय मदनुग्रह एष एव ।
त्वद्भृत्यभृत्यपरिचारकभृत्यभृत्यभृत्यस्य भृत्य इति मां स्मर लोकनाथ ॥ (24)

Kripacharya said, 'O One Who Removed the Burden of Madhu and Kaitabha! O Lord of the Worlds! As a result of my birth, I pray for only this fruit. Please show me your favours and remember me. I want to be the attendant of your servant's servant, the servant of the servant of your servant.'

अश्वत्थामा उवाच

गोविन्द केशव जनार्दन वासुदेव विश्वेश विश्व मधुसूदन विश्वरूप ।
श्रीपद्मनाभ पुरुषोत्तम देहि दास्यं नारायणाच्युत नृसिंह नमो नमस्ते ॥ (25)

Ashvatthama said, 'O Govinda! O Keshava! O Janardana! O Vasudeva! O Lord of the Universe! O Universe! O Madhusudana! O One with the Universe as Your Form! O Shri Padmanabha! O Purushottama! O Narayana! O Achyuta! O Nrisimha! I prostrate myself repeatedly before you. Please make me your servant.'

कर्ण उवाच

नान्यं वदामि न शृणोमि न चिन्तयामि नान्यं
स्मरामि न भजामि न चाश्रयामि ।
भक्त्या त्वदीयचरणाम्बुजमादरेण श्रीश्रीनिवास
पुरुषोत्तम देहि दास्यम् ॥ (26)

Karna said, 'I do not speak of anyone else, hear of anyone else, think of anyone else, remember anyone else, worship anyone else, or seek refuge with anyone else. O Shri Shrinivasa! O Purushottama! Devotedly and lovingly, I seek your lotus feet. Please make me your servant.'

धृतराष्ट्र उवाच

नमो नमः कारणवामनाय नारायणायामितविक्रमाय ।
श्रीशार्ङ्गचक्रासिगदाधराय नमोऽस्तु तस्मै पुरुषोत्तमाय ॥ (27)

Dhritarashtra said, 'I repeatedly prostrate myself before the cause behind vamana, the infinitely valorous Narayana. I prostrate myself before Purushottama, who wields the Shri Sharnga bow, the chakra, the sword and the mace.'

गान्धारी उवाच

त्वमेव माता च पिता त्वमेव त्वमेव बन्धुश्च सखा त्वमेव ।
त्वमेव विद्या द्रविणं त्वमेव त्वमेव सर्वं मम देव देव ॥ (28)

Gandhari said, 'You are the mother and you are the father. You are the relative and you are the friend. You are knowledge and you are wealth. O Lord of the Gods! You are everything to me.'

द्रुपद उवाच

यज्ञेशाच्युत गोविन्द माधवानन्त केशव ।
कृष्ण विष्णो हृषीकेश वासुदेव नमोऽस्तु ते ॥ (29)

Drupada said, 'O Lord of Sacrifices! O Achyuta! O Govinda! O Madhava! O Ananta! O Keshava! O Krishna! O Vishnu! O Hrishikesha! O Vasudeva! I prostrate myself before you.'

जयद्रथ उवाच

नमः कृष्णाय देवाय ब्रह्मणेऽनन्तशक्तये ।
योगेश्वराय योगाय त्वामहं शरणं गतः ॥ (30)

Jayadratha[23] said, 'I prostrate myself before Krishna the divinity, the brahman who is infinite in his powers. You are lord of yoga, you are yoga. I seek refuge with you.'

विकर्ण उवाच

कृष्णाय वासुदेवाय देवकीनन्दनाय च ।
नन्दगोपकुमाराय गोविन्दाय नमो नमः ॥ (31)

Vikarna[24] said, 'O Krishna! O Vasudeva! O Devaki's son! O Son of Nandagopa! O Govinda! I repeatedly prostrate myself before you.'

सोमदत्त उवाच

नमः परमकल्याण नमस्ते विश्वभावन ।
वासुदेवाय शान्ताय पशूनांपतये नमः ॥ (32)

---

[23]Dhritarashtra's son-in-law, Duhshala's husband.
[24]Duryodhana's brother.

Somadatta[25] said, 'O Supremely Beneficial One! I prostrate myself before you. O Creator of the Universe! I prostrate myself before you. I prostrate myself before the serene Vasudeva, the lord of animals.'

विराट उवाच

नमो ब्रह्मण्यदेवाय गोब्राह्मणहिताय च ।
जगद्धिताय कृष्णाय गोविन्दाय नमो नमः ॥ (33)

Virata said, 'I prostrate myself before the divinity of brahmanas, who ensures the welfare of cattle and brahmanas. I repeatedly prostrate myself before Krishna Govinda, who ensures the welfare of the universe.'

शल्य उवाच

अतसीपुष्पसंकाशं पीतवाससमच्युतम् ।
ये नमस्यन्ति गोविन्दं तेषां न विद्यते भयम् ॥ (34)

Shalya[26] said, 'His complexion is like that of the atasi flower.[27] He is attired in yellow garments. Those who prostrate themselves before Govinda have nothing to fear.'

बलभद्र उवाच

कृष्ण कृष्ण कृपालो त्वमगतीनां गतिर्भव ।
संसारार्णवमग्नानां प्रसीद पुरुषोत्तम ॥ (35)

Balabhadra[28] said, 'O Krishna! O Krishna! O Compassionate One! Be the refuge for those who have no refuge. O Purushottama! They are submerged in the ocean that is samsara. Please show your favours.'

---

[25]The king of Bahlika.
[26]The king of Madra, Madri's brother, fought on the side of the Kouravas.
[27]A flower from the linseed family.
[28]Balarama.

श्रीकृष्ण उवाच

कृष्ण कृष्णेति कृष्णेति यो मां स्मरति नित्यशः ।
जलं भित्वा यथा पद्मं नरकादुद्धराम्यहम् ॥ (36)

Shri Krishna said, '"O Krishna!", "O Krishna!", "O Krishna!"—if a person always remembers me in this way, like raising a lotus out of water, I raise him up from hell.'

श्रीकृष्ण उवाच

नित्यं वदामि मनुजाः स्वयमूर्ध्वबाहुर्यो मां मुकुन्द नरसिंह जनार्दनेति ।
जीवो जपत्यनुदिनं मरणे रणे वा पाषाणकाष्ठसदृशाय ददाम्यभीष्टम् ॥ (37)

Shri Krishna said, 'O Men! I raise up my arms and always say that if a being performs japa every day, at the time of death, or in the field of battle, addressing me as Mukunda, Narasimha and Janardana, I will grant him his wishes, even if he is like a block of stone or a piece of wood.'

ईश्वर उवाच

सकृन्नारायणेत्युक्त्वा पुमान् कल्पशतत्रयम् ।
गङ्गादिसर्वतीर्थेषु स्नातो भवति पुत्रक ॥ (38)

Ishvara[29] said, 'O Son! If a man chants the name of Narayana once, he obtains the good merits of bathing in the Ganga and all the other tirthas for three hundred kalpas.'

सूत उवाच

तत्रैव गङ्गा यमुना च तत्र गोदावरी सिन्धु सरस्वती च ।
सर्वाणि तीर्थानि वसन्ति तत्र यत्राच्युतोदार कथाप्रसङ्गः ॥ (39)

Suta[30] said, 'Wherever extensive accounts about Achyuta are recited, Ganga, Yamuna, Godavari, Sindhu, Sarasvati and all the tirthas reside there.'

---

[29] Shiva.
[30] Lomaharshana.

यम उवाच

नरके पच्यमानेतु यमेनं परिभाषितम् ।
किं त्वया नार्चितो देवः केशवः क्लेशनाशनः ॥ (40)

Yama said, 'When a person is cooked in hell, Yama speaks to him—"Did you not worship the divinity Keshava, the destroyer of hardships?"'

नारद उवाच

जन्मान्तरसहस्रेण तपोध्यानसमाधिना ।
नराणां क्षीणपापानां कृष्णे भक्तिः प्रजायते ॥ (41)

Narada said, 'After thousands of births full of austerities, dhyana and samadhi, men destroy their sins and devotion towards Krishna is generated in them.'

प्रह्लाद उवाच

नाथ योनिसहस्रेषु येषु येषु व्रजाम्यहम् ।
तेषु तेष्वचला भक्तिरच्युतास्तु सदा त्वयि ॥ (42)
या प्रीतिरविवेकनां विषयेष्वनुधारिणी ।
त्वदनुस्मरणादेव हृदयादपसर्पति ॥ (43)

Prahlada said, 'O Protector! O Achyuta! Whatever be the thousands of wombs I progress towards, in all those, may I always have unwavering devotion towards you. Those without a sense of discrimination possess love for material objects and nurture it. O Divinity! As soon as I remember you, may these be dispelled from my heart.'

विश्वामित्र उवाच

किं तस्य दानैः किं तीर्थैः किं तपोभिः किमध्वरैः ।
यो नित्यं ध्यायते देवं नारायणमनन्यधीः ॥ (44)

Vishvamitra said, 'If a person constantly performs dhyana on the divinity Narayana, with his mind on nothing else, what will he do with donations, tirthas, austerities and sacrifices?'

जमदग्निरुवाच

नित्योत्सवो भवेत्तेषां नित्यं नित्यं च मङ्गलम् ।
येषां हृदिस्थो भगवान्मङ्गलायतनो हरि: ॥ (45)

Jamadagni[31] said, 'For those in whose hearts Bhagavan Hari, the abode of auspiciousness is present, there are constant festivities and auspiciousness is always present.'

भरद्वाज उवाच

लाभस्तेषां जयस्तेषां कुतस्तेषां पराजय: ।
येषामिन्दीवरश्यामो हृदयस्थो जनार्दन: ॥ (46)

Bharadvaja said, 'For those in whose hearts Janardana, with the complexion of a blue lotus, is present, there is gain and victory. How can they be defeated?'

गौतम उवाच

गोकोटिदानं ग्रहणेषु काशीप्रयागगंगायुतकल्पवास: ।
यज्ञायुतं मेरुसुवर्णदानं गोविन्दनामस्मरणेन तुल्यम् ॥ (47)

Goutama[32] said, 'Donating one crore cows during eclipses, residing in Kashi, Prayaga and the banks of the Ganga for ten thousand kalpas, performing ten thousand sacrifices and donating gold on Meru is equal [in good merits] to remembering Govinda's name.'

अग्निरुवाच

गोविन्देति सदा स्नानं गोविन्देति सदा जप: ।
गोविन्देति सदा ध्यानं सदा गोविन्दकीर्तनम् ॥ (48)
त्र्यक्षरं परमं ब्रह्म गोविन्देति त्र्यक्षरं परम् ।
तस्मादुच्चारितं येन ब्रह्मभूयाय कल्पते ॥ (49)

Agni said, 'Uttering "Govinda" is constant bathing. Uttering "Govinda" is constant japa. Uttering "Govinda" is constant dhyana.

---

[31] A famous sage, descended from the Bhrigu lineage, Parashurama's father.
[32] A famous sage.

One must constantly chant Govinda's name. The supreme three aksharas in "Govinda" are the three aksharas of the supreme brahman.[33] Therefore, anyone who utters it is worthy of merging into the brahman.'

श्रीबादरायणि उवाच

अच्युत: कल्पवृक्षोऽसावनन्त: कामधेनुव: ।
चिन्तामणिस्तु गोविन्दो हरेर्नाम विचिंतयेत् ॥ (50)

Shri Badarayani[34] said, 'Achyuta is the tree that confers every object of desire. Ananta is the cow that confers every object of desire. Govinda is the jewel that confers every object of desire. Think of Hari's name.'

हरिरूवाच

जयतु जयतु देवो देवकीनन्दनोऽयं जयतु जयतु कृष्णो वृष्णिवंशप्रदीप: ।
जयतु जयतु मेघश्यामल: कोमलाङ्गो जयतु जयतु पृथ्वीभारनाशो
मुकुन्द: ॥ (51)

Hari[35] said, 'Victory. Victory to the divinity. Victory to Devaki's son. Victory to Krishna. Victory to the lamp of the Vrishni lineage. Victory. Victory to the one whose complexion is like that of a dark cloud. Victory to the one whose limbs are delicate. Victory to Mukunda, who removes the burdens of the earth.'

पिप्पलायन उवाच

श्रीमन्नृसिंहविभवे गरुडध्वजाय तापत्रयोपशमनाय भवौषधाय ।
कृष्णाय वृश्चिकजलाग्निभुजङ्गरोगक्लेशव्ययाय हरये गुरवे नमस्ते ॥ (52)

---

[33]The three aksharas of the brahman are OUM, and the three aksharas in Govinda are 'go', 'vin' and 'da'.
[34]Identified with Vedavyasa.
[35]This Hari refers to Indra. Hari, the tawny one, is one of Indra's names.

Pippalayana[36] said, 'I prostrate myself before Krishna, Hari, the guru, the prosperous and powerful Nrisimha, the one with Garuda on his banner, the one who pacifies the three kinds of hardship,[37] the medication for this world, the one who takes away difficulties on account of scorpions, water, fire, serpents and disease.'

हविर्होत्र उवाच ।

कृष्ण त्वदीयपदपंकजपिंजरान्ते अद्यैव मे विशतु मानसराजहंसः ।
प्राणप्रयाणसमये कफवातपित्तै: कंठावरोधनविधौ स्मरणं कुतस्ते ॥ (53)

Havirhotra[38] said, 'O Krishna! Please imprison the royal swan that is my mind in the cage of your lotus feet. At the time of the departure of the breath of life, when the throat is obstructed by phlegm, air and bile, how can one possibly remember you?'

विदुर उवाच

हरेर्नामैव नामैव नामैव मम जीवनम् ।
कलौ नास्त्येव नास्त्येव नास्त्येव गतिरन्यथा ॥ (54)

Vidura said, 'My life is only Hari's name, his name and his name. In Kali Yuga, there is no other destination, nothing else, nothing else.'

वसिष्ठ उवाच

कृष्णेति मंगलं नाम यस्य वाचाप्रवर्तते ।
भस्मीभवन्ति तस्याशु महापातककोटयः ॥ (55)

Vasishtha said, 'If a person's speech utters the auspicious name of Krishna, swiftly, crores of his great sins are reduced to ashes.'

---

[36]The son of Rishabha, Vishnu's devotee. His story is recounted in the Bhagavata Purana.
[37]Relating to *adhidaivika* (destiny), *adhibhoutika* (nature) and *adhyatmika* (one's own nature).
[38]Not much is known about him. There was a king with the same name from the Shalihotra lineage much later in the timeline.

अरुन्धत्युवाच

कृष्णाय वासुदेवाय हरये परमात्मने ।
प्रणतक्लेशनाशाय गोविन्दाय नमो नमः ॥ (56)

Arundhati[39] said, 'I prostrate myself before Krishna, Vasudeva, Hari, the paramatman. He destroys the difficulties of those who prostrate themselves. I prostrate myself before Govinda.'

कश्यप उवाच

कृष्णानुस्मरणादेव पापसंघट्टपंजरम् ।
शतधा भेदमाप्नोति गिरिर्वज्रहतो यथा ॥ (57)

Kashyapa said, 'As soon as one remembers Krishna, this cage of sins is shattered into a hundred fragments, like a mountain struck by the *vajra*.'[40]

दुर्योधन उवाच

जानामि धर्मं न च मे प्रवृत्तिर्जानामि पापं न च मे निवृत्तिः ।
केनापि देवेन हृदिस्थितेन यथा नियुक्तोऽस्मि तथा करोमि ॥ (58)
यंत्रस्य मम दोषेण शाम्यतां मधुसूदन ।
अहं यन्त्रं भवान् यन्त्री मम दोषो न दीयताम् ॥ (59)

Duryodhana said, 'I know dharma but do not practise it. I know sin but do not refrain from it. There is a divinity who is established in my heart. I do whatever he engages me in. O Madhusudana! I am only a machine. Please pacify my sins. I am the machine, you are the one who controls the machine. Please do not blame me for my sins.'

भृगुरुवाच

नामैव तव गोविन्द नाम त्वत्तः शताधिकम् ।
ददात्युच्चारणान्मुक्तिः भवानष्टाङ्गयोगतः ॥ (60)

---

[39]Vasishtha's wife.
[40]Indra's weapon.

Bhrigu said, 'O Govinda! Your name has a worth that is a hundred times your worth. You bestow liberation through the eight divisions of yoga, but the mere utterance of your name is sufficient.'

लोमश उवाच

नमामि नारायणपादपङ्कजं करोमि नारायणपूजनं सदा ।
वदामि नारायणनाम निर्मलं स्मरामि नारायणतत्त्वमव्ययम् ॥ (61)

Lomasha[41] said, 'I prostrate myself before Narayana's lotus feet. I constantly worship Narayana. I utter Narayana's sparkling name. I remember Narayana's undecaying principles.'

शौनक उवाच

स्मृते: सकलकल्याणभाजनं यत्र जायते ।
पुरुषस्तमजं नित्यं व्रजामि शरणं हरिम् ॥ (62)

Shounaka said, 'As soon as one remembers him, one becomes a vessel for everything auspicious. He is the eternal Purusha, without birth. I seek refuge with that Hari.'

गर्ग उवाच

नारायणेति मन्त्रोऽस्ति वागस्ति वशवर्तिनी ।
तथापि नरके घोरे पतन्तीत्यद्भुतं महत् ॥ (63)

Garga[42] said, 'The mantra of "Narayana" exists and is within the control of the tongue. Nevertheless, it is extremely surprising that there are those who descend into a terrible hell.'

दाल्भ्य उवाच ।
किं तस्य बहुभिर्मन्त्रैर्भक्तिर्यस्य जनार्दने ।
नमो नारायणायेति मन्त्र: सर्वार्थसाधक: ॥ (64)

---

[41]A sage who was Vishnu's devotee. He figures extensively in the Mahabharata.
[42]A sage who named Krishna and initially taught him.

Dalbhya[43] said, 'For a person who possesses devotion towards Janardana, what is the need for many mantras? "I prostrate myself before Narayana." This mantra accomplishes all the objectives.'

वैशंपायन उवाच ।
यत्र योगेश्वरः कृष्णो यत्र पार्थो धनुर्धरः ।
तत्र श्रीर्विजयो भूतिर्ध्रुवा नीतिर्मतिर्मम ॥ (65)

Vaishampayana said, 'Wherever Krishna, lord of yoga, and Partha, the wielder of the bow, exist, it is my view that wealth, victory, prosperity and good policy certainly exist.'[44]

अग्निरुवाच
हरिर्हरति पापानि दुष्टचित्तैरपि स्मृतः ।
अनिच्छयापि संस्पृष्टो दहत्येव हि पावकः ॥ (66)

Agni said, 'If one remembers Hari, even with a wicked mind, he takes away sins, like a fire burns, even though it is touched involuntarily.'

परमेश्वर उवाच
सकृदुच्चरितं येन हरिरित्यक्षरद्वयम् ।
बद्धः परिकरस्तेन मोक्षाय गमनं प्रति ॥ (67)

Parameshvara[45] said, 'If a person utters the two aksharas[46] "Hari" only once, he has bound up the revenue and dependents required for a journey towards moksha.'

पुलस्त्य उवाच
हे जिह्वे रससारज्ञे सर्वदा मधुरप्रिये ।
नारायणाख्यपीयूषं पिब जिह्वे निरन्तरम् ॥ (68)

---

[43] A sage who figures prominently in the Mahabharata and Puranas.
[44] This is the famous last shloka (18.78) of the Bhagavat Gita, attributed to Sanjaya.
[45] Interpreted as Shiva.
[46] 'Ha' and 'ri'.

Pulastya[47] said, 'O Tongue! O One Who Knows the Essence of Juices! O One Who Always Loves What Is Sweet! O Tongue! Constantly drink the nectar known as "Narayana".'

व्यास उवाच

सत्यं सत्यं पुनः सत्यं सत्यं सत्यं वदाम्यहम् ।
नास्ति वेदात्परं शास्त्रं न देवः केशवात्परः ॥ (69)

Vyasa said, 'This is the truth. This is again the truth. I am speaking the truth, the truth, the truth. There is no sacred text superior to the Vedas. There is no deva superior to Keshava.'

धन्वन्तरिरुवाच ।
अच्युतानन्त गोविन्द नामोच्चारणभेषजम् ।
नश्यन्ति सकला रोगाः सत्यं सत्यं वदाम्यहम् ॥ (70)

Dhanvantari[48] said, 'Chanting the name of Achyuta, Ananta, Govinda is a medication that destroys every kind of disease. I am speaking the truth, the truth.'

मार्कण्डेय उवाच

स्वर्गदं मोक्षदं देवं सुखदं जगतोगुरुम् ।
कथं मुहूर्तमपि तं वासुदेवं न चिन्तयेत् ॥ (71)

Markandeya said, 'He is the one who bestows heaven. He is the one who bestows moksha. He is the divinity who bestows happiness. He is the guru of the universe. How can one spend even a muhurta without thinking of Vasudeva?'

अगस्त्य उवाच

निमिषं निमिषार्धं वा प्राणिनां विष्णुचिन्तनम् ।
तत्र तत्र कुरुक्षेत्रं प्रयागो नैमिषं वनम् ॥ (72)

---

[47]One of the saptarshis.
[48]The physician of the devas.

Agastya said, 'Wherever living beings think of Vishnu for a *nimisha*[49] or half a nimisha, that place becomes like Kuruskhetra, Prayaga or the forest of Naimisha.'

वामदेव उवाच

निमिषं निमिषार्धं वा प्राणिनां विष्णुचिन्तनम् ।
कल्पकोटिसहस्राणि लभते वांछितं फलम् ॥ (73)

Vamadeva said, 'If living beings think of Vishnu for a nimisha or half a nimisha, they obtain their desired fruits for thousands of crores of kalpas.'

शुक उवाच

आलोड्य सर्वशास्त्राणि विचार्य च पुन: पुन: ।
इदमेकं सुनिष्पन्नं ध्येयो नारायण: सदा ॥ (74)

Shuka said, 'After agitating all the sacred texts and reflecting again and again, I have come to a single proper determination—always meditate on Narayana.'

श्रीमहादेव उवाच

शरीरे जर्जरीभूते व्याधिग्रस्ते कलेवरे ।
औषधं जाह्नवीतोयं वैद्यो नारायणो हरि: ॥ (75)

Shri Mahadeva said, 'When the body has become completely old and the limbs are devoured by disease, the water of the Jahnavi is the medicine and Narayana Hari is the physician.'

शौनक उवाच

भोजनाच्छादने चिन्तां वृथा कुर्वन्ति वैष्णवा: ।
योऽसौ विश्वम्भरो देव: स किं भक्तानुपेक्षते ॥ (76)

---

[49]The duration of the blink of an eye. Usually written as 'nimesha'.

Shounaka said, 'Vishnu's devotees unnecessarily worry about food and clothing. How can the divinity who preserves the world ignore his devotees?'

सनत्कुमार उवाच

यस्य हस्ते गदा चक्रं गरुडो यस्य वाहनम् ।
शंखचक्रगदापद्मी स मे विष्णुः प्रसीदतु ॥ (77)

Sanatkumara[50] said, 'His hands wield the mace and the chakra. Garuda is his mount. He holds the conch shell, the chakra, the mace and the lotus. Let that Vishnu show me his favours.'

एवं ब्रह्मादयोदेवाऋषयश्च तपोधनाः ।
कीर्तयन्ति सुरश्रेष्ठमेवं नारायणं विभुम् ॥ (78)

In this way, Brahma and the other devas and the rishis, stores of austerities, chanted about the best of gods, Lord Narayana.[51]

इदं पवित्रमायुष्यं पुण्यं पापप्रणाशनम् ।
दुःस्वप्ननाशनं स्तोत्रं पाण्डवैः परिकीर्तितम् ॥ (79)

This auspicious *stotram*[52] was recited by the Pandavas. It is sacred. It confers a long life and destroys sins. It destroys bad dreams.

यः पठेत्प्रातरुत्थाय शुचिस्तद्गतमानसः ।
गवां शतसहस्रस्य सम्यग्दत्तस्य यत्फलम् ॥ (80)

If a person wakes up in the morning, purifies himself and reads this with single-minded attention, he obtains the fruits of properly donating a hundred thousand cows.

तत्फलं समवाप्नोति यः पठेदिति संस्तवम् ।
सर्वपापविनिर्मुक्तो विष्णुलोकं स गच्छति ॥ (81)

---

[50]One of four sages born to Brahma through the powers of his mind.
[51]These and the succeeding shlokas are naturally not attributed to anyone.
[52]A hymn of praise.

If a person reads this, along with its praise, he obtains the fruits of being freed from all sins and going to Vishnu's world.

गङ्गा गीता च गायत्री गोविन्दोगरुडध्वज: ।
चतुर्गकारसंयुक्त: पुनर्जन्म न विद्यते ॥ (82)

It has four words[53] that start with 'ga'—Ganga, Gita, Gayatri and Govinda, with Garuda on his banner. There is no rebirth for such a person.

गीतां य: पठते नित्यं श्लोकार्ध श्लोकमेव च ।
मुच्यते सर्वपापेभ्यो विष्णुलोकं स गच्छति ॥ (83)

If a person reads half a shloka or a shloka of this Gita every day, he is freed from all sins and goes to Vishnu's world.

Thus ends the Pandava Gita.

---

[53]In some versions, Garudadhvaja (one with Garuda on his banner) is counted as a separate word from Govinda and there are five words with 'ga', instead of four.

Thus ends *Sacred Songs*.

ACKNOWLEDGEMENTS

The Bhagavat Gita is one of the most important texts of Hinduism. It has been read and reread, translated and retranslated. There have been many commentaries. It has influenced the lives of people. There are people who know all 700 verses of the Bhagavat Gita by heart. However, though it is the most important, the Bhagavat Gita is only one of numerous Gitas. The word 'Gita' simply means it was sung, and the entire Itihasa Purana corpus was recited and sung. Therefore, there are other 'Gitas' in the Itihasa Purana corpus, and some outside it too. For instance, the Ashtavakra Gita, which has also influenced a lot of people, is such an independent Gita and not tied to the Itihasa Purana corpus. All these Gitas should be read and reread. If they cannot be read in Sanskrit, they should be translated and retranslated.

This volume has the Gitas from the Mahabharata in Sanskrit as well as their word-for-word English translation. The intention is to have a sequel, with Gitas from the Puranas. Obviously, any publication endeavour has to consider the market and, for a book like this, the market cannot be very large. I am indebted to Kapish Mehra and Yamini Chowdhury of Rupa for thinking that the effort was worth making. Fabulous editing by Aurodeep Mukherjee and Smita Mathur ensured that the book became much more readable. I am grateful to all of them and to the wonderful designer and illustrator.

Dr Subrahmanyam Jaishankar once remarked to me that translating the Itihasa Purana corpus was fine (which I have been extensively involved in), but surely one should focus on governance lessons from the Mahabharata and on how they relate to today's Bharatavarsha. Governance is a broad concept. Indeed, there are governance lessons from the Mahabharata and the Itihasa Purana corpus and that is a broader idea, possibly for a subsequent book. Depending on how one interprets governance, there is plenty about dharma for kings and for individual householders in this collection of Mahabharata Gitas. However, for that chance remark, which triggered this translation, this book owes gratitude to Kyoko and Dr Jaishankar. (The subsequent governance book remains in the works.)

As is always the case, my wife, Suparna Banerjee, has been a *sahadharmini* in all these acts of dharma. I am indebted to her, too, for making all these works of translation easier, by encouraging and providing a conductive environment.